Maddy & Richard
Alex

# A TREASURY OF MODERN MYSTERIES

*Volume 2*

AGATHA CHRISTIE • JOYCE CAROL OATES
GEORGE FOX • HARRY KEMELMAN
BILL PRONZINI • DOROTHY SALISBURY DAVIS
MARGERY ALLINGHAM • DAPHNE du MAURIER

# A TREASURY OF MODERN MYSTERIES

DONALD E. WESTLAKE • ARTHUR PORGES
THOMAS KYD • ROSS MACDONALD
IRA LEVIN • GEORGES SIMENON
JOHN D. MacDONALD • JAMES HOLDING
STANLEY ELLIN • IAN FLEMING • TRUMAN CAPOTE

VOLUME 2

DOUBLEDAY & COMPANY, INC.
Garden City, New York

Library of Congress Catalog Number 73–77298
Printed in the United States of America

# CONTENTS

## *VOLUME 1*

## *VOLUME 2*

# A TREASURY OF MODERN MYSTERIES

*Volume 2*

# A KISS BEFORE DYING

*by Ira Levin*

## PART ONE: DOROTHY

### 1

HIS PLANS HAD been running so beautifully, so goddamned beautifully, and now *she* was going to smash them all. Hate erupted and flooded through him, gripping his face with jaw-aching pressure. That was all right though; the lights were out.

And she, she kept on sobbing weakly in the dark, her cheek pressed against his bare chest, her tears and her breath burning hot. He wanted to push her away.

Finally his face relaxed. He put his arm around her and stroked her back. It was warm, or rather his hand was cold; all of him was cold, he discovered; his armpits were creeping with sweat and his legs were quivering the way they always did when things took a crazy turn and caught him helpless and unprepared. He lay still for a moment, waiting for the trembling to subside. With his free hand he drew the blanket up around her shoulders. "Crying isn't going to do any good," he told her gently.

Obediently, she tried to stop, catching her breath in long choking gasps. She rubbed her eyes with the worn binding of the blanket. "It's just . . . the holding it in for so long. I've known for days . . . weeks. I didn't want to say anything until I was sure . . ."

His hand on her back was warmer. "No mistake possible?" He spoke in a whisper, even though the house was empty.

"No."

"How far?"

"Two months almost." She lifted her cheek from his chest, and in the dark he could sense her eyes on him. "What are we going to do?" she asked.

"You didn't give the doctor your right name did you?"

"No. He knew I was lying though. It was awful . . ."

"If your father ever finds out . . ."

She lowered her head again and repeated the question, speaking against his chest. "What are we going to do?" She waited for his answer.

He shifted his position a bit, partially to give emphasis to what he was about to say, and partially in the hope that it would encourage her to move, for her weight on his chest had become uncomfortable. "Listen, Dorrie," he said, "I know you want me to say we'll get married right away—tomorrow. And I want to marry you. More than anything else in the world. I swear to God I do." He paused, planning his words with care. Her body, curled against his, was motionless, listening. "But if we marry this way, me not even meeting your father first, and then a baby comes seven months later . . . You know what he'd do."

"He couldn't *do* anything," she protested. "I'm over eighteen. Eighteen's all you have to be out here. What could he do?"

"I'm not talking about an annulment or anything like that."

"Then what? What do you mean?" she appealed.

"The money," he said. "Dorrie, what kind of man is he? What did you tell me about him—him and his holy morals? Your mother makes a single slip; he finds out about it eight years later and divorces her, divorces her not caring about you and your sisters, not caring about her bad health. Well what do you think he would do to you? He'd forget you ever existed. You wouldn't see a penny."

"I don't *care,*" she said earnestly. "Do you think I care?"

"But I do, Dorrie." His hand began moving gently on her back again. "Not for me. I swear to God not for me. But for you. What will happen to us? We'll both have to quit school; you for the baby, me to work. And what will I do?—another guy with two years' college and no degree. What will I be? A clerk? Or an oiler in some textile mill or something?"

"It doesn't matter . . ."

"It does! You don't know how much it does. You're only nineteen and you've had money all your life. You don't know what it means not to have it. I do. We'd be at each other's throats in a year."

"No . . . no . . . we wouldn't!"

"All right, we love each other so much we never argue. So where are we? In a furnished room with—with paper drapes? Eating spaghetti seven nights a week? If I saw you living that way and I knew it was my fault . . ."—he paused for an instant, then finished very softly— ". . . I'd take out insurance and jump in front of a car."

She began sobbing again.

He closed his eyes and spoke dreamily, intoning the words in a sedative chant. "I had it planned so beautifully. I would have come to New York this summer and you would have introduced me to him. I could have gotten him to like me. You would have told me what he's interested in, what he likes, what he dislikes—" He stopped short, then continued. "And after graduation we would have been married. Or even this summer. We could have come back here in September for our last two years. A little apartment of our own, right near the campus . . ."

She lifted her head from his chest. "What are you trying to do?" she begged. "Why are you saying these things?"

"I want you to see how beautiful, how wonderful, it could have been."

"I see. Do you think I don't see?" The sobs twisted her voice. "But I'm pregnant. I'm two months pregnant." There was silence, as though unnoticed motors had suddenly stopped. "Are . . . are you trying to get out of it? To get away? Is that what you're trying to do?"

"No! God no, Dorrie!" He grabbed her by the shoulders and pulled her up until her face was next to his. "No!"

"Then what are you doing to me? We *have* to get married now! We don't have any choice!"

"We *do* have a choice, Dorrie," he said.

He felt her body stiffen against his.

She gave a small terrified whisper—"No!"—and began shaking her head violently from side to side.

"Listen, Dorrie!" he pleaded, hands gripping her shoulders, "No operation. Nothing like that." He caught her jaw in one hand, fingers pressing into her cheeks, holding her head rigid. "Listen!" He waited until the wildness of her breathing subsided. "There's a guy on campus, Hermy Godsen. His uncle owns the drugstore on University and Thirty-Fourth. Hermy sells things. He could get some pills."

He let go of her jaw. She was silent.

"Don't you see, baby? We've got to try! It means so much!"

"Pills . . ." she said gropingly, as though it were a new word.

"We've got to try. It could be so wonderful."

She shook her head in desperate confusion. "Oh God, I don't know . . ."

He put his arms around her. "Baby, I *love* you. I wouldn't let you take anything that might hurt you."

She collapsed against him, the side of her head striking his shoulder. "I don't know . . . I don't know . . ."

He said, "It would be so wonderful . . ."—his hand caressing—"A little apartment of our own . . . no waiting for a damn landlady to go to the movies . . ."

Finally she said, "How . . . how do you know they would work? What if they didn't work?"

He took a deep breath. "If they don't work,"—he kissed her forehead, and her cheek, and the corner of her mouth—"If they don't work we'll get married right away and to hell with your father and Kingship Copper Incorporated. I swear we will, baby."

He had discovered that she liked to be called 'baby.' When he called her 'baby' and held her in his arms he could get her to do practically anything. He had thought about it, and decided it had something to do with the coldness she felt towards her father.

He kept kissing her gently, talking to her with warm low words, and in a while she was calm and easy.

They shared a cigarette, Dorothy holding it first to his lips and then to hers, where the pink glow of each puff would momentarily touch the feathery blonde hair and the wide brown eyes.

She turned the burning end of the cigarette towards them and moved it around and around, back and forth, painting circles and lines of vivid orange in the darkness. "I bet you could hypnotize someone this way," she said. Then she swung the cigarette slowly before his eyes. In its wan light her slim-fingered hand moved sinuously. "You are my slave," she whispered, lips close to his ear. "You are my slave and completely in my power! You must obey my every bidding!" She was so cute he couldn't help smiling.

When they finished the cigarette he looked at the luminous dial of his watch. Waving his hand before her, he intoned, "You must get dressed. You must get dressed because it is twenty past ten and you must be back at the dorm by eleven."

## 2

HE WAS BORN in Menasset, on the outskirts of Fall River, Massachusetts; the only child of a father who was an oiler in one of the Fall River textile mills and a mother who sometimes had to take in sewing when the money ran low. They were of English extraction with some French intermixed along the way, and they lived in a neighborhood populated largely by Portuguese. His father found no reason to be bothered by this, but his mother did. She was a bitter and unhappy woman who had married young, expecting her husband to make more of himself than a mere oiler.

At an early age he became conscious of his good looks. On Sundays guests would come and exclaim over him—the blondness of his hair, the clear blue of his eyes—but his father was always there, shaking his head admonishingly at the guests. His parents argued a great deal, usually over the time and money his mother devoted to dressing him.

Because his mother had never encouraged him to play with the children of the neighborhood, his first few days at school were an agony of insecurity. He was suddenly an anonymous member of a large group of boys, some of whom made fun of the perfection of his clothes and the obvious care he took to avoid the puddles in the schoolyard. One day, when he could bear it no longer, he went up to the ringleader of the hazers and spat on his shoes. The ensuing fight was brief but wild, and at the end of it he had the ringleader flat on his back and was kneeling on his chest, banging his head against the ground again and again. A teacher came running and broke up the fight. After that, everything was all right. Eventually he accepted the ringleader as one of his friends.

His marks in school were good, which made his mother glow and even won reluctant praise from his father. His marks became still better when he started sitting next to an unattractive but brilliant girl who was so beholden to him for some awkward cloakroom kisses that she neglected to cover her paper during examinations.

His school-days were the happiest of his life; the girls liked him for his looks and his charm; the teachers liked him because he was polite and attentive, nodding when they stated important facts, smiling when they attempted feeble jokes; and to the boys he showed his dislike of both girls and teachers just enough so that they liked him too. At home, he was a god. His father finally gave in and joined his mother in deferent admiration.

When he started dating, it was with girls from the better part of town. His parents argued again, over his allowance and the amount of money spent on his clothes. The arguments were short though, his father only sparring halfheartedly. His mother began to talk about his marrying a rich man's daughter. She only said it jokingly, of course, but she said it more than once.

He was president of his senior class in high school and was graduated with the third highest average and honors in mathematics and science. In the school yearbook he was named The Best Dancer, The Most Popular, and The Most Likely to Succeed. His parents gave a party for him, which was attended by many young people from the better part of town.

Two weeks later, he was drafted.

For the first few days of Basic Training, he coasted along on the glory he had left behind. But then reality rubbed off the insulation, and he found the impersonal authority of the Army to be a thousand times more degrading than his early schooldays had been. And here, if he went up to the sergeant and spat on his shoes, he'd probably spend the rest of his life in the stockade. He cursed the blind system which had dropped him into the infantry, where he was surrounded by coarse, comic-book-reading idiots. After a while he read comic-books too, but only because it was impossible to concentrate on the copy of *Anna Karenina* he had brought with him. He made friends with some of the men, buying them beers in the PX, and inventing obscene and fantastically funny biographies of all the officers. He was contemptuous of everything that had to be learned and everything that had to be done.

When he was shipped out of San Francisco, he vomited all the way across the Pacific, and he knew it was only partly from the lift and drop of the ship. He was sure he was going to be killed.

On an island still partially occupied by the Japanese, he became separated from the other members of his company and stood terrified in the midst of a silent jungle, desperately shifting this way and that, not knowing in which direction safety lay. A rifle slapped, sent a bullet keening past his ear. Jagged bird screams split the air. He dropped to his stomach and rolled under a bush, sick with the certainty that this was the moment of his death.

The bird sounds fluttered down into silence. He saw a gleam in a tree up ahead, and knew that that was where the sniper waited. He found himself inching forward under the bushes, dragging his rifle with one hand. His body was clammy cold and alive with sweat; his legs were trembling so badly that he was sure the Jap would hear the leaves rustling under them. The rifle weighed a ton.

Finally he was only twenty feet from the tree, and looking up, he could discern the figure crouched in it. He lifted his rifle; he aimed, and fired. The bird chorus shrieked. The tree remained motionless. Then suddenly a rifle dropped from it, and he saw the sniper slide clumsily down a vine and drop to the ground with his hands high in the air; a little yellow man grotesquely festooned with leaves and branches, his lips emitting a terrified sing-song chatter.

Keeping the rifle trained on the Jap, he stood up. The Jap was as scared as he was; the yellow face twitched wildly and the knees shivered; more scared, in fact, for the front of the Jap's pants was dark with a spreading stain.

He watched the wretched figure with contempt. His own legs steadied. His sweating stopped. The rifle was weightless, like an extension of his arms, immobile, aimed at the trembling caricature of a man that confronted him. The Jap's chatter had slowed to a tone of entreaty. The yellow-brown fingers made little begging motions in the air.

Quite slowly, he squeezed the trigger. He did not move with the recoil. Insensate to the kick of the butt in his shoulder, he watched attentively as a black-red hole blossomed and swelled in the chest of the Jap. The little man slid clawing to the jungle floor. Bird screams were like a handful of colored cards thrown into the air.

After looking at the slain enemy for a minute or so, he turned and walked away. His step was as easy and certain as when he had crossed the stage of the auditorium after accepting his diploma.

He received an honorable discharge in January of 1947, and left the Army with the Bronze Star and the Purple Heart, and the record of a shell fragment traced in a vein of thin scar tissue over his dextral ribs. Returning home, he found that his father had been killed in an automobile accident while he was overseas.

He was offered several jobs in Menasset, but rejected them as being of too little promise. His father's insurance money was sufficient to support his mother and she was taking in sewing again besides, so after two months of drawing admiration from the townspeople and twenty dollars a week from the federal government, he decided to go to New York. His mother argued, but he was over twenty-one, if only by a few months, so he had his way. Some of the neighbors expressed surprise that he did not intend to go to college, especially when the government would pay for it. He felt, however, that college would only be an unnecessary stopover on the road to the success he was certain awaited him.

His first job in New York was in a publishing house, where the personnel manager assured him there was a fine future for the right man. Two weeks, however, was all he could take of the shipping room.

His next job was with a department store, where he was a salesclerk in the mens' wear department. The only reason he remained there an entire month was that he was able to buy his clothes on a twenty per cent discount.

By the end of August, when he had been in New York five months and had had six jobs, he was again prey to the awful insecurity of being one among many rather than one alone; unadmired and with no tangible sign of success. He sat in his furnished room and devoted some time to serious self-analysis. If he had not found what he wanted in these six jobs, he decided, it was unlikely that he would find it in the next six. He took out his fountain pen and made what he considered to be a completely objective list of his qualities, abilities and talents.

In September, he enrolled in a dramatic school under the G.I. Bill. The instructors expressed great hopes for him at first; he was handsome, intelligent, and had a fine speaking voice, although the New England accent would have to be eliminated. He had great hopes too, at first. Then he discovered how much work and study were involved in becoming an actor. The exercises the instructors gave—"Look at this photograph and act out the emotions it brings to mind"—struck him as ridiculous, although the other students seemed to take them seriously. The only study to which he applied himself was diction; he had been dismayed to hear the word 'accent' used in relation to himself, having always thought of it as something someone else had.

In December, on his twenty-second birthday, he met a fairly attractive widow. She was in her forties and she had a good deal of money. They met on the corner of Fifth Avenue and Fifty-Fifth Street, —quite romantically, they later agreed. Stepping back onto the curb to avoid a bus, she tripped and fell into his arms. She was embarrassed and terribly shaken. He made some humorous comments on the ability and thoughtfulness of Fifth Avenue bus drivers, and then they went down the street to a dignified bar where they had two Martinis each, for which he paid the check. In the weeks that followed they attended small East Side art movies and dined in restaurants where there were three or four people to be tipped at the end of the meal. He paid many more checks, although not again with his own money.

Their attachment lasted for several months, during which time he weaned himself away from the dramatic school—no painful process—and devoted his afternoons to squiring her on shopping tours, some of which were for him. At first he was somewhat embarrassed at being seen with her because of the obvious discrepancy in their ages, but he soon found himself getting over that. He was, however, dissatisfied with the relationship on two accounts; firstly, while her face was fairly attractive, her body, unfortunately, was not; secondly, and of greater importance, he learned from the elevator operator in her apartment house that he was only one of a series of young men, each of whom had been replaced with equinoctial regularity at the end of six months. It seemed, he reflected humorlessly, that this was another position with no future. At the end of five months, when she began to exhibit less curiosity about how he spent the nights he was not with her, he anticipated her move and told her that he had to return home because his mother was deathly ill.

He did return home, after reluctantly excising the custom tailor's labels from his suits and pawning a Patek Philippe wristwatch. He spent the early part of June lounging around the house, silently lamenting the fact that the widow had not been younger, prettier, and open to a more permanent sort of alliance.

That was when he began to make his plans. He decided he would go to college after all. He took a summer job in a local dry goods store because, while the G.I. Bill would cover his tuition, his living expenses would be quite high; he was going to attend a good school.

He finally chose Stoddard University in Blue River, Iowa, which was supposed to be something of a country club for the children of the Midwestern wealthy. There was no difficulty in his gaining admission. He had such a fine high school record.

In his first year he met a lovely girl, a senior, the daughter of the vice-president of an internationally organized farm equipment concern. They took walks together, cut classes together, and slept together. In May she told him that she was engaged to a boy back home and she hoped he hadn't taken it too seriously.

In his sophomore year, he met Dorothy Kingship.

## 3

HE GOT THE pills, two grayish-white capsules, from Hermy Godsen. They cost him five dollars.

At eight o'clock he met Dorothy at their regular meeting place, a tree-shrouded bench in the center of the wide stretch of lawn between the Fine Arts and Pharmacy buildings. When he left the white concrete path and cut across the darkness of the lawn he saw that Dorothy was already there, sitting stiffly with her fingers locked in her lap, a dark coat cloaking her shoulders against the April coolness. A streetlamp off to the side cast leaf shadows on her face.

He sat down beside her and kissed her cheek. She greeted him softly. From the rectangle of lighted windows in the Fine Arts Building drifted the conflicting themes of a dozen pianos. After a moment he said, "I got them."

A couple crossed the lawn towards them and, seeing the bench occupied, turned back to the white path. The girl's voice said, "My God, they're all taken."

He took the envelope from his pocket and put it into Dorothy's hand. Her fingers felt the capsules through the paper. "You're to take both of them together," he said. "You're liable to get a little fever, and you'll probably feel nauseous."

She put the envelope in her coat pocket. "What's in them?" she asked.

"Quinine, some other things. I'm not sure." He paused. "They can't hurt you."

He looked at her face and saw that she was staring off at something beyond the Fine Arts Building. He turned and followed her gaze to a winking red light miles away. It marked the local radio station's transmitting tower, which stood atop Blue River's tallest structure, the Municipal Building,—where the Marriage License Bureau was. He wondered if she were staring at the light because of that, or only because it was a winking red light in a sky of darkness. He touched her hands and found them cold. "Don't worry, Dorrie. Everything will be all right."

They sat in silence for a few minutes, and then she said, "I'd like to go to a movie tonight. There's a Joan Fontaine picture at the Uptown."

"I'm sorry," he said, "but I've got a ton of Spanish homework."

"Let's go over to the Student Union. I'll help you with it."

"What are you trying to do, corrupt me?"

He walked her back across the campus. Opposite the low modern shape of the Girls' Dormitory, they kissed goodnight. "See you in class tomorrow," he said. She nodded, and kissed him again. She was trembling. "Look, baby, there's nothing to worry about. If they don't work we get married. Haven't you heard?—love conquers all." She was waiting for him to say more. "And I love you very much," he said, and kissed her. When their lips parted, hers were pressed into an unsteady smile.

"Good night, baby," he said.

He returned to his room, but he couldn't do his Spanish. He sat with his elbows planted on the bridge table, his head in his hands, thinking about the pills. Oh God, they must work! They *will* work!

But Hermy Godsen had said: "I can't give you no written guarantee. If this girlfriend of yours is two months gone already . . ."

He tried not to think about it. He got up and went to the bureau and opened the bottom drawer. From under the neatly folded pajamas he took two pamphlets whose supple covers gleamed with a copper finish.

On first meeting Dorothy and discovering, through one of the student-secretaries in the Registrar's office, that she was not merely one of the 'Kingship Copper' Kingships but actually a daughter of the corporation's president, he had written a businesslike letter to the organization's New York office. In it he represented himself as contemplating an investment in Kingship Copper (which was not entirely an untruth), and requested descriptive brochures of its holdings.

Two weeks later, when he was reading *Rebecca* and pretending to love it because it was Dorothy's favorite book, and when she was doggedly knitting him bulky argyle socks because a previous boyfriend had liked them and so the knitting of them had become the badge of her devotion, the pamphlets arrived. He opened their envelope with ceremonial care. They proved wonderful—*Technical Information on Kingship Copper and Copper Alloys* and *Kingship Copper, Pioneer in Peace and War* they were called, and they were crammed with photographs: mines and furnaces, concentrators and converters, reversing mills, rolling mills, rod mills and tube mills. He read them a hundred times and knew every caption by heart. He returned to them at odd moments, a musing smile on his lips, like a woman with a love letter.

Tonight they were no good. "Open-cut mine in Landers, Michigan. From this single mine, a yearly output . . ."

What angered him most was that in a sense the responsibility for the entire situation rested with Dorothy. He had wanted to take her to his room only once—a down-payment guaranteeing the fulfillment of a contract. It was Dorothy, with her gently closed eyes and her passive, orphan hunger, who had wished for further visits. He struck the table. It really was her fault! Damn her!

He dragged his mind back to the pamphlets, but it was no use; after a minute he pushed them away and rested his head in his hands again. If the pills didn't work . . . Leave school? Ditch her? It would be futile; she knew his Menasset address. Even if she should be reluctant to seek him out, her father would hasten to do so. Of course there could be no legal action (or could there?), but Kingship could still cause him plenty of trouble. He imagined the wealthy as a closely knit, mutually protective clan, and he could hear Leo Kingship: "Watch out for this young man. He's no good. I feel it my duty as a parent to warn you . . ." And what would be left for him then? Some shipping room?

Or if he married her. Then she would have the baby and they'd never get a cent out of Kingship. Again the shipping room, only this time saddled with a wife and child. Oh God!

The pills *had* to work. That was all there was to it. If they failed, he didn't know what he'd do.

The book of matches was white, with *Dorothy Kingship* stamped on it in copper leaf. Every Christmas Kingship Copper gave personalized matches to its executives, customers and friends. It took her four strokes to light the match, and when she held it to her cigarette the flame trembled as though in a breeze. She sat back, trying to relax, but she couldn't tear her eyes from the open bathroom door, the white envelope waiting on the edge of the sink, the glass of water . . .

She closed her eyes. If only she could speak to Ellen about it. A letter had come that morning—"The weather has been beautiful . . . president of the refreshment committee for the Junior Prom . . . have you read Marquand's new novel? . . ."—another of the meaningless mechanical notes that had been drifting between them since Christmas and the argument. If only she could get Ellen's advice, talk to her the way they used to talk . . .

Dorothy had been five and Ellen six when Leo Kingship divorced his wife. A third sister, Marion, was ten. When the three girls lost their mother, first through the divorce and then through her death a year later, Marion felt the loss most deeply of all. Recalling clearly the accusations and denunciations which had preceded the divorce, she recounted them in bitter detail to her sisters as they grew up. She exaggerated Kingship's cruelty to some degree. As the years passed she grew apart, solitary and withdrawn.

Dorothy and Ellen, however, turned to each other for the affection which they received neither from their father, who met their coldness with coldness, nor from the series of odorless and precise governesses to whom he transferred the custody the courts had granted him. The two sisters went to the same schools and camps, joined the same clubs and attended the same dances (taking care to return home at the hour designated by their father). Where Ellen led, Dorothy followed.

But when Ellen entered Caldwell College, in Caldwell, Wisconsin, and Dorothy made plans to follow her there the next year, Ellen said no; Dorothy should grow up and become self-reliant. Their father agreed, self-reliance being a trait he valued in himself and in others. A measure of compromise was allowed, and Dorothy was sent to Stoddard, slightly more than a hundred miles from Caldwell, with the understanding that the sisters would visit one another on weekends. A few visits were made, the length of time between them increasing progressively, until Dorothy austerely announced that her first year of college had made her completely self-reliant, and the visits stopped altogether. Finally, this past Christmas, there had been an argument. It had started on nothing—"If you wanted to borrow my blouse you might at least have asked me!"—and had swollen because Dorothy had been in a depressed mood all during her vacation. When the girls returned to school, the letters between them faded to brief, infrequent notes . . .

There was still the telephone. Dorothy found herself staring at it. She could get Ellen on the line in an instant . . . But no; why should she be the one to give in first and chance a rebuff? She squashed her cigarette in an ashtray. Besides, now that she had calmed down, what was there to hesitate about? She would take the pills; if they worked, all well and good. If not; marriage. She thought about how wonderful that would be, even if her father did have a fit. She didn't want any of *his* money anyway.

She went to the hall door and locked it, feeling a slight thrill in the unaccustomed and somewhat melodramatic act.

In the bathroom, she took the envelope from the edge of the sink and tilted the capsules into her palm. They were gray-white, their gelatin coating lustrous, like elongated pearls. Then, as she dropped the envelope into the wastebasket, the thought flashed into her mind—"What if I don't take them?"

They would be married tomorrow! Instead of waiting until the summer, or more likely until graduation—over two years—they'd be married by tomorrow night!

But it wouldn't be fair. She had promised she would try. Still, tomorrow . . .

She lifted the glass, clapped the pills into her mouth, and drained the water in a single draught.

## 4

THE CLASSROOM, IN one of Stoddard's new buildings, was a clean rectangle with one wall of aluminum-framed glass. Eight rows of seats faced the lecturer's platform. There were ten gray metal seats to a row, each with a right arm that curved in and fanned to form a writing surface.

He sat in the back of the room, in the second seat from the window. The seat on his left, the window seat, the empty seat, was hers. It was the first class of the morning, a daily Social Science lecture, and their only class together this semester. The speaker's voice droned in the sun-filled air.

Today of all days she could have made an effort to be on time. Didn't she know he'd be frozen in an agony of suspense? Heaven or hell. Complete happiness, or the awful mess he didn't even want to think about. He looked at his watch; 9:08. Damn her.

He shifted in his seat, fingering his keychain nervously. He stared at the back of the girl in front of him and started to count the polka dots in her blouse.

The door at the side of the room opened quietly. His head jerked around.

She looked awful. Her face was pasty white so that the rouge was like paint. There were gray arcs under her eyes. She was looking at him the instant the door opened, and with a barely perceptible motion, she shook her head.

Oh God! He turned back to the keychain in his fingers and stared at it, numb. He heard her coming around behind him, slipping into the seat on his left. He heard her books being put on the floor in the aisle between them, and then the scratching of a pen on paper, and finally the sound of a page being torn from a spiral-bound pad.

He turned. Her hand was extended towards him, holding a folded piece of blue-lined paper. She was watching him, her wide eyes anxious.

He took the paper and opened it in his lap:

*I had a terrible fever and I*
*threw up. But nothing happened.*

He closed his eyes for a moment, then opened them again and turned to her, his face expressionless. Her lips made a tight nervous smile. He tried to make himself return the smile, but he couldn't. His eyes went back to the note in his hand. He folded the paper in half, then folded it again and again, until it was a tight wad, which he placed in his pocket. Then he sat with his fingers locked firmly together, watching the lecturer.

After a few minutes, he was able to turn to Dorothy, give her a reassuring smile, and form the words "Don't worry" with silent lips.

When the bell sounded at 9:55, they left the room with the other students who were laughing and pushing and complaining about coming exams and overdue papers and broken dates. Outside, they moved from the crowded path and stood in the shadow of the concrete-walled building.

The color was beginning to return to Dorothy's cheeks. She spoke quickly. "It'll be all right. I know it will. You won't have to quit school. You'll get more money from the government, won't you? With a wife?"

"A hundred and five a month." He couldn't keep the sourness out of his voice.

"Others get along on it . . . the ones in the trailer camp. We'll manage."

He put his books down on the grass. The important thing was to get time, time to think. He was afraid his knees were going to start shaking. He took her by the shoulders, smiling. "That's the spirit. You just don't worry about anything." He took a breath. "Friday afternoon we'll go down to the Municipal—"

"Friday?"

"Baby, it's Tuesday. Three days won't make any difference now."

"I thought we'd go today."

He fingered the collar of her coat. "Dorrie, we can't. Be practical. There are so many things to be taken care of. I think I have to take a blood test first. I'll have to check on that. And then, if we get married Friday we can have the weekend for a honeymoon. I'm going to get us a reservation at the New Washington House . . ."

She frowned indecisively.

"What difference will three days make?"

"I guess you're right," she sighed.

"That's my baby."

She touched his hand. "I . . . I know it isn't the way we wanted it, but . . . you're happy, aren't you?"

"Well what do you think? Listen, the money isn't that important. I just thought that for your sake . . ."

Her eyes were warm, reaching.

He looked at his watch. "You have a ten o'clock, don't you?"

"*Solamente el Español.* I can cut it."

"Don't. We'll have better reasons to cut our morning classes." She squeezed his hand. "I'll see you at eight," he said. "At the bench." Reluctantly, she turned to go. "Oh, Dorrie . . ."

"Yes?"

"You haven't said anything to your sister, have you?"

"Ellen? No."

"Well you better not. Not until after we're married."

"I thought I'd tell her before. We've been so close. I'd hate to do it without telling her."

"If she's been so rotten to you the past two years . . ."

"Not rotten."

"That was the word you used. Anyhow, she's liable to tell your father. He might do something to stop us."

"What could he do?"

"I don't know. He would try anyway, wouldn't he?"

"All right. Whatever you say."

"Afterwards you'll call her up right away. We'll tell everybody."

"All right." A final smile, and then she was walking to the sun-bright path, her hair glinting gold. He watched her until she disappeared behind the corner of a building. Then he picked up his books and walked away in the opposite direction. A braking car screeched somewhere, making him start. It sounded like a bird in a jungle.

Without forming a conscious decision he was cutting the rest of the day's classes. He walked all the way through town and down to the river, which was not blue but a dull muddy brown. Leaning on the rail of the black-girdered Morton Street Bridge, he looked into the water and smoked a cigarette.

Here it was. The dilemma had finally caught up with him and engulfed him like the filthy water that pounded the abutments of the bridge. Marry her or leave her. A wife and a child and no money, or be hounded and blackballed by her father. "You don't know me, sir. My name is Leo Kingship. I'd like to speak to you about the young man you have just employed . . . The young man your daughter is going with . . . I think you should know . . ." Then what? There would be no place to go to but home. He thought of his mother. Years of complacent pride, patronizing sneers for the neighbors' children, and then she sees him clerking in a dry goods store, not just for the summer, but permanently. Or even some lousy mill! His father had failed to live up to her expectations, and he'd seen what love she'd had for the old man burn itself into bitterness and contempt. Was that in store for him too?

People talking behind his back. Oh Jesus! Why hadn't the goddamned pills killed the girl?

If only he could get her to undergo an operation. But no, she was determined to get married, and even if he pleaded and argued and called her "baby" from now till doomsday, she'd still want to consult Ellen before taking such a drastic measure. And anyway, where would they get the money? And suppose something happened, suppose she died. He would be involved because he would have been the one who arranged for the operation. He'd be right where he started—with her father out to get him. Her death wouldn't do him a bit of good.

Not if she died that way.

There was a heart scratched into the black paint of the railing, with initials on either side of the arrow that pierced it. He concentrated on the design, picking at it with his fingernail, trying to blank his mind of what had finally welled to the surface. The scratches had exposed cross-sections of paint layers; black, orange, black, orange, black, orange. It reminded him of the pictures of rock strata in a geology text. Records of dead ages.

Dead.

After a while he picked up his books and slowly walked from the bridge. Cars flew towards him and passed with a rushing sound.

He went into a dingy riverside restaurant and ordered a ham sandwich and coffee. He ate the sandwich at a little corner table. While sipping the coffee, he took out his memorandum book and fountain pen.

The first thing that had entered his mind was the Colt .45 he had taken on leaving the Army. Bullets could be obtained with little difficulty. But assuming he wanted to do it, a gun would be no good. It would have to look like an accident, or suicide. The gun would complicate matters too much.

He thought of poison. But where would he get it? Hermy Godsen? No. Maybe the Pharmacy Building. The supply room there shouldn't be too hard to get into. He would have to do some research at the library, to see which poison . . .

It would have to look like an accident or suicide, because if it looked like anything else, he would be the first one the police would suspect.

There were so many details—assuming he wanted to do it. Today was Tuesday; the marriage could be postponed no later than Friday or she might get worried and call Ellen. Friday would be the deadline. It would require a great deal of fast, careful planning.

He looked at the notes he had printed:

1. *Gun* (n.g.)
2. *Poison*
    a) *Selection*
    b) *Obtaining*
    c) *Administering*
    d) *Appearance of* (1) *accident*<br>or (2) *suicide*

Assuming, of course, that he wanted to do it. At present it was all purely speculative; he would explore the details a little. A mental exercise.

But his stride, when he left the restaurant and headed back through town, was relaxed and sure and steady.

## 5

HE REACHED THE campus at three o'clock and went directly to the library. In the card catalogue he found listed six books likely to contain the information he wanted; four of them were general works on toxicology; the other two, manuals of criminal investigation whose file cards indexed chapters on poisons. Rather than have a librarian get the books for him, he registered at the desk and went into the stacks himself.

He had never been in the stacks before. There were three floors filled with bookshelves, a metal staircase spiraling up through them. One of the books on his list was out. He found the other five without difficulty on the shelves on the third floor. Seating himself at one of the small study tables that flanked a wall of the room, he turned on the lamp, arranged his pen and memorandum book in readiness, and began to read.

At the end of an hour, he had a list of five toxic chemicals likely to be found in the Pharmacy supply room, any one of which, by virtue of its reaction time and the symptoms it produced prior to death, would be suitable for the plan whose rudimentary outline he had already formulated during the walk from the river.

He left the library and the campus, and walked in the direction of the house where he roomed. When he had gone two blocks he came upon a dress shop whose windows were plastered with big-lettered sale signs. One of the signs had a sketch of an hourglass with the legend *Last Days of Sale.*

He looked at the hourglass for a moment. Then he turned around and walked back towards the campus.

He went to the University Bookstore. After consulting the mimeographed booklist tacked to the bulletin board, he asked the clerk for a copy of *Pharmaceutical Techniques,* the laboratory manual used by the advanced pharmacy students. "Pretty late in the semester," the clerk commented, returning from the rear of the store with the manual in his hand. It was a large thin book with a distinctive green paper cover. "Lose yours?"

"No. It was stolen."

"Oh. Anything else?"

"Yes. I'd like some envelopes, please."

"What size?"

"Regular envelopes. For letters."

The clerk put a pack of white envelopes on the book. "That's a dollar-fifty and twenty-five. Plus tax—a dollar seventy-nine."

The College of Pharmacy was housed in one of Stoddard's old buildings, three stories of ivy-masked brick. Its front had broad stone steps that led up the main entrance. At either side of the building were steps leading down to a long corridor which cut straight through the basement, where the supply room was located. There was a Yale lock on the supply room door. Keys to this lock were in the possession of the usual university functionaries, the entire faculty of the College of Pharmacy, and those advanced students who had received permission to work without supervision. This was the regular arrangement followed in all departments of the university which used enough equipment to necessitate the maintenance of a supply room. It was an arrangement familiar to almost everyone on campus.

He came in at the main entrance and crossed the hall to the lounge. Two bridge games were in session and some other students sat around, reading and talking. A few of them glanced up when he entered. He went directly to the long clothes rack in the corner and put his books on the shelf above it. Removing his corduroy jacket, he hung it on one of the hooks. He took the pack of envelopes from among his books, removed three of them and folded them into his hip pocket. He put the rest of the envelopes back with the books, took the lab manual, and left the room.

He went downstairs to the basement corridor. There was a men's room to the right of the stairwell. He entered it and after looking under the doors to make sure the booths were empty, dropped the manual on the floor. He stepped on it a few times and then kicked it all the way across the tiled floor. When he picked it up it had lost its blatant newness. He put it on the ledge of a sink. Watching himself in the mirror, he unbuttoned the cuffs of his shirt and rolled the sleeves halfway up his arms. He unfastened his collar and lowered the knot of his tie. Tucking the manual under his arm, he stepped out into the corridor.

The door to the supply room was midway between the central stairwell and one end of the corridor. On the wall a few feet beyond it was a bulletin board. He walked down to the board and stood before it, looking at the notices tacked there. He stood with his back turned slightly towards the end of the corridor, so that from the corner of his eye he could see the stairwell. He held the manual under his left arm. His right arm was at his side, fingers by his keychain.

A girl came out of the supply room, closing the door behind her. She carried one of the green manuals and a beaker half full of a milky fluid. He watched her as she went down the corridor and turned to climb the stairs.

Some people entered from the door behind him. They walked past, talking. Three men. They went straight down the corridor and out the door at the other end. He kept looking at the bulletin board.

At five o'clock bells rang, and for a few minutes there was a great deal of activity in the hallway. It subsided quickly though, and he was alone again. One of the notices on the board was an illustrated folder about summer sessions at the University of Zurich. He began to read it.

A bald-headed man emerged from the stairwell. He had no manual, but it was apparent from the angle at which he approached and the movement of his hand towards his keychain that he was coming to the supply room. There was, however, the look of an instructor . . . Putting his back towards the approaching man, he turned a page of the Zurich pamphlet. He heard the sound of a key in the door, and then the door opening and closing. A minute later, it opened and closed again, and the sound of the man's footsteps diminished and then changed to a stair-climbing rhythm.

He resumed his former position and lighted a cigarette. After one puff he dropped it and ground it under his foot; a girl had appeared, coming towards him. There was a lab manual in her hand. She had lanky brown hair and horn-rimmed glasses. She was taking a brass key from the pocket of her smock.

He lessened the pressure on the manual under his arm, letting it drop down into his left hand, conspicuous with its green cover. With a last casual finger-flick at the Zurich folder, he moved to the supply room door, not looking at the approaching girl. He fumbled with his keychain as though the keys had caught in the pocket's lining. When he finally brought out the bunch of keys the girl was already at the door. His attention was on the keys, shuffling through them, apparently looking for a certain one. It seemed as though he didn't become conscious of the girl's presence until she had inserted her key in the lock, turned it and pushed the door partially open, smiling up at him. "Oh . . . thanks," he said, reaching over her to push the door wide, his other hand tucking the keys back in his pocket. He followed the girl in and closed the door behind them.

It was a small room with counters and shelves filled with labeled bottles and boxes and odd-looking apparatuses. The girl touched a wall switch, making fluorescent tubes wink to life, incongruous among the room's old-fashioned fittings. She went to the side of the room and opened her manual on a counter there. "Are you in Aberson's class?" she asked.

He went to the opposite side. He stood with his back to the girl, facing a wall of bottles. "Yes," he said.

Faint clinkings of glass and metal sounded in the room. "How's his arm?"

"About the same, I guess," he said. He touched the bottles, pushing them against each other, so that the girl's curiosity should not be aroused.

"Isn't that the craziest thing?" she said. "I hear he's practically blind without his glasses." She lapsed into silence.

Each bottle had a white label with black lettering. A few bore an additional label that glared POISON in red. He scanned the rows of bottles quickly, his mind registering only the red-labeled ones. The list was in his pocket, but the names he had written on it shimmered in the air before him as though printed on a gauze screen.

He found one. The bottle was a bit above eye level, not two feet from where he stood. *White Arsenic*—$As_4O_6$—POISON. It was half filled with white powder. His hand moved towards it, stopped.

He turned slowly until he could see the girl from the corner of his eye. She was pouring some yellow powder from the tray of a balance into a glass cup. He turned back to the wall and opened his manual on the counter. He looked at meaningless pages of diagrams and instructions.

At last the girl's movements took on sounds of finality; the balance being put away, a drawer closing. He leaned more closely over the manual, following the lines of print with a careful finger. Her footsteps moved to the door. "So long," she said.

"So long."

The door opened and closed. He looked around. He was alone.

He took his handkerchief and the envelopes from his pocket. With the handkerchief draped over his right hand, he lifted the arsenic bottle from the shelf, put it on the counter and removed the stopper. The powder was like flour. He poured about a tablespoonful into the envelope; it fell in whispering puffs. He folded the envelope into a tight pack, folded that into a second envelope and pocketed it. After he had stoppered and replaced the bottle, he moved slowly around the room, reading the labels on drawers and boxes, the third envelope held open in his hand.

He found what he wanted within several minutes: a box filled with empty gelatin capsules, glittering like oval bubbles. He took six of them, to be on the safe side. He put them in the third envelope and slipped it gently into his pocket, so as not to crush the capsules. Then, when everything appeared as he had found it, he took the manual from the counter, turned out the lights, and left the room.

After retrieving his books and his jacket, he left the campus again. He felt wonderfully secure; he had devised a course of action and had executed its initial steps with speed and precision. Of course it was still only a tentative plan and he was in no way committed to carry it through to its goal. He would see how the next steps worked out. The police would never believe that Dorrie had taken a lethal dose of arsenic by accident. It would have to look like suicide, like obvious, indisputable suicide. There would have to be a note or something equally convincing. Because if they ever suspected that it wasn't suicide and started an investigation, the girl who had let him into the supply room would always be able to identify him.

He walked slowly, conscious of the fragile capsules in the left-hand pocket of his trousers.

He met Dorothy at eight o'clock. They went to the Uptown, where the Joan Fontaine picture was still playing.

The night before, Dorothy had been anxious to go; her world had been as gray as the pills he had given her. But tonight—tonight everything was radiant. The promise of immediate marriage had swirled away her problems the way a fresh wind swirls away dead leaves; not only the looming problem of her pregnancy, but all the problems she had ever had; the loneliness, the insecurity. The only hint of gray remaining was the inevitable day when her father, having already been appalled by a hasty unquestioning marriage, would learn the truth about its cause. But even that seemed of trifling importance tonight. She had always hated his unyielding morality and had defied it only in secrecy and guilt. Now she would be able to display her defiance openly, from the security of a husband's arms. Her father would make an ugly scene of it, but in her heart she looked forward to it a little.

She envisioned a warm and happy life in the trailer camp, still warmer and happier when the baby came. She was impatient with the motion picture, which distracted her from a reality more beautiful than any movie could ever be.

He, on the other hand, had not wanted to see the picture on the previous night. He was not fond of movies, and he especially disliked pictures that were founded on exaggerated emotions. Tonight, however, in comfort and darkness, with his arm about Dorothy and his hand resting lightly on the upper slope of her breast, he relished the first moments of relaxation he had known since Sunday night, when she had told him she was pregnant.

He surrendered all his attention to the picture, as though answers to eternal mysteries were hidden in the windings of its plot. He enjoyed it immensely.

Afterwards he went home and made up the capsules.

He funneled the white powder from a folded sheet of paper into the tiny gelatin cups, and then fitted the slightly larger cups that were the other halves of the capsules over them. It took him almost an hour, since he ruined two capsules, one squashed and the other softened by the moisture of his fingers, before he was able to complete two good ones.

When he was finished, he took the damaged capsules and the remaining capsules and powder into the bathroom and flushed them down the toilet. He did the same with the paper from which he had poured the arsenic and the envelopes in which he had carried it, first tearing them into small pieces. Then he put the two arsenic capsules into a fresh envelope and hid them in the bottom drawer of his bureau, under the pajamas and the Kingship Copper pamphlets, the sight of which brought a wry smile to his face.

One of the books he had read that afternoon had listed the lethal dose of arsenic as varying from one tenth to one half of a gram. By rough computation, he estimated that the two capsules contained a total of five grams.

## 6

HE FOLLOWED HIS regular routine on Wednesday, attending all his classes, but he was no more a part of the life and activity that surrounded him than is the diver in his diving bell a part of the alien world in which he is submerged. All of his energies were turned inward, focused on the problem of beguiling Dorothy into writing a suicide note or, if that could not be contrived, finding some other way to make her death seem self-induced. While in this state of labored concentration he unconsciously dropped the pretense of being undecided as to whether or not he would actually go through with his plans; he was going to kill her; he had the poison and he already knew how he was going to administer it; there was only this one problem left, and he was determined to solve it. At times during the day, when a loud voice or the chalk's screech made him momentarily aware of his surroundings, he looked at his classmates with mild surprise. Seeing their brows contracted over a stanza in Browning or a sentence in Kant, he felt as though he had suddenly come upon a group of adults playing hopscotch.

A Spanish class was his last of the day, and the latter half of it was devoted to a short unannounced examination. Because it was his poorest subject, he forced himself to lower the focus of his concentration to the translating of a page of the florid Spanish novel which the class was studying.

Whether the stimulus was the actual work he was doing or the comparative relaxation which the work offered after a day of more rigorous thinking, he could not say. But in the midst of his writing the idea came to him. It rose up fully formed, a perfect plan, unlikely to fail and unlikely to arouse Dorothy's suspicion. The contemplation of it so occupied his mind that when the period ended he had completed only half the assigned page. The inevitable failing mark in the quiz troubled him very little. By ten o'clock the following morning Dorothy would have written her suicide note.

That evening, his landlady having gone to an Eastern Star meeting, he brought Dorothy back to his room. During the two hours they spent there, he was as warm and tender as she had ever wished him to be. In many ways he liked her a great deal, and he was conscious of the fact that this was to be her last such experience.

Dorothy, noticing his new gentleness and devotion, attributed it to the nearness of their wedding. She was not a religious girl, but she deeply believed that the state of wedlock carried with it something of holiness.

Afterwards they went to a small restaurant near the campus. It was a quiet place and not popular with the students; the elderly proprietor, despite the pains he took to decorate his windows with blue and white crepe paper and Stoddard pennants, was irascible with the noisy and somewhat destructive university crowd.

Seated in one of the blue-painted wall booths, they had cheeseburgers and chocolate malteds, while Dorothy chattered on about a new type of bookcase that opened out into a full-size dining table. He nodded unenthusiastically, waiting for a pause in the monologue.

"Oh, by the way," he said, "do you still have that picture I gave you? The one of me?"

"Of course I do."

"Well let me have it back for a couple of days. I want to have a copy made to send to my mother. It's cheaper than getting another print from the studio."

She took a green wallet from the pocket of the coat folded on the seat beside her. "Have you told your mother about us?"

"No, I haven't."

"Why not?"

He thought for a moment. "Well, as long as you can't tell your family until after, I thought I wouldn't tell my mother. Keep it our secret." He smiled. "You haven't told anyone, have you?"

"No," she said. She was holding a few snapshots she had taken from the wallet. He looked at the top one from across the table. It was of Dorothy and two other girls,—her sisters, he supposed. Seeing his glance, she passed the picture to him. "The middle one is Ellen, and Marion's on the end."

The three girls were standing in front of a car, a Cadillac, he noticed. The sun was behind them, their faces shadowed, but he could still discern a resemblance among them. All had the same wide eyes and prominent cheekbones. Ellen's hair seemed to be of a shade midway between Dorothy's light and Marion's dark. "Who's the prettiest?" he asked. "After you, I mean."

"Ellen," Dorothy said. "And before me. Marion could be very pretty too, only she wears her hair like this." She pulled her hair back severely and frowned. "She's the intellectual. Remember?"

"Oh. The Proust fiend."

She handed him the next snapshot, which was of her father. "Grrrrr," he growled, and they both laughed. Then she said, "And this is my fiancé," and passed him his own picture.

He looked at it speculatively, seeing the symmetry of the clear planes. "I don't know," he drawled, rubbing his chin. "Looks kind of dissolute to me."

"But so handsome," she said. "So very handsome." He smiled and pocketed the picture with a satisfied air. "Don't lose it," she warned seriously.

"I won't." He looked around, his eyes bright. On the wall next to them was a selector for the jukebox at the rear of the restaurant. "Music," he announced, producing a nickel and dropping it into the slot. He traced a finger up and down the twin rows of red buttons as he read the names of the songs. He paused at the button opposite *Some Enchanted Evening*, which was one of Dorothy's favorites, but then his eyes caught *On Top of Old Smoky* further down the row, and he thought a moment and chose that instead. He pushed the button. The jukebox bloomed into life, casting a pink radiance on Dorothy's face.

She looked at her wristwatch, then leaned back, eyes closed rapturously. "Oh gee, just think . . ." she murmured, smiling. "Next week no rushing back to the dorm!" Introductory guitar chords sounded from the jukebox. "Shouldn't we put in an application for one of the trailers?"

"I was down there this afternoon," he said. "It may take a couple of weeks. We can stay at my place. I'll speak to my landlady." He took a paper napkin and began tearing careful bits from its folded edges.

A girl's voice sang:

*On top of old Smoky,*
*All covered with snow,*
*I lost my true loved one,*
*For courtin' too slow . . .*

"Folk songs," Dorothy said, lighting a cigarette. The flame glinted on the copper-stamped matchbook.

"The trouble with you," he said, "is you're a victim of your aristocratic upbringing."

*Now courtin's a pleasure,*
*But partin's a grief,*
*And a falsehearted lover*
*Is worse than a thief . . .*

"Did you take the blood test?"

"Yes. I did that this afternoon too."

"Don't I have to take one?"

"No."

"I looked in the Almanac. It said 'blood test required' for Iowa. Wouldn't that mean for both?"

"I asked. You don't have to." His fingers picked precisely at the napkin.

*A thief he will rob you,*
*And take what you have,*
*But a false-hearted lover*
*Will lead you to the grave . . .*

"It's getting late . . ."

"Just let's stay to the end of the record, okay? I like it." He opened the napkin; the torn places multiplied symmetrically and the paper became a web of intricate lace. He spread his handiwork on the table admiringly.

*The grave will decay you,*
*And turn you to dust.*
*Not one man in a hundred*
*A poor girl can trust . . .*

"See what we women have to put up with?"

"A pity. A real pity. My heart bleeds."

Back in his room, he held the photograph over an ashtray and touched a lighted match to its lowest corner. It was a print of the yearbook photo and a good picture of him; he hated to burn it, but he had written "To Dorrie, with all my love" across the bottom of it.

## 7

AS USUAL SHE was late for the nine o'clock class. Sitting in the back of the room, he watched the rows of seats fill up with students. It was raining outside and ribbons of water sluiced down the wall of windows. The seat on his left was still empty when the lecturer mounted the platform and began talking about the City Manager form of government.

He had everything in readiness. His pen was poised over the notebook opened before him and the Spanish novel, *La Casa de las Flores Negras,* was balanced on his knee. A sudden heart-stopping thought hit him; what if she picked today to cut? Tomorrow was Friday, the deadline. This was the only chance he would have to get the note, and he had to have it by tonight. What would he do if she cut?

At ten past nine, though, she appeared; out of breath, her books in one arm, her raincoat over the other, a smile for him lighting her face the moment she eased through the door. Tiptoeing across the room behind him, she draped the raincoat over the back of her chair and sat down. The smile was still there as she sorted her books, keeping a notebook and a small assignment pad before her and putting the remaining books in the aisle between their seats.

Then she saw the book that he held open on his knee, and her eyebrows lifted questioningly. He closed the book, keeping his finger between the pages, and tilted it towards her so that she could see the title. Then he opened it again and with his pen ruefully indicated the two exposed pages and his notebook, meaning that that was how much translation he had to do. Dorothy shook her head condolingly. He pointed to the lecturer and to her notebook—she should take notes and he would copy them later. She nodded.

After he had worked for a quarter of an hour, carefully following the words of the novel, slowly writing in his notebook, he glanced cautiously at Dorothy and saw that she was intent on her own work. He tore a piece of paper about two inches square from the corner of one of the notebook's pages. One side of it he covered with doodling; words written and crossed out, spirals and zigzagging lines. He turned that side downward. With a finger stabbing the print of the novel, he began shaking his head and tapping his foot in impatient perplexity.

Dorothy noticed. Inquiringly, she turned to him. He looked at her and expelled a troubled sigh. Then he lifted his finger in a gesture that asked her to wait a moment before returning her attention to the lecturer. He began to write, squeezing words onto the small piece of paper, words that he was apparently copying from the novel. When he was through, he passed the paper to her.

*Traducción, por favor,* he had headed it. Translation, please:

> *Querido,*
> *Espero que me perdonares por la infelicidad que causaré. No hay ninguna otra cosa que puedo hacer.*

She gave him a mildly puzzled glance, because the sentences were quite simple. His face was expressionless, waiting. She picked up her pen and turned the paper over, but the back of it was covered with doodling. So she tore a page from her assignment pad and wrote on that.

She handed him the translation. He read it and nodded. "*Muchas gracias,*" he whispered. He hunched forward and wrote in his notebook. Dorothy crumpled the paper on which he had written the Spanish and dropped it to the floor. From the corner of his eye he saw it land. There was another bit of paper near it, and some cigarette butts. At the end of the day they would all be swept together and burned.

He looked at the paper again, at Dorothy's small slanted handwriting:

*Darling,*

*I hope you will forgive me for the unhappiness that I will cause. There is nothing else that I can do.*

He tucked the paper carefully into the pocket on the inner cover of the notebook, and closed it. He closed the novel and placed it on top of the notebook. Dorothy turned, looked at the books and then at him. Her questioning glance asked if he were finished.

He nodded and smiled.

They were not to see each other that evening. Dorothy wanted to wash and set her hair and pack a small valise for their weekend honeymoon at the New Washington House. But at eight-thirty the phone on her desk rang.

"Listen, Dorrie. Something's come up. Something important."

"What do you mean?"

"I've got to see you right away."

"But I can't. I can't come out. I just washed my hair."

"Dorrie, this is important."

"Can't you tell me now?"

"No. I have to see you. Meet me at the bench in half an hour."

"It's *drizzling* out. Can't you come to the lounge downstairs?"

"No. Listen, you know that place where we had the cheeseburgers last night? Gideon's? Well, meet me there. At nine."

"I don't see why you can't come to the lounge . . ."

"Baby, please . . ."

"Is—is it anything to do with tomorrow?"

"I'll explain everything at Gideon's."

"Is it?"

"Well, yes and no. Look, everything's going to be all right. I'll explain everything. You just be there at nine."

"All right."

At ten minutes of nine he opened the bottom drawer of his bureau and took two envelopes from under the pajamas. One envelope was stamped, sealed, and addressed:

*Miss Ellen Kingship*
*North Dormitory*
*Caldwell College*
*Caldwell, Wisconsin*

He had typed the address that afternoon in the Student Union lounge, on one of the typewriters available for general student use. In the envelope was the note that Dorothy had written in class that morning. The other envelope contained the two capsules.

He put one envelope in each of the inner pockets of his jacket, taking care to remember which envelope was on which side. Then he put on his trenchcoat, belted it securely, and with a final glance in the mirror, left the room.

When he opened the front door of the house he was careful to step out with his right foot forward, smiling indulgently at himself as he did so.

## 8

GIDEON'S WAS PRACTICALLY empty when he arrived. Only two booths were occupied; in one, a pair of elderly men sat frozen over a chessboard; in the other, across the room, Dorothy sat with her hands clasped around a cup of coffee, gazing down at it as though it were a crystal ball. She had a white kerchief tied about her head. The hair that showed in front was a series of flattened damp-darkened rings, each transfixed by a bobby pin.

She became aware of him only when he was standing at the head of the booth taking off his coat. Then she looked up, her brown eyes worried. She had no make-up on. Her pallor and the closeness of her hair made her seem younger. He put his coat on a hook beside her raincoat and eased into the seat opposite her. "What is it?" she asked anxiously.

Gideon, a sunken cheeked old man, came to their table. "What's yours?"

"Coffee."

"Just coffee?"

"Yes."

Gideon moved away, his slippered feet dragging audibly. Dorothy leaned forward. "What is it?"

He kept his voice low, matter-of-fact. "When I got back to my place this afternoon there was a message for me. Hermy Godsen called."

Her hands squeezed tighter around the coffee cup. "Hermy Godsen . . ."

"I called him back." He paused for a moment, scratching the tabletop. "He made a mistake with those pills the other day. His uncle—" He cut off as Gideon approached with a cup of coffee rattling in his hand. They sat motionless, eyes locked, until the old man was gone. "His uncle switched things around in the drugstore or something. Those pills weren't what they were supposed to be."

"What were they?" She sounded frightened.

"Some kind of emetic. You said you threw up." Lifting his cup, he put a paper napkin in the saucer to absorb the coffee that Gideon's shaking hand had spilled. He pressed the bottom of the cup into the napkin to wipe it.

She breathed relief. "Well that's all *over* with. They didn't hurt me. The way you spoke on the phone, you got me so worried . . ."

"That's not the point, baby." He put the soggy napkin to one side. "I saw Hermy just before I called you. He gave me the right pills, the ones we should have had last time."

Her face sagged. "No . . ."

"Well there's nothing tragic. We're right where we were Monday, that's all. It's a second chance. If they work, everything's rosy. If not, we can still get married tomorrow." He stirred his coffee slowly, watching it swirl. "I've got them with me. You can take them tonight."

"But . . ."

"But what?"

"I don't *want* a second chance. I don't *want* any more *pills* . . ." She leaned forward, hands knotted white on the table. "All I've been thinking about is tomorrow, how wonderful, how happy . . ." She closed her eyes, the lids pressing out tears.

Her voice had risen. He glanced across the room to where the chess players sat with Gideon watching. Fishing a nickel from his pocket, he pushed it into the jukebox selector and jabbed one of the buttons. Then he clasped her clenched hands, forced them open, held them. "Baby, baby," he soothed, "do we have to go through it all again? It's you I'm thinking of. You, not me."

"No." She opened her eyes, staring at him. "If you were thinking of me you'd want what I want." Music blared up, loud brassy jazz.

"What *do* you want, baby? To starve? This is no movie; this is real."

"We *wouldn't* starve. You're making it worse than it would be. You'd get a good job even if you didn't finish school. You're smart, you're—"

"You don't know," he said flatly. "You just don't know. You're a kid who's been rich all her life."

Her hands tried to clench within his. "Why must everyone always throw that at me? Why must *you*? Why do you think that's so important?"

"It is important, Dorrie, whether you like it or not. Look at you, —a pair of shoes to match every outfit, a handbag to match every pair of shoes. You were brought up that way. You can't—"

"Do you think that matters? Do you think I care?" She paused. Her hands relaxed, and when she spoke again the anger in her voice had softened to a straining earnestness. "I know you smile at me sometimes, at the movies I like . . . at my being romantic . . . Maybe it's because you're five years older than I am, or because you were in the Army, or because you're a man,—I don't know . . . But I believe, I truly believe, that if two people really love each other . . . the way I love you . . . the way you say you love me . . . then nothing else matters very much . . . money, things like that, they just don't matter. I believe that . . . I really do . . ." Her hands pulled away from his and flew to her face.

He drew a handkerchief from his breast pocket and touched it to the back of her hand. She took it and held it against her eyes. "Baby, I believe that too. You know I do," he said gently. "Do you know what I did today?" He paused. "Two things. I bought a wedding ring for you, and I put a classified ad in the Sunday *Clarion.* An ad for a job. Night work." She patted her eyes with the handkerchief. "Maybe I did paint things too black. Sure, we'll manage to get along, and we'll be happy. But let's be just a *little* realistic, Dorrie. We'll be even happier if we can get married this summer with your father's approval. You can't deny that. And all you have to do for us to have a chance at that extra happiness is just take these pills." He reached into his inner pocket and brought out the envelope, pressing it to make sure it was the right one. "There isn't one logical reason why you should refuse."

She folded the handkerchief and turned it in her hands, looking at it. "Since Tuesday morning I've been dreaming about tomorrow. It changed everything . . . the whole world." She pushed the handkerchief over to him. "All my life I've been arranging things to suit my father."

"I know you're disappointed, Dorrie. But you've got to think of the future." He extended the envelope to her. Her hands, folded on the table, made no move to accept it. He put it on the table between them, a white rectangle slightly swollen by the capsules inside. "I'm prepared to take a night job now, to quit school at the end of this term. All I'm asking you to do is to swallow a couple of pills."

Her hands remained folded, her eyes on the sterile whiteness of the envelope.

He spoke with cool authority: "If you refuse to take them, Dorothy, you're being stubborn, unrealistic, and unfair. Unfair more to yourself than to me."

The jazz record ended, the colored lights died, and there was silence.

They sat with the envelope between them.

Across the room there was the whisper of a chessman being placed and an old man's voice said "Check."

Her hands parted slightly and he saw the glisten of sweat in her palms. His own hands were sweating too, he realized. Her eyes lifted from the envelope to meet his.

"Please, baby . . ."

She looked down again, her face rigid.

She took the envelope. She pushed it into the handbag on the bench beside her and then sat gazing at her hands on the table.

He reached across the table and touched her hand, caressed the back of it, clasped it. With his other hand he pushed his untouched coffee over to her. He watched her lift the cup and drink. He found another nickel in his pocket and, still holding her hand, dropped the coin into the selector and pressed the button opposite *Some Enchanted Evening.*

They walked the wet concrete paths in silence, divorced by the privacy of their thoughts, holding hands through habit. The rain had stopped, but face-tingling moisture filled the air, defining the scope of each streetlamp in shifting gray.

Across the street from the dorm, they kissed. Her lips under his were cool and compressed. When he tried to part them she shook her head. He held her for a few minutes, whispering persuasively, and then they exchanged goodnights. He watched as she crossed the street and passed into the yellow-lighted hall of the building.

He went to a nearby bar, where he drank two glasses of beer and tore a paper napkin into a delicate filigreed square of admirable detail. When half an hour had passed, he stepped into the telephone booth and dialed the number of the dorm. He asked the girl at the switchboard for Dorothy's room.

She answered after two rings. "Hello?"

"Hello, Dorrie?" Silence at her end. "Dorrie, did you do it?"

A pause. "Yes."

"When?"

"A few minutes ago."

He drew a deep breath. "Baby, does that girl on the switchboard ever listen in?"

"No. They fired the last girl for—"

"Well listen, I didn't want to tell you before, but . . . they might hurt a little." She said nothing. He continued, "Hermy said you'll probably throw up, like before. And you might get a sort of burning sensation in your throat and some pains in your stomach. Whatever happens, don't get frightened. It'll just mean that the pills are working. Don't call anyone." He paused, waiting for her to say something, but she was silent. "I'm sorry I didn't tell you before but, well, it won't hurt too much. And it'll be over before you know it." A pause. "You're not angry with me, are you, Dorrie?"

"No."

"You'll see, it'll all be for the best."

"I know. I'm sorry I was stubborn."

"That's all right, baby. Don't apologize."

"I'll see you tomorrow."

"Yes."

There was silence for a moment and then she said, "Well, good night."

"Good-by, Dorothy," he said.

## 9

STRIDING INTO THE classroom Friday morning he felt weightless and tall and wonderful. It was a beautiful day; sunlight poured into the room and bounced off the metal chairs to spangle the walls and ceiling. Taking his seat in the back of the room, he stretched his legs all the way out and folded his hands across his chest, watching the other students crowd in. The morning's radiance had inflamed them all, and tomorrow was the first Varsity baseball game, with the Spring Dance in the evening; there was chattering, shouting, grinning and laughter.

Three girls stood off to the side and whispered excitedly. He wondered if they were dorm girls, if they could possibly be talking about Dorothy. She couldn't have been found yet. Why would anyone enter her room? They would think she wanted to sleep late. He was counting on her not being found for several hours; he held his breath until the girls' whispering erupted into laughter.

No, it was unlikely that she would be found before one o'clock or so. "Dorothy Kingship wasn't at breakfast and she wasn't at lunch either"—then they would knock on her door and get no answer. They'd most likely have to get the house mother or someone with a key. Or it might not even happen then. Many of the dorm girls slept through breakfast, and some of them ate lunch out occasionally. Dorrie hadn't had any close friends who would miss her right away. No, if his luck held, they might not find her until Ellen's phone call came.

The night before, after saying good-by to Dorothy on the telephone, he had returned to the dorm. In the mailbox on the corner he had posted the envelope addressed to Ellen Kingship, the envelope containing Dorothy's suicide note. The first mail collection of the morning was at six; Caldwell was only a hundred miles away and so the letter would be delivered this afternoon. If Dorothy were found in the morning, Ellen, notified by her father, might leave Caldwell for Blue River before the letter arrived, which would mean that an investigation of some sort would almost certainly be launched, because the suicide note would not be found until Ellen returned to Caldwell. It was the only risk, but it was a small one and unavoidable; it had been impossible for him to sneak into the Girls' Dormitory to plant the note in Dorothy's room, and impractical to secrete it in the pocket of her coat or in one of her books prior to giving her the pills, in which case there would have been the far greater risk of Dorothy finding the note and throwing it away or, still worse, putting two and two together.

He had decided upon noon as the safety mark. If Dorothy were found after twelve, Ellen would have received the note by the time the school authorities contacted Leo Kingship and Kingship in turn contacted her. If his luck *really* held, Dorothy would not be discovered until late afternoon, a frantic phone call from Ellen leading to the discovery. Then everything would be neat and in its proper order.

There would be an autopsy, of course. It would reveal the presence of a great deal of arsenic and a two-month embryo—the way and the why of her suicide. That and the note would more than satisfy the police. Oh, they would make a perfunctory check of the local drugstores, but it would net them only a fat zero. They might even consider the Pharmacy supply room. They would ask the students, "Did you see this girl in the supply room or anywhere in the Pharmacy Building?"—displaying photograph of the deceased. Which would produce another zero. It would be a mystery, but hardly an important one; even if they couldn't be sure of the source of the arsenic, her death would still be an indisputable suicide.

Would they look for the man in the case, the lover? He considered that unlikely. For all they knew she was as promiscuous as a bunny. That was hardly their concern. But what about Kingship? Would outraged morality inaugurate a private inquiry? "Find the man who ruined my daughter!" Although, from the description of her father that Dorothy had painted, Kingship would be more likely to think "Aha, she was ruined all along. Like mother, like daughter." Still, there might be an inquiry . . .

He would certainly be dragged into that. They had been seen together, though not as frequently as might be expected. In the beginning, when success with Dorothy had been in question, he had not taken her to popular places; there had been that other rich girl last year, and if Dorothy didn't work out as he planned there would be others in the future; he didn't want the reputation of a money-chaser. Then, when Dorothy did work out, they had gone to movies, to his room, and to quiet places like Gideon's. Meeting at the bench rather than in the dorm lounge had become a custom.

He would be involved in any inquiry all right, but Dorothy hadn't told anyone they were going steady, so other men would be involved too. There was the red-headed one she'd been chatting with outside the classroom the day he first saw her and noticed the copper-stamped *Kingship* on her matches, and the one she'd started knitting argyle socks for, and every man she'd dated once or twice,—they would *all* be brought into it, and then it would be anybody's guess as to who had "ruined" her because all would deny it. And as thorough as the investigation might be, Kingship could never be certain that he hadn't completely overlooked the "guilty" party. There would be suspicion directed at all the men, proof against none.

No, everything would be perfect. There would be no quitting school, no shipping clerk's job, no oppressing wife and child, no vengeful Kingship. Only one tiny shadow . . . Suppose he were pointed out around campus as one of the men who'd gone with Dorothy. Suppose that the girl who had let him into the supply room should see him again, hear who he was, learn that he wasn't a Pharmacy student at all . . . But even that was unlikely, out of twelve thousand students . . . But suppose the very worst happened. Suppose she saw him, remembered, and went to the police. Even then, it would be no evidence. So he was in the supply room. He could make up some kind of excuse and they would have to believe him, because there would still be the note, the note in Dorothy's handwriting. How could they explain . . .

The door at the side of the room opened, creating a draft that lifted the pages of his notebook. He turned to see who it was. It was Dorothy.

Shock burst over him, hot as a wave of lava. He half-rose, blood pushing to his face, his chest a block of ice. Sweat dotted his body and crawled like a million insects. He knew it was written on his face in swollen eyes and burning cheeks, written for her to see, but he couldn't stop it. She was looking at him wonderingly, the door closing behind her. Like any other day; books under her arm, green sweater, plaid skirt. Dorothy. Coming to him, made anxious by his face.

His notebook slapped to the floor. He bent down, seizing the momentary escape. He stayed with his face near the side of the seat, trying to breathe. What happened? Oh God! She didn't take the pills! She couldn't have! She lied! The bitch! The lying goddamned bitch! The note on its way to Ellen . . . Oh Jesus, Jesus!

He heard her sliding into her seat. Her frightened whisper—"*What's wrong? What's the matter?*" He picked up the notebook and sat erect, feeling the blood drain from his face, from his entire body, leaving him dead cold with sweat drops moving. "*What's wrong?*" He looked at her. Like any other day. There was a green ribbon in her hair. He tried to speak but it was as if he were empty inside with nothing to make a sound. "*What is it?*" Students were turning to look. Finally he scraped out, "Nothing . . . I'm all right . . ."

"You're sick! Your face is as gray as . . ."

"I'm all right. It's . . . it's this . . ."—touching his side where she knew he had the Army scar. "It gives me a twinge once in a while . . ."

"God, I thought you were having a heart attack or something," she whispered.

"No. I'm all right." He kept looking at her, trying for one good breath, his hands clutching his knees in rigid restraint. Oh God, what could he do? The bitch! She had planned also, planned to get married!

He saw the anxiety for him melt from her face, a flushed tension replacing it. She ripped a page from her assignment pad, scribbled on it and passed it to him:

*The pills didn't work.*

The liar! The goddamned liar! He crumpled the paper and squeezed it in his hand, fingernails biting into his palm. Think! Think! His danger was so enormous he couldn't grasp it all at once. Ellen would receive the note—when? Three o'clock? Four?—and call Dorothy—"What does this mean? Why did you write this?"—"Write what?"—then Ellen would read the note and Dorothy would recognize it . . . Would she come to him? What explanation could he invent? Or would she see the truth—blurt out the whole story to Ellen—call her father. If she had kept the pills—if she hadn't thrown them away, there would be proof! Attempted murder. Would she take them to a drugstore, have them analyzed? There was no figuring her now. She was an unknown quantity. He'd thought he could predict every little twitch of her god-damned brain, and now . . .

He could feel her looking at him, waiting for some kind of reaction to the words she'd written. He tore paper from his notebook and pulled open his pen. He shielded his hand so she couldn't see how it was shaking. He couldn't write. He had to print, digging the point of the pen so hard that it shredded the surface of the paper. Make it sound natural!

*Okay. We tried, that's all.*
*Now we get married as per*
*schedule.*

He handed it to her. She read it and turned to him, and her face was warm and radiant as the sunlight. He pressed a smile back at her, praying she wouldn't notice the stiffness of it.

It still wasn't too late. People wrote suicide notes and then stalled around before actually doing it. He looked at his watch; 9:20. The earliest Ellen could get the note would be . . . three o'clock. Five hours and forty minutes. No step by step planning now. It would have to be quick, positive. No trickery that counted on her doing a certain thing at a certain time. No poison. How else do people kill themselves? In five hours and forty minutes she must be dead.

## 10

AT TEN O'CLOCK they left the building arm in arm, going out into the crystalline air that rang with the shouts of between-class students. Three girls in cheerleaders' uniforms pushed by, one beating a tin pie pan with a wood spoon, the other two carrying a big sign advertising a baseball pep rally.

"Does your side still hurt you?" Dorothy asked, concerned for his grim expression.

"A little," he said.

"Do you get those twinges often?"

"No. Don't worry." He looked at his watch. "You're not marrying an invalid."

They stepped off the path onto the lawn. "When will we go?" She pressed his hand.

"This afternoon. Around four."

"Shouldn't we go earlier?"

"Why?"

"Well, it'll take time, and they probably close around five or so."

"It won't take long. We just fill out the application for the license and then there's someone right on the same floor who can marry us."

"I'd better bring proof that I'm over eighteen."

"Yes."

She turned to him, suddenly serious, remorse flushing her cheeks. Not even a good liar, he thought. "Are you terribly sorry the pills didn't work?" she asked anxiously.

"No, not terribly."

"You *were* exaggerating, weren't you? About how things will be?"

"Yes. We'll make out okay. I just wanted you to try the pills. For your sake."

She flushed more deeply. He turned away, embarrassed by her transparency. When he looked at her again, the joy of the moment had crowded out her compunctions and she was hugging her arms and smiling. "I *can't* go to my classes! I'm cutting."

"Good. I am too. Stay with me."

"What do you mean?"

"Until we go down to the Municipal Building. We'll spend the day together."

"I can't, darling. Not the whole day. I have to get back to the dorm, finish packing, dress . . . Don't you have to pack?"

"I left a suitcase down at the hotel when I made the reservation."

"Oh. Well you have to dress, don't you. I expect to see you in your blue suit."

He smiled. "Yes ma'am. You can give me *some* of your time, anyway. Until lunch."

"What'll we do?" They sauntered across the lawn.

"I don't know," he said. "Maybe go for a walk. Down to the river."

"In these shoes?" She lifted a foot, displaying a soft leather loafer. "I'd get fallen arches. There's no support in these things."

"Okay," he said, "no river."

"I've got an idea." She pointed to the Fine Arts Building ahead of them. "Let's go to the record room in Fine Arts and listen to some records."

"I don't know, it's such a beautiful day I'd like to stay . . ." He paused as her smile faded.

She was looking beyond the Fine Arts Building to where the needle of station KBRI's transmission tower speared the sky. "The last time I was in the Municipal Building it was to see that doctor," she said soberly.

"It'll be different this time," he said. And then he stopped walking.

"What is it?"

"Dorrie, you're right. Why should we wait until four o'clock? Let's go now!"

"Get married *now?*"

"Well, after you pack and dress and everything. Look, you go back to the dorm now and get ready. What do you say?"

"Oh, yes! Yes! Oh, I wanted to go now!"

"I'll call you up in a little while and tell you when I'll pick you up."

"Yes. Yes." She stretched up and kissed his cheek excitedly. "I love you so much," she whispered.

He grinned at her.

She hurried away, flashing a smile back over her shoulder, walking as fast as she could.

He watched her go. Then he turned and looked again at the KBRI tower, which marked the Blue River Municipal Building; the tallest building in the city; fourteen stories above the hard slabs of the sidewalk.

## 11

HE WENT INTO the Fine Arts Building where a telephone booth was jammed under the slope of the main stairway. Calling Information, he obtained the number of the Marriage License Bureau.

"Marriage License Bureau."

"Hello. I'm calling to find out what hours the Bureau is open today."

"Till noon and from one to five-thirty."

"Closed between twelve and one?"

"That's right."

"Thank you." He hung up, dropped another coin into the phone and dialed the dorm. When they buzzed Dorothy's room there was no answer. He replaced the receiver, wondering what could have detained her. At the rate she had been walking she should have been in her room already.

He had no more change, so he went out and crossed the campus to a luncheonette, where he broke a dollar bill and glared at the girl who occupied the phone booth. When she finally abdicated he stepped into the perfume-smelling booth and closed the door. This time Dorothy answered.

"Hello?"

"Hi. What took you so long? I called a couple of minutes ago."

"I stopped on the way. I had to buy a pair of gloves." She sounded breathless and happy.

"Oh. Listen, it's—twenty-five after ten now. Can you be ready at twelve?"

"Well, I don't know. I want to take a shower . . ."

"Twelve-fifteen?"

"Okay."

"Listen, you're not going to sign out for the week end, are you?"

"I have to. You know the rules."

"If you sign out, you'll have to put down where you're going to be, won't you?"

"Yes."

"Well?"

"I'll put down 'New Washington House.' If the house mother asks, I'll explain to her."

"Look, you can sign out later this afternoon. We have to come back here anyway. About the trailer. We have to come back about that."

"We do?"

"Yes. They said I couldn't make the formal application until we were actually married."

"Oh. Well if we're coming back later, I won't take my valise now."

"No. Take it now. As soon as we're through with the ceremony we'll check in at the hotel and have lunch. It's only a block or so from the Municipal Building."

"Then I might as well sign out now too. I don't see what difference it'll make."

"Look, Dorrie, I don't think the school is exactly crazy about having out-of-town girls running off to get married. Your house mother is sure to slow us up somehow. She'll want to know if your father knows. She'll give you a lecture, try to talk you into waiting until the end of the term. That's what house mothers are there for."

"All right. I'll sign out later."

"That's the girl. I'll be waiting for you outside the dorm at a quarter after twelve. On University Avenue."

"On University?"

"Well you're going to use the side door, aren't you?—leaving with a valise and not signing out."

"That's right. I didn't think of that. Gee, we're practically eloping."

"Just like a movie."

She laughed warmly. "A quarter after twelve."

"Right. We'll be downtown by twelve-thirty."

"Good-by, groom."

"So long, bride."

He dressed meticulously in his navy blue suit, with black shoes and socks, a white-on-white shirt, and a pale blue tie of heavy Italian silk patterned with black and silver fleurs-de-lis. On surveying himself in the mirror, however, he decided that the beauty of the tie was a trifle too conspicuous, and so he changed it for a simple pearl gray knit. Viewing himself again as he refastened his jacket, he wished he could as easily exchange his face, temporarily, for one of less distinctive design. There were times, he realized, when being so handsome was a definite handicap. As a step, at least, in the direction of appearing commonplace, he reluctantly donned his one hat, a dove gray fedora, settling the unfamiliar weight cautiously, so as not to disturb his hair.

At five minutes past twelve he was on University Avenue, across the street from the side of the dorm. The sun was almost directly overhead, hot and bright. In the sultry air the occasional sounds of birds and footfalls and grinding streetcars had a rarefied quality, as though coming from behind a glass wall. He stood with his back to the dorm, staring into the window of a hardware store.

At twelve-fifteen, reflected in the window, he saw the door across the street open and Dorothy's green-clad figure appear. For once in her life she was punctual. He turned. She was looking from right to left, her pivoting glance overlooking him completely. In one white-gloved hand she held a purse, in the other, a small valise covered in tan airplane cloth with wide red stripes. He lifted his arm and in a moment she noticed him. With an eager smile she stepped from the curb, waited for a break in the passing traffic, and came towards him.

She was beautiful. Her suit was dark green, with a cluster of white silk sparkling at the throat. Her shoes and purse were brown alligator, and there was a froth of dark green veil floating in her feathery golden hair. When she reached him, he grinned and took the valise from her hand. "All brides are beautiful," he said, "but you especially."

"*Gracias, señor.*" She looked as though she wanted to kiss him.

A taxicab cruised by and slowed in passing. Dorothy looked at him inquiringly, but he shook his head. "If we're going to economize, we'd better get in practice." He peered down the avenue. In the glittering air a streetcar approached.

Dorothy drank in the world as if she had been indoors for months. The sky was a shell of perfect blue. The campus, unfolding at the front of the dorm and stretching seven blocks down University Avenue, was quiet, shaded by freshly-green trees. A few students walked the paths; others sprawled on the lawns. "Just think," she marveled, "when we come back this afternoon, we'll be married."

The streetcar clattered up and groaned to a halt. They got on.

They sat towards the back of the car, saying little, each enfolded in thoughts. The casual observer would have been uncertain as to whether or not they traveled together.

The lower eight floors of the Blue River Municipal Building were given over to the offices of the city and of Rockwell County, of which Blue River was the county seat. The remaining six floors were rented to private tenants, most of whom were lawyers, doctors and dentists. The building itself was a mixture of modern and classical architecture, a compromise between the functional trend of the thirties and resolute Iowa conservatism. Professors teaching the introductory architecture courses at Stoddard's College of Fine Arts referred to it as an architectural abortion, causing freshmen to laugh self-consciously.

Viewed from above, the building was a hollow square, an airshaft plunging down through the core of it. From the side, setbacks at the eighth and twelfth stories gave it the appearance of three blocks of decreasing size piled one atop the other. Its lines were graceless and stark, its window lintels were traced with factitious Grecian designs, and its three bronze and glass revolving doors were squeezed between giant pillars whose capitals were carved into stylized ears of corn. It was a monstrosity, but on alighting from the streetcar Dorothy turned, paused, and gazed up at it as though it were the cathedral at Chartres.

It was twelve-thirty when they crossed the street, mounted the steps, and pushed through the central revolving door. The marble floored lobby was filled with people going to and from lunch, people hurrying to appointments, people standing and waiting. The sound of voices and the surf of shoes on marble hung susurrant under the vaulted ceiling.

He dropped a pace behind Dorothy, letting her lead the way to the directory board at the side of the lobby. "Would it be under R for Rockwell County or M for Marriage?" she asked, her eyes intent on the board as he came up beside her. He looked at the board as though oblivious of her presence. "There it is," she said triumphantly. "Marriage License Bureau—six-oh-four." He turned towards the elevators, which were opposite the revolving doors. Dorothy hurried along beside him. She reached for his hand but the valise was in it. He apparently did not notice her gesture, for he made no move to change hands.

One of the four elevators stood open, half filled with waiting passengers. As they approached it, he stepped back a bit, allowing Dorothy to enter first. Then an elderly woman came up and he waited until she too had gone in before entering. The woman smiled at him, pleased by his air of gallantry, doubly unexpected from a young man in a busy office building. She seemed a bit disappointed when he failed to remove his hat. Dorothy smiled at him also, over the head of the woman, who had somehow got between them. He returned the smile with an almost invisible curving of his lips.

They left the car at the sixth floor, along with two men with briefcases who turned to the right and walked briskly down the corridor. "Hey, wait for me!" Dorothy protested in an amused whisper as the elevator door clanged shut behind her. She had been the last to leave the car, and he the first. He had turned to the left and walked some fifteen feet, for all the world as though he were alone. He turned, appearing flustered, as she caught up with him and gaily took his arm. Over her head he watched the men with the briefcases reach the other end of the corridor, turn to the right and vanish down the side of the square. "Where you running?" Dorothy teased.

"Sorry," he smiled. "Nervous bridegroom." They walked along arm in arm, following the left turn the corridor made. Dorothy recited the numbers painted on the doors as they passed them. "Six-twenty, six-eighteen, six-sixteen . . ." They had to take another left turn before they reached 604, which was at the back of the square, across from the elevators. He tried the door. It was locked. They read the hours listed on the frosted glass panel and Dorothy moaned dejectedly.

"Damn," he said. "I should have called to make sure." He put down the valise and looked at his watch. "Twenty-five to one."

"Twenty-five minutes," Dorothy said. "I guess we might as well go downstairs."

"Those crowds . . ." he muttered, then paused. "Hey, I've got an idea."

"What?"

"The roof. Let's go up on the roof. It's such a beautiful day, I bet we'll be able to see for miles!"

"Are we allowed?"

"If nobody stops us, we're allowed." He picked up the valise. "Come on, get your last look at the world as an unmarried woman."

She smiled and they began walking, retracing their path around the square to the bank of elevators where, in a few moments, there glowed above one of the doors a white arrow pointing upwards.

When they left the car at the fourteenth floor, it happened again that they were separated by the other alighting passengers. In the corridor, they waited until these had hurried around the turns or into offices, and then Dorothy said "Let's go," in a conspiratorial whisper. She was making an adventure of it.

Again they had to make a half-circuit of the building, until, next to room 1402, they found a door marked *Stairway*. He pushed it open and they entered. The door sighed closed behind them. They were on a landing, with black metal stairs leading up and down. Dim light sifted through a dirt-fogged skylight. They walked upwards; eight steps, a turn, and eight more steps. A door confronted them, heavy reddish-brown metal. He tried the knob.

"Is it locked?"

"I don't think so."

He put his shoulder to the door and pushed.

"You're going to get your suit filthy."

The door rested on a ledge, a sort of giant threshold that raised its bottom a foot above the level of the landing. The ledge jutted out, making it difficult for him to apply his weight squarely. He put down the valise, braced his shoulder against the door and tried again.

"We can go downstairs and wait," Dorothy said. "That door probably hasn't been opened in . . ."

He clenched his teeth. With the side of his left foot jammed against the base of the ledge, he swung back and then smashed his shoulder against the door with all his strength. It gave, groaning open. The chain of a counterweight clattered. A slice of electric blue sky hit their eyes, blinding after the obscurity of the stairway. There was the quick flutter of pigeons' wings.

He picked up the valise, stepped over the ledge, and put the valise down again where it would be clear of the door's swing. Pushing the door further open, he stood with his back to it. He extended one hand to Dorothy. With the other he gestured towards the expanse of roof as a head waiter gestures towards his finest table. He gave her a mock bow and his best smile. "Enter, mam'selle," he said.

Taking his hand, she stepped gracefully over the ledge and onto the black tar of the roof.

## 12

HE WASN'T NERVOUS at all. There had been a moment of near-panic when he couldn't get the door open, but it had dissolved the instant the door had yielded to the force of his shoulder, and now he was calm and secure. Everything was going to be perfect. No mistakes, no intruders. He just *knew* it. He hadn't felt so good since—Jesus, since high school!

He swung the door partly closed, leaving a half inch between it and the jamb, so that it wouldn't give him any trouble when he left. He would be in a hurry then. Bending over, he moved the valise so that he would be able to pick it up with one hand while opening the door with the other. As he straightened up he felt his hat shift slightly with the motion. He took it off, looked at it, and placed it on the valise. Christ, he was thinking of everything! A little thing like the hat would probably louse up somebody else. They would push her over and then a breeze or the force of the movement might send their hat sailing down to land beside her body. Bam! They might as well throw themselves over after it. Not he, though; he had anticipated, prepared. An act of God, the crazy kind of little thing that was always screwing up perfect plans,—and he had anticipated it. Jesus! He ran a hand over his hair, wishing there were a mirror.

"Come look at this."

He turned. Dorothy was standing a few feet away, her back towards him, the alligator purse tucked under one arm. Her hands rested on the waist-high parapet that edged the roof. He came up behind her. "Isn't it something?" she said. They were at the back of the building, facing south. The city sprawled before them, clear and sharp in the brilliant sunlight. "Look"—Dorothy pointed to a green spot far away—"I think that's the campus." He put his hands on her shoulders. A white-gloved hand reached up to touch his.

He had planned to do it quickly, as soon as he got her up there, but now he was going to take it slow and easy, drawing it out as long as he safely could. He was entitled to that, after a week of nerve-twisting tension. Not just a week,—years. Ever since high school it had been nothing but strain and worry and self-doubt. There was no need to rush this. He looked down at the top of her head against his chest, the dark green veiling buoyant in the yellow hair. He blew, making the fine net tremble. She tilted her head back and smiled up at him.

When her eyes returned to the panorama, he moved to her side, keeping one arm about her shoulders. He leaned over the parapet. Two stories below, the red tiled floor of a wide balcony extended like a shelf across the width of the building. The top of the twelfth story setback. It would be on all four sides. That was bad; a two story drop wasn't what he wanted. He turned and surveyed the roof.

It was perhaps a hundred and fifty feet square, edged by the brick parapet whose coping was flat white stone, a foot wide. An identical wall rimmed the airshaft, a square hole some thirty feet across, in the center of the roof. On the left side of the roof was a vast stilt-supported water storage tank. On the right, the KBRI tower reared up like a smaller Eiffel, its girdered pattern black against the sky. The staircase entrance, a slant roofed shed, was in front of him and a bit to his left. Beyond the airshaft, at the north side of the building, was a large rectangular structure, the housing of the elevator machinery. The entire roof was dotted with chimneys and ventilator pipes that stuck up like piers from a tarry sea.

Leaving Dorothy, he walked across to the parapet of the airshaft. He leaned over. The four walls funneled down to a tiny areaway fourteen stories below, its corners banked with trash cans and wooden crates. He looked for a moment, then stooped and pried a rain-faded matchbook from the gummy surface of the roof. He held the folder out beyond the parapet—and dropped it, watching as it drifted down, down, down, and finally became invisible. He glanced at the walls of the shaft. Three were striped with windows. The fourth, which faced him and evidently backed on the elevator shafts, was blank, windowless. This was the spot. The south side of the airshaft. Right near the stairway, too. He slapped the top of the parapet, his lips pursed thoughtfully. Its height was greater than he had anticipated.

Dorothy came up behind him and took his arm. "It's so quiet," she said. He listened. At first there seemed to be absolute silence, but then the sounds of the roof asserted themselves: the throbbing of the elevator motors, a gentle wind strumming the cables that guyed the radio tower, the squeak of a slow-turning ventilator cap . . .

They began walking slowly. He led her around the airshaft and past the elevator housing. As they strolled she brushed his shoulder clean of the dust from the door. When they reached the northern rim of the roof they were able to see the river, and with the sky reflected in it, it was really blue, as blue as the rivers painted on maps. "Do you have a cigarette?" she asked.

He reached into his pocket and touched a pack of Chesterfields. Then his hand came out empty. "No, I don't. Do you have any?"

"They're buried in here someplace." She dug into her purse, pushing aside a gold compact and a turquoise handkerchief, and finally produced a crushed pack of Herbert Tareytons. They each took one. He lit them and she returned the pack to her purse.

"Dorrie, there's something I want to tell you . . ."—she was blowing a stream of smoke against the sky, hardly listening—". . . about the pills."

Her face jerked around, going white. She swallowed. "What?"

"I'm glad they didn't work," he said, smiling. "I really am."

She looked at him uncomprehendingly. "You're glad?"

"Yes. When I called you last night, I was going to tell you not to take them, but you already had." Come on, he thought, confess. Get it off your chest. It must be killing you.

Her voice was shaky. "Why? You were so . . . what made you change your mind?"

"I don't know. I thought it over. I suppose I'm as anxious to get married as you are." He examined his cigarette. "Besides, I guess it's really a sin to do something like that." When he looked up again her cheeks were flushed and her eyes glistened.

"Do you mean that?" she asked breathlessly. "Are you really glad?"

"Of course I am. I wouldn't say it if I weren't."

"Oh, thank God!"

"What's the matter, Dorrie?"

"Please . . . don't be angry. I—I didn't take them." He tried to look surprised. The words poured from her lips: "You said you were going to get a night job and I knew we could manage, everything would work out, and I was counting on it so much, *so* much. I knew I was right." She paused. "You aren't angry, are you?" she beseeched. "You understand?"

"Sure, baby. I'm not angry. I told you I was glad they didn't work."

Her lips made a quivering smile of relief. "I felt like a criminal, lying to you. I thought I would never be able to tell you. I . . . I can't believe it!"

He took the neatly folded handkerchief from his breast pocket and touched it to her eyes. "Dorrie, what did you do with the pills?"

"Threw them away." She smiled shamefacedly.

"Where?" he asked casually, replacing the handkerchief.

"The john."

That was what he wanted to hear. There would be no questions about why she had taken such a messy way out when she had already gone to the trouble of obtaining poison. He dropped his cigarette and stepped on it.

Dorothy, taking a final puff, did the same with hers. "Oh gee," she marveled, "everything's perfect now. Perfect."

He put his hands on her shoulders and kissed her gently on the lips. "Perfect," he said.

He looked down at the two stubs, hers edged with lipstick, his clean. He picked his up. Splitting it down the middle with his thumbnail, he let the tobacco blow away and rolled the paper into a tiny ball. He flicked it out over the parapet. "That's the way we used to do it in the Army," he said.

She consulted her watch. "It's ten to one."

"You're fast," he said, glancing at his. "We've got fifteen minutes yet." He took her arm. They turned and walked leisurely away from the edge of the roof.

"Did you speak to your landlady?"

"Wha—? Oh, yes. It's all set." They passed the elevator housing. "Monday we'll move your stuff from the dorm."

Dorothy grinned. "Will they be surprised, the girls in the dorm." They strolled around the parapet of the airshaft. "Do you think your landlady'll be able to give us some more closet space?"

"I think so."

"I can leave some of my stuff, the winter things, in the attic at the dorm. There won't be too much."

They reached the south side of the airshaft. He stood with his back against the parapet, braced his hands on the top of it, and hitched himself up. He sat with his heels kicking against the side of the wall.

"Don't sit there," Dorothy said apprehensively.

"Why not?" he asked, glancing at the white stone coping. "It's a foot wide. You sit on a bench a foot wide and you don't fall off." He patted the stone on his left. "Come on."

"No," she said.

"Chicken."

She touched her rear. "My suit . . ."

He took out his handkerchief, whipped it open and spread it on the stone beside him. "Sir Walter Raleigh," he said.

She hesitated a moment, then gave him her purse. Turning her back to the parapet, she gripped the top on either side of the handkerchief and lifted herself up. He helped her. "There," he said, putting his arm around her waist. She turned her head slowly, peeking over her shoulder. "Don't look down," he warned. "You'll get dizzy."

He put the purse on the stone to his right and they sat in silence for a moment, her hands still fastened upon the front of the coping. Two pigeons came out from behind the staircase shed and walked around, watching them cautiously, their claws ticking against the tar.

"Are you going to call or write when you tell your mother?" Dorothy asked.

"I don't know."

"I think I'll write Ellen and Father. It's an awfully hard thing to just say over the phone."

A ventilator cap creaked. After a minute, he took his arm from her waist and put his hand over hers, which gripped the stone between them. He braced his other hand on the coping and eased himself down from the parapet. Before she could do likewise he swung around and was facing her, his waist against her knees, his hands covering both of hers. He smiled at her and she smiled back. His gaze dropped to her stomach. "Little mother," he said. She chuckled.

His hands moved to her knees, cupped them, his fingertips caressing under the hem of her skirt.

"We'd better be going, hadn't we, darling?"

"In a minute, baby. We still have time."

His eyes caught hers, held them, as his hands descended and moved behind to rest curving on the slope of her calves. At the periphery of his field of vision he could make out her white-gloved hands; they still clasped the front of the coping firmly.

"That's a beautiful blouse," he said, looking at the fluffy silk bow at her throat. "Is it new?"

"New? It's as old as the hills."

His gaze became critical. "The bow is a little off center."

One hand left the stone and rose to finger the bow. "No," he said, "now you've got it worse." Her other had detached itself from the top of the parapet.

His hands moved down over the silken swell of her calves, as low as he could reach without bending. His right foot dropped back, poised on the toe in readiness. He held his breath.

She adjusted the bow with both hands. "Is that any bett—"

With cobra speed he ducked—hands streaking down to catch her heels—stepped back and straightened up, lifting her legs high. For one frozen instant, as his hands shifted from cupping her heels to a flat grip against the soles of her shoes, their eyes met, stupefied terror bursting in hers, a cry rising in her throat. Then, with all his strength, he pushed against her fear-rigid legs.

Her shriek of petrified anguish trailed down into the shaft like a burning wire. He closed his eyes. The scream died. Silence, then a godawful deafening crash. Wincing, he remembered the cans and crates piled far below.

He opened his eyes to see his handkerchief billowing as the breeze pulled it free of the stone's rough surface. He snatched it up. Wheeling, he raced to the stairway door, grabbed hat and valise with one hand and pulled the door open, wiping the knob with the handkerchief as he did so. He stepped quickly over the threshold ledge, pulled the door closed and wiped its inner knob. He turned and ran.

He clattered down flight after flight of black metal steps, the valise banging against his legs, his right hand burning over the bannisters. His heart galloped and the image of whirling walls dizzied him. When he finally stopped he was on the seventh floor landing.

He clung to the newel post, gasping. The phrase 'physical release of tension' danced in his mind. That was why he had run that way—physical release of tension—not panic, not panic. He caught his breath. Putting down the valise, he reshaped his hat, which had been crushed in his grasp. He put it on, his hands trembling slightly. He looked at them. The palms were dirty gray from the soles of . . . he wiped them clean and jammed the handkerchief into his pocket. After a few straightening tugs at his jacket, he picked up the valise, opened the door, and stepped out into the corridor.

Every door was open. People rushed across the corridor from offices on the outer circumference to those on the inner, where windows faced the airshaft. Men in business suits, stenographers with paper cuffs clipped to their blouses, shirtsleeved men with green eyeshades; all with jaws clenched, eyes wide, faces bloodless. He walked towards the elevators at a moderate pace, pausing when someone darted before him, then continuing on his way. Passing the doorway of each inner office, he glanced in and saw the backs of people crammed around the open windows, their voices a murmur of excitement and tense speculation.

Shortly after he reached the bank of elevators, a down car came. He squeezed in and faced the front of the car. Behind him the other passengers avidly exchanged fragments of information, the customary elevator coldness shattered by the violence at their backs.

The easy bustle of normality filled the lobby. Most of the people there, having just entered from outside, were unaware of any disturbance. Swinging the valise lightly, he made his way across the marbled expanse and out into the bright noisy afternoon. As he jogged down the steps that fronted the building, two policemen passed him, going up. He turned and watched the blue uniforms vanish into a revolving door. At the foot of the steps he paused and examined his hands once again. They were steady as rocks. Not a tremor. He smiled. Turning, he looked at the revolving doors, wondering how dangerous it would be for him to go back, mingle with the crowd, see her . . . He decided against it.

A University streetcar rumbled past. He walked double-time to the corner, where the car was detained by a red light. Swinging himself on, he dropped a dime in the box and walked to the rear of the car. He stood looking out the window. When the car had gone about four blocks, a white ambulance clanged by, the pitch of its bell dropping as it passed. He watched it grow smaller and smaller and finally cut through traffic to pull up in front of the Municipal Building. Then the streetcar turned onto University Avenue, and he could see no more.

## 13

THE BASEBALL PEP rally began at nine that night, taking place on an empty lot next to the stadium, but the news of a student's suicide (for how could she have fallen when the *Clarion* clearly stated there was a three and a half foot wall?) put a damper on the entire affair. In the orange glow of the bonfire, the students, the girls especially, spread their blankets and sat huddled in conversation. The business manager of the baseball team and the members of the cheerleading squad tried vainly to make the rally what it should be. They spurred the boys to the gathering of more and more fuel, throwing on crates and cartons until the flaming pillar was so high it threatened to topple, but it was to no avail. Cheers wavered and died before half the school's name was spelled out.

He had not attended many of the pep rallies before, but he attended this one. He walked the dark streets from his rooming house at a slow liturgic pace, bearing a carton in his arms.

In the afternoon he had emptied Dorothy's valise, hiding her clothes under the mattress of his bed. Then, although it was a warm day, he had donned his trenchcoat, and after filling its pockets with the bottles and small containers of cosmetics that had been lodged among the clothes, he left the house with the valise, from which he had stripped the tags bearing Dorothy's New York and Blue River addresses. He had gone downtown and checked the valise in a locker at the bus terminal. From there he had walked to the Morton Street Bridge, where he dropped the locker key and then the bottles, one by one, into the umber water, opening them first so that trapped air would not keep them afloat. Ghosts of pink lotion rode the water and thinned and faded. On his way home from the bridge he stopped at a grocery store, where he secured a tan corrugated carton that had once contained cans of pineapple juice.

He carried the carton to the rally and picked his way through the mass of squatting and reclining figures orange-sketched in the darkness. Stepping gingerly between blanket corners and blue-jeaned legs, he advanced to the flaming center of the field.

The heat and the glare were intense in the clearing that surrounded the roaring twelve foot fire. He stood for a moment, staring at the flames. Suddenly the baseball manager and a cheerleader came dashing around from the other side of the clearing. "That's it! That's the boy!" they cried, and seized the carton from his hands.

"Hey," the manager said, hefting the box. "This isn't empty."

"Books . . . old notebooks."

"Ah! Magnifico!" The manager turned to the encircling crowd. "Attention! Attention! The burning of the books!" A few people looked up from their conversations. The manager and the cheerleader took the carton between them, swinging it back and forth towards the rippling flames. "All the way to the top!" the manager shouted.

"Hey . . ."

"Don't worry, friend. We never miss! Book-burning a specialty!" They swung the carton; one . . . two . . . *three!* It sailed up parallel to the cone shaped pyre, arced over and landed with a gush of sparks at the very top. It teetered a moment, then held. There was a spattering of applause from the onlookers. "Hey, here comes Al with a packing case!" cried the cheerleader. He dashed around to the other side of the fire, the manager running after him.

He stood watching as the carton turned black, sheets of flame sliding up past its sides. Suddenly the foundation of the fire shifted, pushing out showers of sparks. A flaming brand hit his foot. He jumped back. Sparks glowed all over the front of his trousers. Nervously he slapped them out, his hands coppery in the fire's glare.

When the last sparks were extinguished, he looked up to make certain that the carton was still secure. It was. Flames ripped up through its top. Its contents, he thought, were probably completely burned by now.

These had included the Pharmacy lab manual, the Kingship Copper pamphlets, the tags from the valise, and the few articles of clothing that Dorothy had prepared for their brief honeymoon; a cocktail dress of gray taffeta, a pair of black suede pumps, stockings, a half slip, bra and panties, two handkerchiefs, a pair of pink satin mules, a pink negligee, and a nightgown; silk and lace, delicate, scented, white . . .

## 14

*From the Blue River* Clarion-Ledger; *Friday, April 28, 1950:*

# STODDARD COED DIES IN PLUNGE

### MUNICIPAL BUILDING TRAGEDY FATAL TO DAUGHTER OF COPPER MAGNATE

Dorothy Kingship, 19-year-old Stoddard University sophomore, was killed today when she fell or jumped from the roof of the 14 story Blue River Municipal Building. The attractive blonde girl, whose home was in New York City, was a daughter of Leo Kingship, president of Kingship Copper Inc.

At 12:58 PM, workers in the building were startled by a loud scream and a crashing sound from the wide airshaft which runs through the structure. Rushing to their windows, they saw the contorted figure of a young woman. Dr. Harvey C. Hess, of 57 Woodbridge Circle, who was in the lobby at the time, reached the scene seconds later to pronounce the girl dead.

The police, arriving shortly thereafter, found a purse resting on the 3½ foot wall that encircles the airshaft. In the purse were a birth certificate and a Stoddard University registration card which served to identify the girl. Police also found a fresh cigarette stub on the roof, stained with lipstick of the shade Miss Kingship wore, leading them to conclude that she had been on the roof for several minutes prior to the plunge which ended her life . . .

Rex Cargill, an elevator operator, told police that he took Miss Kingship to the 6th or 7th floor half an hour before the tragedy. Another operator, Andrew Vecci, believes he took a woman dressed similarly to Miss Kingship to the 14th floor shortly after

12:30, but is uncertain of the floor at which she entered his car.

According to Stoddard's Dean of Students, Clark D. Welch, Miss Kingship was doing satisfactory work in all her studies. Shocked residents of the dormitory where she lived could offer no reason why she might have taken her own life. They described her as quiet and withdrawn. "Nobody knew her too well," said one girl.

*From the Blue River* Clarion-Ledger; *Saturday, April 29, 1950:*

# COED'S DEATH WAS SUICIDE

## SISTER RECEIVES NOTE IN MAIL

The death of Dorothy Kingship, Stoddard coed who plunged from the roof of the Municipal Building yesterday afternoon, was a suicide, Chief of Police Eldon Chesser told reporters last night. An unsigned note in a handwriting definitely established to be that of the dead girl was received through the mail late yesterday afternoon by her sister, Ellen Kingship, a student in Caldwell, Wisconsin. Although the exact wording of the note has not been made public, Chief Chesser characterized it as "a clear expression of suicidal intent." The note was mailed from this city, postmarked yesterday at 6:30 AM.

On receiving the note, Ellen Kingship attempted to reach her sister by telephone. The call was transferred to Stoddard's Dean of Students, Clark D. Welch, who informed Miss Kingship of the 19-year-old girl's death. Miss Kingship left immediately for Blue River, arriving here yesterday evening. Her father, Leo Kingship, president of Kingship Copper, Inc., is expected to arrive some time today, his plane having been grounded in Chicago because of bad weather.

# *LAST PERSON TO SPEAK TO SUICIDE DESCRIBES HER AS TENSE, NERVOUS*

*by LaVerne Breen*

"She laughed a lot and was smiling the whole time she was in my room. And she kept moving around. I thought at the time that she was very happy about something, but now I realize that those were all symptoms of the terrible nervous strain she was under. Her laughs were tense laughs, not happy ones. I should have recognized that right away, being a psychology major." Thus Annabelle Koch, Stoddard sophomore, describes the behavior of Dorothy Kingship two hours before the latter's suicide.

Miss Koch, a native of Boston, is a petite and charming young lady. Yesterday she was confined to her dormitory room because of a severe head cold. "Dorothy knocked on the door around a quarter past eleven," says Miss Koch. "I was in bed. She came in and I was a little surprised, because we hardly knew each other. As I said, she was smiling and moving around a great deal. She was wearing a bathrobe. She asked if I would loan her the belt to my green suit. I should mention that we both have the same green suit. I got mine in Boston and she got hers in New York, but they're exactly the same. We both wore them to dinner last Saturday night, and it was really embarrassing. Anyway, she asked if I would loan her my belt because the buckle of hers was broken. I hesitated at first, because it's my new spring suit, but she seemed to want it so badly that I finally told her which drawer it was in and she got it. She thanked me very much and left."

Here Miss Koch paused and removed her eyeglasses. "Now here's the strange part. Later, when the police came and searched her room for a note, *they found my belt on her desk!* I recognized it by the way the gold finish was rubbed off the tooth of the buckle. I had been very disappointed about that, because it was an expensive suit. The police kept the belt.

"I was very puzzled by Dorothy's actions. She had pretended to want my belt, but she hadn't used it at all. She was wearing her green suit when . . . when it happened. The police checked and her belt buckle wasn't the least bit broken. It all seemed very mysterious.

"Then I realized that the belt must have been just a pretext to talk to me. Laying out the suit probably reminded her of me, and everyone knew I was incapacitated with a cold, so she came in and pretended she needed the belt. She must have been desperate for someone to talk with. If only I'd recognized the signs at the time. I can't help feeling that if I had gotten her to talk out her troubles, whatever they might have been, maybe all this wouldn't have happened."

. . . As we left Annabelle Koch's room, she added a final word. "Even when the police return the belt to me," she said, "I know I won't be able to wear my green suit again."

## 15

HE FOUND THE last six weeks of the school year disappointingly flat. He had expected the excitement created by Dorothy's death to linger in the air like the glow of a rocket; instead it had faded almost immediately. He had anticipated more campus conversations and newspaper articles, allowing him the luxuriant superiority of the omniscient; instead—nothing. Three days after Dorothy died campus gossip veered away to pounce on a dozen marijuana cigarettes that had been discovered in one of the smaller dormitories. As for the newspapers, a short paragraph announcing Leo Kingship's arrival in Blue River marked the last time the Kingship name appeared in the *Clarion-Ledger*. No word of an autopsy nor of her pregnancy, although surely when an unmarried girl committed suicide without stating a reason, that must be the first thing they looked for. Keeping it out of the papers must have cost Kingship plenty.

He told himself he should be rejoicing. If there had been any kind of inquiry he certainly would have been sought for questioning. But there had been no questions, no suspicion,—hence no investigation. Everything had fallen into place perfectly. Except that business of the belt. That puzzled him. Why on earth had Dorothy taken that Koch girl's belt when she hadn't wanted to wear it? Maybe she really did want to talk to someone—about the wedding—and then had thought better of it. Thank God for that. Or maybe the buckle of her belt had really been broken, but she had managed to fix it after she had already taken Koch's. Either way, though, it was an unimportant incident. Koch's interpretation of it only strengthened the picture of a suicide, added to the flawless success of his plans. He should be walking on air, smiling at strangers, toasting himself with secret champagne. Instead there was this dull, leaden, let-down feeling. He couldn't understand it.

His depression became worse when he returned to Menasset early in June. Here he was, right where he'd been last summer after the daughter of the farm equipment concern had told him about the boy back home, and the summer before, after he had left the widow. Dorothy's death had been a defensive measure; all his planning hadn't advanced him in the slightest.

He became impatient with his mother. His correspondence from school had been limited to a weekly postcard, and now she badgered him for details; did he have pictures of the girls he'd gone out with? —expecting them to be the most beautiful, the most sought after—Did he belong to this club, to that club?—expecting him to be the president of each—What was his standing in philosophy, in English, in Spanish? —expecting him to be the leader in all. One day he lost his temper. "It's about time you realized I'm not the king of the world!" he shouted, storming from the room.

He took a job for the summer; partly because he needed money, partly because being in the house with his mother all day made him uneasy. The job didn't do any good towards taking his mind off things though; it was in a haberdashery shop whose fixtures were of angular modern design; the glass display counters were bound with inch wide strips of burnished copper.

Towards the middle of July, however, he began to slough off his dejection. He still had the newspaper clippings about Dorothy's death, locked in a small gray strongbox he kept in his bedroom closet. He began taking them out once in a while, skimming through them, smiling at the officious certainty of Chief of Police Eldon Chesser and the half-baked theorizing of Annabelle Koch.

He dug up his old library card, had it renewed, and began withdrawing books regularly; Pearson's *Studies in Murder,* Bolitho's *Murder for Profit,* volumes in the *Regional Murder Series.* He read about Landru, Smith, Pritchard, Crippen; men who had failed where he had succeeded. Of course it was only the failures whose stories got written, —God knows how many successful ones there were. Still it was flattering to consider how many had failed.

Until now he had always thought of what happened at the Municipal Building as "Dorrie's death." Now he began to think of it as "Dorrie's murder."

Sometimes, when he had lain in bed and read several accounts in one of the books, the enormous daring of what he had done would overwhelm him. He would get up and look at himself in the mirror over the dresser. I got away with murder, he would think. Once he whispered it aloud: "I got away with murder!"

So what if he wasn't rich yet! Hell, he was only twenty-four.

# PART TWO: ELLEN

## 1

*Letter from Annabelle Koch to Leo Kingship:*

GIRLS' DORMITORY
STODDARD UNIVERSITY
BLUE RIVER, IOWA
*March 5, 1951*

DEAR MR. KINGSHIP,

*I suppose you are wondering who I am, unless you remember my name from the newspapers. I am the young woman who loaned a belt to your daughter Dorothy last April. I was the last person to speak to her. I would not bring up this subject as I am sure it must be a very painful subject to you, except that I have a good reason.*

*As you may recall Dorothy and I had the same green suit. She came to my room and asked to borrow my belt. I loaned it to her and later the police found it (or what I thought was it) in her room. They kept it for over a month until they got around to returning it to me and by that time it was quite late in the season so I did not wear the green suit again last year.*

*Now spring is approaching again and last night I tried on my spring clothes. I tried on my green suit and it fitted perfectly. But when I put on the belt I found to my surprise that it was Dorothy's belt all along. You see, the notch that is marked from the buckle is two notches too big for my waist. Dorothy was quite slender but I am even more so. In fact to be frank I am quite thin. I know that I certainly did not lose any weight because the suit still fits me perfectly, as I said above, so the belt must be Dorothy's. When the police first showed it to me I thought it was mine because the gold finish on the tooth of the buckle was rubbed off. I should have realized that since both suits were made by the same manufacturer the finish would have come off of both buckles.*

*So now it seems that Dorothy could not wear her own belt for some reason, even though it was not broken at all, and took mine instead. I cannot understand it. At the time I thought she only pretended to need my belt because she wanted to speak to me.*

*Now that I know the belt is Dorothy's I would feel funny wearing it. I am not superstitious, but after all it does not belong to me and it did belong to poor Dorothy. I thought of throwing it away but I would feel funny doing that also, so I am sending it to you in a separate package and you can keep it or dispose of it as you see fit.*

*I can still wear the suit because all the girls here are wearing wide leather belts this year anyway.*

*Yours truly,*
ANNABELLE KOCH

*Letter from Leo Kingship to Ellen Kingship:*

*March 8, 1951*

MY DEAR ELLEN,

*I received your last letter and am sorry not to have replied sooner, but the demands of business have been especially pressing of late.*

*Yesterday being Wednesday, Marion came here to dinner. She is not looking too well. I showed her a letter which I received yesterday and she suggested that I send it on to you. You will find it enclosed. Read it now, and then continue with my letter.*

*Now that you have read Miss Koch's letter, I will explain why I forwarded it.*

*Marion tells me that ever since Dorothy's death you have been rebuking yourself for your imagined callousness to her. Miss Koch's unfortunate story of Dorothy's "desperate need of someone to talk with" made you feel, according to Marion, that that someone should have been you and would have been you, had you not pushed Dorothy out on her own too soon. You believe, although this is something which Marion has only deduced from your letters, that had there been a difference in your attitude towards Dorothy, she might not have chosen the path she did.*

*I credit what Marion says since it explains your wishful thinking, for I can only call it that, of last April, when you stubbornly refused to believe that Dorothy's death had been a suicide, despite the incontestable evidence of the note which you yourself received. You felt that if Dorothy had committed suicide you were in some way responsible, and so it was several weeks before you were able to accept her death for what it was, and accept also the burden of an imagined responsibility.*

*This letter from Miss Koch makes it clear that Dorothy went to the girl because, for some peculiar reason of her own, she did want her belt; she was* not *in desperate need of someone to whom she could talk. She had made up her mind to do what she was going to do, and there is absolutely no reason for you to believe that she would have come to you first if you two had not had that argument the previous Christmas. (And don't forget it was* she *who was in a sullen mood and started the argument.) As for the initial coldness on Dorothy's part, remember that I agreed with you that she should go to Stoddard rather than Caldwell, where she would only have become more dependent on you. True, if she had followed you to Caldwell the tragedy would not have happened, but "if" is the biggest word in the world. Dorothy's punishment may have been excessively severe, but she was the one who chose it. I am not responsible, you are not responsible; no one is but Dorothy herself.*

*The knowledge that Miss Koch's original interpretation of Dorothy's behavior was erroneous will, I hope, rid you of any feelings of self-recrimination that may remain.*

*Your loving,*
FATHER

*P.S. Please excuse my indecipherable handwriting. I thought this letter too personal to dictate to Miss Richardson.*

*Letter from Ellen Kingship to Bud Corliss:*

*March 12, 1951*
*8:35 AM*

DEAR BUD,

*Here I sit in the club car with a Coke (at this hour—ugh!) and a pen and paper, trying to keep my writing hand steady against the motion of the train and trying to give a "lucid if not brilliant" explanation—as Prof. Mulholland would say—of why I am making this trip to Blue River.*

*I'm sorry about tonight's basketball game, but I'm sure Connie or Jane will be glad to go in my place, and you can think of me between the halves.*

*Now first of all, this trip* is not *impulsive! I thought about it all last night. You'd think I was running off to Cairo, Egypt! Second of all, I* will not *be missing work, because* you *are going to take complete notes in each class, and anyway I doubt if I'll be gone more than a week. And besides, since when do they flunk seniors for overcuts? Third of all, I won't be wasting my time, because I'll never know until I've tried, and until I try I'll never have a moment's peace.*

*Now that the objections are out of the way, let me explain why I am going. I'll fill in a little background first.*

*From the letter I received from my father Saturday morning, you know that Dorothy originally wanted to come to Caldwell and I op-*

*posed her for her own good, or so I convinced myself at the time. Since her death I've wondered whether it wasn't pure selfishness on my part. My life at home had been restrained both by my father's strictness and Dorothy's dependence on me, although I didn't realize it at the time. So when I got to Caldwell I really let go. During my first three years I was the rah-rah girl; beer parties, hanging around with the Big Wheels, etc. You wouldn't recognize me. So as I say, I'm not sure whether I prevented Dorothy from coming in order to encourage her independence or to avoid losing mine, Caldwell being the everybody-knows-what-everybody-else-is-doing-type place that it is.*

*My father's analysis (probably second-hand via Marion) of my reaction to Dorothy's death is absolutely right. I didn't want to admit it was suicide because that meant that I was partly responsible. I thought I had other reasons for doubt besides emotional ones however. The note she sent me, for instance. It was her handwriting—I can't deny that—but it didn't sound like her. It sounded kind of stilted, and she addressed me as "Darling," when before it had always been "Dear Ellen" or "Dearest Ellen." I mentioned that to the police, but they said that naturally she was under a strain when she wrote the note and couldn't be expected to sound her usual self, which I had to admit seemed logical. The fact that she carried her birth certificate with her also bothered me, but they explained that away too. A suicide will often take pains to make sure he is immediately identified, they said. The fact that other things which she always carried in her wallet (Stoddard registration card, etc.) would have been sufficient identification didn't seem to make any impression on them. And when I told them that she just wasn't the suicidal type, they didn't even bother to answer me. They swept away every point I raised.*

*So there I was. Of course I finally had to accept the fact that Dorothy committed suicide—and that I was partly to blame. Annabelle Koch's story was only the clincher. The motive for Dorothy's suicide made me even more responsible, for rational girls today do not kill themselves if they become pregnant—not, I thought, unless they have been brought up to depend on someone else and then that someone else suddenly isn't there.*

*But Dorothy's pregnancy meant that another person had deserted her too,—the man. If I knew anything about Dorothy it was that she did not treat sex lightly. She wasn't the kind for quick flings. The fact that she was pregnant meant that there was one man whom she had loved and had intended to marry some day.*

*Now early in the December before her death, Dorothy had written me about a man she had met in her English class. She had been going out with him for quite some time, and this was the Real Thing. She said she would give me all the details over Christmas vacation. But we had an argument during Christmas, and after that she wouldn't even give me the right time. And when we returned to school our letters were almost like business letters. So I never even learned his name. All I knew about him was what she had mentioned in that letter; that he had been in her English class in the fall, and that he was handsome and somewhat like Len Vernon—he is the husband of a cousin of ours —which meant that Dorothy's man was tall, blond, and blue-eyed.*

*I told my father about this man, urging him to find out who he was and punish him somehow. He refused, saying that it would be impossible to prove he was the one who had gotten Dorothy into trouble, and futile even if we could prove it. She had punished herself for her sins; it was a closed case as far as he was concerned.*

*That's how things stood until Saturday, when I received my father's letter with the one from Annabelle Koch enclosed. Which brings us to my big scene.*

*The letters did not have the effect my father had hoped for—not at first—because as I said, Annabelle Koch's story was far from the sole cause of my melancholy. But then I began to wonder; if Dorothy's belt was in perfect condition, why had she lied about it and taken Annabelle's instead? Why couldn't Dorothy wear her own belt? My father was content to let it pass, saying she had "some peculiar reason of her own," but I wanted to know what that reason was, because there were three other seemingly inconsequential things which Dorothy did on the day of her death that puzzled me then and that still puzzled me. Here they are:*

*1. At 10:15 that morning she bought an inexpensive pair of white cloth gloves in a shop across the street from her dormitory. (The owner reported it to the police after seeing her picture in the papers.) First she asked for a pair of stockings, but because of a rush of business for the Spring Dance scheduled for the following night, they were out of her size. She then asked for gloves, and bought a pair for $1.50. She was wearing them when she died, yet in the bureau in her room was a beautiful pair of hand-made white cloth gloves, perfectly spotless, that Marion had given her the previous Christmas. Why didn't she wear those?*

*2. Dorothy was a careful dresser. She was wearing her green suit when she died. With it she wore an inexpensive white silk blouse whose floppy out-of-style bow was all wrong for the lines of the suit. Yet in her closet was a white silk blouse, also perfectly spotless, which had been* specially made *to go with the suit. Why didn't she wear that blouse?*

3. *Dorothy was wearing dark green, with brown and white accessories. Yet the handkerchief in her purse was bright turquoise, as wrong as could be for the outfit she wore. In her room were at least a dozen handkerchiefs that would have matched her outfit perfectly. Why didn't she take one of those?*

*At the time of her death I mentioned these points to the police. They dismissed them as quickly as they had dismissed the others I brought up. She was distracted. It was ridiculous to expect her to dress with her ordinary care. I pointed out that the glove incident was the reverse of carelessness; she had gone out of her way to get them. If there was conscious preparation behind one incident, it wasn't unreasonable to assume that all three had some kind of purpose. Their comeback was, "You can't figure a suicide."*

*Annabelle Koch's letter added a fourth incident which followed the pattern of the other three. Her own belt was perfectly all right, but Dorothy wore Annabelle's instead. In each case she rejected an appropriate item for one that was less appropriate. Why?*

*I batted that problem around in my head all day Saturday, and Saturday night too. Don't ask me what I expected to prove. I felt that there had to be some kind of meaning to it all, and I wanted to find out as much as I could about Dorothy's state of mind at the time. Like poking a bad tooth with your tongue, I guess.*

*I'd have to write reams to tell you all the mental steps I went through, searching for some relationship among the four rejected items. Price, where they came from, and a thousand other thoughts, but nothing made sense. The same thing happened when I tried to get common characteristics in the wrong things she had actually worn. I even took sheets of paper and headed them Gloves, Handkerchief, Blouse, and Belt, and put down everything I knew about each, looking for a meaning. Apparently, there just wasn't a meaning. Size, age, ownership, cost, color, quality, place of purchase—none of the significant characteristics appeared on all four lists. I tore up the papers and went to bed. You can't figure a suicide.*

*It came to me about an hour later, so startlingly that I shot up straight in bed, suddenly cold. The out-of-style blouse, the gloves she'd bought that morning. Annabelle Koch's belt, the turquoise handkerchief . . . Something old, something new, something borrowed, and something blue.*

*It might—I keep telling myself—be a coincidence. But in my heart I don't believe that.*

*Dorothy went to the Municipal Building, not because it is the tallest building in Blue River, but because a Municipal Building is where you go when you want to get married. She wore something old, something new, something borrowed and something blue—poor romantic Dorothy —and she carried her birth certificate with her to prove she was over eighteen. And you don't make a trip like that alone. Dorothy can only have gone with one person—the man who made her pregnant, the man she'd been going with for a long time, the man she loved—the handsome blue-eyed blond of her fall English class. He got her up to the roof somehow. I'm almost certain that's the way it was.*

*The note? All it said was "I hope you will forgive me for the unhappiness I will cause. There is nothing else that I can do." Where is there mention of suicide? She was referring to the marriage! She knew Father would disapprove of a hasty step like that, but there was nothing else she could do because she was pregnant. The police were right when they said the stilted tone was the result of strain, only it was the strain of an eloping bride, not of a person contemplating suicide.*

*"Something old, something new" was enough to set me going, but it would never be enough to make the police reclassify a suicide with note as an unsolved murder, especially when they would be prejudiced against me—the crank who pestered them last year. You know that's true. So I'm going to find this man and do some* very cautious *Sherlocking. As soon as I turn up anything that supports my suspicions, anything strong enough to interest the police, I promise to go straight to them. I've seen too many movies where the heroine accuses the murderer in his soundproof penthouse and he says "Yes, I did it, but you'll never live to tell the tale." So don't worry about me, and don't get impatient, and don't write my father as he would probably explode. Maybe it is "crazy and impulsive" to rush into it this way, but how can I sit and wait when I know what has to be done and there is no one else to do it?*

*Perfect timing. We're just entering Blue River now. I can see the Municipal Building from the window.*

*I'll wind this letter up later in the day, when I'll be able to tell you where I'm staying and what progress, if any, I've made. Even though Stoddard is ten times as big as Caldwell, I have a pretty good idea of how to begin. Wish me luck . . .*

## 2

DEAN WELCH WAS plump, with round gray eyes like buttons pressed into the shiny pink clay of his face. He favored suits of clergy-black flannel, single breasted so as to expose his Phi Beta Kappa key. His office was dim and chapel-like, with dark wood and draperies and, in its center, a broad field of meticulously accoutred desktop.

After releasing the button on the inter-office speaker, the Dean rose and faced the door, his customary moist-lipped smile replaced by an expression of solemnity suitable for greeting a girl whose sister had taken her own life while nominally under his care. The ponderous notes of the noonday carillon floated into the chamber, muffled by distance and draperies. The door opened and Ellen Kingship entered.

By the time she had closed the door and approached his desk, the Dean of Students had measured and evaluated her with the complacent certainty of one who has dealt with younger people for many years. She was neat; he liked that. And quite pretty. Red-brown hair in thick bangs, brown eyes, a smile whose restraint acknowledged the unfortunate past . . . Determined looking. Probably not brilliant, but a plodder . . . second quarter of her class. Her coat and dress were shades of dark blue, a pleasant contrast to the usual student polychrome. She seemed a bit nervous, but then, weren't they all?

"Miss Kingship . . ." he murmured with a nod, indicating the visitor's chair. They sat. The Dean folded his pink hands. "Your father is well, I hope."

"Very well, thank you." Her voice was low-pitched and breathy.

The Dean said, "I had the pleasure of meeting him . . . last year." There was a moment of silence. "If there's anything I can do for you . . ."

She shifted in the stiff-backed chair. "We—my father and I—are trying to locate a certain man, a student here." The Dean's eyebrows lifted in polite curiosity. "He lent my sister a fairly large sum of money a few weeks before her death. She wrote me about it. I happened to come across her checkbook last week and it reminded me of the incident. There's nothing in the checkbook to indicate that she ever repaid the debt, and we thought he might have felt awkward about claiming it."

The Dean nodded.

"The only trouble," Ellen said, "is that I don't recall his name. But I do remember Dorothy mentioning that he was in her English class during the fall semester, and that he was blond. We thought perhaps you could help us locate him. It was a fairly large sum of money . . ." She took a deep breath.

"I see," said the Dean. He pressed his hands together as though comparing their size. His lips smiled at Ellen. "Can do," he snapped with military briskness. He held the pose for an instant, then jabbed one of the buttons on the inter-office speaker. "Miss Platt," he snapped, and released the button.

He brought his chair into more perfect alignment with the desk, as if he were preparing for a long campaign.

The door opened and a pale efficient-looking woman stepped into the room. The Dean nodded at her and then leaned back in his chair and stared at the wall beyond Ellen's head, mapping his strategy. Several moments passed before he spoke. "Get the program card of Kingship, Dorothy, fall semester, nineteen forty-nine. See which English section she was in and get the enrollment list for that section. Bring me the folders of all the male students whose names appear on the list." He looked at the secretary. "Got that?"

"Yes, sir."

He made her repeat the instructions.

"Fine," he said. She went out. "On the double," he said to the closed door. He turned back to Ellen and smiled complacently. She returned the smile.

By degrees the air of military efficiency faded, giving way to one of avuncular solicitude. The Dean leaned forward, his fingers softly clustered on the desk. "Surely you haven't come to Blue River solely for this purpose," he said.

"I'm visiting friends."

"Ahh."

Ellen opened her handbag. "May I smoke?"

"By all means." He pushed a crystal ashtray to her side of the desk. "I smoke myself," he admitted graciously. Ellen offered him a cigarette, but he demurred. She lit hers with a match drawn from a white folder on which *Ellen Kingship* was printed in copper letters.

The Dean regarded the matchbook thoughtfully. "Your conscientiousness in financial matters is admirable," he said, smiling. "If only everyone we dealt with were similarly conscientious." He examined a bronze letter opener. "We are at present beginning the construction of a new gymnasium and fieldhouse. Several people who pledged contributions have failed to live up to their words."

Ellen shook her head sympathetically.

"Perhaps your father would be interested in making a contribution," the Dean speculated. "A memorial to your sister . . ."

"I'll be glad to mention it to him."

"Would you? I would certainly appreciate that." He replaced the letter opener. "Such contributions are tax-deductible," he added.

A few minutes later the secretary entered with a stack of Manila folders in her arm. She set them before the Dean. "English fifty-one," she said, "section six. Seventeen male students."

"Fine," said the Dean. As the secretary left he straightened his chair and rubbed his hands, the military man once more. He opened the top folder and leafed through its contents until he came to an application form. There was a photograph pasted in the corner of it. "Dark hair," he said, and put the folder on his left.

When he had gone through all of them, there were two uneven piles. "Twelve with dark hair and five with light," the Dean said.

Ellen leaned forward. "Dorothy once told me he was handsome . . ."

The Dean drew the pile of five folders to the center of his desk blotter and opened the first one. "George Speiser," he said thoughtfully. "I doubt if you'd call Mr. Speiser handsome." He lifted out the application form and turned it towards Ellen. The face in the photograph was a chinless, gimlet-eyed teen-ager. She shook her head.

The second was an emaciated young man with thick eyeglasses.

The third was fifty-three years old and his hair was white, not blond.

Ellen's hands were damp on her purse.

The Dean opened the fourth folder. "Gordon Gant," he said. "Does that sound like the name?" He turned the application form towards her.

He was blond and unarguably handsome; light eyes under full brows, a long firm jaw and a cavalier grin. "I think so . . ." she said. "Yes, I think he . . ."

"Or could it be Dwight Powell?" the Dean asked, displaying the fifth application form in his other hand.

The fifth photograph showed a square-jawed, serious-looking young man, with a cleft chin and pale-toned eyes.

"Which name sounds familiar?" the Dean asked.

Ellen looked impotently from one picture to the other.

They were both blond; they were both blue-eyed; they were both handsome.

She came out of the Administration Building and stood at the head of the stone steps surveying the campus, dull gray under a clouded sky. Her purse was in one hand, a slip of paper from the Dean's memo pad in the other.

Two . . . It would slow her up a little, that's all. It should be simple to find out which was the one . . . and then she would watch him, even meet him perhaps—though not as Ellen Kingship. Watch for the darting eye, the guarded answer. Murder must leave marks. (It *was* murder. It *must* have been murder.)

She was getting ahead of herself. She looked at the paper in her hand:

*Gordon C. Gant*
*1312 West 26th Street*

*Dwight Powell*
*1520 West 35th Street*

## 3

HER LUNCH, EATEN in a small restaurant across the street from the campus, was a hasty mechanical affair, her mind racing with swift thoughts. How to begin? Ask a few discreet questions of their friends? But where do you start? Follow each man, learn the identity of his friends, meet them, find the ones who had known him last year? Time, time, time . . . If she remained in Blue River too long, Bud might call her father. Her fingers tapped impatiently. Who would be *sure* to know about Gordon Gant and Dwight Powell? Their families. Or if they were from out of town, a landlady or a roommate. It would be impetuous to go straight to the center of things, to the people nearest them, but still, no time would be wasted . . . She bit her lower lip, her fingers still tapping.

After a minute she put down her half finished cup of coffee, rose from the table and threaded her way to the phone booth. Hesitantly she ruffled the pages of the thin Blue River book. There was no Gant at all, no Powell on 35th Street. That meant they either had no phones, which seemed unlikely, or they were living with families other than their own.

She called Information and obtained the number of the telephone at 1312 West 26th Street; 2–2014:

"Hello?" The voice was a woman's; dry, middle-aged.

"Hello." Ellen swallowed. "Is Gordon Gant there?"

A pause. "Who's calling?"

"A friend of his. Is he there?"

"No." Snapped out sharply.

"Who is this?"

"His landlady."

"When do you expect him back?"

"Won't be back till late tonight." The woman's voice was quick with annoyance. There was a click as she hung up.

Ellen looked at the dead receiver and placed it on the hook. When she got back to her table the coffee was cold.

He would be gone all day. Go there? . . . A single conversation with the landlady might establish that Gant was the one who had gone with Dorothy. Or, by elimination, it might prove that Powell was the one. Speak to the landlady . . . but under what pretext?

Why, any pretext! Provided the woman believed it, what harm could the wildest story do?—even if its falseness were completely obvious to Gant when the landlady reported it. Either he wasn't the man, in which case let him puzzle over a mysterious questioner pretending to be a friend or a relative, or he *was* the man, in which case: A) He had not killed Dorothy—again let him puzzle over a mysterious questioner, or: B) He *had* killed Dorothy—and the story of a girl seeking information about him would make him uneasy. Yet his uneasiness would not interfere with her plans, for should she later make his acquaintance, he would have no reason to associate her with the girl who had questioned his landlady. Uneasiness on his part might even be a help to her, making him tense, more likely to betray himself. Why, he might even decide to take no chances and leave town—and that would be all she'd need to convince the police that there was a sound basis to her suspicions. They would investigate, find the proof . . .

Go straight to the center of things. Impetuous? When you thought about it, it was really the most logical thing to do.

She looked at her watch. Five past one. Her visit shouldn't be made too soon after the telephone call or the landlady might connect the two and become suspicious. Forcing herself to sit back in the chair, Ellen caught the waitress' eye and ordered another cup of coffee.

At a quarter of two she entered the 1300 block of West 26th Street. It was a quiet, tired-looking street, with pallid two story frame houses sitting behind pocked brown lawns still hard from winter. A few old Fords and Chevvies stood immobile along the curb, some aging naturally, some trying to stay young with unprofessional paint jobs, bright colored but lusterless. Ellen walked with the enforced slowness of attempted nonchalance, the sound of her heels the only sound in the still air.

The house where Gordon Gant lived, 1312, was the third one in from the corner; mustard colored, its brown trim the shade of stale chocolate. After looking at it for a moment, Ellen walked up the cracked concrete path that bisected the dead lawn and led to the porch. There she read the nameplate on the mailbox affixed to one of the posts: *Mrs. Minna Arquette.* She stepped to the door. Its bell was of the old fashioned kind; a fan-shaped metal tab protruded from the center of the door. Drawing a deep initiatory breath, she gave the tab a quick twist. The bell within rang gratingly. Ellen waited.

Presently footsteps sounded inside, and then the door opened. The woman who stood in the doorway was tall and lank, with frizzy gray hair clustered above a long equine face. Her eyes were pink and rheumy. A busily printed housedress hung from her sharp shoulders. She looked Ellen up and down. "Yes?"—the dry Midwestern voice of the telephone.

"You must be Mrs. Arquette," Ellen declared.

"That's right." The woman twitched a sudden smile, displaying teeth of an unnatural perfection.

Ellen smiled back at her. "I'm Gordon's cousin."

Mrs. Arquette arched thin eyebrows. "His cousin?"

"Didn't he mention that I'd be here today?"

"Why, no. He didn't say anything about a cousin. Not a word."

"That's funny. I wrote him I'd be passing through. I'm on my way to Chicago and I purposely came this way so I could stop off and see him. He must have forgotten to—"

"When did you write him?"

Ellen hesitated. "The day before yesterday. Saturday."

"Oh." The smile flashed again. "Gordon leaves the house early in the morning and the first mail don't come till ten. Your letter is probably sitting in his room this minute."

"Ohh . . ."

"He isn't here right—"

"Couldn't I come in for a few minutes?" Ellen cut in quickly. "I took the wrong streetcar from the station and I had to walk about ten blocks."

Mrs. Arquette took a step back into the house. "Of course. Come on in."

"Thank you very much." Ellen crossed the threshold, entering a hallway that was stale-smelling and—once the front door was closed—dimly lighted. A flight of stairs rose along the right wall. On the left an archway opened onto a parlor which had the stiff look of seldom used rooms.

"Miz Arquette?" a voice called from the back of the house.

"Coming!" she answered. She turned to Ellen. "You mind sitting in the kitchen?"

"Not at all," Ellen said. The Arquette teeth shone again, and then Ellen was following the tall figure down the hallway, wondering why the woman, so pleasant now, had been so irritable over the telephone.

The kitchen was painted the same mustard color as the exterior of the house. There was a white porcelain-topped table in the middle of the room, with a set of anagrams laid out on it. An elderly bald-headed man with thick eyeglasses sat at the table, pouring the last of a bottle of Dr. Pepper into a flowered jar that had once held cheese. "This is Mr. Fishback from next door," said Mrs. Arquette. "We play anagrams."

"Nickel a word," added the old man, raising his eyeglasses to look at Ellen.

"This is Miss . . ." Mrs. Arquette waited.

"Gant," said Ellen.

"Miss Gant, Gordon's cousin."

"How do you do," said Mr. Fishback. "Gordon's a nice boy." He dropped his glasses back into place, his eyes swelling up behind them. "It's your go," he said to Mrs. Arquette.

She took the seat opposite Mr. Fishback. "Sit down," she said to Ellen, indicating one of the empty chairs. "You want some pop?"

"No, thank you," Ellen said, sitting. She slipped her arms from the sleeves of her coat and dropped it back over the chair.

Mrs. Arquette stared at the dozen turned up letters in the ring of blank-backed wooden squares. "Where you on your way from?" she inquired.

"California."

"I didn't know Gordon had family in the West."

"No, I was just visiting there. I'm from the East."

"Oh." Mrs. Arquette looked at Mr. Fishback. "Go ahead, I give up. Can't do anything with no vowels."

"It's my turn?" he asked. She nodded. With a grin Mr. Fishback snatched at the turned up letters. "You missed it, you missed it!" he crowed. "C-R-Y-P-T. Crypt. What they bury folks in." He pushed the letters together and added the word to the others ranged before him.

"That's not fair," Mrs. Arquette protested. "You had all that time to think while I was at the door."

"Fair is fair," Mr. Fishback declared. He turned up two more letters and placed them in the center of the ring.

"Oh, shoot," Mrs. Arquette muttered, sitting back in her chair.

"How is Gordon these days?" Ellen asked.

"Oh, fine," said Mrs. Arquette. "Busy as a bee, what with school and the program."

"The program?"

"You mean you don't know about Gordon's program?"

"Well, I haven't heard from him in quite a while . . ."

"Why, he's had it for almost three months now!" Mrs. Arquette drew herself up grandly. "He plays records and talks. A disc jockey. 'The Discus Thrower' he's called. Every night except Sunday, from eight to ten over KBRI."

"That's wonderful!" Ellen exclaimed.

"Why, he's a real celebrity," the landlady continued, turning up a letter as Mr. Fishback nodded to her. "They had an interview on him in the paper a couple of Sundays back. Reporter come here and everything. And girls he don't even know calling him up at all hours. Stoddard girls. They get his number out of the Student Directory and call up just to hear his voice over the telephone. He don't want anything to do with them, so I'm the one's got to answer. It's enough to drive a person crazy." Mrs. Arquette frowned at the anagrams. "Go ahead, Mr. Fishback," she said.

Ellen fingered the edge of the table. "Is Gordon still going out with that girl he wrote me about last year?" she asked.

"Which one's that?"

"A blonde girl, short, pretty. Gordon mentioned her in a few of his letters last year,—October, November, all the way up through April. I thought he was really interested in her. But he stopped writing about her in April."

"Well I'll tell you," Mrs. Arquette said, "I don't ever get to see the girls Gordon goes out with. Before he got the program he used to go out three-four times a week, but he never brought any of the girls here. Not that I'd expect him to. I'm only his landlady. He never talks about them neither. Other boys I had here before him used to tell me all about their girls, but college boys were younger then. Nowadays they're mostly veterans and I guess they get a little older, they don't chatter so much. Least Gordon don't. Not that I'd want to pry, but I'm interested in people." She turned over a letter. "What was that girl's name? You tell me her name I can probably tell you if he's still going out with her, because sometimes when he's using the phone over by the stairs there, I'm in the parlor and can't help hearing part of the conversation."

"I don't remember her name," Ellen said, "but he was going with her last year, so maybe if *you* remember the names of some of the girls he spoke to then, I'll be able to recognize it."

"Let's see," Mrs. Arquette pondered, mechanically arranging anagrams in search of a word. "There was a Louella. I remember that one because I had a sister-in-law by that name. And then there was a . . ." —her watery eyes closed in concentration—". . . a Barbara. No, that was the year before, his first year. Let's see, Louella . . ." She shook her head. "There was others, but I'm hanged if I can remember them."

The game of anagrams went on in silence for a minute. Finally Ellen said, "I think this girl's name was Dorothy."

Mrs. Arquette waved a go-ahead at Mr. Fishback. "Dorothy . . ." Her eyes narrowed. "No . . . if the name's Dorothy, I don't think he's still going out with her. I haven't heard him talking to any Dorothy lately, I'm sure of that. Of course he goes down to the corner sometimes to make a real personal call or a Long Distance."

"But he *was* going with a Dorothy last year?"

Mrs. Arquette looked up at the ceiling. "I don't know . . . I don't *remember* a Dorothy, but I don't *not remember* one either, if you know what I mean."

"Dottie?" Ellen tried.

Mrs. Arquette considered for a moment and then gave a noncommittal shrug.

"Your go," Mr. Fishback said petulantly.

The wooden squares clicked softly as Mrs. Arquette maneuvered them about. "I think," said Ellen, "that he must have broken up with this Dorothy in April when he stopped writing about her. He must have been in a bad mood around the end of April. Worried, nervous . . ." She looked at Mrs. Arquette questioningly.

"Not Gordon," she said. "He had real spring fever last year. Going around humming. I joshed him about it." Mr. Fishback fidgeted impatiently. "Oh, go ahead," Mrs. Arquette said.

Choking over his Dr. Pepper, Mr. Fishback pounced on the anagrams. "You missed one again!" he cried, clawing up letters. "F-A-N-E. Fane!"

"What're you talking about, fane? No such word!" Mrs. Arquette turned to Ellen. "You ever hear of a word 'fane'?"

"You should know better'n to argue with me!" Mr. Fishback shrilled. "I don't know what it means, but I know it's a word. I seen it!" He turned to Ellen. "I read three books a week, regular as clockwork."

"Fane," snorted Mrs. Arquette.

"Well look it up in the dictionary!"

"That little pocket one with nothing in it? Every time I look up one of your words and it ain't there you blame it on the dictionary!"

Ellen looked at the two glaring figures. "Gordon must have a dictionary," she said. She stood up. "I'll be glad to get it if you'll tell me which room is his."

"That's right," Mrs. Arquette said decisively. "He *does* have one." She rose. "You sit down, dear. I know just where it is."

"May I come along then? I'd like to see Gordon's room. He's told me what a nice place . . ."

"Come on," said Mrs. Arquette, stalking out of the kitchen. Ellen hurried after her.

"You'll see," Mr. Fishback's voice chased them, "I know more words than you'll *ever* know, even if you live to be a hundred!"

They sped up the darkwood stairs, Mrs. Arquette in the fore muttering indignantly. Ellen followed her through a door adjacent to the head of the stairway.

The room was bright with flowered wallpaper. There was a green-covered bed, a dresser, easy chair, table . . . Mrs. Arquette, having snatched a book from the top of the dresser, stood by the window ruffling the pages. Ellen moved to the dresser and scanned the titles of the books ranked across its top. A diary maybe. Any kind of notebook. *Prize Stories of 1950, An Outline of History, Radio Announcer's Handbook of Pronunciation, The Brave Bulls, A History of American Jazz, Swann's Way, Elements of Psychology, Three Famous Murder Novels* and *A Sub-Treasury of American Humor.*

"Oh, shoot," said Mrs. Arquette. She stood with her forefinger pressed to the open dictionary. "Fane," she read, "a temple; hence a church." She slammed the book shut. "Where does he get words like that?"

Ellen eased over to the table, where three envelopes were fanned out. Mrs. Arquette, putting the dictionary on the dresser, glanced at her. "The one without a return address is yours, I guess."

"Yes, it is," Ellen said. The two letters with return addresses were from *Newsweek* and the National Broadcasting Company.

Mrs. Arquette was at the door. "Coming?"

"Yes," Ellen said.

They trudged down the stairs and walked slowly into the kitchen, where Mr. Fishback was waiting. As soon as he observed Mrs. Arquette's dejection he burst into gleeful cackling. She gave him a dirty look. "It means a church," she said, slumping into her chair. He laughed some more. "Oh, shut up and get on with the game," Mrs. Arquette grumbled. Mr. Fishback turned over two letters.

Ellen took her purse from the coat-draped chair in which she had sat. "I guess I'll be going now," she said dispiritedly.

"Going?" Mrs. Arquette looked up, the thin eyebrows arching.

Ellen nodded.

"Well for goodness' sake, aren't you going to wait for Gordon?" Ellen went cold. Mrs. Arquette looked at the clock on the refrigerator next to the door. "It's ten after two," she said. "His last class ended at two o'clock. He should be here any minute."

She couldn't speak. The image of Mrs. Arquette's upturned face swayed sickeningly. "You . . . you told me he would be gone all day . . ." she strained out finally.

Mrs. Arquette looked injured. "Why, I never told you no such thing! Why on earth you been sitting here if not waiting for him?"

"The telephone . . ."

The landlady's jaw dropped. "Was that you? Around one o'clock?"

Ellen nodded helplessly.

"Well why didn't you tell me it was you? I thought it was one of those fool girls. Whenever someone calls and won't give me a name I tell them he's gone for the day. Even if he's here. He told me to. He . . ." The expression of earnestness drained from Mrs. Arquette's face. The dull eyes, the thin-lipped mouth became grim, suspicious. "If you thought he was out for the day," she demanded slowly, "then why did you come here at all?"

"I . . . I wanted to meet you. Gordon wrote so much . . ."

"Why were you asking all those questions?" Mrs. Arquette stood up.

Ellen reached for her coat. Suddenly Mrs. Arquette was holding Ellen's arms, the long bony fingers clutching painfully. "Let go of me . . . Please . . ."

"Why were you snooping in his room?" The horselike face pressed close to Ellen's, the eyes swelling with anger, the rough skin red. "What did you want in there? You take something while my back was turned?"

Behind Ellen, Mr. Fishback's chair scraped and his voice piped frightenedly, "Why'd she want to steal anything from her own cousin?"

"Who says she's his cousin?" Mrs. Arquette snapped.

Ellen worked futilely in her grasp. "Please, you're hurting me . . ."

The pale eyes narrowed. "And I don't think she's one of those damn girls looking for a souvenir or something either. Why was she asking all those questions?"

"I'm his cousin! I am!" Ellen tried to steady her voice. "I want to go now. You can't keep me here. I'll see him later."

"You'll see him now," Mrs. Arquette said. "You're staying here until

Gordon comes." She glanced over Ellen's shoulder. "Mr. Fishback, get over by the back door." She waited, her eyes following Mr. Fishback's slow passage, and then she released Ellen. Moving quickly to the front doorway, she blocked it, her arms folded across her chest. "We'll find out what this is all about," she said.

Ellen rubbed her arms where Mrs. Arquette's fingers had clamped them. She looked at the man and woman blocking the doors at either end of the kitchen; Mr. Fishback with his glass-magnified eyes blinking nervously; Mrs. Arquette standing grim, monolithic. "You can't do this." She retrieved her purse from the floor. She took her coat from the chair and put it over her arm. "Let me out of here," she said firmly.

Neither of them moved.

They heard the front door slam and footsteps on the stairs. "Gordon!" Mrs. Arquette shouted, "Gordon!" The footsteps stopped. "What is it, Mrs. Arquette?" The landlady turned and ran down the hallway.

Ellen faced Mr. Fishback. "Please," she implored, "let me out of here. I didn't mean any harm."

He shook his head slowly.

She stood motionless, hearing the excited rasping of Mrs. Arquette's voice far behind her. Footsteps approached and the voice grew louder. "She kept asking all kinds of questions about what girls you were going out with last year, and she even tricked me into taking her to your room. She was looking at your books and the letters on your table . . ." Mrs. Arquette's voice suddenly flooded the kitchen. "There she is!"

Ellen turned. Mrs. Arquette stood to the left of the table, one arm lifted, pointing accusation. Gant was in the doorway leaning against the jamb, tall and spare in a pale-blue topcoat, books in one hand. He looked at her for a moment, then his lips curved a smile over his long jaw and one eyebrow lifted slightly.

He detached himself from the jamb and stepped into the room, putting his books on the refrigerator without taking his eyes from her. "Why, Cousin Hester . . ." he marveled softly, his eyes flicking down then up again in considered appraisal. "You've passed through adolescence magnificently . . ." He ambled around the table, placed his hands on Ellen's shoulders, and kissed her fondly on the cheek.

4

"YOU . . . YOU MEAN she really *is* your cousin?" Mrs. Arquette gasped.

"Arquette, my love," said Gant, moving to Ellen's left, "ours was a communal teething ring." He patted Ellen's shoulder. "Wasn't it, Hester?"

She eyed him crazily, her face flushed, her mouth slack. Her gaze moved to Mrs. Arquette at the left of the table, to the hallway beyond it, to the coat and purse in her hands . . . She darted to the right, sped around the table and through the door and down the hallway hearing Arquette's "Running away!" And Gant's pursuing shout: "She's from the psychotic side of the family!" Wrenching open the heavy front door, she fled from the house, her toes biting the concrete path. At the sidewalk she turned to the right and reined to swift bitter strides, wrestling into her tangled coat. Oh God, everything messed up! She clenched her teeth, feeling the hot pressure of tears behind her eyes. Gant caught up with her and matched her strides with long easy legs. She flung a fiery glance at the grinning face and then glared straight ahead, her whole being compressed with unreasoned fury at herself and him.

"Isn't there a secret word?" he asked. "Aren't you supposed to press a message into my hand and whisper 'Southern Comfort' or something? Or is this the one where the heavy in the dark suit has been following you all day and you sought refuge in the nearest doorway? I like them equally well, so whichever it is . . ." She strode along in acid silence. "You ever read the Saint stories? I used to. Old Simon Templar was *always* running into beautiful women with strange behavior patterns. Once one of them swam onto his yacht in the middle of the night. Said she was a channel swimmer gone astray, I believe. Turned out to be an insurance investigator." He caught her arm. "Cousin Hester, I have the most insatiable curiosity . . ."

She pulled her arm free. They had reached an intersecting avenue along the other side of which a taxi cruised. She waved and the cab began a U turn. "It was a joke," she said tightly. "I'm sorry. I did it on a bet."

"That's what the girl on the yacht told the Saint." His face went serious. "Fun is fun, but why all the questions about my sordid past?"

The cab pulled up. She tried to open the door but he braced his hand against it. "Look here, cousin, don't be fooled by my disc jockey dialogue. I'm not kidding . . ."

"Please," she moaned exhaustedly, tugging at the door handle. The cabbie appeared at the front window, looking up at them and appraising the situation. "Hey mister . . ." he said. His voice was a menacing rumble.

With a sigh, Gant released the door. Ellen opened it, ducked in and slammed it closed. She sank into soft worn leather. Outside Gant was leaning over, his hands on the door, staring in at her through the glass as though trying to memorize the details of her face. She looked away.

She waited until the cab had left the curb before telling the driver her destination.

It took ten minutes to reach the New Washington House, where Ellen had registered before calling on the Dean,—ten minutes of lip-biting and quick-handed smoking and bitter self-denunciation, the release of the tension which had been built up before Gant's arrival and which had been left hanging, unspent, by his anticlimactic asinine banter. Cousin Hester! Oh, she had really messed things up! She had bet half her chips and got nothing in return. Still in the dark as to whether or not he was *the* man, she had made further questioning of him or his landlady completely impossible. If investigation of Powell should show he wasn't the man, proving that Gant was, she might as well give up and go back to Caldwell, because if—always the second, the big "if"—if Gant had killed Dorothy, he would be on guard, knowing Ellen's face and knowing what she was after by the questions she had asked Mrs. Arquette. A killer on guard, ready perhaps to kill again. She wouldn't risk tangling with that—not when he had seen her face. Better to live in doubt than to die in certainty. Her only other course would be to go to the police, and she would still have nothing more to offer them than "something old, something new," so they would nod solemnly and usher her politely from the station.

Oh, she had made a fine start!

The hotel room had beige walls and clumsy brown furniture and the same clean, impersonal, transient air as the miniature paper-wrapped cake of soap in the adjoining bathroom. The only mark of its occupancy was the suitcase with the Caldwell stickers on the rack at the foot of the double bed.

After hanging her coat in the closet, Ellen seated herself at the writing table by the window. She took her fountain pen and the letter to Bud from her purse. Staring down at the addressed but still unsealed envelope, she debated whether or not to mention, in addition to an outline of the interview with Dean Welch, the story of the Gant fiasco. No . . . if Dwight Powell turned out to be the one, then the Gant business meant nothing. It *must* be Powell. Not Gant, she told herself,—

not with that lighthearted chatter. But what had he said?—Don't be fooled by my disc jockey dialogue. I'm not kidding . . .

There was a knock at the door. She jumped to her feet. "Who is it?"

"Towels," a high feminine voice answered.

Ellen crossed the room and grasped the doorknob. "I . . . I'm not dressed. Could you leave them outside please?"

"All right," the voice said.

She stood there for two minutes, hearing occasional passing footsteps and the muffled sound of the elevator down the hall, while the knob grew damp in her hand. Finally she smiled at her nervousness, visualizing herself peering under the bed old-maid fashion before going to sleep. She opened the door.

Gant lounged with one elbow against the jamb, the hand propping up his blond head. "Hi, Cousin Hester," he said. "I believe I mentioned my insatiable curiosity." She tried to close the door, but his foot was in the way, immovable. He smiled. "Much fun. Follow that cab!" His right hand described a zigzag course. "Shades of the Warner Brothers. The driver got such a kick out of it he almost refused the tip. I told him you were running away from my bed and board."

"Get away!" she whispered fiercely. "I'll call the manager!"

"Look, Hester,"—the smile dropped—"I think I could have you arrested for illegal entry or impersonating a cousin or something like that, so why don't you invite me in for a small confab? If you're worried about what the bellhops will think, you can leave the door open." He pushed gently on the door, forcing Ellen to retreat a step. "That's a good girl," he said as he eased through the opening. He eyed her dress with exaggerated disappointment. " 'I'm not dressed,' she says. I should have known you were a habitual liar." He strolled to the bed and sat down on the edge of it. "Well for pity's sake, coz, stop shaking! I'm not going to eat you."

"What . . . what do you want?"

"An explanation."

She swung the door all the way open and remained standing in the doorway, as though it were his room and she the visitor. "It's . . . very simple. I listen to your program all the time . . ."

He glanced at the suitcase. "In Wisconsin?"

"It's only a hundred miles away. We get KBRI. We really do."

"Go ahead."

"I listen to you all the time, and I like your program very much . . . I'm in Blue River, so I thought I'd try to meet you."

"And when you meet me you run away."

"Well what would you have done? I didn't plan it *that* way. I pretended to be your cousin because I . . . I wanted to get information about you—what kind of girls you like . . ."

Rubbing his jaw doubtfully, he stood up. "How did you get my phone number?"

"From the Student Directory."

He moved to the foot of the bed and touched the suitcase. "If you go to Caldwell, how did you get a Stoddard directory?"

"From one of the girls here."

"Who?"

"Annabelle Koch. She's a friend of mine."

"Annabelle . . ." He had recognized the name. He squinted at Ellen incredulously. "Hey, is this really on the level?"

"Yes." She looked down at her hands. "I know it was a crazy thing to do, but I like your program so much . . ." When she looked up again he was by the window.

He said, "Of all the stupid, idiotic . . ."—and suddenly he was staring at the hallway beyond her, his eyes baffled. She turned. There was nothing out of the ordinary to be seen. She looked back at Gant and he was facing the window, his back to her. "Well, Hester," he said, "that was a flattering explanation"—he turned, taking his hand from inside his jacket—"and one I shall long remember." He glanced at the partially open bathroom door. "Do you mind if I utilize your facilities?" he asked, and before she could say anything he had ducked into the bathroom and closed the door. The lock clicked.

Ellen gazed blankly at the door, wondering whether or not Gant had believed her. Her knees quivered. Drawing a deep steadying breath, she crossed the room to the writing table and took a cigarette from her purse. She broke two matches before she got it lighted, and then she stood looking out the window, nervously rolling her fountain pen back and forth over the surface of the table which was bare except for her purse. Bare . . . the letter . . . The letter to Bud! Gant had been standing near the table and he had tricked her into turning towards the hallway and then he had been facing the window and he turned, taking his hand from inside his jacket! . . .

Frantically she hammered on the bathroom door. "Give me that letter! Give it to me!"

Several seconds passed before Gant's deep-toned voice said, "My curiosity is especially insatiable when it comes to phony cousins with flimsy stories."

She stood in the doorway with one hand on the jamb and her coat in the other, looking from the still-closed bathroom door to the hallway and smiling inanely at the occasional passers-by. A bellhop asked if there were anything he could do for her. She shook her head.

Gant finally came out. He was folding the letter carefully into its envelope. He put it on the writing table. "Well," he said. He viewed her ready-to-flee figure. "Well." He smiled somewhat uncomfortably. "As my grandmother said when the man on the phone asked for Lana Turner, 'Boy, have you got the wrong number.' "

Ellen did not move.

"Look," he said. "I didn't even know her. I said hello to her once or twice. There were other blond guys in that class. I didn't even know her name until her picture was in the papers. The teacher had taken attendance by seat numbers, never called the roll. I didn't even know her name."

Ellen didn't move.

"Well for God's sake, if you want to break a speed record that coat's only going to be in the way."

She didn't move.

In two swift strides he was at the bedside table, snatching up the Gideon Bible. He raised his right hand. "I swear on this Bible that I never went out with your sister, or said more than two words to her . . . or anything . . ." He put the Bible down. "Well?"

"If Dorothy was killed," Ellen said, "the man who did it would swear on a dozen Bibles. And if she thought he loved her, then he was a good actor too."

Gant rolled his eyes heavenward and extended his wrists for the handcuffs. "All right," he said, "I'll go quietly."

"I'm glad you think this is something to joke about."

He lowered his hands. "I'm sorry," he said sincerely. "But how the hell am I supposed to convince you that—"

"You can't," Ellen said. "You might as well go."

"There were other blond guys in the class," he insisted. He snapped his fingers. "There was one she used to come in with all the time! Cary Grant chin, tall . . ."

"Dwight Powell?"

"That's right!" He stopped short. "Is he on your list?"

She hesitated a moment, and then nodded.

"He's the one!"

Ellen looked at him suspiciously.

He threw up his hands. "Okay. I give up. You'll see, it was Powell."

He moved towards the door; Ellen backed into the hallway. "I would just like to leave, as you suggested," Gant said loftily.

He came into the hallway. "Unless you want me to go on calling you Hester, you ought to tell me what your name really is."

"Ellen."

Gant seemed reluctant to go. "What are you going to do now?"

After a moment she said, "I don't know."

"If you barge into Powell's place, don't pull a fluff like you did this afternoon. He may be no one to fool around with."

Ellen nodded.

Gant looked her up and down. "A girl on a mission," he mused. "Never thought I'd live to see the day." He started to go and then turned back. "You wouldn't be in the market for a Watson, would you?"

"No, thanks," she said in the doorway. "I'm sorry but . . ."

He shrugged and smiled. "I figured my credentials wouldn't be in order. Well, good luck . . ." He turned and walked down the hallway.

Ellen backed into her room and slowly closed the door.

*. . . It's 7:30 now, Bud, and I'm comfortably settled in a very nice room at the New Washington House—just had dinner and am ready to take a bath and turn in after a full day.*

*I spent most of the afternoon in the waiting room of the Dean of Students. When I finally got to see him I told a fabulous story about an unpaid debt which Dorothy owed to a handsome blond in her fall English class. After much digging through records and examining a rogues gallery of application blank photos, we came up with the man—Mr. Dwight Powell of 1520 West 35th Street, on whom the hunting season opens tomorrow morning.*

*How's that for an efficient start? Never underestimate the power of a woman!*

*Love,*
ELLEN

At eight o'clock she paused in her undressing and dropped a quarter into the coin-operated bedside radio. She pushed the button marked KBRI. There was a low humming and then, smooth and sonorous, Gant's voice swelled into the room. ". . . another session with The Discus Thrower, or as our engineer puts it, 'Puff and Pant with Gordon Gant,' which shows the limitations of a purely scientific education. On to the agenda. The first disc of the evening is an oldie, and it's dedicated to Miss Hester Holmes of Wisconsin . . ."

A jumpy orchestral introduction, nostalgically dated, burst from the radio and faded under the singing of a sugary, little-girl voice:

*Button up your overcoat*
*When the wind is free,*
*Take good care of yourself,*
*You belong to me . . .*

Smiling, Ellen went into the bathroom. The tiled walls rang with the sound of water pounding into the tub. She kicked off her slippers and hung her robe on a hook beside the door. She reached over and turned off the water. In the sudden silence, the wispy voice sifted in from the next room:

*Don't sit on hornets' tails, ooh-ooh,*
*Or on nails, ooh-ooh,*
*Or third rails, ooh-ooh . . .*

## 5

"HELLO?" THE VOICE was a woman's.

"Hello," Ellen said. "Is Dwight Powell there?"

"No, he isn't."

"When do you expect him back?"

"I couldn't say for sure. I know he works over at Folger's between his classes and afterwards, but I don't know to what time he works."

"Aren't you his landlady?"

"No. I'm her daughter-in-law come over to clean. Mrs. Honig is in Iowa City with her foot. She cut it last week and it got infected. My husband had to take her to Iowa City."

"Oh, I'm sorry . . ."

"If you have a message for Dwight, I can leave him a note."

"No, thanks. I have a class with him in a couple of hours, so I'll see him then. It wasn't anything important."

"Okay. Good-by."

"Good-by."

Ellen hung up. She certainly wasn't going to wait to speak to the landlady. She was already more or less convinced that Powell was the man who had been going with Dorothy; checking with the landlady would only have been a sort of formality; verification could be obtained just as easily from Powell's friends. Or from Powell himself . . .

She wondered what kind of place it was where he worked. Folger's. It would have to be near the campus if he went there in free hours between classes. If it were a store of some sort, where he waited on customers . . .

She picked up the telephone book, turned to the F's and skimmed through the listings.

*Folger Drugs 1448 UnivAv. . . . 2–3800*

It was between 28th and 29th Streets across the avenue from the campus; a squat brick structure with a long green sign stretched across its brow: *Folger Drugs* and in smaller letters *Prescriptions* and in still smaller letters *Fountain Service*. Ellen paused outside the glass door and smoothed her bangs. Drawing herself up as though making an entrance onto a stage, she pushed open the door and went in.

The fountain was on the left; mirrors, chrome, gray marble; fronted by a line of round-topped red leatherette stools. It was not yet noon so only a few people were seated at the forward end.

Dwight Powell was behind the counter, wearing a snug white mess jacket and a white cap which rode the waves of his fine blond hair like an overturned ship. His square-jawed face was lean and he had a moustache; a thin carefully trimmed line of almost colorless hairs, visible only when the light gleamed on it; a feature which evidently had been added some time after the taking of the photograph which the Dean had shown. Powell was squirting whipped cream from a metal cannister onto a gummy-looking sundae. There was a sullen set to his lips that made it clear he disliked his job.

Ellen walked towards the far end of the counter. As she passed Powell, who was placing the sundae before a customer, she sensed him glance up. She went on, eyes straight ahead, to the empty section. Taking off her coat, she folded it and put it with her purse on one of the row of empty stools. She seated herself on the next stool. With her hands flat on the cold marble, she examined her reflection in the mirrored wall opposite. Her hands left the marble, dropped to the bottom of her powder blue sweater and pulled it down tight.

Powell approached along the gangway behind the counter. He put a glass of water and a paper napkin before her. His eyes were deep blue, the skin immediately below them gray-shadowed. "Yes, miss?" he said in a low-pitched voice. His eyes met hers and then strayed downwards momentarily.

She looked at the mirrored wall, at the pictures of sandwiches fixed to it. The grill was directly opposite her. "A cheeseburger," she said, looking back at him. His eyes were on hers again. "And a cup of coffee."

"Cheeseburger and coffee," he said, and smiled. It was a stiff smile that vanished quickly, as though his facial muscles were unaccustomed to the exercise. He turned and opened a locker under the grill, taking out a patty of meat on a piece of waxed paper. Kicking the locker door shut, he slapped the meat onto the grill and peeled the waxed paper off its back. The meat sizzled. He took a hamburger roll from a bin next to the grill and began slicing it down the center with a long knife. She watched his face in the mirror. He glanced up and smiled again. She returned the smile faintly; I am not interested, but I am not completely *un*interested. He put the two halves of the roll face down beside the hamburger and turned to Ellen. "Coffee now or later?"

"Now, please."

He produced a tan cup and saucer and a spoon from under the counter. He arranged them before her and then moved a few paces down the gangway, to return with a glass pot of coffee. He poured the steaming liquid slowly into her cup. "You go to Stoddard?" he asked.

"No, I don't."

He rested the coffee pot on the marble and with his free hand brought a jigger of cream up from under the counter.

"You?" Ellen asked.

He nodded.

Down the counter a spoon chinked against glass. Powell answered the call with the sullen compression returning to his lips.

He was back a minute later, picking up a spatula and turning the hamburger. He opened the locker again and took out a slice of American cheese which he put on top of the meat. They looked at each other in the mirror as he arranged the roll and a couple of slices of pickle on a plate. "You haven't been in here before, have you," he said.

"No. I've only been in Blue River a couple of days."

"Oh. Staying or passing through?" He spoke slowly, like a circling hunter.

"Staying. If I can find a job."

"As what?"

"A secretary."

He turned around, the spatula in one hand, the plate in the other. "That should be easy to find."

"Ha," she said.

There was a pause. "Where you from?" he asked.

"Des Moines."

"It should be easier to find a job there than it is here."

She shook her head. "All the girls looking for jobs go to Des Moines."

Turning back to the grill, he lifted the cheeseburger with the spatula and slid it onto the roll. He set the plate before her and produced a bottle of ketchup from below the counter. "You have relatives here?"

She shook her head. "Don't know a soul in town. Except the woman at the employment agency."

A spoon tapped glass again down the counter. "Damn," he muttered. "Maybe you want *my* job?" He stalked away.

In a few minutes he returned. He began scraping the top of the grill with the edge of the spatula. "How's the cheeseburger?"

"Fine."

"You want something else? Some more coffee?"

"No, thanks."

The grill was perfectly clean but he continued scraping it, watching Ellen in the mirror. She dabbed at her lips with the napkin. "Check, please," she said.

He turned, taking a pencil and a green pad from a clip on his belt. "Listen," he said, not looking up from his writing, "there's a very good revival at the Paramount tonight. *Lost Horizon.* You want to see it?"

"I . . ."

"You said you didn't know anybody in town."

She seemed to debate for a moment. "All right," she said finally.

He looked up and smiled, this time effortlessly. "Swell. Where can I meet you?"

"The New Washington House. In the lobby."

"Eight o'clock okay?" He tore the check from the pad. "My name is Dwight," he said. "As in Eisenhower. Dwight Powell." He looked at her, waiting.

"Mine is Evelyn Kittredge."

"Hi," he said, smiling. She flashed a broad smile in return. Something flickered over Powell's face; surprise? . . . memory? . . .

"What's wrong?" Ellen asked. "Why do you look at me that way?"

"Your smile," he said uneasily. "Exactly like a girl I used to know . . ."

There was a pause, then Ellen said decisively, "Joan Bacon or Bascomb or something. I've been in this town only two days and two people have told me I look like this Joan—"

"No," Powell said, "this girl's name was Dorothy." He folded the check. "Lunch is on me." He waved his arm, trying to attract the attention of the cashier up front. Craning his neck, he pointed to the check, to Ellen and to himself, and then tucked the check into his pocket. "All taken care of," he said.

Ellen was standing, putting on her coat. "Eight o'clock in the New

Washington lobby," Powell reiterated. "Is that where you're staying?"

"Yes." She made herself smile. She could see his mind following the path; easy pick-up, stranger in town, staying at a hotel . . . "Thanks for lunch."

"Don't mention it."

She picked up her purse.

"See you tonight, Evelyn."

"Eight o'clock," she said. She turned and walked towards the front of the store, keeping her pace slow, feeling his eyes on her back. At the door she turned. He lifted a hand and smiled. She returned the gesture.

Outside, she found that her knees were shaking.

## 6

ELLEN WAS IN the lobby at seven-thirty, so that Powell would not have the occasion to ask the desk clerk to ring Miss Kittredge's room. He arrived at five of eight, the thin line of his moustache glinting over an edgy smile. (Easy pick-up . . . stranger in town . . .) He had ascertained that *Lost Horizon* went on at 8:06, so they took a cab to the theater although it was only five blocks away. Midway through the picture Powell put his arm around Ellen, resting his hand on her shoulder. She kept seeing it from the corner of her eye, the hand that had caressed Dorothy's body, had pushed powerfully . . . maybe . . .

The Municipal Building was three blocks from the theater and less than two from the New Washington House. They passed it on their way back to the hotel. A few windows were lighted in the upper floors of the looming façade across the street. "Is that the tallest building in the city?" Ellen asked, looking at Powell.

"Yes," he said. His eyes were focused some twenty feet ahead on the sidewalk.

"How high is it?"

"Fourteen stories." The direction of his gaze had not altered. Ellen thought: When you ask a person the height of something that's in his presence, he instinctively turns to look at it, even if he already knows the answer. Unless he has some reason for not wanting to look at it.

They sat in a booth in the hotel's black-walled soft-pianoed cocktail lounge and drank whiskey sours. Their conversation was intermittent, Ellen pushing it against the uphill slope of Powell's slow deliberate speech. The taut buoyancy with which he had begun the evening had faded in passing the Municipal Building, had risen again on entering the hotel, and now was waning steadily the longer they sat in the red-upholstered booth.

They spoke about jobs. Powell disliked his. He had held it for two months and planned to quit as soon as he could find something better. He was saving his money for a summer study tour of Europe.

What was he studying? His major was English. What did he plan to do with it? He wasn't sure. Advertising, maybe, or get into publishing. His plans for the future seemed sketchy.

They spoke about girls. "I'm sick of these college girls," he said. "Immature . . . they take everything too seriously." Ellen thought this was the beginning of a line, the one that leads straight to "You place too much importance on sex. As long as we like each other, what's the harm in going to bed?" It wasn't though. It seemed to be something that was troubling him. He weighed his words carefully, twisting the stem of the third cocktail glass between long restless fingers. "You get one of them on your neck," he said, the blue eyes clouded, "and you can't get her off." He watched his hand. "Not without making a mess . . ."

Ellen closed her eyes, her hands damp on the slick black tabletop.

"You can't help feeling sorry for people like that," he went on, "but you've got to think of yourself first."

"People like what?" she said, not opening her eyes.

"People who throw themselves on other people . . ." There was the loud slap of his hand hitting the tabletop. Ellen opened her eyes. He was taking cigarettes from a pack on the table, smiling. "The trouble with me is too many whiskey sours," he said. His hand, holding a match to her cigarette, was unsteady. "Let's talk about you."

She made up a story about a secretarial school in Des Moines run by an elderly Frenchman who pitched spitballs at the girls when they weren't looking. When it was finished Powell said, "Look, let's get out of here."

"You mean go to another place?" Ellen asked.

"If you want to," he said unenthusiastically.

Ellen reached for the coat beside her. "If you don't mind, I'd just as soon we didn't. I was up very early this morning."

"Okay," Powell said. "I'll escort you to your door." The edgy smile which had begun the evening made its return.

She stood with her back to the door of her room, the brass-tagged key in her hand. "Thank you very much," she said. "It really was a nice evening."

His arm with both their coats over it went around her back. His lips came towards her and she turned away, catching the kiss on her cheek. "Don't be coy," he said flatly. He caught her jaw in his hand and kissed her mouth hard.

"Let's go in . . . have a last cigarette," he said.

She shook her head.

"Evvie . . ." His hand was on her shoulder.

She shook her head again. "Honestly, I'm dead tired." It was a refusal, but the modest curling of her voice implied that things might be different some other night.

He kissed her a second time. She pushed his hand back up to her shoulder. "Please . . . someone might . . ." Still holding her, he drew back a bit and smiled at her. She smiled back, trying to make it the same broad smile she had given him in the drugstore.

It worked. It was like touching a charged wire to an exposed nerve. The shadow flickered across his face.

He drew her close, both arms around her, his chin over her shoulder as if to avoid seeing her smile. "Do I still remind you of that girl?" she asked. And then, "I'll bet she was another girl you went out with just once."

"No," he said, "I went out with her for a long time." He pulled back. "Who says I'm going out with you just once? You doing anything tomorrow night?"

"No."

"Same time, same place?"

"If you'd like."

He kissed her cheek and held her close again. "What happened?" she asked.

"What do you mean?" His words vibrated against her temple.

"That girl. Why did you stop going with her?" She tried to make it light, casual. "Maybe I can profit by her mistakes."

"Oh." There was a pause. Ellen stared at the cloth of his lapel, seeing the precise weaving of the slate blue threads. "It was like I said downstairs . . . we got too involved. Had to break it off." She heard him take a deep breath. "She was very immature," he added.

After a moment Ellen made a withdrawing movement. "I think I'd better . . ."

He kissed her again, a long one. She closed her eyes sickly.

Easing from his arms, she turned and put the key in the door without looking at him. "Tomorrow night at eight," he said. She had to turn around to take her coat, and there was no avoiding his eyes. "Good night, Evvie."

She opened the door behind her and stepped back, forcing a smile to her lips. "Good night." She shut the door.

She was sitting motionlessly on the bed, the coat still in her hands, when the telephone rang five minutes later. It was Gant.

"Keeping late hours, I see."

She sighed. "Is it a relief to talk to you . . ."

"Well!" he said, stretching the word. "Well, well, *well!* I gather that my innocence has been clearly and conclusively established."

"Yes. Powell's the one who was going with her. And I'm right about it not being suicide. I know I am. He keeps talking about girls who throw themselves on other people and take things too seriously and get involved and things like that." The words tumbled quickly, freed of the strain of guarded conversation.

"Good Lord, your efficiency astounds me. Where did you get your information?"

"From him."

"What?"

"I picked him up in the drugstore where he works. I'm Evelyn Kittredge, unemployed secretary, of Des Moines, Iowa. I just tight-roped through the evening with him."

There was a long silence from Gant's end of the line. "Tell all," he said finally, wearily. "When do you plan to beat the written confession out of him?"

She told him of Powell's sudden dejection when passing the Municipal Building, repeating as accurately as she could the remarks he had made under the influence of the doldrums and the whiskey sours.

When Gant spoke again he was serious. "Listen, Ellen, this doesn't sound like anything to play around with."

"Why? As long as he thinks I'm Evelyn Kittredge—"

"How do you know he does? What if Dorothy showed him a picture of you?"

"She had only one, and that was a very fuzzy group snapshot with our faces in the shade. If he did see it, it was almost a year ago. He couldn't possibly recognize me. Besides, if he suspected who I am he wouldn't have said the things he did."

"No, I guess he wouldn't have," Gant admitted reluctantly. "What do you plan to do now?"

"This afternoon I went down to the library and read all the newspaper reports of Dorothy's death. There were a few details that were never mentioned, little things like the color of her hat, and the fact that she was wearing gloves. I have another date with him tomorrow night. If I can get him talking about her 'suicide' maybe he'll let drop one of those things that he couldn't know unless he was with her."

"It wouldn't be conclusive evidence," Gant said. "He could claim he was in the building at the time and he saw her after she . . ."

"I'm not *looking* for conclusive evidence. All I want is something that will prevent the police from thinking that I'm just a crank with an overactive imagination. If I can prove he was anywhere near her at the time, it should be enough to start them digging."

"Well will you please tell me how the hell you expect to get him to talk in such detail without making him suspicious? He's not an idiot, is he?"

"I have to try," she argued. "What else is there to do?"

Gant thought for a moment. "I am the owner of an old ball-peen hammer," he said. "We could beat him over the head, drag him to the scene of the crime, and sweat it out of him."

"You see," Ellen said seriously, "there's no other way to . . ." Her voice faded.

"Hello?"

"I'm still here," she said.

"What happened? I thought we were cut off."

"I was just thinking."

"Oh. Look, seriously . . . be careful, will you? And if it's at all possible, call me tomorrow evening, just to let me know where you are and how things are going."

"Why?"

"Just to be on the safe side."

"He thinks I'm Evelyn Kittredge."

"Well call me anyway. It can't hurt. Besides, my hair grays easily."

"All right."

"Good night, Ellen."

"Good night, Gordon."

She replaced the receiver and remained sitting on the bed, biting her lower lip and drumming her fingers the way she always did when she was toying with an idea.

## 7

SNAPPING SHUT HER purse, Ellen looked up and smiled across the lobby at Powell's approaching figure. He was wearing a gray topcoat and a navy blue suit, and the same smile he had worn the previous evening.

"Hi," he said, dropping down beside her on the leather divan. "You certainly don't keep your dates waiting."

"Some of them I do."

His smile broadened. "How's the job-hunting?"

"Pretty good," she said. "I think I've got something. With a lawyer."

"Swell. You'll be staying in Blue River then, right?"

"It looks that way."

"Swell . . ." he drew the word out caressingly. Then his eyes flicked to his wristwatch. "We'd better get on our horses. I passed the Glo-Ray Ballroom on my way over here and there was a line all the way—"

"Ohh," she lamented.

"What's the matter?"

Her face was apologetic. "I've got an errand to do first. This lawyer. I have to bring him a letter . . . a reference." She tapped her purse.

"I didn't know secretaries needed references. I thought they just tested your shorthand or something."

"Yes, but I mentioned that I had this letter from my last employer and he said he'd like to see it. He's going to be at his office till eight-thirty." She sighed. "I'm awfully sorry."

"That's all right."

Ellen touched his hand. "I'd just as soon not go dancing," she confided. "We can go someplace, have a few drinks . . ."

"Okay," he said more cheerfully. They stood up. "Where is this lawyer?" Powell asked, standing behind her, helping her on with her coat.

"Not far from here," Ellen said. "The Municipal Building."

At the head of the steps that fronted the Municipal Building, Powell stopped. Ellen, in the quadrant of a revolving door, relaxed her about-to-push hand and looked at him. He was pale, but that might have been the grayish light filtering out from the lobby. "I'll wait for you down here, Evvie." His jaw was rigid, the words coming out stiffly.

"I wanted you to come up with me," she said. "I could have brought this letter over here before eight o'clock, but I thought it was kind of odd, his telling me to bring it in the evening. He's a greasy looking character." She smiled. "You're my protection."

"Oh," Powell said.

Ellen pushed around through the door, and after a moment Powell followed her. She had turned and was watching him when he came out of the door. He was breathing through partially opened lips, his face barren of expression.

The vast marbled lobby was silent and empty. Three of the four elevators were black behind latticed metal gates. The fourth was a yellow-lighted cell with wooden walls the color of honey. They walked towards it side by side, their footsteps drawing whispering echoes from the domed ceiling.

In the cell a tan-uniformed Negro operator stood reading a copy of *Look.* He tucked the magazine under his arm, toed the floor button that released the big sliding metal door, and threw the latticed gate across after it. "Floor please," he said.

"Fourteen," Ellen said.

They stood in silence, watching the steadily advancing position of the lighted numeral in the row of unlighted numerals over the door. 7 . . . 8 . . . 9 . . . Powell rubbed his moustache with the side of his forefinger.

When the light jumped from 13 to 14, the car came to a smooth automatic top-floor stop. The operator drew in the gate and pulled down on the jointed bar that opened the outer door.

Ellen stepped out into the deserted corridor, Powell following her. Behind them the door slid shut with a hollow clangor. They heard the gate closing and then the decrescent hum of the car. "It's this way," Ellen said, moving towards the right. "Room fourteen-oh-five." They walked to the bend of the corridor and made the right turn. There was light behind only two of the frosted glass door panels in the stretch of straight-lined corridor before them. There was no sound except their feet on the polished rubber tiles. Ellen groped for something to say . . . "It won't take long. I just have to give him the letter."

"Do you think you'll get the job?"

"I think so. It's a good letter."

They reached the end of the corridor and turned right again. One door was lighted, up ahead in the left wall, and Powell angled towards it. "No, that's not the one," Ellen said. She went to an unlighted door on the right. Its frosted panel was inscribed *Frederic H. Clausen, Attorney at Law.* Powell came up behind her as she futilely tried the knob and looked at her watch. "How do you like that?" she said bitterly. "Not even a quarter after and he said he'd be here till eight-thirty." (The secretary on the telephone had said "The office closes at five.")

"What now?" Powell asked.

"I guess I'll leave it under the door," she said, opening her purse. She took out a large white envelope and her fountain pen. Uncapping the pen, she held the envelope flat against the purse and began to write. "It's a shame about the dancing," she said.

"That's okay," said Powell. "I wasn't too keen on it myself." He was breathing more easily, like a novice aerialist passing the middle of the taut wire and becoming less uncertain of his footing.

"On second thought," Ellen said, glancing up at him, "If I leave the letter now I'll only have to come back for it tomorrow anyway. I might just as well bring it over in the morning." She recapped the pen and put it back in her purse. She held the envelope at an angle to the light, saw that the ink was still wet, and began to wave the envelope with quick fanlike motions. Her gaze drifted to a door across the corridor, the door marked *Stairway*. Her eyes lighted. "You know what I'd like to do?" she asked.

"What?"

". . . Before we go back and have those drinks . . ."

"What?" He smiled.

She smiled back at him, waving the envelope. "Go up to the roof."

The aerialist looked down and saw the net being drawn out from under him. "What do you want to do that for?" he asked slowly.

"Didn't you see the moon? And the stars? It's a perfect night. The view must be tre*men*dous."

"I think we might still be able to get into the Glo-Ray," he said.

"Oh, neither of us are crazy about going." She slipped the envelope into her purse and snapped it shut. "Come on," she said gaily, turning from him and crossing the corridor. "What happened to all that romance you displayed in the hall last night?" His hand reached out for her arm and caught empty air.

She pushed the door open and looked back, waiting for him to follow.

"Evvie, I . . . Heights make me dizzy." He forced a thin smile.

"You don't have to look down," she said lightly. "You don't even have to go near the edge."

"The door's probably locked . . ."

"I don't think they can lock a door to a roof. Fire laws." She frowned in mock disgust. "Oh, come on! You'd think I was asking you to go over Niagara Falls in a barrel or something!" She backed through the doorway onto the landing, holding the door, smiling, waiting for him.

He came with a slow trancelike helplessness, as though there were part of him that perversely wanted to follow her. When he was on the landing she released the door. It swung closed with a soft pneumatic hissing, cutting off the light from the corridor and leaving a 10-watt bulb to fight a losing battle against the shadows of the stairwell.

They climbed eight steps, turned, and climbed eight more. There was a dark metal door with a warning painted on it in large white letters:

*Entrance Strictly Forbidden Except in Emergency.* Powell read it aloud, stressing the words 'strictly forbidden.'

"Signs," Ellen said disdainfully. She tried the knob.

"It must be locked," Powell said.

"If it were locked they wouldn't have *that.*" Ellen indicated the sign. "You try."

He took the knob, pushed. "It's stuck, then."

"Oh, come on. Give a real try."

"Okay," he said, "okay okay," with to-hell-with-it abandon. He drew back and slammed his shoulder against the door full-force. It flew open almost dragging him with it. He stumbled across the high threshold onto the tarred deck. "Okay, Evvie," he said sullenly, straightening himself, holding the door wide, "come look at your gorgeous moon."

"Sourpuss," Ellen said, the light tone of her voice stripping his bitterness of significance. She stepped over the ledge and breezed a few steps past Powell, advancing from the shadow of the staircase housing out onto the expanse of roof like a cold-legged skater pretending not to worry about thin ice. She heard the door closing behind her, and then Powell came up on her left.

"Sorry," he said, "it's just that I almost broke my shoulder on the damn door, that's all." He managed a starchy smile.

They were facing the KBRI tower; skeletal, black against the blue-black star-spattered sky; at the very top of it a slowly flashing red light whose steady pulsing flushed the roof with intermittent rose. Between the red throbs there was the soft light of the quarter moon overhead.

Ellen glanced at Powell's upturned tense-jawed profile; first dim white, then bathed with red, then white again. Beyond him she saw the wall that rimmed the airshaft, its white stone top distinct in the night. She remembered a diagram that had appeared in one of the newspapers; the X at the south side of the square—the side nearest them. Suddenly she was caught by a crazy desire to go there, look over, see where Dorothy . . . A sick wave swept over her. The focus of her vision realigned on Powell's white-edged profile and involuntarily she drew away.

It's all right, she told herself, I'm safe—safer than pushing conversation in some cocktail lounge. I'm all right, I'm Evelyn Kittredge . . .

He became conscious of her gaze. "I thought you wanted to look at the sky," he said, not lowering his own skyward face. She looked up and the sudden lifting of her head heightened the dizziness. The stars wheeled . . .

She broke away, went to the right, to the outer edge of the roof. Abrading her hands against the roughness of the coping, she gasped lungfuls of the cold night air . . . This is where he killed her. He's bound to betray himself—enough to go to the police. I'm safe . . . Finally her head cleared. She looked at the panorama below, the myriad lights glittering off into blackness. "Dwight, come look."

He turned and walked towards the parapet, but he stopped a few feet away.

"Isn't it beautiful?" She spoke without looking back.

"Yes," he said.

He looked for a moment, while a breeze plucked softly at the tower cables, and then he turned slowly around until he was facing the airshaft. He stared at the parapet. Then his right foot extended itself and his legs began to walk. They carried him forward with silent relentless efficiency, like the legs of a reformed alcoholic carrying him to the bar for just one little drink. They carried him straight up to the airshaft parapet and his hands rose and set themselves flat on the cool stone. He leaned over and looked down.

Ellen felt his absence. She turned around and probed the quarter-moon obscurity. Then the tower light flashed on, its crimson glow showing him at the wall of the airshaft, and her heart jumped chokingly. The red glow vanished, but knowing where he was she could still distinguish him in the wan moonlight. She began moving forward, her steps noiseless on the resilient tar.

He looked down. A few yellow beams from lighted windows crisscrossed the square funnel of the shaft. One light was far below, at the very bottom, illuminating the small gray concrete square that was the focus of the converging walls.

"I thought heights made you dizzy."

He whirled.

There were sweat beads on his brow and above his moustache. A nervous smile shot to his lips. "They do," he said, "but I can't help looking. Self-torture . . ." The smile faded. "That's my specialty." He took a deep breath. "You ready to go now?" he asked.

"We just got here," Ellen protested lightly. She turned and walked towards the eastern rim of the roof, threading her way between the gaunt shapes of ventilator pipes. Powell followed reluctantly. Reaching the edge, Ellen stood with her back to the parapet and gazed up at the rearing red-limned tower beside them. "It's nice up here," she said. Powell, looking out over the city, his hands folded on the parapet, said nothing. "Have you ever been here at night?" Ellen asked.

"No," he said. "I've never been here before at all."

She turned to the parapet and leaned over, looking down at the shelf of the setback two stories below. She frowned thoughtfully. "Last year," she said slowly, "I think I read about some girl falling from here . . ."

A ventilator cap creaked. "Yes," Powell said. His voice was dry. "A suicide. She didn't fall."

"Oh." Ellen kept looking at the setback. "I don't see how she could have gotten killed," she said. "It's only two stories."

He lifted a hand, the thumb pointing back over his shoulder. "Over there . . . the shaft."

"Oh, that's right." She straightened up. "I remember now. The Des Moines newspapers gave it a very big write-up." She put her purse on the ledge and held it squarely with both hands, as though testing the rigidity of its frame. "She was a Stoddard girl, wasn't she?"

"Yes," he said. He pointed far out towards the horizon. "You see that roundish building there, with the lights on it? That's the Stoddard Observatory. Had to go out there for a Physical Science project once. They have a—"

"Did you know her?"

The red light stained his face. "Why do you ask?" he said.

"I just thought you might have known her. That's a natural thing to think, both going to Stoddard . . ."

"Yes," he said sharply, "I knew her and she was a very nice girl. Now let's talk about something else."

"The only reason the story stuck in my mind," she said, "was because of the hat."

Powell gave an exasperated sigh. Wearily he said, "What hat?"

"She was wearing a red hat with a bow on it and I had just bought a red hat with a bow on it the day that it happened."

"Who said she was wearing a red hat?" Powell asked.

"Wasn't she? The Des Moines papers said . . ." . . . Tell me they were wrong, she prayed, tell me it was green . . .

There was silence for a moment. "The *Clarion* never mentioned a red hat," Powell said. "I read the articles carefully, knowing her . . ."

"Just because the Blue River paper never mentioned it doesn't mean that it wasn't so," Ellen said.

He didn't say anything. She looked and saw him squinting at his wristwatch. "Look," he said brusquely, "it's twenty-five to nine. I've had enough of this magnificent view." He turned away abruptly, heading for the staircase housing.

Ellen hurried after him. "We can't go yet," she wheedled, catching his arm just outside the slant-roofed shed.

"Why not?"

Behind a smile her mind raced. "I . . . I want a cigarette."

"Oh for . . ." His hand jerked towards a pocket, then stopped short. "I don't have any. Come on, we'll get some downstairs."

"I have some," she said quickly, flashing her purse. She backed away, the position of the airshaft behind her as clear in her mind as if she were looking at the newspaper diagram. X marks the spot. Turning slightly, she sidled back towards it, opening the purse, smiling at Powell, saying inanely "It'll be nice to smoke a cigarette up here." The parapet reared against her hip. X. She fumbled in her purse. "You want one?"

He came towards her with resignation and compressed-lip anger. She shook the crumpled pack of cigarettes until one white cylinder protruded, thinking—it has to be tonight, because he won't ask Evelyn Kittredge for another date. "Here," she offered. He snatched the cigarette grimly.

Her fingertips dug for another one, and as they did her eyes roved and apparently became aware of the airshaft for the first time. She turned towards it slightly. "Is this where . . . ?" She turned back to him.

His eyes were narrowed, his jaw tightened by the last threads of a fast-raveling patience. "Listen, Evvie," he said, "I asked you not to talk about it. Now will you just do me that one favor? Will you please?" He jabbed the cigarette between his lips.

She didn't take her eyes from his face. Drawing a cigarette from the pack, she put it calmly to her lips and dropped the pack back into her purse. "I'm sorry," she said coolly, tucking the purse under her left arm. "I don't know what you're so touchy about."

"Can't you understand? I *know* the girl."

She struck a match and held it to his cigarette, the orange glow lighting his face, showing the blue eyes simmering with about-to-break strain, the jaw muscles tight as piano wires. . . . One more jab, one more jab . . . She withdrew the match from his lighted cigarette, held it before his face. "They never did say why she did it, did they?" His eyes closed painfully. "I'll bet she was pregnant," she said.

His face flared from flame orange to raw red as the match died and the tower light flashed on. The wire-tight muscles burst and the blue eyes shot open like dams exploding. . . . Now!—Ellen thought triumphantly—Now! Let it be something good, something damning! . . .

"All right!" he blazed, "all right! You know why I won't talk about it? You know why I didn't want to come up here at all? Why I didn't even want to come into this goddamn building?"—he flung away his cigarette—"Because the girl who committed suicide here was the girl I told you about last night! The one you smile like!" His eyes dropped from her face. "The girl who I—"

The words cut off guillotine-sharp. She saw his downcast eyes dilate with shock and then the tower light faded and she could see him only as a dim form confronting her. Suddenly his hand caught her left wrist, gripping it with paralyzing pressure. A scream pushed the cigarette from her lips. He was wrenching at the fingers of her captive hand, clawing at them. The purse slid out from under her arm and thudded to her feet. Futilely her right hand flailed his head. He was thumbing the muscles of her hand, forcing the fingers open . . . Releasing her, he stepped back and became a dimly outlined form again.

"What did you do?" she cried. "What did you take?" Dazedly she stooped and retrieved her purse. She flexed her left hand, her jarred senses vainly trying to recall the imprint of the object she had been holding.

Then the red light flashed on again and she saw it resting in the palm of his hand as though he had been examining it even in the dark. The matchbook. With the coppered letters glinting sharp and clear: *Ellen Kingship.*

Coldness engulfed her. She closed her eyes sickly, nauseous fear ballooning in her stomach. She swayed; her back felt the hard edge of the airshaft parapet.

## 8

"HER SISTER . . ." he faltered, "her sister . . ."

She opened her eyes. He was staring at the matchbook with glazed incomprehension. He looked up at her. "What is this?" he asked dully. Suddenly he hurled the matchbook at her feet and his voice flared loud again, "What do you want from me?"

"Nothing, nothing," she said quickly, "nothing." Her eyes darted desperately. He was standing between her and the stairway shed. If only she could circle around him . . . She began inching to her left, her back pulling against the parapet.

He rubbed his forehead. "You . . . you pick me up . . . you ask me questions about her . . . you get me up here . . ." Now his voice was entreating: "What do you *want* from me?"

"Nothing . . . nothing," warily sidestepping.

"Then why did you *do* this?" His body flexed to move forward.

"Stop!" she cried.

The ball-poised feet dropped flat, frozen.

"If anything happens to me," she said, forcing herself to speak slowly, evenly, "there's somebody else who knows all about you. He knows I'm with you tonight, and he knows all about you, so if anything happens, anything at all . . ."

"If anything . . . ?" His brow furrowed. "What are you talking about?"

"You know what I mean. If I fall . . ."

"Why should you . . . ?" He stared unbelievingly. "You think I'd . . . ?" One hand gestured limply towards the parapet. "Jesus!" he whispered. "What are you, crazy?"

She was a good fifteen feet from him. She began edging away from the parapet, cutting across to get on a straight line with the stairway door that was behind him and on his right. He pivoted slowly, following her cautious transverse path. "What's this 'knows all about me'?" he demanded. "Knows what?"

"Everything," she said. "Everything. And he's waiting downstairs. If I'm not down in five minutes he's calling the police."

He slapped his forehead exhaustedly. "I give up," he moaned. "You want to go downstairs? You want to go? Well go ahead!" He turned and backed to the airshaft parapet, to the spot where Ellen had been standing originally, leaving her a clear path to the door. He stood with his elbows resting on the stone behind him. "Go ahead! Go on!"

She moved towards the door slowly, suspiciously, knowing that he could still beat her there, cut her off. He didn't move.

"If I'm supposed to be arrested," he said, "I'd just like to know what for. Or is that too much to ask?"

She made no answer until she had the door open in her hand. Then she said, "I expected you to be a convincing actor. You had to be, to make Dorothy believe you were going to marry her."

"What?" This time his surprise seemed deeper, painful. "Now listen, I never said *anything* to make her believe I was going to marry her. That was all on *her* side, all *her* idea."

"You liar," she clenched hatefully. "You filthy liar." She ducked behind the shield of the open door and stepped over the high threshold.

"Wait!" As though sensing that any forward movement would send her running, he dropped back along the parapet and then cut out from it, following the same path Ellen had taken before. He stopped when he was opposite the doorway, some twenty feet from it. Within the shed Ellen turned to face him, one hand on the doorknob, ready to pull it closed.

"For God's sake," he said earnestly, "will you just tell me what this is all about? Please?"

"You think I'm bluffing. You think we really don't know."

"Jesus . . ." he whispered furiously.

"All right," she glared. "I'll itemize it for you. One; she was pregnant. Two; you didn't want—"

"*Pregnant?*" It hit him like a rock in the stomach. He leaned forward. "Dorothy was *pregnant?* Is *that* why she did it? Is *that* why she killed herself?"

"She didn't kill herself!" Ellen cried. "You killed her!" She pulled the door shut, turned and ran.

She ran clatteringly down the metal steps, her heels ringing, clutching at the bannister and swinging round the turn at each landing and before she had gone two and a half flights she heard him thundering down after her shouting *Evvie! Ellen! Wait!* and then it was too late to take the elevator because by the time she ran all the way around the corridor and it came and took her down he would be waiting there already so there was nothing to do but keep on running with her heart beating and legs aching down the fourteen flights from roof to lobby which were really twenty-eight half-flights spiraling down through the gloomy stairwell with twenty-seven landings to swing out arm-pullingly banging against the wall with him thundering closer behind all the way down to the main floor half-slipping with the damn heels and coming out into a marble corridor and running around clattering echoing into the slippery floored cathedral of a lobby where the startled Negro head popped out of the elevator then pushing exhaustedly out through the heavy revolving door and down more steps of treacherous marble and almost bumping into a woman on the sidewalk and running down to the left down towards Washington Avenue down the smalltown night-deserted street and finally slowing with her heart hard-pumping to snatch one backward look before rounding the corner and there he was running down the marble steps waving and shouting *Wait! Wait!* She wheeled around the corner running again ignoring the couple that turned to stare and the boys in the car shouting *Want a ride?* and seeing the hotel down the block with its glass doors glowing like an ad for hotels getting nearer—he's getting nearer too but don't look back just keep on running—until at last she reached the beautiful glass doors and a man smiling amusedly held one of them open "Thank you, thank you," and finally she was in the lobby, the lobby, the safe warm lobby, with bellhops and loungers and men behind newspapers . . . She was dying to drop into one of the chairs but she went straight to the corner phone booths because if

Gant went to the police with her, Gant who was a local celebrity, then they'd be more inclined to listen to her, believe her, investigate. Panting, she seized the phone book and flipped to the K's—it was five to nine so he'd be at the studio. She slapped away pages, gaspingly catching her breath. There it was: KBRI—5–1000. She opened her purse and hunted for coins. Five-one-thousand, five-one-thousand, as she turned from the phone book rack and looked up.

Powell confronted her. He was flushed and panting, his blond hair wild. She wasn't afraid; there were bright lights and people. Hate leveled her rough breathing like a glacier: "You should have run the other way. It won't do you any good, but I would start running if I were you."

And he looked at her with a sick-dog, pleading, near-tears expression that was so pathetically sad-looking it had to be true, and he said softly, hurtfully,—"Ellen, I loved her."

"I have a phone call to make," she said, "if you'll get out of the way."

"Please, I've got to talk to you," he pleaded. "Was she? Was she really pregnant?"

"I have a phone call to make."

"Was she?" he demanded.

"You know she was!"

"The papers said nothing! Nothing . . ." Suddenly his brow furrowed and his voice dropped low, intense. "What month was she in?"

"Will you please get out of my—"

"What month was she in?" His voice was demanding again.

"Oh God! The second."

He let out a tremendous weight-dropping sigh of relief.

"Now will you *please* get out of my way?"

"Not until you explain what's going on. This Evelyn Kittredge act . . ."

Her glare was acid.

He whispered confusedly, "You mean you really think I killed her?" and saw no change in the narrow stabbing of her eyes. "I was in New York!" he protested. "I can prove it! I was in New York all last spring!"

It shook her, but only for a moment. Then she said, "I suppose you could figure out a way to prove you were in Cairo, Egypt, if you wanted to."

"Jesus . . ." he hissed, exasperated. "Will you just let me speak to you for five minutes? Five minutes?" He glanced around and caught a glimpse of a man's head vanishing behind a quickly lifted newspaper. "People are listening," he said. "Just come into the cocktail lounge for five minutes. What harm can it do? I couldn't 'do anything' to you there, if that's what you're worried about."

"What *good* can it do?" she argued. "If you were in New York and you didn't kill her, then why did you avoid looking at the Municipal Building when we passed it last night? And why didn't you want to go up on the roof tonight? And why did you stare down into the airshaft the way you did?"

He looked at her awkwardly, painfully. "I can explain it," he said haltingly, "only I don't know whether you'll be able to understand it. You see, I felt . . ."—he groped for a word—". . . I felt *responsible* for her suicide."

Most of the booths in the black-walled lounge were empty. Glasses clinked and the soft piano dallied with some Gershwin themes. They took the seats they had occupied the night before, Ellen sitting back stiffly against the upholstered partition as though to repudiate any suggestion of intimacy. When the waiter appeared they ordered whiskey sours, and it wasn't until the drinks were on the table between them and Powell had taken the first sip of his that, realizing Ellen's intention to maintain a noncommittal silence, he began to speak. The words came slowly at first, and with embarrassment.

"I met her a couple of weeks after classes began last year," he said. "Last school year, I mean. Late September. I'd seen her before—she was in two of my classes and she'd been in one of my classes in freshman year—but I never spoke to her until this particular day because I usually wind up with a seat in the first or second row and she always sat in the back, in the corner. Well, on the night before this day when I spoke to her, I'd been talking with some guys and one of them had said how the quiet girls were the ones who . . ." He paused, fingering his glass and looking down at it. "You're more likely to have a good time with a quiet girl. So when I saw her the next day, sitting in the back in the corner where she always sat, I remembered what this guy had said.

"I started a conversation with her, going out of the room at the end of the period. I told her I'd forgotten to take down the assignment and would she give it to me, and she did. I think she knew it was just an excuse to talk, but still she responded so . . . so eagerly it surprised me. I mean, usually a pretty girl will take a thing like that lightly, give you smart answers, you know . . . But she was so . . . unsophisticated, she made me feel a little guilty.

"Well anyway, we went out that Saturday night, went to a movie and to Frank's Florentine Room, and we really had a nice time. I don't mean fooling around or anything. Just a nice time. We went out again the next Saturday night and two times the week after that, and then three times until finally, just before we broke up, we were seeing each other almost every night. Once we got to know each other, she was a lot of fun. Not at all like she'd been in class. Happy. I liked her.

"Early November it turned out that that guy was right, what he said about quiet girls. About Dorothy, anyway." He glanced up, his eyes meeting Ellen's squarely. "You know what I mean?"

"Yes," she said coolly, impassive as a judge.

"This is a hell of a thing to tell a girl's sister."

"Go on."

"She was a *nice* girl," he said, still looking at her. "It was just that she was . . . love-starved. Not sex. Love." His glance fell. "She told me about things at home, about her mother—your mother, about how she'd wanted to go to school with you . . ."

A tremor ran through her; she told herself it was only the vibration caused by someone sitting down in the booth behind her.

"Things went on that way for a while," Powell continued, talking more swiftly now, his shame melting into a confessionary satisfaction. "She was really in love, hanging onto my arm and smiling up at me all the time. I mentioned once I liked argyle socks; she knitted me three pairs of them." He scratched the tabletop carefully. "I loved her too, only it wasn't the same. It was . . . sympathy-love. I felt sorry for her. Very nice of me.

"The middle of December she started to talk about marriage. Very indirectly. It was just before Christmas vacation and I was going to stay here in Blue River. I've got no family and all I've got in Chicago are a couple of cousins and some high school and Navy friends. So she wanted me to go to New York with her. Meet the family. I told her no, but she kept bringing it up again and finally there was a showdown.

"I told her I wasn't ready to get tied down yet, and she said that plenty of men were engaged and even married by twenty-two and if it was the future I was worrying about, her father would find a place for me. I didn't want that though. I had ambitions. I'll have to tell you about my ambitions some day. I was going to revolutionize American advertising. Well anyway, she said we could both get jobs when we finished school, and I said she could never live that way having been rich all her life. She said I didn't love her as much as she loved me, and I said I guessed she was right. That was it, of course, more than any of the other reasons.

"There was a scene and it was terrible. She cried and said I'd be sorry and all the things a girl says. Then after a while she changed her tack and said she was wrong; we would wait and go on the way we had been. But I'd been feeling sort of guilty all along, so I figured that since we'd had this halfway break, we might as well make it complete, and right before a vacation was the best time to do it. I told her it was all over, and there was more crying and more 'You'll be sorry' and that's the way it ended. Couple of days later she left for New York."

Ellen said, "All during that vacation she was in such a bad mood. Sulking . . . picking arguments . . ."

Powell printed wet rings on the table with the bottom of his glass. "After vacation," he said, "it was bad. We still had those two classes together. I would sit in the front of the room not daring to look back. We kept bumping into each other all over campus. So I decided I'd had enough of Stoddard and applied for a transfer to NYU." He saw the downcast expression on Ellen's face. "What's the matter?" he said. "Don't you believe me? I can prove all this. I've got a transcript from NYU and I think I've still got a note that Dorothy sent me when she returned a bracelet I'd given her."

"No," Ellen said dully. "I believe you. That's just the trouble."

He gave her a baffled look, and then continued. "Just before I left, towards the end of January, she was starting to go with another guy. I saw—"

"Another man?" Ellen leaned forward.

"I saw them together a couple of times. It hadn't been such a big blow to her after all, I thought. I left with a nice clean conscience. Even felt a bit noble."

"Who was he?" Ellen asked.

"Who?"

"The other man."

"I don't know. A man. I think he was in one of my classes. Let me finish.

"I read about her suicide the first of May, just a paragraph in the New York papers. I raced up to Times Square and got a *Clarion-Ledger* at that Out-of-Town Newspaper stand. I bought a *Clarion* every day that week, waiting for them to say what was in the note she sent you. They never did. They never said why she did it . . .

"Can you imagine how I felt? I didn't think she had done it just on account of me, but I did think that it was sort of a . . . general despondency. Which I was a major cause of.

"My work fell off after that. I was bucking too hard. I guess I felt

I had to get terrific marks to justify what I'd done to her. I broke into a cold sweat before every exam, and my marks turned out pretty poor. I told myself it was because of the transfer; at NYU I had to make up a lot of required courses that weren't required at Stoddard, and I'd lost about sixteen credits besides. So I decided to come back to Stoddard in September, to get myself straightened out." He smiled wryly. "Also maybe to try to convince myself that I didn't feel guilty.

"Anyway, it was a mistake. Every time I saw one of the places we used to go to, or the Municipal Building . . ." He frowned. "I kept telling myself it was her fault, that any other girl would have been mature enough to shrug it off . . . but it didn't do much good. It got to the point where I found myself going out of my way to walk past the building, needling myself, like looking into the airshaft tonight, visualizing her . . ."

"I know," Ellen said, hurrying him, "I wanted to look too. I guess it's a natural reaction."

"No," Powell said, "you don't know what it means to feel *responsible* . . ." He paused, seeing Ellen's humorless smile. "What are you smiling at?"

"Nothing."

"Well . . . that's it. Now you tell me she did it because she was pregnant . . . two months. It's a rotten thing of course, but it makes me feel a whole lot better. I guess she still wouldn't be dead if I hadn't ditched her, but I couldn't be expected to know how things would turn out, could I? I mean, there's a limit to responsibility. If you keep going back you could blame it on anyone." He drained the rest of his drink. "I'm glad to see you've stopped running for the police," he said. "I don't know where you got the idea that I killed her."

"Someone did kill her," Ellen said. He looked at her wordlessly. The piano paused between selections, and in the sudden stillness she could hear the faint cloth rustlings of the person in the booth behind her.

Leaning forward, she began talking, telling Powell of the ambiguously worded note, of the birth certificate, of something old, something new, something borrowed and something blue.

He was silent until she had finished. Then he said, "My God . . . It *can't* be a coincidence,"—as eager as she to disprove suicide.

"This man you saw her with," Ellen said. "You're sure you don't know who he was?"

"I think he was in one of my classes that semester, but the two times I saw them together were fairly late in January, when exams had started and there were no more classes, so I couldn't make sure or find out his name. And right afterwards I left for New York."

"Haven't you seen him again?"

"I don't know," Powell said. "I'm not sure. Stoddard's a big campus."

"And you're absolutely certain you don't know his name?"

"I don't know it now," Powell said, "but I can find it out in about an hour." He smiled. "You see, I've got his address."

## 9

"I TOLD YOU I saw them together a couple of times," he said. "Well the second time was one afternoon in a luncheonette across from the campus. I never expected to see Dorothy there; it wasn't a very popular place. That's why I was there. I didn't notice them until I'd sat down at the counter and then I didn't want to get up and leave because she'd already seen me in the mirror. I was sitting at the end of the counter, then two girls, then Dorothy and this guy. They were drinking malteds.

"The minute she saw me she started talking to him and touching his arm a lot; you know, trying to show me she had someone new. It made me feel awful, her doing that. Embarrassed for her. Then, when they were ready to leave, she gave a nod to those two girls sitting between us, turned to him and said in a louder-than-necessary voice, 'Come on, we can drop our books at your place.' To show me how chummy they were, I figured.

"As soon as they were gone one of the girls commented to the other about how good-looking he was. The other one agreed, and then she said something like 'He was going with so-and-so last year. It looks as if he's only interested in the ones who have money.'

"Well, I figured that if Dorothy was a sitting duck because she was on the rebound from me, then I ought to make sure that she wasn't being taken in by some gold-digger. So I left the luncheonette and followed them.

"They went to a house a few blocks north of the campus. He rang the bell a couple of times and then he took some keys out of his pocket and unlocked the door and they went in. I walked by on the other side of the street and copied down the address on one of my notebooks. I thought I would call up later, when someone else was there, and find out his name. I had a vague idea about speaking to some of the girls around school about him.

"I never did it though. On the way back to the campus, the . . . presumption of the whole thing hit me. I mean, where did I come off asking questions about this guy just on the basis of some remark made by a girl who probably had a bad case of sour grapes? It was a cinch he couldn't treat Dorothy any worse than I had. And that 'on the rebound' stuff; how did I know they weren't fine for each other?"

"But you still have the address?" Ellen asked anxiously.

"I'm pretty sure I do. I've got all my old notes in a suitcase in my room. We can go over there and get it right now if you want."

"Yes," she agreed quickly. "Then all we'll have to do is call up and find out who he is."

"He isn't necessarily the right one," Powell said, taking out his wallet.

"He must be. It can't be anyone she started going with much later than that." Ellen stood up. "There's still a phone call I'd like to make before we go."

"To your assistant? The one who was waiting downstairs ready to call the police if you didn't show up in five minutes?"

"That's right," she admitted, smiling. "He wasn't waiting downstairs, but there really is someone."

She went to the back of the dimly lit room, where a telephone booth painted black to match the walls stood like an up-ended coffin. She dialed 5–1000:

"KBRI, good evening," a woman's voice chirruped.

"Good evening. May I speak to Gordon Gant please?"

"I'm sorry, but Mr. Gant's program is on the air now. If you call again at ten o'clock you might be able to catch him before he leaves the building."

"Couldn't I speak to him while a record is on?"

"I'm sorry, but no telephone calls may be directed to a studio from which a program is being broadcast."

"Well would you take a message for him?"

The woman sing-songed that she would be glad to take a message, and Ellen told her that Miss Kingship—spelled out—said that Powell—spelled out—was all right but had an idea as to who wasn't, and Miss Kingship was going to Powell's home and would be there at ten o'clock, when Mr. Gant could call her.

"Any telephone number?"

"Darn," Ellen said, opening the purse in her lap. "I don't have the number, but the address"—managing to unfold the slip of paper without dropping the purse—"is Fifteen-Twenty West Thirty-Fifth Street."

The woman read the message back. "That's right," Ellen said. "You'll be sure he gets it?"

"Of course I will," the woman declared frostily.

"Thank you very much."

Powell was feeding coins onto a small silver tray in the hand of a rapt waiter when Ellen returned to their booth. A smile appeared momentarily on the waiter's face and he vanished, trailing a mumbled thank you. "All set," Ellen said. She reached for her coat which was folded on the banquette where she had been sitting. "By the way, what does he look like, our man? Aside from being so handsome that girls comment on it."

"Blond, tall . . ." Powell said, pocketing his wallet.

"Another blond," sighed Ellen.

"Dorothy went for us Nordic types."

Ellen smiled, pulling on her coat. "Our father is blond—or was until he lost his hair. All three of us—" Ellen's empty coatsleeve slapped over the top of the booth partition as her hand groped for it. "Excuse me," she said, glancing back over her shoulder, and then she saw that the next booth had been vacated. There were a cocktail glass and a dollar bill on the table, and a paper napkin which had been carefully torn into a delicate lacework web.

Powell helped her with the obstinate sleeve. "Ready?" he asked, putting on his own coat.

"Ready," she said.

It was 9:50 when the cab pulled up in front of Powell's house. West 35th Street was silent, feebly lighted by streetlamps whose beams had to strain their way through meshing tree branches. Yellow windowed houses faced each other on either side, like timid armies showing flags across no-man's-land.

As the roar of the departing cab faded away, Ellen and Powell mounted the steps of a dark, creaking-floored porch. After a few unsuccessful stabs for the keyhole, Powell unlocked the door and pushed it open. He stepped aside and followed Ellen in, throwing the door closed with one hand and flicking a light switch with the other.

They were in a pleasant-looking living room full of fat chintz-and-maple furniture. "You'd better stay down here," Powell said, going towards a staircase at the left side of the room. "Everything's in a mess upstairs. My landlady is in the hospital and I wasn't expecting company." He paused on the first step. "It'll probably take me a few minutes to find that book. There's some instant coffee in the kitchen back there. You want to fix some?"

"All right," Ellen said, slipping out of her coat.

Powell jogged up the stairs and swung around the newel post. The door to his room was opposite the side of the stairwell. He went in, flipping on the light, and shucked off his coat. The unmade bed, on the right against the windows, was littered with pajamas and discarded clothes. He tossed his coat on top of the whole business and squatted down, about to pull a suitcase from under the bed; but with a sharp fingersnap he straightened up, turned, and stepped over to the bureau, which stood squeezed between a closet door and an armchair. He opened the top drawer and rummaged through papers and small boxes and scarves and broken cigarette lighters. He found the paper he wanted at the bottom of the drawer. Pulling it free with a flourish, he went into the hall and leaned over the stairwell bannister. "Ellen!" he called.

In the kitchen, Ellen adjusted the sighing gas flame under a pan of water. "Coming!" she answered. She hurried through the dining room and into the living room. "Got it already?" she asked, going to the stairs and looking up.

Powell's head and shoulders jutted into the stairwell. "Not yet," he said. "But I thought you'd like to see this." He let go of a stiff sheet of paper that came side-slipping down. "Just in case you have any lingering doubts."

It landed on the stairs before her. Picking it up, she saw that it was a photostat of his NYU record, the words *Student Copy* stamped on it. "If I had any lingering doubts," she said, "I wouldn't be here, would I?"

"True," Powell said, "true,"—and vanished from the stairwell.

Ellen took another look at the transcript and noted that his marks had indeed been pretty poor. Putting the paper on a table, she returned through the dining room to the kitchen. It was a depressing room with old fashioned appliances and cream colored walls that were brown in the corners and behind the stove. There was, however, a pleasant breeze blowing through from the back.

She found cups and saucers and a can of Nescafé in the various cupboards, and while she was spooning the powder into the cups, she noticed a radio with a cracked plastic case on the counter next to the stove. She turned it on, and once it had warmed up, slowly twisted the selector knob until she found KBRI. She almost passed over it because the small celluloid-vibrating set made Gant's voice sound unfamiliarly thin. ". . . and a little too much about things political," he was saying, "so let's get back to music. We've just got time for one more record, and it's the late Buddy Clark singing *If This Isn't Love.*"

Powell, having dropped the transcript down to Ellen, turned around and went back into his room. Squatting before the bed, he shot his hand underneath it—to bang his fingertips painfully against the suitcase, which had been pulled forward from its usual position flush against the wall. He jerked his hand out, waggling the fingers and blowing on them, and cursing his landlady's daughter-in-law who apparently had not been satisfied with only secreting his shoes beneath the bureau.

He reached under the bed again, more cautiously this time, and dragged the heavy-as-lead suitcase all the way out into the open. He took a bunch of keys from his pocket, found the right one and twisted it in the two locks springing them. Replacing the keys, he lifted the lid. The suitcase was filled with textbooks, a tennis racket, a bottle of Canadian Club, golf shoes . . . He took out the larger items and put them on the floor so that it would be easier to get at the notebooks underneath.

There were nine of them; pale green, spiral-bound notebooks. He gathered them into a bundle, stood up with the bundle in his arm and began inspecting them one at a time; examining both covers, dropping the books one by one back into the suitcase.

It was on the seventh one, on the back cover. The penciled address was rubbed and smudged, but it was still legible. He dropped the other two notebooks into the suitcase and turned around, his mouth opening to form Ellen's name in a triumphant shout.

The shout didn't come through. The exultant expression clung to his face for a moment, like a stopped movie, and then it cracked and slid slowly away, like thick snow cracking and sliding from a canted roof.

The closet door was open and a man in a trenchcoat stood framed there. He was tall and blond, and a gun bulked large in his gloved right hand.

## 10

HE WAS SWEATING. Not cold sweat though; hot healthy sweat from standing in the sweatbox of an airless closet in the sweatsuit of an imporous trenchcoat. His hands too; the gloves were brown leather with a fuzzy lining and elastic cuffs that held in the heat even more; his hands were sweating so much that the fuzzy lining was sodden and caked.

But the automatic (weightless now like part of him after dragging heavily in his pocket all evening) was motionless; the inevitable trajectory of the bullet as palpable in the air as a dotted line in a diagram.

Point A: the rock-steady muzzle; Point B: the heart under the lapel of the cheesy-looking probably-bought-in-Iowa suit. He looked down at the Colt .45 as though to verify its blue steel existence, so light it was, and then he took a step forward from the mouth of the closet, reducing by a foot the length of dotted line AB.

Well say something, he thought, enjoying the slow stupid melting of Mister Dwight Powell's face. Start talking. Start pleading. Probably can't. Probably he's all talked out after the—what's that word?—the logorrhea of the cocktail lounge. Good word.

"I bet you don't know what logorrhea means," he said, standing there powerfully with the gun in his hand.

Powell stared at the gun. "You're the one . . . with Dorothy," he said.

"It means what *you*'ve got. Diarrhea of the mouth. Words keep running. I thought my ear would fall off in that cocktail lounge." He smiled at Powell's widening eyes. "I was responsible for poor Dorothy's death," he mimicked. "A pity. A real pity." He stepped closer. "The notebook, *por favor*," he said, extending his left hand. "And don't try anything."

From downstairs, singing came softly:

*If this isn't love,*
*Then winter is summer . . .*

He took the notebook that Powell held out, dropped back a step and pressed it against his side, bending it in half lengthwise, cracking the cover, never taking his eyes or the gun off Powell. "I'm awfully sorry you found this. I was standing in there hoping you wouldn't." He stuck the folded notebook into his coat pocket.

"You really killed her . . ." Powell said.

"Let's keep the voices low." He moved the gun admonishingly. "We don't want to disturb the girl detective, do we?" It annoyed him the way Mister Dwight Powell was standing there so blankly. Maybe he was too stupid to realize . . . "Maybe you don't realize it, but this is a real gun, and it's loaded."

Powell didn't say anything. He just went on looking at the gun, not even staring now,—just looking at it with mildly distasteful interest, as though it were the first ladybug of the year.

"Look, I'm going to kill you."

Powell didn't say anything.

"You're such a great one for analyzing yourself—tell me, how do you feel now? I bet your knees are shaking, aren't they? Cold sweat all over you?"

Powell said, "She thought she was going there to get married . . ."

"Forget about her! You've got yourself to worry about." Why wasn't he trembling? Didn't he have brains enough . . . ?

"Why did you kill her?" Powell's eyes finally lifted from the gun. "If you didn't want to marry her, you could have left her. That would have been better than killing her."

"Shut up about her! What's the matter with you? You think I'm bluffing? Is that it? You think—"

Powell leaped forward.

Before he had gone six inches a loud explosion roared; dotted line AB was solidified and fulfilled by tearing lead.

Ellen had been standing in the kitchen looking out through the closed window and listening to the fading theme of Gordon Gant's program, when she suddenly realized that with the window closed, where was that pleasant breeze coming from?

There was a shadowed alcove in a rear corner of the room. She went to it and saw the back door, with the pane of glass nearest the knob smashed in and lying in fragments on the floor. She wondered if Dwight knew about it. You'd think he would have swept up the—

That was when she heard the shot. It smacked loudly through the house, and as the sound died the ceiling light shivered as if something upstairs had fallen. Then there was silence.

The radio said, "At the sound of the chime, ten PM, Central Standard Time," and a chime toned.

"Dwight?" Ellen said.

There was no answer.

She went into the dining room. She called the name louder: "Dwight?"

In the living room she moved hesitantly to the staircase. There was no sound from overhead. This time she spoke the name with dry-throated apprehension: "Dwight?"

The silence held for another moment. Then a voice said, "It's all right, Ellen. Come on up."

She hurried up the stairs with her heart drumming. "In here," the voice said from the right. She pivoted around the newel post and swept to the lighted doorway.

The first thing she saw was Powell lying on his back in the middle of the room, limbs sprawled loosely. His jacket had fallen away from his chest. On his white shirt blood was flowering from a black core over his heart.

She steadied herself against the jamb. Then she raised her eyes to the man who stood beyond Powell, the man with the gun in his hand.

Her eyes dilated, her face went rigid with questions that couldn't work their way to her lips.

He shifted the gun from the firing position to a flat appraising weight on his gloved palm. "I was in the closet," he said, looking her straight in the eye, answering the unasked questions. "He opened that suitcase and took out this gun. He was going to kill you. I jumped him. The gun went off."

"No . . . Oh God . . ." She rubbed her forehead dizzily. "But how . . . how did you . . . ?"

He put the gun in the pocket of his coat. "I was in the cocktail lounge," he said. "Right behind you. I heard him talking you into coming up here. I left while you were in the phone booth."

"He told me he . . ."

"I heard what he told you. He was a good liar."

"Oh God, I believed him . . . I believed him . . ."

"That's just your trouble," he said with an indulgent smile. "You believe everybody."

"Oh God . . ." she shivered.

He came to her, stepping between Powell's spraddled legs.

She said, "But I still don't understand . . . How were you there, in the lounge . . . ?"

"I was waiting for you in the lobby. I missed you when you went out with him. Got there too late. I kicked myself for that. But I waited around. What else could I do?"

"But how . . . how . . . ?"

He stood before her with his arms wide, like a soldier returning home. "Look, a heroine isn't supposed to question her nick-of-time rescuer. Just be glad you gave me his address. I may have thought you were being a fool, but I wasn't going to take any chances on having you get your head blown off."

She threw herself into his arms, sobbing with relief and retrospective fear. The leather-tight hands patted her back comfortingly. "It's all right, Ellen," he said softly. "Everything's all right now."

She buried her cheek against his shoulder. "Oh Bud," she sobbed, "thank God for you! Thank God for you, Bud!"

## 11

THE TELEPHONE RANG downstairs.

"Don't answer it," he said as she started to draw away.

There was a lifeless glaze to her voice: "I know who it is."

"No, don't answer it. Listen,"—his hands were solid and convincing on her shoulders—"someone is sure to have heard that shot. The police will probably be here in a few minutes. Reporters, too." He let that sink in. "You don't want the papers to make a big story out of this, do you? Dragging up everything about Dorothy, pictures of you . . ."

"There's no way to stop them . . ."

"There is. I have a car downstairs. I'll take you back to the hotel and then come right back here." He turned off the light. "If the police haven't shown up yet, I'll call them. Then you won't be here for the reporters to jump on, and I'll refuse to talk until I'm alone with the police. They'll question you later, but the papers won't know you're involved." He led her out into the hallway. "By that time you'll have called your father; he's got enough influence to keep the police from letting out anything about you or Dorothy. They can say Powell was drunk and started a fight with me, or something like that."

The telephone stopped ringing.

"I wouldn't feel right about leaving . . ." she said as they started down the stairs.

"Why not? I'm the one who did it, not you. It's not as if I'm going to lie about your being here; I'll need you to back up my story. All I want to do is prevent the papers from having a field day with this." He turned to her as they descended into the living room. "Trust me, Ellen," he said, touching her hand.

She sighed deeply, gratefully letting tension and responsibility drop from her shoulders. "All right," she said. "But you don't have to drive me. I can get a cab."

"Not at this hour, not without phoning. And I think the streetcars stop running at ten." He picked up her coat and held it for her.

"Where did you get a car?" she asked dully.

"I borrowed it."—he gave her her purse—"From a friend." Turning off the lights, he opened the door to the porch. "Come on," he said, "we haven't got too much time."

He had parked the car across the street and some fifty feet down the block. It was a black Buick sedan, two or three years old. He opened the door for Ellen, then went around to the other side and slipped in behind the wheel. He fumbled with the ignition key. Ellen sat silently, hands folded in her lap. "You feel all right?" he asked.

"Yes," she said, her voice thin and tired. "It's just that . . . he was going to kill me . . ." She sighed. "At least I was right about Dorothy. I *knew* she didn't commit suicide." She managed a reproachful smile. "And you tried to talk me out of making this trip . . ."

He got the motor started. "Yes," he said. "You were right."

She was silent for a moment. "Anyway, there's a sort of a silver lining to all this," she said.

"What's that?" He shifted gears and the car glided forward.

"Well, you saved my life," she said. "You really saved my life. That should cut short whatever objections my father might have, when you meet him and we speak to him about us."

After they had been driving down Washington Avenue for a few minutes, she moved closer to him and hesitantly took his arm, hoping it wouldn't interfere with his driving. She felt something hard pressing against her hip and realized that it was the gun in his pocket, but she didn't want to move away.

"Listen, Ellen," he said. "This is going to be a lousy business, you know."

"What do you mean?"

"Well, I'll be held for manslaughter."

"But you didn't mean to kill him! You were trying to get the gun away from him."

"I know, but they'll still have to hold me . . . all kinds of red tape . . ." He stole a quick glance at the downcast figure beside him and then returned his gaze to the traffic ahead. "Ellen . . . when we get to the hotel, you could just pick up your things and check out. We could be back in Caldwell in a couple of hours . . ."

"Bud!" Her voice was sharp with surprised reproach. "We couldn't do a thing like that!"

"Why not? He killed your sister, didn't he? He got what was coming to him. Why should we have to get mixed up—"

"We can't do it," she protested. "Aside from its being such a—a *wrong* thing to do, suppose they found out anyway that you . . . killed him. Then they'd never believe the truth, not if you ran away."

"I don't see how they could find out it was me," he said. "I'm wearing gloves, so there can't be any fingerprints. And nobody saw me there, except you and him."

"But suppose they *did* find out! Or suppose they blamed someone else for it! How would you feel then?" He was silent. "As soon as I get to the hotel, I'll call my father. Once he's heard the story, I know he'll take care of lawyers and everything. I guess it *will* be a terrible business. But to run away . . ."

"It was a foolish suggestion," he said. "I didn't really expect you to agree."

"No, Bud, you wouldn't want to do a thing like that, would you?"

"I only tried it as a last resort," he said. Suddenly he swung the car in a wide left turn from the brightly lighted orbit of Washington Avenue to the darkness of a northbound road.

"Shouldn't you stay on Washington?" Ellen asked.

"Quicker this way. Avoid traffic."

"What I can't understand," she said, tapping her cigarette on the edge of the dashboard tray, "is why he didn't do anything to me there, on the roof." She was settled comfortably, turned towards Bud with her left leg drawn up under her, the cigarette suffusing her with sedative warmth.

"You must have been pretty conspicuous, going there at night," he said. "He was probably afraid that an elevator man or someone would remember his face."

"Yes, I suppose so. But wouldn't it have been less risky than taking me back to his house and . . . doing it there?"

"Maybe he didn't intend to do it there. Maybe he was going to force you into a car and drive you out into the country someplace."

"He didn't have a car."

"He could have stolen one. It's not such a hard thing to steal a car." A streetlight flashing by brushed his face with white, then dropped it back into the darkness where the cleanly-hewn features were touched only by the dashboard's nebulous green.

"The lies he told me! 'I loved her. I was in New York. I felt responsible.'" She mashed the cigarette into the ashtray, shaking her head bitterly. "Oh my God!" she gasped.

He flicked a glance at her. "What is it?"

Her voice had taken on the sick glaze again. "He showed me his transcript . . . from NYU. He *was* in New York . . ."

"That was probably a fake. He must have known someone in the registrar's office there. They could fake something like that."

"But suppose it wasn't . . . Suppose he was telling the truth!"

"He was coming after you with a gun. Isn't that proof enough he was lying?"

"Are you sure, Bud? Are you sure he didn't—maybe take the gun out to get at something else? The notebook he mentioned?"

"He was going to the door with the gun."

"Oh God, if he really didn't kill Dorothy . . ." She was silent for a moment. "The police will investigate," she said positively. "They'll prove he was right here in Blue River! They'll prove he killed Dorothy!"

"That's right," he said.

"But even if he didn't, Bud, even if it was a—a terrible mistake,—

they wouldn't blame you for anything. You couldn't know; you saw him with the gun. They could never blame you for anything."

"That's right," he said.

Shifting uncomfortably, she drew her folded leg out from under her. She squinted at her watch in the dashboard's glow. "It's twenty-five after ten. Shouldn't we be there already?"

He didn't answer her.

She looked out the window. There were no more streetlights, no more buildings. There was only the pitch blackness of fields under the star-heightened blackness of the sky. "Bud, this isn't the way into town."

He didn't answer her.

Ahead of the car a white onrush of highway narrowed to implied infinity always beyond the headlights' reach.

"Bud, you're going the wrong way!"

## 12

"WHAT YOU WANT from *me?*" Chief of Police Eldon Chesser asked blandly. He lay supine, his long legs supported beneath the ankles by an arm of the chintz-covered sofa, his hands laced loosely across the front of his red flannel shirt, his large brown eyes vaguely contemplating the ceiling.

"Get after the car. That's what I want," Gordon Gant said, glaring at him from the middle of the living room.

"Ha," said Chesser. "Ha ha. A dark car is all the man next door knows; after he called about the shot he saw a man and a woman go down the block and get into a dark car. A dark car with a man and a woman. You know how many dark cars there is driving around town with a man and woman in them? We didn't even have a description of the girl until you come shooting in. By that time they could've been halfway to Cedar Rapids. Or parked in some garage two blocks from here, for all we know."

Gant paced malevolently. "So what are we supposed to do?"

"Wait, is all. I notified the highway boys, didn't I? Maybe this is bank night. Why don't you sit down?"

"Sure, sit down," Gant snapped. "She's liable to be murdered!" Chesser was silent. "Last year her sister,—now her."

"Here we go again," Chesser said. The brown eyes closed in weariness. "Her sister committed suicide," he articulated slowly. "I saw the note with my own two eyes. A handwriting expert—" Gant made a noise. "And who killed her?" Chesser demanded. "You said Powell was supposed to be the one, only now it couldn't've been him 'cause the girl left a message for you that he was all right, and you found this paper here from New York U. that makes it look like he wasn't even in these parts last spring. So if the only suspect didn't do it, who did? Answer: nobody."

His voice tight with the exasperation of repetition, Gant said, "Her message said that Powell had an idea who it was. The murderer must have known that Powell—"

"There *was* no murderer, until tonight," Chesser said flatly. "The sister committed suicide." His eyes blinked open and regarded the ceiling.

Gant glared at him and resumed his bitter pacing.

After a few minutes Chesser said, "Well, I guess I got it all reconstructed now."

"Yeah?" Gant said.

"Yeah. You didn't think I was laying here just to be lazy, did you? This is the way to think, with your feet higher'n your head. Blood goes to the brain." He cleared his throat. "The guy breaks in about a quarter to ten—man next door heard the glass break but didn't think anything of it. No sign of any of the other rooms having been gone through, so Powell's must have been the first one he hit. A couple minutes later Powell and the girl come in. The guy is stuck upstairs. He hides in Powell's closet—the clothes are all pushed to the side. Powell and the girl go into the kitchen. She starts making coffee, turns on the radio. Powell goes upstairs to hang up his coat, or maybe he heard a noise. The guy comes out. He's already tried to open the suitcase—we found glove smudges on it. He makes Powell unlock it and goes through it. Stuff all over the floor. Maybe he finds something, some money. Anyway, Powell jumps him. The guy shoots Powell. Probably panics, probably didn't intend to shoot him—they never do; they only carry the guns to scare people. Always wind up shooting 'em. Forty-five shell. Most likely an Army Colt. Million of 'em floating around.

"Next thing the girl comes running upstairs—same prints on the door frame up there as on the cups and stuff in the kitchen. The guy is panicky, no time to think . . . He forces her to leave with him."

"Why? Why wouldn't he have left her here . . . the way he left Powell?"

"Don't ask me. Maybe he didn't have the nerve. Or maybe he got ideas. Sometimes they get ideas when they're holding a gun and there's a pretty girl on the other end of it."

"Thanks," Gant said. "That makes me feel a whole lot better. Thanks a lot."

Chesser sighed. "You might as well sit down," he said. "There ain't a damn thing we can do but wait."

Gant sat down. He began rubbing his forehead with the heel of his hand.

Chesser finally turned his face from the ceiling. He watched Gant sitting across the room. "What is she? Your girlfriend?" he asked.

"No," Gant said. He remembered the letter he had read in Ellen's room. "No, there's some guy in Wisconsin."

## 13

BEHIND THE RACING island of the headlights' reach, the car arrowed over the tight line of highway, tarred seams in concrete creating a regular rhythm under the tires. The speedometer's luminous green needle split the figure fifty. The foot on the accelerator was steady as the foot of a statue.

He drove with his left hand, occasionally giving the steering wheel an inappreciable right or left movement to relieve the hypnotic monotony of the highway. Ellen was huddled all the way over against the door, her body knotted tight, her eyes staring brokenly at the handkerchief-twisting hands in her lap. On the seat between them, snakelike, lay his gloved right hand with the gun in it, the muzzle riveted against her hip.

She had cried; long throat-dragging animal moans; more sound and shaking than actual tears.

He had told her everything, in a bitter voice, glancing frequently at her green-touched face in the darkness. There were moments of awkward hesitancy in his narration, as an on-leave soldier telling how he won his medals hesitates before describing to the gentle townsfolk how his bayonet ripped open an enemy's stomach, then goes on and describes it because they asked how he won his medals, didn't they?—describes it with irritation and mild contempt for the gentle townsfolk who never had had to rip open anyone's stomach. So he told Ellen about the pills and the roof and why it had been necessary to kill Dorothy, and why it had then been the most logical course to transfer to Caldwell and go after *her*, Ellen, knowing her likes and dislikes from conversations with Dorothy, knowing how to make himself the man she was waiting for—not only the most logical and inevitable course, going after the girl with whom he had such an advantage, but also the course most ironically satisfying, the course most compensatory for past bad luck—(the course most law-defying, back-slapping, ego-preening)—he told her these things with irritation and contempt; this girl with her hands over her mouth in horror had had everything given her on a silver platter; she didn't know what it was to live on a swaying catwalk over the chasm of failure, stealing perilously inch by inch towards the solid ground of success so many miles away.

She listened with the muzzle of his gun jabbing painfully into her hip; painfully only at first, then numbingly, as though that part of her were already dead, as though death came from the gun not in a swift bullet but in slow radiation from the point of contact. She listened, and then she cried, because she was so sickened and beaten and shocked that there was nothing else she could do to express it all. Her cries were long throat-dragging animal moans; more sound and shaking than actual tears.

And then she sat staring brokenly at the handkerchief-twisting hands in her lap.

"I *told* you not to come," he said querulously. "I *begged* you to stay in Caldwell, didn't I?" He glanced at her as though expecting an affirmation. "But *no.* No, you had to be the girl detective! Well this is what happens to girl detectives." His eyes returned to the highway. "If you only *knew* what I've gone through since Monday," he clenched, remembering how the world had dropped out from under him Monday morning when Ellen had phoned—"Dorothy didn't commit suicide! I'm leaving for Blue River!"—running down to the station, barely catching her, futilely, desperately trying to keep her from leaving but she stepped onto the train—"I'll write you this minute! I'll explain the whole thing!"—leaving him standing there, watching her glide away, sweating, terrified. It made him sick just thinking about it.

Ellen said something faintly.

"What?"

"They'll catch you . . ."

After a moment's silence he said, "You know how many don't get caught? More than fifty per cent, that's how many. Maybe a *lot* more." After another moment he said, "How are they going to catch me? Fingerprints?—none. Witnesses?—none. Motive?—none that they know about. They won't even think of me. The gun?—I have to go over the Mississippi to get back to Caldwell; good-by gun. This car?—two or three in the morning I leave it a couple of blocks from where I took it; they think it was some crazy high school kids. Juvenile delinquents." He smiled. "I did it last night too. I was sitting two rows behind you and Powell in the theater and I was right around a bend in the hall when he kissed you goodnight." He glanced at her to see her reaction; none was visible. His gaze returned to the road and his face clouded again. "That letter of yours—how I sweated till it came! When I first started to read it I thought I was safe; you were looking for someone she'd met in her English class in the fall; I didn't meet her till January, and it was in Philosophy. But then I realized who that guy you were looking for actually was—Old Argyle-Socks, my predecessor. We'd had Math together, and he'd seen me with Dorrie. I thought he might know my name. I knew that if he ever convinced you he didn't have anything to do with Dorrie's murder . . . if he ever mentioned my name to you . . ."

Suddenly he jammed down on the brake pedal and the car screeched to a halt. Reaching left-handed around the steering column, he shifted gears. When he stepped on the gas again, the car rolled slowly backwards. On their right, the dark form of a house slid into view, low-crouching behind a broad expanse of empty parking lot. The headlights of the retreating car caught a large upright sign at the highway's edge: *Lillie and Doane's—The Steak Supreme.* A smaller sign hung swaying from the gallows of the larger one: *Reopening April 15th.*

He shifted back into first, spun the wheel to the right, and stepped on the gas. He drove across the parking lot and pulled up at the side of the low building, leaving the motor running. He pressed the horn ring; a loud blast banged through the night. He waited a minute, then sounded the horn again. Nothing happened. No window was raised, no light went on. "Looks like nobody's home," he said, turning off the headlights.

"Please . . ." she said, "please . . ."

In the darkness the car rolled forward, turned to the left, moved behind the house where the asphalt of the parking lot flowed into a smaller paved area. The car swung around in a wide curve, almost going off the edge of the asphalt into the dirt of a field that swept off to meet the blackness of the sky. It swung all the way around until it was facing the direction from which it had come.

He set the emergency brake and left the motor running.

"Please . . ." she said.

He looked at her. "You think I want to do this? You think I like the idea? We were almost engaged!" He opened the door on his left. "You had to be smart . . ." He stepped out onto the asphalt, keeping the gun aimed at her huddled figure. "Come here," he said. "Come out on this side."

"Please . . ."

"Well what am I supposed to do, Ellen? I can't let you go, can I? I asked you to go back to Caldwell without saying anything, didn't I?" The gun made an irritated gesture. "Come out."

She pulled herself across the seat, clutching her purse. She stepped out onto the asphalt.

The gun directed her in a semicircular path until she stood with the field at her back, the gun between her and the car.

"Please . . ." she said, holding up the purse in a futile shielding gesture, "please . . ."

## 14

*From the Blue River* Clarion-Ledger; *Thursday, March 15, 1951:*

### DOUBLE SLAYING HERE

#### POLICE SEEK MYSTERY GUNMAN

Within a period of two hours last night, an unknown gunman committed two brutal murders. His victims were Ellen Kingship, 21, of New York City, and Dwight Powell, 23, of Chicago, a junior at Stoddard University . . .

Powell's slaying occurred at 10:00 PM, in the home of Mrs. Elizabeth Honig, 1520 West 35th St., where Powell was a roomer. As police reconstruct the events, Powell, entering the house at 9:50 in the company of Miss Kingship, went to his second-floor room where he encountered an armed burglar who had earlier broken into the house through the back door . . .

. . . the medical examiner established the time of Miss Kingship's death as somewhere near midnight. Her body, however, was not discovered until 7:20 this morning, when Willard Herne, 11, of nearby Randalia, crossed through a field adjacent to the restaurant . . . Police learned from Gordon Gant, KBRI announcer and a friend of Miss Kingship, that she was the sister of Dorothy Kingship who last April committed suicide by jumping from the roof of the Blue River Municipal Building . . .

Leo Kingship, president of Kingship Copper, Inc., and father of the slain girl, is expected to arrive in Blue River this afternoon, accompanied by his daughter, Marion Kingship.

*An Editorial from the* Clarion-Ledger; *Thursday, April 19, 1951:*

## DISMISSAL OF GORDON GANT

In dismissing Gordon Gant from their employ (story on p. 5) the management of KBRI points out that "despite frequent warnings, he has persisted in using (KBRI's) microphones to harass and malign the Police Department in a manner bordering on the slanderous." The matter involved was the month-old Kingship-Powell slayings, in which Mr. Gant has taken a personal and somewhat acrimonious interest. His public criticism of the police was, to say the least, indiscreet, but considering that no progress has been made towards reaching a solution of the case, we find ourselves forced to agree with the appropriateness of his remarks, if not with their propriety.

## 15

AT THE END of the school year he returned to Menasset and sat around the house in somber depression. His mother tried to combat his sullenness and then began to reflect it. They argued, like hot coals boosting each other into flame. To get out of the house and out of himself, he reclaimed his old job at the haberdashery shop. From nine to five-thirty he stood behind a glass display counter not looking at the binding-strips of gleaming burnished copper.

One day in July he took the small gray strongbox from his closet. Unlocking it on his desk, he took out the newspaper clippings about Dorothy's murder. He tore them into small pieces and dropped them into the wastebasket. He did the same with the clippings on Ellen and Powell. Then he took out the Kingship Copper pamphlets; he had written away for them a second time when he started to go with Ellen. As his hands gripped them, ready to tear, he smiled ruefully. Dorothy, Ellen . . .

It was like thinking "Faith, Hope . . ." "Charity" pops into the mind to fulfill the sequence.

Dorothy, Ellen . . . Marion.

He smiled at himself and gripped the pamphlets again.

But he found that he couldn't tear them. Slowly he put them down on the desk, mechanically smoothing the creases his hands had made.

He pushed the strongbox and the pamphlets to the back of the desk and sat down. He headed a sheet of paper *Marion* and divided it into two columns with a vertical line. He headed one column *Pro;* the other *Con.*

There were so many things to list under *Pro:* Months of conversations with Dorothy, months of conversations with Ellen; all studded with passing references to Marion; her likes, her dislikes, her opinions, her past. He knew her like a book without even having met her; lonely, bitter, living alone . . . A perfect set-up.

Emotion was on the *Pro* side too. Another chance. Hit a home run and the two strikes that preceded it are washed away. And three was the lucky number . . . third time lucky . . . all the childhood fairy tales with the third try and the third wish and the third suitor . . .

He couldn't think of a thing to list under *Con.*

That night he tore up the *Pro* and *Con* list and began another one, of Marion Kingship's characteristics, opinions, likes and dislikes. He made several notations and, in the weeks that followed, added regularly to the list. In every spare moment he pushed his mind back to conversations with Dorothy and Ellen; conversations in luncheonettes, between classes, while walking, while dancing; dredging words, phrases and sentences up from the pool of his memory. Sometimes he spent entire evenings flat on his back, remembering, a small part of his mind probing the larger, less conscious part like a Geiger counter that clicked on *Marion.*

As the list grew, his spirits swelled. Sometimes he would take the paper from the strongbox even when he had nothing to add,—just to admire it; the keenness, the planning, the potence displayed. It was almost as good as having the clippings on Dorothy and Ellen.

"You're crazy," he told himself aloud one day, looking at the list. "You're a crazy nut," he said affectionately. He didn't really think that; he thought he was daring, audacious, brilliant, intrepid and bold.

"I'm not going back to school," he told his mother one day in August.

"What?" She stood small and thin in the doorway of his room, one hand frozen in mid-passage over her straggly gray hair.

"I'm going to New York in a few weeks."

"You got to finish *school,*" she said plaintively. He was silent. "What is it, you got a job in New York?"

"I don't but I'm going to get one. I've got an idea I want to work on. A—a project, sort of."

"But you got to finish school, Bud," she said hesitantly.

"I don't 'got to' do anything!" he snapped. There was silence. "If this idea flops, which I don't think it will, I can always finish school next year."

Her hands wiped the front of her housedress nervously. "Bud, you're past twenty-five. You got to—have to finish school and get yourself started someplace. You can't keep—"

"Look, will you just let me live my own life?"

She stared at him. "That's what your father used to give me," she said quietly, and went away.

He stood by his desk for a few moments, hearing the angry clanking of cutlery in the kitchen sink. He picked up a magazine and looked at it, pretending he didn't care.

A few minutes later he went into the kitchen. His mother was at the sink, her back towards him. "Mom," he said pleadingly, "you know I'm as anxious as you are to see myself get someplace." She didn't turn around. "You know I wouldn't quit school if this idea wasn't something important." He went over and sat down at the table, facing her back. "If it doesn't work, I'll finish school next year. I *promise* I will, Mom."

Reluctantly, she turned. "What kind of idea is it?" she asked slowly. "An invention?"

"No. I can't tell you," he said regretfully. "It's only in the—the planning stage. I'm sorry . . ."

She sighed and wiped her hands on a towel. "Can't it wait till next year? When you'd be through with school?"

"Next year might be too late, Mom."

She put down the towel. "Well I wish you could tell me what it is."

"I'm sorry, Mom. I wish I could too. But it's one of those things that you just can't explain."

She went around behind him and laid her hands on his shoulders. She stood there for a moment, looking down at his anxiously upturned face. "Well," she said, pressing his shoulders, "I guess it must be a *good* idea."

He smiled up at her happily.

# PART THREE: MARION

## 1

WHEN MARION KINGSHIP was graduated from college (Columbia University, an institution demanding long hours of earnest study; unlike that Midwestern Twentieth Century-Fox playground that Ellen was entering), her father offhandedly mentioned the fact to the head of the advertising agency which handled the Kingship Copper account, and Marion was offered a job as a copy writer. Although she wanted very much to write advertising copy, she refused the offer. Eventually she managed to find a position with a small agency where Kingship was a name stamped in the washroom plumbing and where Marion was assured that in the not-too-distant future she would be permitted to submit copy for some of the smaller accounts, provided that the writing of the copy did not interfere with her secretarial duties.

A year later, when Dorothy inevitably followed Ellen's lead and went off to football cheers and campus kisses, Marion found herself alone in an eight-room apartment with her father, the two of them like charged metal pellets that drift and pass but never touch. She decided, against her father's obvious though unvoiced disapproval, to find a place of her own.

She rented a two-room apartment on the top floor of a converted brownstone in the East Fifties. She furnished it with a great deal of care. Because the two rooms were smaller than those she had occupied in her father's home, she could not take all her possessions with her. Those that she did take, therefore, were the fruit of a thoughtful selection. She told herself she was choosing the things she liked best, the things that meant the most to her, which was true; but as she hung each picture and placed each book upon the shelf, she saw it not only through her own eyes but also through the eyes of a visitor who would some day come to her apartment, a visitor as yet unidentified except as to his sex. Every article was invested with significance, an index to her self; the furniture and the lamps and the ashtrays (modern but not modernistic), the reproduction of her favorite painting (Charles Demuth's *My Egypt;* not quite realistic; its planes accentuated and enriched by the eye of the artist), the records (some of the jazz and some of the Stravinsky and Bartók, but mostly the melodic listen-in-the-dark themes of Grieg and Brahms and Rachmaninoff), and the books—especially the books, for what better index of the personality is there?—(the novels and plays, the non-fiction and verse, all chosen in proportion and representation of her tastes). It was like the concentrated abbreviation of a Help Wanted ad. The egocentricity which motivated it was not that of the spoiled, but of the too little spoiled; the lonely. Had she been an artist she would have painted a self-portrait; instead she decorated two rooms, charging them with objects which some visitor, some day, would recognize and understand. And through that understanding he would divine all the capacities and longings she had found in herself and was unable to communicate.

The map of her week was centered about two landmarks; on Wednesday evenings she had dinner with her father, and on Saturdays she thorough-cleaned her two rooms. The first was a labor of duty; the second, of love. She waxed wood and polished glass, and dusted and replaced objects with sacramental care.

There were visitors. Dorothy and Ellen came when they were home on vacation, unconvincingly envying Marion as a woman of the world. Her father came, puffing from the three flights of stairs, looking dubiously at the small living-bedroom and smaller kitchen and shaking his head. Some girls from the office came, playing Canasta as though life and honor were at stake. And a man came once; the bright young junior account executive; very nice, very intelligent. His interest in the apartment manifested itself in sidelong glances at the studio couch.

When Dorothy committed suicide, Marion returned to her father's apartment for two weeks, and when Ellen died, she stayed with him for a month. They could no more get close to each other than could charged metal pellets, no matter how they tried. At the end of the month, he suggested with a diffidence unusual in him that she move back permanently. She couldn't; the thought of relinquishing her own apartment was unimaginable, as though she had locked too much of herself into it. After that though, she had dinner at her father's three evenings a week instead of only one.

On Saturdays she cleaned the rooms, and once each month she opened all the books to prevent their bindings from growing stiff.

One Saturday morning in September, the telephone rang. Marion, on her knees in the act of polishing the underside of a plate glass coffee table, froze at the sound of the bell. She gazed down through the blue-toned glass at the flattened dustcloth, hoping that it was a mistake, that someone had dialed the wrong number, had realized it at the last moment and hung up. The phone rang again. Reluctantly she rose to her feet and went over to the table beside the studio couch, still holding the dustcloth in her hand.

"Hello," she said flatly.

"Hello." It was a man's voice, unfamiliar. "Is this Marion Kingship?"

"Yes."

"You don't know me. I was . . . a friend of Ellen's." Marion felt suddenly awkward; a friend of Ellen's; someone handsome and clever and fast-talking . . . Someone dull underneath, someone *she* wouldn't care for anyway. The awkwardness retreated. "My name," the man continued, "is Burton Corliss . . . Bud Corliss."

". . . Oh, yes. Ellen told me about you . . ." ('I love him so much,' Ellen had said during the visit that had proved to be her last, 'and he loves me too,'—and Marion, though happy for her, had for some reason been somber the rest of the evening.)

"I wonder if I could see you," he said. "I have something that belonged to Ellen. One of her books. She lent it to me just before . . . before she went to Blue River, and I thought you might like to have it."

Probably some Book-of-the-Month novel, Marion thought, and then, hating herself for her smallness, said, "Yes, I'd like very much to have it. Yes, I would."

For a moment there was silence from the other end of the wire. "I could bring it over now," he said. "I'm in the neighborhood."

"No," she said quickly, "I'm going out."

"Well then, sometime tomorrow . . ."

"I . . . I won't be in tomorrow either." She shifted uncomfortably, ashamed of her lying, ashamed that she didn't want him in her apartment. He was probably likeable enough, and he'd loved Ellen and Ellen was dead, and he was going out of his way to give her Ellen's book . . . "We could meet someplace this afternoon," she offered.

"Fine," he said. "That would be fine."

"I'm going to be . . . around Fifth Avenue."

"Then suppose we meet, say, in front of the statue at Rockefeller Center, the one of Atlas holding up the world."

"All right."

"At three o'clock?"

"Yes. Three o'clock. Thank you very much for calling. It's very nice of you."

"Don't mention it," he said. "Good-by, Marion." There was a pause. "I'd feel funny calling you Miss Kingship. Ellen spoke about you so much."

"That's all right . . ." She felt awkward again, and self-conscious. "Good-by . . ." she said, unable to decide whether to call him Bud or Mr. Corliss.

"Good-by," he repeated.

She replaced the receiver and stood looking at the telephone for a moment. Then she turned and went to the coffee table. Kneeling, she resumed her work, sweeping the dustcloth in unaccustomedly hurried arcs, because now the whole afternoon was broken up.

## 2

IN THE SHADOW of the towering bronze statue, he stood with his back to the pedestal, immaculate in gray flannel, a paper-wrapped package under his arm. Before him passed intermeshing streams of oppositely-bound people, slow-moving against a backdrop of roaring busses and impatient taxis. He watched their faces carefully. The Fifth Avenue set; men with unpadded shoulders and narrowly knotted ties; women self-consciously smart in tailored suits, kerchiefs crisp at their throats, their beautiful heads lifted high, as though photographers might be waiting farther down the street. And, like transient sparrows tolerated in an aviary, the pink rural faces gawking at the statue and the sun-sharpened spires of Saint Patrick's across the street. He watched them all carefully, trying to recall the snapshot Dorothy had shown him so long ago. "Marion could be very pretty, only she wears her hair like this." He smiled, remembered Dorrie's fierce frown as she pulled her hair back primly. His fingers toyed with a fold in the wrapping of the package.

She came from the north, and he recognized her when she was still a hundred feet away. She was tall and thin, a bit too thin, and dressed much like the women around her; a brown suit, a gold kerchief, a small Vogue-looking felt hat, a shoulder-strap handbag. She seemed stiff and uncomfortable in the outfit, though, as if it had been made to someone else's measure. Her pulled-back hair was brown. She had Dorothy's large brown eyes, but in her drawn face they were too large, and the high cheekbones that had been so beautiful in her sisters were, in Marion, too sharply defined. As she came nearer, she saw him. With an uncertain, questioning smile, she approached, appearing ill at ease in the spotlight of his gaze. Her lipstick, he noticed, was the pale rose he associated with timorously experimenting adolescents.

"Marion?"

"Yes." She offered her hand hesitantly. "How do you do," she said, directing a too-quick smile at a point somewhere below his eyes.

Her hand in his was long-fingered and cold. "Hello," he said. "I've been looking forward to meeting you."

They went to a determinedly Early American cocktail lounge around the corner. Marion, after some indecision, ordered a Daiquiri.

"I . . . I can't stay long, I'm afraid," she said, sitting erect on the edge of her chair, her fingers stiff around the cocktail glass.

"Where are they always running, these beautiful women?" he inquired smilingly—and immediately saw that it was the wrong approach; she smiled tensely and seemed to grow more uncomfortable. He looked at her curiously, allowing the echo of his words to fade. After a moment he began again. "You're with an advertising agency, aren't you?"

"Camden and Galbraith," she said. "Are you still at Caldwell?"

"No."

"I thought Ellen said you were a junior."

"I was, but I had to quit school." He sipped his Martini. "My father is dead. I didn't want my mother to work any more."

"Oh. I'm sorry . . ."

"Maybe I'll be able to finish up next year. Or I may go to night school. Where did you go to school?"

"Columbia. Are you from New York?"

"Massachusetts."

Every time he tried to steer the conversation around to her, she turned it back towards him. Or to the weather. Or to a waiter who bore a startling resemblance to Claude Raines.

Eventually she asked, "Is that the book?"

"Yes. *Dinner at Antoine's.* Ellen wanted me to read it. There are some personal notes she scribbled on the flyleaf, so I thought you might like to have it." He passed the package to her.

"Personally," he said, "I go for books that have a little more meaning."

Marion stood up. "I'll have to be leaving now," she said apologetically.

"But you haven't finished your drink yet."

"I'm sorry," she said quickly, looking down at the package in her hands, "I have an appointment. A business appointment. I couldn't possibly be late."

He rose. "But . . ."

"I'm sorry." She looked at him uncomfortably.

He put money on the table.

They walked back to Fifth Avenue. At the corner she offered her hand again. It was still cold. "It's been very nice meeting you, Mr. Corliss," she said. "Thank you for the drink. And the book. I appreciate it . . . very thoughtful . . ." She turned and melted into the stream of people.

Emptily, he stood on the corner for a moment. Then his lips clenched and he started walking.

He followed her. The brown felt hat had a gold ornament that glittered brightly. He stayed some thirty feet behind it.

She walked up to Fifty-Fourth Street, where she crossed the avenue, heading east towards Madison. He knew where she was going; he remembered the address from the telephone book. She crossed Madison and Park. He stopped on the corner and watched her climb the steps of the brownstone house.

"Business appointment," he muttered. He waited around for a few minutes, not knowing exactly why he waited, and then he turned and walked slowly back towards Fifth Avenue.

## 3

SUNDAY AFTERNOON MARION went to the Museum of Modern Art. The main floor was still occupied by an automobile exhibit which she had seen before and found uninteresting, and the second floor was unusually crowded, so she continued up the turning stairway to the third floor, there to wander among the pleasantly familiar paintings and sculptures; the arched white smoothness of the *Girl Washing Her Hair*, the perfect spear of *Bird In Space*.

Two men were in the room that held the Lehmbruck sculptures, but they went out soon after Marion entered, leaving her alone in the cool gray cube with the two statues, the male and female, he standing and she kneeling in opposite quarters of the room, their bodies elongated and gauntly beautiful. The attenuation of the statues gave them an unearthly air, almost like religious art, so that Marion had always been able to look at them with none of the slight embarrassment she usually felt on viewing nude sculptures. She moved slowly around the figure of the young man.

"Hello." The voice was behind her, pleasantly surprised.

It must be for me, she thought, there's no one else here. She turned around.

Bud Corliss smiled in the doorway.

"Hello," Marion said confusedly.

"It really *is* a small world," he said, coming to her. "I came in right behind you downstairs, only I wasn't sure it was you. How are you?"

"Fine, thank you." There was an uncomfortable pause. "How are you?" she added.

"Fine, thanks."

They turned to the statue. Why did she feel so clumsy? Because he was handsome? Because he had been part of Ellen's circle?—had shared football cheers and campus kisses and love . . .

"Do you come here often?" he asked.

"Yes."

"So do I."

The statue embarrassed her now, because Bud Corliss was standing beside her. She turned away and moved towards the figure of the kneeling woman. He followed at her side. "Did you make that appointment on time?"

"Yes," she said. What brought him here? You'd think he'd be strolling in Central Park with some poised flawless Ellen on his arm . . .

They looked at the statue. After a moment, he said, "I really didn't think it was you downstairs."

"Why not?"

"Well, Ellen wasn't the museum type . . ."

"Sisters aren't exactly alike," she said.

"No, I guess not." He began to circle around the kneeling figure. "The Fine Arts department at Caldwell had a small museum," he said. "Mostly reproductions and copies. I dragged Ellen there once or twice. Thought I'd indoctrinate her." He shook his head. "No luck."

"She wasn't interested in art."

"No," he said. "It's funny the way we try to push our tastes on people we like."

Marion looked at him, facing her on the other side of the statue. "I once took Ellen and Dorothy—Dorothy was our youngest sister—"

"I know . . ."

"I took them here once when they were just going into their teens. They were bored, though. I guess it was too young."

"I don't know," he said, retracing his semicircular path towards her. "If there'd been a museum in my home town when I was that age . . . Did *you* come here when you were twelve or thirteen?"

"Yes."

"See?" he said. His smile made them fellow members of a group to which Ellen and Dorothy had never belonged.

A man and woman with two children in tow came bursting into the room.

"Let's move on," he suggested, at her side again.

"I . . ."

"It's Sunday," he said. "No business appointments to run to." He smiled at her; a very nice smile, soft and lenitive. "I'm alone; you're alone . . ." He took her elbow gently. "Come on," he said, with the persuasive smile.

They went through the third floor and half of the second, commenting on the works they saw, and then they went down to the main floor, past the gleaming automobiles incongruous within a building, and out through the glass doors to the garden behind the museum. They strolled from statue to statue, pausing before each. They came to the Maillol woman, full-bodied, strident.

"The last of the red-hot mammas," Bud said.

Marion smiled. "I'll tell you something," she said. "I always get a little embarrassed looking at . . . statues like this."

"This one embarrasses *me* a little," he said, smiling. "It's not a nude; it's a naked." They both laughed.

When they had looked at all the statues, they sat down on one of the benches at the back of the garden and lighted cigarettes.

"You and Ellen were going steady, weren't you."

"Not exactly."

"I thought . . ."

"Not officially, I mean. Anyway, going steady in college doesn't always mean as much as going steady outside of college."

Marion smoked in silence.

"We had a great many things in common, but they were mainly surface things; having the same classes, knowing the same people . . . things having to do with Caldwell. Once we were through with college though, I don't think we would've . . . I don't think we would've gotten married." He stared at his cigarette. "I was fond of Ellen. I liked her better than any girl I've ever known. I was miserable when she died. But . . . I don't know . . . she wasn't a very *deep* person." He paused. "I hope I'm not offending you."

Marion shook her head, watching him.

"Everything was like that museum business. I thought I could at least get her interested in some of the uncomplicated artists, like Hopper or Wood. But it didn't work. She wasn't interested at all. And it was the same thing with books or politics—anything serious. She always wanted to be *doing* something."

"She'd led a restricted life at home. I guess she was making up for it."

"Yes," he said. "And then, she was four years younger than I." He put out his cigarette. "But she was the sweetest girl I've ever known."

There was a pause.

"Didn't they ever find out *anything* about who did it?" he asked incredulously.

"Nothing. Isn't it awful . . ."

They sat in silence for a moment. Then they began to talk again; about how many interesting things there were to do in New York, what a pleasant place the museum was, about the Matisse exhibit that was coming soon.

"Do you know who I like?" he asked.

"Who?"

"I don't know if you're familiar with his work," he said. "Charles Demuth."

## 4

LEO KINGSHIP SAT with his elbows propped on the table, his fingers interlocked around a cold-frosted glass of milk which he studied as though it were a beautifully colored wine. "You've been seeing him frequently, haven't you," he said, trying to sound casual.

With elaborate care, Marion placed her coffee cup in the indentation of the blue and gold Aynsley saucer, and then looked across the crystal and silver and damask at her father. His full red face was bland. Reflected light blanked the lenses of his eyeglasses, masking his eyes. "Bud?" she said, knowing it was Bud he meant.

Kingship nodded.

"Yes," Marion said squarely, "I've been seeing him frequently." She paused. "He's calling for me tonight, in about fifteen minutes." She watched her father's expressionless face with waiting eyes, hoping that there would not be an argument because it would tarnish the entire evening, and hoping that there *would* be one because it would try the strength of what she felt for Bud.

"This job of his," Kingship said, setting down the milk. "What are its prospects?"

After a cold moment Marion said, "He's on the executive training squad. He should be a section manager in a few months. Why all the questions?" She smiled with her lips only.

Kingship removed his glasses. His blue eyes wrestled uncomfortably with Marion's cool stare. "You brought him here to dinner, Marion," he said. "You never brought anyone to dinner before. Doesn't that entitle me to ask a few questions?"

"He lives in a rooming house," Marion said. "When he doesn't eat with me, he eats alone. So I brought him to dinner one night."

"The nights you don't dine here, you dine with him?"

"Yes, most of them. Why should we both eat alone? We work only five blocks from each other." She wondered why she was being evasive; she hadn't been caught doing something wrong. "We eat together because we enjoy each other's company," she said firmly. "We like each other very much."

"Then I do have a right to ask some questions, don't I," Kingship pointed out quietly.

"He's someone I like. Not someone applying for a job with Kingship Copper."

"Marion . . ."

She plucked a cigarette from a silver cup and lighted it with a silver table lighter. "You don't like him, do you?"

"I didn't say that."

"Because he's poor," she said.

"That's not true, Marion, and you know it."

There was silence for a moment.

"Oh yes," Kingship said, "he's poor all right. He took pains to mention it exactly three times the other night. And that anecdote he dragged in, about the woman his mother did sewing for."

"What's wrong with his mother taking in sewing?"

"Nothing, Marion, nothing. It's the way he alluded to it so casually, so very casually. Do you know who he reminded me of? There's a man at the club who has a bad leg, limps a little. Every time we play golf he says, 'You boys go on ahead. Old Peg-leg'll catch up with you.' So everyone walks extra slowly and you feel like a heel if you beat him."

"I'm afraid the similarity escapes me," Marion said. She rose from the table and went out towards the living room, leaving Kingship to rub a hand despairingly over the few yellow-white hairs that thinly crossed his scalp.

In the living room there was a large window that looked out over the East River. Marion stood before it, one hand on the thick cloth of the draperies. She heard her father come into the room behind her.

"Marion, believe me, I only want to see you happy." He spoke awkwardly. "I know I haven't always been so . . . concerned, but haven't I . . . done better since Dorothy and Ellen . . ."

"I know," she admitted reluctantly. She fingered the drapes. "But I'm practically twenty-five . . . a grown woman. You don't have to treat me as if—"

"I just don't want you rushing into anything, Marion."

"I'm not," she said softly.

"That's all I want."

Marion stared out the window. "Why do you dislike him?" she asked.

"I don't dislike him. He—I don't know, I . . ."

"Is it that you're afraid I'll go away from you?" She spoke the question slowly, as though the idea surprised her.

"You're already away from me, aren't you? In that apartment."

She turned from the window and faced Kingship at the side of the room. "You know, you really should be grateful to Bud," she said. "I'll tell you something. I didn't want him to have dinner here. As soon as I suggested it, I was sorry. But he insisted. 'He's your father,' he said. 'Think of his feelings.' You see, Bud is strong on family ties, even if I'm not. So you should be grateful to him, not antagonistic. Because if he does anything, it will be to bring us closer together." She faced the window again.

"All right," Kingship said. "He's probably a wonderful boy. I just want to make sure you don't make any mistakes."

"What do you mean?" She turned from the window again, this time more slowly, her body stiffening.

"I just don't want you to make any mistakes, that's all," Kingship said uncertainly.

"Are you asking other questions about him?" Marion demanded. "Asking other people? Do you have someone checking on him?"

"No!"

"Like you did with Ellen?"

"Ellen was seventeen at the time! And I was right, wasn't I? Was that boy any good?"

"Well I'm twenty-five and I know my own mind! If you have anyone checking on Bud—"

"The idea never entered my mind!"

Marion's eyes stung him. "I like Bud," she said slowly, her voice tight. "I like him very much. Do you know what that means, to finally find someone you like?"

"Marion, I—"

"So if you do *anything*, anything at all, to make him feel unwelcome or unwanted, to make him feel that he's not good enough for me . . . I'll never forgive you. I swear to God I'll never speak to you again as long as I live."

She turned back to the window.

"The idea never entered my mind. Marion, I swear . . ." He looked futilely at her rigid back and then sank into a chair with a weary sigh.

A few minutes later the chimes of the front door sounded. Marion left the window and crossed the room towards the double door that led to the foyer.

"Marion." Kingship stood up.

She paused and looked back at him. From the foyer came the sound of the front door opening and the murmur of voices in conversation.

"Ask him to stay a few minutes . . . have a drink."

A moment passed. "All right," she said. At the doorway she hesitated for a second. "I'm sorry I spoke the way I did." She went out.

Kingship watched her go. Then he turned and faced the fireplace. He took a step back and regarded himself in the mirror tilted over the mantel. He looked at the well-fed man in the three hundred and forty dollar suit in the seven hundred dollar a month living-room.

Then he straightened up, put a smile on his face, turned and walked towards the doorway, extending his right hand. "Good evening, Bud," he said.

## 5

MARION'S BIRTHDAY FELL on a Saturday early in November. In the morning she cleaned her apartment hastily. At one o'clock she went to a small building in a quiet tributary of Park Avenue, where a discreet silver plaque beside a white door confided that the premises were occupied, not by a psychiatrist nor an interior decorator, but by a restaurant. Leo Kingship was waiting within the white door, sitting gingerly on a Louis Quinze sofa and scanning a management-owned copy of *Gourmet*. He put down the magazine, rose, kissed Marion on the cheek and wished her a happy birthday. A maître d'hôtel with fluttering fingers and neon teeth ushered them to their table, swooped away a Reserved placard and seated them with Gallic effusion. There was a centerpiece of roses on the table, and, at Marion's place, a small box wrapped in white paper and clouds of gold ribbon. Kingship pretended not to be aware of it. While he was occupied with the wine card and "If I may suggest, Monsieur," Marion freed the box of its gold entanglement, excitement coloring her cheeks and shining her eyes. Nested between layers of cotton was a golden disc, its surface constellated with tiny pearls. Marion exclaimed over the brooch and, when the maître d' had gone, thanked her father happily, squeezing his hand, which lay as if by chance near hers on the table.

The brooch was not one which she would have chosen herself; its design was too elaborate for her taste. Her happiness, however, was genuine, inspired by the giving if not by the gift. In the past, Leo Kingship's standard birthday present to his daughters had been a one hundred dollar gift certificate redeemable at a Fifth Avenue department store, a matter automatically attended to by his secretary.

After leaving her father, Marion spent some time at a beauty salon and then returned to her apartment. Late in the afternoon the buzzer sounded. She pressed the button that released the door downstairs. A few minutes later a messenger appeared at her door, panting dramatically, as though he had been carrying something much heavier than a florist's box. The receipt of a quarter soothed his respiration.

In the box, under green waxed paper, was a white orchid arranged in a corsage. The card with it said simply, "—Bud." Standing before a mirror, Marion held the bloom experimentally to her hair, her wrist, and her shoulder. Then she went into the kitchen and placed the flower in its box and in the waist-high refrigerator, first sprinkling a few drops of water on its thick-veined tropical petals.

He arrived promptly at six. He gave the button next to Marion's nameplate two quick jabs and stood waiting in the stuffy hallway, removing a gray suede glove to pick a speck of lint from the lapel of his navy blue coat. Soon footsteps sounded on the stairs. The dingily curtained door opened and Marion appeared, radiant, the orchid bursting whitely on her black coat. They clasped each other's hands. Wishing her the happiest of birthdays, he kissed her on the cheek so as not to smudge her lipstick, which he noticed was of a deeper shade than she had worn when first he met her.

They went to a steak house on Fifty-Second Street. The prices on the menu, although considerably lower than those on the one from which she had selected her lunch, seemed exorbitant to Marion, because she was seeing them through Bud's eyes. She suggested that he order for both of them. They had black onion soup and sirloin steaks, preceded by champagne cocktails—"To you, Marion." At the end of the meal, placing eighteen dollars on the waiter's salver, Bud caught Marion's faint frown. "Well, it's your birthday, isn't it?" he said, smiling.

From the restaurant they took a taxi to the theater where *Saint Joan* was playing. They sat in the orchestra, sixth row center. During the intermission Marion was unusually voluble, her doelike eyes glittering brightly as she talked of Shaw and the acting and a celebrity who was seated in the row in front of them. During the play their hands were warm in each other's.

Afterwards—because, she told herself, Bud had already spent so much money that evening—Marion suggested that they go to her apartment.

"I feel like a pilgrim who's finally being permitted to enter the shrine," he said as he slipped the key into the slit of the lock. He turned the key and doorknob simultaneously.

"It's nothing fancy," Marion said, her voice quick. "Really. They call it two rooms but it's more like one, the kitchen is so tiny."

He pushed the door open, withdrawing the key which he handed to Marion. She stepped into the apartment and reached for a wall switch beside the door. Lamps filled the room with diffused light. He entered, closing the door behind him. Marion turned to watch his face. His eyes were ranging over the deep gray walls, the blue and white striped drapes, the limed oak furniture. He gave an appreciative murmur.

"It's very small," Marion said.

"But nice," he said. "*Very* nice."

"Thank you." She turned away from him, unpinning the orchid from her coat, suddenly as ill at ease as when they first met. She put the corsage on a sideboard and started to remove her coat. His hands helped her. "Beautiful furniture," he said over her shoulder.

She hung their coats in the closet mechanically, and then turned to the mirror over the sideboard. With fumbling fingers, she pinned the orchid to the shoulder of her russet dress, her eyes focused beyond her own reflection, on Bud's image. He had walked down to the center of the room. Standing before the coffee table, he picked up a square copper plate. His face, in profile, was expressionless, giving no indication whether he liked or disliked the piece. Marion found herself motionless. "Mmmm," he said at last, liking it. "A present from your father, I bet."

"No," Marion said into the mirror, "Ellen gave it to me."

"Oh." He looked at it for a moment and then put it down.

Fingering the collar of her dress, Marion turned from the mirror and watched as he crossed the room with three easy strides. He stood before the low bookcase and looked at the picture on the wall above it. Marion watched him. "Our old friend Demuth," he said. He glanced at her, smiling. She smiled back. He looked at the picture again.

After a moment, Marion moved forward and went to his side.

"I never could figure out why he called a picture of a grain elevator 'My Egypt,'" Bud said.

"Is that what it is? I was never sure."

"It's a beautiful picture, though." He turned to Marion. "What's the matter? Have I got some dirt on my nose or something?"

"What?"

"You were looking—"

"Oh. No. Would you like something to drink?"

"Mmm-hmm."

"There's nothing but wine."

"Perfect."

Marion turned towards the kitchen.

"Before you go . . ." He took a small tissue-wrapped box from his pocket. "Happy Birthday."

"Oh, Bud, you shouldn't have!" "I shouldn't have," he mimicked simultaneously. "But aren't you glad I did?"

There were silver earrings in the box, simple polished triangles. "Oh, thank you! They're lovely!" Marion exclaimed, and kissed him.

She hurried to the sideboard to try them on. He came up behind her, looking at her in the mirror. When she had fastened both earrings, he turned her around. "Lovely is right," he said.

When the kiss ended he said, "Now where's that wine we were talking about?"

Marion came out of the kitchen with a raffia-covered bottle of Bardolino and two glasses on a tray. Bud, his jacket off, was sitting cross-legged on the floor in front of the bookcase, a book opened on his lap. "I didn't know you liked Proust," he said.

"Oh, I do!" She set the tray on the coffee table.

"Here," he said, pointing to the bookcase. Marion transferred the tray to the bookcase. She filled the two glasses and handed one to Bud. Holding the other, she worked her feet out of her shoes and lowered herself to the floor beside him. He leafed through the pages of the book. "I'll show you the part I'm crazy about," he said.

He pressed the switch. The tone arm swung slowly and dipped down to touch with its serpent's head the rim of the spinning record. Closing the cover of the phonograph, he crossed the room and sat beside Marion on the blue-covered studio couch. The first deep piano notes of the Rachmaninoff Second Concerto sounded. "Just the right record," Marion said.

Leaning back against the thick bolster that ran along the wall, Bud scanned the room, now softly lighted by a single lamp. "Everything's so perfect here," he said. "Why haven't you asked me up before?"

She picked at a filament of raffia that had got caught on one of the buttons on the front of her dress. "I don't know . . ." she said. "I . . . I thought maybe you wouldn't like it."

"How could I not like it?" he asked.

His fingers worked dexterously down the row of buttons. Her hands, warm, closed over his, restraining them between her breasts.

"Bud, I've never . . . done anything before."

"I know that, darling. You don't have to tell me that."

"I've never loved anyone before."

"Neither have I. I've never loved anyone. Not until you."
"Do you mean that? Do you?"
"Only you."
"Not even Ellen?"
"Only you. I swear it."
He kissed her again.
Her hands freed his and rose to find his cheeks.

## 6

*From* The New York Times; *Monday, December 24, 1951:*

### MARION J. KINGSHIP TO BE WED SATURDAY

Miss Marion Joyce Kingship, daughter of Mr. Leo Kingship of Manhattan and the late Phyllis Hatcher, will be married to Mr. Burton Corliss, son of Mrs. Joseph Corliss of Menasset, Mass., and the late Mr. Corliss, on the afternoon of Saturday, December 29, in the home of her father.

Miss Kingship was graduated from the Spence School in New York and is an alumna of Columbia University. Until last week she was with the advertising agency of Camden and Galbraith.

The prospective bridegroom, who served with the Army during the second World War and attended Caldwell College in Caldwell, Wis., has recently joined the domestic sales division of the Kingship Copper Corporation.

## 7

SEATED AT HER desk, Miss Richardson stretched out her right hand in a gesture she considered quite graceful and squinted at the gold bracelet that constricted the plumpness of her wrist. It was definitely too young looking for her mother, she decided. She would get something else for mother and keep the bracelet for herself.

Beyond her hand the background suddenly turned blue. With white pin-stripes. She looked up, starting to smile, but stopped when she saw that it was the pest again.

"Hello," he said cheerfully.

Miss Richardson opened a drawer and busily ruffled the edges of some blank typing paper. "Mr. Kingship is still at lunch," she said frigidly.

"Dear lady, he was at lunch at twelve o'clock. It is now three o'clock. What is he, a rhinoceros?"

"If you wish to make an appointment for later in the week . . ."

"I would like an audience with His Eminence this afternoon."

Miss Richardson closed the drawer grimly. "Tomorrow is Christmas," she said. "Mr. Kingship is interrupting a four day weekend by coming in today. He wouldn't do that unless he were very busy. He gave me strict orders not to disturb him on any account. On no account whatsoever."

"Then he isn't at lunch."

"He gave me strict orders . . ."

The man sighed. Slinging his folded coat over one shoulder, he drew a slip of paper from the rack next to Miss Richardson's telephone. "May I?" he asked, already having taken the paper. Placing it on a large blue book which he held in the crook of his arm, he removed Miss Richardson's pen from its onyx holder and began to write.

"Well I never!" said Miss Richardson. "Honestly!" she said.

Finished writing, the man replaced the pen and blew on the paper. He folded it carefully into quarters and handed it to Miss Richardson. "Give him this," he said. "Slip it under the door, if need be."

Miss Richardson glared at him. Then she calmly unfolded the paper and read it.

Uncomfortably, she looked up. "Dorothy and Ellen—?"

His face was expressionless.

She hoisted herself from the chair. "He told me not to disturb him on any account," she repeated softly, as though seeking guidance in the incantation. "What's your name?"

"Just give him that, please, like the angel you are."

"Now look . . ."

He was doing just that; looking at her quite seriously, despite the lightness of his voice. Miss Richardson frowned, glanced again at the paper, and refolded it. She moved to a heavily paneled door. "All right," she said darkly, "but you'll see. He gave me strict orders." Gingerly she tapped on the door. Opening it, she slipped in with the paper held appeasingly before her.

She reappeared a minute later with a betrayed expression on her face. "Go ahead," she said sharply, holding the door open.

The man breezed past her, his coat over his shoulder, the book under his arm. "Keep smiling," he whispered.

At the faint sound of the door closing, Leo Kingship looked up from the slip of paper in his hand. He was standing behind his desk in his shirtsleeves, his jacket draped on the back of the chair behind him. His eyeglasses were pushed up on his pink forehead. Sunlight, sliced by a Venetian blind, striped his stocky figure. He squinted anxiously at the man approaching him across the paneled and carpeted room.

"Oh," he said, when the man came close enough to block the sunlight, enabling Kingship to recognize his face. "You." He looked down at the slip of paper and crumpled it, his expression of anxiety turning to relief and then to annoyance.

"Hello, Mr. Kingship," the man said, offering his hand.

Kingship took it halfheartedly. "No wonder you wouldn't give your name to Miss Richardson."

Smiling, the man dropped into the visitor's chair. He settled his coat and the book in his lap.

"But I'm afraid I've forgotten it," Kingship said. "Grant?" he ventured.

"Gant." The long legs crossed comfortably. "Gordon Gant."

Kingship remained standing. "I'm extremely busy, Mr. Gant," he said firmly, indicating the paper-strewn desk. "So if this 'information about Dorothy and Ellen' "—he held up the crumpled slip of paper—"consists of the same 'theories' you were expounding back in Blue River . . ."

"Partially," Gant said.

"Well, I'm sorry. I don't want to listen."

"I gathered that I wasn't number one on your Hit Parade."

"You mean I didn't like you? That isn't so. Not at all. I realized your motives were of the best; you had taken a liking to Ellen; you showed a—a youthful enthusiasm . . . But it was misdirected, misdirected in a way that was extremely painful to me. Barging into my hotel room so soon after Ellen's death . . . bringing up the past at such a moment . . ." He looked at Gant appealingly. "Do you think I wouldn't have liked to believe that Dorothy didn't take her own life?"

"She didn't."

"The note," he said wearily, "the note . . ."

"A couple of ambiguously worded sentences that could have referred to a dozen things beside suicide. Or that she could have been tricked into writing." Gant leaned forward. "Dorothy went to the Municipal Building to get married. Ellen's theory was right; the fact that she was killed proves it."

"It does no such thing," Kingship snapped. "There was no connection. You heard the police—"

"A housebreaker!"

"Why not? Why not a housebreaker?"

"Because I *don't* believe in coincidences. Not that kind."

"A sign of immaturity, Mr. Gant."

After a moment Gant said flatly, "It was the same person both times."

Kingship braced his hands tiredly on the desk, looking down at the papers there. "Why do you have to revive all this?" he sighed. "Intruding in other people's business. How do you think I feel . . . ?" He pushed his eyeglasses down into place and fingered the pages of a ledger. "Would you please go now."

Gant made no move to rise. "I'm home on vacation," he said. "Home is White Plains. I didn't spend an hour on the New York Central just to rehash what was already said last March."

"What then?" Kingship looked warily at the long-jawed face.

"There was an article in this morning's *Times* . . . the society page."

"My daughter?"

Gant nodded. He took a pack of cigarettes from his breast pocket. "What do you know about Bud Corliss?" he asked.

Kingship eyed him in silence. "Know about him?" he said slowly. "He's going to be my son-in-law. What do you mean, know about him?"

"Do you know that he and Ellen were going together?"

"Of course." Kingship straightened up. "What are you driving at?"

"It's a long story," Gant said. The blue eyes were sharp and steady under the thick blond brows. He gestured towards Kingship's chair. "And my delivery is bound to suffer if you stand towering over me."

Kingship sat down. He kept his hands on the edge of the desk before him, as though ready to rise again in an instant.

Gant lit his cigarette. He sat silently for a moment, regarding it thoughtfully and working his lower lip with his teeth, as though awaiting a time signal. Then he began to speak in the easy, fluid, announcer's voice.

"When she left Caldwell," he said, "Ellen wrote a letter to Bud Corliss. I happened to read that letter soon after Ellen arrived in Blue River. It made quite an impression on me, since it described a murder suspect whom I resembled much too closely for comfort." He smiled. "I read the letter twice, and carefully, as you can imagine.

"On the night Ellen was killed, Eldon Chesser, that lover of prima-facie evidence, asked me if Ellen were my girlfriend. It was probably the only constructive thing he ever did during his entire detectival career, because it set me thinking of friend Corliss. Partly to take my mind off Ellen, who was God-knows-where with an armed killer, and partly because I liked her and wondered what kind of a man she liked, I thought about that letter which was still fresh in my mind and which was my only source of information about my 'rival,' Bud Corliss."

Gant paused for a second, and then continued. "At first it seemed to contain nothing; a name—Dear Bud—and an address on the envelope—Burton Corliss, something-or-other Roosevelt Street, Caldwell, Wisconsin. No other clues. But on further reflection I found several bits of information in Ellen's letter, and I was able to fit them together into an even bigger piece of information about Bud Corliss; it seemed insignificant at the time; a purely external fact about him rather than an indication of his personality, which was what I was really looking for. But that fact stayed with me, and today it seems significant indeed."

"Go ahead," Kingship said as Gant drew on his cigarette.

Gant leaned back comfortably. "First of all: Ellen wrote Bud that she wouldn't fall behind in her work while away from Caldwell because she would be able to get all the notes from him. Now, Ellen was a senior, which meant that she was taking advanced courses. In every college senior courses are closed to freshmen and often to sophomores. If Bud shared *all* Ellen's classes—they probably made out their programs together—it meant that he was conceivably a sophomore, but in all probability a junior or a senior.

"Secondly: at one point in the letter Ellen described her behavior during her first three years at Caldwell, which apparently differed from her behavior after Dorothy's death. She described how she had been 'the rah-rah girl,' and then she said, and I think I remember the exact words, 'You wouldn't recognize me.' Which meant, as clearly as could possibly be, that Bud had not seen her during those first three years. This would be highly conceivable at a good-sized university like Stoddard, but we come to thirdly.

"Thirdly: Caldwell is a very small college; one tenth the size of Stoddard, Ellen wrote, and she was giving it the benefit of the doubt. I checked in the Almanac this morning; Stoddard has over twelve thousand students; Caldwell, barely eight hundred. Furthermore, Ellen mentioned in the letter that she hadn't wanted Dorothy to come to Caldwell precisely because it was the kind of place where everyone knew everybody else and knew what they were doing.

"So, we add one, two, and three: Bud Corliss, who is at least in his third year of college, was a stranger to Ellen at the beginning of her fourth year, despite the fact that they both attended a very small school where, I understand, the social side of life plays hob with the scholastic. All of which can be explained in only one way and can be condensed to a simple statement of fact; the fact which seemed insignificant last March, but today seems like the most important fact in Ellen's letter: *Bud Corliss was a transfer student, and he transferred to Caldwell in September of 1950, at the beginning of Ellen's fourth year and after Dorothy's death.*"

Kingship frowned. "I don't see what—"

"We come now to today, December 24, 1951," Gant said, crushing his cigarette in an ashtray, "when my mother, bless her, brings the prodigal son breakfast in bed, along with *The New York Times.* And there, on the society page, is the name of Kingship. Miss Marion Kingship to wed Mr. Burton Corliss. Imagine my surprise. Now, my mind, in addition to being insatiably curious and highly analytical, is also very dirty. It looks to me, says I, as though the new member of the domestic sales division was determined not to be disqualified from the Kingship Copper sweepstakes."

"Now look here, Mr. Gant—"

"I considered," Gant went on, "how when one sister was killed he proceeded directly to the next one. Beloved of two of the Kingship daughters. Two out of three. Not a bad score.

"And then the analytical side and the dirty side of my brain blended, and I thought: three out of three would have been an even better score for Mr. Burton Corliss who transferred to Caldwell College in September of 1950."

Kingship stood up, staring at Gant.

"A random thought," Gant said. "Wildly improbable. But easily removed from the realm of doubt. A simple matter of sliding out from under the breakfast tray, going to the bookcase, and taking therefrom *The Stoddard Flame,* yearbook for 1950." He displayed the large blue leatherette book with its white-lettered cover. "In the sophomore section," he said, "there are several interesting photographs. One of Dorothy Kingship and one of Dwight Powell, both of whom are now dead. None of Gordon Gant; didn't have five spare bucks to have my face recorded for posterity. But many sophomores did, among them—" He opened the book to a page marked by a strip of newsprint, turned the volume around and put it down on the desk, his finger stabbing one of the checkerboard photographs. He recited the inscription beside it from memory: "Corliss, Burton quote Bud unquote, Menasset, Mass., Liberal Arts."

Kingship sat down again. He looked at the photograph, hardly larger than a postage stamp. Then he looked at Gant. Gant reached forward, turned a few pages, and pointed to another picture. It was Dorothy. Kingship looked at that, too. Then he looked up again.

Gant said, "It struck me as awfully odd. I thought you should know."

"Why?" Kingship asked stolidly. "What is this supposed to be leading up to?"

"May I ask you one question, Mr. Kingship, before I answer that?"

"Go ahead."

"He never told you he went to Stoddard, did he?"

"No. But we've never discussed things like that," he explained quickly. "He must have told Marion. Marion must know."

"I don't think she does."

"Why not?" Kingship demanded.

"*The Times.* Marion gave them the information for that article, didn't she? The bride-to-be usually does."

"Well?"

"Well there's no mention of Stoddard. And in the other wedding and engagement articles, it's mentioned when someone's attended more than one school."

"Maybe she just didn't bother to tell them."

"Maybe. Or maybe she doesn't know. Maybe Ellen didn't know either."

"All right, now what are you saying, mister?"

"Don't be sore at *me,* Mr. Kingship. The facts speak for themselves; I didn't invent them." Gant closed the yearbook and put it in his lap. "There are two possibilities," he said. "Either Corliss told Marion that he attended Stoddard, in which case it might conceivably be a coincidence; he went to Stoddard and he transferred to Caldwell; he might not have known Dorothy any more than he knew me." He paused. "Or else, he *didn't* tell Marion he went there."

"Which means?" Kingship challenged.

"Which means that he must have been involved with Dorothy in some way. Why else would he conceal it?" Gant looked down at the book in his lap. "There was a man who wanted Dorothy out of the way because he had gotten her pregnant . . ."

Kingship stared at him. "You're back to the same thing! Someone killed Dorothy, then killed Ellen . . . You've got this—this cockeyed moving picture theory and you don't want to admit . . ." Gant was silent. "Bud?" Kingship asked incredulously. He sat back. He shook his head, smiling pityingly. "Come on, now," he said. "That's crazy. Just crazy." He kept shaking his head—"What do you think that boy is, a maniac?"—and smiling—"You've got this crazy idea . . ."

"All right," Gant said, "it's crazy. For the time being. But if he didn't tell Marion he went to Stoddard, then in some way he must have been involved with Dorothy. And if he was involved with Dorothy, and then Ellen, and now with Marion,—then he was goddamned good and determined to marry one of your daughters! Any one!"

The smile left Kingship's face slowly, draining it of expression. His hands were motionless on the edge of the desk.

"That *isn't* so crazy, I take it."

Kingship removed his glasses. He blinked a couple of times and then straightened up. "I have to speak to Marion," he said.

Gant looked at the telephone.

"No," Kingship said emptily. "She's had her phone disconnected. She's giving up her apartment, staying with me until the wedding." His voice faltered. "After the honeymoon they're moving into an apartment I'm furnishing for them . . . Sutton Terrace . . . Marion didn't want to accept it at first, but he convinced her. He's been so good with her . . . made the two of us get along so much better . . ." They looked at each other for a moment; Gant's eyes steady and challenging, Kingship's apprehensive.

Kingship stood up.

"Do you know where she is?" Gant asked.

"At her place . . . packing things." He put on his jacket. "He *must* have told her about Stoddard . . ."

When they came out of the office Miss Richardson looked up from a magazine.

"That's all for today, Miss Richardson. If you'll just clear my desk."

She frowned with frustrated curiosity. "Yes, Mr. Kingship. Merry Christmas."

"Merry Christmas, Miss Richardson."

They walked down a long corridor, on the walls of which were black and white photographs, matted and mounted between plates of glass held together by copper brackets at top and bottom. There were photographs of underground and open-pit mines, smelters, refineries, furnaces, rolling mills, and artistic close-ups of tubing and copper wire.

Waiting for the elevator Kingship said, "I'm sure he told her."

## 8

"GORDON GANT?" Marion said, exploring the name, when they had shaken hands. "Don't I know that name?" She backed into the room, smiling, one hand finding Kingship's and drawing him with her, the other rising to the collar of her blouse and fingering the golden pearl-starred brooch.

"Blue River." Kingship's voice was wooden as when he had performed the introduction, and his eyes were not quite on Marion's. "I think I told you about him."

"Oh, yes. You knew Ellen, wasn't that it?"

"That's right," Gant said. He shifted his hand farther down the spine of the book at his side, to a spot where the leatherette wasn't damp, wishing he hadn't been so damned eager when Kingship had asked him to come up; the *Times* photo of Marion had offered no hint in its dotted grays of the lucency of her eyes, the radiance of her cheeks, the halo of I'm-getting-married-Saturday that glowed all over her.

She gestured at the room despairingly. "I'm afraid there isn't even a place to sit down." She moved towards a chair on which some shoe boxes were piled.

"Don't bother," Kingship said. "We just stopped by. Only for a minute. A lot of work waiting for me at the office."

"You haven't forgotten tonight, have you?" Marion asked. "You can expect us at seven or so. She's arriving at five, and I guess she'll want to stop at her hotel first." She turned to Gant. "My prospective mother-in-law," she said significantly.

Oh Lord, Gant thought, I'm supposed to say 'You're getting married?'—'Yes, Saturday.'—'Congratulations, good luck, best wishes!' He smiled wanly and didn't say anything. Nobody said anything.

"To what do I owe the pleasure of this visit?" Marion inquired, a curtsey in her voice.

Gant looked at Kingship, waiting for him to speak.

Marion looked at both of them. "Anything special?"

After a moment, Gant said, "I knew Dorothy, too. Very slightly."

"Oh," Marion said. She looked down at her hands.

"She was in one of my classes. I go to Stoddard." He paused. "I don't think Bud was ever in any of my classes though."

She looked up. "Bud?"

"Bud Corliss. Your . . ."

She shook her head, smiling. "Bud was never at Stoddard," she corrected him.

"He was, Miss Kingship."

"No," she insisted amusedly, "he went to Caldwell."

"He went to Stoddard, *then* to Caldwell."

Marion smiled quizzically at Kingship, as though expecting him to offer some explanation for the obstinacy of the caller he had brought.

"He was at Stoddard, Marion," Kingship said heavily. "Show her the book."

Gant opened the yearbook and handed it to Marion, pointing to the picture.

"Well for goodness' sake," she said. "I have to apologize. I never knew . . ." She glanced at the cover of the book. "Nineteen-fifty."

"He's in the forty-nine yearbook too," Gant said. "He went to Stoddard for two years and then transferred to Caldwell."

"For goodness' sake," she said. "Isn't that funny? Maybe he knew Dorothy." She sounded pleased, as though this were yet another bond between her and her fiancé. Her eyes slipped back to his picture.

"He never mentioned it to you at all?" Gant asked, despite Kingship's prohibitive headshakings.

"Why, no, he never said a . . ."

Slowly she looked up from the book, becoming aware for the first time of the strain and discomfort of the two men. "What's the matter?" she asked curiously.

"Nothing," Kingship said. He glanced at Gant, seeking corroboration.

"Then why are the two of you standing there as if . . ." She looked at the book again, and then at her father. There was a tightening movement in her throat. "Is this why you came up here, to tell me this?" she asked.

"We . . . we only wondered if you knew, that's all."

"Why?" she asked.

"We just wondered, that's all."

Her eyes cut to Gant. "Why?"

"Why should Bud conceal it," Gant asked, "unless—"

Kingship said, "Gant!"

"*Conceal* it?" Marion said. "What kind of a word is that? He didn't *conceal* it; we never talk about school much, because of Ellen; it just didn't come up."

"Why should the girl he's marrying not know he spent two years at Stoddard," Gant rephrased implacably, "unless he was involved with Dorothy?"

"*Involved?* With *Dorothy?*" Her eyes, wide with incredulity, probed into Gant's, and then swung slowly, narrowing, to Kingship. "What is this?"

Kingship's face flickered with small uneasy movements, as though dust were blowing at it.

"How much are you paying him?" Marion asked coldly.

"Paying him?"

"For snooping!" she flared. "For digging up dirt! For *inventing* dirt!"

"He came to me of his own accord, Marion!"

"Oh yes, he just *happened* to pop up!"

Gant said, "I saw the article in *The Times*."

Marion glared at her father. "You swore you wouldn't do this," she said bitterly. "Swore! It would *never* enter your mind to ask *ques*tions, to in*ves*tigate, treat him like a *crim*inal. Oh no, not much!"

"I *haven't* been asking questions," Kingship protested.

Marion turned her back. "I thought you changed," she said. "I really did. I thought you liked Bud. I thought you liked *me*. But you can't . . ."

"Marion . . ."

"No, not if you're doing this. The apartment, the job . . . and all along *this* has been going on."

"*Nothing* is going on, Marion. I swear . . ."

"Nothing? I'll tell you *exactly* what's going on." She faced him again. "You think I don't know you? He was 'involved' with Dorothy—is he supposed to be the one who got her in trouble?—and he was 'involved' with Ellen, and now he's 'involved' with me—all for the money, all for your precious money. That's what's going on—*in your mind!*" She thrust the yearbook into his hands.

"You've got it wrong, Miss Kingship," Gant said. "That's what's going on in *my* mind, not your father's."

"See?" Kingship said. "He came to me of his own accord."

Marion stared at Gant. "Just who are you? What makes this your business?"

"I knew Ellen."

"So I understand," she snapped. "Do you know Bud?"

"I've never had the pleasure."

"Then will you please explain to me what you're doing here, making accusations against him behind his back!"

"It's quite a story—"

"You've said enough, Gant," Kingship interrupted.

Marion said, "Are you jealous of Bud? Is that it? Because Ellen preferred him to you?"

"That's right," Gant said drily. "I'm consumed with jealousy."

"And have you heard of the slander laws?" she demanded.

Kingship edged towards the door, signaling Gant with his eyes. "Yes," Marion said, "you'd better go."

"Wait a minute," she said as Gant opened the door. "Is this going to stop?"

Kingship said, "There's nothing *to* stop, Marion."

"Whoever's behind it,"—she looked at Gant—"it's got to stop. We never talked about school. Why should we, with Ellen? It just never came up."

"All right, Marion," Kingship said, "all right." He followed Gant into the hall and turned to pull the door closed.

"It's got to stop," she said.

"All right." He hesitated, and his voice dropped. "You're still coming tonight, aren't you, Marion?"

Her lips clenched. She thought for a moment. "Because I don't want to hurt Bud's mother's feelings," she said finally.

Kingship closed the door.

They went to a drugstore on Lexington Avenue, where Gant ordered coffee and cherry pie, and Kingship, a glass of milk.

"So far, so good," Gant said.

Kingship was gazing at a paper napkin he held. "What do you mean?"

"At least we know where we stand. He didn't tell her about Stoddard. That makes it practically certain that—"

"You heard Marion," Kingship said. "They don't talk about school because of Ellen."

Gant regarded him with slightly lifted eyebrows. "Come on," he said slowly, "that may satisfy *her;* she's in love with him. But for a man not to tell his fiancée where he went to college . . ."

"It isn't as if he lied to her," Kingship protested.

Sardonically Gant said, "They just didn't talk about school."

"Considering the circumstances, I think that's understandable."

"Sure. The circumstances being that he was mixed up with Dorothy."

"That's an assumption you have no right to make."

Gant stirred his coffee slowly and sipped it. He added more cream and stirred it again. "You're afraid of her, aren't you," he said.

"Of Marion? Don't be ridiculous." Kingship set his glass of milk down firmly. "A man is innocent until he's proved guilty."

"Then we've got to find proof, don't we?"

"You see? You're assuming he's a fortune hunter before you've started."

"I'm assuming a hell of a lot more than that," Gant said, lifting a forkful of pie to his mouth. When he had swallowed it he said, "What are you going to do?"

Kingship was looking at the napkin again. "Nothing."

"You're going to let them get married?"

"I couldn't stop them even if I wanted to. They're both over twenty-one, aren't they?"

"You could hire detectives. There are four days yet. They might find something."

"Might," Kingship said. "If there's anything to find. Or Bud might get wind of it and tell Marion."

Gant smiled. "I thought I was being ridiculous about you and Marion."

Kingship sighed. "Let me tell you something," he said, not looking at Gant. "I had a wife and three daughters. Two daughters were taken from me. My wife I pushed away myself. Maybe I pushed one of the daughters too. So now I have only one daughter. I'm fifty-seven years old and I have one daughter and some men I play golf and talk business with. That's all."

After a moment Kingship turned to Gant, his face set rigidly. "What about you?" he demanded. "What *is* your real interest in this affair? Maybe you just enjoy chattering about your analytical brain and showing people what a clever fellow you are. You didn't have to go through that whole rigamarole, you know. In my office, about Ellen's letter. You could have just put the book on my desk and said 'Bud Corliss went to Stoddard.' Maybe you just like to show off."

"Maybe," Gant said lightly. "Also maybe I think he might have killed your daughters and I've got this quixotic notion that murderers should be punished."

Kingship finished his milk. "I think you'd better just go back to Yonkers and enjoy your vacation."

"White Plains." Gant scraped together the syrupy remains of the pie with the side of his fork. "Do you have ulcers?" he asked, glancing at the empty milk glass.

Kingship nodded.

Gant leaned back on his stool and surveyed the man beside him. "And about thirty pounds overweight, I'd say." He put the red-clotted fork in his mouth and drew it out clean. "I should estimate that Bud has you figured for ten more years, tops. Or maybe he'll get impatient in three or four years and try to hurry you on."

Kingship got off his stool. He pulled a dollar from a money-clipped roll and put it on the counter. "Good-by, Mr. Gant," he said, and strode away.

The counterman came over and took the dollar. "Anything else?" he asked.

Gant shook his head.

He caught the 5:19 for White Plains.

## 9

IN WRITING TO his mother, Bud had made only the most vague allusions to Kingship's money. Once or twice he had mentioned *Kingship Copper,* but never with any clarifying phrases, and he was certain that she, whose poverty-formed conception of wealth was as hazy and inexact as a pubert's visions of orgies, had not the slightest real comprehension of the luxuriance of living into which the presidency of such a corporation could be translated. He had looked forward eagerly, therefore, to the moment when he could introduce her to Marion and her father, and to the surrounding magnificence of Kingship's duplex apartment, knowing that in light of the coming marriage her awe-widened eyes would regard each inlaid table and glittering chandelier as evidence, not of Kingship's capabilities, but of his own.

The evening, however, was a disappointment.

Not that his mother's reaction was anything less than he had anticipated; with mouth partially opened and teeth lightly touching her lower lip, she drew in her breath with soft sibilance, as though seeing not one but a series of miracles; the formally attired servant—a butler!—the velvety depth of the carpets, the wallpaper that wasn't paper at all but intricately textured cloth, the leather-bound books, the golden clock, the silver tray from which the butler served champagne—champagne!—in crystal goblets . . . Vocally, she restrained her admiration to a gently smiling "Lovely, lovely," accompanied by a slight nodding of the stiff newly-waved gray hair, giving the impression that such surroundings were by no means completely alien to her,—but when her eyes met Bud's as the toast was drunk, the bursting pride she felt leaped out to him like a thrown kiss, while one work-roughened hand surreptitiously marveled at the cloth of the couch on which she sat.

No, his mother's reaction was warming and wonderful. What made the evening a disappointment was the fact that Marion and Leo had apparently had an argument; Marion spoke to her father only when appearances made it inescapable. And furthermore, the argument must have been about him, since Leo addressed him with hesitant unfocused eyes, while Marion was determinedly, defiantly effusive, clinging to him and calling him 'dear' and 'darling,' which she had never done before when others were present. The first faint worry began to sting him like a pebble in his shoe.

Dinner, then, was dismal. With Leo and Marion at the ends of the table and his mother and he at the sides, conversation passed only around the edges; father and daughter would not talk; mother and son could not talk, for anything they had to say would be personal and exclusive-sounding before these people who were still in a sense outsiders. So Marion called him 'darling' and told his mother about the Sutton Terrace apartment, and his mother spoke to Leo about 'the children,' and Leo asked him to pass the bread please, not quite looking at him.

And he was silent, lifting each fork and spoon slowly as he selected it, so that his mother could see and do likewise; an affectionate conspiracy fallen into without word or signal, dramatizing the bond between them and forming the one enjoyable aspect of the meal—that and the smiles that passed across the table when Marion and Leo were looking down at their food, smiles prideful and loving and all the more pleasing to him because of the unsuspecting heads whose path they slipped across.

At the end of the meal, although there was a silver lighter on the table, he lit Marion's and his own cigarette with his matches, afterwards tapping the folder absentmindedly on the cloth until his mother had noticed the white cover on which *Bud Corliss* was stamped in copper leaf.

But all along there was the pebble in his shoe.

Later, it being Christmas Eve, they went to church, and after church Bud expected to take his mother back to her hotel while Marion returned home with Leo. But Marion, to his annoyance, assumed an unfamiliar coquetry and insisted on accompanying them to the hotel, so Leo went off by himself as Bud squired the two women into a taxi. He sat between them, reciting to his mother the names of what landmarks they passed. The cab, at his direction, departed from its course so that Mrs. Corliss, who had never been to New York before, might see Times Square at night.

He left her in the lobby of her hotel, outside the elevator. "Are you very tired?" he asked, and when she said she was, he seemed disappointed. "Don't go to sleep right away," he said. "I'll call you later." They kissed goodnight and, still holding Bud's hand, Mrs. Corliss kissed Marion happily on the cheek.

During the taxi ride back to Leo's, Marion was silent.

"What's the matter, darling?"

"Nothing," she said, smiling unconvincingly. "Why?"

He shrugged.

He had intended to leave her at the door of the apartment, but the pebble of worry was assuming the proportions of a sharp stone; he went in with her. Kingship had already retired. They went into the living room where Bud lighted cigarettes while Marion turned on the radio. They sat on the couch.

She told him that she liked his mother very much. He said he was glad, and he could tell that his mother liked her too. They began to speak of the future, and he sensed from the stiff casualness of her voice that she was working up to something. He leaned back with his eyes half closed, one arm around her shoulders, listening as he had never listened before, weighing every pause and inflection, fearful all the while of what it was leading up to. It couldn't be anything important! It couldn't be! He had slighted her somehow, forgotten something he'd promised to do, that was all. What could it be? . . . He paused before each reply, examining his words before he spoke them, trying to determine what response they would bring, like a chess player touching pieces before making his move.

She worked the conversation around to children. "Two," she said.

His left hand, on his knee, pinched the crease of his trousers. He smiled. "Or three," he said. "Or four."

"Two," she said. "Then one can go to Columbia and one to Caldwell."

Caldwell. Something about Caldwell. Ellen? "They'll probably both wind up at Michigan or someplace," he said.

"Or if we only have one," Marion went on, "he can go to Columbia and then transfer to Caldwell. Or vice-versa." She leaned forward, smiling, and pressed her cigarette into an ashtray. Much more carefully than she usually put out her cigarettes, he observed. Transfer to Caldwell. Transfer to Caldwell . . . He waited in silence. "No," she said, "I really wouldn't want him to do that,"—following up her statement with a tenacity she never would have applied to mere idle chatter—"because he would lose credits. Transferring must be very involved."

They sat side by side, silently for a moment.

"No it isn't," he said.

"Isn't it?" she asked.

"No," he said. "I didn't lose any credits."

"You didn't transfer, did you?" She sounded surprised.

"Of course," he said. "I told you."

"No you didn't. You never said—"

"I did, honey. I'm sure I told you. I went to Stoddard University, and then to Caldwell."

"Why, that's where my sister Dorothy went, Stoddard!"

"I know. Ellen told me."

"Don't tell me you *knew* her."

"No. Ellen showed me her picture though, and I think I remember seeing her around. I'm sure I told you, that first day, in the museum."

"No, you didn't. I'm positive."

"Well sure, I was at Stoddard two years. And you mean to say you didn't—" Marion's lips stopped the rest of the sentence, kissing him fervidly, atoning for doubt.

A few minutes later he looked at his watch. "I'd better be leaving," he said. "I want to get as much sleep as I can this week, because I have an idea I won't be getting much sleep at all next week."

It only meant that Leo had somehow learned he'd been at Stoddard. There was no real danger. There wasn't! Trouble maybe; the wedding plans might be blown up—oh Jesus!—but there was no *danger*, no police danger. There's no law against going after a rich girl, is there?

But why so late? If Leo wanted to check on him, why hadn't he done it sooner? Why today? . . . The announcement in *The Times* . . . of course! Someone had seen it, someone who'd been at Stoddard. The son of one of Leo's friends or someone like that. "My son and your future son-in-law were at Stoddard together." So Leo puts two and two together; Dorothy, Ellen, Marion—gold-digger. He tells Marion, and that was their argument.

God damn, if only it had been possible to mention Stoddard at the beginning! That would have been crazy though; Leo would have suspected right off, and Marion would have listened to him then. But why did it have to come up now!

Still, what could Leo do, with only suspicions? They must be only suspicions; the old man couldn't know for sure that he'd known Dorothy, or else Marion wouldn't have been so happy when he himself told her he hadn't known her. Or could Leo have withheld part of his information from Marion? No, he would have tried to convince her, given her all the evidence he had. So Leo wasn't certain. Could he *make* certain? How? The kids at Stoddard, mostly seniors now, would they remember who Dorothy had gone with? They might. But it's Christmas! Vacation. They're scattered all over the country. Only four days to the wedding. Leo could never talk Marion into postponing.

All he had to do was sit tight and keep his fingers crossed. Tuesday, Wednesday, Thursday, Friday . . . *Saturday*. If worst came to worst, so he was after the money; that was all Leo could ever prove. He couldn't prove that Dorothy didn't commit suicide. He couldn't drag the Mississippi for a gun that was probably buried under twenty feet of mud.

And if best came to best, the wedding would go off as per schedule. Then what could Leo do even if the kids at Stoddard did remember? Divorce? Annulment? Not nearly enough grounds for either, even if Marion could be persuaded to seek one, which she probably couldn't. What then? Maybe Leo would try to buy him off . . .

Now *there* was a thought . . . How much would Leo be willing to pay to free his daughter from the big bad gold-digger? Quite a lot, probably.

But not nearly as much as Marion would have some day.

Bread now or cake later?

When he got back to his rooming house, he telephoned his mother. "I hope I didn't wake you. I walked back from Marion's."

"That's all right, darling. Oh Bud, she's a lovely girl! Lovely! So sweet . . . I'm so happy for you!"

"Thanks, Mom."

"And Mr. Kingship, such a fine man! Did you notice his hands?"

"What about them?"

"So clean!" He laughed. "Bud," her voice lowered, "they must be rich, very rich . . ."

"I guess they are, Mom."

"That apartment . . . like a movie! My goodness . . . !"

He told her about the Sutton Terrace apartment—"Wait till you see it, Mom!"—and about the visit to the smelter—"He's taking me there Thursday. He wants me to be familiar with the whole set-up!"—and towards the end of the conversation, she said:

"Bud, what ever happened to that idea of yours?"

"What idea?"

"The one why you didn't go back to school."

"Oh, that," he said. "It didn't pan out."

"Oh . . ." She was disappointed.

"You know that shaving cream?" he said. "Where you press the button and it comes out of the can like whipped cream?"

"Yes?"

"Well that was it. Only they beat me to it."

She breathed a drawn-out "Oh" of commiseration. "If that isn't a shame . . . You didn't talk to anyone about it, did you?"

"No. They just beat me to it."

"Well," she said with a sigh, "things like that happen. It certainly is a shame though. An idea like that . . ."

When he had finished talking to her, he went into his room and stretched out on the bed, feeling good all over. Leo and his suspicions, nuts to him! Everything was going to be perfect.

Jesus, that was one thing he was going to do—see that she got some of the money.

## 10

THE TRAIN, HAVING passed through Stamford, Bridgeport, New Haven and New London, continued grinding eastward along the southern border of Connecticut, passing between flat snow on the left and flat water on the right; a segmented serpent from whose body trapped people vapidly gazed. Inside, aisles and vestibules were clogged with the Christmas Day overflow.

In one of the vestibules, facing a dirt-smeared window, Gordon Gant occupied himself by counting codfish-cake billboards. It was, he reflected, a hell of a way to spend Christmas Day.

Shortly after six o'clock the train reached Providence.

In the station, Gant addressed several questions to the bored oracle of the information booth. Then, regarding his watch, he left the building. It was already dark outside. Crossing a wide and slushy thoroughfare, he entered an establishment which called itself a 'spa,' where he made quick work of a steak sandwich, mincemeat pie and coffee. Christmas dinner. He left the spa and went to a drugstore two doors away, where he purchased an inch-wide roll of Scotch Tape. He returned to the station. He sat on an uncomfortable bench and read a Boston tabloid. At ten minutes of seven he left the station again, proceeding to a nearby place where three busses stood waiting. He boarded a blue and yellow one marked *Menasset—Somerset—Fall River.*

At twenty minutes past seven the bus paused midway down Menasset's four block Main Street, discharging several passengers, Gant among them. After a brief acclimatizing glance, he entered a 1910-looking pharmacy where he consulted a thin directory, from which he copied an address and a telephone number. He tried the number in the phone booth and, when the phone on the other end of the line had rung ten times without answer, hung up.

The house was a shabby gray box, one story, the sills of its darkened windows furred with snow. Gant looked at it closely as he passed. It was set back only a few yards from the sidewalk; the snow between door and sidewalk was undisturbed.

He walked to the end of the deserted block, turned and came back, passing the gray house again, this time paying more attention to the houses on either side of it. In one, framed in the window's homemade Christmas wreath, a Spanish-looking family was dining in an atmosphere of magazine cover warmth. In the house on the other side of the gray one, a solitary man was holding a globe of the world in his lap, spinning it in its frame and then stopping it with his finger and looking to see which country his finger had chosen. Gant passed, walked to the other end of the block, turned and came back. This time, as he passed the gray house, he turned sharply, cutting between it and the Spanish-family house. He went around to the back.

There was a small porch. Facing it, across a little yard laced with stiff clotheslines, was a high board fence. Gant went up on the porch. There were a door and a window, a garbage can and a basket of clothespins. He tried the door; it was locked. The window was locked also. Propped on the sill within was an ice company sign, a square placard with *5, 10, 25,* and *X* printed around the four sides. The *X* side was uppermost. Gant took the roll of Scotch Tape from his pocket. Tearing off a ten inch length, he pressed it across one of the window's dozen panes, the one below the central latch. He fitted the ends of the tape over the pane's molding and tore off another ten inch strip.

In a few minutes he had crosshatched the rectangular pane with cellophane strips. He struck it with his gloved fist. There was a cracking sound; the broken glass sagged, held in place by the tape. Gant began to pull the tape ends from the molding. When that was done he drew the rectangle of cellophane and broken glass from the window and lowered it noiselessly to the bottom of the garbage can. Reaching through the window, he unfastened the latch and raised the lower section. The ice placard fell back into the darkness.

He took a pencil flashlight from his pocket and leaned through the open window. There was a chair piled with folded newspapers before it. He pushed the chair aside and climbed in, closing the window after him.

The flashlight's disc of pallid light glided swiftly over a cramped and shabby kitchen. Gant moved forward, treading softly on worn-through linoleum.

He came to a living room. The chairs were fat and velvet, rubbed bald at the arms. Cream colored shades were drawn down over the windows, flanked by floral-patterned paper drapes. There were pictures of Bud all over; Bud as a child in short pants, Bud at high school graduation, Bud in a private's uniform, Bud in a dark suit, smiling. Snapshots were tucked in the frames of the portraits, surrounding the large smiling faces with smaller faces also smiling.

Gant went through the living room to a hallway. The first room off the hallway was a bedroom; a bottle of lotion on the dresser, an empty dress box and tissue paper on the bed, a wedding picture and a picture of Bud on the night table. The second room was the bathroom; the flashlight caught decals of swans on moisture-faded walls.

The third room was Bud's. It might have been a room in a second class hotel; aside from the high school diploma over the bed, it was barren of anything suggesting the occupant's individuality. Gant went in.

He inspected the titles of some books on a shelf; they were mainly college texts and a few classic novels. No diaries, no engagement books. He sat behind the desk and went through the drawers one at a time. There were stationery and blank scratch pads, back issues of *Life* and the *New Yorker,* term papers from college, road maps of New England. No letters, no calendars with appointments written in, no address books with names crossed out. He rose from the desk and went to the dresser. Half the drawers were empty. The others contained summer shirts and swimming trunks, a couple of pairs of argyle socks, underwear, tarnished cufflinks, celluloid collar stays, bow ties with broken clips. No papers lost in corners, no forgotten pictures.

Perfunctorily he opened the closet. On the floor in the corner there was a small gray strongbox.

He took it out and put it on the desk. It was locked. He lifted and shook it. Its contents shifted, sounding like packets of paper. He put the box down again and picked at its lock with the blade of a small knife he carried on his keychain. Then he took it into the kitchen. He found a screwdriver in one of the drawers and tried that. Finally he wrapped the box in newspaper, hoping that it didn't contain Mrs. Corliss' life's savings.

He opened the window, took the ice placard from the floor, and climbed out onto the porch. When he had closed and locked the window, he tore the placard to size and fitted it in the open pane, blank side out. With the strongbox under his arm, he moved quietly between the houses to the sidewalk.

## 11

LEO KINGSHIP RETURNED to his apartment at ten o'clock on Wednesday night, having worked late in order to compensate for some of the lost hours Christmas had entailed. "Is Marion in?" he asked the butler, giving him his coat.

"Out with Mr. Corliss. She said she'd be in early though. There's a Mr. Dettweiler waiting in the living room."

"Dettweiler?"

"He said Miss Richardson sent him about the securities. He has a little strongbox with him."

"Dettweiler?" Kingship frowned.

He went into the living room.

Gordon Gant rose from a comfortable chair adjacent to the fireplace. "Hello," he said pleasantly.

Kingship looked at him for a moment. "Didn't Miss Richardson make it clear this afternoon that I don't want—" His hands fisted at his sides. "Get out of here," he said. "If Marion comes in . . ."

"Exhibit A," Gant pronounced, raising a pamphlet in each hand, "in the case against Bud Corliss."

"I don't want to—" The sentence hung unfinished. Apprehensively, Kingship came forward. He took the pamphlets from Gant's hands. "Our publications . . ."

"In the possession of Bud Corliss," Gant said. "Kept in a strongbox which until last night resided in a closet in Menasset, Massachusetts." He gave a light kick to the strongbox on the floor beside him. The open lid was bent out of shape. There were four oblong Manila envelopes inside. "I stole it," Gant said.

"*Stole* it?"

He smiled. "Fight fire with fire. I don't know where he's staying in New York, so I decided to sally forth to Menasset."

"You crazy . . ." Kingship sat heavily on a couch that faced the fireplace. He stared at the pamphlets. "Oh God," he said.

Gant resumed his seat next to the couch. "Observe the condition of Exhibit A, if you will. Frayed around the edges, soiled by many fingermarks, center pages worked loose from the staples. I would say he had them for quite some time. I would say he drooled over them considerably."

"That . . . that son of a bitch . . ." Kingship spoke the phrase distinctly, as though not accustomed to using it.

Gant prodded the strongbox with his toe. "The History of Bud Corliss, a drama in four envelopes," he said. "Envelope one: newspaper clippings of the high school hero; class president, chairman of the prom committee, Most Likely To Succeed and so on and so forth. Envelope two: honorable discharge from the Army, Bronze Star, Purple Heart, several interesting though obscene photographs and a pawn ticket which I have discovered may be exchanged for a wristwatch if you have a couple of hundred dollars you don't need. Envelope three: college days; transcripts from Stoddard and Caldwell. Envelope four: two well-read brochures describing the magnitude of Kingship Copper Incorporated, and this . . ."—he drew a folded sheet of blue-lined yellow paper from his pocket and passed it to Kingship—"which I can't make head or tail of."

Kingship unfolded the paper. He read halfway down it. "What is it?"

"I'm asking you."

He shook his head.

"It must have some bearing on this," Gant said. "It was in with the pamphlets."

Kingship shook his head and handed the paper back to Gant, who returned it to his pocket. Kingship's gaze dropped to the pamphlets. The grip of his hands crackled the thick paper. "How am I going to tell Marion?" he said. "She *loves* him . . ." He looked at Gant dismally. Then slowly his face smoothed out. He glanced at the pamphlets and back at Gant, his eyes narrowing. "How do I know these were in the strongbox? How do I know that you didn't put them there yourself?"

Gant's jaw dropped. "Oh, for . . ."

Kingship went around the end of the couch and across the room. There was a telephone on a carved table. He dialed a number.

"Come on now," Gant chided.

In the silence of the room the buzzing and the clicks of the phone were audible. "Hello? Miss Richardson? This is Mr. Kingship. I'd like to ask a favor of you. A big favor, I'm afraid. And absolutely confidential." An unintelligible twittering emanated from the phone. "Would you please go down to the office—yes, now. I wouldn't ask you, only it's terribly important, and I—" There was more twittering. "Go to the public relations department," Kingship said. "Go through the files and see whether we've ever sent any promotional publications to . . . Bud Corliss."

"Burton Corliss," Gant said.

"Or Burton Corliss. Yes, that's right—Mr. Corliss. I'm at my home, Miss Richardson. Call me as soon as you find out. Thank you. Thank you very much, Miss Richardson. I appreciate this . . ." He hung up.

Gant shook his head wryly. "We're really grasping at straws, aren't we."

"I have to be sure," Kingship said. "You have to be sure of your evidence in a thing like this." He came back across the room and stood behind the couch.

"You're sure already, and you know damn well you are," Gant said.

Kingship braced his hands on the couch, looking down at the pamphlets in the hollow of the cushion where he had been sitting.

"You know damn well you are," Gant repeated.

After a moment Kingship's breath sighed out tiredly. He came around the couch, picked up the pamphlets, and sat down. "How am I supposed to tell Marion?" he asked. He rubbed his knee. "That son of a bitch . . . that God-damned son of a bitch . . ."

Gant leaned towards him, his elbows on his knees. "Mr. Kingship, I was right about this much. Will you admit I might be right all the way?"

"What 'all the way'?"

"About Dorothy and Ellen." Kingship drew an irritated breath. Gant spoke quickly: "He didn't tell Marion he went to Stoddard. He *must* have been mixed up with Dorothy. He *must* be the one who got her pregnant. He killed her, and Powell and Ellen somehow found out it was him and he had to kill them too."

"The note . . ."

"He could have tricked her into writing it! It's been done before—there was a case in the papers just last month about a guy who did it, and for the same reason; the girl was pregnant."

Kingship shook his head. "I'd believe it of him," he said. "After what he's done to Marion, I'd believe anything of him. But there's a flaw in your theory, a big flaw."

"What?" Gant demanded.

"He's after the money, isn't he?" Gant nodded. "And you 'know' Dorothy was murdered because she was wearing something old, something new, something borrowed, something blue?" Gant nodded again. "Well," Kingship said, "if he were the one who'd gotten her into trouble, and if she were ready to marry him that day, then why would he have killed her? He would have gone ahead and married her, wouldn't he? He would have married her and gotten in on the money."

Gant looked at him wordlessly.

"You were right about this," Kingship said, lifting the pamphlets, "but you're wrong about Dorothy. All wrong."

After a moment Gant rose. He turned and paced up to the window. He looked through it dully, gnawing his lower lip. "I may jump," he announced.

When the door chimes toned, Gant turned from the window. Kingship had risen and was standing before the fireplace, gazing at the birch logs neatly pyramided there. He turned reluctantly, holding the rolled pamphlets at his side, his face averted from Gant's watching eyes.

They heard the front door open, and then voices: ". . . come in for a while?"

"I don't think so, Marion. We'll have to get up early tomorrow." There was a long silence. "I'll be in front of my place at seven-thirty."

"You'd better wear a dark suit. A smelter must be a filthy place." Another silence. "Good night, Bud . . ."

"Good night."

The door closed.

Kingship wound the pamphlets into a tighter cylinder. "Marion," he called, but it came out too low. "Marion," he called again, louder.

"Coming," her voice answered cheerfully.

The two men waited, suddenly conscious of a clock's ticking.

She appeared in the wide doorway, perking up the collar of her crisp white full-sleeved blouse. Her cheeks were luminous from the cold outside. "Hi," she said. "We had a—"

She saw Gant. Her hands froze, dropped.

"Marion, we . . ."

She whirled and was gone.

"Marion!" Kingship hurried to the doorway and into the foyer. "Marion!" She was halfway up the curving white staircase, her legs driving furiously. "Marion!" he shouted grimly, commanding.

She stopped, facing rigidly up the stairs, one hand on the bannister. "Well?"

"Come down here," he said. "I have to speak to you. This is extremely important." A moment passed. "Come down here," he said.

"All right." She turned and descended the stairs with regal coldness. "You can speak to me. Before I go upstairs and pack and get out of here."

Kingship returned to the living room. Gant was standing uncomfortably in the middle of the room, his hand on the back of the couch. Kingship, shaking his head dolefully, went to his side.

She came into the room. Their eyes followed her as, without looking at them, she came up to the chair across from the one in which Gant had sat, at the end of the couch nearer the door. She sat down. She crossed her legs carefully, smoothing the red wool of her skirt. She put her hands on the arms of the chair. She looked up at them, standing behind the couch to her left. "Well?" she said.

Kingship shifted uneasily, withering under her gaze. "Mr. Gant went to . . . Yesterday he . . ."

"Yes?"

Kingship turned to Gant helplessly.

Gant said: "Yesterday afternoon, absolutely without your father's knowledge, I went to Menasset. I broke into your fiancé's home—"

"No!"

"—and I took from it a strongbox I found in the closet in his room—"

She pressed back into the chair, her knuckles gripping white, her mouth clamped to a lipless line, her eyes shut.

"I brought it home and jimmied the cover—"

Her eyes shot open, flashing. "What did you find? The plans of the atom bomb?"

They were silent.

"What did you find?" she repeated, her voice lowering, growing wary.

Kingship moved down to the end of the couch and handed her the pamphlets, awkwardly unrolling them.

She took them slowly and looked at them.

"They're old," Gant said. "He's had them for some time."

Kingship said, "He hasn't been back to Menasset since you started going with him. He had them before he met you."

She smoothed the pamphlets carefully in her lap. Some of the corners were folded over. She bent them straight. "Ellen must have given them to him."

"Ellen never had any of our publications, Marion. You know that. She was as little interested as you are."

She turned the pamphlets over and examined their backs. "Were you there when he broke open the box? Do you know for certain they were in the box?"

"I'm checking on that," Kingship said. "But what reason would Mr. Gant have for . . ."

She began turning the pages of one of the pamphlets; casually, as though it were a magazine in a waiting room. "All right," she said stiffly, after a moment, "maybe it *was* the money that attracted him at first." Her lips formed a strained smile. "For once in my life I'm grateful for your money." She turned a page. "What is it they say?—it's as easy to fall in love with a rich girl as with a poor."—and another page—"You really can't blame him too much, coming from such a poor family. Environmental influence . . ." She stood up and tossed the pamphlets on the couch. "Is there anything else you wanted?" Her hands were trembling slightly.

"Anything else?" Kingship stared. "Isn't that enough?"

"Enough?" she inquired. "Enough for what? Enough for me to call off the wedding? No."—she shook her head—"No, it isn't enough."

"You *still* want to—"

"He *loves* me," she said. "Maybe it was the money that attracted him at first, but—well, suppose I were a very pretty girl; I wouldn't call off the wedding if I found out it was my looks that attracted him, would I?"

"At first?" Kingship said. "The money is still what attracts him."

"You have no right to say that!"

"Marion, you *can't* marry him now . . ."

"No? Come down to City Hall Saturday morning!"

"He's a no-good scheming—"

"Oh yes! You always know just who's good and who's bad, don't you! You knew Mom was bad and you got rid of her, and you knew Dorothy was bad and that's why she killed herself because you brought us up with your good and bad, your right and wrong! Haven't you done enough with your good and bad?"

"You're *not* going to marry a man who's only after you for your money!"

"He *loves* me! Don't you understand English? He loves me! I love him! I don't care *what* brought us together! We think alike! Feel alike! We like the same books, the same plays, the same music, the same—"

"The same food?" Gant cut in. "Would you both be fond of Italian and Armenian food?" She turned to him, her mouth ajar. He was unfolding a sheet of blue-lined yellow paper he had taken from his pocket. "And those books," he said, looking at the paper, "would they include the works of Proust, Thomas Wolfe, Carson McCullers?"

Her eyes widened. "How did you . . . ? What is that?"

He came around the end of the couch. She turned to face him. "Sit down," he said.

"What are you . . . ?" She moved back. The edge of the couch pressed against the back of her knees.

"Sit down, please," he said.

She sat down. "What is that?"

"This was in the strongbox with the pamphlets," he said. "In the same envelope. The printing is his, I presume." He handed her the yellow paper. "I'm sorry," he said.

She looked at him confusedly, and then looked down at the paper.

*Proust, T. Wolfe, C. McCullers, "Madame Bovary," "Alice in Wonderland," Eliz. B. Browning—READ!*

*ART (Mostly modern)–Hopley or Hopper, DeMeuth (sp?)*
*READ general books on mod. art*
*Pink phase in high school.*
*Jealous of E.?*
*Renoir, VanGogh*
*Italian & Armenian food–LOOK UP restaurants in NYC.*
*Theater: Shaw, T. Williams,–serious stuff . . .*

She read barely a quarter of the closely printed page, her cheeks draining of color. Then she folded the paper with trembling care. "Well," she said, folding it again, not looking up, "haven't I been the . . . trusting soul . . ." She smiled crazily at her father coming gently around the end of the couch to stand helplessly beside her. "I should have known, shouldn't I?" The blood rushed back to her cheeks, burning red. Her eyes were swimming and her fingers were suddenly mashing and twisting the paper with steel strength. "Too good to be true," she smiled, tears starting down her cheeks, her fingers plucking at the paper. "I really should have known . . ." Her hands released the yellow fragments and flew to her face. She began to cry.

Kingship sat beside her, his arm about her bended shoulders. "Marion . . . Marion . . . Be glad you didn't find out too late . . ."

Her back was shaking under his arm. "You don't understand," she sobbed through her hands, "you can't understand . . ."

When the tears had stopped she sat numbly, her fingers knotted around the handkerchief Kingship had given her, her eyes on the pieces of yellow paper on the carpet.

"Do you want me to take you upstairs?" Kingship asked.

"No. Please . . . just . . . just let me sit here . . ."

He rose and joined Gant at the window. They were silent for a while, looking at the lights beyond the river. Finally Kingship said, "I'll do *something* to him. I swear to God, I'll do *something*."

A minute passed. Gant said, "She referred to your 'good and bad.' Were you very strict with your daughters?"

Kingship thought for a moment. "Not very," he said.

"I thought you were, the way she spoke."

"She was angry," Kingship said.

Gant stared across the river at a Pepsi-Cola sign. "In the drugstore the other day, after we left Marion's apartment, you said something about maybe having pushed one of your daughters away. What did you mean?"

"Dorothy," Kingship said. "Maybe if I hadn't been . . ."

"So strict?" Gant suggested.

"No. I *wasn't* very strict. I taught them right from wrong. Maybe I . . . overemphasized a little, because of their mother . . ." He sighed. "Dorothy shouldn't have felt that suicide was the only way out," he said.

Gant took out a pack of cigarettes and removed one. He turned it between his fingers. "Mr. Kingship, what would you have done if Dorothy had married without first consulting you, and then had had a baby . . . too soon?"

After a moment Kingship said, "I don't know."

"He would have thrown her out," Marion said quietly. The two men turned. She was sitting motionlessly on the couch, as she had been before. They could see her face in the canted mirror over the mantel. She was still looking at the papers on the floor.

"Well?" Gant said to Kingship.

"I don't think I would have thrown her out," he protested.

"You would have," Marion said tonelessly.

Kingship turned back to the window. "Well," he said finally, "under those circumstances, shouldn't a couple be expected to assume the responsibilities of marriage, as well as the . . ." He left the sentence unfinished.

Gant lit his cigarette. "There you are," he said. "That's why he killed her. She must have told him about you. He knew he wouldn't get near the money even if he did marry her, and if he didn't marry her he would get into trouble, so . . . Then he decides to have a second try, with Ellen, but she starts to investigate Dorothy's death and gets too close to the truth. So close that he has to kill her and Powell. And then he tries a third time."

"Bud?" Marion said. She spoke the name blankly, her face in the mirror showing the barest flicker of surprise, as though her fiancé had been accused of having imperfect table manners.

Kingship stared narrow-eyed out the window. "I'd believe it," he said intently. "I'd believe it . . ." But as he turned to Gant the resolution faded from his eyes. "You're basing it all on his not telling Marion he went to Stoddard. We're not even sure he *knew* Dorothy, let alone he was the one she was . . . seeing. We have to be *sure*."

"The girls at the dorm," Gant said. "Some of them must have known who she was going with."

Kingship nodded. "I could hire someone to go out there, speak to them . . ."

Gant pondered and shook his head. "It's no good. It's vacation; by the time you managed to find one of the girls who knew, it would be too late."

"Too late?"

"Once he knows the wedding is off,"—he glanced at Marion; she was silent—"he's not going to wait around to find out why, is he?"

"We'd find him," Kingship said.

"Maybe. And maybe not. People disappear." Gant smoked thoughtfully. "Didn't Dorothy keep a diary or anything?"

The telephone rang.

Kingship went to the carved table and lifted the receiver. "Hello?" There was a long pause. Gant looked at Marion; she was leaning forward, picking up the pieces of paper from the floor. "When?" Kingship asked. She put the pieces of paper in her left hand and squeezed them together. She looked at them, not knowing what to do with them. She put them on the couch beside her, on top of the two pamphlets. "Thank you," Kingship said. "Thank you very much." There was the sound of the receiver being replaced, and then silence. Gant turned to look at Kingship.

He was standing beside the table, his pink face rigid. "Miss Richardson," he said. "Promotional literature was sent to Burton Corliss in Caldwell, Wisconsin, on October 16, 1950."

"Just when he must have started his campaign with Ellen," Gant said.

Kingship nodded. "But that was the second time," he said slowly. "Promotional literature was also sent to Burton Corliss on February 6, 1950, in Blue River, Iowa."

Gant said, "Dorothy . . ."

Marion moaned.

Gant remained after Marion had gone upstairs. "We're still in the same boat Ellen was in," he said. "The police have Dorothy's 'suicide note' and all we have are suspicions and a flock of circumstantial evidence."

Kingship held one of the pamphlets. "I'll make sure," he said.

"Didn't they find *anything* at Powell's place? A fingerprint, a thread of cloth . . . ?"

"Nothing," Kingship said. "Nothing at Powell's place, nothing at that restaurant where Ellen . . ."

Gant sighed. "Even if you could get the police to arrest him, a first year law student could get him released in five minutes."

"I'll get him somehow," Kingship said. "I'll make sure, and I'll get him."

Gant said, "We've either got to find out how he got her to write that note, or else find the gun he used on Powell and Ellen. And before Saturday."

Kingship looked at the photograph on the pamphlet's cover. "The smelter . . ." Sorrowfully he said, "We're supposed to fly out there tomorrow. I wanted to show him around. Marion too. She was never interested before."

"You'd better see that she doesn't let him know the wedding is off until the last possible moment."

Kingship smoothed the pamphlet on his knee. He looked up. "What?"

"I said you should see that she doesn't let him know the wedding is off until the last possible moment."

"Oh," Kingship said. His eyes returned to the pamphlet. A moment passed. "He picked the wrong man," he said softly, still looking at the photograph of the smelter. "He should have picked on somebody else's daughters."

## 12

WAS THERE EVER such a perfect day? That was all he wanted to know,—was there? He grinned at the plane; it looked as impatient as he; it craned forward at the runway, its compact body gleaming, the coppered KINGSHIP and the crown trademark on its side emblazoned by the early morning sun. He grinned at the busy scene further down the field, where *commercial* planes stood, there waiting passengers herded behind wire fences like dumb animals. Well, we all can't have private planes at our disposal! He grinned at the ceramic blue of the sky, then stretched and pounded his chest happily, watching his breath plume upwards. No, he decided judicially, there really never was such a perfect day. What, never? No, never! What, *never?* Well . . . hardly ever! He turned and strode back to the hangar, humming Gilbert and Sullivan.

Marion and Leo were standing in the shade, having one of their tight-lipped arguments. "I'm going!" Marion insisted.

"What's the dif*few*culty?" he smiled, coming up to them.

Leo turned and walked away.

"What's the matter?" he asked Marion.

"Nothing's the matter. I don't feel well, so he doesn't want me to go." Her eyes were on the plane beyond him.

"Bridal nerves?"

"No. I just don't feel well, that's all."

"Oh," he said knowingly.

They stood in silence for a minute, watching a pair of mechanics fuss with the plane's fuel tank, and then he moved towards Leo. Leave it to Marion to be off on a day like this. Well, it was probably all for the good; maybe she'd keep quiet for a change. "All set to go?"

"A few minutes," Leo said. "We're waiting for Mr. Dettweiler."

"Who?"

"Mr. Dettweiler. His father is on the board of directors."

A few minutes later a blond man in a gray overcoat approached from the direction of the commercial hangars. He had a long jaw and heavy eyebrows. He nodded at Marion and came up to Leo. "Good morning, Mr. Kingship."

"Good morning, Mr. Dettweiler." They shook hands. "I'd like you to meet my prospective son-in-law, Bud Corliss. Bud, this is Gordon Dettweiler."

"How do you do."

"Well," Dettweiler said—he had a handshake like a mangle—"I've certainly been looking forward to meeting you. Yes sir, I certainly have." A character, Bud thought, or maybe he was trying to get in good with Leo.

"Ready, sir?" a man asked from within the plane.

"Ready," Leo said. Marion came forward. "Marion, I honestly wish you wouldn't . . ."—but she marched right past Leo, up the three-step platform and into the plane. Leo shrugged and shook his head. Dettweiler followed Marion in. Leo said, "After you, Bud."

He jogged up the three steps and entered the plane. It was a six-seater, its interior done in pale blue. He took the last seat on the right, behind the wing. Marion was across the aisle. Leo took the front seat, across from Dettweiler.

When the engine coughed and roared to life, Bud fastened his seat-belt. Son of a gun, if it didn't have a copper buckle! He shook his head, smiling. He looked out the window at the people waiting behind fences, and wondered if they could see him . . .

The plane began to roll forward. On the way . . . Would Leo be taking him to the smelter if he were still suspicious? Never! What, never? No, never! He leaned over, tapped Marion's elbow and grinned at her. She smiled back, looking ill all right, and returned to her window. Leo and Dettweiler were talking softly to each other over the aisle. "How long will it take, Leo?" he asked cheerfully. Leo turned—"Three hours. Less if the wind's good."—and turned back to Dettweiler.

Well, he hadn't wanted to talk to anyone anyway. He returned to his window and watched the ground slide past.

At the edge of the field the plane turned slowly around. The engine whined higher, building up power . . .

He stared out the window, fingering the copper buckle. On the way to the smelter . . . The smelter! The grail! The fountainhead of wealth!

Why the hell did his mother have to be afraid of flying? Christ, it would have been *terrific* having her along!

The plane roared forward.

He was the first to spot it; far ahead and below, a small black geometric cluster on the bedsheet of snow; a small black cluster like a twig on the end of a curving stem of railroad tracks. "There it is," he heard Leo saying, and he was faintly conscious of Marion crossing the aisle and taking the seat in front of him. His breath fogged the window; he wiped it clean.

The twig vanished under the wing. He waited. He swallowed and his ears popped as the plane soared lower.

The smelter reappeared directly below him, sliding out from under the wing. There were half a dozen rectilinear brown roofs with thick tails of smoke dragging from their centers. They crowded together, huge and shadowless in the overhead sun, beside the glittering chain-mail patch of a filled parking lot. Railroad tracks looped and encircled them, merging below into a multi-veined stem, down which a freight train crawled, its smudge of smoke dwarfed by the giant black plumes behind it, its chain of cars scintillating with salmon-colored glints.

His head turned slowly, his eyes locked to the smelter that slid towards the tail of the plane. Fields of snow followed it. Scattered houses appeared. The smelter was gone. There were more houses, then roads separating them into blocks. Still more houses, closer now, and stores and signs and creeping cars and dot-like people, a park, the cubist pattern of a housing development . . .

The plane banked, circling. The ground tilted away, then leveled, swept closer, and finally came slicing up under the wing of the plane. A jolt; the seatbelt's buckle bit his stomach. Then the plane rolled smoothly. He drew the pale blue webbing from the copper clamp.

There was a limousine waiting when they descended from the plane; a custom-built Packard, black and polished. He sat on a jump-seat next to Dettweiler. He leaned forward, looking over the driver's shoulder. He peered down the long perspective of the town's main street to a white hill far away on the horizon. At its summit, from the far side, columns of smoke arose. They were curving and black against the sky, like the cloud-fingers of a genie's hand.

The main street became a two lane highway that speared between fields of snow, and the highway became an asphalt road that embraced the curve of the hill's base, and the asphalt road became a gravel one that jounced over the serried ribs of railroad tracks and turned to the left, rising up the hillside parallel to the tracks. First one slowly climbing train was overtaken, and then another. Sparks of hidden metal winked from ore-heaped gondola cars.

Ahead, the smelter rose up. Brown structures merged into a crude pyramid, their belching smokestacks ranked around the largest one. Nearer, the buildings swelled and clarified; their clifflike walls were streaky brown metal, laced in spots with girdered fretwork and irregularly patched with soot-stained glass; the shapes of the buildings were hard, geometric; they were bound together by chutes and catwalks. Still nearer, the buildings merged again, the sky space between them lost behind projecting angles. They became a single massive form, large hulks buttressing larger ones into an immense smoke-spired industrial cathedral. It loomed up mountainously, and then suddenly swept off to the side as the limousine veered away.

The car pulled up before a low brick building, at the door of which waited a lean, white-haired, unctuously smiling man in a dark gray suit.

He forgot what he was eating, that's how interested he was in lunch. He pulled his eyes from the window across the room, the window through which could be seen the buildings wherein heaps of gray-brown dirt were purified to gleaming copper, and looked down at his plate. Creamed chicken. He started eating more quickly, hoping the others would follow suit.

The carefully dressed white-haired man had turned out to be a Mr. Otto, the manager of the smelter. Leo having introduced him, Mr. Otto had led them into a conference room and begun apologizing for things. He apologized smilingly for the tablecloth that left bare one end of the long table—"We're not in the New York office, you know"—and he apologized suavely for cool food and warm wine—"I'm afraid we lack the facilities of our big city brethren." Mr. Otto longed transparently for the New York office. Over the soup he spoke of the copper shortage and disparaged the suggestions of the National Production Authority for its mitigation. Occasionally he referred to copper as "the red metal."

"Mr. Corliss." He looked up. Dettweiler was smiling at him across the table. "You'd better be careful," Dettweiler said. "I found a bone in mine."

Bud glanced at his nearly empty plate and smiled back at Dettweiler. "I'm anxious to see the smelter," he said.

"Aren't we all," Dettweiler remarked, still smiling.

"You found a bone in yours?" Mr. Otto inquired. "That woman! I told her to take care. These people can't even cut up a chicken properly."

Now that they had at long last left the brick building and were crossing the asphalt yard to the buildings of the smelter itself, he walked slowly. The others, coatless, hurried ahead, but he drifted behind, savoring the climactic sweetness of the moment. He watched an ore-laden train disappear behind a steel wall at the left of the buildings. At the right, a train was being loaded; cranes swung copper into the cars; great square slabs like solidified flame that must have weighed five or six hundred pounds each. A heart! he thought, gazing up at the monstrous brown form that filled more and more of the sky,—a giant heart of American industry, drawing in bad blood, pumping out good! Standing so close to it, about to enter it, it was impossible not to share the surging of its power!

The others had vanished into a doorway at the base of the towering steel mass. Now Mr. Otto smiled within the doorway, beckoning.

He moved forward less slowly, like a lover going to a long awaited tryst. Success rewarded! Promise fulfilled! There should be a fanfare! he thought. There should be a fanfare!

A whistle screamed.

Thank you. *Muchas gracias.*

He went into the darkness of the doorway. The door closed after him.

The whistle screamed again, piercingly, like a bird in a jungle.

## 13

HE STOOD ON a chain-railed catwalk staring fascinatedly at an army of huge cylindrical furnaces ranked before him in diminishing perspective like an ordered forest of giant redwood trunks. At their bases men moved methodically, regulating incomprehensible controls. The air was hot and sulphurous.

"There are six hearths, one above the other, in each furnace," Mr.

Otto lectured. "The ore is introduced at the top. It's moved steadily downward from hearth to hearth by rotating arms attached to a central shaft. The roasting removes excess sulphur from the ore."

He listened intently, nodding. He turned to the others to express his awe, but only Marion stood on his right, wooden-faced as she had been all day. Leo and that Dettweiler were gone. "Where'd your father and Dettweiler go?" he asked her.

"I don't know. Dad said he wanted to show him something."

"Oh." He turned back to the furnaces. What would Leo want to show Dettweiler? Well . . . "How many are there?"

"Furnaces?" Mr. Otto dabbed perspiration from his upper lip with a folded handkerchief. "Fifty-four."

Fifty-four! Jesus! "How much ore goes through them in a day?" he asked.

It was wonderful! He'd never been so interested in anything in his whole life! He asked a thousand questions and Mr. Otto, visibly reacting to his fascination, answered them in detail, speaking only to him, while Marion trailed unseeingly behind.

In another building there were more furnaces; brick walled, flat, and over a hundred feet long. "The reverberatory furnaces," Mr. Otto said. "The ore that comes from the roasting furnaces is about ten per cent copper. Here it's melted down. The lighter minerals flow off as slag. What's left is iron and copper—we call it 'matte'—forty per cent copper."

"What do you use for fuel?"

"Pulverized coal. The waste heat is used to generate steam for making power."

He shook his head, whistling between his teeth.

Mr. Otto smiled. "Impressed?"

"It's wonderful," Bud said. "Wonderful." He gazed down the endless stretch of furnaces. "It makes you realize what a great country this is."

"This," Mr. Otto said, pushing his voice over a roaring tide of sound, "is probably the most spectacular part of the entire smelting process."

"Jesus!"

"The converters," Mr. Otto said loudly.

The building was a vast steel shell, percussant with the sustained thunder of machines and men. A greenish haze obscured its far reaches, swimming around shafts of yellow-green sunlight that pillared down through crane tracks and catwalks from windows in the peaked roof dim and high above.

At the near end of the building, on either side, lay six massive dark cylindroid vessels, end to end, like giant steel barrels on their sides, dwarfing the workmen on railed platforms between them. Each vessel had an opening in its uppermost surface. Flames burst forth from these mouths; yellow, orange, red, blue; roaring up into funnel-like hoods overhead that swallowed and bore them away.

One of the converters was turned forward on the cogged rollers that supported it, so that its round mouth, scabrous with coagulated metal, was at the side; liquid fire rushed from the radiant throat, pouring down into an immense crucible on the floor. The molten flow, heavy and smoking, filled the steel container. The converter rolled back groaningly, its mouth dripping. The yoke of the crucible lifted, caught by a great blunt hook from whose block a dozen cables rose in unwavering ascension, rose higher than the converters, higher than the central spine of catwalk, up to the underbelly of a grimy cab that hung from a single-railed track below the dimness of the roof. The cables contracted; the crucible lifted in slow, weightless levitation. It rose until it was higher than the converters, some twenty-five feet above the ground, and then cab, cables and crucible began to draw away, retreating towards the cuprous haze at the northern end of the building.

The center of it all! The heart of the heart! With rapt eyes Bud followed the heat-shimmering column of air over the departing crucible.

"Slag," Mr. Otto said. They stood on an island of railed platform against the south wall, a few feet above the floor and midway between the two banks of converters. Mr. Otto touched his handkerchief to his forehead. "The molten matte from the reverberatory furnaces is poured into these converters. Silica is added, and then compressed air is blown in through pipes at the back. The impurities are oxidized; slag forms and is poured off, as you just saw. More matte is added, more slag forms, and so on. The copper keeps getting richer and richer until, after about five hours, it's ninety-nine per cent pure. Then it's poured out in the same way as the slag."

"Will they be pouring copper soon?"

Mr. Otto nodded. "The converters are operated on a stagger system, so that there's a continuous output."

"I'd like to see them pour the copper," Bud said. He watched one of the converters on the right pouring off slag. "Why are the flames different colors?" he asked.

"The color changes as the process advances. That's how the operators tell what's going on inside."

Behind them a door closed. Bud turned. Leo was standing beside Marion. Dettweiler leaned against a ladder that climbed the wall beside the door. "Are you enjoying the tour?" Leo asked over the thunder.

"It's wonderful, Leo! Overpowering!"

"They're going to pour copper over there," Mr. Otto said loudly.

Before one of the converters on the left, a crane had lowered a steel vat, larger than the crucible into which the slag had been poured. Its steep sides were a three inch thickness of dull gray metal, as high as a man. Its rim was seven feet across.

The mammoth cylinder of the converter began to turn, rumbling, rolling forward in its place. A wraith of blue flame flickered over its clotted mouth. It turned further; a volcanic radiance blasted from its interior, veils of white smoke arose, and then a flood of racing incandescence came bursting out. It spilled forward and fell gleamingly into the giant bowl. The steady molten flow seemed motionless, a solid, shining shaft between the converter and the depths of the vat. The converter turned further; new ribs twisted fluidly down the shaft, and again it was motionless. Within the vat the surface of the liquid appeared, slowly rising, clouded by whorls of smoke. The bitter smell of copper singed the air. The streaming shaft thinned, twisting, as the converter began rolling back. The thin stream petered out, its last few drops rolling over the swell of the cylinder and sparkling to the cement floor.

The smoke above the vat dissolved to vaporous wisps. The surface of the molten copper, a few inches below the vessel's rim, was an oblique disc of glistening oceanic green.

"It's green," Bud said, surprised.

"When it cools it regains its usual color," Mr. Otto said.

Bud stared at the restless pool. Blisters formed, swelled, and popped glutinously on its surface. "What's the matter, Marion?" he heard Leo ask. The heated air above the vat trembled as though sheets of cellophane were being shaken. "Matter?" Marion said. Leo said, "You look pale."

Bud turned around. Marion seemed no paler than usual. "I'm all right," she was saying.

"But you're pale," Leo insisted, and Dettweiler nodded agreement.

"It must be the heat or something," Marion said.

"The fumes," Leo said. "Some people can't stand the fumes. Mr. Otto, why don't you take my daughter back to the administration building. We'll be along in a few minutes."

"Honestly, Dad," she said tiredly, "I feel—"

"No nonsense," Leo smiled stiffly. "We'll be with you in a few minutes."

"But . . ." She hesitated a moment, looking annoyed, and then shrugged and turned to the door. Dettweiler opened it for her.

Mr. Otto followed after Marion. He paused in the doorway and turned back to Leo. "I hope you're going to show Mr. Corliss how we mold the anodes." He turned to Bud. "Very impressive," he said, and went out. Dettweiler closed the door.

"Anodes?" Bud said.

"The slabs they were loading on the train outside," Leo said. Bud noticed an odd mechanical quality in his voice, as though he were thinking of something else. "They're shipped to the refinery in New Jersey. Electrolytic refining."

"My God," Bud said, "it's some involved process." He turned back to the converters on the left. The vat of copper, its angular handle hooked by the crane overhead, was about to be raised. The dozen cables tensed, vibrating, and then rigidified sharply. The vat lifted from the floor.

Behind him Leo said, "Did Mr. Otto take you up on the catwalk?"

"No," Bud said.

"You get a much better view," Leo said. "Would you like to go up?"

Bud turned. "Do we have the time?"

"Yes," Leo said.

Dettweiler, his back against the ladder, stepped aside. "After you," he smiled.

Bud went to the ladder. He grasped one of the metal rungs and looked upwards. The rungs, like oversize staples, ran narrowingly up the brown wall. They focused at a trap in the floor of the catwalk, which projected perpendicularly from the wall some fifty feet above.

"Bottleneck," Dettweiler murmured beside him.

He began to climb. The rungs were warm, their upper surfaces polished smooth. He climbed in a steady rhythm, keeping his eyes on the descending wall before him. He heard Dettweiler and Leo following after him. He tried to visualize the sight the catwalk would offer. To look down on that scene of industrial power . . .

He climbed the ladder up through the trap and stepped off onto the ridged metal floor of the catwalk. The thunder of the machines was diminished up here, but the air was hotter and the smell of copper stronger. The narrow runway, railed by heavy chain between iron stanchions, extended in a straight line down the spine of the building. It ended halfway down the building's length, where it was cut off by a broad strip of steel partition wall that hung from roof to floor, some twelve feet wider than the catwalk. Overhead, on either side, crane tracks paralleled the runway. They passed clear of the partition that ended the catwalk and continued into the northern half of the building.

He peered over the left side of the catwalk, his hands folded over the top of one of the waist-high stanchions. He looked down upon the six converters, the men scurrying between them . . .

His eyes shifted. To his right, twenty feet below and ten feet out from the catwalk, hung the vat of copper, a steel rimmed pool of green on its slow procession towards the far end of the building. Ghosts of smoke rose from the liquid sheen of its surface.

He followed it, walking slowly, his left hand tracing over the dipping curves of the chain railing. He stayed far enough behind the vat so that he could just feel the fringe of its radiant heat. He heard Leo and Dettweiler following. His eyes climbed the vat's cables, six and six on either side of the block, up to the cab a dozen feet above him. He could see the shoulder of the operator inside. His eyes dropped back to the copper. How much is in there? How many tons? What was it worth? One thousand? Two thousand? Three? Four? Five? . . .

He was nearing the steel partition, and now he saw that the catwalk didn't end there after all; instead it branched six feet to right and left, following the partition to its edges like the head of a long-stemmed T. The vat of copper vanished beyond the partition. He turned onto the left wing of the T. A three-foot chain swung across the catwalk's end. He put his left hand on the corner stanchion and his right on the edge of the partition, which was quite warm. He leaned forward a bit and peered around the partition at the receding vat. "Where does it go now?" he called out.

Behind him Leo said, "Refining furnaces. Then it's poured into molds."

He turned around. Leo and Dettweiler faced him shoulder to shoulder, blocking the stem of the T. Their faces were oddly inflexible. He patted the partition on his left. "What's behind here?" he asked.

"The refining furnaces," Leo said. "Any more questions?"

He shook his head, puzzled by the grimness of the two men.

"Then I've got one for you," Leo said. His eyes were like blue marbles behind his glasses. "How did you get Dorothy to write that suicide note?"

## 14

EVERYTHING FELL AWAY; the catwalk, the smelter, the whole world; everything melted away like sand castles sucked into the sea, leaving him suspended in emptiness with two blue marbles staring at him and the sound of Leo's question swelling and reverberating like being inside an iron bell.

Then Leo and Dettweiler confronted him again; the smelter's rumble welled up; the plates of the partition materialized slippery against his left hand, the knob of the stanchion damp under his right, the floor of the catwalk . . . but the floor didn't come back completely; it swayed anchorless and undulant beneath his feet, because his knees—Oh God!—were jelly, trembling and shaking. "What're you—" he started to say, but nothing came out. He swallowed air. "What're you . . . talking about . . ."

"Dorothy," Dettweiler told him. Slowly he said, "You wanted to marry her. For the money. But then she was pregnant. You knew you wouldn't get the money. You killed her."

He shook his head in confused protest. "No," he said, "No! She committed suicide! She sent a note to Ellen! You know that, Leo!"

"You tricked her into writing it," Leo said.

"How . . . Leo, how could I do that? How the hell could I do *that?*"

"That's what you're going to tell us," Dettweiler said.

"I hardly knew her!"

"You didn't know her at all," Leo said. "That's what you told Marion."

"That's right! I didn't know her at all!"

"You just said you *hardly* knew her."

"I didn't know her *at all!*"

Leo's fists clenched. "You sent for our publications in February nineteen hundred and fifty!"

Bud stared, his hand bracing tightly against the partition. "What publications?" It was a whisper; he had to say it again: "What publications?"

Dettweiler said, "The pamphlets I found in the strongbox in your room in Menasset."

The catwalk dipped crazily. The strongbox! Oh, Jesus Christ! The pamphlets and what else? The clippings?—he'd thrown them out, thank God! The pamphlets . . . *and the list on Marion!* Oh, Jesus! "Who are you?" he exploded. "Where the hell do you come off breaking into a person's—"

"Stay back!" Dettweiler warned.

Withdrawing the single step he had advanced, Bud gripped the stanchion again. "Who are you?" he shouted.

"Gordon Gant," Dettweiler said.

Gant! The one on the radio, the one who'd kept needling the police! How the hell did he—

"I knew Ellen," Gant said. "I met her a few days before you killed her."

"I—" He felt the sweat running. "Crazy!" he shouted. "You're crazy! Who else did I kill?" To Leo—"You listen to him? Then you're crazy too! I never killed anybody!"

Gant said, "You killed Dorothy and Ellen and Dwight Powell!"

"And almost killed Marion," Leo said. "When she saw that list . . ."

She saw the list! Oh God almighty! "I never killed anybody! Dorrie committed suicide and Ellen and Powell were killed by a burglar!"

"Dorrie?" Gant snapped.

"I— Everybody called her Dorrie! I . . . I never killed anybody! Only a Jap, and that was in the Army!"

"Then why are your legs shaking?" Gant asked. "Why is the sweat dripping down your cheek?"

He swiped at his cheek. Control! Self-control! He dragged a deep breath into his chest . . . Slow up, slow up . . . They can't prove a thing, not a goddamn thing! They know about the list, about Marion, about the pamphlets—okay—but they can't prove a thing about . . . He drew another breath . . .

"You can't prove a thing," he said. "Because there isn't anything to prove. You're crazy, both of you." His hands wiped against his thighs. "Okay," he said, "I knew Dorrie. So did a dozen other guys. And I've had my eyes on the money all along the way. Where's the law against that? So there's no wedding Saturday. Okay." He straightened his jacket with stiff fingers. "I'm probably better off poor than having a bastard like you for a father-in-law. Now get out of the way and let me pass. I don't feel like standing around talking to a couple of crazy lunatics."

They didn't move. They stood shoulder to shoulder six feet away.

"Move," he said.

"Touch the chain behind you," Leo said.

"Get out of the way and let me pass!"

"Touch the chain behind you!"

He looked at Leo's stonelike face for a moment and then turned slowly.

He didn't have to touch the chain; he just had to look at it; the metal eye of the stanchion had been bent open into a loose C that barely engaged the first of the heavy links.

"We were up here when Otto was showing you around," Leo said. "Touch it."

His hand came forward, brushed the chain. It collapsed. The free end clanked to the floor; it slid rattlingly off and swung down, striking noisily against the partition.

Fifty feet below cement floor yawned, seemed to sway . . . "Not as much as Dorothy got," Gant was saying, "but enough."

He turned to face them, clutching the stanchion and the edge of the partition, trying not to think of the void behind his heels. "You wouldn't . . . dare . . ." he heard himself saying.

"Don't I have reason enough?" Leo asked. "You killed my daughters!"

"I didn't, Leo! I swear to God I didn't!"

"Is that why you were sweating and shaking the minute I mentioned Dorothy's name? Is that why you didn't think it was a bad joke, react the way an innocent person would have reacted?"

"Leo, I swear on the soul of my dead father . . ."

Leo stared at him coldly.

He shifted his grip on the stanchion. It was slick with sweat. "You wouldn't do it . . ." he said. "You'd never get away with it . . ."

"Wouldn't I?" Leo said. "Do you think you're the only one who can plan something like this?" He pointed to the stanchion. "The jaws of the wrench were wrapped in cloth; there are no marks on that ring. An accident, a terrible accident; a piece of iron, old, continually subjected to intense heat, weakens and bends when a six foot man stumbles against the chain attached to it. A terrible accident. And how can you prevent it? Yell?; no one will hear you over the noise. Wave your arms?; the men down there have jobs to attend to, and even if they should look up, there's the haze and the distance. Attack us?; one push and you're finished." He paused. "So tell me, why won't I get away with it? Why?

"Of course," he continued after a moment, "I would rather not do it. I would rather hand you over to the police." He looked at his watch. "So I'll give you three minutes. From now. I want something that will convince a jury, a jury that won't be able to take you by surprise and see the guilt written all over you."

"Tell us where the gun is," Gant said.

The two of them stood side by side; Leo with his left wrist lifted and his right hand holding back the cuff to expose his watch; Gant with his hands at his sides.

"How did you get Dorothy to write the note?" Gant asked.

His own hands were so tight against the partition and the stanchion that they throbbed with a leaden numbness. "You're bluffing," he said. They leaned forward to hear him. "You're trying to scare me into admitting—to something I never did."

Leo shook his head slowly. He looked at the watch. A moment passed. "Two minutes and thirty seconds," he said.

Bud whirled to the right, catching the stanchion with his left hand and shouting to the men over at the converters. "Help!" he cried, "Help! Help!"—bellowing as loud as he could, waving his right arm furiously, clutching the stanchion. "Help!"

The men far off and below might as well have been painted figures; their attention was centered on a converter pouring copper.

He turned back to Leo and Gant.

"You see?" Leo said.

"You'll be killing an innocent man, that's what you'll be doing!"

"Where's the gun?" Gant asked.

"There is no gun! I never had a gun!"

Leo said, "Two minutes."

They were bluffing! They must be! He looked around desperately; the main shaft of the catwalk, the roof, the crane tracks, the few windows, the . . . the crane tracks!

Slowly, trying not to make it too obvious, he glanced to the right again. The converter had rolled back. The vat before it was full and smoking, cables trailing slackly up to the cab above. The vat would be lifted; the cab, now over two hundred feet away, would bear the vat forward, approaching along the track that passed behind and above him; and the man in the cab—a dozen feet up? four feet out?—would be able to hear! To see!

If only they could be stalled! If only they could be stalled until the cab was near enough!

The vat lifted . . .

"One minute, thirty seconds," Leo said.

Bud's eyes flicked back to the two men. He met their stares for a few seconds, and then risked another glance to the right, cautiously, so that they should not guess his plan. (Yes, a plan! Even now, at this moment, a plan!) The distant vat hung between floor and catwalk, its skein of cables seeming to shudder in the heat-vibrant air. The boxlike cab was motionless under the track—and then it began to come forward, bearing the vat, growing imperceptibly larger. So slowly! Oh God, make it come faster!

He turned back to them.

"We aren't bluffing, Bud," Leo said. And after a moment: "One minute."

He looked again; the cab was nearer—a hundred and fifty feet? One thirty? He could distinguish a pale shape behind the black square of its window.

"Thirty seconds."

How could time race by so fast? "Listen," he said frantically, "listen, I want to tell you something—something about Dorrie. She . . ." He groped for something to say—and then stopped wide-eyed; there had been a flicker of movement in the dimness at the far end of the catwalk. Someone else was up here! Salvation!

"Help!" he cried, his arm semaphoring. "You! Come here! Help!"

The flicker of movement became a figure hurrying along the catwalk, speeding towards them.

Leo and Gant looked over their shoulders in confusion.

Oh dear God, thank you!

Then he saw that it was a woman.

Marion.

Leo cried out, "What are you— Get out of here! For God's sake, Marion, go back down!"

She seemed not to hear him. She came up behind them, her face flushed and large-eyed above their compacted shoulders.

Bud felt her gaze rake his face and then descend to his legs. Legs that were trembling again . . . If he only had a gun . . . "Marion," he pleaded, "stop them! They're crazy! They're trying to kill me! Stop them! They'll listen to you! I can explain about that list, I can explain everything! I swear I wasn't lying—"

She kept looking at him. Finally she said, "The way you explained why you didn't tell me about Stoddard?"

"I love you! I swear to God I do! I started out thinking about the money, I admit that, but I love you! You know I wasn't lying about that!"

"*How* do I know?" she asked.

"I swear it!"

"You swore so many things . . ." Her fingers appeared curving over the men's shoulders; long, white, pink-nailed fingers; they seemed to be pushing.

"Marion! You wouldn't! Not when we . . . after we . . ."

Her fingers pressed forward into the cloth of the shoulders, pushing . . .

"Marion," he begged futilely.

Suddenly he became aware of a swelling in the smelter's thunder, an added rumble. A wave of heat was spreading up his right side. The cab! He wheeled, catching the stanchion with both hands. There it was! —not twenty feet away, grinding closer on the overhead track with the cables shooting down from its belly. Through the opening in its front end he could see a bent head in a visored gray cap. "You!" he bellowed, his jaw muscles cording. "You in the cab! Help! You!" Heat from the oncoming vat pressed heavily against his chest. "Help! You! In the cab!" The gray cap, coming closer, never lifted. *Deaf?* Was the stupid bastard *deaf?* "Help!" he roared chokingly again and again, but it was no use.

He turned from the swelling heat, wanting to cry in despair.

Leo said, "The noisiest place in the smelter, up there in those cabs." As he said it, he took a step forward. Gant moved up beside him. Marion followed behind.

"Look," Bud said placatingly, clutching the partition in his left hand again. "Please . . ." He stared at their faces, masklike except for burning eyes.

They came another step closer.

The catwalk dipped and bucked like a shaken blanket. The baking heat on his right began extending itself across his back. They meant it! They weren't bluffing! They were going to kill him! Moisture trickled all over him.

"All right!" he cried. "All right! She thought she was doing a Spanish translation! I wrote out the note in Spanish! I asked her to translate—" His voice faded and stopped.

What was the matter with them? Their faces . . . the masklike blankness was gone, warped into—into embarrassment and sick contempt, and they were looking down at . . .

He looked down. The front of his pants was dark with a spreading stain that ran in a series of island blotches down his right trouser leg. Oh God! The Jap . . . the Jap he had killed—that wretched, trembling, chattering, pants-wetting caricature of a man—was that *him?* Was that *himself?*

The answer was in their faces.

"No!" he cried. He clapped his hands over his eyes, but their faces were still there. "No! I'm not like him!" He wheeled away from them. His foot slipped on wetness and kicked out from under him. His hands flew from his face and flailed the air. Heat blasted up at him. Falling, he saw a giant disc of glistening green sliding into place below; gaseous, restless, shimmering—

Hardness in his hands! The cables! The weight of his body swung down and around, pulling at his armpits and tearing his hands on protruding steel threads. He hung with his legs swinging against the taut cables and his eyes staring at one of them, seeing the frayed fibers that were stabbing like needles into his hands above. A chaos of sound; a whistle shrieking, a woman screaming, voices above, voices below . . . He squinted up at his hands—blood was starting to trickle down the insides of his wrists—the ovenlike heat was smothering, dizzying, engulfing him with the noxious stench of copper—voices shouted to him—he saw his hands starting to open—he was letting go because he wanted to, it wasn't the burning suffocation or the needles in his hands, he was letting go because he wanted to, just as he had jumped from the catwalk but instinct had made him grab the cables and now he was overcoming instinct—his left hand opened and fell—he hung by his right, turning slightly in the furnace heat—there was oil on the back of his hand from the stanchion or the chain or something—and they wouldn't have pushed him either—you think *anyone* can kill?—he had jumped and now he was letting go because he wanted to, that's all, and everything was all right and his knees weren't shaking any more, not that they had been shaking so much anyway, his knees weren't shaking any more because he was in command again—he hadn't noticed his right hand open but it must have opened because he was dropping into the heat, cables were shooting up, someone was screaming like Dorrie going into the shaft and Ellen when the first bullet wasn't enough—this person was screaming this god-awful scream and suddenly it was himself and he couldn't stop! Why was he screaming? Why? Why on earth should he be—

The scream, which had knifed through the sudden stillness of the smelter, ended in a viscous splash. From the other side of the vat a sheet of green leaped up. Arcing, it sheared down to the floor where it splattered into a million pools and droplets. They hissed softly on the cement and slowly dawned from green to copper.

## 15

KINGSHIP REMAINED AT the smelter. Gant accompanied Marion back to New York. In the plane they sat silent and immobile with the aisle between them.

After a while Marion took out a handkerchief and pressed it to her eyes. Gant turned to her, his face pale. "We only wanted him to confess," he said defensively. "We weren't going to *do* it. And he *did* confess. What did he have to turn away like that for?"

The words took a long time to reach her. Almost inaudibly she said, "Don't . . ."

He looked at her downcast face. "You're crying," he told her gently.

She gazed at the handkerchief in her hands, saw the damp places in it. She folded it and turned to the window at her side. Quietly she said, "Not for him."

They went to the Kingship apartment. When the butler took Marion's coat—Gant kept his—he said, "Mrs. Corliss is in the living room."

"Oh God," Marion said.

They went into the living room. In the late afternoon sunlight, Mrs. Corliss was standing by a curio cabinet looking at the underside of a porcelain figurine. She put it down and turned to them. "So soon?" she smiled. "Did you enjoy—" She squinted through the light at Gant. "Oh, I thought you were . . ." She came across the room, peering beyond them into the empty hallway.

Her eyes returned to Marion. Her eyebrows lifted and she smiled. "Where's Bud?" she asked.

# STAN THE KILLER

*by Georges Simenon*

MAIGRET PUFFED AT his pipe as he walked along slowly, hands clasped behind his back. It was not a simple matter to push his heavy body through the morning mob on Rue Saint Antoine, where a bright sun poured down on carts and baskets of fruits and vegetables, blocking almost the entire width of the sidewalk.

It was marketing time—the time for feeling artichokes and tasting cherries, the time for scallops and chops to take turns in the scales.

"Fine asparagus, five francs a bundle!"

"Get your fresh whiting, just come in!"

Clerks in white aprons, butchers in fine checks; the smell of cheese from a dairy shop and farther off a whiff of roasting coffee; the ping of cash registers and the rumble of a bus; the distrustful glances of housewives—all the agitated business of alimentation . . . and in the midst of it the slow heavy progress of Maigret, on one of his most tormenting cases.

Across from Rue de Birague there's a little café, with a scant three tables in front of it, called the Barrel of Burgundy. There Maigret settled himself, like any other weary passer-by. He did not even look up at the tall thin waiter who came for his order. "Small white Mâcon," he muttered—and who was to guess that this occasionally inept new waiter at the Barrel of Burgundy was otherwise known as Detective Janvier?

The waiter returned with the wine precariously balanced on a tray. He wiped the table with a questionable cloth, and was even so clumsy as to drop a scrap of paper on the floor. Maigret picked it up as he left, and read:

*The woman's gone out marketing. No sign of One-Eye. The Beard left early. The three others must be still in the hotel.*

At ten in the morning the crowd was getting even worse. Next to the Barrel a grocery was having a sale and barkers kept entreating the passers-by to sample cookies at two francs a box.

At the corner of Rue de Biragues you could see the sign of a dingy hotel, "Rooms by the month, the week or the day. Payment in advance." With doubtless intentional irony this rattrap had chosen to call itself the Beauséjour.

Maigret sipped at his light dry white wine and stared apparently aimlessly at the teeming crowd in the spring sun. But his gaze soon settled on a window in the second floor of a house on Rue de Birague opposite the hotel. At that window a little old man sat by a canary's cage and seemed to have no interest in life but to bask in the sun as long as the Lord should deign to leave him alive.

And this old gentleman, who took no notice of Maigret, was Sergeant Lucas, deftly aged some twenty years.

All this constituted a state of siege that is more vulgarly known to the police as a stake-out. It had lasted six days, and at least twice a day the inspector came around for the latest news. At night his men were relieved by a patrolman who was actually a detective from the Police Judiciaire, and a streetwalker who contrived to walk the streets without ever picking up a customer.

Maigret would have Lucas's report in a moment, by telephone; it would undoubtedly prove to be no more sensational than Janvier's.

The crowd shoved by so close to the tiny terrace of the Barrel of Burgundy that Maigret found himself constantly obliged to pull his legs back under his chair. And now, as he made one of these shifts, he suddenly realized that a man had sat down unnoticed at the same table. He was a little man, with red hair and sad eyes, whose mournful face had something of the clown about it.

"You again?" the inspector grunted.

"I beg you to forgive me, Monsieur Maigrette, but I am certain that you will eventually come to understand me and to accept the proposition that I—" He broke off to say to the waiterly Janvier, "The same as my friend."

He had an extremely marked Polish accent. He presumably suffered from throat trouble; he constantly chewed at a "cigar" impregnated with creosote, which emphasized the clownishness of his appearance.

"You're getting on my nerves!" Maigret burst out. "Will you kindly tell me how you knew I'd come here this morning?"

"I did not know."

"Then why are you here? Are you going to try to convince me that this is an accidental meeting?"

"No."

The little man's reflexes were as leisurely as those of the slow-motion acrobats in vaudeville. His yellow eyes gazed around him, staring into emptiness. He spoke in a sad voice, unvarying in pitch, as though perpetually offering condolences.

"You are not nice to me, Monsieur Maigrette."

"That isn't answering my question. How do you happen to be here this morning?"

"I followed you."

"From Headquarters?"

"Long before that. From your home."

"So you admit you're spying on me?"

"I am not spying on you, Monsieur Maigrette. I have far too much respect and admiration for you! I have already stated to you that I shall one day be your collaborator. . . ."

And he sighed nostalgically, contemplating the artificial ash of painted wood that tipped his creosote cigar.

THERE'D BEEN NOTHING about it in any of the papers save one; and that one, which got the tip the Lord knows where, uniquely complicated the Inspector's task.

*The police have reason to believe that the Polish bandits, including Stan the Killer, are at this moment in Paris.*

It was true enough, but silence would have been more helpful.

In four years a gang of unknown Poles had attacked five farms, always in the North of France, always with the same methods.

In each case it was an isolated farm run by elderly people. The crime invariably took place the night of a market day, and the chosen victims were always those who had sold a good number of fowls and animals and had a large sum of cash on hand.

Nothing scientific about the procedure. Brutal attack, as in the days of the highway robbers. Absolute contempt for human life. These Poles were killers. They killed every human being they found on the farm, even down to the children; it was the one way of making sure that they could never be identified.

Were there two of them? Or five or eight?

In every case neighbors had noticed a small truck. One twelve-year-old claimed that he had seen a one-eyed man. Some asserted that the bandits wore black masks.

Whatever the facts, one thing was certain: Every inhabitant of each farm had had his throat sliced.

This was no business of the Paris police. This was up to the mobile units in the provinces, who worked on it for two years without remotely clarifying the mystery—a failure that did not reassure the countryside.

Then a report came in from Lille, where whole villages are Polish enclaves in French territory. The report was vague enough; it was impossible even to establish its ultimate source.

"The Poles say that this is Stan the Killer's gang. . . ."

But when the police tried to question the coal miners one by one, the men had never heard of it, or muttered, "Well, they told me . . ."

"Who's 'they'?"

"I don't know. I forget . . ."

Then came the crime near Rheims. There the gang overlooked a servant girl sleeping in the attic, who became the first survivor. She had heard the murderers talking in a language she thought was Polish. She had seen their masks through a hole in the boards; and had noticed that one of the men had only one eye and that another, a giant of a man, was extraordinarily hairy.

And so the police had come to refer to them as "Stan the Killer," "The Beard," and "One-Eye."

For months nothing more turned up, until a detective on the hotel squad made a discovery. His territory was the Saint Antoine district, which teems with Poles. And in a hotel on Rue de Birague he observed a suspicious group that included a one-eyed man and a giant whose face was literally covered with hair.

They were seemingly poor people. The bearded giant and his wife rented a room by the week, but almost every night they gave shelter to several compatriots, sometimes two, sometimes as many as five, and often other Poles rented the adjoining room.

"You want to take this over, Maigret?" the director of the Police Judiciaire suggested.

Everything was strictly hush-hush—and so the next day one newspaper printed the story. The day after that Maigret found a letter in his mail—clumsily written in an almost childish hand, full of misspellings, on the cheap sort of paper sold in grocery stores:

*You won't ever get Stan. Look out. Before you can take him, he'll have time to kill off plenty more.*

The letter was no hoax, Maigret was certain; it *felt* right. It had the filthy aftertaste of the underworld.

"Be careful," the chief recommended. "Don't rush into an arrest.

The man who's cut sixteen throats in four years won't hesitate to scatter a few bullets around him when he sees he's done for."

Which was why Janvier had become a waiter and Lucas a basking old man.

The noisy life of the quarter went on with no suspicion that a desperate man might at any moment start firing in all directions. . . .

And then Michael Ozep appeared.

His first meeting with Maigret had been four days ago. He had arrived at Headquarters and insisted on seeing the inspector personally. Maigret had let him wait a good two hours, but the little man was undaunted. He entered the office, clicked his heels, bowed, and extended his hand:

"Michael Ozep, former officer in the Polish Army, now professor of gymnastics in Paris—"

"Sit down. I'm listening."

The Pole spoke so volubly and with so pronounced an accent that it was sometimes impossible to follow him. He explained that he came of very good family, that he had been forced to leave Poland because of unmentionably intimate misfortunes (he allowed his listener to gather that he had been in love with his colonel's wife), and that he had now sunk to worse depths of despair than ever because he could not accustom himself to leading a mediocre life.

"You understand, Monsieur Maigrette . . ." (it was impossible to wean him from that pronunciation) ". . . I am a gentleman. Here I am forced to give lessons to individuals of no culture and no education. I am a poor man . . . I have decided to commit suicide."

"A nut . . ." Maigret thought to himself. An astonishing number of the unbalanced feel the need of confiding their problems to the police; he was used to such visits.

"I tried it three weeks ago. I threw myself into the Seine from the Austerlitz Bridge, but the river squad saw me and pulled me out."

Maigret invented a pretext to step into the next office and phone the river squad. The story was true.

"Six days later I tried to kill myself with gas, but the postman came with a letter and opened the door. . . ."

A phone call to the police station in Ozep's district. And again the story was true.

"I truly *want* to kill myself, do you understand? My existence has lost all value. A gentleman cannot consent to live in poverty and mediocrity. Therefore I thought that you might have need of a man like me . . ."

"For what?"

"To help you to arrest Stan the Killer."

Maigret frowned. "You know him?"

"No. I have only heard talk about him. As a Pole, I am indignant that a man of my people should so violate the laws of hospitality. I should like to see Stan and his gang arrested. I know that he is resolved to sell his life dearly. Among those who go to arrest him, some will certainly be killed. Is it not better then that it should be I, since I already desire to die? Tell me where Stan is. I shall go and disarm him. If need be, I shall wound him so that he can do no more harm."

All Maigret found himself capable of saying was the traditional formula, "Leave your address. I'll write you a letter."

Michael Ozep had a furnished room on Rue des Tournelles, not far from Rue de Birague. The report of the investigating detective was in his favor. He had indeed been a second lieutenant in the Polish Army when it was organized after Poland gained her independence. Then his trail vanished. In Paris he tried to teach gymnastics to the sons and daughters of small merchants. His suicide attempts were genuine.

Nevertheless Maigret sent him, with the chief's approval, an official letter ending:

> *. . . deeply regret that I cannot take advantage of your generous proposition, for which my most sincere thanks . . .*

Twice since then Ozep had appeared at the Quai des Orfèvres and insisted on seeing the inspector. The second time he had even refused to leave, claiming that he could wait as long as he was obliged to, and thus almost forcibly occupying, hour after hour, one of the green plush armchairs in the waiting room.

And now Ozep sat there, at Maigret's table, in front of the Barrel of Burgundy.

"I wish to prove to you, Monsieur Maigrette, that I am of some use and that you can accept my services. It is now three days that I have been following you, and I am in a position to tell you everything that you have done during that time. I know too that the waiter who just brought my wine is one of your detectives and that there is another at the window across from us, near a canary cage."

Maigret clenched the bit of his pipe furiously between his teeth and kept his eyes turned away from the Pole, who kept on and on in his monotonous voice:

"I understand that when a strange man comes to you and says, 'I am a former officer of the Polish Army and I wish to kill myself'—I understand why you would think, 'This may not be true.' But you have verified everything that I have told you. You have seen that I do not stoop to lies. . . ."

He was a mill grinding out words, rapidly, jerkily. It wore Maigret out merely to listen to him, especially since the accent so distorted each syllable that Maigret had to concentrate to follow the sense.

"You are not a Pole, Monsieur Maigrette. You do not speak the language; you do not comprehend the mentality. I earnestly desire to help you; for I cannot see the good name of my native land tarnished by . . ."

The inspector was beginning to choke with anger. The former second lieutenant could hardly fail to observe the fact, but he continued nevertheless:

"If you try to capture Stan, what will he do? He has maybe two, maybe three, revolvers in his pockets. He fires at everybody. Who knows how many ladies he wounds? How many little babies he kills? Then people will say that the police—"

"Will you shut up?"

"Now as for me, I am resolved to die. No one will weep for poor Ozep. You say to me, 'There is Stan!' And I follow him as I have followed you. I wait for the moment when there is no one near us and I say, 'You are Stan the Killer!' Then he fires at me and I shoot him in the leg. By the fact that he shoots me, you have your proof that he is Stan and you are not making a blunder. And since he is crippled by my shot . . ."

There was no stopping him. He would have gone on in spite of the entire universe.

"Supposing I have you arrested?" Maigret broke in crudely.

"Why?"

"To get a little peace!"

"What would you say? What has poor Ozep done in violation of the laws of France, which he wishes only to defend and for which he is offering up his life?"

"Stuff it!"

"I beg your pardon? Are you agreeing?"

"Not in the least."

At that moment a woman went by, a woman with blond hair and clear complexion, recognizably a foreigner. She was carrying a shopping bag and was headed for a butcher shop.

Maigret was following her with his eyes when he noticed that his companion had suddenly set to mopping his brow with an enormous handkerchief that all but swallowed up his small-featured face.

"That is the mistress of Stan, is it not?" Ozep asked.

"Will you leave me alone?"

"You have convinced yourself that this is the mistress of Stan, but you do not know which one is Stan. You think it is the one with the beard. Now the bearded one is called Boris. And the man with one eye is Sasha. He is not a Pole, but a Russian. If you should investigate them yourself you will learn nothing. In the hotel there are only Poles; they will refuse to answer or they will lie to you. Whereas I . . ."

No housewife shopping in the confusion of Rue Saint Antoine could suspect the subjects being discussed on the tiny terrace of the Barrel of Burgundy. The blond foreigner was buying chops at a nearby butcher's stall; in her eyes there was something of that same lassitude that lay in the eyes of Michael Ozep.

"Perhaps you are angry with me because you fear that you may be called to account if I am killed? In the first place, I have no family. In the second place, I have written a letter in which I state that I alone, and purely of my own volition, have sought this death. . . ."

Poor Janvier stood on the threshold trying to figure out a way of telling Maigret that there was a telephone message for him. Maigret noticed the ambiguous pantomime, but went on watching the Pole and puffing forth little clouds of pipe smoke.

"Listen, Ozep."

"Yes, Monsieur Maigrette?"

"If you're seen again anywhere around Rue Saint Antoine, I'll have you arrested!"

"But I live only—"

"You'd better move."

"You are refusing this offer which I—"

"Get out!"

"But—"

"Get out, or I'll arrest you here and now!"

The little man rose, clicked his heels, bowed almost double, and executed a dignified retreat. Maigret had noticed one of his detectives near by; now he signaled the man to follow the peculiar professor of gymnastics.

At last Janvier could deliver his message. "Lucas just phoned. He's spotted that they have guns in the room. Five Poles slept in the next room last night, leaving the door open between. Some of them had to sleep on the floor. Who the devil was that character you were talking to?"

"Nothing . . . How much?"

Janvier slipped back into character, pointing at Ozep's glass. "You're paying Monsieur's check? One franc twenty and one twenty makes two forty."

Maigret took a taxi to Headquarters. At the door of his office he found the detective who had set out after Ozep.

"You lost him?" he roared. "Aren't you ashamed of yourself? I give you the most childish job of shadowing and you—"

"I didn't lose him," the detective murmured humbly.

"Where is he?"

"Here."

"You pulled him in?"

"He pulled me."

For Ozep had, indeed, headed directly for Headquarters, where he had placidly installed himself and his sandwich in the waiting room, after announcing that he had an appointment with Inspector "Maigrette."

THERE'RE NO KUDOS in paper work, but there may be the solution of a case.

Unwillingly, irritatedly, Maigret was adding up in one report in his own large handwriting the various information obtained in the two weeks' siege of the Polish gang.

When he set down the facts in order, he could see even more easily how very little they had learned. They did not even know precisely how many individuals belonged to the gang. The earlier reports, from the people who had seen or thought they had seen the bandits near the time of the attacks, stated that there were four of them, sometimes five. It was probable that they had other accomplices, who cased the farms and markets beforehand. That brought the number to six or seven, which seemed to correspond roughly with the number who hung around the nucleus on Rue de Birague.

There were only three regular tenants, all of whom had filled out their cards according to regulations and displayed passports in perfect order:

1. Boris Saft, the one the police called The Beard, who seemed to live as man and wife with the pale blonde.

2. Olga Tzerewski, 28, born in Vilna.

3. Sasha Vorontsov, known as One-Eye.

Boris the Beard and Olga occupied one room, Sasha One-Eye the next; the door between was always left open.

The young woman did the shopping every morning and cooked the meals on an alcohol stove.

The Beard rarely went out, but spent most of his days stretched on the iron bedstead, reading Polish newspapers that he had one of the gang buy for him at the newspaper kiosk in Place de la Bastille. Once the errand boy brought back an American detective magazine in addition to the Polish periodicals. They all read that.

One-Eye went out often, always followed by one of Maigret's detectives. A fact of which he was probably aware, since he never did more than take long walks through Paris, stopping in many bars but never speaking to a soul.

As for the rest, they were what Lucas called "the floating population." People came and went, always the same lot, four or five of them. Olga fed them, and sometimes they slept on the floor overnight. There was nothing odd about this; it happens in all hotels with poor tenants—exiles who get together to rent a room and then put up any of their compatriots they come across.

On the floating population Maigret had a few notes:

1. The Chemist, so called because he had twice visited the Work Exchange to apply for a job in a chemical plant. His clothes were badly worn but rather well cut. For hours he would wander around the streets of Paris like a man looking for any way to earn a little money; and once, for a whole day, he was employed as a sandwich man.

2. Spinach, named after the implausible spinach-green hat that seemed even more unlikely in view of his faded pink shirt. Spinach went out particularly in the evenings, when he picked up tips opening car doors in front of the Montmartre bars.

3. Puffy, a fat, wheezy little man, better dressed than the others even if his shoes were not mates.

And there were two others who visited the hotel less regularly; it was hard to say if they belonged to the gang.

Maigret stared at the notes with the exasperated feeling that the most important detail was somehow eluding him. Finally he picked up his pen again and wrote: "These people give the impression of penniless foreigners, looking for any kind of work at all. But there's always vodka in the rooms, and sometimes impressive spreads of food. Maybe the gang knows it's being watched, and is putting on an act for the police. If one of them is Stan the Killer, it is probably either The Beard or One-Eye. But this is only guesswork."

It was without the least enthusiasm that he brought his report to the chief.

"Nothing new?"

"Nothing specific. I'd swear the devils have spotted one of our men and are just amusing themselves seeing how often they can come in and go out on innocent errands. They know we can't keep a large section of the force mobilized on their account forever. Time's on their side; they have lots of it. . . ."

"You have a plan?"

"Look, Chief. You know that ideas and I haven't been on speaking terms for a long time. I come and I go and I sniff around. You'll hear people say I'm waiting for inspiration; they're way off the track. What I'm waiting for is the one significant happening that never fails to turn up. The whole thing is being there when it does turn up so that I can take advantage of it."

"So you're waiting for a . . . happening?" the chief smiled. He knew his man.

"This much I'm convinced of: This *is* the Polish gang. Because of that fool of an informer who keeps hanging around here picking up scraps of conversation, they're on their guard. Now what I want to know is, why did Stan write to me? Maybe because he knows the police always hesitate to make a forcible arrest. More probably out of sheer bravado. These killers have their pride—you might almost say, professional pride. But which of them is Stan? And why that nickname? It's more American than Polish.

"You know how I take my time before I reach any conclusions. Well, it's beginning to come . . . The last two or three days I've begun to get the feel of the psychology of these boys. Very different from French murderers.

"They need money, not to retire to the country, or to have a fling in the night spots, or to clear out to foreign parts—but just simply to live their own lives, which to them means doing nothing—eating, drinking, sleeping, spending your days stretched out on a bed, smoking cigarettes, and killing bottles of vodka. And they have this longing to be together—to dream together, gossip together, some nights sing together.

"The way I see it, after their first crime they lived like this until the money ran out; then they got ready for another job. Whenever the funds are low, they start in again, coldly, without remorse, without a trace of pity for the old people whose throats they cut—and whose life's savings they eat up in a few weeks or months . . . And now that I've got the feel of it, I'm waiting——"

"I know. For the happening . . ." the director smiled.

"Joke about it all you want. Just the same the happening may be here already."

"Where?"

"In the waiting room. The little man who calls me Maigrette and who wants at all costs to help in the arrest, even if it costs him his skin. He claims it's just another method of suicide."

"A crackpot?"

"Could be. Or an accomplice of Stan's who's using this method of keeping in touch with what we're doing. Any hypothesis fits; that's what makes my character with the creosote cigar so fascinating."

Maigret emptied his pipe by tapping it gently on the window ledge, so that the ashes fell somewhere on the Quai des Orfèvres, perhaps on the hat of a passer-by.

"He bothers me, that little man," he added. "I've seen his face somewhere. It's not in our files, but I've seen it. And I've seen the girl, too, the blonde; she's worth remembering. None of the others. Just those two."

The director of the Police Judiciaire leaned forward. "We've been going on the assumption that the blonde is Stan's mistress. You associate her and the little man. You see the possible implication?"

"That my little man is Stan himself? Could be."

"Are you going to accept this man's offer?"

"I think so." The inspector headed for the door. He felt that he'd said enough. "You'll see, Chief. I'll be amazed if we still need the stake-out by the end of this week."

And this was Thursday afternoon.

"SIT DOWN! Doesn't it get on your nerves to suck at that filthy creosote cigar all day?"

"No, Monsieur Maigrette."

"That 'Maigrette' of yours is beginning to get me . . . But anyway, let's get down to business. Are you still set on dying?"

"Yes, Monsieur Maigrette."

"And you still want to be entrusted with a perilous mission?"

"I wish to help you to arrest Stan the Killer."

"So if I told you to go up to One-Eye and fire a bullet into his leg, you'd do it?"

"Yes, Monsieur Maigrette. But you would first have to give me a revolver. I am a poor man and——"

"Now suppose I tell you to go to The Beard or One-Eye and say that you have important information—that the police are coming to arrest them?"

"Gladly, Monsieur Maigrette. I shall wait until One-Eye passes by in the street and then I shall perform my commission."

The lowering gaze of the inspector had no effect on the little Pole.

Rarely had Maigret seen a man who combined such self-assurance with such utter serenity. Michael Ozep spoke of killing himself or of visiting the Polish gang as simply, as naturally, as he might refer to brushing his teeth. He was as much at ease in police headquarters as in the Barrel of Burgundy.

"You've never met either of them?"

"No, Monsieur Maigrette."

"All right. I'm going to give you the job. And if there's any trouble, it's on your head." Maigret lowered his eyelids to conceal his too sharp interest in the other's reaction. "In a minute we'll go together to Rue Saint Antoine. I'll wait for you outside. You'll go up to the room, picking a time when the woman is there alone. You'll tell her you're a fellow Pole and you happened by chance to learn that the police are raiding the hotel tonight. . . ."

Ozep said nothing.

"You understand?"

"Yes."

"It's all set?"

"I must confess something to you, Monsieur Maigrette . . ."

"You're turning yellow?"

"Yellow? I do not under–ah! yes. No, I am not turning yellow. But I should prefer to arrange the matter in a different way. You may think that I am taking much upon myself . . . is that how I say it? But I am a timid man with the ladies. And the ladies are intelligent, far more intelligent than we men. Therefore, she will see that I am lying. And because I know that she will see that I am lying, I shall blush. And when I blush . . ."

Maigret sat motionless, absorbing this unlikely explanation.

"I should prefer to talk to a man. To the one with the beard, if you like, or the one you call One-Eye, or anyone at all. . . ."

A ray of sunlight pierced slantwise through the office and lit full on Maigret's face. He seemed to be dozing, like a man whose injudiciously heavy lunch obliges him to take a siesta at his desk.

"It is exactly the same thing, Monsieur Maigrette . . ."

But Monsieur Maigrette did not answer. The only sign that he was still alive was the slim blue spiral that rose from his pipe.

"I am desolated. You can ask of me what you wish; but you demand precisely the one thing which——"

"Stuff it!"

"I beg your pardon?"

"I say, 'Stuff it!' Which means, in French, to shut up. Where did you know the woman Olga Tzerewski?"

"I?"

"Answer me!"

"I do not understand what you mean . . ."

"Answer me!"

"I do not know this woman. If I knew her, I would tell you so. I am a former officer of the Polish Army and if I had not suffered misfortunes——"

"Where did you know her?"

"I swear to you, Monsieur Maigrette, by the head of my sainted mother and my poor father——"

"*Where did you know her?*"

"Why have you suddenly stopped being nice to me? You talk to me so brutally! To me, who came here to place myself at your disposal, to prevent Frenchmen from being murdered by a compatriot——"

"Cut the pitch!"

"Pitch?"

"Sales talk, to you. You aren't selling me."

"Ask anything of me, no matter what——"

"That's what I'm doing!"

"Ask me anything else—to throw myself under a subway train——"

"I'm asking you to go see that woman and tell her that we'll make a raid tonight."

"You insist?"

"Take it or leave it."

"And if I refuse?"

"Then you'd better see to it that I never lay eyes on you again."

"Are you really going to arrest the gang tonight?"

"Probably."

"And you will allow me to help you?"

"Possibly. We'll see about that when you've finished your first job."

"At what time?"

"Your job?"

"No. At what time will you make the raid?"

"Let's say one in the morning."

"I am going."

"Where?"

"To find the woman."

"Just a minute! We're going together."

"It is better that I go alone. If one of them sees us, he will understand that I am assisting the police. . . ."

The Pole had hardly left the office, of course, before the inspector had set a detective at his heels.

"Should I keep under cover?" the detective asked.

"No use. He's smarter than you are and he knows very well I'll have him followed."

And without losing a moment Maigret hurried downstairs and leaped into a taxi.

"Corner of Rue de Birague and Rue Saint Antoine, as fast as you can make it!"

IT WAS A RADIANT AFTERNOON. Striped awnings lent a note of color to the shops. In their shadows dogs sprawled and napped, and all life seemed to run in slow motion. You felt that even the buses had a hard time making headway in the hot heavy air. Their wheels left tracks in the heated asphalt.

Maigret sprang out of the taxi into the house on the corner. On the second floor he opened a door without bothering to knock and found Lucas sitting at the window, still in the role of a quiet and curious elderly gentleman.

The room was shabby but clean. On the table lay the remains of a cold meal that Lucas had had sent up from a delicatessen.

"Anything new, Inspector?"

"Anybody at home across the way?"

The room had been chosen for its strategic position; you could see straight into the two rooms of the Hôtel Beauséjour that the Poles occupied.

In this heat all the windows stood wide open, including the window of another room, which revealed a young girl asleep and scantily clad.

"Well, well, Lucas! Looks like you don't find your job too boring . . ."

A pair of field glasses on a chair gave evidence that Lucas attended to his work conscientiously and missed no detail, however slight.

"At the moment," said the sergeant, "there are two of them in the rooms, but there'll be only one in a minute. The man's getting dressed. He stayed in bed all morning, as usual."

"That's The Beard?"

"Yes. There were three of them for lunch: The Beard, the woman, and One-Eye. One-Eye left as soon as he'd eaten. Then The Beard got up and began to dress . . . Well! He's just put on a clean shirt. That doesn't happen very often."

Maigret came to the window to take his turn watching. The hairy giant was knotting his tie. The white shirt made an unexpected and therefore all the more dazzling splotch in the gray room.

You could see the man's lips move as he looked at himself in the mirror. Behind him the blond woman was cleaning up, gathering gray papers and rolling them into a ball, turning off the alcohol stove, dusting the frame of a bright-colored picture on the wall.

"If only we knew what they're saying!" Lucas sighed. "There are times when it drives me crazy. I watch them talking and talking and they never stop. They wave their arms around and I can't even guess what it's all about."

"The limitless resources of the police," said Maigret dryly, "do not include a lip reader who knows Polish."

"It gets on my nerves. I'm beginning to understand the torture it must be to be deaf. I'm beginning to see why people afflicted that way are generally so cranky."

"Don't talk so much! Do you think the woman will stay there?"

"This isn't the time she usually goes out. And if she meant to, she would have put on her gray suit."

Olga was wearing the same dark wool dress in which she had done her marketing that morning. While she cleaned up her bohemian establishment, she kept smoking a cigarette without ever taking it from her lips, in the fashion of the true smoker who needs tobacco from morning till night.

"She never talks," Maigret observed.

"This isn't the time she does that, either. It's in the evenings that she gets to talking, when they're all gathered around her. Or a few times when she's alone with the one I call Spinach—which doesn't happen very often. Either I'm badly mistaken or she has a weakness for Spinach. He's the best-looking of the lot."

It was a strange sensation to be in an unknown room like this, to look into the lives of people and come to know their smallest gestures.

"You're getting as snoopy as a concierge, Lucas."

"That's what I'm here for, isn't it? I can even tell you that the little girl over there—the one who's sleeping so soundly—was making love last night until three in the morning with a young man with an Ascot tie who left at dawn, undoubtedly so he could get into his family's house unnoticed—— Hold on! Now The Beard's leaving."

"Look at that, will you! He's practically elegant!"

"You might say so. But he looks more like a foreign wrestler than a man of the world."

"Well, let's say a wrestler who's doing good business," Maigret conceded.

No good-by kiss across the way. The man just went—that is, he disappeared from the part of the room visible from the police observatory.

A little later he emerged onto the sidewalk and set off toward Place de la Bastille.

"Derain will pick him up," Lucas announced, sitting there like a huge spider at the center of its web. "But he knows he's being followed. He won't do anything but walk around and maybe pick up a drink somewhere."

As for the woman, she had taken a road map out of a drawer and spread it on the table.

Ozep couldn't have taken a taxi, Maigret calculated; he must have come by subway, in which case he should arrive at any moment. "*If* he's coming . . ." he corrected himself.

And he did come. They saw him arrive, hesitate, wander up and down the sidewalk, while the detective trailing him displayed great interest in a fish stall on Rue Saint Antoine.

Seen from above like this, the tiny Pole seemed even thinner, even more insignificant. Maigret experienced, for a moment, a pang of remorse. He could hear the poor devil's voice repeating a hundred times, in involved explanation, his famous "Monsieur Maigrette . . ."

He was hesitating; that was obvious. He seemed even to be afraid, to stare around him with a visible anguish.

"Do you know what he's looking for?" the inspector asked Lucas.

"The little pale fellow? No. Maybe some money to get into the hotel?"

"He's looking for me. He's saying to himself that I must be somewhere around and if by some miracle I've changed my mind . . ."

Too late to change now; Michael Ozep had plunged into the dark hallway of the hotel. They could follow him in their minds. He would be climbing the stairs, reaching the second floor. . . .

"He's still stalling," Maigret announced. The door should have opened before this. "He's on the landing. He's going to knock. He's knocked—look!"

The blond girl trembled, shoved the map, with an instinctive movement, back in the dresser, and went toward the door. For a moment they could see nothing. The two were in the invisible part of the room. Then suddenly the woman appeared. Something about her had changed. Her steps were fast, decisive. She went straight to the window, closed it, then drew the dark curtains.

Lucas turned to the inspector with a quizzical smile. "Think of that!" he laughed. But his smile faded as he noticed that Maigret was far more concerned than he had expected.

"What time is it, Lucas?"

"Three-ten."

"In your opinion, what are the chances that one of the gang will come back to the hotel in the next hour?"

"I doubt it. Unless, as I was telling you, Spinach, if he knows The Beard is out of the way. You don't look very happy about things."

"I don't like the way she closed that window."

"Are you afraid for your little Pole?"

Maigret made no answer.

"Have you thought," Lucas went on, "that we haven't any real proof that he is in that room? It's true we saw him go into the hotel. But he might perfectly well have gone to some other room, while somebody else came——"

Maigret shrugged his shoulders and sighed.

"WHAT TIME IS IT, LUCAS?"

"Three-twenty."

"Do you know what's going to happen?"

"Do you want to go over and see what's happening across the way?"

"Not yet. But I'm probably going to make a fool of myself . . . Where can you telephone?"

"In the next room. He's a tailor who does piecework for one of the big houses, so he has to have a phone."

"Go to your tailor, then. Try not to let him listen in. Telephone the chief, and tell him I want him to send me twenty armed men at once. They're to spread a cordon around the Hôtel Beauséjour and wait for my signal."

Lucas's expression indicated the seriousness of this order, so out of character for Maigret, who usually laughed at police mobilization. "You think there'll be dirty work going on?"

"If it hasn't already gone on . . ."

His eyes remained fixed on the window, on the filthy glass panes, on the crimson velvet curtains of the time of Louis Philippe.

When Lucas came back from the telephone, he found the inspector still in the same place, still frowning thoughtfully.

"The boss says please be careful. There was a detective killed only last week, and now if there should be another accident——"

"Shut up, will you?"

"Do you think that Stan the Killer——"

"I don't think anything! I've thought so much about this case since this morning that I've got a headache. Now I'm satisfied just to have impressions; and if you want to know, I have the impression that some disagreeable things are happening or are about to happen. What time is it?"

"Twenty-three after."

In the neighboring room the young girl was still asleep, her mouth open, her legs bent back. Higher up, on the fifth or sixth floor, somebody was trying to play an accordion, incessantly repeating, with the same false notes, the same fox-trot refrain.

"Do you want me to go over?" Lucas suggested.

Maigret gave him a harsh look, as if his subordinate had reproached him for lack of courage. "Just what do you mean by that?"

"Nothing. I can't help seeing you're worried about what may be going on over there, and I thought I could go and check——"

"And you think I'd hesitate to go myself? You're forgetting one thing: Once we're over there, it's too late. If we go and find nothing, we'll never pin anything on that gang. That's why I'm hesitating . . . If only that wench hadn't closed the window!" He suddenly lifted his eyebrows. "Tell me: The other times, when she's been alone with a man, she's never closed the window, has she?"

"Never."

"Then she hadn't any suspicion of your presence here."

"She probably took me for just another foolish old man."

"So it isn't the girl who had the idea of closing the window, but the character who came in."

"Ozep?"

"Ozep or somebody else. It's the one who came in who told the girl to close the window before he showed himself."

He took his hat from the chair, emptied his pipe, scraped the bowl with his index finger.

"Where are you going, Chief?"

"I'm waiting for our men to get here . . . Look! There are two of them by the bus stop. And I recognize some others in that parked taxi . . . If I stay inside five minutes without opening that window, you'll come in with our men."

"You have your gun?"

A few moments later Lucas could see Maigret crossing the street, could see Detective Janvier notice him and break off his task of wiping the tables on the terrace.

After what seemed a miraculously short interval, the window across the way opened. Maigret signaled to his sergeant to join him.

From across the street Lucas had gathered that the room was empty save for the inspector. He stumbled up a dark staircase through the stench of bad cooking and worse plumbing and entered the room, only to start back as he found the body of a woman stretched out at his feet.

"Dead, of course," Maigret grunted.

It was as if the murderer had wished to leave his signature on his crime. The woman's throat had been cut, as with all the other victims of Stan. There was blood everywhere.

The bright picture on the wall turned out, on closer inspection, to be a portrait of Olga—even blonder, even more fresh-skinned than she had been in life. Lucas looked from the lushly alluring portrait to the unappetizing sight on the floor. He felt oddly like a drinking man who sees a bottle of fine brandy smashed.

"It was your Pole?"

Maigret shrugged his shoulders, still standing rooted in the middle of the room.

"Shall I give his description to our men so they can see that he doesn't leave the hotel?"

"If you wish."

"I'd like to put a man on the roof, just in case——"

"Go ahead."

"Shall I call the chief?"

"In a minute."

It was no easy job to talk with Maigret when he was like this. Lucas tried to put himself in his shoes. Maigret himself had said that he'd make a fool of himself. But this was worse than looking foolish. He had mobilized a large body of police when it was too late, when the crime had already been committed under Maigret's very eyes—almost with his consent, since he'd been the one who had sent Ozep into the Hôtel Beauséjour.

"And if any of the gang come back, shall I arrest them?"

An affirmative nod. Or rather a gesture of indifference. And at last Lucas went out.

"WHERE'S MAIGRET?" the chief demanded of Lucas before he was halfway out of his car.

"In the room. Number Nineteen on the second floor. The people in the hotel don't know about it yet."

A few minutes later the director of the Police Judiciaire found Maigret sitting in a chair in the middle of the room, two steps from the body.

"Well, my friend! It looks to me as though we were in a pretty fix!"

For answer he received a grunt.

"So the notorious killer was none other than the little man who offered you his services! You must admit, Maigret, you might have been somewhat less trustful; Ozep's attitude was, to say the least, suspicious . . ."

A heavy vertical furrow seamed Maigret's brow and his jaws jutted out, giving his whole face a striking quality of power.

"You think he hasn't managed to slip out of the hotel yet?"

"I'm sure of it," the inspector replied, as if he attached not the least importance to the matter.

"You haven't searched the hotel?"

"Not yet."

"You think he'll let himself be captured easily?"

Then Maigret's gaze detached himself slowly from the window, shifted toward the director.

"If I'm wrong, the man will try to kill as many people as he can before he's arrested. If I'm not wrong, things will take care of themselves."

"I don't understand, Maigret."

"I tell you again, Chief: I can be wrong. Anybody can be wrong. In that case, I beg your pardon, because there's going to be trouble. The way this case seems to have solved itself doesn't satisfy me. There's something that doesn't fit, I can feel it. If Ozep was Stan, there was no reason why . . ." His voice trailed off.

"You're staying here, Maigret?"

"Pending further instructions, yes."

"Meanwhile, I'll go see what our men are doing outside."

They had arrested Spinach when, as Lucas had foreseen, he had come to pay his call on the young woman. When they told him that Olga had been killed, he turned pale, but he showed no reaction when they spoke of Ozep.

When this arrest was announced to Maigret, he merely mumbled, "What's it to me?" and resumed his strange tête-à-tête with the dead woman.

A half hour later it was One-Eye's turn to come home and be arrested on the threshold. He submitted impassively, but when they told him of the woman's death, he tried to break free from his handcuffs and leap upstairs.

"Who did it?" he shouted. "Who killed her? One of you, wasn't it?"

"It was Ozep, alias Stan the Killer."

The man quieted down as if by magic. He frowned as he repeated, "Ozep?"

"You aren't going to tell us you didn't know your boss's real name?"

It was the chief in person who conducted this hasty questioning in a corridor, and he had the impression that a faint smile crossed the prisoner's lips.

Then came another of the gang, the one they called The Chemist. He simply answered all questions with an air of absolute confusion, as if he had never heard of the woman or of Ozep or of Stan.

Maigret was still upstairs, mulling over the same problem, hunting for the key that would at last enable him to understand what had happened.

"All right . . ." he murmured when Lucas told him of the arrest of The Beard, who had begun by raging like a fiend and ended by bawling like a calf.

Suddenly he raised his head. "Do you notice something, Lucas? That's four that they've arrested, and not one of them's put up any real resistance. Whereas a man like Stan——"

"But since Stan is Ozep——"

"Have you found him?"

"Not yet. We had to let all the accomplices come home before we turned the hotel upside down. If they got a whiff of anything wrong, they'd never come into the mousetrap. Now that we have almost all of them, the big boss is laying siege to the establishment. Our men are downstairs and they're going to go through everything."

"Listen, Lucas . . ."

The sergeant had been about to leave. He paused, feeling for Maigret something akin to pity.

"One-Eye is not Stan. Spinach is not Stan. The Beard is not Stan. But I'm convinced that Stan lived in this hotel and was the focus around which the others gathered."

Lucas thought it better to say nothing. Let the inspector have his monomania.

"If Ozep was Stan, he had no reason to come here to kill an accomplice. If he was not Stan . . ."

Suddenly Maigret rose, crossed to the wall and pulled down the brightly colored picture of Olga. He tore away the tape that framed it, revealing lines of lettering above and below the face. He handed it to Lucas.

The sergeant knew enough English to make out both the line above:

REAL LIFE DETECTIVE CASES

and the lines below:

THE PRETTY POLE AND THE
TERROR OF TERRE HAUTE

Maigret was smiling now. "Vanity," he said. "They can't ever resist it. They had to buy the magazine when they saw it on the stands, and she had to frame the picture.

"I knew I'd seen her face before. I do remember the case roughly. I kept some clippings on it. Very similar to ours. In the Middle West of America, four or five years ago. A gang attacking lonely farms, cutting throats . . . just like ours . . . and they had a woman leader. The American press took great pleasure in describing her atrocities."

"Then Stan . . . ?"

". . . was Olga. Almost certainly. I'll be positive in an hour, now that I know what to look for in the office. Are you coming with me, Lucas?"

"But Ozep?" Lucas asked as they settled back in the cab.

"It's Ozep I especially want to look up. That is, I'm hoping I'll find something about him. If he killed this woman, he must have had a motive . . . Listen, Lucas: When I wanted to send him to the others, he agreed at once. But when I gave him an errand to the woman, he refused, and I was forced to use pressure, even to threaten him. In other words, the rest of the gang did not know him—*but the woman did.*"

It took a good half hour to find the clippings in question. Order was not Maigret's dominant attribute.

"Read this! Always allowing for the exaggeration of the American press—they like to give the readers their money's worth. 'The Female Fiend . . .' 'The Deadly Pole . . .' 'Girl, 23, Heads Murder Gang . . .' "

The press reveled in the exploits of the Polish girl and furnished many proofs of her photogenic qualities.

At eighteen Stephanie Polintskaja was already known to the Warsaw police. Around this time she met a man who married her and strove to curb her evil instincts. She had a child by him. One day the man came home from work to find that his wife had vanished with all the money and jewelry. The child's throat had been cut.

"You know who that man was?" Maigret asked.

"Ozep?"

"Here's his picture, and a good likeness. You understand now? Stephanie, nicknamed Stan, ran wild in America. How she escaped the American prisons I do not know. In any case she took refuge in France, surrounded herself with a fresh lot of brutes, and took up her old career.

"Her husband learns from the papers that she is in Paris, that the police are on her trail. Does he want to rescue her once more? I doubt it. I'm rather inclined to think that he wants to make sure that the detestable murderess of his child shall not escape punishment. That's why he offers me his services. He hasn't the guts to work alone. He's too much of a weakling. He needs the police to help him. And then, this afternoon, I force his hand . . .

"Face to face with his former wife, what can he do? Kill or be killed! She certainly would not hesitate to destroy the only man outside the gang who could testify against her.

"So he killed . . . And do you want to know what I think? I'm betting that they'll find him somewhere in the hotel, more or less seriously wounded. After muffing two attempts at suicide, it would amaze me if he muffed the third. Now you can go back to the hotel and—"

"No use!" It was the chief's voice. "Stan the Killer hanged himself in a vacant room on the sixth floor. Good riddance!"

"He made it," Maigret sighed. "Poor devil!"

"You're sorry for him?"

"Indeed I am. Especially since I'm somewhat responsible for his death . . . I don't know if it means I'm getting old, but I certainly took long enough to find the solution—"

"What solution?" the director asked suspiciously.

"The solution to the whole problem!" Lucas intervened happily. "The inspector has reconstructed the case in all its details."

"That so, Maigret?"

"It is . . . You know, if you keep mulling over the same question . . . I don't think I've ever been so mad at myself in my life. I felt that the solution was there, within reach, that just one little touch . . . And you all kept buzzing around me like horseflies, telling me about arrests that didn't mean a thing . . . And then I remembered the American detective magazine and the woman's face on the cover . . ."

Maigret took a deep breath, loaded his pipe, and asked Lucas for matches. The afternoon vigil had used up all his own.

"What do you say, Chief? It's seven o'clock. Suppose we three settle down to a nice glass of beer? Provided that Lucas gets rid of his wig and makes himself respectable again."

# HIT AND RUN

*by John D. MacDonald*

TWENTY-EIGHT DAYS after the woman died, Walter Post, special investigator for the Traffic Division, squatted on his heels in a big parking lot and ran his fingertips lightly along the front-right fender of the car which had killed her. It was a blue and gray four-door sedan, three years old, in the lower price range.

The repair job had probably been done in haste and panic. But it had been competently done. The blue paint was an almost perfect match. Some of it had got on the chrome stripping and had been wiped off, but not perfectly. The chrome headlight ring was a replacement, with none of the minute pits and rust flecks of the ring on the left headlight. He reached up into the fender well and brushed his fingers along the area where the undercoating had been flattened when the fender had been hammered out.

He stood up and looked toward the big insurance-company office building, large windows and aluminum panels glinting in the morning sun, and wondered where Mr. Wade Adams was, which window was his. A vice-president, high up, looking down on the world.

It had been a long hunt. Walter Post had examined many automobiles. The killing had occurred on a rainy Tuesday morning in September at 9:30, in the 1200 block of Harding Avenue. It was an old street of big elms and frame houses. It ran north and south. Residents in the new suburban areas south of the city used Harding Avenue in preference to Wright Boulevard when they drove to the center of the city. Harding Avenue had been resurfaced a year ago. There were few traffic lights. The people who lived on Harding Avenue had complained about fast traffic before Mary Berris was killed.

Mr. and Mrs. Steve Berris and their two small children had lived at 1237 Harding Avenue. He was the assistant manager of a supermarket. On that rainy morning she had put on her plastic rain cape to hurry across the street, apparently to see a neighbor on some errand. It was evident she had not intended to be gone long, as her two small children were left untended. The only witness was a thirteen-year-old girl, walking from her home to the bus stop.

Through careful and repeated interrogations of that girl after she had quieted down, authorities were able to determine that the street had been momentarily empty of traffic, that the death car had been proceeding toward the center of town at a high rate of speed, that Mary Berris had started to cross from right to left in front of the car, hurrying. Apparently, when she realized she had misjudged the speed and distance of the car, she had turned and tried to scamper back to the protection of the curb.

Walter Post guessed that the driver, assuming the young woman would continue across, had swerved to the right to go behind her. When she had turned back, the driver had hit the brakes. There were wet leaves on the smooth asphalt. The car had skidded. Mary Berris was struck and thrown an estimated twenty feet through the air, landing close to the curb. The car had swayed out of its skid and then accelerated.

The child had not seen the driver of the car. She said it was a pale car, a gray or blue, not a big car and not shiny new. Almost too late she realized she should look at the license number. But by then it was so far away that she could only tell that it was not an out-of-state license and that it ended, in her words, "in two fat numbers. Not sharp numbers like ones and sevens. Fat ones like sixes and eights and nines."

Mary Berris lived for nearly seventy hours with serious brain injuries, ugly contusions and abrasions, and a fractured hip. She lived long enough for significant bruises to form, indicating from their shape and placement that the vehicle had struck her a glancing blow on the right hip and thigh, the curve of the bumper striking her right leg just below the knee. The fragments of glass from the lens of the shattered sealed-beam headlamp indicated three possible makes of automobile. No shellac or enamel was recovered from her clothing. It was believed that, owing to the glancing inpact, the vehicle had not been seriously damaged. She did not regain consciousness before death.

For the first two weeks of the investigation Walter Post had the assistance of sufficient manpower to cover all places where repairs could have been made. The newspapers cooperated. Everyone in the metropolitan area was urged to look for the death car. But as in so many other instances, the car seemed to disappear without a trace. Walter

Post was finally left alone to continue the investigation, in addition to his other duties.

And this time, he devoted more time to it than he planned. It seemed more personal. This was not a case of one walking drunk lurching into the night path of a driving drunk. This was a case of a young, pretty housewife—very pretty, according to the picture of her he had seen—mortally injured on a rainy Tuesday by somebody who had been in a hurry, somebody too callous to stop and clever enough to hide. He had talked to the broken husband and seen the small, puzzled kids, and heard the child witness say, "It made a terrible noise. A kind of—thick noise. And then she just went flying in the air, all loose in the air. And the car tried to go away so fast the wheels were spinning."

Walter Post would awaken in the night and think about Mary Berris and feel a familiar anger. This was his work, and he knew the cost of it and realized his own emotional involvement made him better at what he did. But this was a very small comfort in the bitter mood of the wakeful night. And he knew there would be no joy in solving the case because he would find at the end of his search not some monster, some symbol of evil, but merely another victim, a trembling human animal.

His wife Carolyn endured this time of his involvement as she had those which had gone before, knowing the cause of his remoteness, his brutal schedule of self-assigned work hours. Until this time of compulsion was ended, she and the children would live with—and rarely see—a weary man who kept pushing himself to the limit of his energy, who returned and ate and slept and went out again.

Operating on the assumption that the killer was a resident of the suburban areas south of the city, he had driven the area until he was able to block off one large section where, if you wanted to drive down into the center of the city, Harding Avenue was the most efficient route to take. With the cooperation of the clerks at the State Bureau of Motor Vehicle Registration, he compiled a discouragingly long list of all medium and low-priced sedans from one to four years old registered in the name of persons living in his chosen area, where the license numbers ended in 99, 98, 89, 88, 96, 69, 86, 68, and 66. He hoped he would not have to expand it to include threes and fives, which could also have given that impression of "fatness," in spite of the child witness's belief that the numbers were not threes or fives.

With his list of addresses he continued the slow process of elimination. He could not eliminate the darker or brighter colors until he was certain the entire car had not been repainted. He worked with a feeling of weary urgency, suspecting the killer would feel more at ease once the death car was traded in. He lost weight. He accomplished his other duties in an acceptable manner.

At nine on this bright October tenth, a Friday, just twenty-eight days and a few hours after Mary Berris had died, he had checked the residence of a Mr. Wade Adams. It was a long and impressive house on a wide curve of Saylor Lane. A slim, dark woman of about forty answered the door. She wore slacks and a sweater. Her features were too strong for prettiness, and her manner and expression were pleasant and confident.

"Yes?"

He smiled and said, "I just want to take up a few moments of your time. Are you Mrs. Adams?"

"Yes, but really, if you're selling something, I just—"

He took out his notebook. "This is a survey financed by the automotive industry. People think we're trying to sell cars, but we're not. This is a survey about how cars are used."

She laughed. "I can tell you one thing. There aren't enough cars in this family. My husband drives to work. We have a son eighteen, in his last year of high school, and a daughter, fourteen who needs a lot of taxi service. The big car is in for repairs, and today my husband took the little car to work. So you can see how empty the garage is. If Gary's marks are good at midyear, Wade is going to get him a car of his own."

"Could I have the make and year and model and color of your two cars, Mrs. Adams?"

She gave him the information on the big car first. And then she told him the make of the smaller car and said, "It's three years old. A four-door sedan. Blue and gray."

"Who usually drives it, Mrs. Adams?"

"It's supposed to be mine, but my husband and Gary and I all drive it. So I'm always the one who has it when it runs out of gas. I *never* can remember to take a look at the gauge."

"What does your husband do, Mrs. Adams?"

"He's a vice-president at Surety Insurance."

"How long has your boy been driving?"

"Since it was legal. Don't they all? A junior license when he was sixteen, and his senior license last July when he turned eighteen. It makes me nervous, but what can you do? Gary is really quite a reliable boy. I shudder to think of what will happen when Nancy can drive. She's a scatterbrain. All you can do is depend on those young reflexes, I guess."

He closed his notebook. "Thanks a lot, Mrs. Adams. Beautiful place you have here."

"Thank you." She smiled at him. "I guess the automobile people are in a tizzy, trying to decide whether to make big cars or little cars."

"It's a problem," he said. "Thanks for your cooperation."

He had planned to check two more registrations in that immediate area. But he had a hunch about the Adams's car. Obviously Mrs. Adams hadn't been driving. He had seen too many of the guilty ones react. They had been living in terror. When questioned, they broke quickly and completely. And questions always brought on the unmistakable guilt reactions of the amateur criminal.

So he had driven back into the city, shown his credentials to the guard at the gate of the executive parking area of the Surety Insurance Company and inspected the blue-gray car with the license that ended in 89.

He walked slowly back to his own car and stood beside it, thinking, a tall man in his thirties, dark, big-boned, a man with a thoughtful, slow-moving manner. The damage to the Adams car could be coincidence. But he was certain he had located the car. The old man or the boy had done it. Probably the boy. The public schools hadn't opened until the fifteenth.

He thought of the big job and the fine home and the pleasant, attractive woman. It was going to blow up that family as if you stuck a bomb under it. It would be hell, but not one-tenth, one-hundredth the hell Steve Berris was undergoing.

He went over his facts and assumptions. The Adamses lived in the right area to use Harding Avenue as the fast route to town. The car had been damaged not long ago in precisely the way he had guessed it would be. It fitted the limited description given.

He went into the big building. The information center in the lobby sent him up to the twelfth-floor receptionist. He told her his name, said he did not have an appointment but did not care to state his business. She raised a skeptical eyebrow, phoned Adams's secretary and asked him to wait a few minutes. He sat in a deep chair amid an efficient hush. Sometimes, when a door opened, he could hear a chattering drone of tabulating equipment.

Twenty minutes later a man walked quickly into the reception room. He was in his middle forties, a trim balding man with heavy glasses, a nervous manner, and a weathered golfing tan. Walter stood as he approached.

"Mr. Post? I'm Wade Adams. I can spare a few minutes."

"You might want to make it more than a few minutes, Mr. Adams."

"I don't follow you."

"When and how did you bash in the front-right fender of your car down there in the lot?"

Adams stared at him. "If that fender is bashed in, Mr. Post, it happened since I parked it there this morning."

"It has been bashed in and repaired."

"That's nonsense!"

"Why don't we go down and take a look at it?" He kept his voice low.

Wade Adams was visibly irritated. "You'd better state your business in a—a less cryptic way, Mr. Post. I certainly have more to do than go down and stare at the fender of my own car."

"Do you happen to remember that hit-and-run on Harding Avenue? Mary Berris?"

"Of course I rem—" Wade Adams suddenly stopped talking. He stared beyond Post, frowning into the distance. "Surely you can't have any idea that—" He paused again, and Post saw his throat work as he swallowed. "This is some mistake."

"Let's go down and look at the fender."

Adams told the receptionist to tell his secretary he was leaving the building for a few moments. They went down to the lot. Post pointed out the unmistakable clues. There was a gleam of perspiration on Adams's forehead and upper lip. "I never noticed this. Not at all. My gosh, you don't look this carefully at a car."

"You have no knowledge of this fender's being bashed since you've owned the car?"

"Let's go back to my office, Mr. Post."

Adams had a big corner office, impressively furnished. Once they were alone, and Adams was seated behind his desk, he seemed better able to bring himself under control.

"Why have you—picked that car?"

Post explained the logic of his search and told of the subterfuge he had used with Mrs. Adams.

"Janet would know nothing about—"

"I know that, from talking to her."

"My wife is incapable of deceit. She considers it her great social handicap," he said, trying to smile.

"You didn't kill that woman either."

"No, I—"

"We're thinking of the same thing, Mr. Adams."

Adams got up quickly and walked restlessly over to the window. He turned suddenly, with a wide, confident smile. "Damn stupid of me, Mr. Post. I remember now. Completely slipped my mind. I drove that car over to Mercer last July. I—uh—skidded on a gravel road and had it fixed in a little country garage . . . hit it against a fence post when I went in the ditch."

Walter Post looked at him and shook his head slowly. "It won't work."

"I swear it's—"

"Mr. Adams, this is not a misdemeanor. In this state a hit-and-run killing is a mandatory murder charge. Second degree. The only way out of it is a valid insanity plea. In either case the criminal has to spend plenty of time locked up. You'd have to prove the date of the trip, show police officers exactly where you skidded, take them to the country garage, find people to back up the story. No, Mr. Adams. Not even a good try."

Adams went behind his desk and sat down heavily. "I don't know what to do. Get hold of a lawyer, I guess. All of a sudden I'm a hundred years old. I want to make myself believe that Gary bashed a fender and had it repaired on his own so he wouldn't lose his driving privilege."

"Why can't you believe that?"

"He has—changed, Mr. Post. In the last month. The teen-age years are strange, murky years, if what I remember of my own is any clue. He's a huge youngster, Mr. Post. They all seem to grow so big lately. I've had trouble with him. The normal amount. If a kid doesn't have a streak of rebellion against authority in him—authority as represented by his male parent—then he isn't worth a damn. Gary has been a sunny type, usually. Reliable. Honest. He's traveled with a nice pack of kids. He's a pretty fair athlete and a B student. His contemporaries seem to like and respect him. Here's his picture. Taken last June."

Crew cut and broad smiling face, a pleasant, rugged-looking boy, a good-looking kid.

"He's changed. Janet and I have discussed it, and we've tried to talk to him, but he won't talk. He's sour and moody and gloomy. Off his feed. He doesn't seem interested in dates or athletics or his studies. He spends a lot of time in his room with the door closed. He grunts at us and barks at his sister. We thought it was a phase and have hoped it would end soon. We've wondered if he's in some kind of trouble that he can't or won't tell us about."

"I appreciate your being so frank, Mr. Adams."

"I can't, in my heart, believe him capable of this. But I've read about all the polite, decent, popular kids from good homes who have got into unspeakable trouble. You know—you can live with them and not understand them at all."

"Were you here in the office on the ninth?"

"Yes, if it was a weekday."

"What time did you get in?"

Adams looked back in his appointment calendar. "A Tuesday. I'd called a section meeting for nine. I was in at eight thirty, earlier than usual. I can't believe Gary—"

"A kid can panic, Mr. Adams. A good kid can panic just as quick as a bad kid. And once you run, it's too late to go back. Maybe he loaned the car to some other kid. Maybe your wife loaned it."

Adams looked across the desk at Walter Post, a gleam of hope apparent. "It's against orders for him to let any of his friends drive it. But it could have happened that way."

"That's what we have to find out, Mr. Adams."

"Can we—talk to my boy? Can we go together and talk to Gary?"

"Of course."

Wade Adams phoned the high school. He said he would be out in twenty minutes to speak to his son on a matter of importance, and he would appreciate their informing him and providing a place where they could talk privately.

When they arrived at the high school, they went to the administration office and were directed to a small conference room. Gary Adams was waiting for them and stood up when they came in and closed the door. He was big. He had a completely closed expression, watchful eyes.

"What's up, dad? I phoned the house to find out, but mom didn't know a thing. I guess I just got her worried."

Wade Adams said, "I was going to let Mr. Post here ask you some questions, Gary, but with his permission I think I would like to ask you myself."

Walter Post had to admire the man. The answers he would get would very probably shatter a good life, and unless the kid was one in ten thousand, his future would be ruined beyond repair. Yet Wade Adams was under control.

"Go ahead," Post said.

"You have acted strange for a month, Gary. You know that. Your mother and I have spoken to you. Now I'm desperately afraid I know what has been wrong."

"Do you?" the boy said with an almost insolent indifference.

"Will you sit down?"

"I'd just as soon stand, thanks."

Wade Adams sighed. "You'd better tell us about the front-right fender on the small car, Gary. You'd better tell us the whole thing."

Post saw the flicker of alarm in the boy's light-colored eyes as he glanced sideways at Post. He had hunted a killer, and now he felt sick at heart, as in all the times that had gone before.

"You better clue me, dad. That question is far out."

"Did you repair it yourself? Were you driving or was one of your friends driving when you hit that woman? Does that—clue you enough?" he asked bitterly.

The boy stiffened and stared at his father with a wild, naked astonishment. "No!" the boy said in an almost inaudible voice. "You couldn't possibly—you couldn't be trying to—"

"To what? I'm ordering you to tell me about that fender."

The boy changed visibly in a way Walter Post had seen once before and would always remember. It takes a curious variety of shock to induce that look of boneless lethargy. Once, at a major fire, he had seen a man who believed his whole family had perished, had seen that man confronted by his family. There was the same look of heavy, brooding wonder.

Gary Adams slid heavily into one of the wooden armchairs at the small conference table. He looked at the scarred table and said in a dull voice, "I'll tell you about that fender. The fourteenth of September was a Sunday. You can look it up. You and mom had gone to the club. Nancy was off some place. School started the next day. I played tennis. I got back about four in the afternoon, dad. I decided to wash the car. I hadn't washed it in two weeks, and I figured you'd start to give me a hard time about it any day. That was when I found out somebody had bashed the right fender and had it fixed since the last time I'd washed it. You wash a car, and you can spot something like that right away."

"But, Gary, you didn't say anything."

"If anybody'd been home, I'd have gone right in and asked who clobbered the fender. You know, like a joke. But there wasn't anybody home. And it—it kept coming into my mind. About that woman."

Wade Adams had moved to stand beside his son. The boy looked up at him with a dull agony. "Dad, I just couldn't stop thinking about it. We always go down Harding Avenue. Our car matches the description. And if—if you or mom had bashed a fender in some kind of harmless way, you wouldn't have kept it a secret. I couldn't imagine you or mom doing such a terrible thing, but I kept thinking about it, and it got worse and worse. I thought I was going to throw up. And ever since then, I haven't known what to—"

"Where were you on the day that woman was hit, son," Walter Post asked.

The boy frowned at him. "Where was I? Oh, a guy picked me up real early, about dawn, and a bunch of us went up to his folks' place at the lake and swam and skied all day and got back late."

Wade Adams spoke to his son in a strange voice. "Let me get this straight. For the last month, Gary, you've been living with the idea that either your mother or I could have killed that woman and driven away?"

Walter Post could see how strongly the man's hand was grasping the boy's shoulder.

"But nobody else ever drives the car!" the boy cried. "Nobody else."

Walter Post watched Wade Adams's face and saw the fierce indignation of the falsely accused change to a sudden understanding of what the boy had been enduring.

In a trembling voice Wade Adams said, "We didn't do it, boy. Neither of us. Not one of the three of us. Believe me, son. You can come out of your nightmare. You can come home again."

When the boy began to cry, to sob in the hoarse clumsy way of the man-child years, Walter Post stepped quietly out into the corridor and closed the door and leaned against the wall and smoked a cigarette, tasting his own gladness, a depth of satisfaction he had never before experienced in this deadly occupation. It made him yearn for some kind of work where this could happen more often. And he now knew the probable answer to the killing.

When Adams and his son came out of the room, they had an identical look of pride and exhaustion. The boy shook hands with Post and went back to class.

"Now we go to your house and talk to your wife," Walter Post said. "We were too quick to think it was the boy. We should have talked to her first."

"I'm glad we did it just this way, Mr. Post. Very glad. About the car. I think now I can guess what happened—"

"Let's see your wife and let her confirm it."

At 3:30 that afternoon Walter Post sat in the small office of Stewart Partchman, owner of Partchman Motors. With him were Partchman and a redheaded service manager named Finnigan and a mechanic named Dawes.

Finnigan was saying, "The reason I didn't let Thompson go, Mr. Partchman, is that he's always been a reliable little guy, and this is the first time he goofs. Dawes drove him out there to bring back the Adams job, around nine o'clock, and figured Thompson was following him right on back into town, and Thompson doesn't show up with the car until after lunch. He had some story about his wife being sick and stopping by his house to see how she was."

Partchman said angrily, "So it gave him time to take it some place and hammer that fender out, then come back here and sneak the headlamp and chrome ring out of stock and get some paint onto it."

"It was in for a tune-up," Finnigan said, looking at the service sheet on the job, "new muffler, lube, and oil change. It got in so late we couldn't deliver it back out there until the next day. I remember apologizing to Mrs. Adams over the phone. I didn't tell her why it was late. She was pretty decent about it."

The mechanic said, "Tommy has been jumpy lately. He's been making mistakes."

"How do you want to handle it?" Partchman asked Walter Post.

"Bring him in here right now and everybody stay here and keep quiet and let me do the talking," Post said wearily.

Thompson was brought in, small, pallid, worried. His restless eyes kept glancing quickly at Post.

Post let the silence become long and heavy after Thompson asked what was wanted of him. At last he said, "How did you feel during those three days, while you were wondering whether she was going to die?"

Thompson stared at him and moistened his lips. He started twice to speak. The tears began to run down his smudged cheeks.

"I felt terrible," he whispered. "I felt just plain terrible." And he ground his fists into his eyes like a guilty child.

Walter Post took him in and turned him over to the experts from the Homicide Section and accomplished his share of the paperwork. He was home by six o'clock. He told Carolyn about it that evening, when he was lethargic with emotional reaction to the case. He talked to her about trying to get into some other line of investigatory work and tried to explain his reasons to her.

But they woke him up at three in the morning and told him to go out to River Road. He got there before the lab truck. He squatted in a floodlighted ditch and looked at the broken old body of a bearded vagrant and at the smear of green automotive enamel ground into the fabric of a shabby coat.

He straightened up slowly, bemused by his own ready acceptance of the fact it was not yet time to leave this work. Somebody was driving in a personal terror through the misty night, in a car so significantly damaged it would wear—for Walter Post—the signs and stains of a sudden murder.

# SECOND TALENT

*by James Holding*

MANUEL ANDRADAS WALKED to the back of the mansion through the formal gardens that encircled it. Senhor Martinho was sitting at ease on the patio overlooking his lily pond. He was sipping an iced drink and reading a pamphlet.

He glanced up in surprise as Manuel appeared. To his knowledge, he had never seen this small unremarkable fellow with the muddy brown eyes before. "Who are you?" he asked sharply. "I didn't hear you ring." He put his drink down on the glass-topped table beside him.

The intruder had a camera case slung by a strap across his shoulders, and he presented his card with a half bow.

"Manuel Andradas, photographer," Martinho read aloud. "Oh, yes." He looked up at Manuel. "I know your work, Senhor. I've admired it often in *Rio Illustrated.*" With the casual politeness of the very rich, he invited Manuel to sit down.

Manuel thanked him and took a straight chair directly facing his host's chaise. He was very pleased that Martinho knew his work and recognized his name. He said obliquely, "Since your servants are evidently out, I took the liberty of coming straight back, Senhor Martinho." Behind him, sunlight glinted brightly on the surface of the lily pond, where a pair of swans floated in stately silence.

"Ah, yes, the servants' picnic, a little treat I arrange for them annually. I had forgotten I am here alone today." Martinho leaned back. "Well, what do you wish of me then, Senhor Andradas? Permission to photograph my collection?" His collection of pre-Columbian artifacts was world famous.

Manuel shook his head, then took a gun out of his jacket pocket. "No, Senhor," he said quietly. "I am here to kill you."

Aside from a startled flicker of the eyes, Martinho's lined face remained surprisingly calm. "Indeed," he said. "How extraordinary. I thought you were a photographer."

"I am," said Andradas. "A good one, I hope. Yet I have a second talent which pays better than photography."

"Killing for money, you mean?"

"I prefer to call it nullification," Manuel said with dignity. "There is no malice in it, you understand. With me, it is purely a matter of business. I make a living, you might say, out of your dying."

Martinho thought this might be intended as a joke. The photographer's thin lips, however, were not smiling, nor were his eyes. "I see," said Luis Martinho. "You are a professional, then?"

"Exactly."

"A professional would not sit here talking for two minutes before administering the *coup de grace*. Therefore I think you bluff, Senhor. You attempt to put the fear of death in me so that you may thereby gain other ends. Am I not right?"

"Not even remotely right. I am here to kill you, and I shall do so. Never doubt it."

"Then why not get it over?" Martinho reached out an arm and placed his pamphlet on the table beside his drink.

That question had been troubling Manuel, too. This was a job like any other, so why dawdle over it? Could the explanation lie in the empathy of one artist for another? Was he obscurely reluctant to nullify Martinho because the collector was a man of artistic judgment who admired his, Manuel's, work? He said to Martinho, "I am in no hurry if you are not."

Martinho licked his lips. "Do you do this sort of thing frequently? Kill people, I mean?"

"Only occasionally, Senhor."

"Who hired you to kill me?"

"I don't know. I know only the middleman, as it were. The broker." Manuel paused. It was against his rule to mention his employers. Yet what harm could it do when Martinho was virtually a dead man? "Have you ever heard of the Corporation? The Big Ones?"

"Isn't it some sort of criminal organization?"

Manuel nodded. "It was the Corporation that arranged for me to nullify you . . . on behalf of some client unknown to me who will pay them generously for the service."

"Oh." Martinho sat quietly for a moment, then reached into his shirt pocket and drew out a packet of cigarettes. He offered one to Manuel. When the photographer refused with a shake of the head, the collector lit one for himself and returned the packet to his pocket. "A broker, indeed. Well, there is no doubt in my mind," Martinho said thoughtfully, "who is paying this Corporation of yours for my removal." He was very thoughtful.

"We all have enemies," Manuel said sententiously.

Martinho ignored him. "My nephew!" he said. "Who else would wish me dead?" A certain frenetic excitement came into his voice. "Of course. He is the poor relation. I am rich. He covets my collection for the second-rate museum of which he is curator. He knows he is my sole heir, but I am still quite robust, although old, as you see. So perhaps he has grown tired of waiting for me to die in the usual fashion, eh, in the natural way? And he is attempting to expedite matters with your help? Then he inherits my money and my collection now, not sometime in the uncertain future, but immediately. What do you think of that hypothesis? Can you find a flaw in it?"

Manuel sat like a stone. "There are many reasons why men seek the Corporation's help."

"The ingrate!" Martinho was at last in the grip of violent emotion. "I refuse to die for him!"

"I'm afraid you have no choice, Senhor." Manuel's gun pointed unwaveringly at his middle.

The collector jerked upright in his lounge chair. "Wait! You said your killings pay better than your photography. Didn't you?"

The photographer nodded.

"Then you like money, quite obviously. Lots of it."

"I like it." An understatement.

"Look," said Martinho, pointing. "Those two Mochica vases beside the door over there are Peruvian antiquities. They are worth five thousand *novo* cruzeiros each."

Manuel's eyes went to the vases for a moment, then switched back to Martinho. The gun didn't budge. He said nothing.

"And over on that table near you," Martinho said, "that's a piece of molded black-ware pottery of the Chimu empire. It's worth three thousand."

Shocked into speech, Manuel said, "If they are so valuable, you display them very carelessly, Senhor."

"Oh, they are locked safely away behind my numerous burglar alarms at night, with the rest of my collection. I bring a few treasures to the patio here each day for my own pleasure, you understand. I love to look at them."

"They don't look like much," Manuel said.

"No, they don't, do they? You'd rather have the money they'd bring?"

Manuel's expression did not change. "You are trying to buy your life with them."

"Well . . ."

"You can't. I told you I am a professional. When I make a contract, I do the work."

"That's a pity." Martinho reached out for his drink, brought the glass to his lips and took a sip. He was perspiring. "This thing I am using for an ashtray, do you know what it is?" he asked as he ground out his cigarette in it. "It is a polychrome eating plate of the Incas, five hundred years old, and worth ten thousand cruzeiros."

The photographer allowed his eyes to flash to the plate on the table. Impossible, such a shabby thing! Ten thousand! Martinho choked on his drink and went into a paroxysm of coughing. Manuel looked back at him quickly. The old man was red in the face. His left hand was pressed against his chest. Finally he stopped coughing.

Manuel said, "I am grateful to you for pointing out these valuable objects. I plan to take several of them with me when I leave."

"To make my shooting seem the work of burglars? Art thieves?"

Andradas shrugged. "Why not?"

Martinho's thin face took on an expression of resignation. He rubbed a hand over his white hair. "In that case," he said wryly, "you'd better steal something that will make your stratagem credible." His lips curved in a half-smile. "I misled you about these objects on the patio. They're worthless."

"I suspected as much."

"Yes, trash. If you really want the authorities to believe I've been murdered by art thieves, you should steal my ear of corn."

"Ear of corn?" Manuel tried to conceal his bewilderment.

"The treasure of my collection. A solid gold, hand-carved ear of corn, the only extant fragment of the famous golden cornfield planted by Inca goldsmiths in Cuzco's *Curi-canchi*, the Golden Enclosure, in the fifteenth century . . ." Martinho looked into the photographer's dull eyes, saw none of his own enthusiasm for Inca culture reflected there. "But never mind. The main thing is, my golden corn is literally priceless. Any collector, museum or dealer would give his soul to possess it."

Manuel said, "I don't doubt you, Senhor. Yet an ear of corn . . ."

Martinho stood up. "I'll show it to you," he said.

Manuel moved the gun muzzle a fraction of an inch. "Where is it?"

"In my study, through the doors there. I have never shown it to a stranger. But since I am to die, I would like to see it once more myself?" His voice rose at the end.

Manuel Andradas came to his feet like a cat. "I will be right behind you." What harm to indulge Martinho's whim? Besides, he was faintly curious about the ear of corn.

He followed Martinho across the patio and through the French doors into the collector's study, a large room lined with glass-fronted cases. On velvet-clad shelves inside the cases reposed the age-darkened objects that comprised Martinho's collection. Manuel gave them only a glance.

Martinho went directly to a waist-high steel safe of massive construction at one end of the room. Kneeling before it, he raised his eyes to the ceiling in momentary thought, then made mysterious movements with his hands before the safe door, above it, and on each side. "I keep the corn here," he said over his shoulder. "This is a truly burglar-proof safe. It operates on a complex system of electrical impulses, activated and interrupted at specific points and intervals. No one can open it except me and my confidential secretary, you know."

The safe door whispered open. Martinho removed from it a cylindrical-shaped object encased in padded velvet. He squatted on his heels and held the velvet bundle up toward Manuel. "Here it is, Senhor Andradas. The ear of corn."

Manuel stepped back a pace. His gun was steady. "Unwrap it yourself," he said.

Martinho did so. He put the velvet case on the floor before the open safe, and laid the golden ear of corn upon it. "There," he said, in a voice so low Manuel could scarcely hear him, "is a finer piece than Pizarro ever plundered!" His eyes rested reverently upon the corn. "Isn't it a marvel?" he asked. He took his packet of cigarettes from his shirt pocket and lit one, inhaling luxuriously, waiting for the photographer's comment.

Manuel said, "Yes, it is handsome. To photograph it and get that exact sheen of ancient gold, the detail of each kernel of corn, would be . . ." He stopped. "Close the safe. Pick up the corn and bring it to the patio."

Martinho nodded. He pushed the door of the safe firmly shut, then picked up the ear of corn and preceded Manuel to the patio, where he once more sank into his chaise. He set the golden relic on the table beside the pamphlet he had been reading.

Manuel resumed his chair. He said, "It is well known that you own this unique ear of corn?"

"Certainly. It is the finest item I possess."

"Very well. I shall take it with me, as you suggest."

"For verisimilitude only, I warn you. You cannot sell it without giving yourself away as my murderer. It is too well known."

"I'll drop it off Sugar Loaf into the sea," Manuel said. "No one else shall own it. I promise you that." The gun came up. "Are you ready?"

"May I have a last cigarette? And a last look at my ear of corn?"

Out of respect for the old man's courage, Manuel said, "Go ahead."

"Can you give me a cigarette?"

"I don't smoke," Manuel answered. "I confine myself to cashew juice." Then, "But where are your own cigarettes? You had some in your shirt pocket."

Martinho said, "I locked those up in my safe just now."

"Why?"

"The packet of cigarettes contained my new Japanese camera," Martinho said. "The Banzai Miniature. It is advertised as no bigger than a cigarette. You know it?" His tone was bland.

"I know it. I prefer the Minox, however." Manuel paused. "It was in your packet of cigarettes?"

"It was in my left hand until I snapped your picture with it," said Martinho. "I choked on my drink to cover the sound of the shutter-click. Remember? Then I slipped the camera into my packet of cigarettes."

"You took a photograph of me?"

"Exactly. A medium close-up, I think you call it. It should show your features and your gun very clearly."

Patiently Manuel said, "Let us not joke, Senhor. You are telling me you had a miniature camera in your hand when I arrived here? That you took my photograph with it? That you then locked the camera in your burglar-proof safe?"

"A very precise summary."

"Of an excellent bluff only. Oh, I take your intention: to make me suppose that when your secretary opens your safe in the course of the police investigation of your murder, they find a camera in the safe instead of this precious ear of corn. They will develop the film in the camera and will thus be presented with a picture of your murderer . . . who can be readily identified by hundreds of people as Manuel Andradas, the photographer. Is that it?"

"Precisely. Your analysis is masterly."

"And your idea ingenious," Manuel said, "to lay a photographic trap for a photographer. I do not, however, believe you."

"Why not?" Martinho was relaxed, smiling a little.

"I have watched you every moment since I arrived. You couldn't have taken my picture."

"You looked at my Mochica vases, my Chimu black-ware and my Inca dinner plate, did you not?"

Manuel, suddenly finding it difficult to breathe, said, "Perhaps, as you say. But that you had a miniature camera in your hand when I came upon you, that is stretching coincidence too far."

Martinho shrugged. "I do not usually lie yet I might, to save my life. Perhaps this will convince you?" He handed Manuel the pamphlet he had been reading when the photographer arrived upon his patio.

A single glance revealed it was an instruction manual on how to use the new Banzai Miniature Camera.

With the air of a man who has just lost a wager larger than he can afford to lose, Manuel put away his gun. "The police, I suppose?" he asked after a painful pause.

"Not necessarily. Another idea occurs to me." The creases in Martinho's face leading from nose to mouth corners momentarily deepened. "My nephew's perfidy in this affair concerns me far more than your own purely mechanical involvement, Senhor Andradas." Then he asked, "How do you get your assignments from the Corporation?"

"A jackal named Rodolfo—"

"No, no. Do they point out your victims to you in the flesh, I mean?"

"I get only a name and address from my contact. Correct identification is entirely up to me."

"In that case, the matter simplifies itself, I think." Senhor Martinho nodded. "The name and address only, eh?"

"That's all."

"Then I suggest that what has happened, Senhor Andradas, is that you have made an unfortunate mistake in identification today. The right name, the right address, yes, but the wrong man. Do you see?"

Manuel shook his head. "I do not."

Martinho's faded blue eyes narrowed. "My nephew," he said softly, "happens to be my brother's son. His name is therefore Martinho, like mine. Luis Martinho, indeed, since he is my namesake."

"Ah." Manuel saw where the trail led now. "But the address, Senhor?"

Martinho waved a hand at a building beyond the lily pond. "That is my carriage house over there. I permit my nephew to live in it, rent-free. The same address, therefore, as mine."

Manuel remained silent.

Martinho said, "One does not arrange the sudden death of rich uncles with impunity, even in these corrupt days. My nephew must be taught a lesson."

After a moment Manuel said without inflection, "A permanent lesson, Senhor?"

"A permanent lesson, by all means. Will you see to it, then?"

"When?"

"Tonight? He will be at home, I know. The servants will not return from their picnic before eleven."

"Where will you be?"

Martinho smiled. "Across the city, dining with friends, from eight until midnight."

"Very well," said Manuel. "*Va bem.*"

"Then that is settled."

"Except," said Manuel, "that the Corporation will withhold my money if I nullify the wrong man, especially their own client, and my reputation with them will no doubt suffer damage."

Martinho shrugged. "We must all pay for our mistakes—my nephew, you, I, everyone."

Manuel sighed. "I can think of no mistake that you have made, Senhor. For me, on the other hand, the day has been a disaster. I lose the money I was to earn for your removal. I am forced to nullify your nephew without recompense. I lose my anonymity as a Corporation employee. I, a professional photographer, am photographically tricked by an amateur. I also lose, I presume, this ear of golden corn."

"You do, indeed." Martinho picked up the corn and fondled it. "However, once you have taught my nephew his lesson, I will give you the incriminating film."

Manuel stared. "Even though retaining it might prevent me from making another attempt on your life?"

"Even so. I'll guarantee to send the film, undeveloped, to your studio tomorrow—if you are successful tonight."

It was evident from the blankness of the photographer's eyes that he failed to comprehend this quixotic gesture. Martinho laughed. "You must understand that I bear you no ill will over this business. Instead, I'm grateful to you for opening my eyes to my own nephew's character. So I shall send you the film."

"*Obrigado,*" murmured Manuel. "Thanks."

Martinho waved a hand at his vases, his black-ware, his ashtray. "When you leave, you may wish to take one of these antiquities with you," he said, "as a slight token of my appreciation." He rose, cradling his golden ear of corn in his hands as tenderly as one might hold a baby bird with a broken wing. "I must say good-day to you now, Senhor Andradas. I tire rather easily these days. Thank you for relieving my tedium, however." He shook his head. "It is ironic that my nephew was so impatient. A few short weeks would have made all the difference to him."

"How so?" asked Manuel.

Martinho flashed him a brilliant smile. "My doctors assured me yesterday that I am incurably ill," he said. "They give me, at the most, two months to live."

The old man walked into the house. Manuel watched him, hitching the strap of his camera case to ease its weight on his shoulder. When Martinho was gone, he thoughtfully dumped into a handy flowerpot the cigarette stubs and powdered ashes from Martinho's polychrome ashtray. Then he slipped it into his pocket.

With a trickster like Senhor Martinho, one never knew what to believe. The ashtray just might be worth something.

# THE HOUSE PARTY

*by Stanley Ellin*

*"He's coming around," said the voice.*

He was falling. His hands were outflung against the stone cold blackness of space, and his body tilted head over heels, heels over head as he fell. If there were only a way of knowing what was below, of bracing himself against the moment of impact, the terror might not have been so great. This way he was no more than a lump of terror flung into a pit, his mind cowering away from the inevitable while his helpless body descended toward it.

"Good," the voice said from faraway, and it sounded to him as if someone were speaking to him quite calmly and cheerfully from the bottom of the pit. "Very good."

He opened his eyes. A glare of light washed in on him suddenly and painfully, and he squinted against it at the figures standing around him, at the faces, partly obscured by a sort of milky haze, looking down at him. He was lying on his back, and from the thrust of the cushions under him he knew he was on the familiar sofa. The milky haze was fading away now, and with it the panic. This was the old house at Nyack, the same living room, the same Utrillo on the wall, the same chandelier glittering over his head. *The same everything,* he thought bitterly, even to the faces around him.

That was Hannah, her eyes bright with tears—she could turn on tears like a faucet—and her hand was gripping his so hard that his fingers were numb under the pressure. Hannah with the overdeveloped maternal instinct, and only a husband to exercise it on . . . That was Abel Roth chewing on a cigar—even at a time like this, that reeking cigar!—and watching him worriedly. Abel with his first successful production in five years, worrying about his investment . . . And that was Ben Thayer and Harriet, the eternal bumpkins . . . And Jake Hall . . . And Tommy McGowan . . . All the old familiar faces, the sickening familiar faces.

But there was a stranger, too. A short stout man with a look of amiable interest on his face, and splendidly bald, with only a tonsure of graying hair to frame his gleaming scalp. He ran his fingers reflectively over his scalp, and nodded at Miles.

"How do you feel now?" he asked.

"I don't know," Miles said. He pulled his hand free of Hannah's, and gingerly tried to raise himself to a sitting position. Halfway there he was transfixed by a shocking pain that was driven like a white-hot needle between his ribs. He heard Hannah gasp, and then the stranger's blunt fingers were probing deep into the pain, turning it to liquid, melting it away.

"See?" the man said. "It's nothing. Nothing at all."

Miles swung his legs around so that he sat erect on the sofa. He took a deep breath, then another. "For a second I thought it was my heart," he said. "The way it hit me—"

"No, no," the man said. "I know what you thought. You can believe me when I say it is of no concern." And then, as if it explained everything, he said, "I am Dr. Maas. Dr. Victor Maas."

"It was a miracle, darling," Hannah said breathlessly. "Dr. Maas was the one who found you outside and brought you in. And he's been an absolute angel. If it weren't for him—"

Miles looked at her, and then looked at all the others standing there and watching him with concern. "Well," he demanded, "what *did* happen? What was it? Heart? Stroke? Amnesia? I'm not a child, for God's sake. You don't have to play games with me."

Abel Roth rolled his cigar from the left-hand corner of his mouth to the right-hand corner. "You can't blame him for feeling that way, can you, doc? After all, the man is out cold for fifteen minutes, he wants to know where he stands. Maybe there's some kind of checkup you could give him, like blood pressure and stuff like that. Maybe we'd all feel better for it."

Miles relished that, and relished even more the thought of what he had in store for Abel Roth. "Maybe we would, Abel," he said. "Maybe we've got a theater sold out sixteen weeks in advance, and the SRO sign up every night. Maybe we've got a real little gold mine to dig so long as I can keep swinging the shovel eight performances a week."

Abel's face turned red. "Ah, now, Miles," he said. "The way you talk—"

"Yes?" Miles said. "What about the way I talk?"

Ben Thayer shook his head slowly and solemnly. "If you'd only take the chip off your shoulder for one minute, Miles," he drawled. "If you'd try to understand—"

"Please!" Dr. Maas said sharply. "Gentlemen, please!" He frowned at them. "There is one thing I must make clear. Actually, I am not a medical physician. My interests, so to speak, lie more in the field of psychiatrics, and while I am, perhaps, qualified to make the examination of Mr. Owen that you suggest, I have no intention of doing so. For Mr. Owen's benefit I will also say that there is no need for me or anyone else to do so. He has my word on that."

"And Dr. Maas, I am sure," said Miles, "is an honorable man." He stood up flexing his knees gingerly, and noting the relief on the faces around him. "If you want to make yourself at home, doctor, go right ahead. There seems to be some kind of buffet over there, and while I can't vouch for the food I can promise that the liquor is very, very good."

The doctor's grin gave him a surprising resemblance to a plump and mischievous boy. "A delightful suggestion," he said, and immediately made his way toward the buffet. Abel followed, and, Miles observed, before the doctor had even reached the buffet, the cigar was perilously close to his ear. Abel spent three hours a week on a psychoanalyst's couch, and at least as much time pouring out lists of frightening and inconsequential symptoms to a sleek and well-fed Park Avenue practitioner. Dr. Maas, Miles thought with a wry sympathy, was in for some heavy going, whether he knew it or not.

The rest of the circle around the sofa broke up and eddied off, until only Hannah was left. She caught his arm in a panicky grip.

"Are you *sure* you're all right?" she demanded. "You know you can tell me if there's anything wrong."

There was something wrong. Every time she caught hold of him like that, tried to draw him close, he had the feeling of a web ensnaring him, closing over him so that he had to fight it savagely.

It had not been like that at the start. She had been so beautiful that he thought in her case it might be different. The rising together, the eating together, the talking together, the endless routine of marriage looked as if it might somehow be bearable as long as it was shared with that loveliness. But then after a year the loveliness had become too familiar, the affection too cloying, the routine too much of a crushing burden.

He had been unconscious for fifteen minutes. He wondered if he had babbled during that time, said something about Lily that could be seized on as a clue. It wasn't of much concern if he had; in fact, it might have been a good way of preparing Hannah for the blow. It was going to be quite a blow, too. He could picture it falling, and it wasn't a pleasant picture.

He shrugged off Hannah's hand. "There's nothing wrong," he said, and then could not resist adding, "unless it's this business of your throwing a house party the one time of the week when I might expect a little peace and quiet."

"I?" Hannah said uncertainly. "What did *I* have to do with it?"

"Everything, as long as you've got that damn yen to be the perfect hostess and everybody's friend."

"They're *your* friends," she said.

"You ought to know by now that they're not my friends either. I thought I made it clear a hundred different ways that I hate them all, individually and collectively. They're nobody's friends. Why is it my obligation to feed them and entertain them the one time of the week I can get rid of them?"

"I don't understand you," Hannah said. She looked as if she were about to break into tears. "I know you bought the house up here so you could get away from everybody, but you were the one—"

The web was closing in again. "All *right*," he said. "All *right!*"

The whole thing didn't matter, anyhow. After he cleared out she could throw a house party every night of the week if she wanted to. She could burn the damn house down if that suited her. It wasn't of any concern to him. He'd had enough of this country-squire life between every Saturday and Monday performance to last him the rest of his life, and, as Lily had once remarked, Central Park had all the trees she wanted to see. Just the realization that he would soon be packed and out of here made any arguments pointless.

He shouldered his way to the buffet past Bob and Liz Gregory who were mooning at each other as if doing it on the radio six mornings a week wasn't enough; past Ben Thayer who was explaining to Jake Hall the trouble he was having with the final act of his new play; past Abel who was saying something to Dr. Maas about psychosomatic factors. The doctor had a tall glass in one hand, and a sandwich in the other. "Interesting," he was saying. "Very interesting."

Miles tried to close his ears to all of them as he poured down two fingers of bourbon. Then he looked at his glass with distaste. The stuff was as flat as warm water, and as unpleasant to the palate. Obviously, one of the local help who took turns cleaning up the house had found the key to the liquor cabinet, and, after nearly emptying the bottle, had done a job on it at the kitchen tap. Damn fool. If you're going to sneak a drink, do it and forget it. But to ruin the rest of the bottle this way . . .

Abel poked him in the ribs. "I was just telling the doctor here," Abel said, "if he gets an evening off I'll fix him up with a house seat for

*Ambuscade.* I was telling him, if he hasn't seen Miles Owen in *Ambuscade* he hasn't seen the performance of all time. How does that sound to you, Miles?"

Miles was lifting another bottle after making sure its seal was unbroken. He looked at Abel, and then set the bottle down with great care.

"As a matter of fact," he said, "I don't know how it sounds to me, Abel. It's something I've wanted to talk to you about, and maybe this is as good a time as any."

"Talk about what?" said Abel cheerfully, but there was a sudden worry in his eyes, a flickering of premonition on his face.

"It's private business, Abel," Miles said, and nodded to Dr. Maas who stood by interestedly. "That is, if the doctor will excuse us."

"Of course, of course," the doctor said quickly. He waved his glass enthusiastically toward Miles. "And you were altogether right about the liquor, Mr. Owen. It is superb."

"Fine," Miles said. "This way, Abel."

He pushed his way through the crowd and crossed the room to the library, Abel trailing after him. When he closed the door of the library and switched on a lamp, the chill dampness of the room seemed to soak right into him, and he shivered. Logs and kindling had been laid on the fireplace, and he held a match to it until the wood crackled and caught. Then he lit a cigarette and drew deeply on it. He looked at the cigarette in surprise. There was a flatness about it, a lack of sensation which made him run his tongue over his lips questioningly. He drew again on the cigarette, and then flung it into the fire. First the liquor, he thought, and now this. Dr. Maas might be a handy man with Freudian complexes, but the first thing Monday an honest-to-God M.D. would be checking up on this little problem. It is discomforting to find out suddenly that you've lost your capacity to taste anything. Ridiculous maybe, but still discomforting.

Abel was standing at the window. "Look at that fog, will you. When I brought *Coxcomb* over to London I thought I saw the real thing there, but this makes it look like nothing. You could cut your way through this with a shovel."

The fog was banked solidly outside the window, stirring in slow waves, sending threads of damp smoke against the glass. Where the threads clung, little beads of water trickled down the pane.

"You get that around here a couple of times a year," Miles said impatiently. "And I didn't come in here to talk about the weather."

Abel turned away from the window and sat down reluctantly in an armchair. "No, I guess you didn't. All right, Miles, what's bothering you?"

"*Ambuscade*," Miles said. "*Ambuscade* is what's bothering me."

Abel nodded wearily. "It figured. It figured. Well, what particular thing? Your billing? We're using the biggest letters they make. Your publicity? All you have to do is name the time and you have your pick of any TV or radio guest spot in town. Remember what I told you after opening night, Miles? You name it, and if I can get it for you, I will."

Miles found himself suddenly enjoying the scene. Ordinarily, he had a genuine horror of such scenes. "Funny," he said. "I didn't hear you say anything about money just now, did I? I mean, in all that pretty speech it couldn't have slipped past me, could it?"

Abel sank down in his chair and sighed like a man deeply stricken. "I thought it would come down to this. Even if I'm paying you twice as much as the biggest star I ever had, I could see it coming, Miles. All right, what's the beef?"

"As a matter of fact," Miles said, "there's no beef."

"No?"

"None at all."

"What are you getting at?" Abel demanded. "What's all this about?"

Miles smiled. "I'm not getting *at* anything, Abel. I'm getting *out*. I'm leaving the show."

Miles had seen Abel meet more than one crisis before; he could have predicted every action before it took place. The face becoming an impassive mask, the hand searching for a match, the thumbnail flicking the match into a light, the elaborate drawing on the cigar stump, the neat flick of the match across the room. Abel fooled him. The match was snapped with sudden violence between the fingers, and then slowly rolled back and forth, back and forth.

"You're a cute boy, Miles," Abel said. "This wouldn't be your idea of a joke, would it?"

"I'm getting out, Abel. Tonight was positively the last appearance. That gives you all day tomorrow to line up another boy for the Monday-night curtain."

"What other boy?"

"Well, you've got Jay Welker on tap, haven't you? He's been understudying me for five months, and hoping I'd break a leg every night of it."

"Jay Welker couldn't carry *Ambuscade* one week, and you know it, Miles. Nobody can carry that show but you, and you know that, too."

Abel leaned forward in his chair and shook his head from side to side unbelievingly. "And knowing that, you don't give a damn. You'd close the biggest thing on Broadway just like that, and to hell with the whole world, is that it?"

Miles felt his heart starting to pound heavily, his throat tightening. "Wait a second, Abel, before you start on the dirty words. One thing has already come through pretty well. In all this, you haven't yet asked me why I'm leaving. For all you know I might have some condition that's going to kill me an hour from now, but that would bother you less than keeping your show running! Have you thought about that side of it?"

"What side of it? I was standing right there when the doctor said you were in good shape. What am I supposed to do now? Get affidavits from the American Medical Association?"

"Then it's your idea that I'm pulling out because of a whim?"

"Let's not kid each other, Miles. You did this to Barrow five years ago, you did it to Goldschmidt after that, you did it to Howie Freeman last year, and I know, because that's how I got my chance to grab you for *Ambuscade*. But all the time I figured these others didn't know how to handle you, they didn't see just how much you meant to a show. Now I tell you they were right all along, and I was a prize sucker. They told me you would be going along fine, and then all of a sudden you would get a bug in your ear, and that was it. Bug in your ear, Miles. That's my low, ignorant way of saying whim, which is what it adds up to."

Abel paused. "The difference between me and them, Miles, is that I didn't take chances, and that's why you signed the first run-of-the-play contract you ever got since you were a nobody. You think you're walking out on that contract? Think again, my friend."

Miles nodded. "All right," he said thickly, "I'm thinking. Do you want to know about what?"

"They're your dice, my friend."

"I'm thinking about eight performances a week, Abel. Eight times a week I say the same lines, walk the same steps, make the same faces. I've done it for five months, which is the biggest break you ever got in your life, but if you had your way I'd be doing it for five years! Right now it's turned into one of those nightmares where you do the same thing over and over without being able to stop, but you wouldn't know about that because *you're* a guy in love with routine! But *I'm* not! After a while it's like being in jail with the key thrown away. What do you tell a man when he can walk out of jail? To stay there and like it?"

"Jail!" Abel cried. "Tell me somebody in this country who wouldn't give his right eye to be in the kind of jail you're in!"

"Listen," Miles said. He leaned forward urgently. "Do you remember before the show opened when we were rehearsing that kitchen scene? Do you remember when we ran through it that night ten times, fifteen times, twenty times? Do you know how I felt then? I felt as if I was plunked right down in hell, and all I would do for eternity was just play that scene over and over again. That's my idea of hell, Abel: a sweet little place where you do the same thing over and over, and they won't even let you go nuts at it, because that would spoil the fun for them. Do you get that? Because if you do, you can see just how I feel about *Ambuscade!*"

"I get it," Abel said. "I also get a certain little run-of-the-play contract tucked away in my safe deposit box. If you think rehearsing a scene a few times is hell you'll find out different when Equity lands on you. They look at this a little different from you."

"Don't try to scare me, Abel."

"Scare you, hell. I'm going to sue you black and blue, and I'm going to make it stick. I'm dead serious about that, Miles."

"Maybe. But isn't it hard to sue a man who's too sick to work?"

Abel nodded with grim understanding. "I figured you'd get around to that angle. I'm the patsy, because to the rest of the world you're sick." His eyes narrowed. "And that explains something else, too. That little business of your little blackout on the front doorstep, with a doctor handy, and twenty witnesses to swear to it. I have to hand it to you, Miles, you don't miss a trick. Only it'll take more than a smart trick and a quack doctor to work things your way."

Miles choked down the rage rising in him. "If you think that was a trick—!"

"What was a trick?" Harriet Thayer's voice said gaily behind him. Harriet and Ben were standing in the doorway, regarding him with a sort of cheerful curiosity. They made an incongruous couple, Ben's gauntness towering high over Harriet's little-girl fragility, and they had an eager, small-town friendliness that grated on Miles's nerves like a fingernail drawn down a slate. "It sounds terribly exciting and interesting," Harriet said. "Don't let us stop you."

Abel pointed at Miles with a shaking forefinger. "This'll stop you all right," he said, "and I'll give it to you in one line. Our friend here is walking out on *Ambuscade*. Maybe *you* can do something to change his mind!"

Ben stared with slow incredulity, and Miles had to marvel, as he had done so many times before, that any man who could write even the few good lines to be found in *Ambuscade* could be so slow on his feet.

"But you can't," Ben said. "Your contract runs as long as the play does."

"Sure," Abel jeered, "but he's a sick man. He falls down and has fits. You saw him, didn't you?"

Harriet nodded dumbly. "Yes, but I never thought—"

"And you were right," Abel said. "He's faking it. He's just fed up with making all that money and having all those nice things printed about him, so he's going to close the show. That's all. Just fold it up tight."

Miles slammed his hand down hard on the arm of Abel's chair. "All right," he said, "now that you've made everything so clear I'll ask you something. Do you think if *Ambuscade* was really a good play that any one person could close it up? Did it ever strike you that no one comes to see your crummy play; they come to see me walk through it? If you gave me *Jabberwocky* to read up there they'd come to see me! Who's to tell a one-man show that he has to keep playing when he doesn't want to!"

"It *is* a good play!" Harriet shouted at him. "It's the best play you ever acted in, and if you don't know that—"

Miles was shouting himself now. "Then get someone else to play it! It might be even better that way!"

Ben held his hands out, palms up, in a pleading gesture. "Now, Miles, you know you've been identified with that part so no one else could take it over," he said. "And try to see it my way, Miles. I've been writing fifteen years, and this is the first real break—"

Miles walked up to him slowly. "You clown," he said softly. "Don't you have any self-respect at all?"

When he walked out of the library he quickly slammed the door behind him to forestall any belated answer to that.

The party had broken into several small knots of people scattered around the room, a deafening rise and fall of voices, a haze of blue smoke which lay like a transparent blanket midway between floor and ceiling. Someone, Miles observed, had overturned a drink on the piano; the puddle ran down in a glittering string along the side of the mahogany and was leaving a damp stain on the Wilton rug beneath. Tommy McGowan and his latest, an overripe blonde—Norma or Alma or something—sat on the floor shuffling through piles of phonograph records, arranging some into a dangerously high stack, and carelessly tossing the others aside. The buffet looked as if a cyclone had hit it; only some empty platters and broken pieces of bread remained amidst the wreckage. From the evidence, Miles thought sardonically, the party would have to be rated a roaring success.

But even the sense of heat and excitement in the room could not erase the chill that he seemed to have brought with him from the library. He rubbed his hands together hard, but this didn't help any, and he felt a small pang of fright at the realization. What if there really were something wrong with him? Lily was not the kind of woman to take gracefully to the role of nursemaid to an invalid. Not that she was wrong about that, as far as he was concerned; if the shoe were on the other foot he couldn't see himself playing any Robert Browning to her Elizabeth Barrett either. Not for Lily or anyone else in the world. In that case it was better not to even bother about a checkup. If there was something, he didn't even want to know about it!

"You are disturbed about something, I think."

It was Dr. Maas. He was leaning casually against the wall, not an arm's length away, his hands thrust into his pockets, his eyes fixed reflectively on Miles. Taking in everything, Miles thought angrily, like some damn scientist looking at a bug under a microscope.

"No," Miles snapped. Then he thought better of it. "Yes," he said. "As a matter of fact, I am."

"Ah?"

"I don't feel right. I know you told me I was fine, but I don't feel fine."

"Physically?"

"Of course, physically! What are you trying to tell me? That it's all in my mind, or some claptrap like that?"

"I am not trying to tell you anything, Mr. Owen. You are telling me."

"All right. Then I want to know what makes you so sure of yourself. No examination, no X-ray, no anything, and you come up with your answer just like that. What's the angle here? Do we somehow get around to the idea that there's nothing wrong physically, but if I put myself in your hands for a nice long expensive psychoanalysis—"

"Stop right there, Mr. Owen," Dr. Maas said coldly. "I will take for granted that your manners are abominable because you are clearly under some pressure. But you should rein in your imagination. I do not practice psychoanalysis, and I never said I did. I am not a healer of any sort. The people I deal with are, unfortunately, always past the point of any cure, and my interest in them, as you can see, must be wholly academic. To be taken for some kind of sharper seeking a victim—"

"Look," Miles said abruptly, "I'm sorry. I'm terribly sorry. I don't know what made me go off like that. Maybe it's this party. I hate these damn parties; they always do things to me. Whatever it is, I'm honestly sorry for taking it out on you."

The doctor nodded gravely. "Of course," he said. "Of course." Then he nervously ran his fingers over his shining scalp. "There is something else I should like to say. I am afraid, however, I would risk offending you."

Miles laughed. "I think you owe it to me."

The doctor hesitated, and then gestured toward the library. "As it happens, Mr. Owen, I heard much of what went on in there. I am not an eavesdropper, but the discussion got a little—well, heated shall we say?—and it was impossible not to overhear it from outside the door here."

"Yes?" Miles said warily.

"The clue to your condition, Mr. Owen, lies in that discussion. To put it bluntly, you are running away. You find what you call routine unbearable, and so you are fleeing from it."

Miles forced himself to smile. "What do you mean, what *I* call routine? Is there another word for it in your language?"

"I think there is. I think I would call it responsibility. And since your life, Mr. Owen—both your profession and your private life—are very much an open book to the world, I will draw on it and say that most of this life has also been spent fleeing from responsibility of one sort or another. Does it strike you as strange, Mr. Owen, that no matter how far and fast you run you always find yourself facing the same problem over and over again?"

Miles clenched and unclenched his fist. "After all," he said, "it's my problem."

"That is where you're wrong, Mr. Owen. When you suddenly leave your role in a play, it affects everyone concerned with that play, and, in turn, everyone concerned with those people. In your relations with women you may move on, but they do not stay motionless either. They move on, too, dangerous to themselves and perhaps to others. Forgive me if I seem sententious, Mr. Owen, but you cannot cast pebbles in the water without sending ripples to the far shore.

"That is why when you say *routine,* it is because you are thinking only of yourself caught in a situation. And when I say *responsibility,* I am thinking of everyone else concerned with it."

"And what's the prescription, Doctor?" Miles demanded. "To stay sunk in a private little hell because if you try to get away you might step on somebody's toes in the process?"

"Get away?" the doctor said in surprise. "Do you really think you can get away?"

"You've got a lot to learn, Doctor. Watch me and see."

"I am watching you, Mr. Owen, and I do see. In a wholly academic way, as I said. It is both fascinating and bewildering to see a man trying to flee, as he calls it, his private little hell, while all the time he is carrying it with him."

Miles's hand was half raised, and then it dropped limp at his side. "In other words, Doctor," he said mockingly, "you're replacing the good old-fashioned sulphur and brimstone hell with something even bigger and better."

The doctor shrugged. "Of course, you don't believe that."

"No," Miles said. "I don't."

"I have a confession to make, Mr. Owen." The doctor smiled, and suddenly he was the plump and mischievous boy again. "I knew you wouldn't. In fact, that is why I felt free to discuss the matter with you."

"In an academic way, of course."

"Of course."

Miles laughed. "You're quite a man, Doctor. I think I'd like to see more of you."

"I am sure you will, Mr. Owen. But right now I believe that someone is trying to attract your notice. There, by the door."

Miles followed the doctor's gesturing finger, and his heart stopped. All he could do was pray that no one else had noticed, as he swiftly crossed the room and blocked off the woman who was entering it from the hallway that led to the front door. He thrust her back against the door, and catching hold of her shoulders he shook her once, sharply and angrily.

"Are you crazy?" he demanded. "Don't you have any more sense than to show up here like this?"

She twisted her shoulders away from his grasp, and carefully brushed at the collar of her coat with her fingertips. The coat had cost Miles a month's pay.

"Aren't you sweet, Miles. Do you invite all your guests in this way?"

Even in the dimness of the hallway she was startling to look at. The sulky lips against the gardenia pallor of the face, the high cheek bones, the slanted eyes darting fire at him. He quailed.

"All right, I'm sorry. I'm sorry. But, my God, Lily, there are two dozen of the biggest mouths on Broadway in that room. If you want the whole world to know about this, why don't you just tip off Winchell!"

She knew when she had him beaten. "I don't like that, darling. I don't like that at all. I mean, to make it sound as obscene and disgusting as all that. It really isn't supposed to be like that, is it?"

"You know damn well it isn't like that, Lily. But use your head, will you? There is such a thing as discretion."

"There's also such a thing as working a word to death, darling. And I don't mind telling you that in the last two months you've filled me up to here with that one."

Miles said angrily, "I've been trying to make it clear that we'd work this thing out in the right way at the right time. I've already told Abel I was leaving the show. I was going to talk to Hannah, too, but this party has fouled everything up. Tomorrow, when I can be alone with her—"

"Ah, but tomorrow may be a long time away, darling. Much longer than you realize."

"What exactly does that mean?"

She fumbled through her purse and drew an envelope from it. She waved the envelope back and forth under his nose with a fine air of triumph.

"It means this, Miles. Two pretty little reservations, outward bound, for tomorrow's sailing. You see, you don't have nearly as much time as you thought, do you, darling?"

"Tomorrow! The agent said he couldn't possibly have anything for us within a month!"

"He didn't count on cancellations. This one came through just two hours ago, which is exactly how long it took me to get here. And if it wasn't for that awful fog on the road I would have been here that much sooner. I have the car outside, Miles. You can pack whatever is handy, and get the rest of what you need on the boat. When I go back I expect you to be with me, Miles, because whether you are or not I'll be sailing tomorrow. You can't really blame me for that, can you, darling? After all, none of us are getting any younger."

He tried to straighten out the aching confusion of his thoughts. He wanted to escape Hannah's web, and now it seemed, somehow or other, there was another waiting to be dropped around him. Running, the doctor had said. Always running and never getting anywhere. There was a great weight of weariness in his arms, his legs, his whole body. Running did that to you.

"Well," Lily said, "make up your mind, darling."

He rubbed his hand over his forehead. "Where's the car?"

"Right across the road."

"All right," Miles said, "you wait in it. Just stay there, and don't blow the horn for me, or anything like that. I'll be down in ten minutes.

Fifteen minutes at the most. Most of my stuff is in town, anyhow. We'll pick it up on the way to the boat."

He opened the door and gently pushed her toward it.

"You'll have to feel your way to the car, Miles. I've never seen anything like what's outside."

"I'll find it," he said. "You just wait there."

He closed the door, then leaned against it fighting the sickness that kept rising to his throat. The loud voices in the next room, the shrieks of idiot laughter that now and then cut through it, the roar of music from the phonograph tuned at its greatest volume—everything seemed conspiring against him, not allowing him to be alone, not allowing him to think things out.

He went up the stairs almost drunkenly, and into the bedroom. He pulled out his valise, and then at random started cramming it full. Shirts, socks, the contents of the jewel case on his dresser. He thrust down hard with all his weight, making room for more.

"What are you doing, Miles?"

He didn't look up. He knew exactly what the expression on her face would be, and he didn't want to meet it then. It would have been too much.

"I'm leaving, Hannah."

"With that woman?" Her voice was a vague, uncomprehending whisper.

He had to look at her then. Her eyes stared at him, enormous against the whiteness of her skin. Her hand fumbled with the ornament at her breast. It was the silver mask of comedy he had picked up for her on Fifth Avenue a week before their marriage.

She said wonderingly, "I saw you with her in the hallway. I wasn't prying or anything like that, Miles, but when I asked the doctor where you were—"

"Stop it!" Miles shouted. "What do you have to apologize for!"

"But she's the one, isn't she?"

"Yes, she's the one."

"And you want to go away with her?"

His hands were on the lid of the valise. He rested his weight on them, head down, eyes closed.

"Yes," he said at last. "That's what it comes to."

"No!" she cried with a sudden fervor. "You don't really want to. You know she's not good for you. You know there's nobody in the whole world as good for you as I am!"

He pressed the lid of the valise down. The lock caught with a tiny click.

"Hannah, it would have been better for you not to have come up just now. I would have written to you, explained it somehow—"

"Explained it? When it would be too late? When you'd know what a mistake you made? Miles, listen to me. Listen to me, Miles. I'm talking to you out of all my love. It would be a terrible mistake."

"I'll have to be the judge of that, Hannah."

He stood up, and she came toward him, her fingers digging into his arms frantically. "Look at me, Miles," she whispered. "Can't you see how I feel? Can't you understand that I'd rather have the both of us dead than to have you go away like this and leave the whole world empty for me!"

It was horrible. It was the web constricting around him so hard that it was taking all his strength to pull himself free. But he did, with a brutal effort, and saw her fall back against the dresser. Then she suddenly wheeled toward it, and when she faced him again he saw the pistol leveled at him. It shone a cold, deadly blue in her hand, and then he realized that her hand was trembling so violently that the gun must be frightening her as much as it did him. The whole grotesquerie of the scene struck him full force, melting away the fear, filling him with a sense of outrage.

"Put that thing down," he said.

"No." He could hardly hear her. "Not unless you tell me that you're not going."

He took a step toward her, and she shrank farther back against the dresser, but the gun remained leveled at him. She was like a child afraid someone was going to trick her out of a toy. He stopped short, and then shrugged with exaggerated indifference.

"You're making a fool of yourself, Hannah. People are paid for acting like this on the stage. They're not supposed to make private shows of themselves."

Her head moved from side to side in a slow, aimless motion. "You still don't believe me, do you, Miles?"

"No," he said. "I don't."

He turned his back on her, half expecting to hear the sudden explosion, feel the impact between his shoulder blades, but there was nothing. He picked up the valise and walked to the door.

"Goodbye, Hannah," he said. He didn't turn his head to look at her.

The weakness in his knees made each step a trial. He stopped at the foot of the staircase to shift the valise from one hand to the other, and saw Dr. Maas standing there, hat in hand, a topcoat thrown over his arm.

"Ah?" said the doctor inquiringly. "So you, too, are leaving the party, Mr. Owen?"

"Party?" Miles said, and then laughed short and sharp. "Leaving the nightmare, if you don't mind, Doctor. I hate to tell this to a guest, but I think you'll understand me when I say that this past hour has been a nightmare that gets thicker and thicker. That's what I'm leaving, Doctor, and you can't blame me for being happy about it."

"No, no," said the Doctor. "I quite understand."

"The car is waiting for me outside. If I can give you a lift anywhere—?"

"Not at all," the doctor said. "I really do not have far to go."

They went to the doorway together and stepped outside. The fog moved in on them, cold and wet, and Miles turned up his jacket collar against it.

"Rotten weather," he said.

"Terrible," the doctor agreed. He glanced at his watch, and then lumbered down the steps to the walk like a walrus disappearing into a snowbank. "I'll be seeing you, Mr. Owen," he called.

Miles watched him go, then lifted the valise and went down the steps himself, burying his nose in his collar against the smothering dampness all around him. He was at the bottom step when he heard the sibilance of the door opening behind him, the faraway whisper of danger in his bones.

He turned, and, as he knew it would be, there was Hannah standing at the open door, still holding the gun. But the gun was gripped tightly in both hands now, and the menace of it was real and overwhelming.

"I tried to make you understand, Miles," she said, like a child saying the words. "I tried to make you understand."

He flung his arms out despairingly.

"No!" he cried wildly. "No!"

And then there was the roar of the explosion in his ears, the gout of flame leaping out toward him, the crushing impact against his chest, and the whole world dissolving. In it, only one thing stood sharp and definable: the figure of the doctor bending over him, the face strangely Satanic in its cruel indifference.

For that single moment Miles understood everything. He had been here before. He had lived this hour a thousand times before, and would live it again and again for all eternity. The curtain was falling now, but when it rose again the stage would be set once more for the house party. Because he was in Hell, and the most terrible thing of all, the terror which submerged all others, was this moment of understanding given him so that he could know this, and could see himself crawling the infinite treadmill of his doom. Then the darkness closed in with a rush, blotting out all understanding–until next time . . .

*"He's coming around," said the voice.*

He was falling. His hands were outflung . . .

# THE PROPERTY OF A LADY

*by Ian Fleming*

IT WAS, EXCEPTIONALLY, a hot day in early June. James Bond put down the dark-gray chalk pencil that was the marker for the dockets routed to the Double-O Section and took off his coat. He didn't bother to hang it over the back of his chair, let alone take the trouble to get up and drape the coat over the hanger Mary Goodnight had suspended, at her own cost (damn women!), behind the Office of Works' green door of his connecting office. He dropped the coat on the floor.

There was no reason to keep the coat immaculate, the creases tidy. There was no sign of any work to be done. All over the world there was quiet. The In and Out signals had, for weeks, been routine. The daily top secret SITREP, even the newspapers, yawned vacuously—in the latter case scratchings at domestic scandals for readership, for bad news, the only news that makes such sheets readable, whether top secret or on sale for pennies.

Bond hated these periods of vacuum. His eyes, his mind, were barely in focus as he turned the pages of a jaw-breaking dissertation by the Scientific Research Station on the Russian use of cyanide gas, propelled by the cheapest bulb-handled children's water pistol, for assassination. The spray, it seemed, directed at the face, took instantaneous effect. It was recommended for victims from 25 years upward, on ascending stairways or inclines. The verdict would then probably be heart failure.

The harsh burr of the red telephone sprayed into the room so suddenly that James Bond, his mind elsewhere, reached his hand automatically toward his left armpit in self-defense. The edges of his mouth turned down as he recognized the reflex. On the second burr he picked up the receiver.

"Sir?"

"Sir."

He got up from his chair and picked up his coat. He put on the coat and at the same time put on his mind. He had been dozing in his bunk. Now he had to go up on the bridge. He walked through into the connecting office and resisted the impulse to ruffle up the inviting nape of Mary Goodnight's golden neck.

He told her "M." and walked out into the close-carpeted corridor and along, between the muted whiz and zing of the Communications Section, of which his Section was a neighbor, to the lift and up to the eighth.

Miss Moneypenny's expression conveyed nothing. It usually conveyed something if she knew something—private excitement, curiosity, or, if Bond was in trouble, encouragement or even anger. Now the smile of welcome showed disinterest. Bond registered that this was going to be some kind of routine job, a bore, and he adjusted his entrance through that fateful door accordingly.

There was a visitor—a stranger. He sat on M.'s left. He only briefly glanced up as Bond came in and took his usual place across the red-leather-topped desk.

M. said, stiffly, "Dr. Fanshawe, I don't think you've met Commander Bond of my Research Department."

Bond was used to these euphemisms.

He got up and held out his hand. Dr. Fanshawe rose, briefly touched Bond's hand, and sat quickly down as if he had touched paws with a Gila monster.

If he looked at Bond, inspected him, and took him in as anything more than an anatomical silhouette, Bond thought that Dr. Fanshawe's eyes must be fitted with a thousandth-of-a-second shutter. So this was obviously some kind of expert—a man whose interests lay in facts, things, theories—not in human beings.

Bond wished that M. had given him some kind of brief, hadn't got this puckish, rather childishly malign desire to surprise—to spring the jack-in-a-box on his staff. But Bond, remembering his own boredom of ten minutes ago, and putting himself in M.'s place, had the intuition to realize that M. himself might have been subject to the same June heat, the same oppressive vacuum in his duties, and, faced by the unexpected relief of an emergency, a small one perhaps, had decided to extract the maximum effect, the maximum drama, out of it to relieve his own tedium.

The stranger was middle-aged, rosy, well-fed, and clothed rather foppishly in the neo-Edwardian fashion—turned-up cuffs to his dark blue, four-buttoned coat, a pearl pin in a heavy silk cravat, spotless wing collar, cuff links formed of what appeared to be antique coins, pince-nez on a thick black ribbon. Bond summed him up as something literary, a critic perhaps, a bachelor—possibly with homosexual tendencies.

M. said, "Dr. Fanshawe is a noted authority on antique jewelry. He is also, though this is confidential, adviser to H.M. Customs and to the C.I.D. on such things. He has in fact been referred to me by our friends at M.I.5. It is in connection with our Miss Freudenstein."

Bond raised his eyebrows. Maria Freudenstein was a secret agent working for the Soviet KGB in the heart of the Secret Service. She was in the Communications Department, but in a watertight compartment of it that had been created especially for her, and her duties were confined to operating the Purple Cipher—a cipher which had also been created especially for her. Six times a day she was responsible for encoding and dispatching lengthy SITREPS in this cipher to the C.I.A. in Washington. These messages were the out-put of Section 100 which was responsible for running double agents. They were an ingenious mixture of true fact, harmless disclosures, and an occasional nugget of the grossest misinformation.

Maria Freudenstein, who had been known to be a Soviet agent when she was taken into the Service, had been allowed to steal the key to the Purple Cipher with the intention that the Russians should have complete access to these SITREPS—be able to intercept and decipher them—and thus, when appropriate, be fed false information. It was a highly secret operation which needed to be handled with extreme delicacy; but it had now been running smoothly for three years and, if Maria Freudenstein also picked up a certain amount of canteen gossip at Headquarters, that was a necessary risk, and she was not attractive enough to form liaisons which could be a security risk.

M. turned to Dr. Fanshawe. "Perhaps, Doctor, you would care to tell Commander Bond what it is all about."

"Certainly, certainly." Dr. Fanshawe looked quickly at Bond and then away again. He addressed his boots. "You see, it's like this, er, Commander. You've heard of a man called Faberge, no doubt. Famous Russian jeweler."

"Made fabulous Easter eggs for the Czar and Czarina before the revolution."

"That was indeed one of his specialties. He made many other exquisite pieces of what we may broadly describe as objects of vertu. Today, in the sale rooms, the best examples fetch truly fabulous prices—£50,000 and more. And recently there entered this country the most amazing specimen of all—the so-called Emerald Sphere, a work of supreme art hitherto known only from a sketch by the great man himself. This treasure arrived by registered post from Paris and it was addressed to this woman of whom you know, Miss Maria Freudenstein."

"Nice little present. Might I ask how you learned of it, Doctor?"

"I am, as your Chief has told you, an adviser to H.M. Customs and Excise in matters concerning antique jewelry and similar works of art. The declared value of the package was £100,000. This was unusual. There are methods of opening such packages clandestinely. The package was opened—under a Home Office Warrant, of course—and I was called in to examine the contents and give a valuation. I immediately recognized the Emerald Sphere from the account and sketch of it given in Mr. Kenneth Snowman's definitive work on Faberge. I said that the declared price might well be on the low side. But what I found of particular interest was the accompanying document which gave, in Russian and French, the provenance of this priceless object."

Dr. Fanshawe gestured toward a photostat of what appeared to be a brief family tree that lay on the desk in front of M. "That is a copy I had made. Briefly, it states that the Sphere was commissioned by Miss Freudenstein's grandfather directly from Faberge in 1917—no doubt as a means of turning some of his rubles into something portable and of great value. On his death in 1918 it passed to his brother and thence, in 1950, to Miss Freudenstein's mother. She, it appears, left Russia as a child and lived in White Russian emigre circles in Paris. She never married, but gave birth to this girl, Maria, illegitimately. It seems that she died last year and that some friend or executor, the paper is not signed, has forwarded the Sphere to its rightful owner, Miss Maria Freudenstein.

"I had no reason to question this girl, although as you can imagine my interest was most lively, until last month Sotheby's announced that they would auction the piece, described as 'the property of a lady,' a week from today. On behalf of the British Museum and, er, other interested parties, I then made discreet inquiries and met the lady, who, with perfect composure, confirmed the rather unlikely story contained in the provenance. It was then that I learned that she worked for the Ministry of Defense and it crossed my rather suspicious mind that it was, to say the least of it, odd that a junior clerk, engaged presumably on sensitive duties, should suddenly receive a gift to the value of £100,000 or more from abroad. I spoke to a senior official in M.I.5 with whom I have some contact through my work for H.M. Customs and I was in due course referred to this, er, department." Dr. Fanshawe spread his hands and gave Bond a brief glance. "And that, Commander, is all I have to tell you."

M. broke in, "Thank you, Doctor. Just one or two final questions and I won't detain you any further. You have examined this emerald ball thing and you pronounce it genuine?"

Dr. Fanshawe ceased gazing at his boots. He looked up and spoke to a point somewhere above M.'s left shoulder. "Certainly. So does Mr. Snowman of Wartski's, the greatest Faberge experts and dealers in the world. It is undoubtedly the missing masterpiece of which hitherto Carl Faberge's sketch was the only record."

"What about the provenance? What do the experts say about that?"

"It stands up adequately. The greatest Faberge pieces were nearly always privately commissioned. Miss Freudenstein says that her grandfather was a vastly rich man before the revolution—a porcelain manufacturer. Ninety-nine percent of all Faberge's output has found its way abroad. There are only a few pieces left in the Kremlin—described simply as 'pre-revolutionary examples of Russian jewelry.' The official Soviet view has always been that they are merely capitalist baubles. Officially they despise them as they officially despise their superb collection of French Impressionists."

"So the Soviet still retain some examples of the work of this man Faberge. Is it possible that this emerald affair could have lain secreted somewhere in the Kremlin through all these years?"

"Certainly. The Kremlin treasure is vast. No one knows what they keep hidden. They have only recently put on display what they have wanted to put on display."

M. drew on his pipe. His eyes through the smoke were bland, scarcely interested. "So that, in theory, there is no reason why this emerald ball should not have been unearthed from the Kremlin, furnished with a faked history to establish ownership, and transferred abroad as a reward to some friend of Russia for services rendered?"

"None at all. It would be an ingenious method of greatly rewarding the beneficiary without the danger of paying large sums into his, or her, bank account."

"But the final monetary reward would of course depend on the amount realized by the sale of the object—the auction price for instance?"

"Exactly."

"And what do you expect this object to fetch at Sotheby's?"

"Impossible to say. Wartski's will certainly bid very high. But of course they wouldn't be prepared to tell anyone just how high—either on their own account for stock, so to speak, or acting on behalf of a customer. Much would depend on how high they are forced up by an underbidder. Anyway, not less than £100,000 I'd say."

"Hm." M.'s mouth turned down at the corners. "Expensive hunk of jewelry."

Dr. Fanshawe was aghast at this barefaced revelation of M.'s philistinism. He actually looked M. straight in the face. "My dear sir," he expostulated, "do you consider the stolen Goya, sold at Sotheby's for £140,000, that went to the National Gallery, just an expensive hunk, as you would put it, of canvas and paint?"

M. said placatingly, "Forgive me, Dr. Fanshawe. I expressed myself clumsily. I have never had the leisure to interest myself in works of art nor, on a naval officer's pay, the money to acquire any. I was just registering my dismay at the runaway prices being fetched at auction these days."

"You are entitled to your views, sir," said Dr. Fanshawe stuffily.

Bond thought it was time to rescue M. He also wanted to get Dr. Fanshawe out of the room so that they could get down to the professional aspects of this odd business. He got to his feet. He said to M., "Well, sir, I don't think there is anything else I need to know. No doubt this will turn out to be perfectly straight-forward (like hell it would!) and just a matter of one of your staff turning out to be a very lucky woman. But it's very kind of Dr. Fanshawe to have gone to so much trouble." He turned to Dr. Fanshawe. "Would you care to have a staff car take you where you're going?"

"No, thank you, thank you very much. It will be pleasant to walk across the park."

Hands were shaken, goodbyes said, and Bond showed the doctor out. Bond came back into the room. M. had taken a bulky file, stamped with the top-secret red star, out of a drawer and was already immersed in it. Bond took his seat again and waited. The room was silent save for the riffling of paper. This also stopped as M. extracted a foolscap sheet of blue cardboard used for Confidential Staff Records and carefully read through the forest of close type on both sides.

Finally he slipped it back in the file and looked up. "Yes," he said and the blue eyes were bright with interest. "It fits all right. The girl was born in Paris in 1935. Mother very active in the Resistance during the war. Helped run the Tulip Escape Route and got away with it. After the war the girl went to the Sorbonne and then got a job in the Embassy, in the Naval Attache's office, as an interpreter. You know the rest. She was compromised—some unattractive sexual business—by some of her mother's old Resistance friends who by then were working for the NKVD, and from then on she has been working under Control. She applied, no doubt on instruction, for British citizenship.

"Her clearance from the Embassy and her mother's Resistance record helped her to get that by 1959, and she was then recommended to us by the FO. But it was there that she made her big mistake. She asked for a year's leave before coming to us and was next reported by the Hutchinson network in the Leningrad espionage school. There she presumably received the usual training and we had to decide what to do about her. Section 100 thought up the Purple Cipher operation and you know the rest. She's been working for three years inside headquarters for the KGB and now she's getting her reward—this emerald ball thing worth £100,000.

"And that's interesting on two counts. First, it means that the KGB is totally hooked on the Purple Cipher or they wouldn't be making this fantastic payment. That's good news. It means that we can hot up the material we're passing over—put across some Grade 3 deception material and perhaps even move up to Grade 2. Secondly, it explains something we've never been able to understand—that this girl hasn't hitherto received a single payment for her services. We were worried by that. She had an account at Glyn, Mills that only registered her monthly paycheck of around £50. And she's consistently lived within it. Now she's getting her payoff in one large lump sum via this bauble we've been learning about. All very satisfactory."

M. reached for the ashtray made out of a twelve-inch shell base and rapped out his pipe with the air of a man who has done a good afternoon's work.

Bond shifted in his chair. He badly needed a cigarette, but he wouldn't have dreamed of lighting one. He wanted one to help him focus his thoughts. He felt that there were some ragged edges to this problem—one particularly. He said mildly, "Have we ever caught up with her local Control, sir? How does she get her instructions?"

"Doesn't need to," said M. impatiently, busying himself with his pipe. "Once she'd got hold of the Purple Cipher all she needed to do was hold down her job. Damn it man, she's pouring the stuff into their lap six times a day. What sort of instructions would they need to give her? I doubt if the KGB men in London even know of her existence—perhaps the Resident Director does, but as you know we don't even know who he is. Give my eyes to find out."

Bond suddenly had a flash of intuition. It was as if a camera had started grinding in his skull, grinding out a length of clear film. He said quietly, "It might be that this business at Sotheby's could show him to us—show us who he is."

"What the devil are you talking about, 007? Explain yourself."

"Well, sir," Bond's voice was calm with certainty, "you remember what this Dr. Fanshawe said about an underbidder—someone to make these Wartski merchants go to their very top price. If the Russians don't seem to know or care very much about Faberge, as Dr. Fanshawe says, they may have no very clear idea what this thing's really worth. The KGB wouldn't be likely to know about such things anyway. They may imagine it's only worth its breakup value—say ten or twenty thousand pounds for the emerald. That sort of sum would make more sense than the small fortune the girl's going to get if Dr. Fanshawe's right.

"Well, if the Resident Director is the only man who knows about this girl he will be the only man who knows she's been paid. So he'll be the underbidder. He'll be sent to Sotheby's and told to push the sale through the roof. I'm certain of it. So we'll be able to identify him and we'll have enough on him to have him sent home. He just won't know what's hit him. Nor will the KGB. If I can go to the sale and bowl him out and we've got the place covered with cameras, and the auction records, we can get the FO to declare him *persona non grata* inside a week. And Resident Directors don't grow on trees. It may be months before the KGB can appoint a replacement."

M. said thoughtfully, "Perhaps you've got something there." He swiveled his chair round and gazed out of the big window toward the jagged skyline of London. Finally he said, over his shoulder, "All right, 007. Go and see the Chief of Staff and set the machinery up. I'll square things with Five. It's their territory, but it's our bird. There won't be any trouble. But don't go and get carried away and bid for this bit of rubbish yourself. I haven't got the money to spare."

Bond said, "No, sir." He got to his feet and went quickly out of the room. He thought he had been very clever and he wanted to see if he had. He didn't want M. to change his mind.

Wartski has a modest, ultramodern frontage at 138 Regent Street. The window, with a restrained show of modern and antique jewelry, gave no hint that these were the greatest Faberge dealers in the world. The interior—gray carpet, walls paneled in sycamore, a few unpretentious vitrines—held none of the excitement of Cartier's, Boucheron, or Van Cleef, but the group of famed Royal Warrants from Queen Mary, the Queen Mother, the Queen, King Paul of Greece, and the unlikely King Frederick IX of Denmark, suggested that this was no ordinary jeweler.

James Bond asked for Mr. Kenneth Snowman. A good-looking, very well-dressed man of about 40 rose from a group of men sitting with their heads together at the back of the room and came forward.

Bond said quietly, "I'm from the C.I.D. Can we have a talk? Perhaps you'd like to check my credentials first. My name's James Bond. But you'll have to go direct to Sir Ronald Vallance or his P.A. I'm not directly on the strength at Scotland Yard. Sort of liaison job."

The intelligent, observant eyes didn't appear even to look him over. The man smiled. "Come on downstairs. Just having a talk with some American friends—sort of correspondents really. From 'Old Russia' on Fifth Avenue."

"I know the place," said Bond. "Full of rich-looking icons and so on. Not far from the Pierre."

"That's right." Mr. Snowman seemed even more reassured. He led the way down a narrow, thickly carpeted stairway into a large and glittering showroom which was obviously the real treasurehouse of the shop. Gold and diamonds and cut stones winked from lit cases round the walls.

"Have a seat. Cigarette?"

Bond took one of his own. "It's about this Faberge that's coming up at Sotheby's tomorrow—this Emerald Sphere."

"Ah, yes." Mr. Snowman's clear brow furrowed anxiously. "No trouble about it, I hope?"

"Not from your point of view. But we're very interested in the actual sale. We know about the owner, Miss Freudenstein. We think there may be an attempt to raise the bidding artificially. We're interested in the underbidder—assuming, that is, that your firm will be leading the field, so to speak."

"Well, er, yes," said Mr. Snowman with rather careful candor. "We're certainly going to go after it. But it'll sell for a huge price. Between you and me, we believe the V and A are going to bid, and probably the Metropolitan. But is it some crook you're after? If so you needn't worry. This is out of their class."

Bond said, "No. We're not looking for a crook." He wondered how far to go with this man. Because people are very careful with the secrets of their own business doesn't mean that they'll be careful with the secrets of yours. Bond picked up a wood and ivory plaque that lay on the table. It said:

> It is naught, it is naught, saith the buyer.
> But when he is gone his way, he boasteth.
>
> Proverbs XX, 14

Bond was amused. He said so. "You can read the whole history of the bazaar, of the dealer and the customer, behind the quotation," he said. He looked Mr. Snowman straight in the eyes. "I need that sort of nose, that sort of intuition in this case. Will you give me a hand?"

"Certainly. If you'll tell me how I can help." He waved a hand. "If it's secrets you're worried about, please don't worry. Jewelers are used to them. Scotland Yard will probably give my firm a clean bill in that respect. Heaven knows we've had enough to do with them over the years."

"And if I told you that I'm from the Ministry of Defense?"

"Same thing," said Mr. Snowman. "You can naturally rely absolutely on my discretion."

Bond made up his mind. "All right. Well, all this comes under the Official Secrets Act, of course. We suspect that the underbidder, presumably to you, will be a Soviet Agent. My job is to establish his identity. Can't tell you any more, I'm afraid. And you don't actually need to know any more. All I want is to go with you to Sotheby's tomorrow night and for you to help me spot the man. No medals, I'm afraid, but we'd be extremely grateful."

Mr. Kenneth Snowman's eyes glinted with enthusiasm. "Of course. Delighted to help in any way. But," he looked doubtful, "you know it's not necessarily going to be all that easy. Peter Wilson, the head of Sotheby's, who'll be taking the sale, would be the only person who could tell us for sure—that is, if the bidder wants to stay secret. There are dozens of ways of bidding without making any movement at all. But if the bidder fixes his method, his code so to speak, with Peter Wilson before the sale, Peter wouldn't think of letting anyone in on the code. It would give the bidder's game away to reveal his limit. And that's a close secret, as you can imagine, in the rooms. And a thousand times not if you come with me.

"I shall probably be setting the pace. I already know how far I'm going to go—for a client, by the way—but it would make my job vastly easier if I could tell how far the underbidder's going to go. As it is, what you've told me has been a great help. I shall warn my man to put his sights even higher. If this chap of yours has got a strong nerve he may push me very hard indeed. And there will be others in the field, of course. It sounds as if this is going to be quite a night. They're putting it on television and asking all the millionaires and dukes and duchesses for the sort of gala performance Sotheby's do rather well. Wonderful publicity, of course. By jove, if they knew there was cloak-and-dagger stuff mixed up with the sale, there'd be a riot! Now then, is there anything else to go into? Just spot this man and that's all?"

"That's all. How much do you think this thing will go for?"

Mr. Snowman tapped his teeth with a gold pencil. "Well, now, you see that's where I have to keep quiet. I know how high I'm going to go, but that's my client's secret." He paused and looked thoughtful. "Let's say that if it goes for less than £100,000 we'll be surprised."

"I see," said Bond. "Now then, how do I get into the sale?"

Mr. Snowman produced an elegant alligator-skin notecase and extracted two engraved bits of pasteboard. He handed one over. "That's my wife's. I'll get her one somewhere else in the rooms. B.5—well placed in the center front. I'm B.6."

Bond took the ticket. It said:

Sotheby & Co.
Sale of
A Casket of Magnificent Jewels
and
A Unique Object of Vertu by
Carl Faberge
The Property of a Lady
Admit one to the Main Sale Room
Tuesday, 20 June, at 9.30 p.m.
precisely
ENTRANCE IN ST. GEORGE STREET

"It's not the old Georgian entrance in Bond Street," commented Mr. Snowman. "They have an awning and red carpet out from their back door now that Bond Street's one way. Now," he got up from his chair, "would you care to see some Faberge? We've got some pieces here my father bought from the Kremlin around 1927. It'll give you some idea what all the fuss is about, though of course the Emerald Sphere's incomparably finer than anything I can show you by Faberge apart from the Imperial Easter Eggs."

Later, dazzled by the diamonds, the multicolored gold, the silken sheen of translucent enamels, James Bond walked up and out of the Aladdin's Cave under Regent Street and went off to spend the rest of the day in drab offices around Whitehall planning drearily minute arrangements for the identification and photographing of a man in a crowded room who did not yet possess a face or an identity but who was certainly the top Soviet spy in London.

Through the next day Bond's excitement mounted. He found an excuse to go into the Communications Section and wander into the little room where Miss Maria Freudenstein and two assistants were working the cipher machines that handled the Purple Cipher dispatches. He picked up the *en clair* file—he had freedom of access to most material at headquarters—and ran his eye down the carefully edited paragraphs that, in half an hour or so, would be spiked, unread, by some junior

C.I.A. clerk in Washington and, in Moscow, be handed, with reverence, to a top-ranking officer of the KGB. He joked with the two junior girls, but Maria Freudenstein only looked up from her machine to give him a polite smile and Bond's skin crawled minutely at this proximity to treachery and at the black and deadly secret locked up beneath the frilly white blouse.

She was an unattractive girl with a pale, rather pimply skin, black hair, and a vaguely unwashed appearance. Such a girl would be unloved, make few friends, have chips on her shoulder—more particularly in view of her illegitimacy—and a grouse against society. Perhaps her only pleasure in life was the triumphant secret she harbored in that flattish bosom—the knowledge that she was cleverer than all those around her, that she was, every day, hitting back against the world—the world that despised, or just ignored her, because of her plainness—with all her might. One day they'd be sorry! It was a common neurotic pattern—the revenge of the ugly duckling on society.

Bond wandered off down the corridor to his own office. By tonight that girl would have made a fortune, been paid her thirty pieces of silver a thousandfold. Perhaps the money would change her character, bring her happiness. She would be able to afford the best beauty specialists, the best clothes, a pretty flat. But M. had said he was now going to hot up the Purple Cipher Operation, try a more dangerous level of deception. This would be dicey work. One false step, one incautious lie, an ascertainable falsehood in a message, and the KGB would smell a rat. Once more, and they would know they were being hoaxed and probably had been ignominiously hoaxed for three years. Such a shameful revelation would bring quick revenge. It would be assumed that Maria Freudenstein had been acting as a double agent, working for the British as well as the Russians. She would inevitably and quickly be liquidated—perhaps with the cyanide pistol that Bond had been reading about only the day before.

James Bond, looking out of the window across the trees in Regent's Park, shrugged. Thank God it was none of his business. The girl's fate wasn't in his hands. She was caught in the grimy machine of espionage and she would be lucky if she lived to spend a tenth of the fortune she was going to gain in a few hours at the auction.

There was a line of cars and taxis blocking George Street behind Sotheby's. Bond paid off his taxi and joined the crowd filtering under the awning and up the steps. He was handed a catalogue by the uniformed Commissionaire who inspected his ticket, and went up the broad stairs with the fashionable, excited crowd and along a gallery and into the main auction room that was already thronged. He found his seat next to Mr. Snowman, who was writing figures on a pad on his knee, and looked round him.

The lofty room was perhaps as large as a tennis court. It had the look and the smell of age, and the two large chandeliers, to fit in with the period, blazed warmly in contrast to the strip lighting along the vaulted ceiling whose glass roof was partly obscured by a blind, still halfdrawn against the sun that would be blazing down on the afternoon's sale. Miscellaneous pictures and tapestries hung on the olive-green walls and batteries of television and other cameras (among them the M.I.5 cameraman with a press pass from *The Sunday Times*) were clustered with their handlers on a platform built out from the middle of a giant tapestried hunting scene.

There were perhaps a hundred dealers and spectators sitting attentively on small gilt chairs. All eyes were focused on the slim good-looking auctioneer talking quietly from the raised wooden pulpit. He was dressed in an immaculate dinner jacket with a red carnation in the buttonhole. He spoke unemphatically and without gestures.

"Fifteen thousand pounds. And sixteen"—a pause. A glance at someone in the front row. "Against you, sir." The flick of a catalogue being raised. "Seventeen thousand pounds I am bid. Eighteen. Nineteen. I am bid twenty thousand pounds." And so the quiet voice went, calmly, unhurriedly on while down among the audience the equally impassive bidders signaled their responses to the litany.

"What is he selling?" asked Bond, opening his catalogue.

"Lot 40," said Mr. Snowman. "That diamond riviere the porter's holding on the black velvet tray. It'll probably go for about twenty-five. An Italian is bidding against a couple of Frenchmen. Otherwise they'd have got it for twenty. I only went to fifteen. Liked to have got it. Wonderful stones. But there it is."

Sure enough, the price stuck at twenty-five thousand and the hammer, held by its head and not by its handle, came down with soft authority. "Yours, sir," said Mr. Peter Wilson and a salesclerk hurried down the aisle to confirm the identity of the bidder.

"I'm disappointed," said Bond.

Mr. Snowman looked up from his catalogue. "Why is that?"

"I've never been to an auction before and I always thought the auctioneer banged his gavel three times and said going, going, gone, so as to give the bidders a last chance."

Mr. Snowman laughed. "You might still find that operating in the

Shires or in Ireland, but it hasn't been the fashion at London salerooms since I've been attending them."

"Pity. It adds to the drama."

"You'll get plenty of that in a minute. This is the last lot before the curtain goes up on the Emerald Sphere."

One of the porters had reverently uncoiled a glittering mass of rubies and diamonds on his black velvet tray. Bond looked at the catalogue. It said "Lot 41" which the luscious prose described as:

> A PAIR OF FINE AND IMPORTANT RUBY AND DIAMOND BRACELETS, the front of each in the form of an elliptical cluster composed of one larger and two smaller rubies within a border of cushion-shaped diamonds, the sides and back formed of simpler clusters alternating with diamond openwork scroll motifs springing from single-stone ruby centers millegriffe-set in gold, running between chains of rubies and diamonds linked alternately, the clasp also in the form of an elliptical cluster.
>
> According to family tradition, this lot was formerly the property of Mrs. Fitzherbert (1756-1837) whose marriage to the Prince of Wales, afterwards Geo. IV, was definitely established when in 1905 a sealed packet deposited at Coutts Bank in 1833 and opened by Royal permission disclosed the marriage certificate and other conclusive proofs.
>
> These bracelets were probably given by Mrs. Fitzherbert to her niece, who was described by the Duke of Orleans as "the prettiest girl in England."

While the bidding progressed, Bond slipped out of his seat and went down the aisle to the back of the room where the overflow audience spread out into the New Gallery and the Entrance Hall to watch the sale on closed-circuit television. He casually inspected the crowd, seeking any face he could recognize from the 200 members of the Soviet Embassy staff whose photographs, clandestinely obtained, he had been studying during the past day. But in an audience that defied classification—a mixture of dealers, amateur collectors, and what could be broadly classified as rich pleasure-seekers—there was not a face that he could recognize except from the gossip columns.

One or two sallow faces might have been Russian, but equally they might have belonged to half a dozen European races. There was a scattering of dark glasses, but dark glasses are no longer a disguise. Bond went back to his seat. Presumably the man would have to divulge himself when the bidding began.

"Fourteen thousand I am bid. And fifteen. Fifteen thousand." The hammer came down. "Yours, sir."

There was a hum of excitement and a fluttering of catalogues. Mr. Snowman wiped his forehead with a white silk handkerchief. He turned to Bond. "Now I'm afraid you are more or less on your own. I've got to pay attention to the bidding and anyway for some unknown reason it's considered bad form to look over one's shoulder to see who's bidding against you—if you're in the trade, that's to say—so I'll only be able to spot him if he's somewhere up front here, and I'm afraid that's unlikely. Pretty much all dealers, but you can stare around as much as you like. What you've got to do is to watch Peter Wilson's eyes and then try and see who he's looking at, or who's looking at him.

"If you can spot the man, which may be quite difficult, note any movement he makes, even the very smallest. Whatever the man does—scratching his head, pulling at the lobe of his ear, or whatever, will be a code he's arranged with Peter Wilson. I'm afraid he won't do anything obvious like raising his catalogue. Do you get me? And don't forget that he may make absolutely no movement at all until right at the end when he's pushed me as far as he thinks I'll go, then he'll want to sign off. Mark you," Mr. Snowman smiled, "when we get to the last lap I'll put plenty of heat on him and try and make him show his hand. That's assuming, of course, that we are the only two bidders left in." He looked enigmatic. "And I think you can take it that we shall be."

From the man's certainty James Bond felt pretty sure that Mr. Snowman had been given instructions to get the Emerald Sphere at any cost.

A sudden hush fell as a tall pedestal draped in black velvet was brought in with ceremony and positioned in front of the auctioneer's rostrum. Then a handsome oval case of what looked like white velvet was placed on top of the pedestal and, with reverence, an elderly porter in gray uniform with wine-red sleeves, collar, and back belt, unlocked it and lifted out Lot 42, placed it on the black velvet, and removed the case.

The cricket ball of polished emerald on its exquisite base glowed with a supernatural green fire and the jewels on its surface and on the opalescent meridian winked their various colors.

There was a gasp of admiration from the audience and even the clerks and experts behind the rostrum and sitting at the tall counting-house desk beside the auctioneer, accustomed to the Crown Jewels of Europe parading before their eyes, leaned forward to get a better look.

James Bond turned to his catalogue. There it was, in heavy type and in prose as stickily luscious as a butterscotch sundae:

THE TERRESTRIAL GLOBE
DESIGNED IN 1917 BY CARL FABERGE FOR A RUSSIAN GENTLEMAN AND NOW THE PROPERTY OF
HIS GRANDDAUGHTER

42 A VERY IMPORTANT FABERGE TERRESTRIAL GLOBE. A sphere carved from an extraordinarily large piece of Siberian emerald matrix weighing approximately one thousand three hundred carats, and of a superb color and vivid translucence, represents a terrestrial globe supported upon an elaborate *rocaille* scroll mount finely chased in *quatre-couleur* gold and set with a profusion of rose-diamonds and small emeralds of intense color, to form a table clock.

Around this mount six gold *putti* disport themselves among cloud forms which are naturalistically rendered in carved rock-crystal finished matt and veined with fine lines of tiny rose-diamonds. The globe itself, the surface of which is meticulously engraved with a map of the world with the principal cities indicated by brilliant diamonds embedded within gold collets, rotates mechanically on an axis controlled by a small clock movement, by *G. Moser,* signed, which is concealed in the base, and is girdled by a fixed gold belt enameled opalescent oyster along a reserved path in *champleve* technique over a moire *guillochage* with painted Roman numerals in pale sepia enamel serving as the dial of the clock, and a single triangular pigeon-blood Burma ruby of about five carats set into the surface of the orb, pointing the hour. Height: *7½in. Workmaster, Henrik Wigstrom.* In the original double-opening white velvet, satin-lined, oviform case with the gold key fitted in the base.

The theme of this magnificent sphere is one that had inspired Faberge some fifteen years earlier, as evidenced in the miniature terrestrial globe which forms part of the Royal Collection at Sandringham. (See plate 280 in *The Art of Carl Faberge,* by A. Kenneth Snowman.)

After a brief and searching glance round the room Mr. Wilson banged his hammer softly. "Lot 42—an object of vertu by Carl Faberge." A pause. "Twenty thousand pounds I am bid."

Mr. Snowman whispered to Bond, "That means he's probably got a bid of at least fifty. This is simply to get things moving."

Catalogues fluttered. "And thirty, forty, fifty thousand pounds I am bid. And sixty, seventy, and eighty thousand pounds. And ninety." A pause and then: "One hundred thousand pounds I am bid."

There was a rattle of applause round the room. The cameras had swiveled to a youngish man, one of three on a raised platform to the left of the auctioneer who were speaking softly into telephones. Mr. Snowman commented, "That's one of Sotheby's young men. He'll be on an open line to America. I should think that's the Metropolitan bidding, but it might be anybody. Now it's time for me to get to work." Mr. Snowman flicked up his rolled catalogue.

"And ten," said the auctioneer. The man spoke into his telephone and nodded. "And twenty."

Again a flick from Mr. Snowman.

"And thirty."

The man on the telephone seemed to be speaking rather more words than before into his mouthpiece—perhaps giving his estimate of how much higher the price was likely to go. He gave a slight shake of his head in the direction of the auctioneer and Peter Wilson looked away from him and round the room.

"One hundred and thirty thousand pounds I am bid," he repeated quietly.

Mr. Snowman said softly to Bond, "Now you'd better watch out. America seems to have signed off. It's time for your man to start pushing me."

James Bond slid out of his place and went and stood among a group of reporters in a corner to the left of the rostrum. Peter Wilson's eyes were directed toward the far right-hand corner of the room. Bond could detect no movement, but the auctioneer announced, "And forty thousand pounds." He looked down at Mr. Snowman. After a long pause Mr. Snowman raised five fingers. Bond guessed that this was part of his process of putting the heat on. He was showing reluctance, hinting that he was near the end of his tether.

"One hundred and forty-five thousand." Again the piercing glance toward the back of the room. Again no movement. But again some signal had been exchanged. "One hundred and fifty thousand pounds."

There was a buzz of comment and some desultory clapping. This time Mr. Snowman's reaction was even slower and the auctioneer twice repeated the last bid. Finally he looked directly at Mr. Snowman. "Against you, sir." At last Mr. Snowman raised five fingers.

James Bond was beginning to sweat. He had got absolutely nowhere and the bidding must surely be coming to an end. The auctioneer repeated the bid.

And now there was the tiniest movement. At the back of the room a chunky-looking man in a dark suit reached up and unobtrusively took off his dark glasses. It was a smooth nondescript face—the sort of face that might belong to a bank manager, a member of Lloyd's, or a doctor. This must have been the prearranged code with the auctioneer. So long as the man wore his dark glasses he would raise in tens of thousands. When he took them off, he had quit.

Bond shot a quick glance toward the bank of cameramen. Yes, the M.I.5 photographer was on his toes. He had also seen the movement. He lifted his camera deliberately and there was the quick glare of a flash. Bond got back to his seat and whispered to Snowman, "Got him. Be in touch with you tomorrow. Thanks a lot." Mr. Snowman only nodded. His eyes remained glued on the auctioneer.

Bond slipped out of his place and walked swiftly down the aisle as the auctioneer said for the third time, "One hundred and fifty-five thousand pounds I am bid," and then softly brought down his hammer. "Yours, sir."

Bond got to the back of the room before the audience had risen, applauding, to its feet. His quarry was hemmed in among the gilt chairs. He had now put on his dark glasses again and Bond put on a pair of his own. He contrived to slip into the crowd and get behind the man as the chattering crowd streamed down the stairs. The hair grew low on the back of the man's rather squat neck and the lobes of his ears were pinched in close to his head. He had a slight hump, perhaps only a bone deformation, high up on his back.

Bond suddenly remembered. This was Piotr Malinowski, with the official title on the Embassy staff of "Agricultural Attache." So!

Outside, the man began walking swiftly toward Conduit Street. James Bond got unhurriedly into a taxi with its engine running and its flag down. He said to the driver, "That's him. Take it easy."

"Yes, sir," said the M.I.5 driver, pulling away from the curb.

The man picked up a taxi in Bond Street. The tail in the mixed evening traffic was easy. Bond's satisfaction mounted as the Russian's taxi turned up north of the Park and along Bayswater. It was just a question whether he would turn down the private entrance into Kensington Palace Gardens, where the first mansion on the left is the massive building of the Soviet Embassy. If he did, that would clinch matters. The two patrolling policemen, the usual Embassy guards, had been specially picked that night. It was their job just to confirm that the occupant of the leading taxi actually entered the Soviet Embassy.

Then, with the Secret Service evidence and the evidence of Bond and of the M.I.5 cameraman, there would be enough for the Foreign Office to declare Comrade Piotr Malinowski *persona non grata* on the grounds of espionage activity and send him packing. In the grim chess game that is secret service work the Russians would have lost a queen. It would have been a very satisfactory visit to the auction rooms.

The leading taxi *did* turn in through the big iron gates.

Bond smiled with grim satisfaction. He leaned forward. "Thanks, driver. Headquarters please."

# IN COLD BLOOD

*by Truman Capote*

## 1

### *The Last To See Them Alive*

THE VILLAGE OF Holcomb stands on the high wheat plains of western Kansas, a lonesome area that other Kansans call "out there." Some seventy miles east of the Colorado border, the countryside, with its hard blue skies and desert-clear air, has an atmosphere that is rather more Far West than Middle West. The local accent is barbed with a prairie twang, a ranch-hand nasalness, and the men, many of them, wear narrow frontier trousers, Stetsons, and high-heeled boots with pointed toes. The land is flat, and the views are awesomely extensive; horses, herds of cattle, a white cluster of grain elevators rising as gracefully as Greek temples are visible long before a traveler reaches them.

Holcomb, too, can be seen from great distances. Not that there is much to see—simply an aimless congregation of buildings divided in the center by the main-line tracks of the Santa Fe Railroad, a haphazard hamlet bounded on the south by a brown stretch of the Arkansas (pronounced "Ar-kan-sas") River, on the north by a highway, Route 50, and on the east and west by prairie lands and wheat fields. After rain, or when snowfalls thaw, the streets, unnamed, unshaded, unpaved, turn from the thickest dust into the direst mud. At one end of the town stands a stark old stucco structure, the roof of which supports an electric sign—DANCE—but the dancing has ceased and the advertisement has been dark for several years. Nearby is another building with an irrelevant sign, this one in flaking gold on a dirty window—HOLCOMB BANK. The bank closed in 1933, and its former counting rooms have been converted into apartments. It is one of the town's two "apartment houses," the second being a ramshackle mansion known, because a good part of the local school's faculty lives there, as the Teacherage. But the majority of Holcomb's homes are one-story frame affairs, with front porches.

Down by the depot, the postmistress, a gaunt woman who wears a rawhide jacket and denims and cowboy boots, presides over a falling-apart post office. The depot itself, with its peeling sulphur-colored paint, is equally melancholy; the Chief, the Super-Chief, the El Capitan go by every day, but these celebrated expresses never pause there. No passenger trains do—only an occasional freight. Up on the highway, there are two filling stations, one of which doubles as a meagerly supplied grocery store, while the other does extra duty as a café—Hartman's Café, where Mrs. Hartman, the proprietress, dispenses sandwiches, coffee, soft drinks, and 3.2 beer. (Holcomb, like all the rest of Kansas, is "dry.")

And that, really, is all. Unless you include, as one must, the Holcomb School, a good-looking establishment, which reveals a circumstance that the appearance of the community otherwise camouflages: that the parents who send their children to this modern and ably staffed "consolidated" school—the grades go from kindergarten through senior high, and a fleet of buses transport the students, of which there are usually around three hundred and sixty, from as far as sixteen miles away—are, in general, a prosperous people. Farm ranchers, most of them, they are outdoor folk of very varied stock—German, Irish, Norwegian, Mexican, Japanese. They raise cattle and sheep, grow wheat, milo, grass seed, and sugar beets. Farming is always a chancy business, but in western Kansas its practitioners consider themselves "born gamblers," for they must contend with an extremely shallow precipitation (the annual average is eighteen inches) and anguishing irrigation problems. However, the last seven years have been years of droughtless beneficence. The farm ranchers in Finney County, of which Holcomb is a part, have done well; money has been made not from farming alone but also from the exploitation of plentiful natural-gas resources, and its acquisition is reflected in the new school, the comfortable interiors of the farmhouses, the steep and swollen grain elevators.

Until one morning in mid-November of 1959, few Americans—in fact, few Kansans—had ever heard of Holcomb. Like the waters of the river, like the motorists on the highway, and like the yellow trains streaking down the Santa Fe tracks, drama, in the shape of exceptional happenings, had never stopped there. The inhabitants of the village, numbering two hundred and seventy, were satisfied that this should be so, quite content to exist inside ordinary life—to work, to hunt, to watch television, to attend school socials, choir practice, meetings of the 4-H Club. But then, in the earliest hours of that morning in November, a Sunday morning, certain foreign sounds impinged on the normal nightly Holcomb noises—on the keening hysteria of coyotes, the dry scrape of scuttling tumbleweed, the racing, receding wail of locomotive whistles. At the time not a soul in sleeping Holcomb heard them—four shotgun blasts that, all told, ended six human lives. But afterward the townspeople, theretofore sufficiently unfearful of each other to seldom trouble to lock their doors, found fantasy re-creating them over and again—those somber explosions that stimulated fires of mistrust in the glare of which many old neighbors viewed each other strangely, and as strangers.

The master of River Valley Farm, Herbert William Clutter, was forty-eight years old, and as a result of a recent medical examination for an insurance policy, knew himself to be in first-rate condition. Though he wore rimless glasses and was of but average height, standing just under five feet ten, Mr. Clutter cut a man's-man figure. His shoulders were broad, his hair had held its dark color, his square-jawed, confident face retained a healthy-hued youthfulness, and his teeth, unstained and strong enough to shatter walnuts, were still intact. He weighed a hundred and fifty-four—the same as he had the day he graduated from Kansas State University, where he had majored in agriculture. He was not as rich as the richest man in Holcomb—Mr. Taylor Jones, a neighboring rancher. He was, however, the community's most widely known citizen, prominent both there and in Garden City, the close-by county seat, where he had headed the building committee for the newly completed First Methodist Church, an eight-hundred-thousand-dollar edifice. He was currently chairman of the Kansas Conference of Farm Organizations, and his name was everywhere respectfully recognized among Midwestern agriculturists, as it was in certain Washington offices, where he had been a member of the Federal Farm Credit Board during the Eisenhower administration.

Always certain of what he wanted from the world, Mr. Clutter had in large measure obtained it. On his left hand, on what remained of a finger once mangled by a piece of farm machinery, he wore a plain gold band, which was the symbol, a quarter-century old, of his marriage to the person he had wished to marry—the sister of a college classmate, a timid, pious, delicate girl named Bonnie Fox, who was three years younger than he. She had given him four children—a trio of daughters, then a son. The eldest daughter, Eveanna, married and the mother of a boy ten months old, lived in northern Illinois but visited Holcomb frequently. Indeed, she and her family were expected within the fortnight, for her parents planned a sizable Thanksgiving reunion of the Clutter clan (which had its beginnings in Germany; the first immigrant Clutter—or Klotter, as the name was then spelled—arrived here in 1880); fifty-odd kinfolk had been asked, several of whom would be traveling from places as far away as Palatka, Florida. Nor did Beverly, the child next in age to Eveanna, any longer reside at River Valley Farm; she was in Kansas City, Kansas, studying to be a nurse. Beverly was engaged to a young biology student, of whom her father very much approved; invitations to the wedding, scheduled for Christmas Week, were already printed. Which left, still living at home, the boy, Kenyon, who at fifteen was taller than Mr. Clutter, and one sister, a year older—the town darling, Nancy.

In regard to his family, Mr. Clutter had just one serious cause for disquiet—his wife's health. She was "nervous," she suffered "little spells"—such were the sheltering expressions used by those close to her. Not that the truth concerning "poor Bonnie's afflictions" was in the least a secret; everyone knew she had been an on-and-off psychiatric patient the last half-dozen years. Yet even upon this shadowed terrain sunlight had very lately sparkled. The past Wednesday, returning from two weeks of treatment at the Wesley Medical Center in Wichita, her customary place of retirement, Mrs. Clutter had brought scarcely credible tidings to tell her husband; with joy she informed him that the source of her misery, so medical opinion had at last decreed, was not in her head but in her spine—it was *physical*, a matter of misplaced vertebrae. Of course, she must undergo an operation, and afterward—well, she would be her "old self" again. Was it possible—the tension, the withdrawals, the pillow-muted sobbing behind locked doors, all due to an out-of-order backbone? If so, then Mr. Clutter could, when addressing his Thanksgiving table, recite a blessing of unmarred gratitude.

Ordinarily, Mr. Clutter's mornings began at six-thirty; clanging milk pails and the whispery chatter of the boys who brought them, two sons of a hired man named Vic Irsik, usually roused him. But today he lingered, let Vic Irsik's sons come and leave, for the previous evening, a Friday the thirteenth, had been a tiring one, though in part exhilarating. Bonnie had resurrected her "old self"; as if serving up a preview of the normality, the regained vigor, soon to be, she had rouged her lips, fussed with her hair, and, wearing a new dress, accompanied him to the Holcomb School, where they applauded a student production of *Tom Sawyer*, in which Nancy played Becky Thatcher. He had enjoyed it, seeing Bonnie out in public, nervous but nonetheless smiling, talking to people, and they both had been proud of Nancy; she had done so well, remembering all her lines, and looking, as he had said to her in the course of backstage congratulations, "Just beautiful, honey—a real Southern belle." Whereupon Nancy had behaved like one; curtsying in her hoop-skirted costume, she had asked if she might drive into Garden City. The State Theatre was having a *special,* eleven-thirty, Friday-the-thirteenth "Spook Show," and *all* her friends were going. In other circumstances Mr. Clutter would have refused. His laws were laws, and one of them was: Nancy—and Kenyon, too—must be home by ten on week nights, by twelve on Saturdays. But weakened by the genial events of the evening, he had consented. And Nancy had not returned home until almost two. He had heard her come in, and had called to her, for though he was not a man ever really to raise his voice, he had some plain things to say to her, statements that concerned less the lateness of the hour than the youngster who had driven her home—a school basketball hero, Bobby Rupp.

Mr. Clutter liked Bobby, and considered him, for a boy his age, which was seventeen, most dependable and gentlemanly; however, in the three years she had been permitted "dates," Nancy, popular and pretty as she was, had never gone out with anyone else, and while Mr. Clutter understood that it was the present national adolescent custom to form couples, to "go steady" and wear "engagement rings," he disapproved, particularly since he had not long ago, by accident, surprised his daughter and the Rupp boy kissing. He had then suggested that Nancy discontinue "seeing so much of Bobby," advising her that a slow retreat now would hurt less than an abrupt severance later—for, as he reminded her, it was a parting that must eventually take place. The Rupp family were Roman Catholics, the Clutters, Methodist—a fact that should in itself be sufficient to terminate whatever fancies she and this boy might have of some day marrying. Nancy had been reasonable—at any rate, she had not argued—and now, before saying good night, Mr. Clutter secured from her a promise to begin a gradual breaking off with Bobby.

Still, the incident had lamentably put off his retiring time, which was ordinarily eleven o'clock. As a consequence, it was well after seven when he awakened on Saturday, November 14, 1959. His wife always slept as late as possible. However, while Mr. Clutter was shaving, showering, and outfitting himself in whipcord trousers, a cattleman's leather jacket, and soft stirrup boots, he had no fear of disturbing her; they did not share the same bedroom. For several years he had slept alone in the master bedroom, on the ground floor of the house—a two-story, fourteen-room frame-and-brick structure. Though

Mrs. Clutter stored her clothes in the closets of this room, and kept her few cosmetics and her myriad medicines in the blue-tile-and-glass-brick bathroom adjoining it, she had taken for serious occupancy Eveanna's former bedroom, which, like Nancy's and Kenyon's rooms, was on the second floor.

The house—for the most part designed by Mr. Clutter, who thereby proved himself a sensible and sedate, if not notably decorative, architect—had been built in 1948 for forty thousand dollars. (The resale value was now sixty thousand dollars.) Situated at the end of a long, lanelike driveway shaded by rows of Chinese elms, the handsome white house, standing on an ample lawn of groomed Bermuda grass, impressed Holcomb; it was a place people pointed out. As for the interior, there were spongy displays of liver-colored carpet intermittently abolishing the glare of varnished, resounding floors; an immense modernistic living-room couch covered in nubby fabric interwoven with glittery strands of silver metal; a breakfast alcove featuring a banquette upholstered in blue-and-white plastic. This sort of furnishing was what Mr. and Mrs. Clutter liked, as did the majority of their acquaintances, whose homes, by and large, were similarly furnished.

Other than a housekeeper who came in on weekdays, the Clutters employed no household help, so since his wife's illness and the departure of the elder daughters, Mr. Clutter had of necessity learned to cook; either he or Nancy, but principally Nancy, prepared the family meals. Mr. Clutter enjoyed the chore, and was excellent at it—no woman in Kansas baked a better loaf of salt-rising bread, and his celebrated coconut cookies were the first item to go at charity cake sales—but he was not a hearty eater; unlike his fellow-ranchers, he even preferred Spartan breakfasts. That morning an apple and a glass of milk were enough for him; because he touched neither coffee or tea, he was accustomed to begin the day on a cold stomach. The truth was he opposed all stimulants, however gentle. He did not smoke, and of course he did not drink; indeed, he had never tasted spirits, and was inclined to avoid people who had—a circumstance that did not shrink his social circle as much as might be supposed, for the center of that circle was supplied by the members of Garden City's First Methodist Church, a congregation totaling seventeen hundred, most of whom were as abstemious as Mr. Clutter could desire. While he was careful to avoid making a nuisance of his views, to adopt outside his realm an externally uncensoring manner, he enforced them within his family and among the employees at River Valley Farm. "Are you a drinking man?" was the first question he asked a job applicant, and even though the fellow gave a negative answer, he still must sign a work contract containing a clause that declared the agreement instantly void if the employee should be discovered "harboring alcohol." A friend—an old pioneer rancher, Mr. Lynn Russell—had once told him, "You've got no mercy. I swear, Herb, if you caught a hired man drinking, out he'd go. And you wouldn't care if his family was starving." It was perhaps the only criticism ever made of Mr. Clutter as an employer. Otherwise, he was known for his equanimity, his charitableness, and the fact that he paid good wages and distributed frequent bonuses; the men who worked for him—and there were sometimes as many as eighteen—had small reason to complain.

After drinking the glass of milk and putting on a fleece-lined cap, Mr. Clutter carried his apple with him when he went outdoors to examine the morning. It was ideal apple-eating weather; the whitest sunlight descended from the purest sky, and an easterly wind rustled, without ripping loose, the last of the leaves on the Chinese elms. Autumns reward western Kansas for the evils that the remaining seasons impose: winter's rough Colorado winds and hip-high, sheep-slaughtering snows; the slushes and the strange land fogs of spring; and summer, when even crows seek the puny shade, and the tawny infinitude of wheatstalks bristle, blaze. At last, after September, another weather arrives, an Indian summer that occasionally endures until Christmas. As Mr. Clutter contemplated this superior specimen of the season, he was joined by a part-collie mongrel, and together they ambled off toward the livestock corral, which was adjacent to one of three barns on the premises.

One of these barns was a mammoth Quonset hut; it brimmed with grain—Westland sorghum—and one of them housed a dark, pungent hill of milo grain worth considerable money—a hundred thousand dollars. That figure alone represented an almost four-thousand-percent advance over Mr. Clutter's entire income in 1934—the year he married Bonnie Fox and moved with her from their home town of Rozel, Kansas, to Garden City, where he had found work as an assistant to the Finney County agricultural agent. Typically, it took him just seven months to be promoted; that is, to install himself in the head man's job. The years during which he held the post—1935 to 1939—encompassed the dustiest, the down-and-outest the region had known since white men settled there, and young Herb Clutter, having, as he did, a brain expertly racing with the newest in streamlined agricultural practices, was quite qualified to serve as middleman between the government and the despondent farm ranchers; these men could well use the optimism and the educated instruction of a likable young fellow who seemed to know his business. All the same, he was not doing what he wanted to do; the son of a farmer, he had from the beginning aimed at operating a property of his own. Facing up to it, he resigned as county agent after four years and, on land leased with borrowed money, created, in embryo, River Valley Farm (a name justified by the Arkansas River's meandering presence but not, certainly, by any evidence of valley). It was an endeavor that several Finney County conservatives watched with show-us amusement—old-timers who had been fond of baiting the youthful county agent on the subject of his university notions: "That's fine, Herb. You always know what's best to do on the other fellow's land. Plant this. Terrace that. But you might say a sight different if the place was your own." They were mistaken; the upstart's experiments succeeded—partly because, in the beginning years, he labored eighteen hours a day. Setbacks occurred—twice the wheat crop failed, and one winter he lost several hundred head of sheep in a blizzard; but after a decade Mr. Clutter's domain consisted of over eight hundred acres owned outright and three thousand more worked on a rental basis—and that, as his colleagues admitted, was "a pretty good spread." Wheat, milo seed, certified grass seed—these were the crops the farm's prosperity depended upon. Animals were also important—sheep, and especially cattle. A herd of several hundred Hereford bore the Clutter brand, though one would not have suspected it from the scant contents of the livestock corral, which was reserved for ailing steers, a few milking cows, Nancy's cats, and Babe, the family favorite—an old fat workhorse who never objected to lumbering about with three and four children astride her broad back.

Mr. Clutter now fed Babe the core of his apple, calling good morning to a man raking debris inside the corral—Alfred Stoecklein, the sole resident employee. The Stoeckleins and their three children lived in a house not a hundred yards from the main house; except for them, the Clutters had no neighbors within half a mile. A long-faced man with long brown teeth, Stoecklein asked, "Have you some particular work in mind today? Cause we got a sick-un. The baby. Me and Missis been up and down with her most the night. I been thinking to carry her to doctor." And Mr. Clutter, expressing sympathy, said by all means to take the morning off, and if there was any way he or his wife could help, please let them know. Then, with the dog running ahead of him, he moved southward toward the fields, lion-colored now, luminously golden with after-harvest stubble.

The river lay in this direction; near its bank stood a grove of fruit trees—peach, pear, cherry, and apple. Fifty years ago, according to native memory, it would have taken a lumberjack ten minutes to axe all the trees in western Kansas. Even today, only cottonwoods and

Chinese elms—perennials with a cactuslike indifference to thirst—are commonly planted. However, as Mr. Clutter often remarked, "an inch more of rain and this country would be paradise—Eden on earth." The little collection of fruit-bearers growing by the river was his attempt to contrive, rain or no, a patch of the paradise, the green, apple-scented Eden, he envisioned. His wife once said, "My husband cares more for those trees than he does for his children," and everyone in Holcomb recalled the day a small disabled plane crashed into the peach trees: "Herb was fit to be tied! Why, the propeller hadn't stopped turning before he'd slapped a lawsuit on the pilot."

Passing through the orchard, Mr. Clutter proceeded along beside the river, which was shallow here and strewn with islands—midstream beaches of soft sand, to which, on Sundays gone by, hot-weather Sabbaths when Bonnie had still "felt up to things," picnic baskets had been carted, family afternoons whiled away waiting for a twitch at the end of a fishline. Mr. Clutter seldom encountered trespassers on his property; a mile and a half from the highway, and arrived at by obscure roads, it was not a place that strangers came upon by chance. Now, suddenly a whole party of them appeared, and Teddy, the dog, rushed forward roaring out a challenge. But it was odd about Teddy. Though he was a good sentry, alert, ever ready to raise Cain, his valor had one flaw: let him glimpse a gun, as he did now—for the intruders were armed—and his head dropped, his tail turned in. No one understood why, for no one knew his history, other than that he was a vagabond Kenyon had adopted years ago. The visitors proved to be five pheasant hunters from Oklahoma. The pheasant season in Kansas, a famed November event, lures hordes of sportsmen from adjoining states, and during the past week plaid-hatted regiments had paraded across the autumnal expanses, flushing and felling with rounds of birdshot great coppery flights of the grain-fattened birds. By custom, the hunters, if they are not invited guests, are supposed to pay the landowner a fee for letting them pursue their quarry on his premises, but when the Oklahomans offered to hire hunting rights, Mr. Clutter was amused. "I'm not as poor as I look. Go ahead, get all you can," he said. Then, touching the brim of his cap, he headed for home and the day's work, unaware that it would be his last.

Like Mr. Clutter, the young man breakfasting in a café called the Little Jewel never drank coffee. He preferred root beer. Three aspirin, cold root beer, and a chain of Pall Mall cigarettes—that was his notion of a proper "chow-down." Sipping and smoking, he studied a map spread on the counter before him—a Phillips 66 map of Mexico—but it was difficult to concentrate, for he was expecting a friend, and the friend was late. He looked out a window at the silent small-town street, a street he had never seen until yesterday. Still no sign of Dick. But he was sure to show up; after all, the purpose of their meeting was Dick's idea, his "score." And when it was settled—Mexico. The map was ragged, so thumbed that it had grown as supple as a piece of chamois. Around the corner, in his room at the hotel where he was staying, were hundreds more like it—worn maps of every state in the Union, every Canadian province, every South American country—for the young man was an incessant conceiver of voyages, not a few of which he had actually taken: to Alaska, to Hawaii and Japan, to Hong Kong. Now, thanks to a letter, an invitation to a "score," here he was with all his worldly belongings: one cardboard suitcase, a guitar, and two big boxes of books and maps and songs, poems and old letters, weighing a quarter of a ton. (Dick's face when he saw those *boxes!* "Christ, Perry. You carry that junk *every*where?" And Perry had said, "*What* junk? One of them books cost me thirty bucks.") Here he was in little Olathe, Kansas. Kind of funny, if you thought about it; imagine being back in Kansas, when only four months ago he had sworn, first to the State Parole Board, then to himself, that he would never set foot within its boundaries again. Well, it wasn't for long.

Ink-circled names populated the map. COZUMEL, an island off the coast of Yucatán, where, so he had read in a men's magazine, you could "shed your clothes, put on a relaxed grin, live like a Rajah, and have all the women you want for $50-a-month!" From the same article he had memorized other appealing statements: "Cozumel is a hold-out against social, economic, and political pressure. No official pushes any private person around on *this* island," and "Every year flights of parrots come over from the mainland to lay their eggs." ACAPULCO connoted deep-sea fishing, casinos, anxious rich women; and SIERRA MADRE meant gold, meant *Treasure of the Sierra Madre,* a movie he had seen eight times. (It was Bogart's best picture, but the old guy who played the prospector, the one who reminded Perry of his father, was terrific, too. Walter Huston. Yes, and what he had told Dick was true: He *did* know the ins and outs of hunting gold, having been taught them by his father, who was a professional prospector. So why shouldn't they, the two of them, buy a pair of pack horses and try their luck in the Sierra Madre? But Dick, the practical Dick, had said, "Whoa, honey, whoa. I seen that show. Ends up everybody nuts. On account of fever and bloodsuckers, mean conditions all around. Then, when they got the gold—remember, a big wind came along and blew it all away?") Perry folded the map. He paid for the root beer and stood up. Sitting, he had seemed a more than normal-sized man, a powerful man, with the shoulders, the arms, the thick, crouching torso of a weight lifter—weight lifting was, in fact, his hobby. But some sections of him were not in proportion to others. His tiny feet, encased in short black boots with steel buckles, would have neatly fitted into a delicate lady's dancing slippers; when he stood up, he was no taller than a twelve-year-old child, and suddenly looked, strutting on stunted legs that seemed grotesquely inadequate to the grown-up bulk they supported, not like a well-built truck driver but like a retired jockey, overblown and muscle-bound.

Outside the drugstore, Perry stationed himself in the sun. It was a quarter to nine, and Dick was a half hour late; however, if Dick had not hammered home the every-minute importance of the next twenty-four hours, he would not have noticed it. Time rarely weighed upon him, for he had many methods of passing it—among them, mirror gazing. Dick had once observed, "Every time you see a mirror you go into a trance, like. Like you was looking at some gorgeous piece of butt. I mean, my God, don't you ever get tired?" Far from it; his own face enthralled him. Each angle of it induced a different impression. It was a changeling's face, and mirror-guided experiments had taught him how to ring the changes, how to look now ominous, now impish, now soulful; a tilt of the head, a twist of the lips, and the corrupt gypsy became the gentle romantic. His mother had been a full-blooded Cherokee; it was from her that he had inherited his coloring—the iodine skin, the dark, moist eyes, the black hair, which he kept brilliantined and was plentiful enough to provide him with sideburns and a slippery spray of bangs. His mother's donation was apparent; that of his father, a freckled, ginger-haired Irishman, was less so. It was as though the Indian blood had routed every trace of the Celtic strain. Still, pink lips and a perky nose confirmed its presence, as did a quality of roguish animation, of uppity Irish egotism, which often activated the Cherokee mask and took control completely when he played the guitar and sang. Singing, and the thought of doing so in front of an audience, was another mesmeric way of whittling hours. He always used the same mental scenery—a night club in Las Vegas, which happened to be his home town. It was an elegant room filled with celebrities excitedly focused on the sensational new star rendering his famous, backed-by-violins version of "I'll Be Seeing You" and encoring with his latest self-composed ballad:

> Every April flights of parrots
> Fly overhead, red and green,

Green and tangerine.
I see them fly, I hear them high,
Singing parrots bringing April spring . . .

(Dick, on first hearing this song, had commented, "Parrots don't sing. Talk, maybe. Holler. But they sure as hell don't sing." Of course, Dick was very literal-minded, *very*—he had no understanding of music, poetry—and yet when you got right down to it, Dick's literalness, his pragmatic approach to every subject, was the primary reason Perry had been attracted to him, for it made Dick seem, compared to himself, so authentically tough, invulnerable, "totally masculine.")

Nevertheless, pleasant as this Las Vegas reverie was, it paled beside another of his visions. Since childhood, for more than half his thirty-one years, he had been sending off for literature ("FORTUNES IN DIVING! Train at Home in Your Spare Time. Make Big Money Fast in Skin and Lung Diving. FREE BOOKLETS . . ."), answering advertisements ("SUNKEN TREASURE! Fifty Genuine Maps! Amazing Offer . . .") that stoked a longing to realize an adventure his imagination swiftly and over and over enabled him to experience: the dream of drifting downward through strange waters, of plunging toward a green sea-dusk, sliding past the scaly, savage-eyed protectors of a ship's hulk that loomed ahead, a Spanish galleon—a drowned cargo of diamonds and pearls, heaping caskets of gold.

A car horn honked. At last—Dick.

"Good grief, Kenyon! I *hear* you."

As usual, the devil was in Kenyon. His shouts kept coming up the stairs: "Nancy! Telephone!"

Barefoot, pajama-clad, Nancy scampered down the stairs. There were two telephones in the house—one in the room her father used as an office, another in the kitchen. She picked up the kitchen extension: "Hello? Oh, yes, good morning, Mrs. Katz."

And Mrs. Clarence Katz, the wife of a farmer who lived on the highway, said, "I *told* your daddy not to wake you up. I said Nancy must be *tired* after all that wonderful acting she did last night. You were lovely, dear. Those white ribbons in your hair! And that part when you thought Tom Sawyer was dead—you had real tears in your eyes. Good as anything on TV. But your daddy said it was time you got up; well, it *is* going on for nine. Now, what I wanted, dear—my little girl, my little Jolene, she's just dying to bake a cherry pie, and seeing how you're a champion cherry-pie maker, always winning prizes, I wondered could I bring her over there this morning and you show her?"

Normally, Nancy would willingly have taught Jolene to prepare an entire turkey dinner; she felt it her duty to be available when younger girls came to her wanting help with their cooking, their sewing, or their music lessons—or, as often happened, to confide. Where she found the time, and still managed to "practically run that big house" and be a straight-A student, the president of her class, a leader in the 4-H program and the Young Methodists League, a skilled rider, an excellent musician (piano, clarinet), an annual winner at the county fair (pastry, preserves, needlework, flower arrangement)—how a girl not yet seventeen could haul such a wagonload, and do so without "brag," with, rather, merely a radiant jauntiness, was an enigma the community pondered, and solved by saying, "She's got *character*. Gets it from her old man." Certainly her strongest trait, the talent that gave support to all the others, derived from her father: a fine-honed sense of organization. Each moment was assigned; she knew precisely, at any hour, what she would be doing, how long it would require. And that was the trouble with today: she had overscheduled it. She had committed herself to helping another neighbor's child, Roxie Lee Smith, with a trumpet solo that Roxie Lee planned to play at a school concert; had promised to run three complicated errands for her mother; and had arranged to attend a 4-H meeting in Garden City with her father. And then there was lunch to make and, after lunch, work to be done on the bridesmaids' dresses for Beverly's wedding, which she had designed and was sewing herself. As matters stood, there was no room for Jolene's cherry-pie lesson. Unless something could be canceled.

"Mrs. Katz? Will you hold the line a moment, please?"

She walked the length of the house to her father's office. The office, which had an outside entrance for ordinary visitors, was separated from the parlor by a sliding door; though Mr. Clutter occasionally shared the office with Gerald Van Vleet, a young man who assisted him with the management of the farm, it was fundamentally his retreat—an orderly sanctuary, paneled in walnut veneer, where, surrounded by weather barometers, rain charts, a pair of binoculars, he sat like a captain in his cabin, a navigator piloting River Valley's sometimes risky passage through the seasons.

"Never mind," he said, responding to Nancy's problem. "Skip 4-H. I'll take Kenyon instead."

And so, lifting the office phone, Nancy told Mrs. Katz yes, fine, bring Jolene right on over. But she hung up with a frown. "It's so peculiar," she said as she looked around the room and saw in it her father helping Kenyon add a column of figures, and, at his desk by the window, Mr. Van Vleet, who had a kind of brooding, rugged good looks that led her to call him Heathcliff behind his back. "But I keep smelling cigarette smoke."

"On your breath?" inquired Kenyon.

"No, funny one. Yours."

That quieted him, for Kenyon, as he knew she knew, did once in a while sneak a puff—but, then, so did Nancy.

Mr. Clutter clapped his hands. "That's all. This is an office."

Now, upstairs, she changed into faded Levis and a green sweater, and fastened round her wrist her third-most-valued belonging, a gold watch; her closest cat friend, Evinrude, ranked above it, and surmounting even Evinrude was Bobby's signet ring, the cumbersome proof of her "going-steady" status, which she wore (*when* she wore it; the least flare-up and off it came) on a thumb, for even with the use of adhesive tape its man-size girth could not be made to fit a more suitable finger. Nancy was a pretty girl, lean and boyishly agile, and the prettiest things about her were her short-bobbed, shining chestnut hair (brushed a hundred strokes each morning, the same number at night) and her soap-polished complexion, still faintly freckled and rose-brown from last summer's sun. But it was her eyes, wide apart, darkly translucent, like ale held to the light, that made her immediately likable, that at once announced her lack of suspicion, her considered and yet so easily triggered kindliness.

"Nancy!" Kenyon called. "Susan on the phone."

Susan Kidwell, her confidante. Again she answered in the kitchen.

"Tell," said Susan, who invariably launched a telephone session with this command. "And, to begin, tell why you were flirting with Jerry Roth." Like Bobby, Jerry Roth was a school basketball star.

"Last night? Good grief, I wasn't flirting. You mean because we were holding hands? He just came backstage during the show. And I was so nervous. So he held my hand. To give me courage."

"Very sweet. Then what?"

"Bobby took me to the spook movie. And *we* held hands."

"Was it scary? Not Bobby. The movie."

"He didn't think so; he just laughed. But you know me. Boo!—and I fall off the seat."

"What are you eating?"

"Nothing."

"I know—your fingernails," said Susan, guessing correctly. Much as Nancy tried, she could not break the habit of nibbling her nails, and, whenever she was troubled, chewing them right to the quick. "Tell. Something wrong?"

"No."

"Nancy. *C'est moi . . .*" Susan was studying French.

"Well—Daddy. He's been in an awful mood the last three weeks. Awful. At least, around me. And when I got home last night he started *that* again."

*"That"* needed no amplification; it was a subject that the two friends had discussed completely, and upon which they agreed. Susan, summarizing the problem from Nancy's viewpoint, had once said, "You love Bobby now, and you need him. But deep down even Bobby knows there isn't any future in it. Later on, when we go off to Manhattan, everything will seem a new world." Kansas State University is in Manhattan, and the two girls planned to enroll there as art students, and to room together. "Everything will change, whether you want it to or not. But you can't change it now, living here in Holcomb, seeing Bobby every day, sitting in the same classes—and there's no *reason* to. Because you and Bobby are a very happy thing. And it will be something happy to think back about—if you're left alone. Can't you make your father understand that?" No, she could not. "Because," as she explained it to Susan, "whenever I start to *say* something, he looks at me as though I must not love him. Or as though I loved him *less*. And suddenly I'm tongue-tied; I just want to be his daughter and do as he wishes." To this Susan had no reply; it embodied emotions, a relationship, beyond her experience. She lived alone with her mother, who taught music at the Holcomb School, and she did not remember her own father very clearly, for years ago, in their native California, Mr. Kidwell had one day left home and not come back.

"And, anyway," Nancy continued now, "I'm not sure it's *me*. That's making him grouchy. Something else—he's really worried about something."

"Your mother?"

No other friend of Nancy's would have presumed to make such a suggestion. Susan, however, was privileged. When she had first appeared in Holcomb, a melancholy, imaginative child, willowy and wan and sensitive, then eight, a year younger than Nancy, the Clutters had so ardently adopted her that the fatherless little girl from California soon came to seem a member of the family. For seven years the two friends had been inseparable, each, by virtue of the rarity of similar and equal sensibilities, irreplaceable to the other. But then, this past September, Susan had transferred from the local school to the vaster, supposedly superior one in Garden City. It was the usual procedure for Holcomb students who intended going on to college, but Mr. Clutter, a die-hard community booster, considered such defections an affront to community spirit; the Holcomb School was good enough for his children, and there they would remain. Thus, the girls were no longer always together, and Nancy deeply felt the daytime absence of her friend, the one person with whom she need be neither brave nor reticent.

"Well. But we're all so happy about Mother—you heard the wonderful news." Then Nancy said, "Listen," and hesitated, as if summoning nerve to make an outrageous remark. "*Why* do I keep smelling smoke? Honestly, I think I'm losing my mind. I get into the car, I walk into a room, and it's as though somebody had just been there, smoking a cigarette. It isn't Mother, it can't be Kenyon. Kenyon wouldn't dare . . ."

Nor, very likely, would any visitor to the Clutter home, which was pointedly devoid of ashtrays. Slowly, Susan grasped the implication, but it was ludicrous. Regardless of what his private anxieties might be, she could not believe that Mr. Clutter was finding secret solace in tobacco. Before she could ask if this was really what Nancy meant, Nancy cut her off: "Sorry, Susie. I've got to go. Mrs. Katz is here."

Dick was driving a black 1949 Chevrolet sedan. As Perry got in, he checked the back seat to see if his guitar was safely there; the previous night, after playing for a party of Dick's friends, he had forgotten and left it in the car. It was an old Gibson guitar, sandpapered and waxed to a honey-yellow finish. Another sort of instrument lay beside it—a twelve-gauge pump-action shotgun, brand-new, blue-barreled, and with a sportsman's scene of pheasants in flight etched along the stock. A flashlight, a fishing knife, a pair of leather gloves, and a hunting vest fully packed with shells contributed further atmosphere to this curious still life.

"You wearing that?" Perry asked, indicating the vest.

Dick rapped his knuckles against the windshield. "Knock, knock. Excuse me, sir. We've been out hunting and lost our way. If we could use the phone . . ."

*"Si, señor. Yo comprendo."*

"A cinch," said Dick. "I promise you, honey, we'll blast hair all over them walls."

"'Those' walls," said Perry. A dictionary buff, a devotee of obscure words, he had been intent on improving his companion's grammar and expanding his vocabulary ever since they had celled together at Kansas State Penitentiary. Far from resenting these lessons, the pupil, to please his tutor, once composed a sheaf of poems, and though the verses were very obscene, Perry, who thought them nevertheless hilarious, had had the manuscript leather-bound in a prison shop and its title, *Dirty Jokes*, stamped in gold.

Dick was wearing a blue jumper suit; lettering stitched across the back of it advertised Bob Sands' Body Shop. He and Perry drove along the main street of Olathe until they arrived at the Bob Sands establishment, an auto-repair garage, where Dick had been employed since his release from the penitentiary in mid-August. A capable mechanic, he earned sixty dollars a week. He deserved no salary for the work he planned to do this morning, but Mr. Sands, who left him in charge on Saturdays, would never know he had paid his hireling to overhaul his own car. With Perry assisting him, he went to work. They changed the oil, adjusted the clutch, recharged the battery, replaced a throw-out bearing, and put new tires on the rear wheels—all necessary undertakings, for between today and tomorrow the aged Chevrolet was expected to perform punishing feats.

"Because the old man was around," said Dick, answering Perry, who wanted to know why he had been late in meeting him at the Little Jewel. "I didn't want him to see me taking the gun out of the house. Christ, then he would have knowed I wasn't telling the truth."

" 'Known.' But what did you say? Finally?"

"Like we said. I said we'd be gone overnight—said we was going to visit your sister in Fort Scott. On account of she was holding money for you. Fifteen hundred dollars." Perry had a sister, and had once had two, but the surviving one did not live in Fort Scott, a Kansas town eighty-five miles from Olathe; in fact, he was uncertain of her present address.

"And was he sore?"

"Why should he be sore?"

"Because he hates me," said Perry, whose voice was both gentle and prim—a voice that, though soft, manufactured each word exactly, ejected it like a smoke ring issuing from a parson's mouth. "So does your mother. I could see—the ineffable way they looked at me."

Dick shrugged. "Nothing to do with you. As such. It's just they don't like me seeing anybody from The Walls." Twice married, twice divorced, now twenty-eight and the father of three boys, Dick had received his parole on the condition that he reside with his parents; the family, which included a younger brother, lived on a small farm near Olathe. "Anybody wearing the fraternity pin," he added, and touched a blue dot tattooed under his left eye—an insigne, a visible password, by which certain former prison inmates could identify him.

"I understand," said Perry. "I sympathize with that. They're good people. She's a real sweet person, your mother."

Dick nodded; he thought so, too.

At noon they put down their tools, and Dick, racing the engine, listening to the consistent hum, was satisfied that a thorough job had been done.

Nancy and her protégée, Jolene Katz, were also satisfied with their morning's work; indeed, the latter, a thin thirteen-year-old, was agog with pride. For the longest while she stared at the blue-ribbon winner, the oven-hot cherries simmering under the crisp lattice crust, and then she was overcome, and hugging Nancy, asked, "Honest, did I really make it myself?" Nancy laughed, returned the embrace, and assured her that she had—with a little help.

Jolene urged that they sample the pie at once—no nonsense about leaving it to cool. "Please, let's both have a piece. And you, too," she said to Mrs. Clutter, who had come into the kitchen. Mrs. Clutter smiled—attempted to; her head ached—and said thank you, but she hadn't the appetite. As for Nancy, she hadn't the time; Roxie Lee Smith, and Roxie Lee's trumpet solo, awaited her, and afterward those errands for her mother, one of which concerned a bridal shower that some Garden City girls were organizing for Beverly, and another the Thanksgiving gala.

"You go, dear, I'll keep Jolene company until her mother comes for her," Mrs. Clutter said, and then, addressing the child with unconquerable timidity, added, "If Jolene doesn't mind keeping *me* company." As a girl she had won an elocution prize; maturity, it seemed, had reduced her voice to a single tone, that of apology, and her personality to a series of gestures blurred by the fear that she might give offense, in some way displease. "I hope you understand," she continued after her daughter's departure. "I hope you won't think Nancy rude?"

"Goodness, no. I just love her to death. Well, everybody does. There isn't anybody like Nancy. Do you know what Mrs. Stringer says?" said Jolene, naming her home-economics teacher. "One day she told the class, 'Nancy Clutter is always in a hurry, but she always has time. And that's one definition of a lady.'"

"Yes," replied Mrs. Clutter. "All my children are very efficient. They don't need me."

Jolene had never before been alone with Nancy's "strange" mother, but despite discussions she had heard, she felt much at ease, for Mrs. Clutter, though unrelaxed herself, had a relaxing quality, as is generally true of defenseless persons who present no threat; even in Jolene, a very childlike child, Mrs. Clutter's heart-shaped, missionary's face, her look of helpless, homespun ethereality aroused protective compassion.

But to think that she was Nancy's mother! An aunt—that seemed possible; a visiting spinster aunt, slightly odd, but *nice.*

"No, they don't need me," she repeated, pouring herself a cup of coffee. Though all the other members of the family observed her husband's boycott of this beverage, she drank two cups every morning and often as not ate nothing else the rest of the day. She weighed ninety-eight pounds; rings—a wedding band and one set with a diamond modest to the point of meekness—wobbled on one of her bony hands.

Jolene cut a piece of pie. "Boy!" she said, wolfing it down. "I'm going to make one of these every day seven days a week."

"Well, you have all those little brothers, and boys can eat a lot of pie. Mr. Clutter and Kenyon, I know they never get tired of them. But the cook does—Nancy just turns up her nose. It'll be the same with you. No, no—why do I say that?" Mrs. Clutter, who wore rimless glasses, removed them and pressed her eyes. "Forgive me, dear. I'm sure you'll never know what it is to be tired. I'm sure you'll always be happy . . ."

Jolene was silent. The note of panic in Mrs. Clutter's voice had caused her to have a shift of feeling; Jolene was confused, and wished that her mother, who had promised to call back for her at eleven, would come.

Presently, more calmly, Mrs. Clutter asked, "Do you like miniature things? Tiny things?" and invited Jolene into the dining room to inspect the shelves of a whatnot on which were arranged assorted Lilliputian gewgaws—scissors, thimbles, crystal flower baskets, toy figurines, forks and knives. "I've had some of these since I was a child. Daddy and Mama—all of us—spent part of most years in California. By the ocean. And there was a shop that sold such precious little things. These cups." A set of doll-house teacups, anchored to a diminutive tray, trembled in the palm of her hand. "Daddy gave them to me; I had a lovely childhood."

The only daughter of a prosperous wheat grower named Fox, the adored sister of three older brothers, she had not been spoiled but spared, led to suppose that life was a sequence of agreeable events—Kansas autumns, California summers, a round of teacup gifts. When she was eighteen, inflamed by a biography of Florence Nightingale, she enrolled as a student nurse at St. Rose's Hospital in Great Bend, Kansas. She was not meant to be a nurse, and after two years she confessed it: a hospital's realities—scenes, odors—sickened her. Yet to this day she regretted not having completed the course and received her diploma—"just to prove," as she had told a friend, "that I once succeeded at something." Instead, she had met and married Herb, a college classmate of her oldest brother, Glenn; actually, since the two families lived within twenty miles of each other, she had long known him by sight, but the Clutters, plain farm people, were not on visiting terms with the well-to-do and cultivated Foxes. However, Herb was handsome, he was pious, he was strong-willed, he wanted her—and she was in love.

"Mr. Clutter travels a great deal," she said to Jolene. "Oh, he's always headed somewhere. Washington and Chicago and Oklahoma and Kansas City—sometimes it seems like he's never home. But wherever he goes, he remembers how I dote on tiny things." She unfolded a little paper fan. "He brought me this from San Francisco. It only cost a penny. But isn't it pretty?"

The second year of the marriage, Eveanna was born, and three years later, Beverly; after each confinement the young mother had experienced an inexplicable despondency—seizures of grief that sent her wandering from room to room in a hand-wringing daze. Between the births of Beverly and Nancy, three more years elapsed, and these were the years of the Sunday picnics and of summer excursions to Colorado, the years when she really ran her own home and was the happy center of it. But with Nancy and then with Kenyon, the pattern of postnatal depression repeated itself, and following the birth of her son, the mood of misery that descended never altogether lifted; it lingered like a cloud that might rain or might not. She knew "good days," and occasionally they accumulated into weeks, months, but even on the best of the good days, those days when she was otherwise her "old self," the affectionate and charming Bonnie her friends cherished, she could not summon the social vitality her husband's pyramiding activities required. He was a "joiner," a "born leader"; she was not, and stopped attempting to be. And so, along paths bordered by tender regard, by total fidelity, they began to go their semi-separate ways—his a public route, a march of satisfying conquests, and hers a private one that eventually wound through hospital corridors. But she was not without hope. Trust in God sustained her, and from time to time secular sources supplemented her faith in His forthcoming mercy; she read of a miracle medicine, heard of a new therapy, or, as most recently, decided to believe that a "pinched nerve" was to blame.

"Little things really belong to you," she said, folding the fan. "They don't have to be left behind. You can carry them in a shoebox."

"Carry them where to?"

"Why, wherever you go. You might be gone for a long time."

Some years earlier Mrs. Clutter had traveled to Wichita for two weeks of treatment and remained two months. On the advice of a doctor, who had thought the experience would aid her to regain "a sense of adequacy and usefulness," she had taken an apartment, then found a job—as a file clerk at the Y.W.C.A. Her husband, entirely sympathetic, had encouraged the adventure, but she had liked it too well, so much that it seemed to her unchristian, and the sense of guilt she in consequence developed ultimately outweighed the experiment's therapeutic value.

"Or you might never go home. And—it's important always to have with you something of your own. That's really yours."

The doorbell rang. It was Jolene's mother.

Mrs. Clutter said, "Goodbye, dear," and pressed into Jolene's hand the paper fan. "It's only a penny thing—but it's pretty."

Afterward Mrs. Clutter was alone in the house. Kenyon and Mr. Clutter had gone to Garden City; Gerald Van Vleet had left for the day; and the housekeeper, the blessed Mrs. Helm to whom she could confide anything, did not come to work on Saturdays. She might as well go back to bed—the bed she so rarely abandoned that poor Mrs. Helm had to battle for the chance to change its linen twice a week.

There were four bedrooms on the second floor, and hers was the last at the end of a spacious hall, which was bare except for a baby crib that had been bought for the visits of her grandson. If cots were brought in and the hall was used as a dormitory, Mrs. Clutter estimated, the house could accommodate twenty guests during the Thanksgiving holidays; the others would have to lodge at motels or with neighbors. Among the Clutter kinfolk the Thanksgiving get-together was an annual, turnabout to-do, and this year Herb was the appointed host, so it had to be done, but coinciding, as it did, with the preparations for Beverly's wedding, Mrs. Clutter despaired of surviving either project. Both involved the necessity of making decisions—a process she had always disliked, and had learned to dread, for when her husband was off on one of his business journeys she was continually expected, in his absence, to supply snap judgments concerning the affairs of the farm, and it was unendurable, a torment. What if she made a mistake? What if Herb should be displeased? Better to lock the bedroom door and pretend not to hear, or say, as she sometimes did, "I can't. I don't know. Please."

The room she so seldom left was austere; had the bed been made, a visitor might have thought it permanently unoccupied. An oak bed, a walnut bureau, a bedside table—nothing else except lamps, one curtained window, and a picture of Jesus walking on the water. It was as though by keeping this room impersonal, by not importing her intimate belongings but leaving them mingled with those of her husband, she lessened the offense of not sharing his quarters. The only used drawer in the bureau contained a jar of Vick's Vaporub, Kleenex, an electric heating pad, a number of white nightgowns, and white cotton socks. She always wore a pair of these socks to bed, for she was always cold. And, for the same reason, she habitually kept her windows closed. Summer before last, on a sweltering August Sunday, when she was secluded here, a difficult incident had taken place. There were guests that day, a party of friends who had been invited to the farm to pick mulberries, and among them was Wilma Kidwell, Susan's mother. Like most of the people who were often entertained by the Clutters, Mrs. Kidwell accepted the absence of the hostess without comment, and assumed, as was the custom, that she was either "indisposed" or "away in Wichita." In any event, when the hour came to go to the fruit orchard, Mrs. Kidwell declined; a city-bred woman, easily fatigued, she wished to remain indoors. Later, while she was awaiting the return of the mulberry pickers, she heard the sound of weeping, heartbroken, heartbreaking. "Bonnie?" she called, and ran up the stairs, ran down the hall to Bonnie's room. When she opened it, the heat gathered inside the room was like a sudden, awful hand over her mouth; she hurried to open a window. "Don't!" Bonnie cried. "I'm not hot. I'm cold. I'm freezing. Lord, Lord, Lord!" She flailed her arms. "Please, Lord, don't let anybody see me this way." Mrs. Kidwell sat down on the bed; she wanted to hold Bonnie in her arms, and eventually Bonnie let herself be held. "Wilma," she said, "I've been listening to you, Wilma. All of you. Laughing. Having a good time. I'm missing out on everything. The best years, the children—everything. A little while, and even Kenyon will be grown up—a man. And how will he remember me? As a kind of ghost, Wilma."

Now, on this final day of her life, Mrs. Clutter hung in the closet the calico housedress she had been wearing, and put on one of her trailing nightgowns and a fresh set of white socks. Then, before retiring, she exchanged her ordinary glasses for a pair of reading spectacles. Though she subscribed to several periodicals (the *Ladies' Home Journal, McCall's, Reader's Digest,* and *Together: Midmonth Magazine for Methodist Families*), none of these rested on the bedside table—only a Bible. A bookmark lay between its pages, a stiff piece of watered silk upon which an admonition had been embroidered: "Take ye heed, watch and pray: for ye know not when the time is."

The two young men had little in common, but they did not realize it, for they shared a number of surface traits. Both, for example, were fastidious, very attentive to hygiene and the condition of their fingernails. After their grease-monkey morning, they spent the better part of an hour sprucing up in the lavatory of the garage. Dick stripped to his briefs was not quite the same as Dick fully clothed. In the latter state, he seemed a flimsy dingy-blond youth of medium height, fleshless and perhaps sunken-chested; disrobing revealed that he was nothing of the sort, but, rather, an athlete constructed on a welterweight scale. The tattooed face of a cat, blue and grinning, covered his right hand; on one shoulder a blue rose blossomed. More markings, self-designed and self-executed, ornamented his arms and torso: the head of a dragon with a human skull between its open jaws; bosomy nudes; a gremlin brandishing a pitchfork; the word PEACE accompanied by a cross radiating, in the form of crude strokes, rays of holy light; and two sentimental concoctions—one a bouquet of flowers dedicated to MOTHER-DAD, the other a heart that celebrated the romance of DICK and CAROL, the girl whom he had married when he was nineteen, and from whom he had separated six years later in order to "do the right thing" by another young lady, the mother of his youngest child. ("I have three boys who I will definitely take care of," he had written in applying for parole. "My wife is remarried. I have been married twice, only I don't want anything to do with my second wife.")

But neither Dick's physique nor the inky gallery adorning it made as remarkable an impression as his face, which seemed composed of mismatching parts. It was as though his head had been halved like an apple, then put together a fraction off center. Something of the kind had happened; the imperfectly aligned features were the outcome of a car collision in 1950—an accident that left his long-jawed and narrow face tilted, the left side rather lower than the right, with the results that the lips were slightly aslant, the nose askew, and his eyes not only situated at uneven levels but of uneven size, the left eye being truly serpentine, with a venomous, sickly-blue squint that although it was involuntarily acquired, seemed nevertheless to warn of bitter sediment at the bottom of his nature. But Perry had told him, "The eye doesn't matter. Because you have a wonderful smile. One of those smiles that really work." It was true that the tightening action of a smile contracted his face into its correct proportions, and made it possible to discern a less unnerving personality—an American-style "good kid" with an outgrown crew cut, sane enough but not too bright. (Actually, he was very intelligent. An I.Q. test taken in prison gave him a rating of 130; the average subject, in prison or out, scores between 90 and 110.)

Perry, too, had been maimed, and his injuries, received in a motorcycle wreck, were severer than Dick's; he had spent half a year in a State of Washington hospital and another six months on crutches, and though the accident had occurred in 1952, his chunky, dwarfish legs, broken in five places and pitifully scarred, still pained him so severely that he had become an aspirin addict. While he had fewer tattoos than his companion, they were more elaborate—not the self-inflicted work of an amateur but epics of the art contrived by Honolulu and Yokohama masters. COOKIE, the name of a nurse who had been friendly to him when he was hospitalized, was tattooed on his right biceps. Blue-furred, orange-eyed, red-fanged, a tiger snarled upon his left biceps; a spitting snake, coiled around a dagger, slithered down his arm; and elsewhere skulls gleamed, a tombstone loomed, a chrysanthemum flourished.

"O.K., beauty. Put away the comb," said Dick, dressed now and ready to go. Having discarded his work uniform, he wore gray khakis, a matching shirt, and, like Perry, ankle-high black boots. Perry, who could never find trousers to fit his truncated lower half, wore blue jeans rolled up at the bottom and a leather windbreaker. Scrubbed, combed, as tidy as two dudes setting off on a double date, they went out to the car.

The distance between Olathe, a suburb of Kansas City, and Holcomb, which might be called a suburb of Garden City, is approximately four hundred miles.

A town of eleven thousand, Garden City began assembling its founders soon after the Civil War. An itinerant buffalo hunter, Mr. C. J. (Buffalo) Jones, had much to do with its subsequent expansion from a collection of huts and hitching posts into an opulent ranching center with razzle-dazzle saloons, an opera house, and the plushiest hotel anywhere between Kansas City and Denver—in brief, a specimen of frontier fanciness that rivaled a more famous settlement fifty miles east of it, Dodge City. Along with Buffalo Jones, who lost his money and then his mind (the last years of his life were spent haranguing street groups against the wanton extermination of the beasts he himself had so profitably slaughtered), the glamours of the past are today entombed. Some souvenirs exist; a moderately colorful row of commercial buildings is known as the Buffalo Block, and the once splendid Windsor Hotel, with its still splendid high-ceilinged saloon and its atmosphere of spittoons and potted palms, endures amid the variety stores and supermarkets as a Main Street landmark—one comparatively unpatronized, for the Windsor's dark, huge chambers and echoing hallways, evocative as they are, cannot compete with the air-conditioned amenities offered at the trim little Hotel Warren, or with the Wheat Lands Motel's individual television sets and "Heated Swimming Pool."

Anyone who has made the coast-to-coast journey across America, whether by train or by car, has probably passed through Garden City, but it is reasonable to assume that few travelers remember the event. It seems just another fair-sized town in the middle—almost the exact middle—of the continental United States. Not that the inhabitants would tolerate such an opinion—perhaps rightly. Though they may overstate the case ("Look all over the world, and you won't find friendlier people or fresher air or sweeter drinking water," and "I could go to Denver at triple the salary, but I've got five kids, and I figure there's no better place to raise kids than right here. Swell schools with every kind of sport. We even have a junior college," and "I came out here to practice law. A temporary thing, I never planned to stay. But when the chance came to move, I thought, Why go? What the hell for? Maybe it's not New York—but who wants New York? Good neighbors, people who care about each other, that's what counts. And everything else a decent man needs—we've got that, too. Beautiful churches. A golf course"), the newcomer to Garden City, once he has adjusted to the nightly after-eight silence of Main Street, discovers much to support the defensive boastings of the citizenry: a well-run public library, a competent daily newspaper, green-lawned and shady squares here and there, placid residential streets where animals and children are safe to run free, a big, rambling park complete with a small menagerie ("See the Polar Bears!" "See Penny the Elephant!"), and a swimming pool that consumes several acres ("World's Largest FREE Swimpool!"). Such accessories, and the dust and the winds and the ever-calling train whistles, add up to a "home town" that is probably remembered with nostalgia by those who have left it, and that, for those who have remained, provides a sense of roots and contentment.

Without exception, Garden Citians deny that the population of the town can be socially graded ("No, sir. Nothing like that here. All equal, regardless of wealth, color, or creed. Everything the way it ought to be in a democracy; that's us"), but, of course, class distinctions are as clearly observed, and as clearly observable, as in any other human hive. A hundred miles west and one would be out of the "Bible Belt," that gospel-haunted strip of American territory in which a man must, if only for business reasons, take his religion with the straightest of faces, but in Finney County one is still within the Bible Belt borders, and therefore a person's church affiliation is the most important factor influencing his class status. A combination of Baptists, Methodists, and

Roman Catholics would account for eighty percent of the county's devout, yet among the elite—the businessmen, bankers, lawyers, physicians, and more prominent ranchers who tenant the top drawer—Presbyterians and Episcopalians predominate. An occasional Methodist is welcomed, and once in a while a Democrat infiltrates, but on the whole the Establishment is composed of right-wing Republicans of the Presbyterian and Episcopalian faiths.

As an educated man successful in his profession, as an eminent Republican and church leader—even though of the Methodist church—Mr. Clutter was entitled to rank among the local patricians, but just as he had never joined the Garden City Country Club, he had never sought to associate with the reigning coterie. Quite the contrary, for their pleasures were not his; he had no use for card games, golf, cocktails, or buffet suppers served at ten—or, indeed, for any pastime that he felt did not "accomplish something." Which is why, instead of being part of a golfing foursome on this shining Saturday, Mr. Clutter was acting as chairman of a meeting of the Finney County 4-H Club. (4-H stands for "Head, Heart, Hands, Health," and the club motto claims "We learn to do by doing." It is a national organization, with overseas branches, whose purpose is to help those living in rural areas—and the children particularly—develop practical abilities and moral character. Nancy and Kenyon had been conscientious members from the age of six.) Toward the end of the meeting, Mr. Clutter said, "Now I have something to say concerning one of our adult members." His eyes singled out a chubby Japanese woman surrounded by four chubby Japanese children. "You all know Mrs. Hideo Ashida. Know how the Ashidas moved here from Colorado—started farming out to Holcomb two years ago. A fine family, the kind of people Holcomb's lucky to have. As anyone will tell you. Anyone who has been sick and had Mrs. Ashida walk nobody can calculate how many miles to bring them some of the wonderful soups she makes. Or the flowers she grows where you wouldn't expect a flower could grow. And last year at the county fair you will recall how much she contributed to the success of the 4-H exhibits. So I want to suggest we honor Mrs. Ashida with an award at our Achievement Banquet next Tuesday."

Her children tugged at her, punched her; the oldest boy shouted, "Hey, Ma, that's you!" But Mrs. Ashida was bashful; she rubbed her eyes with her baby-plump hands and laughed. She was the wife of a tenant farmer; the farm, an especially wind-swept and lonesome one, was halfway between Garden City and Holcomb. After 4-H conferences, Mr. Clutter usually drove the Ashidas home, and he did so today.

"Gosh, that was a jolt," said Mrs. Ashida as they rolled along Route 50 in Mr. Clutter's pickup truck. "Seems like I'm always thanking you, Herb. But thanks." She had met him on her second day in Finney County; it was the day before Halloween, and he and Kenyon had come to call, bringing a load of pumpkins and squash. All through that first hard year, gifts had arrived, of produce that the Ashidas had not yet planted—baskets of asparagus, lettuce. And Nancy often brought Babe by for the children to ride. "You know, in most ways, this is the best place we've ever lived. Hideo says the same. We sure hate to think about leaving. Starting all over again."

"Leaving?" protested Mr. Clutter, and slowed the car.

"Well, Herb. The farm here, the people we're working for—Hideo thinks we could do better. Maybe in Nebraska. But nothing's settled. It's just talk so far." Her hearty voice, always on the verge of laughter, made the melancholy news sound somehow cheerful, but seeing that she had saddened Mr. Clutter, she turned to other matters. "Herb, give me a man's opinion," she said. "Me and the kids, we've been saving up, we want to give Hideo something on the grand side for Christmas. What he needs is teeth. Now, if your wife was to give you three gold teeth, would that strike you as a wrong kind of present? I mean, asking a man to spend Christmas in the dentist's chair?"

"You beat all. Don't ever try to get away from here. We'll hogtie you," said Mr. Clutter. "Yes, yes, by all means gold teeth. Was me, I'd be tickled."

His reaction delighted Mrs. Ashida, for she knew he would not approve her plan unless he meant it; he was a gentleman. She had never known him to "act the Squire," or to take advantage or break a promise. She ventured to obtain a promise now. "Look, Herb. At the banquet—no speeches, huh? Not for me. You, you're different. The way you can stand up and talk to hundreds of people. Thousands. And be so easy—convince anybody about whatever. Just nothing scares you," she said, commenting upon a generally recognized quality of Mr. Clutter's: a fearless self-assurance that set him apart, and while it created respect, also limited the affections of others a little. "I can't imagine you afraid. No matter what happened, you'd talk your way out of it."

By midafternoon the black Chevrolet had reached Emporia, Kansas —a large town, almost a city, and a safe place, so the occupants of the car had decided, to do a bit of shopping. They parked on a side street, then wandered about until a suitably crowded variety store presented itself.

The first purchase was a pair of rubber gloves; these were for

Perry, who, unlike Dick, had neglected to bring old gloves of his own.

They moved on to a counter displaying women's hosiery. After a spell of indecisive quibbling, Perry said, "I'm for it."

Dick was not. "What about my eye? They're all too light-colored to hide that."

"Miss," said Perry, attracting a salesgirl's attention. "You got any black stockings?" When she told him no, he proposed that they try another store. "Black's foolproof."

But Dick had made up his mind: stockings of any shade were unnecessary, an encumbrance, a useless expense ("I've already invested enough money in this operation"), and, after all, anyone they encountered would not live to bear witness. "*No* witnesses," he reminded Perry, for what seemed to Perry the millionth time. It rankled in him, the way Dick mouthed those two words, as though they solved every problem; it was stupid not to admit that there might be a witness they hadn't seen. "The ineffable happens, things *do* take a turn," he said. But Dick, smiling boastfully, boyishly, did not agree: "Get the bubbles out of your blood. Nothing can go wrong." No. Because the plan was Dick's, and from first footfall to final silence, flawlessly devised.

Next they were interested in rope. Perry studied the stock, tested it. Having once served in the Merchant Marine, he understood rope and was clever with knots. He chose a white nylon cord, as strong as wire and not much thicker. They discussed how many yards of it they required. The question irritated Dick, for it was part of a greater quandary, and he could not, despite the alleged perfection of his over-all design, be certain of the answer. Eventually, he said, "Christ, how the hell should I know?"

"You damn well better."

Dick tried. "There's him. Her. The kid and the girl. And maybe the other two. But it's Saturday. They might have guests. Let's count on eight, or even twelve. The only *sure* thing is every one of them has got to go."

"Seems like a lot of it. To be so sure about."

"Ain't that what I promised you, honey—plenty of hair on them-those walls?"

Perry shrugged. "Then we'd better buy the whole roll."

It was a hundred yards long—quite enough for twelve.

Kenyon had built the chest himself: a mahogany hope chest, lined with cedar, which he intended to give Beverly as a wedding present. Now, working on it in the so-called den in the basement, he applied a last coat of varnish. The furniture of the den, a cement-floored room that ran the length of the house, consisted almost entirely of examples of his carpentry (shelves, tables, stools, a ping-pong table) and Nancy's needlework (chintz slip covers that rejuvenated a decrepit couch, curtains, pillows bearing legends: HAPPY? and YOU DON'T HAVE TO BE CRAZY TO LIVE HERE BUT IT HELPS). Together, Kenyon and Nancy had made a paint-splattered attempt to deprive the basement room of its unremovable dourness, and neither was aware of failure. In fact, they both thought their den a triumph and a blessing—Nancy because it was a place where she could entertain "the gang" without disturbing her mother, and Kenyon because here he could be alone, free to bang, saw, and mess with his "inventions," the newest of which was an electric deep-dish frying pan. Adjoining the den was a furnace room, which contained a tool-littered table piled with some of his other works-in-progress—an amplifying unit, an elderly wind-up Victrola that he was restoring to service.

Kenyon resembled neither of his parents physically; his crew-cut hair was hemp-colored, and he was six feet tall and lanky, though hefty enough to have once rescued a pair of full-grown sheep by carrying them two miles through a blizzard—sturdy, strong, but cursed with a lanky boy's lack of muscular coordination. This defect, aggravated by an inability to function without glasses, prevented him from taking more than a token part in those team sports (basketball, baseball) that were the main occupation of most of the boys who might have been his friends. He had only one close friend—Bob Jones, the son of Taylor Jones, whose ranch was a mile west of the Clutter home. Out in rural Kansas, boys start driving cars very young; Kenyon was eleven when his father allowed him to buy, with money he had earned raising sheep, an old truck with a Model A engine—the Coyote Wagon, he and Bob called it. Not far from River Valley Farm there is a mysterious stretch of countryside known as the Sand Hills; it is like a beach without an ocean, and at night coyotes slink among the dunes, assembling in hordes to howl. On moonlit evenings the boys would descend upon them, set them running, and try to outrace them in the wagon; they seldom did, for the scrawniest coyote can hit fifty miles an hour, whereas the wagon's top speed was thirty-five, but it was a wild and beautiful kind of fun, the wagon skidding across the sand, the fleeing coyotes framed against the moon—as Bob said, it sure made your heart hurry.

Equally intoxicating, and more profitable, were the rabbit roundups the two boys conducted: Kenyon was a good shot and his friend a better one, and between them they sometimes delivered half a hundred rabbits to the "rabbit factory"—a Garden City processing plant that paid ten cents a head for the animals, which were then quick-frozen and shipped to mink growers. But what meant most to Kenyon—and Bob, too—was their weekend, overnight hunting hikes along the shores of the river: wandering, wrapping up in blankets, listening at sunrise for the noise of wings, moving toward the sound on tiptoe, and then, sweetest of all, swaggering homeward with a dozen duck dinners swinging from their belts. But lately things had changed between Kenyon and his friend. They had not quarreled, there had been no overt falling-out, nothing had happened except that Bob, who was sixteen, had started "going with a girl," which meant that Kenyon, a year younger and still very much the adolescent bachelor, could no longer count on his companionship. Bob told him, "When you're my age, you'll feel different. I used to think the same as you: Women—so what? But then you get to talking to some woman, and it's mighty nice. You'll see." Kenyon doubted it; he could not conceive of ever wanting to waste an hour on any girl that might be spent with guns, horses, tools, machinery, even a book. If Bob was unavailable, then he would rather be alone, for in temperament he was not in the least Mr. Clutter's son but rather Bonnie's child, a sensitive and reticent boy. His contemporaries thought him "stand-offish," yet forgave him, saying, "Oh, *Ken*yon. It's just that he lives in a world of his own."

Leaving the varnish to dry, he went on to another chore—one that took him out-of-doors. He wanted to tidy up his mother's flower garden, a treasured patch of disheveled foliage that grew beneath her bedroom window. When he got there, he found one of the hired men loosening earth with a spade—Paul Helm, the husband of the housekeeper.

"Seen that car?" Mr. Helm asked.

Yes, Kenyon had seen a car in the driveway—a gray Buick, standing outside the entrance to his father's office.

"Thought you might know who it was."

"Not unless it's Mr. Johnson. Dad said he was expecting him."

Mr. Helm (the late Mr. Helm; he died of a stroke the following March) was a somber man in his late fifties whose withdrawn manner veiled a nature keenly curious and watchful; he liked to know what was going on. "Which Johnson?"

"The insurance fellow."

Mr. Helm grunted. "Your dad must be laying in a stack of it. That car's been here I'd say three hours."

The chill of oncoming dusk shivered through the air, and though the sky was still deep blue, lengthening shadows emanated from the garden's tall chrysanthemum stalks; Nancy's cat frolicked among them, catching its paws in the twine with which Kenyon and the old man were now tying plants. Suddenly, Nancy herself came jogging across the fields aboard fat Babe—Babe, returning from her Saturday treat, a bathe in the river. Teddy, the dog, accompanied them, and all three were water-splashed and shining.

"You'll catch cold," Mr. Helm said.

Nancy laughed; she had never been ill—not once. Sliding off Babe, she sprawled on the grass at the edge of the garden and seized her cat, dangled him above her, and kissed his nose and whiskers.

Kenyon was disgusted. "*Kissing* animals on the mouth."

"You used to kiss Skeeter," she reminded him.

"Skeeter was a *horse.*" A beautiful horse, a strawberry stallion he had raised from a foal. How that Skeeter could take a fence! "You use a horse too hard," his father had cautioned him. "One day you'll ride the life out of Skeeter." And he had; while Skeeter was streaking down a road with his master astride him, his heart failed, and he stumbled and was dead. Now, a year later, Kenyon still mourned him, even though his father, taking pity on him, had promised him the pick of next spring's foals.

"Kenyon?" Nancy said. "Do you think Tracy will be able to talk? By Thanksgiving?" Tracy, not yet a year old, was her nephew, the son of Eveanna, the sister to whom she felt particularly close. (Beverly was Kenyon's favorite.) "It would thrill me to pieces to hear him say 'Aunt Nancy.' Or 'Uncle Kenyon.' Wouldn't you like to hear him say that? I mean, don't you *love* being an uncle? Kenyon? Good grief, why can't you *ever* answer me?"

"Because you're silly," he said, tossing her the head of a flower, a wilted dahlia, which she jammed into her hair.

Mr. Helm picked up his spade. Crows cawed, sundown was near, but his home was not; the lane of Chinese elms had turned into a tunnel of darkening green, and he lived at the end of it, half a mile away. "Evening," he said, and started his journey. But once he looked back. "And that," he was to testify the next day, "was the last I seen them. Nancy leading old Babe off to the barn. Like I said, nothing out of the ordinary."

The black Chevrolet was again parked, this time in front of a Catholic hospital on the outskirts of Emporia. Under continued needling ("That's your trouble. You think there's only one right way—Dick's way"), Dick had surrendered. While Perry waited in the car, he had gone into the hospital to try and buy a pair of black stockings from a nun. This rather unorthodox method of obtaining them had been Perry's inspiration; nuns, he had argued, were certain to have a supply. The notion presented one drawback, of course: nuns, and anything pertaining to them, were bad luck, and Perry was most respectful of his superstitions. (Some others were the number 15, red hair, white flowers, priests crossing a road, snakes appearing in a dream.) Still, it couldn't be helped. The compulsively superstitious person is also very often a serious believer in fate; that was the case with Perry. He was here, and embarked on the present errand, not because he wished to be but because fate had arranged the matter; he could *prove* it—though he had no intention of doing so, at least within Dick's hearing, for the proof would involve his confessing the true and secret motive behind his return to Kansas, a piece of parole violation he had decided upon for a reason quite unrelated to Dick's "score" or Dick's summoning letter. The reason was that several weeks earlier he had learned that on Thursday, November 12, another of his former cellmates was being released from Kansas State Penitentiary at Lansing, and "more than anything in the world," he desired a reunion with this man, his "real and only friend," the "brilliant" Willie-Jay.

During the first of his three years in prison, Perry had observed Willie-Jay from a distance, with interest but with apprehension; if one wished to be thought a tough specimen, intimacy with Willie-Jay seemed unwise. He was the chaplain's clerk, a slender Irishman with prematurely gray hair and gray, melancholy eyes. His tenor voice was the glory of the prison's choir. Even Perry, though he was contemptuous of any exhibition of piety, felt "upset" when he heard Willie-Jay sing "The Lord's Prayer"; the hymn's grave language sung in so credulous a spirit moved him, made him wonder a little at the justice of his contempt. Eventually, prodded by a slightly alerted religious curiosity, he approached Willie-Jay, and the chaplain's clerk, at once responsive, thought he divined in the cripple-legged body builder with the misty gaze and the prim, smoky voice "a poet, something rare and savable." An ambition to "bring this boy to God" engulfed him. His hopes of succeeding accelerated when one day Perry produced a pastel drawing he had made—a large, in no way technically naïve portrait of Jesus. Lansing's Protestant chaplain, the Reverend James Post, so valued it that he hung it in his office, where it hangs still: a slick and pretty Savior, with Willie-Jay's full lips and grieving eyes. The picture was the climax of Perry's never very earnest spiritual quest, and, ironically, the termination of it; he adjudged his Jesus "a piece of hypocrisy," an attempt to "fool and betray" Willie-Jay, for he was as unconvinced of God as ever. Yet should he admit this and risk forfeiting the one friend who had ever "truly understood" him? (Hod, Joe,

Jesse, travelers straying through a world where last names were seldom exchanged, these had been his "buddies"—never anyone like Willie-Jay, who was in Perry's opinion, "way above average intellectually, perceptive as a *well*-trained psychologist." How was it possible that so gifted a man had wound up in Lansing? That was what amazed Perry. The answer, which he knew but rejected as "an evasion of the deeper, the human question," was plain to simpler minds: the chaplain's clerk, then thirty-eight, was a thief, a small-scale robber who over a period of twenty years had served sentences in five different states.) Perry decided to speak out: he was sorry, but it was not for him—heaven, hell, saints, divine mercy—and if Willie-Jay's affection was founded on the prospect of Perry's some day joining him at the foot of the Cross, then he was deceived and their friendship false, a counterfeit, like the portrait.

As usual, Willie-Jay understood; disheartened but not disenchanted, he had persisted in courting Perry's soul until the day of its possessor's parole and departure, on the eve of which he wrote Perry a farewell letter, whose last paragraph ran: "You are a man of extreme passion, a hungry man not quite sure where his appetite lies, a deeply frustrated man striving to project his individuality against a backdrop of rigid conformity. You exist in a half-world suspended between two superstructures, one self-expression and the other self-destruction. You are strong, but there is a flaw in your strength, and unless you learn to control it the flaw will prove stronger than your strength and defeat you. The flaw? *Explosive emotional reaction out of all proportion to the occasion.* Why? Why this unreasonable anger at the sight of others who are happy or content, this growing contempt for people and the desire to hurt them? All right, you think they're fools, you despise them because their morals, their happiness is the source of *your* frustration and resentment. But these are dreadful enemies you carry within yourself—in time destructive as bullets. Mercifully, a bullet kills its victim. This other bacteria, permitted to age, does not kill a man but leaves in its wake the hulk of a creature torn and twisted; there is still fire within his being but it is kept alive by casting upon it faggots of scorn and hate. He may successfully accumulate, but he does not accumulate success, for he is his own enemy and is kept from truly enjoying his achievements."

Perry, flattered to be the subject of this sermon, had let Dick read it, and Dick, who took a dim view of Willie-Jay, had called the letter "just more of Billy Grahamcracker's hooey," adding, "'Faggots of scorn!' *He's* the faggot." Of course, Perry had expected this reaction, and secretly he welcomed it, for his friendship with Dick, whom he had scarcely known until his final few months in Lansing, was an outgrowth of, and counterbalance to, the intensity of his admiration for the chaplain's clerk. Perhaps Dick *was* "shallow," or even, as Willie-Jay claimed, "a vicious blusterer." All the same, Dick was full of fun, and he was shrewd, a realist, he "cut through things," there were no clouds in his head or straw in his hair. Moreover, unlike Willie-Jay, he was not critical of Perry's exotic aspirations; he was willing to listen, catch fire, share with him those visions of "guaranteed treasure" lurking in Mexican seas, Brazilian jungles.

After Perry's parole, four months elapsed, months of rattling around in a fifth-hand, hundred-dollar Ford, rolling from Reno to Las Vegas, from Bellingham, Washington, to Buhl, Idaho, and it was in Buhl, where he had found temporary work as a truck driver, that Dick's letter reached him: "Friend P., Came out in August, and after you left I Met Somcone, you do not know him, but he put me on to Something we could bring off Beautiful. A cinch, the Perfect score . . ." Until then Perry had not imagined that he would ever see Dick again. *Or* Willie-Jay. But they had both been much in his thoughts, and especially the latter, who in memory had grown ten feet tall, a gray-haired wise man haunting the hallways of his mind. "You pursue the negative," Willie-Jay had informed him once, in one of his lectures. "You want not to give a damn, to exist without responsibility, without faith or friends or warmth."

In the solitary, comfortless course of his recent driftings, Perry had over and over again reviewed this indictment, and had decided it was unjust. He *did* give a damn—but who had ever given a damn about him? His father? Yes, up to a point. A girl or two—but that was "a long story." No one else except Willie-Jay himself. And only Willie-Jay had ever recognized his worth, his potentialities, had acknowledged that he was not just an undersized, overmuscled half-breed, had seen him, for all the moralizing, as he saw himself—"exceptional," "rare," "artistic." In Willie-Jay his vanity had found support, his sensibility shelter, and the four-month exile from this high-carat appreciation had made it more alluring than any dream of buried gold. So when he received Dick's invitation, and realized that the date Dick proposed for his coming to Kansas more or less coincided with the time of Willie-Jay's release, he knew what he must do. He drove to Las Vegas, sold his junk-heap car, packed his collection of maps, old letters, manuscripts, and books, and bought a ticket for a Greyhound bus. The journey's aftermath was up to fate; if things didn't "work out with Willie-Jay," then he might "consider Dick's proposition." As it turned out, the choice was between Dick and nothing, for when Perry's bus reached

Kansas City, on the evening of November 12, Willie-Jay, whom he'd been unable to advise of his coming, had already left town—left, in fact, only five hours earlier, from the same terminal at which Perry arrived. That much he had learned by telephoning the Reverend Mr. Post, who further discouraged him by declining to reveal his former clerk's exact destination. "He's headed East," the chaplain said. "To fine opportunities. A decent job, and a home with some good people who are willing to help him." And Perry, hanging up, had felt "dizzy with anger and disappointment."

But what, he wondered when the anguish subsided, had he really expected from a reunion with Willie-Jay? Freedom had separated them; as free men, they had nothing in common, were opposites, who could never have formed a "team"—certainly not one capable of embarking on the skin-diving south-of-the-border adventures he and Dick had plotted. Nevertheless, if he had not missed Willie-Jay, if they could have been together for even an hour, Perry was quite convinced—just "knew"—that he would not now be loitering outside a hospital waiting for Dick to emerge with a pair of black stockings.

Dick returned empty-handed. "No go," he announced, with a furtive casualness that made Perry suspicious.

"Are you sure? Sure you even asked?"

"Sure I did."

"I don't believe you. I think you went in there, hung around a couple of minutes, and came out."

"O.K., sugar—whatever you say." Dick started the car. After they had traveled in silence awhile, Dick patted Perry on the knee. "Aw, come on," he said. "It was a puky idea. What the hell would they have thought? Me barging in there like it was a goddam five-'n'-dime . . ."

Perry said, "Maybe it's just as well. Nuns are a bad-luck bunch."

The Garden City representative of New York Life Insurance smiled as he watched Mr. Clutter uncap a Parker pen and open a checkbook. He was reminded of a local jest: "Know what they say about you, Herb? Say, 'Since haircuts went to a dollar-fifty, Herb writes the barber a check.'"

"That's correct," replied Mr. Clutter. Like royalty, he was famous for never carrying cash. "That's the way I do business. When those tax fellows come poking around, canceled checks are your best friend."

With the check written but not yet signed, he swiveled back in his desk chair and seemed to ponder. The agent, a stocky, somewhat bald, rather informal man named Bob Johnson, hoped his client wasn't having last-minute doubts. Herb was hard-headed, a slow man to make a deal; Johnson had worked over a year to clinch this sale. But, no, his customer was merely experiencing what Johnson called the Solemn Moment—a phenomenon familiar to insurance salesmen. The mood of a man insuring his life is not unlike that of a man signing his will; thoughts of mortality must occur.

"Yes, yes," said Mr. Clutter, as though conversing with himself. "I've plenty to be grateful for—wonderful things in my life." Framed documents commemorating milestones in his career gleamed against the walnut walls of his office: a college diploma, a map of River Valley Farm, agricultural awards, an ornate certificate bearing the signatures of Dwight D. Eisenhower and John Foster Dulles, which cited his services to the Federal Farm Credit Board. "The kids. We've been lucky there. Shouldn't say it, but I'm real proud of them. Take Kenyon. Right now he kind of leans toward being an engineer, or a scientist, but you can't tell me my boy's not a born rancher. God willing, he'll run this place some day. You ever met Eveanna's husband? Don Jarchow? Veterinarian. I can't tell you how much I think of that boy. Vere, too. Vere English—the boy my girl Beverly had the good sense to settle on. If anything ever happened to me, I'm sure I could trust those fellows to take responsibility; Bonnie by herself—Bonnie wouldn't be able to carry on an operation like this . . ."

Johnson, a veteran at listening to ruminations of this sort, knew it was time to intervene. "Why, Herb," he said. "You're a *young* man. Forty-eight. And from the looks of you, from what the medical report tells us, we're likely to have you around a couple of weeks more."

Mr. Clutter straightened, reached again for his pen. "Tell the *truth*, I feel pretty good. And pretty optimistic. I've got an idea a man could make some real money around here the next few years." While outlining his schemes for future financial betterment, he signed the check and pushed it across his desk.

The time was ten past six, and the agent was anxious to go; his wife would be waiting supper. "It's been a pleasure, Herb."

"Same here, fellow."

They shook hands. Then, with a merited sense of victory, Johnson picked up Mr. Clutter's check and deposited it in his billfold. It was the first payment on a forty-thousand-dollar policy that in the event of death by accidental means, paid double indemnity.

"And He walks with me, and He talks with me,
And He tells me I am His own,

And the joy we share as we tarry there,
None other has ever known . . ."

With the aid of his guitar, Perry had sung himself into a happier humor. He knew the lyrics of some two hundred hymns and ballads—a repertoire ranging from "The Old Rugged Cross" to Cole Porter—and, in addition to the guitar, he could play the harmonica, the accordion, the banjo, and the xylophone. In one of his favorite theatrical fantasies, his stage name was Perry O'Parsons, a star who billed himself as "The One-Man Symphony."

Dick said, "How about a cocktail?"

Personally, Perry didn't care what he drank, for he was not much of a drinker. Dick, however, was choosy, and in bars his usual choice was an Orange Blossom. From the car's glove compartment Perry fetched a pint bottle containing a ready-mixed compound of orange flavoring and vodka. They passed the bottle to and fro. Though dusk had established itself, Dick, doing a steady sixty miles an hour, was still driving without headlights, but then the road was straight, the country was as level as a lake, and other cars were seldom sighted. This was "out there"—or getting near it.

"Christ!" said Perry, glaring at the landscape, flat and limitless under the sky's cold, lingering green—empty and lonesome except for the far-between flickerings of farmhouse lights. He hated it, as he hated the Texas plains, the Nevada desert; spaces horizontal and sparsely inhabited had always induced in him a depression accompanied by agoraphobic sensations. Seaports were his heart's delight—crowded, clanging, ship-clogged, sewage-scented cities, like Yokohama, where as an American Army private he'd spent a summer during the Korean War. "Christ—and they told me to keep away from Kansas! Never set my pretty foot here again. As though they were barring me from heaven. And just look at it. Just feast your eyes."

Dick handed him the bottle, the contents reduced by half. "Save the rest," Dick said. "We may need it."

"Remember, Dick? All that talk about getting a boat? I was thinking—we could buy a boat in Mexico. Something cheap but sturdy. And we could go to Japan. Sail right across the Pacific. It's been done—thousands of people have done it. I'm not conning you, Dick—you'd go for Japan. Wonderful, gentle people, with manners like flowers. Really considerate—not just out for your dough. And the women. You've never met a real woman . . ."

"Yes, I have," said Dick, who claimed still to be in love with his honey-blond first wife though she had remarried.

"There are these baths. One place called the Dream Pool. You stretch out, and beautiful, knockout-type girls come and scrub you head to toe."

"You told me." Dick's tone was curt.

"So? Can't I repeat myself?"

"Later. Let's talk about it later. Hell, man, I've got plenty on my mind."

Dick switched on the radio; Perry switched it off. Ignoring Dick's protest, he strummed his guitar:

"I came to the garden alone, while the dew was still on the roses,
And the voice I hear, falling on my ear,
The Son of God discloses . . ."

A full moon was forming at the edge of the sky.

The following Monday, while giving evidence prior to taking a lie-detector test, young Bobby Rupp described his last visit to the Clutter home: "There was a full moon, and I thought maybe, if Nancy wanted to, we might go for a drive—drive out to McKinney Lake. Or go to the movies in Garden City. But when I called her—it must have been about ten of seven—she said she'd have to ask her father. Then she came back, and said the answer was no—because we'd stayed out so late the night before. But said why didn't I come over and watch television. I've spent a lot of time at the Clutters' watching television. See, Nancy's the only girl I ever dated. I'd known her all my life; we'd gone to school together from the first grade. Always, as long as I can remember, she was pretty and popular—a *person*, even when she was a little kid. I mean, she just made everybody feel good about themselves. The first time I dated her was when we were in the eighth grade. Most of the boys in our class wanted to take her to the eighth-grade graduation dance, and I was surprised—I was pretty proud—when she said she would go with me. We were both twelve. My dad lent me the car, and I drove her to the dance. The more I saw her, the more I liked her; the whole family, too—there wasn't any other family like them, not around here, not that I know of. Mr. Clutter may have been more strict about some things—religion, and so on—but he never tried to make you feel he was right and you were wrong.

"We live three miles west of the Clutter place. I used to walk it back and forth, but I always worked summers, and last year I'd saved enough to buy my own car, a '55 Ford. So I drove over there, got there a little after seven. I didn't see anybody on the road or on the lane that leads up to the house, or anybody outside. Just old Teddy. He barked at me. The lights were on downstairs—in the living room and in Mr. Clutter's office. The second floor was dark, and I figured Mrs. Clutter must be asleep—if she was home. You never knew whether she was or not, and I never asked. But I found out I was right, because later in the evening Kenyon wanted to practice his horn, he played baritone horn in the school band—and Nancy told him not to, because he would wake up Mrs. Clutter. Anyway, when I got there they had finished supper and Nancy had cleaned up, put all the dishes in the dishwasher, and the three of them—the two kids and Mr. Clutter—were in the living room. So we sat around like any other night—Nancy and I on the couch, and Mr. Clutter in his chair, that stuffed rocker. He wasn't watching the television so much as he was reading a book—a 'Rover Boy,' one of Kenyon's books. Once he went out to the kitchen and came back with two apples; he offered one to me, but I didn't want it, so he ate them both. He had very white teeth; he said apples were why. Nancy—Nancy was wearing socks and soft slippers, blue jeans, I think a green sweater; she was wearing a gold wristwatch and an I.D. bracelet I gave her last January for her sixteenth birthday—with her name on one side and mine on the other—and she had on a ring, some little silver thing she bought a summer ago, when she went to Colorado with the Kidwells. It wasn't my ring—*our* ring. See, a couple of weeks back she got sore at me and said she was going to take off our ring for a while. When your girl does that, it means you're on probation. I mean, sure, we had fusses—everybody does, all the kids that go steady. What happened was I went to this friend's wedding, the reception, and drank a beer, one bottle of beer, and Nancy got to hear about it. Some tattle told her I was roaring drunk. Well, she was stone, wouldn't say hello for a week. But lately we'd been getting on good as ever, and I believe she was about ready to wear our ring again.

"O.K. The first show was called 'The Man and the Challenge.' Channel 11. About some fellows in the Arctic. Then we saw a Western, and after that a spy adventure—'Five Fingers.' 'Mike Hammer' came on at nine-thirty. Then the news. But Kenyon didn't like anything, mostly because we wouldn't let him pick the programs. He criticized everything and Nancy kept telling him to hush up. They always quibbled, but actually they were very close—closer than most brothers and sisters. I guess partly it was because they'd been alone together so much, what with Mrs. Clutter away and Mr. Clutter gone to Washington, or wherever. I know Nancy loved Kenyon very specially, but I don't think even she, or anybody, exactly understood him. He seemed to be off somewhere. You never knew what he was thinking, never even knew if he was looking at you—on account of he was slightly cockeyed. Some people said he was a genius, and maybe it was true. He sure did read a lot. But, like I say, he was restless; he didn't want to watch the TV, he wanted to practice his horn, and when Nancy wouldn't let him, I remember Mr. Clutter told him why didn't he go down to the basement, the recreation room, where nobody could hear him. But he didn't want to do that, either.

"The phone rang once. Twice? Gosh, I can't remember. Except that once the phone rang and Mr. Clutter answered it in his office. The door was open—that sliding door between the living room and the office—and I heard him say 'Van,' so I knew he was talking to his partner, Mr. Van Vleet, and I heard him say that he had a headache but that it was getting better. And said he'd see Mr. Van Vleet on Monday. When he came back—yes, the Mike Hammer was just over. Five minutes of news. Then the weather report. Mr. Clutter always perked up when the weather report came on. It's all he ever really waited for. Like the only thing that interested me was the sports—which came on next. After the sports ended, that was ten-thirty, and I got up to go. Nancy walked me out. We talked a while, and made a date to go to the movies Sunday night—a picture all the girls were looking forward to, *Blue Denim*. Then she ran back in the house, and I drove away. It was as clear as day—the moon was so bright—and cold and kind of windy; a lot of tumbleweed blowing about. But that's all I saw. Only now when I think back, I think somebody must have been hiding there. Maybe down among the trees. Somebody just waiting for me to leave."

The travelers stopped for dinner at a restaurant in Great Bend. Perry, down to his last fifteen dollars, was ready to settle for root beer and a sandwich, but Dick said no, they needed a solid "tuck-in," and never mind the cost, the tab was his. They ordered two steaks medium rare, baked potatoes, French fries, fried onions, succotash, side dishes of macaroni and hominy, salad with Thousand Island dressing, cinnamon rolls, apple pie and ice cream, and coffee. To top it off, they visited a drugstore and selected cigars; in the same drugstore, they also bought two thick rolls of adhesive tape.

As the black Chevrolet regained the highway and hurried on across a countryside imperceptibly ascending toward the colder, cracker-dry climate of the high wheat plains, Perry closed his eyes and dozed off into a food-dazed semi-slumber, from which he woke to hear a voice reading the eleven-o'clock news. He rolled down a window and bathed his face in the flood of frosty air. Dick told him they were in Finney County. "We crossed the line ten miles back," he said. The car was going very fast. Signs, their messages ignited by the car's headlights, flared up, flew by: "See the Polar Bears," "Burtis Motors," "World's Largest FREE Swimpool," "Wheat Lands Motel," and, finally, a bit before street lamps began, "Howdy, Stranger! Welcome to Garden City. A Friendly Place."

They skirted the northern rim of the town. No one was abroad at this nearly midnight hour, and nothing was open except a string of desolately brilliant service stations. Dick turned into one—Hurd's Phillips 66. A youngster appeared, and asked, "Fill her up?" Dick nodded, and Perry, getting out of the car, went inside the station, where he locked himself in the men's room. His legs pained him, as they often did; they hurt as though his old accident had happened five minutes before. He shook three aspirins out of a bottle, chewed them slowly (for he liked the taste), and then drank water from the basin tap. He sat down on the toilet, stretched out his legs and rubbed them, massaging the almost unbendable knees. Dick had said they were almost there—"only seven miles more." He unzippered a pocket of his windbreaker and brought out a paper sack; inside it were the recently purchased rubber gloves. They were glue-covered, sticky and thin, and as he inched them on, one tore—not a dangerous tear, just a split between the fingers, but it seemed to him an omen.

The doorknob turned, rattled. Dick said, "Want some candy? They got a candy machine out here."

"No."

"You O.K.?"

"I'm fine."

"Don't be all night."

Dick dropped a dime in a vending machine, pulled the lever, and picked up a bag of jelly beans; munching, he wandered back to the car and lounged there watching the young attendant's efforts to rid the windshield of Kansas dust and the slime of battered insects. The attendant, whose name was James Spor, felt uneasy. Dick's eyes and sullen expression and Perry's strange, prolonged sojourn in the lavatory disturbed him. (The next day he reported to his employer, "We had some tough customers in here last night," but he did not think, then or for the longest while, to connect the visitors with the tragedy in Holcomb.)

Dick said, "Kind of slow around here."

"Sure is," James Spor said. "You're the only body stopped here since two hours. Where you coming from?"

"Kansas City."

"Here to hunt?"

"Just passing through. On our way to Arizona. We got jobs waiting there. Construction work. Any idea the mileage between here and Tucumcari, New Mexico?"

"Can't say I do. Three dollars six cents." He accepted Dick's money, made change, and said, "You'll excuse me, sir? I'm doing a job. Putting a bumper on a truck."

Dick waited, ate some jelly beans, impatiently gunned the motor, sounded the horn. Was it possible that he had misjudged Perry's character? That Perry, of all people, was suffering a sudden case of "blood bubbles"? A year ago, when they first encountered each other, he'd thought Perry "a good guy," if a bit "stuck on himself," "sentimental," too much "the dreamer." He had liked him but not considered him especially worth cultivating until, one day, Perry described a murder, telling how, simply for "the hell of it," he had killed a colored man in Las Vegas—beaten him to death with a bicycle chain. The anecdote elevated Dick's opinion of Little Perry; he began to see more of him, and, like Willie-Jay, though for dissimilar reasons, gradually decided that Perry possessed unusual and valuable qualities. Several murderers, or men who boasted of murder or their willingness to commit it, circulated inside Lansing; but Dick became convinced that Perry was that rarity, "a natural killer"—absolutely sane, but conscienceless, and capable of dealing, with or without motive, the coldest-blooded deathblows. It was Dick's theory that such a gift could, under his supervision, be profitably exploited. Having reached this conclusion, he had proceeded to woo Perry, flatter him—pretend, for example, that he believed all the buried-treasure stuff and shared his beachcomber yearnings and seaport longings, none of which appealed to Dick, who wanted "a regular life," with a business of his own, a house, a horse to ride, a new car, and "plenty of blond chicken." It was important, however, that Perry not suspect this—not until Perry, with his gift, had helped further Dick's ambitions. But perhaps it was Dick who had miscalculated, been duped; if so—if it developed that Perry was, after all, only an "ordinary punk"—then "the party" was over, the months of planning were wasted, there was nothing to do but turn and go. It mustn't happen; Dick returned to the station.

The door to the men's room was still bolted. He banged on it: "For Christsake, Perry!"

"In a minute."

"What's the matter? You sick?"

Perry gripped the edge of the washbasin and hauled himself to a standing position. His legs trembled; the pain in his knees made him perspire. He wiped his face with a paper towel. He unlocked the door and said, "O.K. Let's go."

Nancy's bedroom was the smallest, most personal room in the house —girlish, and as frothy as a ballerina's tutu. Walls, ceiling, and everything else except a bureau and a writing desk, were pink or blue or white. The white-and-pink bed, piled with blue pillows, was dominated by a big pink-and-white Teddy bear—a shooting-gallery prize that Bobby had won at the county fair. A cork bulletin board, painted pink, hung above a white-skirted dressing table; dry gardenias, the remains of some ancient corsage, were attached to it, and old valentines, newspaper recipes, and snapshots of her baby nephew and of Susan Kidwell and of Bobby Rupp, Bobby caught in a dozen actions—swinging a bat, dribbling a basketball, driving a tractor, wading, in bathing trunks, at the edge of McKinney Lake (which was as far as he dared go, for he had never learned to swim). And there were photographs of the two together—Nancy and Bobby. Of these, she liked best one that showed them sitting in a leaf-dappled light amid picnic debris and looking at one another with expressions that, though unsmiling, seemed mirthful and full of delight. Other pictures, of horses, of cats deceased but unforgotten—like "poor Boobs," who had died not long ago and most mysteriously (she suspected poison)—encumbered her desk.

Nancy was invariably the last of the family to retire; as she had once informed her friend and home-economics teacher, Mrs. Polly Stringer, the midnight hours were her "time to be selfish and vain." It was then that she went through her beauty routine, a cleansing, creaming ritual, which on Saturday nights included washing her hair. Tonight, having dried and brushed her hair and bound it in a gauzy bandanna, she set out the clothes she intended to wear to church the next morning: nylons, black pumps, a red velveteen dress—her prettiest, which she herself had made. It was the dress in which she was to be buried.

Before saying her prayers, she always recorded in a diary a few occurrences ("Summer here. Forever, I hope. Sue over and we rode Babe down to the river. Sue played her flute. Fireflies") and an occasional outburst ("I love him, I do"). It was a five-year diary; in the four years of its existence she had never neglected to make an entry, though the splendor of several events (Eveanna's wedding, the birth of her nephew) and the drama of others (her "first REAL quarrel with Bobby"—a page literally tear-stained) had caused her to usurp space allotted to the future. A different-tinted ink identified each year:

1956 was green and 1957 a ribbon of red, replaced the following year by bright lavender, and now, in 1959, she had decided upon a dignified blue. But as in every manifestation, she continued to tinker with her handwriting, slanting it to the right or to the left, shaping it roundly or steeply, loosely or stingily—as though she were asking, "Is this Nancy? Or that? Or that? Which is me?" (Once Mrs. Riggs, her English teacher, had returned a theme with a scribbled comment: "Good. But why written in three styles of script?" To which Nancy had replied: "Because I'm not grown-up enough to be one person with one kind of signature.") Still, she had progressed in recent months, and it was in a handwriting of emerging maturity that she wrote, "Jolene K. came over and I showed her how to make a cherry pie. Practiced with Roxie. Bobby here and we watched TV. Left at eleven."

"This is it, this is it, this has to be it, there's the school, there's the garage, now we turn south." To Perry, it seemed as though Dick were muttering jubilant mumbo-jumbo. They left the highway, sped through a deserted Holcomb, and crossed the Santa Fe tracks. "The bank, that must be the bank, now we turn west—see the trees? This is it, this has to be it." The headlights disclosed a lane of Chinese elms; bundles of wind-blown thistle scurried across it. Dick doused the headlights, slowed down, and stopped until his eyes were adjusted to the moon-illuminated night. Presently, the car crept forward.

Holcomb is twelve miles east of the mountain time-zone border, a circumstance that causes some grumbling, for it means that at seven in the morning, and in winter at eight or after, the sky is still dark and the stars, if any, are still shining—as they were when the two sons of Vic Irsik arrived to do their Sunday-morning chores. But by nine, when the boys finished work—during which they noticed nothing amiss—the sun had risen, delivering another day of pheasant-season perfection. As they left the property and ran along the lane, they waved at an incoming car, and a girl waved back. She was a classmate of Nancy Clutter's, and her name was also Nancy—Nancy Ewalt. She was the only child of the man who was driving the car, Mr. Clarence Ewalt, a middle-aged sugar-beet farmer. Mr. Ewalt was not himself a churchgoer, nor was his wife, but every Sunday he dropped his daughter at River Valley Farm in order that she might accompany the Clutter family to Methodist services in Garden City. The arrangement saved him "making two back-and-forth trips to town." It was his custom to wait until he had seen his daughter safely admitted to the house. Nancy, a clothes-conscious girl with a film-star figure, a bespectacled countenance, and a coy, tiptoe way of walking, crossed the lawn and pressed the front-door bell. The house had four entrances, and when, after repeated knockings, there was no response at this one, she moved on to the next—that of Mr. Clutter's office. Here the door was partly open; she opened it somewhat more—enough to ascertain that the office was filled only with shadow—but she did not think the Clutters would appreciate her "barging right in." She knocked, rang, and at last walked around to the back of the house. The garage was there, and she noted that both cars were in it: two Chevrolet sedans. Which meant they *must* be home. However, having applied unavailingly at a third door, which led into a "utility room," and a fourth, the door to the kitchen, she rejoined her father, who said, "Maybe they're asleep."

"But that's *im*possible. Can you imagine Mr. Clutter missing church? Just to *sleep*?"

"Come on, then. We'll drive down to the Teacherage. Susan ought to know what's happened."

The Teacherage, which stands opposite the up-to-date school, is an out-of-date edifice, drab and poignant. Its twenty-odd rooms are separated into grace-and-favor apartments for those members of the faculty unable to find, or afford, other quarters. Nevertheless, Susan Kidwell and her mother had managed to sugar the pill and install a cozy atmosphere in their apartment—three rooms on the ground floor. The very small living room incredibly contained—aside from things to sit on—an organ, a piano, a garden of flowering flowerpots, and usually a darting little dog and a large, drowsy cat. Susan, on this Sunday morning, stood at the window of this room watching the street. She is a tall, languid young lady with a pallid, oval face and beautiful pale-blue-gray eyes; her hands are extraordinary—long-fingered, flexible, nervously elegant. She was dressed for church, and expected momentarily to see the Clutters' Chevrolet, for she too, always attended services chaperoned by the Clutter family. Instead, the Ewalts arrived to tell their peculiar tale.

But Susan knew no explanation, nor did her mother, who said, "If there was some change of plan, why, I'm sure they would have telephoned. Susan, why don't you call the house? They *could* be asleep —I suppose."

"So I did," said Susan, in a statement made at a later date. "I called the house and let the phone ring—at least, I had the *impression* it was ringing—oh, a minute or more. Nobody answered, so Mr. Ewalt suggested that we go to the house and try to 'wake them up.' But when we got there—I didn't want to do it. Go inside the house. I was frightened, and I don't know why, because it never occurred to me—well, something like that just doesn't. But the sun was so bright, everything looked too bright and quiet. And then I saw that all the cars were there, even Kenyon's old coyote wagon. Mr. Ewalt was wearing work clothes; he had mud on his boots; he felt he wasn't properly dressed to go calling on the Clutters. Especially since he never had. Been in the house, I mean. Finally, Nancy said she would go with me. We went around to the kitchen door, and, of course, it wasn't locked; the only person who ever locked doors around there was Mrs. Helm—the family never did. We walked in, and I saw right away that the Clutters hadn't eaten breakfast; there were no dishes, nothing on the stove. Then I noticed something funny: Nancy's purse. It was lying on the floor, sort of open. We passed on through the dining room, and stopped at the bottom of the stairs. Nancy's room is just at the top. I called her name, and started up the stairs, and Nancy Ewalt followed. The sound of our footsteps frightened me more than anything, they were so loud and everything else was so silent. Nancy's door was open. The curtains hadn't been drawn, and the room was full of sunlight. I don't remember screaming. Nancy Ewalt says I did—screamed and screamed. I only remember Nancy's Teddy bear staring at me. And Nancy. And running . . ."

In the interim, Mr. Ewalt had decided that perhaps he ought not to have allowed the girls to enter the house alone. He was getting out of the car to go after them when he heard the screams, but before he could reach the house, the girls were running toward him. His daughter shouted, "She's dead!" and flung herself into his arms. "It's true, Daddy! Nancy's dead!"

Susan turned on her. "No, she isn't. And don't you say it. Don't you dare. It's only a nosebleed. She has them all the time, terrible nosebleeds, and that's all it is."

"There's too much blood. There's blood on the walls. You didn't really look."

"I couldn't make head nor tails," Mr. Ewalt subsequently testified. "I thought maybe the child was hurt. It seemed to me the first thing to do was call an ambulance. Miss Kidwell—Susan—she told me there was a telephone in the kitchen. I found it, right where she said. But the receiver was off the hook, and when I picked it up, I saw the line had been cut."

Larry Hendricks, a teacher of English, aged twenty-seven, lived on the top floor of the Teacherage. He wanted to write, but his apartment was not the ideal lair for a would-be author. It was smaller than the Kidwells', and, moreover, he shared it with a wife, three active children, and a perpetually functioning television set. ("It's the only way we can keep the kids pacified.") Though as yet unpublished, young Hendricks, a he-mannish ex-sailor from Oklahoma who smokes a pipe and has a mustache and a crop of untamed black hair, at least looks literary—in fact, remarkably like youthful photographs of the writer he most admires, Ernest Hemingway. To supplement his teacher's salary, he also drove a school bus.

"Sometimes I cover sixty miles a day," he said to an acquaintance. "Which doesn't leave much time for writing. Except Sundays. Now, *that* Sunday, November fifteenth, I was sitting up here in the apartment going through the papers. Most of my ideas for stories, I get them out of the newspapers—you know? Well, the TV was on and the kids were kind of lively, but even so I could hear *voices*. From downstairs. Down at Mrs. Kidwell's. But I didn't figure it was my concern, since I was new here—only came to Holcomb when school began. But then Shirley—she'd been out hanging up some clothes—my wife, Shirley, rushed in and said, 'Honey, you better go downstairs. They're all hysterical.' The two girls—now, they really were hysterical. Susan never has got over it. Never will, ask me. And poor Mrs. Kidwell. Her health's not too good, she's high-strung to begin with. She kept saying —but it was only later I understood what she meant—she kept saying, 'Oh, Bonnie, Bonnie, what happened? You were so happy, you told me it was all over, you said you'd never be sick again.' Words to that effect. Even Mr. Ewalt, he was about as worked up as a man like that ever gets. He had the sheriff's office on the phone—the Garden City sheriff—and he was telling him that there was 'something *radically* wrong over at the Clutter place.' The sheriff promised to come straight out, and Mr. Ewalt said fine, he'd meet him on the highway. Shirley came downstairs to sit with the women, try and calm them—as if anybody could. And I went with Mr. Ewalt—drove with him out to the highway to wait for Sheriff Robinson. On the way, he told me what had happened. When he came to the part about finding the wires cut, right then I thought, Uh-uh, and decided I'd better keep my eyes open. Make a note of every detail. In case I was ever called on to testify in court.

"The sheriff arrived; it was nine thirty-five—I looked at my watch. Mr. Ewalt waved at him to follow our car, and we drove out to the Clutters'. I'd never been there before, only seen it from a distance. Of course, I knew the family. Kenyon was in my sophomore English class, and I'd directed Nancy in the 'Tom Sawyer' play. But they were such exceptional, unassuming kids you wouldn't have known they were rich or lived in such a big house—and the trees, the lawn, everything so tended and cared for. After we got there, and the sheriff had heard Mr. Ewalt's story, he radioed his office and told them to send reinforcements, and an ambulance. Said, 'There's been some kind of accident.' Then we went in the house, the three of us. Went through the kitchen and saw a lady's purse lying on the floor, and the phone where the wires had been cut. The sheriff was wearing a hip pistol, and when we started up the stairs, going to Nancy's room, I noticed he kept his hand on it, ready to draw.

"Well, it was pretty bad. That wonderful girl—but you would never have known her. She'd been shot in the back of the head with a shotgun held maybe two inches away. She was lying on her side, facing the wall, and the wall was covered with blood. The bedcovers were drawn up to her shoulders. Sheriff Robinson, he pulled them back, and we saw that she was wearing a bathrobe, pajamas, socks, and slippers—like, whenever it happened, she hadn't gone to bed yet. Her hands were tied behind her, and her ankles were roped together with the kind of cord you see on Venetian blinds. Sheriff said, 'Is this Nancy Clutter?'—he'd never seen the child before. And I said, 'Yes. Yes, that's Nancy.'

"We stepped back into the hall, and looked around. All the other doors were closed. We opened one, and that turned out to be a bathroom. Something about it seemed wrong. I decided it was because of the chair—a sort of dining-room chair, that looked out of place in a bathroom. The next door—we all agreed it must be Kenyon's room. A lot of boy-stuff scattered around. And I recognized Kenyon's glasses—saw them on a bookshelf beside the bed. But the bed was empty, though it looked as if it had been slept in. So we walked to the end of the hall, the last door, and there, on her bed, that's where we found Mrs. Clutter. She'd been tied, too. But differently—with her hands in front of her, so that she looked as though she were praying—and in one hand she was holding, *gripping*, a handkerchief. Or was it Kleenex? The cord around her wrists ran down to her ankles, which were bound together, and then ran on down to the bottom of the bed, where it was tied to the footboard—a very complicated, artful piece of work. Think how long it took to do! And her lying there, scared out of her wits. Well, she was wearing some jewelry, two rings—which is one of the reasons why I've always discounted robbery as a motive—and a robe, and a white nightgown, and white socks. Her mouth had been taped with adhesive, but she'd been shot point-blank in the side of the head, and the blast—the impact—had ripped the tape loose. Her eyes were open. Wide open. As though she were still looking at the killer. Because she must have had to watch him do it—aim the gun. Nobody said anything. We were too stunned. I remember the sheriff searched around to see if he could find the discharged cartridge. But whoever had done it was much too smart and cool to have left behind any clues like that.

"Naturally, we were wondering where was Mr. Clutter? And Kenyon? Sheriff said, 'Let's try downstairs.' The first place we tried was the master bedroom—the room where Mr. Clutter slept. The bedcovers were drawn back, and lying there, toward the foot of the bed, was a billfold with a mess of cards spilling out of it, like somebody had shuffled through them hunting something particular—a note, an I.O.U., who knows? The fact that there wasn't any money in it didn't signify one way or the other. It was Mr. Clutter's billfold, and he never did carry cash. Even I knew that, and I'd only been in Holcomb a little more than two months. Another thing I knew was that neither Mr. Clutter nor Kenyon could see a darn without his glasses. And there were Mr. Clutter's glasses sitting on a bureau. So I figured, wherever they were, they weren't there of their own accord. We looked all over, and everything was just as it should be—no sign of a struggle, nothing disturbed. Except the office, where the telephone was off the hook, and the wires cut, same as in the kitchen. Sheriff Robinson, he found some shotguns in a closet, and sniffed them to see if they had been fired recently. Said they hadn't, and—I never saw a more bewildered man—said, 'Where the devil can Herb *be*?' About then we heard footsteps. Coming up the stairs from the basement. 'Who's that?' said the sheriff, like he was ready to shoot. And a voice said, 'It's me. Wendle.' Turned out to be Wendle Meier, the undersheriff. Seems he had come to the house and hadn't seen us, so he'd gone investigating down in the basement. The sheriff told him—and it was sort of pitiful: 'Wendle, I don't know what to make of it. There's two bodies upstairs.' 'Well,' he said, Wendle did, 'there's another one down here.' So we followed him down to the basement. Or playroom, I guess you'd call it. It wasn't dark—there were windows that let in plenty of light. Kenyon was over in a corner, lying on a couch. He was gagged with adhesive tape and bound hand and foot, like the mother—the same intricate process of the cord leading from the hands to the feet, and finally tied to an arm of the couch. Somehow he haunts me the most, Kenyon does. I think it's because he was the most recognizable, the one that looked the most like himself—even though he'd been shot in the face, directly, head-on. He was wearing a T-shirt and blue jeans, and he was barefoot—as though he'd dressed in a hurry, just put on the first thing that came to hand. His head was propped by a couple of pillows, like they'd been stuffed under him to make an easier target.

"Then the sheriff said, 'Where's this go to?' Meaning another door there in the basement. Sheriff led the way, but inside you couldn't see your hand until Mr. Ewalt found the light switch. It was a furnace room, and very warm. Around here, people just install a gas furnace and pump the gas smack out of the ground. Doesn't cost them a nickel—that's why all the houses are overheated. Well, I took one look at Mr. Clutter, and it was hard to look again. I knew plain shooting couldn't account for that much blood. And I wasn't wrong. He'd been shot, all right, the same as Kenyon—with the gun held right in front of his face. But probably he was dead before he was shot. Or, anyway, dying. Because his throat had been cut, too. He was wearing striped pajamas—nothing else. His mouth was taped; the tape had been wound plumb around his head. His ankles were tied together, but not his hands—or, rather, he'd managed, God knows how, maybe in rage or pain, to break the cord binding his hands. He was sprawled in front of the furnace. On a big cardboard box that looked as though it had been laid there specially. A mattress box. Sheriff said, 'Look here, Wendle.' What he was pointing at was a bloodstained footprint. On the mattress box. A half-sole footprint with circles—two holes in the center like a pair of eyes. Then one of us—Mr. Ewalt? I don't recall—pointed out something else. A thing I can't get out of my mind. There was a steampipe overhead, and knotted to it, dangling from it, was a piece of cord—the kind of cord the killer had used. Obviously, at some point Mr. Clutter had been tied there, strung up by his hands, and then cut down. But why? To torture him? I don't guess we'll ever know. Ever know who did it, or why, or what went on in that house that night.

"After a bit, the house began to fill up. Ambulances arrived, and the coroner, and the Methodist minister, a police photographer, state troopers, fellows from the radio and the newspaper. Oh, a bunch. Most of them had been called out of church, and acted as though they were still there. Very quiet. Whispery. It was like nobody could believe it. A state trooper asked me did I have any official business there, and said if not, then I'd better leave. Outside, on the lawn, I saw the undersheriff talking to a man—Alfred Stoecklein, the hired man. Seems Stoecklein lived not a hundred yards from the Clutter house, with nothing between his place and theirs except a barn. But he was saying as to how he hadn't heard a sound—said, 'I didn't know a thing about it till five minutes ago, when one of my kids come running in and told us the sheriff was here. The Missis and me, we didn't sleep two hours last night, was up and down the whole time, on account of we got a sick baby. But the only thing we heard, about ten-thirty, quarter to eleven, I heard a car drive away, and I made the remark to Missis, "There goes Bob Rupp."' I started walking home, and on the way, about halfway down the lane, I saw Kenyon's old collie, and that dog was scared. Stood there with its tail between its legs, didn't bark or move. And seeing the dog—somehow that made me *feel* again. I'd been too dazed, too numb, to feel the full viciousness of it. The suffering. The horror. They were dead. A whole family. Gentle, kindly people, people *I* knew—*murdered.* You had to believe it, because it was really true."

Eight non-stop passenger trains hurry through Holcomb every twenty-four hours. Of these, two pick up and deposit mail—an operation that, as the person in charge of it fervently explains, has its tricky side. "Yessir, you've got to keep on your toes. Them trains come through here, sometimes they're going a hundred miles an hour. The breeze alone, why, it's enough to knock you down. And when those mail sacks come flying out—sakes alive! It's like playing tackle on a football team: Wham! *Wham!* WHAM! Not that I'm complaining, mind you. It's honest work, *government* work, and it keeps me young." Holcomb's mail messenger, Mrs. Sadie Truitt—or Mother Truitt, as the townspeople call her—does seem younger than her years, which amount to seventy-five. A stocky, weathered widow who wears babushka bandannas and cowboy boots ("Most comfortable things you can put on your feet, soft as a loon feather"), Mother Truitt is the oldest native-born Holcombite. "Time was wasn't anybody here wasn't my kin. Them days, we called this place Sherlock. Then along came this stranger. By the name Holcomb. A *hog* raiser, he was. Made money, and decided the town ought to be called after him. Soon as it was, what did he do? Sold out. Moved to California. Not us. I was born here, my children was born here. And! Here! We! Are!" One of her children is Mrs. Myrtle Clare, who happens to be the local postmistress. "Only, don't go thinking that's how I got this position with the government. Myrt didn't even want me to have it. But it's a job you *bid* for. Goes to whoever puts in the lowest bid. And I always do—so low a caterpillar could peek over it. Ha-ha! That sure does rile the boys. Lots of boys would like to be mail messenger, yes*sir*. But I don't know how much they'd like it when the snow's high as old Mr. Primo Carnera, and the wind's blowing blue-hard, and those sacks come sailing—Ugh! Wham!"

In Mother Truitt's profession, Sunday is a workday like any other. On November 15, while she was waiting for the westbound ten-thirty-two, she was astonished to see two ambulances cross the railroad tracks and turn toward the Clutter property. The incident provoked her into doing what she had never done before—abandon her duties. Let the mail fall where it may, this was news that Myrt must hear at once.

The people of Holcomb speak of their post office as "the Federal Building," which seems rather too substantial a title to confer on a drafty and dusty shed. The ceiling leaks, the floor boards wobble, the mailboxes won't shut, the light bulbs are broken, the clock has stopped. "Yes, it's a disgrace," agrees the caustic, somewhat original, and entirely imposing lady who presides over this litter. "But the stamps work, don't they? Anyhow, what do I care? Back here in *my* part is real cozy. I've got my rocker, and a nice wood stove, and a coffee pot, and plenty to read."

Mrs. Clare is a famous figure in Finney County. Her celebrity derives not from her present occupation but a previous one—dance-hall hostess, an incarnation not indicated by her appearance. She is a gaunt, trouser-wearing, woolen-shirted, cowboy-booted, ginger-colored, gingery-tempered woman of unrevealed age ("That's for me to know, and you to guess") but promptly revealed opinions, most of which are announced in a voice of rooster-crow altitude and penetration. Until 1955 she and her late husband operated the Holcomb Dance Pavilion, an enterprise that owing to its uniqueness in the area, attracted from a hundred miles around a fast-drinking, fancy-stepping clientele, whose behavior, in turn, attracted the interest of the sheriff now and then. "We had some tough times, all right," says Mrs. Clare, reminiscing. "Some of those bowlegged country boys, you give 'em a little hooch and they're like redskins—want to scalp everything in sight. Course, we only sold setups, never the hard stuff itself. Wouldn't have, even if it was legal. My husband, Homer Clare, he didn't hold with it; neither did I. One day Homer Clare—he passed on seven months and twelve days ago today, after a five-hour operation out in Oregon—he said to me, 'Myrt, we've lived all our lives in hell, now we're going to die in heaven.' The next day we closed the dance hall. I've never regretted it. Oh, along at first I missed being a night owl—the tunes, the jollity. But now that Homer's gone, I'm just glad to do my work here at the Federal Building. Sit a spell. Drink a cup of coffee."

In fact, on that Sunday morning Mrs. Clare had just poured herself a cup of coffee from a freshly brewed pot when Mother Truitt returned.

"Myrt!" she said, but could say no more until she had caught her breath. "Myrt, there's two ambulances gone to the Clutters'."

Her daughter said, "Where's the ten-thirty-two?"

"Ambulances. Gone to the Clutters'—"

"Well, what about it? It's only Bonnie. Having one of her spells. Where's the ten-thirty-two?"

Mother Truitt subsided; as usual, Myrt knew the answer, was enjoying the last word. Then a thought occurred to her. "But Myrt, if it's only Bonnie, why would there be *two* ambulances?"

A sensible question, as Mrs. Clare, an admirer of logic, though a curious interpreter of it, was driven to admit. She said she would telephone Mrs. Helm. "Mabel will know," she said.

The conversation with Mrs. Helm lasted several minutes, and was most distressing to Mother Truitt, who could hear nothing of it except the noncommittal monosyllabic responses of her daughter. Worse, when the daughter hung up, she did not quench the old woman's curiosity; instead, she placidly drank her coffee, went to her desk, and began to postmark a pile of letters.

"Myrt," Mother Truitt said. "For heaven's sake. What did Mabel *say?*"

"I'm not surprised," Mrs. Clare said. "When you think how Herb Clutter spent his whole life in a hurry, rushing in here to get his mail with never a minute to say good-morning-and-thank-you-dog, rushing around like a chicken with its head off—joining clubs, running everything, getting jobs maybe other people wanted. And now look—it's all caught up with him. Well, he won't be rushing *any* more."

"Why, Myrt? Why won't he?"

Mrs. Clare raised her voice. "BECAUSE HE'S DEAD. And Bonnie, too. And Nancy. And the boy. Somebody shot them."

"Myrt—don't say things like that. Who shot them?"

Without a pause in her postmarking activities, Mrs. Clare replied, "The man in the airplane. The one Herb sued for crashing into his fruit trees. If it wasn't him, maybe it was you. Or somebody across the street. All the neighbors are rattlesnakes. Varmints looking for a chance to slam the door in your face. It's the same the whole world over. You know that."

"I don't," said Mother Truitt, who put her hands over her ears. "I don't know any such thing."

"Varmints."

"I'm scared, Myrt."

"Of what? When your time comes, it comes. And tears won't save you." She had observed that her mother had begun to shed a few. "When Homer died, I used up all the fear I had in me, and all the grief, too. If there's somebody loose around here that wants to cut my throat, I wish him luck. What difference does it make? It's all the same in eternity. Just remember: If one bird carried every grain of sand, grain by grain, across the ocean, by the time he got them all on the other side, that would only be the beginning of eternity. So blow your nose."

The grim information, announced from church pulpits, distributed over telephone wires, publicized by Garden City's radio station, KIUL ("A tragedy, unbelievable and shocking beyond words, struck four members of the Herb Clutter family late Saturday night or early today. Death, brutal and without apparent motive . . ."), produced in the average recipient a reaction nearer that of Mother Truitt than that of Mrs. Clare: amazement, shading into dismay; a shallow horror sensation that cold springs of personal fear swiftly deepened.

Hartman's Café, which contains four roughly made tables and a lunch counter, could accommodate but a fraction of the frightened gossips, mostly male, who wished to gather there. The owner, Mrs. Bess Hartman, a sparsely fleshed, unfoolish lady with bobbed gray-and-gold hair and bright, authoritative green eyes, is a cousin of Postmistress Clare, whose style of candor Mrs. Hartman can equal, perhaps surpass. "Some people say I'm a tough old bird, but the Clutter business sure took the fly out of me," she later said to a friend. "Imagine anybody pulling a stunt like that! Time I heard it, when everybody was pouring in here talking all kinds of wild-eyed stuff, my first thought was Bonnie. Course, it was silly, but we didn't know the facts, and a lot of people thought *maybe*—on account of her spells. Now we don't know what to think. It must have been a grudge killing. Done by somebody who knew the house inside out. But who hated the Clutters? I never heard a word against them; they were about as popular as a family can be, and if something like this could happen to *them*, then who's safe, I ask you? One old man sitting here that Sunday, he put his finger right on it, the reason nobody can sleep; he said, 'All we've got out here are our friends. There isn't anything else.' In a way, that's the worst part of the crime. What a terrible thing when neighbors can't look at each other without kind of wondering! Yes, it's a hard fact to live with, but if they ever do find out who done it, I'm sure it'll be a bigger surprise than the murders themselves."

Mrs. Bob Johnson, the wife of the New York Life Insurance agent, is an excellent cook, but the Sunday dinner she had prepared was not eaten—at least, not while it was warm—for just as her husband was plunging a knife into the roast pheasant, he received a telephone call from a friend. "And that," he recalls, rather ruefully, "was the first I heard of what had happened in Holcomb. I didn't believe it. I couldn't afford to. Lord, I had Clutter's check right here in my pocket. A piece of paper worth eighty thousand dollars. If what I'd heard was true. But I thought, It can't be, there must be some mistake, things like that don't happen, you don't sell a man a big policy one minute and he's dead the next. Murdered. Meaning double indemnity. I didn't know what to do. I called the manager of our office in Wichita. Told him how I had the check but hadn't put it through, and asked what was his advice? Well, it was a *del*icate situation. It appeared that *legally* we weren't obliged to pay. But *morally*—that was another matter. Naturally, we decided to do the moral thing."

The two persons who benefited by this honorable attitude—Eveanna Jarchow and her sister Beverly, sole heirs to their father's estate—were, within a few hours of the awful discovery, on their way to Garden City, Beverly traveling from Winfield, Kansas, where she had been visiting her fiancé, and Eveanna from her home in Mount Carroll, Illinois. Gradually, in the course of the day, other relatives were notified, among them Mr. Clutter's father, his two brothers, Arthur and Clarence, and his sister, Mrs. Harry Nelson, all of Larned, Kansas, and a second sister, Mrs. Elaine Selsor, of Palatka, Florida. Also, the parents of Bonnie Clutter, Mr. and Mrs. Arthur B. Fox, who live in Pasadena, California, and her three brothers—Harold, of Visalia, California; Howard, of Oregon, Illinois; and Glenn, of Kansas City, Kansas. Indeed, the better part of those on the Clutters' Thanksgiving guest list were either telephoned or telegraphed, and the majority set forth at once for what was to be a family reunion not around a groaning board but at the graveside of a mass burial.

At the Teacherage, Wilma Kidwell was forced to control herself in order to control her daughter, for Susan, puffy-eyed, sickened by spasms of nausea, argued, inconsolably insisted, that she must go—must run—the three miles to the Rupp farm. "Don't you see, Mother?" she said. "If Bobby just *hears* it? He loved her. We both did. I *have* to be the one to tell him."

But Bobby already knew. On his way home, Mr. Ewalt had stopped at the Rupp farm and consulted with his friend Johnny Rupp, a father of eight, of whom Bobby is the third. Together, the two men went to the bunkhouse—a building separate from the farmhouse proper, which is too small to shelter all the Rupp children. The boys live in the bunkhouse, the girls "at home." They found Bobby making his bed. He listened to Mr. Ewalt, asked no questions, and thanked him for coming. Afterward, he stood outside in the sunshine. The Rupp property is on a rise, an exposed plateau, from which he could see the harvested, glowing land of River Valley Farm—scenery that occupied him for perhaps an hour. Those who tried to distract him could not. The dinner bell sounded, and his mother called to him to come inside—called until finally her husband said, "No. I'd leave him alone."

Larry, a younger brother, also refused to obey the summoning bell. He circled around Bobby, helpless to help but wanting to, even though he was told to "go away." Later, when his brother stopped standing and started to walk, heading down the road and across the fields toward Holcomb, Larry pursued him. "Hey, Bobby. Listen. If we're going somewhere, why don't we go in the car?" His brother wouldn't answer. He was walking with purpose, running, really, but Larry had no difficulty keeping stride. Though only fourteen, he was the taller of the two, the deeper-chested, the longer-legged, Bobby being, for all his athletic honors, rather less than medium-size—compact but slender, a finely made boy with an open, homely-handsome face. "Hey, Bobby. Listen. They won't let you see her. It won't do any good." Bobby turned on him, and said, "Go back. Go home." The younger brother fell behind, then followed at a distance. Despite the pumpkin-season temperature, the day's arid glitter, both boys were sweating as they approached a barricade that state troopers had erected at the entrance to River Valley Farm. Many friends of the Clutter family, and strangers from all over Finney County as well, had assembled at the site, but none was allowed past the barricade, which, soon after the arrival of the Rupp brothers, was briefly lifted to permit the exit of four ambulances, the number finally required to remove the victims, and a car filled with men from the sheriff's office—men who, even at that moment, were mentioning the name of Bobby Rupp. For Bobby, as he was to learn before nightfall, was their principal suspect.

From her parlor window, Susan Kidwell saw the white cortege glide past, and watched until it had rounded the corner and the unpaved street's easily airborne dust had landed again. She was still contemplating the view when Bobby, shadowed by his large little brother, became a part of it, a wobbly figure headed her way. She went out on the porch to meet him. She said, "I wanted so much to tell you." Bobby began to cry. Larry lingered at the edge of the Teacherage yard, hunched against a tree. He couldn't remember ever seeing Bobby cry, and he didn't want to, so he lowered his eyes.

Far off, in the town of Olathe, in a hotel room where window shades darkened the midday sun, Perry lay sleeping, with a gray portable radio murmuring beside him. Except for taking off his boots, he had not troubled to undress. He had merely fallen face down across the bed, as though sleep were a weapon that had struck him from behind. The boots, black and silver-buckled, were soaking in a washbasin filled with warm, vaguely pink-tinted water.

A few miles north, in the pleasant kitchen of a modest farmhouse, Dick was consuming a Sunday dinner. The others at the table—his mother, his father, his younger brother—were not conscious of anything uncommon in his manner. He had arrived home at noon, kissed his mother, readily replied to questions his father put concerning his supposed overnight trip to Fort Scott, and sat down to eat, seeming quite his ordinary self. When the meal was over, the three male members of the family settled in the parlor to watch a televised basketball game. The broadcast had only begun when the father was startled to hear Dick snoring; as he remarked to the younger boy, he never thought he'd live to see the day when Dick would rather sleep than watch basketball. But, of course, he did not understand how very tired Dick was, did not know that his dozing son had, among other things, driven over eight hundred miles in the past twenty-four hours.

## 2

## *Persons Unknown*

THAT MONDAY, THE sixteenth of November, 1959, was still another fine specimen of pheasant weather on the high wheat plains of western Kansas—a day gloriously bright-skied, as glittery as mica. Often, on such days in years past, Andy Erhart had spent long pheasant-hunting afternoons at River Valley Farm, the home of his good friend Herb Clutter, and often, on these sporting expeditions, he'd been accompanied by three more of Herb's closest friends: Dr. J. E. Dale, a veterinarian; Carl Myers, a dairy owner; and Everett Ogburn, a businessman. Like Erhart, the superintendent of the Kansas State University Agricultural Experiment Station, all were prominent citizens of Garden City.

Today this quartet of old hunting companions had once again gathered to make the familiar journey, but in an unfamiliar spirit and armed with odd, non-sportive equipment—mops and pails, scrubbing brushes, and a hamper heaped with rags and strong detergents. They were wearing their oldest clothes. For, feeling it their duty, a Christian task, these men had volunteered to clean certain of the fourteen rooms in the main house at River Valley Farm: rooms in which four members of the Clutter family had been murdered by, as their death certificates declared, "a person or persons unknown."

Erhart and his partners drove in silence. One of them later remarked, "It just shut you up. The strangeness of it. Going out there, where we'd always had such a welcome." On the present occasion a highway patrolman welcomed them. The patrolman, guardian of a barricade that the authorities had erected at the entrance to the farm, waved them on, and they drove a half mile more, down the elm-shaded lane leading to the Clutter house. Alfred Stoecklein, the only employee who actually lived on the property, was waiting to admit them.

They went first to the furnace room in the basement, where the pajama-clad Mr. Clutter had been found sprawled atop the cardboard mattress box. Finishing there, they moved on to the playroom in which Kenyon had been shot to death. The couch, a relic that Kenyon had rescued and mended and that Nancy had slipcovered and piled with mottoed pillows, was a blood-splashed ruin; like the mattress box, it would have to be burned. Gradually, as the cleaning party progressed from the basement to the second-floor bedrooms where Nancy and her mother had been murdered in their beds, they acquired additional fuel for the impending fire—blood-soiled bedclothes, mattresses, a bedside rug, a Teddy-bear doll.

Alfred Stoecklein, not usually a talkative man, had much to say as he fetched hot water and otherwise assisted in the cleaning-up. He wished "folks would stop yappin' and try to understand" why he and his wife, though they lived scarcely a hundred yards from the Clutter home, had heard "nary a nothin'"—not the slightest echo of gun thunder—of the violence taking place. "Sheriff and all them fellas been out here fingerprintin' and scratchin' around, they got good sense, *they* understand how it was. How come we didn't hear. For one thing, the wind. A west wind, like it was, would carry the sound t'other way. Another thing, there's that big milo barn 'tween this house and our'n. That old barn 'ud soak up a lotta racket 'fore it reached us. And did you ever think of this? Him that done it, he must've *knowed* we wouldn't hear. Else he wouldn't have took the chance—shootin' off a shotgun four times in the middle of the night! Why, he'd be crazy. Course, you might say he must be crazy anyhow. To go doing what he did. But my opinion, him that done it had it figured out to the final T. He *knowed.* And there's one thing I know, too. Me and the Missis, we've slept our last night on this place. We're movin' to a house alongside the highway."

The men worked from noon to dusk. When the time came to burn what they had collected, they piled it on a pickup truck and, with

Stoecklein at the wheel, drove deep into the farm's north field, a flat place full of color, though a single color—the shimmering tawny yellow of November wheat stubble. There they unloaded the truck and made a pyramid of Nancy's pillows, the bedclothes, the mattresses, the playroom couch; Stoecklein sprinkled it with kerosene and struck a match.

Of those present, none had been closer to the Clutter family than Andy Erhart. Gentle, genially dignified, a scholar with work-calloused hands and sunburned neck, he'd been a classmate of Herb's at Kansas State University. "We were friends for thirty years," he said some time afterward, and during those decades Erhart had seen his friend evolve from a poorly paid County Agricultural Agent into one of the region's most widely known and respected farm ranchers: "Everything Herb had, he earned—with the help of God. He was a modest man but a proud man, as he had a right to be. He raised a fine family. He made something of his life." But that life, and what he'd made of it—how could it happen, Erhart wondered as he watched the bonfire catch. How was it possible that such effort, such plain virtue, could overnight be reduced to this—smoke, thinning as it rose and was received by the big, annihilating sky?

The Kansas Bureau of Investigation, a state-wide organization with headquarters in Topeka, had a staff of nineteen experienced detectives scattered through the state, and the services of these men are available whenever a case seems beyond the competence of local authorities. The Bureau's Garden City representative, and the agent responsible for a sizable portion of western Kansas, is a lean and handsome fourth-generation Kansan of forty-seven named Alvin Adams Dewey. It was inevitable that Earl Robinson, the sheriff of Finney County, should ask Al Dewey to take charge of the Clutter case. Inevitable, and appropriate. For Dewey, himself a former sheriff of Finney County (from 1947 to 1955) and, prior to that, a Special Agent of the F.B.I. (between 1940 and 1945 he had served in New Orleans, in San Antonio, in Denver, in Miami, and in San Francisco), was professionally qualified to cope with even as intricate an affair as the apparently motiveless, all but clueless Clutter murders. Moreover, his attitude toward the crime made it, as he later said, "a personal proposition." He went on to say that he and his wife "were real fond of Herb and Bonnie," and "saw them every Sunday at church, visited a lot back and forth," adding, "But even if I hadn't known the family, and liked them so well, I wouldn't feel any different. Because I've seen some bad things, I sure as hell have. But nothing so vicious as this.

However long it takes, it may be the rest of my life, I'm going to know what happened in that house: the why and the who."

Toward the end, a total of eighteen men were assigned to the case full time, among them three of the K.B.I.'s ablest investigators—Special Agents Harold Nye, Roy Church, and Clarence Duntz. With the arrival in Garden City of this trio, Dewey was satisfied that "a strong team" had been assembled. "Somebody better watch out," he said.

The sheriff's office is on the third floor of the Finney County courthouse, an ordinary stone-and-cement building standing in the center of an otherwise attractive tree-filled square. Nowadays, Garden City, which was once a rather raucous frontier town, is quite subdued. On the whole, the sheriff doesn't do much business, and his office, three sparsely furnished rooms, is ordinarily a quiet place popular with courthouse idlers; Mrs. Edna Richardson, his hospitable secretary, usually has a pot of coffee going and plenty of time to "chew the fat." Or did, until, as she complained, "this Clutter thing came along," bringing with it "all these out-of-towners, all this *news*paper fuss." The case, then commanding headlines as far east as Chicago, as far west as Denver, had indeed lured to Garden City a considerable press corps.

On Monday, at midday, Dewey held a press conference in the sheriff's office. "I'll talk facts but not theories," he informed the assembled journalists. "Now, the big fact here, the thing to remember, is we're not dealing with one murder but four. And we don't know which of the four was the main target. The primary victim. It could have been Nancy or Kenyon, or either of the parents. Some people say, Well, it must have been Mr. Clutter. Because his throat was cut; he was the most abused. But that's theory, not fact. It would help if we knew in what order the family died, but the coroner can't tell us that; he only knows the murders happened sometime between eleven P.M. Saturday and two A.M. Sunday." Then, responding to questions, he said no, neither of the women had been "sexually molested," and no, as far as was presently known, nothing had been stolen from the house, and yes, he did think it a "queer coincidence" that Mr. Clutter should have taken out a forty-thousand-dollar life-insurance policy, with double indemnity, within eight hours of his death. However, Dewey was "pretty darn sure" that no connection existed between this purchase and the crime; how could there be one, when the only persons who benefited financially were Mr. Clutter's two surviving children, the elder daughters, Mrs. Donald Jarchow and Miss Beverly Clutter? And yes, he told the reporters, he did have an opinion on whether the murders were the work of one man or two, but he preferred not to disclose it.

Actually, at this time, on this subject, Dewey was undecided. He still entertained a pair of opinions—or, to use his word, "concepts"—and, in reconstructing the crime, had developed both a "single-killer concept" and a "double-killer concept." In the former, the murderer was thought to be a friend of the family, or, at any rate, a man with more than casual knowledge of the house and its inhabitants—someone who knew that the doors were seldom locked, that Mr. Clutter slept alone in the master bedroom on the ground floor, that Mrs. Clutter and the children occupied separate bedrooms on the second floor. This person, so Dewey imagined, approached the house on foot, probably around midnight. The windows were dark, the Clutters asleep, and as for Teddy, the farm's watchdog—well, Teddy was famously gun-shy. He would have cringed at the sight of the intruder's weapon, whimpered, and crept away. On entering the house, the killer first disposed of the telephone installations—one in Mr. Clutter's office, the other in the kitchen—and then, after cutting the wires, he went to Mr. Clutter's bedroom and awakened him. Mr. Clutter, at the mercy of the gun-bearing visitor, was forced to obey instructions—forced to accompany him to the second floor, where they aroused the rest of the family. Then, with cord and adhesive tape supplied by the killer, Mr. Clutter bound and gagged his wife, bound his daughter (who, inexplicably, had not been gagged), and roped them to their beds. Next, father and son were escorted to the basement, and there Mr. Clutter was made to tape Kenyon and tie him to the playroom couch. Then Mr. Clutter was taken into the furnace room, hit on the head, gagged, and trussed. Now free to do as he pleased, the murderer killed them one by one, each time carefully collecting the discharged shell. When he had finished, he turned out all the lights and left.

It might have happened that way; it was *just* possible. But Dewey had doubts: "If Herb had thought his family was in danger, mortal danger, he would have fought like a tiger. And Herb was no ninny—a strong guy in top condition. Kenyon too—big as his dad, bigger, a big-shouldered boy. It's hard to see how one man, armed or not, could have handled the two of them." Moreover, there was reason to suppose that all four had been bound by the same person: in all four instances the same type of knot, a half hitch, was used.

Dewey—and the majority of his colleagues, as well—favored the second hypothesis, which in many essentials followed the first, the important difference being that the killer was not alone but had an accomplice, who helped subdue the family, tape, and tie them. Still, as a theory, this, too, had its faults. Dewey, for example, found it difficult to understand "how two individuals could reach the same degree of rage, the kind of psychopathic rage it took to commit such a crime." He went on to explain: "Assuming the murderer was someone known to the family, a member of this community; assuming that he was an ordinary man, ordinary except that he had a quirk, an insane grudge against the Clutters, or one of the Clutters—where did he find a partner, someone crazy enough to help him? It doesn't add up. It doesn't make sense. But then, come right down to it, nothing does."

After the news conference, Dewey retired to his office, a room that the sheriff had temporarily lent him. It contained a desk and two straight chairs. The desk was littered with what Dewey hoped would some day constitute courtroom exhibits: the adhesive tape and the yards of cord removed from the victims and now sealed in plastic sacks (as clues, neither item seemed very promising, for both were common-brand products, obtainable anywhere in the United States), and photographs taken at the scene of the crime by a police photographer—twenty blown-up glossy-print pictures of Mr. Clutter's shattered skull, his son's demolished face, Nancy's bound hands, her mother's death-dulled, still-staring eyes, and so on. In days to come, Dewey was to spend many hours examining these photographs, hoping that he might "suddenly see something," that a meaningful detail would declare itself: "Like those puzzles. The ones that ask, 'How many animals can you find in this picture?' In a way, that's what I'm trying to do. Find the hidden animals. I feel they must be there—if only I could see them." As a matter of fact, one of the photographs, a close-up of Mr. Clutter and the mattress box upon which he lay, had already provided a valuable surprise: footprints, the dusty trackings of shoes with diamond-patterned soles. The prints, not noticeable to the naked eye, registered on film; indeed, the delineating glare of a flashbulb had revealed their presence with superb exactness. These prints, together with another footmark found on the same cardboard cover—the bold and bloody impression of a Cat's Paw half sole—were the only "serious clues" the investigators could claim. Not that they *were* claiming them; Dewey and his team had decided to keep secret the existence of this evidence.

Among the other articles on Dewey's desk was Nancy Clutter's diary. He had glanced through it, no more than that, and now he settled down to an earnest reading of the day-by-day entries, which began on her thirteenth birthday and ended some two months short of her seventeenth; the unsensational confidings of an intelligent child who adored animals, who liked to read, cook, sew, dance, ride horseback—a popular, pretty, virginal girl who thought it "fun to flirt" but was nevertheless "only really and truly in love with Bobby." Dewey read the final entry first. It consisted of three lines written an hour or two before she died: "Jolene K. came over and I showed her how to make a cherry pie. Practiced with Roxie. Bobby here and we watched TV. Left at eleven."

Young Rupp, the last person known to have seen the family alive, had already undergone one extensive interrogation, and although he'd told a straightforward story of having passed "just an ordinary evening" with the Clutters, he was scheduled for a second interview, at which time he was to be given a polygraph test. The plain fact was that the police were not quite ready to dismiss him as a suspect. Dewey himself did not believe the boy had "anything to do with it"; still, it was true that at this early stage of the investigation, Bobby was the only person to whom a motive, however feeble, could be attributed. Here and there in the diary, Nancy referred to the situation that was supposed to have created the motive: her father's insistence that she and Bobby "break off," stop "seeing so much of each other," his objection being that the Clutters were Methodist, the Rupps Catholic—a circumstance that in his view completely canceled any hope the young couple might have of one day marrying. But the diary notation that most tantalized Dewey was unrelated to the Clutter-Rupp, Methodist-Catholic impasse. Rather, it concerned a cat, the mysterious demise of Nancy's favorite pet, Boobs, whom, according to an entry dated two weeks prior to her own death, she'd found "lying in the barn," the victim, or so she suspected (without saying why), of a poisoner: "Poor Boobs. I buried him in a special place." On reading this, Dewey felt it could be "very important." If the cat had been poisoned, might not this act have been a small, malicious prelude to the murders? He determined to find the "special place" where Nancy had buried her pet, even though it meant combing the vast whole of River Valley Farm.

While Dewey was occupying himself with the diary, his principal assistants, the Agents Church, Duntz, and Nye, were crisscrossing the countryside, talking, as Duntz said, "to anyone who could tell us anything": the faculty of the Holcomb School, where both Nancy and Kenyon had been honor-roll, straight-A students; the employees of River Valley Farm (a staff that in spring and summer sometimes amounted to as many as eighteen men but in the present fallow season consisted of Gerald Van Vleet and three hired men, plus Mrs. Helm); friends of the victims; their neighbors; and, very particularly, their relatives. From far and near, some twenty of the last had arrived to attend the funeral services, which were to take place Wednesday morning.

The youngest of the K.B.I. group, Harold Nye, who was a peppy little man of thirty-four with restless, distrustful eyes and a sharp nose, chin, and mind, had been assigned what he called "the damned delicate business" of interviewing the Clutter kinfolk: "It's painful for you and it's painful for them. When it comes to murder, you can't respect grief. Or privacy. Or personal feelings. You've got to ask the questions. And some of them cut deep." But none of the persons he questioned, and none of the questions he asked ("I was exploring the emotional background. I thought the answer might be another woman—a triangle. Well, consider: Mr. Clutter was a fairly young, very healthy man, but his wife, she was a semi-invalid, she slept in a separate bedroom . . ."), produced useful information; not even the two surviving daughters could suggest a cause for the crime. In brief, Nye learned only this: "Of all the people in all the world, the Clutters were the least likely to be murdered."

At the end of the day, when the three agents convened in Dewey's office, it developed that Duntz and Church had had better luck than Nye—Brother Nye, as the others called him. (Members of the K.B.I. are partial to nicknames; Duntz is known as Old Man—unfairly, since he is not quite fifty, a burly but light-footed man with a broad, tomcat face, and Church, who is sixty or so, pink-skinned and professorial-looking, but "*tough,*" according to his colleagues, and "the fastest draw in Kansas," is called Curly, because his head is partly hairless.) Both men, in the course of their inquiries, had picked up "promising leads."

Duntz's story concerned a father and son who shall here be known as John Senior and John Junior. Some years earlier John Senior had conducted with Mr. Clutter a minor business transaction, the outcome of which angered John Senior, who felt that Clutter had thrown him "a queer ball." Now, both John Senior and his son "boozed"; indeed, John Junior was an often incarcerated alcoholic. One unfortunate day father and son, full of whiskey courage, appeared at the Clutter home intending to "have it out with Herb." They were denied the chance, for Mr. Clutter, an abstainer aggressively opposed to drink and drunkards, seized a gun and marched them off his property. This discourtesy the Johns had not forgiven; as recently as a month ago, John Senior had told an acquaintance, "Every time I think of that bastard, my hands start to twitch. I just want to choke him."

Church's lead was of a similar nature. He, too, had heard of someone admittedly hostile to Mr. Clutter: a certain Mr. Smith (though that is not his true name), who believed that the squire of River Valley Farm had shot and killed Smith's hunting dog. Church had inspected Smith's farm home and seen there, hanging from a barn rafter, a length of rope tied with the same kind of knot that was used to bind the four Clutters.

Dewey said, "One of those, maybe that's our deal. A personal thing—a grudge that got out of hand."

"Unless it was robbery," said Nye, though robbery as the motive had been much discussed and then more or less dismissed. The arguments against it were good, the strongest being that Mr. Clutter's aversion to cash was a county legend; he had no safe and never carried large sums of money. Also, if robbery were the explanation, why hadn't the robber removed the jewelry that Mrs. Clutter was wearing—a gold wedding band and a diamond ring? Yet Nye was not convinced: "The whole setup has that robbery smell. What about Clutter's wallet? Someone left it open and empty on Clutter's bed—I *don't* think it was the owner. And Nancy's purse. The purse was lying on the kitchen floor. How did it get there? Yes, and not a dime in the house. Well—two dollars. We found two dollars in an envelope on Nancy's desk. And we *know* Clutter cashed a check for sixty bucks just the day before. We figure there ought to have been at least fifty of that left. So some say, 'Nobody would kill four people for fifty bucks.' And say, 'Sure, maybe the killer did take the money—but just to try and mislead us, make us think robbery was the reason.' I wonder."

As darkness fell, Dewey interrupted the consultation to telephone his wife, Marie, at their home, and warn her that he wouldn't be home for dinner. She said, "Yes. All right, Alvin," but he noticed in her tone an uncharacteristic anxiety. The Deweys, parents of two young boys, had been married seventeen years, and Marie, a Louisiana-born former F.B.I. stenographer, whom he'd met while he was stationed in New Orleans, sympathized with the hardships of his profession—the eccentric hours, the sudden calls summoning him to distant areas of the state.

He said, "Anything the matter?"

"Not a thing," she assured him. "Only, when you come home tonight, you'll have to ring the bell. I've had all the locks changed."

Now he understood, and said, "Don't worry, honey. Just lock the doors and turn on the porch light."

After he'd hung up, a colleague asked, "What's wrong? Marie scared?"

"Hell, yes," Dewey said. "Her, and everybody else."

Not everybody. Certainly not Holcomb's widowed postmistress, the intrepid Mrs. Myrtle Clare, who scorned her fellow townsmen as "a lily-livered lot, shaking in their boots afraid to shut their eyes," and said of herself, "This old girl, she's sleeping good as ever. Anybody wants to play a trick on me, let 'em try." (Eleven months later a gun-toting team of masked bandits took her at her word by invading the post office and relieving the lady of nine hundred and fifty dollars.) As usual, Mrs. Clare's notions conformed with those of very few. "Around here," according to the proprietor of one Garden City hardware store, "locks and bolts are the fastest-going item. Folks ain't particular what brand they buy; they just want them to *hold.*" Imagination, of course, can open any door—turn the key and let terror walk right in. Tuesday, at dawn, a carload of pheasant hunters from Colorado—strangers, ignorant of the local disaster—were startled by what they saw as they crossed the prairies and passed through Holcomb: windows ablaze, almost every window in almost every house, and, in the brightly lit rooms, fully clothed people, even entire families, who had sat the whole night wide awake, watchful, listening. Of what were they frightened? "It might happen again." That, with variations, was the customary response. However, one woman, a schoolteacher, observed, "Feeling wouldn't run half so high if this had happened to anyone *except* the Clutters. Anyone *less* admired. Prosperous. Secure. But that family represented everything people hereabouts really value and respect, and that such a thing could happen to them—well, it's like being told there is no God. It makes life seem pointless. I don't think people are so much frightened as they are deeply depressed."

Another reason, the simplest, the ugliest, was that this hitherto peaceful congregation of neighbors and old friends had suddenly to endure the unique experience of distrusting each other; understandably, they believed that the murderer was among themselves, and, to the last man, endorsed an opinion advanced by Arthur Clutter, a brother of the deceased, who, while talking to journalists in the lobby of a Garden City hotel on November 17, had said, "When this is cleared up, I'll wager whoever did it was someone within ten miles of where we now stand."

Approximately four hundred miles east of where Arthur Clutter then stood, two young men were sharing a booth in the Eagle Buffet, a Kansas City diner. One—narrow-faced, and with a blue cat tattooed on his right hand—had polished off several chicken-salad sandwiches and was now eying his companion's meal: an untouched hamburger and a glass of root beer in which three aspirin were dissolving.

"Perry, baby," Dick said, "you don't want that burger. I'll take it."

Perry shoved the plate across the table. "Christ! Can't you let me concentrate?"

"You don't have to read it fifty times."

The reference was to a front-page article in the November 17 edition of the Kansas City *Star*. Headlined CLUES ARE FEW IN SLAYING OF 4, the article, which was a follow-up of the previous day's initial announcement of the murders, ended with a summarizing paragraph:

> The investigators are left faced with a search for a killer or killers whose cunning is apparent if his (or their) motive is not. For this killer or killers: *Carefully cut the telephone cords of the home's two telephones. *Bound and gagged their victims expertly, with no evidence of a struggle with any of them. *Left nothing in the house amiss, left no indication they had searched for anything with the possible exception of [Clutter's] billfold. *Shot four persons in different parts of the house, calmly picking up the expended shotgun shells. *Arrived and left the home, presumably with the murder weapon, without being seen. *Acted without a motive, if you care to discount an abortive robbery attempt, which the investigators are wont to do.

" 'For this killer or killers,' " said Perry, reading aloud. "That's incorrect. The grammar is. It ought to be 'For this killer or *these* killers.' " Sipping his aspirin-spiked root beer, he went on, "Anyway, I don't believe it. Neither do you. Own up, Dick. Be honest. You don't believe this no-clue stuff?"

Yesterday, after studying the papers, Perry had put the same question, and Dick, who thought he'd disposed of it ("Look. If those cowboys could make the slightest connection, we'd have heard the sound of hoofs a hundred miles off"), was bored at hearing it again. Too bored to protest when Perry once more pursued the matter: "I've always played my hunches. That's why I'm alive today. You know Willie-Jay? He said I was a natural-born 'medium,' and he knew about things like that, he was interested. He said I had a high degree of 'extrasensory perception.' Sort of like having built-in radar—you see things before you see them. The outlines of coming events. Take, like, my brother and his wife. Jimmy and his wife. They were crazy about each other, but he was jealous as hell, and he made her so miserable, being jealous and always thinking she was passing it out behind his back, that she shot herself, and the next day Jimmy put a bullet through his head. When it happened—this was 1949, and I was in Alaska with Dad up around Circle City—I told Dad, 'Jimmy's dead.' A week later we got the news. Lord's truth. Another time, over in Japan, I was helping load a ship, and I sat down to rest a minute. Suddenly a voice inside me said, 'Jump!' I jumped I guess maybe ten feet, and just then, right where I'd been sitting, a ton of stuff came crashing down. I could give you a hundred examples. I don't care if you believe me or not. For instance, right before I had my motorcycle accident I saw the whole thing happen: saw it in my mind—the rain, the skid tracks, me lying there bleeding and my legs broken. That's what I've got now. A *pre*monition. Something tells me this is a trap." He tapped the newspaper. "A lot of *pre*varications."

Dick ordered another hamburger. During the past few days he'd known a hunger that nothing—three successive steaks, a dozen Hershey bars, a pound of gumdrops—seemed to interrupt. Perry, on the other hand, was without appetite; he subsisted on root beer, aspirin, and cigarettes. "No wonder you got leaps," Dick told him. "Aw, come on, baby. Get the bubbles out of your blood. We scored. It was perfect."

"I'm surprised to hear that, all things considered," Perry said. The quietness of his tone italicized the malice of his reply. But Dick took it, even smiled—and his smile was a skillful proposition. Here, it said, wearing a kid grin, was a very personable character, clean-cut, affable, a fellow any man might trust to shave him.

"O.K.," Dick said. "Maybe I had some wrong information."

"Hallelujah."

"But on the whole it was perfect. We hit the ball right out of the park. It's lost. And it's gonna stay lost. There isn't a single connection."

"I can think of one."

Perry had gone too far. He went further: "Floyd—is that the name?" A bit below the belt, but then Dick deserved it, his confidence was like a kite that needed reeling in. Nevertheless, Perry observed with some misgiving the symptoms of fury rearranging Dick's expression: jaw, lips, the whole face slackened; saliva bubbles appeared at the corners of his mouth. Well, if it came to a fight, Perry could defend himself. He was short, several inches shorter than Dick, and his runty, damaged legs were unreliable, but he outweighed his friend, was thicker, had arms that could squeeze the breath out of a bear. To prove it, however—have a fight, a real falling-out—was far from desirable. Like Dick or not (and he didn't dislike Dick, though once he'd liked him better, respected him more), it was obvious they could not now safely separate. On that point they were in accord, for Dick had said, "If we get caught, let's get caught together. Then we can back each other up. When they start pulling the confession crap, saying you said and I said." Moreover, if he broke with Dick, it meant the end of plans still attractive to Perry, and still, despite recent reverses, deemed possible by both—a skin-diving, treasure-hunting life lived together among islands or along coasts south of the border.

Dick said, "*Mr.* Wells!" He picked up a fork. "It'd be worth it. Like if I was nabbed on a check charge, it'd be worth it. Just to get back in there." The fork came down and stabbed the table. "Right through the heart, honey."

"I'm not saying he would," said Perry, willing to make a concession now that Dick's anger had soared past him and struck elsewhere. "He'd be too scared."

"Sure," said Dick. "Sure. He'd be too scared." A marvel, really, the ease with which Dick negotiated changes of mood; in a trice, all trace of meanness, of sullen bravura, had evaporated. He said, "About that premonition stuff. Tell me this: If you were so damn sure you were gonna crack up, why didn't you call it quits? It wouldn't have happened if you'd stayed off your bike—right?"

That was a riddle that Perry had pondered. He felt he'd solved it, but the solution, while simple, was also somewhat hazy: "No. Because once a thing is set to happen, all you can do is hope it won't. Or will—depending. As long as you live, there's always something waiting, and even if it's bad, and you know it's bad, what can you do? You can't stop living. Like my dream. Since I was a kid, I've had this same dream. Where I'm in Africa. A jungle. I'm moving through the trees toward a tree standing all alone. Jesus, it smells bad, that tree; it kind of makes me sick, the way it stinks. Only, it's beautiful to look at—it has blue leaves and diamonds hanging everywhere. Diamonds like oranges. That's why I'm there—to pick myself a bushel of diamonds. But I know the minute I try to, the minute I reach up, a snake is gonna fall on me. A snake that guards the tree. This fat son of a bitch living in the branches. I know this beforehand, see? And Jesus, I don't know how to fight a snake. But I figure, Well, I'll take my chances. What it comes down to is I want the diamonds more than I'm afraid of the snake. So I go to pick one, I have the diamond in my hand, I'm pulling at it, when the snake lands on top of me. We wrestle around, but he's a slippery sonofabitch and I can't get a hold, he's crushing me, you can hear my legs cracking. Now comes the part it makes me sweat even to think about. See, he starts to swallow me. Feet first. Like going down in quicksand." Perry hesitated. He could not help noticing that Dick, busy gouging under his fingernails with a fork prong, was uninterested in his dream.

Dick said, "So? The snake swallows you? Or what?"

"Never mind. It's not important." (But it was! The finale was of great importance, a source of private joy. He'd once told it to his friend Willie-Jay; he had described to him the towering bird, the yellow "sort of parrot." Of course, Willie-Jay was different—delicate-minded, "a saint." He'd understood. But Dick? Dick might laugh. And that Perry could not abide: anyone's ridiculing the parrot, which had first flown into his dreams when he was seven years old, a hated, hating half-breed child living in a California orphanage run by nuns—shrouded disciplinarians who whipped him for wetting his bed. It was after one of these beatings, one he could never forget ("She woke me up. She had a flashlight, and she hit me with it. Hit me and hit me. And when the flashlight broke, she went on hitting me in the dark"), that the parrot appeared, arrived while he slept, a bird "taller than Jesus, yellow like a sunflower," a warrior-angel who blinded the nuns with its beak, fed upon their eyes, slaughtered them as they "pleaded for mercy," then so gently lifted him, enfolded him, winged him away to "paradise."

As the years went by, the particular torments from which the bird delivered him altered; others—older children, his father, a faithless girl, a sergeant he'd known in the Army—replaced the nuns, but the parrot remained, a hovering avenger. Thus, the snake, that custodian of the diamond-bearing tree, never finished devouring him but was itself always devoured. And afterward the blessed ascent! Ascension to a paradise that in one version was merely "a feeling," a sense of power, of unassailable superiority—sensations that in another version were transposed into "A real place. Like out of a movie. Maybe that's where I *did* see it—remembered it from a movie. Because where else would I have seen a garden like that? With white marble steps? Fountains? And away down below, if you go to the edge of the garden, you can see the ocean. Terrific! Like around Carmel, California. The best thing, though—well, it's a long, long table. You never imagined so much food. Oysters. Turkeys. Hot dogs. Fruit you could make into a million fruit cups. And, listen—it's every bit *free.* I mean, I don't have to be afraid to touch it. I can eat as much as I want, and it won't cost a cent. That's how I know where I am."

Dick said, "I'm a normal. I only dream about blond chicken. Speaking of which, you hear about the nanny goat's nightmare?" That was Dick—always ready with a dirty joke on any subject. But he told the joke well, and Perry, though he was in some measure a prude, could not help laughing, as always.

Speaking of her friendship with Nancy Clutter, Susan Kidwell said: "We were like sisters. At least, that's how I felt about her—as though she were my sister. I couldn't go to school—not those first few days. I stayed out of school until after the funeral. So did Bobby Rupp. For a while Bobby and I were always together. He's a nice boy—he has a good heart—but nothing very terrible had ever happened to him before. Like losing anyone he'd loved. And then, on top of it, having to take a lie-detector test. I don't mean he was bitter about that; he realized the police were doing what they had to do. Some hard things, two or three, had already happened to me, but not to him, so it was a shock when he found out maybe life isn't one long basketball game. Mostly, we just drove around in his old Ford. Up and down the highway. Out to the airport and back. Or we'd go to the Cree-Mee—that's a drive-in—and sit in the car, order a Coke, listen to the radio. The radio was always playing; *we* didn't have anything to say ourselves. Except once in a while Bobby said how much he'd loved Nancy, and how he could never care about another girl. Well, I was sure Nancy wouldn't have wanted that, and I told him so. I remember—I think it was Monday—we drove down to the river. We parked on the bridge. You can see the house from there—the Clutter house. And part of the land—Mr. Clutter's fruit orchard, and the wheat fields going away. Way off in one of the fields a bonfire was burning; they were burning stuff from the house. Everywhere you looked, there was something to remind you. Men with nets and poles were fishing along the banks of the river, but not fishing for fish. Bobby said they were looking for the weapons. The knife. The gun.

"Nancy loved the river. Summer nights we used to ride double on Nancy's horse, Babe—that old fat gray? Ride straight to the river and right into the water. Then Babe would wade along in the shallow part while we played our flutes and sang. Got cool. I keep wondering, Gosh, what will become of her? Babe. A lady from Garden City took Kenyon's dog. Took Teddy. He ran away—found his way back to Holcomb. But she came and got him again. And I have Nancy's cat—Evinrude. But Babe. I suppose they'll sell her. Wouldn't Nancy hate that? Wouldn't she be *furious?* Another day, the day before the funeral, Bobby and I were sitting by the railroad tracks. Watching the trains go by. Real stupid. Like sheep in a blizzard. When suddenly Bobby woke up and said, 'We ought to go see Nancy. We ought to be with her.' So we drove to Garden City—went to the Phillips' Funeral Home, there on Main Street. I think Bobby's kid brother was with us. Yes, I'm sure he was. Because I remember we picked him up after school. And I remember he said how there wasn't going to be any school the next day, so all the Holcomb kids could go to the funeral. And he kept telling us what the kids thought. He said the kids were convinced it was the work of 'a hired killer.' I didn't want to hear about it. Just gossip and talk—everything Nancy despised. Anyway, I don't much care who did it. Somehow it seems beside the point. My friend is gone. Knowing who killed her isn't going to bring her back. What else matters? They wouldn't let us. At the funeral parlor, I mean. They said no one could 'view the family.' Except the relatives. But Bobby insisted, and finally the undertaker—he knew Bobby, and, I guess, felt sorry for him—he said all right, be quiet about it, but come on in. Now I wish we hadn't."

The four coffins, which quite filled the small, flower-crowded parlor, were to be sealed at the funeral services—very understandably, for despite the care taken with the appearance of the victims, the effect achieved was disquieting. Nancy wore her dress of cherry-red velvet, her brother a bright plaid shirt; the parents were more sedately attired, Mr. Clutter in navy-blue flannel, his wife in navy-blue crepe; and—and it was this, especially, that lent the scene an awful aura—the head of each was completely encased in cotton, a swollen cocoon twice the size of an ordinary blown-up balloon, and the cotton, because it had been sprayed with a glossy substance, twinkled like Christmas-tree snow.

Susan at once retreated. "I went outside and waited in the car," she recalled. "Across the street a man was raking leaves. I kept looking at him. Because I didn't want to close my eyes. I thought, If I do I'll faint. So I watched him rake leaves and burn them. Watched, without really seeing him. Because all I could see was the dress. I knew it so well. I helped her pick the material. It was her own design, and she sewed it herself. I remember how excited she was the first time she wore it. At a party. All I could see was Nancy's red velvet. And Nancy in it. Dancing."

The Kansas City *Star* printed a lengthy account of the Clutter funeral, but the edition containing the article was two days old before Perry, lying abed in a hotel room, got around to reading it. Even so, he merely skimmed through, skipped about among the paragraphs: "A thousand persons, the largest crowd in the five-year history of the First Methodist Church, attended services for the four victims today. . . . Several classmates of Nancy's from Holcomb High School wept as the Reverend Leonard Cowan said: 'God offers us courage, love and hope even though we walk through the shadows of the valley of death. I'm sure he was with them in their last hours. Jesus has never promised us we would not suffer pain or sorrow but He has always said He would be there to help us bear the sorrow and the pain.' . . . On the unseasonably warm day, about six hundred persons went to the Valley View

Cemetery on the north edge of this city. There, at graveside services, they recited the Lord's Prayer. Their voices, massed together in a low whisper, could be heard throughout the cemetery."

A thousand people! Perry was impressed. He wondered how much the funeral had cost. Money was greatly on his mind, though not as relentlessly as it had been earlier in the day—a day he'd begun "without the price of a cat's miaow." The situation had improved since then; thanks to Dick, he and Dick now possessed "a pretty fair stake"—enough to get them to Mexico.

Dick! Smooth. Smart. Yes, you had to hand it to him. Christ, it was incredible how he could "con a guy." Like the clerk in the Kansas City, Missouri, clothing store, the first of the places Dick had decided to "hit." As for Perry, he'd never tried to "pass a check." He was nervous, but Dick told him, "All I want you to do is stand there. Don't laugh, and don't be surprised at anything I say. You got to play these things by ear." For the task proposed, it seemed, Dick had perfect pitch. He breezed in, breezily introduced Perry to the clerk as "a friend of mine about to get married," and went on, "I'm his best man. Helping him kind of shop around for the clothes he'll want. Ha-ha, what you might say his—ha-ha—trousseau." The salesman "ate it up," and soon Perry, stripped of his denim trousers, was trying on a gloomy suit that the clerk considered "ideal for an informal ceremony." After commenting on the customer's oddly proportioned figure—the oversized torso supported by the undersized legs—he added, "I'm afraid we haven't anything that would fit without alteration." Oh, said Dick, that was O.K., there was plenty of time—the wedding was "a week tomorrow." That settled, they then selected a gaudy array of jackets and slacks regarded as appropriate for what was to be, according to Dick, a Florida honeymoon. "You know the Eden Roc?" Dick said to the salesman. "In Miami Beach? They got reservations. A present from her folks—two weeks at forty bucks a day. How about that? An ugly runt like him, he's making it with a honey she's not only built but loaded. While guys like you and me, good-lookin' guys . . ." The clerk presented the bill. Dick reached in his hip pocket, frowned, snapped his fingers, and said, "Hot damn! I forgot my wallet." Which to his partner seemed a ploy so feeble that it couldn't possibly "fool a day-old nigger." The clerk, apparently, was not of that opinion, for he produced a blank check, and when Dick made it out for eighty dollars more than the bill totaled, instantly paid over the difference in cash.

Outside, Dick said, "So you're going to get married next week? Well, you'll need a ring." Moments later, riding in Dick's aged Chevrolet, they arrived at a store named *Best Jewelry*. From there, after purchasing by check a diamond engagement ring and a diamond wedding band, they drove to a pawnshop to dispose of these items. Perry was sorry to see them go. He'd begun to half credit the make-believe bride, though in his conception of her, as opposed to Dick's, she was not rich, not beautiful; rather, she was nicely groomed, gently spoken, was conceivably "a college graduate," in any event "a very intellectual type"—a sort of girl he'd always wanted to meet but in fact never had.

Unless you counted Cookie, the nurse he'd known when he was hospitalized as a result of his motorcycle accident. A swell kid, Cookie, and she had liked him, pitied him, babied him, inspired him to read "serious literature"—*Gone with the Wind, This Is My Beloved.* Sexual episodes of a strange and stealthy nature had occurred, and love had been mentioned, and marriage, too, but eventually, when his injuries had mended, he'd told her goodbye and given her, by way of explanation, a poem he pretended to have written:

> There's a race of men that don't fit in,
> A race that can't stay still;
> So they break the hearts of kith and kin;
> And they roam the world at will.
> They range the field and they rove the flood,
> And they climb the mountain's crest;
> Theirs is the curse of the gypsy blood,
> And they don't know how to rest.
> If they just went straight they might go far;
> They are strong and brave and true;
> But they're always tired of the things that are,
> And they want the strange and new.

He had not seen her again, or ever heard from or of her, yet several years later he'd had her name tattooed on his arm, and once, when Dick asked who "Cookie" was, he'd said, "Nobody. A girl I almost married." (That Dick had been married—married twice—and had fathered three sons was something he envied. A wife, children—those were experiences "a man ought to have," even if, as with Dick, they didn't "make him happy or do him any good.")

The rings were pawned for a hundred and fifty dollars. They visited another jewelry store, Goldman's, and sauntered out of there with a man's gold wristwatch. Next stop, an Elko Camera Store, where they "bought" an elaborate motion-picture camera. "Cameras are your best investment," Dick informed Perry. "Easiest thing to hock or sell. Cameras and TV sets." This being the case, they decided to obtain several of the latter, and, having completed the mission, went on to attack a few more clothing emporiums—Sheperd & Foster's, Rothschild's, Shopper's Paradise. By sundown, when the stores were closing, their pockets were filled with cash and the car was heaped with salable, pawnable wares. Surveying this harvest of shirts and cigarette lighters, expensive machinery and cheap cuff links, Perry felt elatedly tall—now Mexico, a new chance, a "really living" life. But Dick seemed depressed. He shrugged off Perry's praises ("I mean it, Dick. You were amazing. Half the time I believed you myself"). And Perry was puzzled; he could not fathom why Dick, usually so full of himself, should suddenly, when he had good cause to gloat, be meek, look wilted and sad. Perry said, "I'll stand you a drink."

They stopped at a bar. Dick drank three Orange Blossoms. After the third, he abruptly asked, "What about Dad? I feel—oh, Jesus, he's such a good old guy. And my mother—well, you saw her. What about *them*? Me, I'll be off in Mexico. Or wherever. But they'll be right here when those checks start to bounce. I know Dad. He'll want to make them good. Like he tried to before. And he can't—he's old and he's sick, he ain't got anything."

"I sympathize with that," said Perry truthfully. Without being kind, he was sentimental, and Dick's affection for his parents, his professed concern for them, did indeed touch him. "But hell, Dick. It's very simple," Perry said. "*We* can pay off the checks. Once we're in Mexico, once we get started down there, we'll make money. Lots of it."

"How?"

"How?"—what could Dick mean? The question dazed Perry. After all, such a rich assortment of ventures had been discussed. Prospecting for gold, skin-diving for sunken treasure—these were but two of the projects Perry had ardently proposed. And there were others. The boat, for instance. They had often talked of a deep-sea-fishing boat, which they would buy, man themselves, and rent to vacationers—this though neither had ever skippered a canoe or hooked a guppy. Then, too, there was quick money to be made chauffeuring stolen cars across South American borders. ("You get paid five hundred bucks a trip," or so Perry had read somewhere.) But of the many replies he might have made, he chose to remind Dick of the fortune awaiting them on Cocos Island, a land speck off the coast of Costa Rica. "No fooling, Dick," Perry said. "This is authentic. I've got a map. I've got the whole history. It was buried there back in 1821—Peruvian bullion, jewelry. Sixty million dollars—that's what they say it's worth. Even if we didn't find all of it, even if we found only some of it— Are you with me, Dick?" Heretofore, Dick had always encouraged him, listened attentively to his talk of maps, tales of treasure, but now—and it had not occurred to him before—he wondered if all along Dick had only been *pretending,* just kidding him.

The thought, acutely painful, passed, for Dick, with a wink and a playful jab, said, "Sure, honey. I'm with you. All the way."

It was three in the morning, and the telephone rang again. Not that the hour mattered. Al Dewey was wide awake anyway, and so were Marie and their sons, nine-year-old Paul and twelve-year-old Alvin Adams Dewey, Jr. For who could sleep in a house—a modest one-story house—where all night the telephone had been sounding every few minutes? As he got out of bed, Dewey promised his wife, "This time I'll leave it off the hook." But it was not a promise he dared keep. True, many of the calls came from news-hunting journalists, or would-be humorists, or theorists ("Al? Listen, fella, I've got this deal figured. It's suicide and murder. I happen to *know* Herb was in a bad way financially. He was spread pretty thin. So what does he do? He takes out this big insurance policy, shoots Bonnie and the kids, and kills himself with a bomb. A hand grenade stuffed with buckshot"), or anonymous persons with poison-pen minds ("Know them Ls? Foreigners? Don't work? Give parties? Serve *cock*tails? Where's the money come from? Wouldn't surprise me a darn if they ain't at the roots of this Clutter trouble"), or nervous ladies alarmed by the gossip going around, rumors that knew neither ceiling nor cellar ("Alvin, now, I've known you since you were a boy. And I want you to tell me straight out whether it's so. I loved and respected Mr. Clutter, and I *refuse* to believe that that man, that Christian—I refuse to believe he was chasing after women . . .").

But most of those who telephoned were responsible citizens wanting to be helpful ("I wonder if you've interviewed Nancy's friend, Sue Kidwell? I was talking to the child, and she said something that struck me. She said the last time she ever spoke to Nancy, Nancy told her Mr. Clutter was in a real bad mood. Had been the past three weeks. That she thought he was very worried about something, so worried he'd taken to smoking cigarettes . . ."). Either that or the callers were people officially concerned—law officers and sheriffs from other parts of the state ("This may be something, may not, but a bartender here says he overheard two fellows discussing the case in terms made it sound like they had a lot to do with it . . ."). And while none of these conversations had as yet done more than make extra work for the investigators, it was always possible that the next one might be, as Dewey put it, "the break that brings down the curtain."

On answering the present call, Dewey immediately heard "I want to confess."

He said, "To whom am I speaking, please?"

The caller, a man, repeated his original assertion, and added, "I did it. I killed them all."

"Yes," said Dewey. "Now, if I could have your name and address . . ."

"Oh, no, you don't," said the man, his voice thick with inebriated indignation. "I'm not going to tell you anything. Not till I get the reward. You send the reward, then I'll tell you who I am. That's final."

Dewey went back to bed. "No, honey," he said. "Nothing important. Just another drunk."

"What did he want?"

"Wanted to confess. Provided we sent the reward first." (A Kansas paper, the Hutchinson *News,* had offered a thousand dollars for information leading to the solution of the crime.)

"Alvin, are you lighting another cigarette? Honestly, Alvin, can't you at least *try* to sleep?"

He was too tense to sleep, even if the telephone could be silenced—too fretful and frustrated. None of his "leads" had led anywhere, except, perhaps, down a blind alley toward the blankest of walls. Bobby Rupp? The polygraph machine had eliminated Bobby. And Mr. Smith, the farmer who tied rope knots identical with those used by the murderer—he, too, was a discarded suspect, having established that on the night of the crime he'd been "off in Oklahoma." Which left the Johns, father and son, but they had also submitted provable alibis. "So," to quote Harold Nye, "it all adds up to a nice round number. Zero." Even the hunt for the grave of Nancy's cat had come to nothing.

Nevertheless, there had been one or two meaningful developments. First, while sorting Nancy's clothes, Mrs. Elaine Selsor, her aunt, had found tucked in the toe of a shoe a gold wristwatch. Second, accompanied by a K.B.I. agent, Mrs. Helm had explored every room at River Valley Farm, toured the house in the expectation that she might notice something awry or absent, and she had. It happened in Kenyon's room. Mrs. Helm looked and looked, paced round and round the room with pursed lips, touching this and that—Kenyon's old baseball mitt, Kenyon's mud-spattered work boots, his pathetic abandoned spectacles. All the while she kept whispering, "Something here is wrong, I feel it, I know it, but I don't know what it is." And then she did know. "It's the *radio!* Where is Kenyon's little radio?"

Taken together, these discoveries forced Dewey to consider again the possibility of "plain robbery" as a motive. Surely that watch had not tumbled into Nancy's shoe by accident? She must, lying there in the dark, have heard sounds—footfalls, perhaps voices—that led her to suppose thieves were in the house, and so believing must have hurriedly hidden the watch, a gift from her father that she treasured. As for the radio, a gray portable made by Zenith—no doubt about it, the radio was gone. All the same, Dewey could not accept the theory that the family had been slaughtered for paltry profit—"a few dollars and a radio." To accept it would obliterate his image of the killer—or, rather, killers. He and his associates had definitely decided to pluralize the term. The expert execution of the crimes was proof enough that at least one of the pair commanded an immoderate amount of coolheaded slyness, and was—*must* be—a person too clever to have done such a deed without calculated motive. Then, too, Dewey had become aware of several particulars that reinforced his conviction that at least one of the murderers was emotionally involved with the victims, and felt for them, even as he destroyed them, a certain twisted tenderness. How else explain the mattress box?

The business of the mattress box was one of the things that most tantalized Dewey. Why had the murderers taken the trouble to move the box from the far end of the basement room and lay it on the floor in front of the furnace, unless the intention had been to make Mr. Clutter more comfortable—to provide him, while he contemplated the approaching knife, with a couch less rigid than cold cement? And in studying the death-scene photographs Dewey had distinguished other details that seemed to support his notion of a murderer now and again moved by considerate impulses. "Or"—he could never quite find the word he wanted—"something fussy. And soft. Those bedcovers. Now, what kind of person would do that—tie up two women, the way Bonnie and the girl were tied, and then draw up the bedcovers, *tuck* them in, like sweet dreams and good night? Or the pillow under Kenyon's head. At first I thought maybe the pillow was put there to make his head a simpler target. Now I think, No, it was done for the same reason the mattress box was spread on the floor—to make the victim more comfortable."

But speculations such as these, though they absorbed Dewey, did not gratify him or give him a sense of "getting somewhere." A case was seldom solved by "fancy theories"; he put his faith in facts—"sweated for and sworn to." The quantity of facts to be sought and sifted, and the agenda planned to obtain them, promised perspiration aplenty, entailing, as it did, the tracking down, the "checking out," of hundreds of people, among them all former River Valley Farm employees, friends and family, anyone with whom Mr. Clutter had done business, much or little—a tortoise crawl into the past. For, as Dewey had told his team, "we have to keep going till we know the Clutters better than they ever knew themselves. Until we see the connection between what we found last Sunday morning and something that happened maybe five years ago. The link. Got to be one. Got to."

Dewey's wife dozed, but she awakened when she felt him leave their bed, heard him once more answering the telephone, and heard, from the nearby room where her sons slept, sobs, a small boy crying. "Paul?" Ordinarily, Paul was neither troubled nor troublesome—not a whiner, ever. He was too busy digging tunnels in the backyard or practicing to be "the fastest runner in Finney County." But at breakfast that morning he'd burst into tears. His mother had not needed to ask him why; she knew that although he understood only hazily the reasons for the uproar round him, he felt endangered by it—by the harassing telephone, and the strangers at the door, and his father's worry-wearied eyes. She went to comfort Paul. His brother, three years older, helped. "Paul," he said, "you take it easy now, and tomorrow I'll teach you to play poker."

Dewey was in the kitchen; Marie, searching for him, found him there, waiting for a pot of coffee to percolate and with the murder-scene photographs spread before him on the kitchen table—bleak stains, spoiling the table's pretty fruit-patterned oilcloth. (Once he had offered to let her look at the pictures. She had declined. She had said, "I want to remember Bonnie the way Bonnie was—and all of them.") He said, "Maybe the boys ought to stay with Mother." His mother, a widow, lived not far off, in a house she thought too spacious and silent; the grandchildren were always welcome. "For just a few days. Until—well, until."

"Alvin, do you think we'll ever get back to normal living?" Mrs. Dewey asked.

Their normal life was like this: both worked, Mrs. Dewey as an office secretary, and they divided between them the household chores, taking turns at the stove and the sink. ("When Alvin was sheriff, I know some of the boys teased him. Used to say, 'Looka-yonder! Here comes Sheriff Dewey! Tough guy! Totes a six-shooter! But once he gets home, off comes the gun and on goes the apron!'") At that time they were saving to build a house on a farm that Dewey had bought in 1951—two hundred and forty acres several miles north of Garden City. If the weather was fine, and especially when the days were hot and the wheat was high and ripe, he liked to drive out there and practice his draw—shoot crows, tin cans—or in his imagination roam through the house he hoped to have, and through the garden he meant to plant, and under trees yet to be seeded. He was very certain that some day his own oasis of oaks and elms would stand upon those shadeless plains: "*Some* day. God willing."

A belief in God and the rituals surrounding that belief—church every Sunday, grace before meals, prayers before bed—were an important part of the Deweys' existence. "I don't see how anyone can sit down to table without wanting to bless it," Mrs. Dewey once said. "Sometimes, when I come home from work—well, I'm tired. But there's always coffee on the stove, and sometimes a steak in the icebox. The boys make a fire to cook the steak, and we talk, and tell each other our day, and by the time supper's ready I know we have good cause to be happy and grateful. So I say, Thank you, Lord. Not just because I should—because I want to."

Now Mrs. Dewey said, "Alvin, answer me. Do you think we'll ever have a normal life again?"

He started to reply, but the telephone stopped him.

The old Chevrolet left Kansas City November 21, Saturday night. Luggage was lashed to the fenders and roped to the roof; the trunk was so stuffed it could not be shut; inside, on the back seat, two television sets stood, one atop the other. It was a tight fit for the passengers: Dick, who was driving, and Perry, who sat clutching the old Gibson guitar, his most beloved possession. As for Perry's other belongings—a cardboard suitcase, a gray Zenith portable radio, a gallon jug of root-beer syrup (he feared that his favorite beverage might not be available in Mexico), and two big boxes containing books, manuscripts, cherished memorabilia (and hadn't Dick raised hell! Cursed, kicked the boxes, called them "five hundred pounds of pig slop!")—these, too, were part of the car's untidy interior.

Around midnight they crossed the border into Oklahoma. Perry, glad to be out of Kansas, at last relaxed. Now it was true—they were on their way— On their way, and never coming back—without regret, as far as he was concerned, for he was leaving nothing behind, and no one who might deeply wonder into what thin air he'd spiraled. The same could not be said of Dick. There were those Dick claimed to love: three sons, a mother, a father, a brother—persons he hadn't dared confide his plans to, or bid goodbye, though he never expected to see them again—not in this life.

Clutter-English Vows Given in Saturday Ceremony: that headline, appearing on the social page of the Garden City *Telegram* for November 23, surprised many of its readers. It seemed that Beverly, the second of Mr. Clutter's surviving daughters, had married Mr. Vere Edward English, the young biology student to whom she had long been engaged. Miss Clutter had worn white, and the wedding, a full-scale affair ("Mrs. Leonard Cowan was soloist, and Mrs. Howard Blanchard organist"), had been "solemnized at the First Methodist Church"—the church in which, three days earlier, the bride had formally mourned her parents, her brother, and her younger sister. However, according to the *Telegram*'s account, "Vere and Beverly had planned to be married at Christmastime. The invitations were printed and her father had reserved the church for that date. Due to the unexpected tragedy and because of the many relatives being here from distant places, the young couple decided to have their wedding Saturday."

The wedding over, the Clutter kinfolk dispersed. On Monday, the day the last of them left Garden City, the *Telegram* featured on its front page a letter written by Mr. Howard Fox, of Oregon, Illinois, a brother of Bonnie Clutter. The letter, after expressing gratitude to the townspeople for having opened their "homes and hearts" to the bereaved family, turned into a plea. "There is much resentment in this community [that is, Garden City]," wrote Mr. Fox. "I have even heard on more than one occasion that the man, when found, should be hanged from the nearest tree. Let us not feel this way. The deed is done and taking another life cannot change it. Instead, let us forgive as God would have us do. It is not right that we should hold a grudge in our hearts. The doer of this act is going to find it very difficult indeed to live with himself. His only peace of mind will be when he goes to God for forgiveness. Let us not stand in the way but instead give prayers that he may find his peace."

The car was parked on a promontory where Perry and Dick had stopped to picnic. It was noon. Dick scanned the view through a pair of binoculars. Mountains. Hawks wheeling in a white sky. A dusty road winding into and out of a white and dusty village. Today was his second day in Mexico, and so far he liked it fine—even the food. (At this very moment he was eating a cold, oily tortilla.) They had crossed the border at Laredo, Texas, the morning of November 23, and spent the first night in a San Luis Potosí brothel. They were now two hundred miles north of their next destination, Mexico City.

"Know what I think?" said Perry. "I think there must be something wrong with us. To do what we did."

"Did what?"

"Out there."

Dick dropped the binoculars into a leather case, a luxurious receptacle initialed H.W.C. He was annoyed. Annoyed as hell. Why the hell couldn't Perry shut up? Christ Jesus, what damn good did it do, always dragging the goddam thing up? It really was *annoying*. Especially since they'd agreed, sort of, not to talk about the goddam thing. Just forget it.

"There's got to be something wrong with somebody who'd do a thing like that," Perry said.

"Deal me out, baby," Dick said. "I'm a normal." And Dick meant what he said. He thought himself as balanced, as sane as anyone—maybe a bit smarter than the average fellow, that's all. But Perry—there *was*, in Dick's opinion, "something wrong" with Little Perry. To say the least. Last spring, when they had celled together at Kansas State Penitentiary, he'd learned most of Perry's lesser peculiarities: Perry could be "such a kid," always wetting his bed and crying in his sleep ("Dad, I been looking everywhere, where you been, Dad?"), and often Dick had seen him "sit for hours just sucking his thumb and poring over them phony damn treasure guides." Which was one side; there were others. In some ways old Perry was "spooky as hell." Take, for instance, that temper of his. He could slide into a fury "quicker than ten drunk Indians." And yet you wouldn't know it. "He might be ready to kill you, but you'd never know it, not to look at or listen to," Dick once said. For however extreme the inward rage, outwardly Perry remained a cool young tough, with eyes serene and slightly sleepy. The time had been when Dick had thought he could control, could regulate the temperature of these sudden cold fevers that burned and chilled his friend. He had been mistaken, and in the aftermath of that discovery, had grown very unsure of Perry, not at all certain what to think—except that he felt he ought to be afraid of him, and wondered really why he wasn't.

"Deep down," Perry continued, "way, way rock-bottom, I never thought I could do it. A thing like that."

"How about the nigger?" Dick said. Silence. Dick realized that Perry was staring at him. A week ago, in Kansas City, Perry had bought a pair of dark glasses—fancy ones with silver-lacquered rims and mirrored lenses. Dick disliked them; he'd told Perry he was ashamed to be seen with "anyone who'd wear that kind of flit stuff." Actually, what irked him was the mirrored lenses; it was unpleasant having Perry's eyes hidden behind the privacy of those tinted, reflecting surfaces.

"But a nigger," said Perry. "That's different."

The comment, the reluctance with which it was pronounced, made Dick ask, "Or did you? Kill him like you said?" It was a significant question, for his original interest in Perry, his assessment of Perry's character and potentialities, was founded on the story Perry had once told him of how he had beaten a colored man to death.

"Sure I did. Only—a nigger. It's not the same." Then Perry said, "Know what it is that really bugs me? About the other thing? It's just I don't believe it—that anyone can get away with a thing like that. Because I don't see how it's possible. To do what we did. And just one hundred percent get away with it. I mean, that's what bugs me—I can't get it out of my head that something's got to happen."

Though as a child he had attended church, Dick had never "come near" a belief in God; nor was he troubled by superstitions. Unlike Perry, he was not convinced that a broken mirror meant seven years' misfortune, or that a young moon if glimpsed through glass portended evil. But Perry, with his sharp and scratchy intuitions, had hit upon Dick's one abiding doubt. Dick, too, suffered moments when that question circled inside his head: Was it possible—were the two of them "honest to God going to get away with doing a thing like that"? Suddenly, he said to Perry, "Now, just shut up!" Then he gunned the motor and backed the car off the promontory. Ahead of him, on the dusty road, he saw a dog trotting along in the warm sunshine.

Mountains. Hawks wheeling in a white sky.

When Perry asked Dick, "Know what I think?" he knew he was beginning a conversation that would displease Dick, and one that, for that matter, he himself would just as soon avoid. He agreed with Dick: Why go on talking about it? But he could not always stop himself. Spells of helplessness occurred, moments when he "remembered things"—blue light exploding in a black room, the glass eyes of a big toy bear—and when voices, a particular few words, started nagging his mind: "Oh, no! Oh, please! No! No! No! No! Don't! Oh, please don't, please!" And certain sounds returned—a silver dollar rolling across a floor, boot steps on hardwood stairs, and the sounds of breathing, the gasps, the hysterical inhalations of a man with a severed windpipe.

When Perry said, "I think there must be something wrong with us," he was making an admission he "hated to make." After all, it was "painful" to imagine that one might be "not just right"—particularly if whatever was wrong was not your own fault but "maybe a thing you were born with." Look at his family! Look at what had happened there! His mother, an alcoholic, had strangled to death on her own vomit. Of her children, two sons and two daughters, only the younger girl, Barbara, had entered ordinary life, married, begun raising a family. Fern, the other daughter, jumped out of a window of a San Francisco hotel. (Perry had ever since "tried to believe she slipped," for he'd loved

Fern. She was "such a sweet person," so "artistic," a "terrific" dancer, and she could sing, too. "If she'd ever had any luck at all, with her looks and all, she could have got somewhere, been somebody." It was sad to think of her climbing over a window sill and falling fifteen floors.) And there was Jimmy, the older boy—Jimmy, who had one day driven his wife to suicide and killed himself the next.

Then he heard Dick say, "Deal me out, baby. I'm a normal." Wasn't that a horse's laugh? But never mind, let it pass. "Deep down," Perry continued, "way, way rock-bottom, I never thought I could do it. A thing like that." And at once he recognized his error: Dick would, of course, answer by asking, "How about the nigger?" When he'd told Dick that story, it was because he'd wanted Dick's friendship, wanted Dick to "respect" him, think him "hard," as much "the masculine type" as he had considered Dick to be. And so one day after they had both read and were discussing a *Reader's Digest* article entitled "How Good a Character Detective Are You?" ("As you wait in a dentist's office or a railway station, try studying the give-away signs in people around you. Watch the way they walk, for example. A stiff-legged gait can reveal a rigid, unbending personality; a shambling walk a lack of determination"), Perry had said "I've always been an outstanding character detective, otherwise I'd be dead today. Like if I couldn't judge when to trust somebody. You never can much. But I've come to trust you, Dick. You'll see I do, because I'm going to put myself in your power. I'm going to tell you something I never told anybody. Not even Willie-Jay. About the time I fixed a guy." And Perry saw, as he went on, that Dick was interested; he was really listening. "It was a couple of summers ago. Out in Vegas. I was living in this old boarding house—it used to be a fancy cathouse. But all the fancy was gone. It was a place they should have torn down ten years back; anyway, it was sort of coming down by itself. The cheapest rooms were in the attic, and I lived up there. So did this nigger. His name was King; he was a transient. We were the only two up there—us and a million *cucarachas*. King, he wasn't too young, but he'd done roadwork and other outdoor stuff—he had a good build. He wore glasses, and he read a lot. He never shut his door. Every time I passed by, he was always lying there buck-naked. He was out of work, and said he'd saved a few dollars from his last job, said he wanted to stay in bed awhile, read and fan himself and drink beer. The stuff he read, it was just junk—comic books and cowboy junk. He was O.K. Sometimes we'd have a beer together, and once he lent me ten dollars. I had no cause to hurt him. But one night we were sitting in the attic, it was so hot you couldn't sleep, so I said, 'Come on, King, let's go for a drive.' I had an old car I'd stripped and souped and painted silver—the Silver Ghost, I called it. We went for a long drive. Drove way out in the desert. Out there it was cool. We parked and drank a few more beers. King got out of the car, and I followed after him. He didn't see I'd picked up this chain. A bicycle chain I kept under the seat. Actually, I had no real idea to do it till I did it. I hit him across the face. Broke his glasses. I kept right on. Afterward, I didn't feel a thing. I left him there, and never heard a word about it. Maybe nobody ever found him. Just buzzards."

There was some truth in the story. Perry had known, under the circumstances stated, a Negro named King. But if the man was dead today it was none of Perry's doing; he'd never raised a hand against him. For all he knew, King might still be lying abed somewhere, fanning himself and sipping beer.

"Or did you? Kill him like you said?" Dick asked.

Perry was not a gifted liar, or a prolific one; however, once he had told a fiction he usually stuck by it. "Sure I did. Only—a nigger. It's not the same." Presently, he said, "Know what it is that really bugs me? About that other thing? It's just I don't believe it—that anyone can get away with a thing like that." And he suspected that Dick didn't, either. For Dick was at least partly inhabited by Perry's mystical-moral apprehensions. Thus: "Now, just shut up!"

The car was moving. A hundred feet ahead, a dog trotted along the side of the road. Dick swerved toward it. It was an old half-dead mongrel, brittle-boned and mangy, and the impact, as it met the car, was little more than what a bird might make. But Dick was satisfied. "Boy!" he said—and it was what he always said after running down a dog, which was something he did whenever the opportunity arose. "Boy! We sure splattered him!"

Thanksgiving passed, and the pheasant season came to a halt, but not the beautiful Indian summer, with its flow of clear, pure days. The last of the out-of-town newsmen, convinced that the case was never going to be solved, left Garden City. But the case was by no means closed for the people of Finney County, and least of all for those who patronized Holcomb's favorite meeting place, Hartman's Café.

"Since the trouble started, we've been doing all the business we can handle," Mrs. Hartman said, gazing around her snug domain, every scrap of which was being sat or stood or leaned upon by tobacco-scented, coffee-drinking farmers, farm helpers, and ranch hands. "Just a bunch of old women," added Mrs. Hartman's cousin, Postmistress Clare, who happened to be on the premises. "If it was spring and work to be done, they wouldn't be here. But wheat's in, winter's on the way, they got nothing to do but sit around and scare each other. You know Bill Brown, down to the *Telegram*? See the editorial he wrote? That one he called it 'Another Crime'? Said, 'It's time for everyone to stop wagging loose tongues.' Because that's a crime, too—telling plain-out lies. But what can you expect? Look around you. Rattlesnakes. Varmints. *Rumor*mongers. See anything else? Ha! Like dash you do."

One rumor originating in Hartman's Café involved Taylor Jones, a rancher whose property adjoins River Valley Farm. In the opinion of a good part of the café's clientele, Mr. Jones and his family, not the Clutters, were the murderer's intended victims. "It makes harder sense," argued one of those who held this view. "Taylor Jones, he's a richer man than Herb Clutter ever was. Now, pretend the fellow who done it wasn't anyone from hereabouts. Pretend he'd been maybe hired to kill, and all he had was instructions on how to get to the house. Well, it would be mighty easy to make a mistake—take a wrong turn—and end up at Herb's place 'stead of Taylor's." The "Jones Theory" was much repeated—especially to the Joneses, a dignified and sensible family, who refused to be flustered.

A lunch counter, a few tables, an alcove harboring a hot grill and an icebox and a radio—that's all there is to Hartman's Café. "But our customers like it," says the proprietress. "Got to. Nowhere else for them to go. 'Less they drive seven miles one direction or fifteen the other. Anyway, we run a friendly place, and the coffee's good since Mabel came to work"—Mabel being Mrs. Helm. "After the tragedy, I said, 'Mabel, now that you're out of a job, why don't you come give me a hand at the café. Cook a little. Wait counter.' How it turned out—the only bad feature is, everybody comes in here, they pester her with questions. About the tragedy. But Mabel's not like Cousin Myrt. Or me. She's shy. Besides, she doesn't know anything special. No more than anybody else." But by and large the Hartman congregation continued to suspect that Mabel Helm knew a thing or two that she was holding back. And, of course, she did. Dewey had had several conversations with her and had requested that everything they said be kept secret. Particularly, she was not to mention the missing radio or the watch found in Nancy's shoe. Which is why she said to Mrs. Archibald William Warren-Browne, "Anybody reads the papers knows as much as I do. More. Because I don't read them."

Square, squat, in the earlier forties, an Englishwoman fitted out with an accent almost incoherently upper-class, Mrs. Archibald William Warren-Browne did not at all resemble the café's other frequenters, and seemed, within that setting, like a peacock trapped in a turkey pen. Once, explaining to an acquaintance why she and her husband had abandoned "family estates in the North of England," exchanging the hereditary home—"the jolliest, oh, the prettiest old priory"—for an old and highly unjolly farmhouse on the plains of western Kansas, Mrs. Warren-Browne said: "Taxes, my dear. Death duties. E*nor*mous, *crim*inal death duties. That's what drove us out of England. Yes, we left a year ago. Without regrets. None. We love it here. *Just* adore it. Though, of course, it's very *dif*ferent from our other life. The life we've always known. Paris and Rome. Monte. London. I do—oc*cas*ionally—think of London. Oh, I don't *really* miss it—the frenzy, and never a cab, and always worrying how one looks. Positively not. We love it here. I suppose some people—those aware of our past, the life we've led—wonder aren't we the tiniest bit *lone*ly, out there in the wheat fields. Out West is where we meant to settle. Wyoming or Neveda—*la vraie chose*. We hoped when we got there some oil might stick to us. But on our way we stopped to visit friends in Garden City—friends *of* friends, *ac*tually. But they couldn't have been kinder. In*sis*ted we linger on. And we thought, Well, why not? Why not hire a bit of land and start ranching? Or farming. Which is a decision we still haven't come to—whether to ranch or farm. Dr. Austin asked if we didn't find it perhaps too quiet. *Ac*tually, no. *Ac*tually, I've never known such bedlam. It's noisier than a bomb raid. *Train* whistles. *Coyo*tes. Monsters *howl*ing the bloody night long. A horrid racket. And since the murders it seems to bother me more. So many things do. Our house—what an old creaker it is! Mark you, I'm not complaining. Really, it's quite a serviceable house—has all the mod. cons.—but, oh, how it coughs and grunts! And after dark, when the wind commences, that *hate*ful prairie wind, one hears the most ap*pall*ing moans. I mean, if one's a bit nervy, one can't help imagining—silly things. Dear God! That poor family! No, we never met them. I *saw* Mr. Clutter once. In the Federal Building."

Early in December, in the course of a single afternoon, two of the café's steadiest customers announced plans to pack up and leave not merely Finney County but the state. The first was a tenant farmer who worked for Lester McCoy, a well-known western-Kansas landowner and businessman. He said, "I had myself a talk with Mr. McCoy. Tried to let him know what's going on out here in Holcomb and hereabouts. How a body can't sleep. My wife can't sleep, and she won't allow me. So I told Mr. McCoy I like his place fine but he better hunt up another man. 'Count of we're movin' on. Down to east Colorado. Maybe then I'll get some rest."

The second announcement was made by Mrs. Hideo Ashida, who stopped by the café with three of her four red-cheeked children. She lined them up at the counter and told Mrs. Hartman, "Give Bruce a box of Cracker Jack. Bobby wants a Coke. Bonnie Jean? We know how you feel, Bonnie Jean, but come on, have a treat." Bonnie Jean shook her head, and Mrs. Ashida said, "Bonnie Jean's sort of blue. She don't want to leave here. The school here. And all her friends."

"Why, say," said Mrs. Hartman, smiling at Bonnie Jean. "That's nothing to be sad over. Transferring from Holcomb to Garden City High. Lots more boys—"

Bonnie Jean said, "You don't understand. Daddy's taking us away. To Nebraska."

Bess Hartman looked at the mother, as if expecting her to deny the daughter's allegation.

"It's true, Bess," Mrs. Ashida said.

"I don't know what to say," said Mrs. Hartman, her voice indignantly astonished, and also despairing. The Ashidas were a part of the Holcomb community everyone appreciated—a family likably high-spirited, yet hard-working and neighborly and generous, though they didn't have much to be generous with.

Mrs. Ashida said, "We've been talking on it a long time. Hideo, he thinks we can do better somewhere else."

"When you plan to go?"

"Soon as we sell up. But anyway not before Christmas. On account of a deal we've worked out with the dentist. About Hideo's Christmas present. Me and the kids, we're giving him three gold teeth. For Christmas."

Mrs. Hartman sighed. "I don't know what to say. Except I wish you wouldn't. Just up and leave us." She sighed again. "Seems like we're losing everybody. One way and another."

"Gosh, you think I want to leave?" Mrs. Ashida said. "Far as people go, this is the nicest place we ever lived. But Hideo, he's the man, and he says we can get a better farm in Nebraska. And I'll tell you something, Bess." Mrs. Ashida attempted a frown, but her plump, round, smooth face could not quite manage it. "We used to argue about it. Then one night I said, 'O.K., you're the boss, let's go.' After what happened to Herb and his family, I felt something around here had come to an end. I mean personally. For me. And so I quit arguing. I said O.K." She dipped a hand into Bruce's box of Cracker Jack. "Gosh, I can't get over it. I can't get it off my mind. I *liked* Herb. Did you know I was one of the last to see him alive? Uh-huh. Me and the kids. We been to the 4-H meeting in Garden City and he gave us a ride home. The last thing I said to Herb, I told him how I couldn't imagine his ever being afraid. That no matter what the situation was, he could talk his way out of it." Thoughtfully she nibbled a kernel of Cracker Jack, took a swig of Bobby's Coke, then said, "Funny, but you know, Bess, I'll bet he *wasn't* afraid. I mean, however it happened, I'll bet right up to the last he didn't believe it would. Because it couldn't. Not to him."

The sun was blazing. A small boat was riding at anchor in a mild sea: the *Estrellita,* with four persons aboard—Dick, Perry, a young Mexican, and Otto, a rich middle-aged German.

"Please. Again," said Otto, and Perry, strumming his guitar, sang in a husky sweet voice a Smoky Mountains song:

"In this world today while we're living
Some folks say the worst of us they can,
But when we're dead and in our caskets,
They always slip some lilies in our hand.
Won't you give me flowers while I'm living . . ."

A week in Mexico City, and then he and Dick had driven south—Cuernavaca, Taxco, Acapulco. And it was in Acapulco, in a "jukebox honky-tonk," that they had met the hairy-legged and hearty Otto. Dick had "picked him up." But the gentleman, a vacationing Hamburg lawyer, "already had a friend"—a young native Acapulcan who called himself the Cowboy. "He proved to be a trustworthy person," Perry once said of the Cowboy. "Mean as Judas, some ways, but oh, man, a funny boy, a real fast jockey. Dick liked him, too. We got on great."

The Cowboy found for the tattooed drifters a room in the house of an uncle, undertook to improve Perry's Spanish, and shared the benefits of his liaison with the holidaymaker from Hamburg, in whose company and at whose expense they drank and ate and bought women. The host seemed to think his pesos well spent, if only because he relished Dick's jokes. Each day Otto hired the *Estrellita,* a deep-sea-fishing craft, and the four friends went trolling along the coast. The Cowboy skippered the boat; Otto sketched and fished; Perry baited hooks, daydreamed, sang, and sometimes fished; Dick did nothing—only moaned, complained of the motion, lay about sun-drugged and listless, like a lizard at siesta. But Perry said, "This is finally it. The way it ought to be." Still, he knew that it couldn't continue—that it was, in fact, destined to stop that very day. The next day Otto was returning to Germany, and Perry and Dick were driving back to Mexico City—at Dick's insistence. "Sure, baby," he'd said when they were debating the matter. "It's nice and all. With the sun on your back. But the dough's going-going-gone. And after we've sold the car, what have we got left?"

The answer was that they had very little, for they had by now mostly disposed of the stuff acquired the day of the Kansas City check-passing spree—the camera, the cuff links, the television sets. Also, they had sold, to a Mexico City policeman with whom Dick had got acquainted, a pair of binoculars and a gray Zenith portable radio. "What we'll do is, we'll go back to Mex, sell the car, and maybe I can get a garage job. Anyway, it's a better deal up there. Better opportunities. Christ, I sure could use some more of that Inez." Inez was a prostitute who had accosted Dick on the steps of the Palace of Fine Arts in Mexico City (the visit was part of a sightseeing tour taken to please Perry). She was eighteen, and Dick had promised to marry her. But he had also promised to marry Maria, a woman of fifty, who was the widow of a "very prominent Mexican banker." They had met in a bar, and the next morning she had paid him the equivalent of seven dollars. "So how about it?" Dick said to Perry. "We'll sell the wagon. Find a job. Save our dough. And see what happens." As though Perry couldn't predict precisely what would happen. Suppose they got two or three hundred for the old Chevrolet. Dick, if he knew Dick, and he did—*now* he did—would spend it right away on vodka and women.

While Perry sang, Otto sketched him in a sketchbook. It was a passable likeness, and the artist perceived one not very obvious aspect of the sitter's countenance—its mischief, an amused, babyish malice that suggested some unkind cupid aiming envenomed arrows. He was naked to the waist. (Perry was "ashamed" to take off his trousers, "ashamed" to wear swimming trunks, for he was afraid that the sight of his injured legs would "disgust people," and so, despite his underwater reveries, all the talk about skindiving, he hadn't once gone into the water.) Otto reproduced a number of the tattoos ornamenting the subject's overmuscled chest, arms, and small and calloused but girlish hands. The sketchbook, which Otto gave Perry as a parting gift, contained several drawings of Dick—"nude studies."

Otto shut his sketchbook, Perry put down his guitar, and the Cowboy raised anchor, started the engine. It was time to go. They were ten miles out, and the water was darkening.

Perry urged Dick to fish. "We may never have another chance," he said.

"Chance?"

"To catch a big one."

"Jesus, I've got the bastard kind," Dick said. "I'm sick." Dick often had headaches of migraine intensity—"the bastard kind." He thought they were the result of his automobile accident. "Please, baby. Let's be very, very quiet."

Moments later Dick had forgotten his pain. He was on his feet, shouting with excitement. Otto and the Cowboy were shouting, too. Perry had hooked "a big one." Ten feet of soaring, plunging sailfish, it leaped, arched like a rainbow, dived, sank deep, tugged the line taut, rose, flew, fell, rose. An hour passed, and part of another, before the sweat-soaked sportsman reeled it in.

There is an old man with an ancient wooden box camera who hangs around the harbor in Acapulco, and when the *Estrellita* docked, Otto commissioned him to do six portraits of Perry posed beside his catch. Technically, the old man's work turned out badly—brown and streaked. Still, they were remarkable photographs, and what made them so was Perry's expression, his look of unflawed fulfillment, of beatitude, as though at last, and as in one of his dreams, a tall yellow bird had hauled him to heaven.

One December afternoon Paul Helm was pruning the patch of floral odds and ends that had entitled Bonnie Clutter to membership in the Garden City Garden Club. It was a melancholy task, for he was reminded of another afternoon when he'd done the same chore. Kenyon had helped him that day, and it was the last time he'd seen Kenyon alive, or Nancy, or any of them. The weeks between had been hard on Mr. Helm. He was "in poor health" (poorer than he knew; he had less than four months to live), and he was worried about a lot of things. His job, for one. He doubted he would have it much longer. Nobody seemed really to know, but he understood that "the girls," Beverly and Eveanna, intended to sell the property—though, as he'd heard one of the boys at the café remark, "ain't nobody gonna buy that spread, long as the mystery lasts." It "didn't do" to think about—strangers here, harvesting "our" land. Mr. Helm minded—he minded for Herb's sake. This was a place, he said, that "ought to be kept in a man's family." Once Herb had said to him, "I hope there'll always be a Clutter here, and a Helm, too." It was only a year ago Herb had said that. Lord, what was he to do if the farm got sold? He felt "too old to fit in somewhere different."

Still, he must work, and he wanted to. He wasn't, he said, the kind to kick off his shoes and sit by the stove. And yet it was true that the farm nowadays made him uneasy: the locked house, Nancy's horse forlornly waiting in a field, the odor of windfall apples rotting under the apple trees, and the absence of voices—Kenyon calling Nancy to the telephone, Herb whistling, his glad "*Good* morning, Paul." He and

Herb had "got along grand"—never a cross word between them. Why, then, did the men from the sheriff's office continue to question him? Unless they thought he had "something to hide"? Maybe he ought never to have mentioned the Mexicans. He had informed Al Dewey that at approximately four o'clock on Saturday, November 14, the day of the murders, a pair of Mexicans, one mustachioed and the other pockmarked, appeared at River Valley Farm. Mr. Helm had seen them knock on the door of "the office," seen Herb step outside and talk to them on the lawn, and, possibly ten minutes later, watched the strangers walk away, "looking sulky." Mr. Helm figured that they had come asking for work and had been told there was none. Unfortunately, though he'd been called upon to recount his version of that day's events many times, he had not spoken of the incident until two weeks after the crime, because, as he explained to Dewey, "I just suddenly recalled it." But Dewey, and some of the other investigators, seemed not to credit his story, and behaved as though it were a tale he'd invented to mislead them. They preferred to believe Bob Johnson, the insurance salesman, who had spent all of Saturday afternoon conferring with Mr. Clutter in the latter's office, and who was "absolutely positive" that from two to ten past six he had been Herb's sole visitor. Mr. Helm was equally definite: Mexicans, a mustache, pockmarks, four o'clock. Herb would have told them that he was speaking the truth, convinced them that he, Paul Helm, was a man who "said his prayers and earned his bread." But Herb was gone.

Gone. And Bonnie, too. Her bedroom window overlooked the garden, and now and then, usually when she was "having a bad spell," Mr. Helm had seen her stand long hours gazing into the garden, as though what she saw bewitched her. ("When I was a girl," she had once told a friend, "I was terribly sure trees and flowers were the same as birds or people. That they thought things, and talked among themselves. And we could hear them if we really tried. It was just a matter of emptying your head of all other sounds. Being very quiet and listening very hard. Sometimes I still believe that. But one can never get quiet enough . . .")

Remembering Bonnie at the window, Mr. Helm looked up, as though he expected to see her, a ghost behind the glass. If he had, it could not have amazed him more than what he did in fact discern—a hand holding back a curtain, and eyes. "But," as he subsequently described it, "the sun was hitting that side of the house"—it made the window glass waver, shimmeringly twisted what hung beyond it—and by the time Mr. Helm had shielded his eyes, then looked again, the curtains had swung closed, the window was vacant. "My eyes aren't too good, and I wondered if they had played me a trick," he recalled. "But I was pretty darn certain that they hadn't. And I was pretty darn certain it wasn't any spook. Because I don't believe in spooks. So who could it be? Sneaking around in there. Where nobody's got a right to go, except the law. And how did they get in? With everything locked up like the radio was advertising tornadoes. That's what I wondered. But I wasn't expecting to find out—not by myself. I dropped what I was doing, and cut across the fields to Holcomb. Soon as I got there, I phoned Sheriff Robinson. Explained that there was somebody prowling around inside the Clutter house. Well, they came raring right on out. State troopers. The sheriff and his bunch. The K.B.I. fellows. Al Dewey. Just as they were stringing themselves around the place, sort of getting ready for action, the front door opened." Out walked a person no one present had ever seen before—a man in his middle thirties, dull-eyed, wild-haired, and wearing a hip holster stocked with a .38-caliber pistol. "I guess all of us there had the identical idea—this was him, the one who came and killed them," Mr. Helm continued. "He didn't make a move. Stood quiet. Kind of blinking. They took the gun away, and started asking questions."

The man's name was Adrian—Jonathan Daniel Adrian. He was on his way to New Mexico, and at present had no fixed address. For what purpose had he broken into the Clutter house, and how, incidentally, had he managed it? He showed them how. (He had lifted a lid off a water well and crawled through a pipe tunnel that led into the basement.) As for why, he had read about the case and was curious, just wanted to see what the place looked like. "And then," according to Mr. Helm's memory of the episode, "somebody asked him was he a hitchhiker? Hitchhiking his way to New Mexico? No, he said, he was driving his own car. And it was parked down the lane a piece. So everybody went to look at the car. When they found what was inside it, one of the men—maybe it was Al Dewey—said to him, told this Jonathan Daniel Adrian, 'Well, mister, seems like we've got something to discuss.' Because, inside the car, what they'd found was a .12-gauge shotgun. And a hunting knife."

A room in a hotel in Mexico City. In the room was an ugly modern bureau with a lavender-tinted mirror, and tucked into a corner of the mirror was a printed warning from the Management:

SU DÍA TERMINA A LAS 2 P.M.
YOUR DAY ENDS AT 2 P.M.

Guests, in other words, must vacate the room by the stated hour or expect to be charged another day's rent—a luxury that the present occupants were not contemplating. They wondered only whether they could settle the sum already owed. For everything had evolved as Perry had prophesied: Dick had sold the car, and three days later the money, slightly less than two hundred dollars, had largely vanished. On the fourth day Dick had gone out hunting honest work, and that night he had announced to Perry, "Nuts! You know what they pay? What the *wages* are? For an *expert* mechanic? Two bucks a day. Mexico! Honey, I've had it. We got to make it out of here. Back to the States. No, now, I'm *not* going to listen. Diamonds. *Buried* treasure. Wake up, little boy. There ain't no caskets of gold. No sunken ship. And even if there was—hell, you can't even *swim*." And the next day, having borrowed money from the richer of his two fiancées, the banker's widow, Dick bought bus tickets that would take them, via San Diego, as far as Barstow, California. "After that," he said, "we walk."

Of course, Perry could have struck out on his own, stayed in Mexico, let Dick go where he damn well wanted. Why not? Hadn't he always been "a loner," and without any "real friends" (except the gray-haired, gray-eyed, and "brilliant" Willie-Jay)? But he was afraid to leave Dick; merely to consider it made him feel "sort of sick," as though he were trying to make up his mind to "jump off a train going ninety-nine miles an hour." The basis of his fear, or so he himself seemed to believe, was a newly grown superstitious certainty that "whatever had to happen won't happen" as long as he and Dick "stick together." Then, too, the severity of Dick's "wake-up" speech, the belligerence with which he'd proclaimed his theretofore concealed opinion of Perry's dreams and hopes—all this, perversity being what it is, appealed to Perry, hurt and shocked him but charmed him, almost revived his former faith in the tough, the "totally masculine," the pragmatic, the decisive Dick he'd once allowed to boss him. And so, since a sunrise hour on a chilly Mexico City morning in early December, Perry had been prowling about the unheated hotel room assembling and packing his possessions—stealthily, lest he waken the two sleeping shapes lying on one of the room's twin beds: Dick, and the younger of his betrotheds, Inez.

There was one belonging of his that need no longer concern him. On their last night in Acapulco, a thief had stolen the Gibson guitar—absconded with it from a waterfront café where he, Otto, Dick, and the Cowboy had been bidding one another a highly alcoholic goodbye. And Perry was bitter about it. He felt, he later said, "real mean and low," explaining, "You have a guitar long enough, like I had that one, wax and shine it, fit your voice to it, treat it like it was a girl you really had some use for—well, it gets to be kind of holy." But while the purloined guitar presented no ownership problem, his remaining property did. As he and Dick would now be traveling by foot or thumb, they clearly could not carry with them more than a few shirts and socks. The rest of their clothing would have to be shipped—and, indeed, Perry had already filled a cardboard carton (putting into it—along with some bits of unlaundered laundry—two pairs of boots, one pair with soles that left a Cat's Paw print, the other pair with diamond-pattern soles) and addressed it to himself, care of General Delivery, Las Vegas, Nevada.

But the big question, and source of heartache, was what to do with his much-loved memorabilia—the two huge boxes heavy with books and maps, yellowing letters, song lyrics, poems, and unusual souvenirs (suspenders and a belt fabricated from the skins of Nevada rattlers he himself had slain; an erotic *netsuke* bought in Kyoto; a petrified dwarf tree, also from Japan; the foot of an Alaskan bear). Probably the best solution—at least, the best Perry could devise—was to leave the stuff with "Jesus." The "Jesus" he had in mind tended bar in a café across the street from the hotel, and was, Perry thought, *muy simpático*, definitely someone he could trust to return the boxes on demand. (He intended to send for them as soon as he had a "fixed address.")

Still, there were some things too precious to chance losing, so while the lovers drowsed and time dawdled on toward 2:00 P.M., Perry looked through old letters, photographs, clippings, and selected from them those mementos he meant to take with him. Among them was a badly typed composition entitled "A History of My Boy's Life." The author of this manuscript was Perry's father, who in an effort to help his son obtain a parole from Kansas State Penitentiary, had written it the previous December and mailed it to the Kansas State Parole Board. It was a document that Perry had read at least a hundred times, never with indifference:

> CHILDHOOD—Be glad to tell you, as I see it, both good and bad. Yes, Perry birth was *normal.* Healthy—yes. Yes, I was able to care for him properly until my wife turned out to be a disgraceful drunkard when my children were at school age. Happy disposition—*yes* and *no*, very serious if mistreated he never forgets. I also keep my promises and make him do so. My wife was different. We lived in the country. We are all truly outdoor people. I taught my children the Golden Rule. Live & let live and in many cases

my children would tell on each other when doing wrong and the guilty one would always admit, and come forward, willing for a spanking. And promise to be good, and always done their work quickly and willing so they could be free to play. Always wash themselves first thing in the morning, dress in clean clothes, I was very strict about that, and wrong doings to others, and if wrong was done to them by other kids I made them quit playing with them. Our children were no trouble to us as long as we were together. It all started when my wife wanted to go to the City and live a wild life—and ran away to do so. I let her go and said goodby as she took the car and left me behind (this was during depression). My children all cryed at the top of their voices. She only cussed them saying they would run away to come to me later. She got mad and then said she would turn the children to hate me, which she did, all but *Perry*. For the love of my children after several months I went to find them, located them in San Francisco, my wife not knowing. I tryed to see them in school. My wife had given orders to the teacher not to let me see them. However, I managed to see them while playing in the school yard and was surprised when they told me, "Mama told us not to talk to you." All but *Perry*. He was different. He put his arms around me and wanted to run away with me rite then. I told him *No*. But right after school was out, he ran away to my lawyers office Mr. *Rinso Turco*. I took my boy back to his mother and left the City. Perry later told me, his mother told him to find a new home. While my children were with her they run around as they pleased, I understand Perry got into trouble. I wanted *her* to ask for divorce, which she did after about a year or so. Her drinkin and stepin out, living with a young man. I contested the divorce and was granted full custody of the children. I took Perry to my home to live with me. The other children were put in homes as I could not manage to take them all in my home and them being part indian blood and welfare took care of them as I requested.

This was during depression time. I was working on W.P.A. very small wages. I owned some property and small home at the time. Perry and I lived together peacefully. My heart was hurt, as I still loved my other children also. So I took to roaming to forget it all. I made a livin for us both. I sold my property and we lived in a "house car." Perry went to school often as possible. He didn't like school very well. He learns quick and never got into trouble with the other kids. Only when the *Bully Kid* picked on him. He was short and stocky a new kid in school they tried to mistreat him. They found him willing to fight for his rights. That was the way I raised my kids. I always told them dont start a fight, if you do, I'll give you a beaten when I find out. But if the other kids start a fight, do your best. One time a kid twice his age at school, run up and hit him, to his surprise Perry got him down and give him a good beating. I had given him some advice in wrestling. As I once used to Box & Wrestle. The lady principal of the school and all the kids watched this fight. The lady principal loved the big kid. To see him get whipped by my little boy Perry was more than she could take. After that Perry was King of the Kids at school. If any big kid tried to mistreat a small one, Perry would settle that rite now. Even the Big Bully was afraid of Perry now, and had to be good. But that hurt the lady principal so she came to me complaining about Perry fighting in school. I told her I knew all about it and that I didnt intend to let my boy get beat up by kids twice his size. I also asked her why she let that Bully Kid beat up on other kids. I told her that Perry had a rite to defend himself. Perry never started the trouble and that I would take a hand in this affair myself. I told her my son was well liked by all the neighbors, and their kids. I also told her I was going to take Perry out of her school real soon, move away to another state. Which I did. Perry is no Angel he has done wrong many times same as so many other kids. Rite is Rite and wrong is wrong. I dont stick up for his wrong doings. He must pay the *Hardway* when he does wrong, law is Boss he knows that by now.

YOUTH—Perry joined the merchant Marines in second war. I went to Alaska, he came later and joined me there. I trapped furs and Perry worked with the Alaska Road Commission the first winter then he got work on the railroad for a short while. He couldn't get the work he liked to do. Yes—he give me $ now and then when he had it. He also sent me $30.00 a month while in Korea war while he was there from beginning until the end and was dischard in Seattle, Wash. Honorable as far as I know. He is mechanically inclined. Bulldozers, draglines, shovels, heavy duty trucks of all type is his desire. For the experience he has had he is real good. Somewhat reckless and speed crazy with motorcycles and light cars. But since he has had a good taste of what speed will do, and his both legs Broke & hip injury he now has slowed down on that I'm sure.

RECREATION—INTERESTS. Yes he had several girl friends, soon as he found a girl to mistreat him or trifle, he would quit her. He never was married as far as I know. My troubles with his mother made him afraid of marriage somewhat. Im a *Sober man* and as far as I know Perry is also a person that dont like drunks. Perry is like myself a great deal. He likes Company of decent type—outdoors people, he like myself, likes to be by himself also he likes best to work for himself. As I do. I'm a jack of all trades, so to speak, master of few and so is Perry. I showed him how to make a living working for himself as a fur trapper, prospector, carpenter, woodsman, horses, etc. I know how to cook and so does he, not a professional cook just plane cooking for himself. Bake bread, etc. hunt, and fish, trap, do most anything else. As I said before, Perry likes to be his own Boss & if he is given a chance to work at a job he likes, tell him how you want it done, then leave him alone, he will take great pride in doing his work. If he sees the Boss appreciates his work he will go out of his way for him. But dont get *tuff with him.* Tell him in a pleasant way how you want to have it done. He is very *touchie,* his feeling is very easily hurt, and so are mine. I have quit several jobs & so has Perry on account of Bully Bosses. Perry does not have much schooling I dont either, I only had *second reader.* But dont let that make you think we are not *sharp.* Im a self taught man & so is Perry. A *White Colar* job is not for *Perry or me.* But outdoors jobs we can master & if we cant, show him or me how its done & in just a couple of days we can master a job or machine. Books are out. Actual experience we both catch on rite now, if we like to work at it. First of all we must like the job. But now hes a Cripple and almost middle-aged man. Perry knows he is not wanted now by Contracters, cripples can't get jobs on heavy equiptment, unless you are well know to the Contracter. He is beginning to realize that, he is beginning to think of a more easier way of supporting himself in line with my life. Im sure Im *correct.* I also think speed is no longer his desire. I notice all that now in his letters to me. He says "be careful Dad. Don't drive if you feel sleepy, better stop & rest by the road side." These are the same words I used to tell him. Now he's telling me. He's learned a lesson.

As I see it—Perry has learned a lesson he will never forget. Freedom means everything to him you will never get him behind bars again. Im quite sure Im rite. I notice a big change in the way he talks. He deeply regrets his mistake he told me. I also know he feels ashamed to meet people he knows he will not tell them he was behind bars. He asked me not to mention where he is to his friends. When he wrote & told me he was behind bars, I told him let that be a lesson—that I was glad that it happened that way when it could have been worse. Someone could have shot him. I also told him to take his term behind bars with a smile U done it yourself. U know better. I didn't raise you to steal from others, so dont complain to me how tuff it is in prison. Be a good boy in prison. & he promised that he would. I hope he is a good prisoner. Im sure no one will talk him into stealing anymore. The *law is boss,* he knows that. He loves his Freedom.

How well I know that Perry is goodhearted if you treat him rite. Treat him mean & you got a buzz saw to fight. You can trust him with any amount of $ if your his friend. He will do as you say he wont steal a cent from a friend or anyone else. Before this happened. And I sincerely hope he will live the rest of his life a honest man. He did steal something in Company with others when he was a little kid. Just ask Perry if I was a good father to him ask him if his mother was good to him in Frisco. Perry knows whats good for him. U got him whipped forever. He knows when he's beat. He's not a dunce. He knows life is too short to sweet to spend behind bars ever again.

RELATIVES. One sister *Bobo* married, and me his father is all that is living of Perry. Bobo & her husband are self-supporting. Own their own home & I'm able & active to take care of myself also. I sold my lodge in Alaska two years ago. I intend to have another small place of my own next year. I located several mineral claims & hope to get something out of them. Besides that I have not given up prospecting. I am also asked to write a book on artistic wood carving, and the famous Trappers Den Lodge I build in Alaska once my homestead known by all tourists that travel by car to Anchorage and maybe I will. I'll share all I have with Perry. Anytime I eat he eats. As long as Im alive. & when I die Ive got life insurance that will be paid to him so he can start LIFE *Anew* when he gets free again. In case Im not alive then.

This biography always set racing a stable of emotions—self-pity in the lead, love and hate running evenly at first, the latter ultimately pulling ahead. And most of the memories it released were unwanted, though not all. In fact, the first part of his life that Perry could remember was treasurable—a fragment composed of applause, glamour. He was perhaps three, and he was seated with his sisters and his older brother in the grandstand at an open-air rodeo; in the ring, a lean Cherokee girl rode a wild horse, a "bucking bronc," and her loosened hair whipped back and forth, flew about like a flamenco dancer's. Her name was Flo Buckskin, and she was a professional rodeo performer, a "champion bronc-rider." So was her husband, Tex John Smith; it was while touring the Western rodeo circuit that the handsome Indian girl and the homely-handsome Irish cowboy had met, married, and had the four children sitting in the grandstand. (And Perry could remember many another rodeo spectacle—see again his father skipping about inside a circle of spinning lassos, or his mother, with silver and turquoise bangles jangling on her wrists, trick-riding at a desperado speed that thrilled her youngest child and caused crowds in towns from Texas to Oregon to "stand up and clap.")

Until Perry was five, the team of "Tex & Flo" continued to work the rodeo circuit. As a way of life, it wasn't "any gallon of ice cream," Perry once recalled: "Six of us riding in an old truck, sleeping in it, too, sometimes, living off mush and Hershey kisses and condensed milk. Hawks Brand condensed milk it was called, which is what weakened my kidneys—the *sugar* content—which is why I was always wetting the bed." Yet it was not an unhappy existence, especially for a little boy proud of his parents, admiring of their showmanship and courage—a happier life, certainly, than what replaced it. For Tex and Flo, both forced by ailments to retire from their occupation, settled near Reno, Nevada. They fought, and Flo "took to whiskey," and then, when Perry was six, she departed for San Francisco, taking the children with her. It was exactly as the old man had written: "I let her go and said goodby as she took the car and left me behind (this was during depression). My children all cryed at the top of their voices. She only cursed them saying they would run away to come to me later." And, indeed, over the course of the next three years Perry had on several occasions run off, set out to find his lost father, for he had lost his mother as well, learned to "despise" her; liquor had blurred the face, swollen the figure of the once sinewy, limber Cherokee girl, had "soured her soul," honed her tongue to the wickedest point, so dissolved her self-respect that generally she did not bother to ask the names of the stevedores and trolley-car conductors and such persons who accepted what she offered without charge (except that she insisted they drink with her first, and dance to the tunes of a wind-up Victrola).

Consequently, as Perry recalled, "I was always thinking about Dad, hoping he could come take me away, and I remember, like a second ago, the time I saw him again. Standing in the schoolyard. It was like when the ball hits the bat really solid. Di Maggio. Only Dad wouldn't help me. Told me to be good and hugged me and went away. It was not long afterward my mother put me to stay in a Catholic orphanage. The one where the Black Widows were always at me. Hitting me. Because of wetting the bed. Which is one reason I have an aversion to nuns. *And* God. *And* religion. But later on I found there are people even more evil. Because, after a couple of months, they tossed me out of the orphanage, and she [his mother] put me some place worse. A children's shelter operated by the Salvation Army. They hated me, too. For wetting the bed. And being half-Indian. There was this one nurse, she used to call me 'nigger' and say there wasn't any difference between niggers and Indians. Oh, Jesus, was she an Evil Bastard! Incarnate. What she used to do, she'd fill a tub with ice-cold water, put me in it, and hold me under till I was blue. Nearly drowned. But she got found out, the bitch. Because I caught pneumonia. I almost conked. I was in the hospital two months. It was while I was so sick that Dad came back. When I got well, he took me away."

For almost a year father and son lived together in the house near Reno, and Perry went to school. "I finished the third grade," Perry recalled. "Which *was* the finish. I never went back. Because that summer Dad built a primitive sort of trailer, what he called a 'house car.' It had two bunks and a little cooking galley. The stove was good. You could cook anything on it. Baked our own bread. I used to put up preserves—pickled apples, crab-apple jelly. Anyway, for the next six years we shifted around the country. Never stayed nowhere too long. When we stayed some place too long, people would begin to look at Dad, act like he was a character, and I hated that, it hurt me. Because I loved Dad then. Even though he could be rough on me. Bossy as hell. But I loved Dad then. So I was always glad when we moved on." Moved on—to Wyoming, Idaho, Oregon, eventually Alaska. In Alaska, Tex taught his son to dream of gold, to hunt for it in the sandy beds of snow-water streams, and there, too, Perry learned to use a gun, skin a bear, track wolves and deer.

"Christ, it was cold," Perry remembered. "Dad and I slept hugged together, rolled up in blankets and bearskins. Mornings, before daylight, I'd hustle our breakfast, biscuits and syrup, fried meat, and off we went to scratch a living. It would have been O.K. if only I hadn't grown up; the older I got, the less I was able to appreciate Dad. He knew everything, one way, but he didn't know anything, another way. Whole sections of me Dad was ignorant of. Didn't understand an iota of. Like I could play a harmonica first time I picked one up. Guitar, too. I had this great natural musical ability. Which Dad didn't recognize. Or care about. I liked to read, too. Improve my vocabulary. Make up songs. And I could draw. But I never got any encouragement—from him or anybody else. Nights I used to lie awake—trying to control my bladder, partly, and partly because I couldn't stop thinking. Always, when it was too cold hardly to breathe, I'd think about Hawaii. About a movie I'd seen. With Dorothy Lamour. I wanted to go there. Where the sun was. And all you wore was grass and flowers."

Wearing considerably more, Perry, one balmy evening in wartime 1945, found himself inside a Honolulu tattoo parlor having a snake-and-dagger design applied to his left forearm. He had got there by the following route: a row with his father, a hitchhike journey from Anchorage to Seattle, a visit to the recruiting offices of the Merchant Marine. "But I never would have joined if I'd known what I was going up against," Perry once said. "I never minded the work, and I liked being a sailor—seaports, and all that. But the queens on ship wouldn't leave me alone. A sixteen-year-old kid, and a small kid. I could handle myself, sure. But a lot of queens aren't effeminate, you know. Hell, I've known queens could toss a pool table out the window. And the piano after it. Those kind of girls, they can give you an evil time, especially when there's a couple of them, they get together and gang up on you, and you're just a kid. It can make you practically want to kill yourself. Years later, when I went into the Army—when I was stationed in Korea—the same problem came up. I had a good record in the Army, good as anybody; they gave me the Bronze Star. But I never got promoted. After four years, and fighting through the whole goddam Korean war, I ought at least to have made corporal. But I never did. Know why? Because the sergeant we had was tough. Because I wouldn't roll over. Jesus, I hate that stuff. I can't stand it. Though—*I* don't know. Some queers I've really liked. As long as they didn't try anything. The most worthwhile friend I ever had, really sensitive and intelligent, he turned out to be queer."

In the interval between quitting the Merchant Marine and entering the Army, Perry had made peace with his father, who, when his son left him, drifted down to Nevada, then back to Alaska. In 1952, the year Perry completed his military service, the old man was in the midst of plans meant to end his travels forever. "Dad was in a fever," Perry recalled. "Wrote me he had bought some land on the highway outside Anchorage. Said he was going to have a hunting lodge, a place for tourists. 'Trapper's Den Lodge'—that was to be the name. And asked me to hurry on up there and help him build it. He was sure we'd make a fortune. Well, while I was still in the Army, stationed at Fort Lewis, Washington, I'd bought a motorcycle (murdercycles, they ought to call them), and as soon as I got discharged I headed for Alaska. Got as far as Bellingham. Up there on the border. It was raining. My bike went into a skid."

The skid delayed for a year the reunion with his father. Surgery and hospitalization account for six months of that year; the remainder he spent recuperating in the forest home, near Bellingham, of a young Indian logger and fisherman. "Joe James. He and his wife befriended me. The difference in our age was only two or three years, but they took me into their home and treated me like I was one of their kids. Which was O.K. Because they took trouble with their kids and liked them. At the time they had four; the number finally went to seven. They were very good to me, Joe and his family. I was on crutches, I was pretty helpless. Just had to sit around. So to give me something to do, try to make myself useful, I started what became a sort of school. The pupils were Joe's kids, along with some of their friends, and we held classes in the parlor. I was teaching harmonica and guitar. Drawing. And penmanship. Everybody always remarks what a beautiful handwriting I have. I do, and it's because once I bought a book on the subject and practiced till I could write same as in the book. Also, we used to read stories—the kids did, each one in turn, and I'd correct them as we went along. It was fun. I like kids. *Little* kids. And that was a nice time. But then the spring came. It hurt me to walk, but I could walk. And Dad was still waiting for me."

Waiting, but not idly. By the time Perry arrived at the site of the proposed hunting lodge, his father, working alone, had finished the hardest chores—had cleared the ground, logged the necessary timber, cracked and carted wagonloads of native rock. "But he didn't commence to build till I got there. We did every damn piece of it ourselves. With once in a while an Indian helper. Dad was like a maniac. It didn't matter what was happening—snowstorms, rainstorms, winds that could split a tree—we kept right at it. The day the roof was finished, Dad danced all over it, shouting and laughing, doing a regular jig. Well, it turned out quite an exceptional place. That could sleep twenty people. Had a big fireplace in the dining room. And there was a cocktail lounge. The Totem Pole Cocktail Lounge. Where I was to entertain the customers. Singing and so forth. We opened for business end of 1953."

But the expected huntsmen did not materialize, and though ordinary tourists—the few that trickled along the highway—now and again paused to photograph the beyond-belief rusticity of Trapper's Den Lodge, they seldom stopped overnight. "For a while we fooled ourselves. Kept thinking it would catch on. Dad tried to trick up the place. Made a Garden of Memories. With a Wishing Well. Put painted signs up and down the highway. But none of it meant a nickel more. When Dad realized that—saw it wasn't any use, all we'd done was waste ourselves and all our money—he began to take it out on me. Boss me around. Be spiteful. Say I didn't do my proper share of the work. It wasn't his fault, any more than it was mine. A situation like that, with no money and the grub getting low, we couldn't help but be on each other's nerves. The point came we were downright hungry. Which is what we fell out over. Ostensibly. A biscuit. Dad snatched a biscuit out of my hand, and said I ate too much, what a greedy, selfish bastard I was, and why didn't I get out, he didn't want me there no more. He carried on like that till I couldn't stand it. My hands got hold of his throat. *My* hands—but I couldn't control them. They wanted to choke him to death. Dad, though, he's slippery, a smart wrestler. He tore loose and ran to get his gun. Came back pointing it at me. He said, 'Look at me, Perry. I'm the last thing living you're ever gonna see.' I just stood my ground. But then he realized the gun wasn't even loaded, and he started to cry. Sat down and bawled like a kid. Then I guess I wasn't mad at him any more. I was sorry for him. For both of us. But it wasn't a bit of use—there wasn't anything I could say. I went out for a walk. This was April, but the woods were still deep in snow. I walked till it was almost night. When I got back, the lodge was dark, and all the doors were locked. And everything I owned was lying out there in the snow. Where Dad had thrown it. Books. Clothes. Everything. I just let it lie. Except my guitar. I picked up my guitar and started on down the highway. Not a dollar in my pocket. Around midnight a truck stopped to give me a lift. The driver asked where I was going. I told him, 'Wherever you're headed, that's where I'm going.'"

Several weeks later, after again sheltering with the James family, Perry decided on a definite destination—Worcester, Massachusetts, the home town of an "Army buddy" he thought might welcome him and help him find "a good-paying job." Various detours prolonged the eastward journey; he washed dishes in an Omaha restaurant, pumped gas at an Oklahoma garage, worked a month on a ranch in Texas. By July of 1955 he had reached, on the trek to Worcester, a small Kansas town, Phillipsburg, and there "fate," in the form of "bad company," asserted itself. "His name was Smith," Perry said. "Same as me. I don't even recall his first name. He was just somebody I'd picked up with somewhere, and he had a car, and he said he'd give me a ride as far as Chicago. Anyway, driving through Kansas we came to this little Phillipsburg place and stopped to look at a map. Seems to me like it was a Sunday. Stores shut. Streets quiet. My friend there, bless his heart, he looked around and made a suggestion." The suggestion was that they burglarize a nearby building, the Chandler Sales Company. Perry agreed, and they broke into the deserted premises and removed a quantity of office equipment (typewriters, adding machines). That might have been that if only, some days afterward, the thieves hadn't ignored a traffic signal in the city of Saint Joseph, Missouri. "The junk was still in the car. The cop that stopped us wanted to know where we got it. A little checking was done, and, as they say, we were 'returned' to Phillipsburg, Kansas. Where the folks have a real cute jail. If you like jails." Within forty-eight hours Perry and his companion had discovered an open window, climbed out of it, stolen a car, and driven northwest to McCook, Nebraska. "Pretty soon we broke up, me and Mr. Smith. I don't know what ever became of him. We both made the F.B.I.'s Wanted list. But far as I know, they never caught up with *him*."

One wet afternoon the following November, a Greyhound bus deposited Perry in Worcester, a Massachusetts factory town of steep, up-and-down streets that even in the best of weathers seem cheerless and hostile. "I found the house where my friend was supposed to live. My Army friend from Korea. But the people there said he'd left six months back and they had no idea where he'd gone. Too bad, big disappointment, end of the world, all that. So I found a liquor store and bought a half gallon of red wop and went back to the bus depot and sat there drinking my wine and getting a little warmer. I was really enjoying myself till a man came along and arrested me for vagrancy." The police booked him as "Bob Turner"—a name he'd adopted because of being listed by the F.B.I. He spent fourteen days in jail, was fined ten dollars, and departed from Worcester on another wet November afternoon. "I went down to New York and took a room in a hotel on Eighth Avenue," Perry said. "Near Forty-second Street. Finally, I got a night job. Doing odd jobs around a penny arcade. Right there on Forty-second Street, next to an Automat. Which is where I ate—*when* I ate. In over three months I practically never left the Broadway area. For one thing, I didn't have the right clothes. Just Western clothes—jeans and boots. But there on Forty-second Street nobody cares, it all rides—*any*thing. My whole life, I never met so many freaks."

He lived out the winter in that ugly, neon-lit neighborhood, with its air full of the scent of popcorn, simmering hot dogs, and orange drink. But then, one bright March morning on the edge of spring, as he remembered it, "two F.B.I. bastards woke me up. Arrested me at the hotel. Bang!—I was extradited back to Kansas. To Phillipsburg. That same cute jail. They nailed me to the cross—larceny, jailbreak, car theft. I got five to ten years. In Lansing. After I'd been there awhile, I wrote Dad. Let him know the news. And wrote Barbara, my sister.

By now, over the years, that was all I had left me. Jimmy a suicide. Fern out the window. My mother dead. Been dead eight years. Everybody gone but Dad and Barbara."

A letter from Barbara was among the sheaf of selected matter that Perry preferred not to leave behind in the Mexico City hotel room. The letter, written in a pleasingly legible script, was dated April 28, 1958, at which time the recipient had been imprisoned for approximately two years:

Dearest Bro. Perry,

We got your 2nd letter today & forgive me for not writing sooner. Our weather here, as yours is, is turning warmer & maybe I am getting spring fever but I am going to try and do better. Your first letter was very disturbing, as I'm sure you must have suspected but that was not the reason I haven't written—it's true the children do keep me busy & it's hard to find time to sit and concentrate on a letter as I have wanted to write you for some time. Donnie has learned to open the doors and climb on the chairs & other furniture & he worries me constantly about falling.

I have been able to let the children play in the yard now & then—but I always have to go out with them as they can hurt themselves if I don't pay attention. But nothing is forever & I know I will be sorry when they start running the block & I don't know where they're at. Here are some statistics if you're interested—

| | Height | Weight | Shoe Size |
|---|---|---|---|
| Freddie | 36-1/2″ | 26-1/2 lbs. | 7-1/2 narrow |
| Baby | 37-1/2″ | 29-1/2 lbs. | 8 narrow |
| Donnie | 34″ | 26 lbs. | 6-1/2 wide |

You can see that Donnie is a pretty big boy for 15 months & with his 16 teeth and his sparkling personality—people just can't help loving him. He wears the same size clothes as Baby and Freddie but the pants are too long as yet.

I am going to try & make this letter a long one so it will probably have a lot of interruptions such as right now it's time for Donnie's bath—Baby & Freddie had theirs this A.M. as it's quite cold today & I have had them inside. Be back soon—

About my typing—First—I cannot tell a lie! I am not a typist. I use from 1 to 5 fingers & although I can manage & do help Big Fred with his business affairs, what it takes me 1 hr. to do would probably take someone with the Know How—15 minutes— Seriously, I do not have the time nor the *will* to learn professionally. But I think it is wonderful how you have stuck with it and become such an excellent typist. I do believe we all were very adaptable (Jimmy, Fern, you and myself) & we had all been blessed with a basic flair for the artistic—among other things. Even Mother & Dad were artistic.

I truthfully feel none of us have *any one* to blame for *whatever* we have done with our own personal lives. It has been proven that at the age of 7 most of us have reached the *age of reason*—which means we *do*, at this age, *understand* & *know* the difference between right & wrong. Of course—environment plays an awfully important part in our lives such as the Convent in mine & in my case I am grateful for that influence. In Jimmy's case—he was the strongest of us all. I remember how he worked & went to school when there was no one to tell him & it was his own WILL to make something of himself. We will never know the reasons for what eventually happened, why he did what he did, but I still hurt thinking of it. It was such a waste. But we have very little control over our human weaknesses, & this applies also to Fern & the hundreds of thousands of other people including ourselves—for *we all* have weaknesses. In your case—I don't know what *your* weakness is but I do feel—IT IS NO SHAME TO HAVE A DIRTY FACE—THE SHAME COMES WHEN YOU KEEP IT DIRTY.

In all truthfulness & with love for you Perry, for you are my only living brother and the uncle of my children, I cannot say or feel your attitude towards our father or your imprisonment JUST or healthy. If you are getting your back up—better simmer down as I realize there are none of us who take criticism cheerfully & it is natural to feel a certain amount of resentment towards the one giving this criticism so I am prepared for one or two things —a) Not to hear from you at all, or b) a letter telling me exactly what you think of me.

I hope I'm wrong & I sincerely hope you will give this letter a lot of thought & *try* to see—how someone else feels. Please understand I know I am not an authority & I do not boast great intelligence or education but I do believe I am a normal individual with basic reasoning powers & the will to live my life according to the laws of God & Man. It is also true that I have "fallen" at times, as is normal—for as I said I am human & therefore I too have human weaknesses but the point is, again, There is no shame—having a dirty face—the shame comes when you keep it dirty. No one is more aware of my shortcomings and mistakes than myself so I won't bore you further.

Now, first, & most important—Dad is *not* responsible for your wrong doings *or* your good deeds. What you have done, whether *right* or *wrong*, is *your own doing*. From what I personally know, you have lived your life exactly as you pleased *without* regard to circumstances or persons who loved you—who might be hurt. Whether you realize it or not—your present confinement is embarrassing to me as well as Dad—not because of what you did but the fact that you don't show me any signs of SINCERE regret and seem to show no *respect* for any laws, people or anything. Your letter implies that the blame of all your problems is that of someone else, but never you. I do admit that you are intelligent & your vocabulary is excellent & I do feel you can do anything you decide to do & do it well but what exactly do you want to do & are you willing to *work* & make an *honest* effort to attain whatever it is you choose to do? Nothing good comes easy & I'm sure you've heard this many times but once more won't hurt.

In case you want the truth about Dad—his heart is broken because of you. He would give anything to get you out so he can have his son back—but I am afraid you would only hurt him worse if you could. He is not well and is getting older &, as the saying goes, he cannot "Cut the Mustard" as in the old days. He has been wrong at times & he realizes this but whatever he had and wherever he went he shared his life & belongings with you when he wouldn't do this for anyone else. Now I don't say you owe him *undying gratitude* or your *life* but you do owe him RESPECT and COMMON DECENCY. I, personally, am proud of Dad. I love him & Respect him as my Dad & I am only sorry he chose to be the Lone Wolf with his son, or he might be living with us and share our love instead of alone in his little trailer & longing & waiting & lonesome for you, his son. I worry for him & when I say *I* I mean my husband too for my husband respects our Dad. Because he is a MAN. It's true that Dad did not have a great extensive education but in school we only learn to recognize the words and to spell but the *application* of these words to *real life* is another thing that only LIFE & LIVING can give us. Dad has lived & you show ignorance in calling him uneducated & unable to understand "the scientific meaning etc" of life's problems. A mother is still the only one who can kiss a boo-boo and make it all well—explain that *scientifically*.

I'm sorry to let you have it so strong but I feel I must speak my piece. I am sorry that this must be censored [by the prison authorities], & I sincerely hope this letter is not detrimental towards your eventual release but I feel you should know & realize what terrible hurt you have done. Dad is the important one as I am dedicated to my family but you are the only one Dad loves—in short, his "family." He knows I love him, of course, but the closeness is not there, as you know.

Your confinement is nothing to be proud of and you will have to live with it & try & live it down & it can be done but not with your attitude of feeling everyone is stupid & uneducated & un-understanding. You are a human being with a *free will.* Which puts you above the animal level. But if you live your life without feeling and compassion for your fellow-man—you are as an animal—"an eye for an eye, a tooth for a tooth" & happiness & peace of mind is not attained by living thus.

As far as responsibility goes, no one really wants it—but all of us are responsible to the community we live in & its laws. When the time comes to assume the responsibility of a home and children or business, this is the seeding of the boys from the Men—for surely you can realize what a mess the world would be if everyone in it said, "I want to be an individual, without responsibilities, & be able to speak my mind freely & do as *I* alone will." We are all free to speak & do as we individually will—*providing* this "freedom" of Speech & Deed are not injurious to our fellow-man.

Think about it, Perry. You are above average in intelligence, but somehow your reasoning is off the beam. Maybe it's the strain of your confinement. Whatever it is—remember—you & only you are responsible and it is up to you and you alone to overcome this part of your life. Hoping to hear from you soon.

With Love & Prayers,
Your sister & Bro. in Law
Barbara & Frederic & Family

In preserving this letter, and including it in his collection of particular treasures, Perry was not moved by affection. Far from it. He "loathed" Barbara, and just the other day he had told Dick, "The only *real* regret I have—I wish the hell my sister had been in that house." (Dick had laughed, and confessed to a similar yearning: "I keep thinking what fun if my second wife had been there. Her, and all her goddam family.") No, he valued the letter merely because his prison friend, the "super-intelligent" Willie-Jay, had written for him a "very sensitive" analysis of it, occupying two single-spaced typewritten pages, with the title "Impressions I Garnered from the Letter" at the top:

Impressions I Garnered from the Letter

1.) When she began this letter, she intended that it should be a compassionate demonstration of Christian principles. That is to say that in return for your letter to her, which apparently annoyed her, she meant to turn the other cheek hoping in this way to incite regret for your previous letter and to place you on the defensive in your next.

However few people can successfully demonstrate a principle in common ethics when their deliberation is festered with emotionalism. Your sister substantiates this failing for as her letter progresses her judgment gives way to temper—her thoughts are good, lucid, the products of intelligence, but it is not now an unbiased, impersonal intelligence. It is a mind propelled by emotional response to memory and frustration; consequently, however wise her admonishments might be, they fail to inspire resolve, unless it would be the resolve to retaliate by hurting her in your next letter. Thus commencing a cycle that can only culminate in further anger and distress.

2.) It is a foolish letter, but born of human failing.

Your letter to her, and this, her answer to you, failed in their objectives. Your letter was an attempt to explain your outlook on life, as you are necessarily affected by it. It was destined to be misunderstood, or taken too literally because your ideas are opposed to conventionalism. What could be *more* conventional than a housewife with three children, who is "dedicated" to her family???? What could be more natural than that she would resent an unconventional person. There is considerable hypocrisy in conventionalism. Any thinking person is aware of this paradox; but in dealing with conventional people it is advantageous to treat them as though they were not hypocrites. It isn't a question of faithfulness to your own concepts; it is a matter of compromise so that you *can* remain an individual without the constant threat of conventional pressures. Her letter failed because she couldn't conceive of the profundity of your problem—she couldn't fathom the pressures brought to bear upon you because of environment, intellectual frustration and a growing tendency toward isolationism.

3.) She feels that:

a) You are leaning too heavily towards self-pity.

b) That you are too calculating.

c) That you are really undeserving of an 8 page letter written in between motherly duties.

4.) On page 3 she writes: "I truthfully feel none of us has anyone to blame etc." Thus vindicating those who bore influence in her formative years. But is this the whole truth? She is a wife and mother. Respectable and more or less secure. It is easy to ignore the rain if you have a raincoat. But how would she feel if she were compelled to hustle her living on the streets? Would she still be all-forgiving about the people in her past? Absolutely not. Nothing is more usual than to feel that others have shared in our failures, just as it is an ordinary reaction to forget those who have shared in our achievements.

5.) Your sister respects your Dad. She also resents the fact that you have been preferred. Her jealousy takes a subtle form in this letter. Between the lines she is registering a question: "I love Dad and have tried to live so he could be proud to own me as his daughter. But I have had to content myself with the crumbs of his affection. Because it is you he loves, and why should it be so?"

Obviously over the years your Dad has taken advantage of your sister's emotional nature via the mails. Painting a picture that justifies her opinion of him—an underdog cursed with an ungrateful son upon whom he has showered love and concern, only to be infamously treated by that son in return.

On page 7 she says she is sorry that her letter must be censored. But she is really not sorry at all. She is glad it passes through a censor. Subconsciously she has written it with the censor in mind, hoping to convey the idea that the Smith family is really a well-ordered unit: *"Please do not judge us all by Perry."*

About the mother kissing away her child's boo-boo. This is a woman's form of sarcasm.

6.) You write to her because:

a) You love her after a fashion.

b) You feel a need for this contact with the outside world.

c) You can use her.

Prognosis: Correspondence between you and your sister cannot serve anything but a purely social function. Keep the theme of your letters within the scope of her understanding. Do not unburden your private conclusions. Do not put her on the defensive and do not permit her to put you on the defensive. Respect her limitations to comprehend your objectives, and remember that she is touchy towards criticism of your Dad. Be consistent in your attitude towards her and do not add anything to the impression she has that you are weak, not because you need her good-will but because you can expect more letters like this, and *they can only serve to increase your already dangerous anti-social instincts.*

FINISH

As Perry continued to sort and choose, the pile of material he thought too dear to part with, even temporarily, assumed a tottering height. But what was he to do? He couldn't risk losing the Bronze Medal earned in Korea, or his high-school diploma (issued by the Leavenworth County Board of Education as a result of his having, while in prison, resumed his long-recessed studies). Nor did he care to chance the loss of a manila envelope fat with photographs—primarily of himself, and ranging in time from a pretty-little-boy portrait made when he was in the Merchant Marine (and on the back of which he had scribbled, "16 yrs. old. Young, happy-go-lucky & Innocent") to the recent Acapulco pictures. And there were half a hundred other items he had decided he must take with him, among them his treasure maps, Otto's sketchbook, and two thick notebooks, the thicker of which constituted his personal dictionary, a non-alphabetically listed miscellany of words he believed "beautiful" or "useful," or at least "worth memorizing." (Sample page: "Thanatoid = deathlike; Omnilingual = versed in languages; Amerce = punishment, amount fixed by court; Nescient = ignorance; Facinorous = atrociously wicked; Hagiophobia = a morbid fear of holy places & things; Lapidicolous = living under stones, as certain blind beetles; Dyspathy = lack of sympathy, fellow feeling; Psilopher = a fellow who fain would pass as a philosopher; Omophagia = eating raw flesh, the rite of some savage tribes; Depredate = to pillage, rob, and prey upon; Aphrodisiac = a drug or the like which excites sexual desire; Megalodactylous = having abnormally large fingers; Myrtophobia = fear of night and darkness.")

On the cover of the second notebook, the handwriting of which he was so proud, a script abounding in curly, feminine flourishes, proclaimed the contents to be "The Private Diary of Perry Edward Smith" —an inaccurate description, for it was not in the least a diary but, rather, a form of anthology consisting of obscure facts ("Every fifteen years Mars gets closer. 1958 is a close year"), poems and literary quotations ("No man is an island, Entire of itself"), and passages for newspapers and books paraphrased or quoted. For example:

> My acquaintances are many, my friends are few; those who really know me fewer still.
>
> Heard about a new rat poison on the market. Extremely potent, odorless, tasteless, is so completely absorbed once swallowed that no trace could ever be found in a dead body.
>
> If called upon to make a speech: "I can't remember what I was going to say for the life of me—I don't think that ever before in my life have so many people been so directly responsible for my being so very, very glad. It's a wonderful moment and a rare one and I'm certainly indebted. Thank you!"
>
> Read interesting article Feb. issue of *Man to Man:* "I Knifed My Way to a Diamond Pit."
>
> "It is almost impossible for a man who enjoys freedom with all its prerogatives, to realize what it means to be deprived of that freedom."—Said by Erle Stanley Gardner.
>
> "What is life? It is the flash of a firefly in the night. It is a breath of a buffalo in the wintertime. It is as the little shadow that runs across the grass and loses itself in the sunset."—Said by Chief Crowfoot, Blackfoot Indian Chief.

This last entry was written in red ink and decorated with a border of green-ink stars; the anthologist wished to emphasize its "personal significance." "A breath of a buffalo in the wintertime"—that exactly evoked his view of life. Why worry? What was there to "sweat about"? Man was nothing, a mist, a shadow absorbed by shadows.

But, damn it, you do worry, scheme, fret over your fingernails and the warnings of hotel managements: "SU DÍA TERMINA A LAS 2 P.M."

"Dick? You hear me?" Perry said. "It's almost one o'clock."

Dick was awake. He was rather more than that; he and Inez were making love. As though reciting a rosary, Dick incessantly whispered: "Is it good, baby? Is it good?" But Inez, smoking a cigarette, remained silent. The previous midnight, when Dick had brought her to the room and told Perry that she was going to sleep there, Perry, though disapproving, had acquiesced, but if they imagined that their conduct stimulated him, or seemed to him anything other than a "nuisance," they were wrong. Nevertheless, Perry felt sorry for Inez. She was such a "stupid kid"—she really believed that Dick meant to marry her, and had no idea he was planning to leave Mexico that very afternoon.

"Is it good, baby? Is it good?"

Perry said: "For Christsake, Dick. Hurry it up, will you? Our day ends at two P.M."

It was Saturday, Christmas was near, and the traffic crept along Main Street. Dewey, caught in the traffic, looked up at the holly garlands that hung above the street—swags of gala greenery trimmed with scarlet paper bells—and was reminded that he had not yet bought a single gift for his wife or his sons. His mind automatically rejected problems not concerned with the Clutter case. Marie and many of their friends had begun to wonder at the completeness of his fixation.

One close friend, the young lawyer Clifford R. Hope, Jr., had spoken plainly: "Do you know what's happening to you, Al? Do you realize you never talk about anything else?" "Well," Dewey had replied, "that's all I think about. And there's the chance that just while talking the thing over, I'll hit on something I haven't thought of before. Some new angle. Or maybe *you* will. Damn it, Cliff, what do you suppose my life will be if this thing stays in the Open File? Years from now I'll still be running down tips, and every time there's a murder, a case anywhere in the country even remotely similar, I'll have to horn right in, check, see if there could be any possible connection. But it isn't only that. The real thing is I've come to feel I know Herb and the family better than they ever knew themselves. I'm haunted by them. I guess I always will be. Until I know what happened."

Dewey's dedication to the puzzle had resulted in an uncharacteristic absent-mindedness. Only that morning Marie had asked him please, would he please, *please,* not forget to . . . But he couldn't remember, or didn't, until, free of the shopping-day traffic and racing along Route 50 toward Holcomb, he passed Dr. I. E. Dale's veterinarian establishment. Of *course*. His wife had asked him to be sure and collect the family cat, Courthouse Pete. Pete, a tiger-striped tom weighing fifteen pounds, is a well-known character around Garden City, famous for his pugnacity, which was the cause of his current hospitalization; a battle lost to a boxer dog had left him with wounds necessitating both stitches and antibiotics. Released by Dr. Dale, Pete settled down on the front seat of his owner's automobile and purred all the way to Holcomb.

The detective's destination was River Valley Farm, but wanting something warm—a cup of hot coffee—he stopped off at Hartman's Café.

"Hello, handsome," said Mrs. Hartman. "What can I do for you?"

"Just coffee, ma'am."

She poured a cup. "Am I wrong? Or have you lost a lot of weight?"

"Some." In fact, during the past three weeks Dewey had dropped twenty pounds. His suits fitted as though he had borrowed them from a stout friend, and his face, seldom suggestive of his profession, was now not at all so; it could have been that of an ascetic absorbed in occult pursuits.

"How do you feel?"

"Mighty fine."

"You *look* awful."

Unarguably. But no worse than the other members of the K.B.I. entourage—Agents Duntz, Church, and Nye. Certainly he was in better shape than Harold Nye, who, though full of flu and fever, kept reporting for duty. Among them, the four tired men had "checked out" some seven hundred tips and rumors. Dewey, for example, had spent two wearying and wasted days trying to trace that phantom pair, the Mexicans sworn by Paul Helm to have visited Mr. Clutter on the eve of the murders.

"Another cup, Alvin?"

"Don't guess I will. Thank you, ma'am."

But she had already fetched the pot. "It's on the house, Sheriff. How you look, you need it."

At a corner table two whiskery ranch hands were playing checkers. One of them got up and came over to the counter where Dewey was seated. He said, "Is it true what we heard?"

"Depends."

"About that fellow you caught? Prowling in the Clutter house? He's the one responsible. That's what we heard."

"I think you heard wrong, old man. Yes, sir, I do."

Although the past life of Jonathan Daniel Adrian, who was then being held in the county jail on a charge of carrying a concealed weapon, included a period of confinement as a mental patient in Topeka State Hospital, the data assembled by the investigators indicated that in relation to the Clutter case he was guilty only of an unhappy curiosity.

"Well, if he's the wrong un, why the hell don't you find the right un? I got a houseful of women won't go to the *bath*room alone."

Dewey had become accustomed to this brand of abuse; it was a routine part of his existence. He swallowed the second cup of coffee, sighed, smiled.

"Hell, I'm not cracking jokes. I mean it. Why don't you arrest somebody? That's what you're paid for."

"Hush your meanness," said Mrs. Hartman. "We're all in the same boat. Alvin's doing good as he can."

Dewey winked at her. "You tell him, ma'am. And much obliged for the coffee."

The ranch hand waited until his quarry had reached the door, then fired a farewell volley: "If you ever run for sheriff again, just forget my vote. 'Cause you *ain't* gonna get it."

"Hush your meanness," said Mrs. Hartman.

A mile separates River Valley Farm from Hartman's Café. Dewey decided to walk it. He enjoyed hiking across wheat fields. Normally, once or twice a week he went for long walks on his own land, the well-loved piece of prairie where he had always hoped to build a house, plant trees, eventually entertain great-grandchildren. That was the dream, but it was one his wife had lately warned him she no longer shared; she had told him that never now would she consider living all alone "way out there in the country." Dewey knew that even if he were to snare the murderers the next day, Marie would not change her mind—for once an awful fate had befallen friends who lived in a lonely country house.

Of course, the Clutter family were not the first persons ever murdered in Finney County, or even in Holcomb. Senior members of that small community can recall "a wild goings-on" of more than forty years ago—the Hefner Slaying. Mrs. Sadie Truitt, the hamlet's septuagenarian mail messenger, who is the mother of Postmistress Clare, is expert on this fabled affair: "August, it was. 1920. Hot *as* Hades. A fellow called Tunif was working on the Finnup ranch. *Walter* Tunif. He had a car, turned out to be stolen. Turned out he was a soldier AWOL from Fort Bliss, over there in Texas. He was a rascal, sure enough, and a lot of people suspected him. So one evening the sheriff—them days that was Orlie Hefner, such a fine singer, don't you know he's part of the Heavenly Choir?—one evening he rode out to the Finnup ranch to ask Tunif a few straightforward questions. Third of August. Hot *as* Hades. Outcome of it was, Walter Tunif shot the sheriff right through the heart. Poor Orlie was gone 'fore he hit the ground. The devil who done it, he lit out of there on one of the Finnup horses, rode east along the river. Word spread, and men for miles around made up a posse. Along about the next morning, they caught up with him; old *Wal*ter Tunif. He didn't get the chance to say how d'you do? On account of the boys were pretty irate. They just let the buckshot fly."

Dewey's own initial contact with foul play in Finney County occurred in 1947. The incident is noted in his files as follows: "John Carlyle Polk, a Creek Indian, 32 years of age, resident Muskogee,

Okla., killed Mary Kay Finley, white female, 40 years of age, a waitress residing in Garden City. Polk stabbed her with the jagged neck of a beer bottle in a room in the Copeland Hotel, Garden City, Kansas, 5-9-47." A cut-and-dried description of an open-and-shut case. Of three other murders Dewey had since investigated, two were equally obvious (a pair of railroad workers robbed and killed an elderly farmer, 11-1-52; a drunken husband beat and kicked his wife to death, 6-17-56), but the third case, as it was once conversationally narrated by Dewey, was not without several original touches: "It all started out at Stevens Park. Where they have a bandstand, and under the bandstand a men's room. Well, this man named Mooney was walking around the park. He was from North Carolina somewhere, just a stranger passing through town. Anyway, he went to the rest room, and somebody followed him inside—a boy from hereabouts, Wilmer Lee Stebbins, twenty years old. Afterward, Wilmer Lee always claimed Mr. Mooney made him an unnatural suggestion. And that was why he robbed Mr. Mooney, and knocked him down, and banged his head on the cement floor, and why, when *that* didn't finish him, he stuck Mr. Mooney's head in a toilet bowl and kept on flushing till he drowned him. Maybe so. But nothing can explain the rest of Wilmer Lee's behavior. First off, he buried the body a couple of miles northeast of Garden City. Next day he dug it up and put it down fourteen miles the other direction. Well, it went on like that, burying and reburying. Wilmer Lee was like a dog with a bone—he just wouldn't let Mr. Mooney rest in peace. Finally, he dug one grave too many; somebody saw him." Prior to the Clutter mystery, the four cases cited were the sum of Dewey's experience with murder, and measured against the case confronting him, were as squalls preceding a hurricane.

Dewey fitted a key into the front door of the Clutter house. Inside, the house was warm, for the heat had not been turned off, and the shiny-floored rooms, smelling of a lemon-scented polish, seemed only temporarily untenanted; it was as though today were Sunday and the family might at any moment return from church. The heirs, Mrs. English and Mrs. Jarchow, had removed a vanload of clothing and furniture, yet the atmosphere of a house still humanly inhabited had not thereby been diminished. In the parlor, a sheet of music, "Comin' Thro' the Rye," stood open on the piano rack. In the hall, a sweat-stained gray Stetson hat—Herb's—hung on a hat peg. Upstairs in Kenyon's room, on a shelf above his bed, the lenses of the dead boy's spectacles gleamed with reflected light.

The detective moved from room to room. He had toured the house many times; indeed, he went out there almost every day, and, in one sense, could be said to find these visits pleasurable, for the place, unlike his own home, or the sheriff's office, with its hullabaloo, was peaceful. The telephones, their wires still severed, were silent. The great quiet of the prairies surrounded him. He could sit in Herb's parlor rocking chair, and rock and think. A few of his conclusions were unshakable: he believed that the death of Herb Clutter had been the criminals' main objective, the motive being a psychopathic hatred, or possibly a combination of hatred and thievery, and he believed that the commission of the murders had been a leisurely labor, with perhaps two or more hours elapsing between the entrance of the killers and their exit. (The coroner, Dr. Robert Fenton, reported an appreciable difference in the body temperatures of the victims, and, on this basis, theorized that the order of execution had been: Mrs. Clutter, Nancy, Kenyon, and Mr. Clutter.) Attendant upon these beliefs was his conviction that the family had known very well the persons who destroyed them.

During this visit Dewey paused at an upstairs window, his attention caught by something seen in the near distance—a scarecrow amid the wheat stubble. The scarecrow wore a man's hunting-cap and a dress of weather-faded flowered calico. (Surely an old dress of Bonnie Clutter's?) Wind frolicked the skirt and made the scarecrow sway—made it seem a creature forlornly dancing in the cold December field. And Dewey was somehow reminded of Marie's dream. One recent morning she had served him a bungled breakfast of sugared eggs and salted coffee, then blamed it all on "a silly dream"—but a dream the power of daylight had not dispersed. "It was so real, Alvin," she said. "As real as this kitchen. That's where I was. Here in the kitchen. I was cooking supper, and suddenly Bonnie walked through the door. She was wearing a blue angora sweater, and she looked so sweet and pretty. And I said, 'Oh, Bonnie . . . Bonnie, dear . . . I haven't seen you since that terrible thing happened.' But she didn't answer, only looked at me in that shy way of hers, and I didn't know how to go on. Under the circumstances. So I said, 'Honey, come see what I'm making Alvin for his supper. A pot of gumbo. With shrimp and fresh crabs. It's just about ready. Come on, honey, have a taste.' But she wouldn't. She stayed by the door looking at me. And then—I don't know how to tell you exactly, but she shut her eyes, she began to shake her head, very slowly, and wring her hands, *very* slowly, and to whimper, or whisper. I couldn't understand *what* she was saying. But it broke my heart, I never felt so sorry for anyone, and I hugged her. I said, 'Please, Bonnie! Oh, don't, darling, don't! If ever anyone was prepared to go to God, it was you, Bonnie.' But I couldn't comfort her. She shook her head, and wrung her hands, and then I heard what she was saying. She was saying, 'To be murdered. To be murdered. No. No. There's nothing worse. Nothing worse than that. Nothing.'"

It was midday deep in the Mojave Desert. Perry, sitting on a straw suitcase, was playing a harmonica. Dick was standing at the side of a black-surfaced highway, Route 66, his eyes fixed upon the immaculate emptiness as though the fervor of his gaze could force motorists to materialize. Few did, and none of those stopped for the hitchhikers. One truck driver, bound for Needles, California, had offered a lift, but Dick had declined. That was not the sort of "setup" he and Perry wanted. They were waiting for some solitary traveler in a decent car and with money in his billfold—a stranger to rob, strangle, discard on the desert.

In the desert, sound often precedes sight. Dick heard the dim vibrations of an oncoming, not yet visible car. Perry heard it, too; he put the harmonica in his pocket, picked up the straw suitcase (this, their only luggage, bulged and sagged with the weight of Perry's souvenirs, plus three shirts, five pairs of white socks, a box of aspirin, a bottle of tequila, scissors, a safety razor, and a fingernail file; all their other belongings had either been pawned or been left with the Mexican bartender or been shipped to Las Vegas), and joined Dick at the side of the road. They watched. Now the car appeared, and grew until it became a blue Dodge sedan with a single passenger, a bald, skinny man. Perfect. Dick raised his hand and waved. The Dodge slowed down, and Dick gave the man a sumptuous smile. The car almost, but not quite, came to a stop, and the driver leaned out the window, looking them up and down. The impression they made was evidently alarming. (After a fifty-hour bus ride from Mexico City to Barstow, California, and half a day of trekking across the Mojave, both hikers were bearded, stark, dusty figures.) The car leaped forward and sped on. Dick cupped his hands around his mouth and called out, "You're a lucky bastard!" Then he laughed and hoisted the suitcase to his shoulder. Nothing could get him really angry, because, as he later recalled, he was "too glad to be back in the good ol' U.S.A." Anyway, another man in another car would come along.

Perry produced his harmonica (his since yesterday, when he stole it from a Barstow variety store) and played the opening bars of what had come to be their "marching music"; the song was one of Perry's favorites, and he had taught Dick all five stanzas. In step, and side by side, they swung along the highway, singing, "Mine eyes have seen the glory of the coming of the Lord; He is trampling out the vintage where the grapes of wrath are stored." Through the silence of the desert, their hard, young voices rang: "Glory! Glory! Hallelujah! Glory! Glory! Hallelujah!"

## 3

## *Answer*

THE YOUNG MAN's name was Floyd Wells, and he was short and nearly chinless. He had attempted several careers, as soldier, ranch hand, mechanic, thief, the last of which had earned him a sentence of three to five years in Kansas State Penitentiary. On the evening of Tuesday, November 17, 1959, he was lying in his cell with a pair of radio earphones clamped to his head. He was listening to a news broadcast, but the announcer's voice and the drabness of the day's events ("Chancellor Konrad Adenauer arrived in London today for talks with Prime Minister Harold Macmillan. . . . President Eisenhower put in seventy minutes going over space problems and the budget for space exploration with Dr. T. Keith Glennan") were luring him toward sleep. His drowsiness instantly vanished when he heard, "Officers investigating the tragic slaying of four members of the Herbert W. Clutter family have appealed to the public for any information which might aid in solving this baffling crime. Clutter, his wife, and their two teen-age children were found murdered in their farm home near Garden City early last Sunday morning. Each had been bound, gagged, and shot through the head with a .12-gauge shotgun. Investigating officials admit they can discover no motive for the crime, termed by Logan Sanford, Director of the Kansas Bureau of Investigation, as the most vicious in the history of Kansas. Clutter, a prominent wheat grower and former Eisenhower appointee to the Federal Farm Credit Board . . ."

Wells was stunned. As he was eventually to describe his reaction, he "didn't hardly believe it." Yet he had good reason to, for not only had he known the murdered family, he knew very well who had murdered them.

It had begun a long time ago—eleven years ago, in the autumn of 1948, when Wells was nineteen. He was "sort of drifting around the country, taking jobs as they came," as he recalled it. "One way and another, I found myself out there in western Kansas. Near the Colorado border. I was hunting work, and asking round, I heard maybe they could use a hand over to River Valley Farm—that's how he called his place, Mr. Clutter did. Sure enough, he put me on. I stayed there I guess a year—all that winter, anyway—and when I left it was just 'cause I was feeling kind of footy. Wanted to move on. Not account of any quarrel with Mr. Clutter. He treated me fine, same as he treated everybody that worked for him; like, if you was a little short before payday, he'd always hand you a ten or a five. He paid good wages, and if you deserved it he was quick to give you a bonus. The fact is, I liked Mr. Clutter much as any man I ever met. The whole family. Mrs. Clutter and the four kids. When I knew them, the youngest two, the ones that got killed—Nancy and the little boy what wore glasses—they were only babies, maybe five or six years old. The other two—one was called Beverly, the other girl I don't remember her name—they were already in high school. A nice family, *real* nice. I never forgot them. When I left there, it was sometime in 1949. I got married, I got divorced, the Army took me, other stuff happened, time went by, you might say, and in 1959—June, 1959, ten years since I last seen Mr. Clutter—I got sent to Lansing. Because of breaking into this appliance store. Electrical appliances. What I had in mind was, I wanted to get hold of some electrical lawn mowers. Not to sell. I was going to start a lawn-mower rental service. That way, see, I'd have had my own permanent little business. Course nothing come of it—'cept I drew a three-to-five. If I hadn't, then I never would have met Dick, and maybe Mr. Clutter wouldn't be in his grave. But there you are. There it is. I come to meet Dick.

"He was the first fellow I celled with. We celled together I guess a month. June and part of July. He was just finishing a three-to-five—due for parole in August. He talked a lot about what he planned to do when he got out. Said he thought he might go to Nevada, one of them missile-base towns, buy hisself a uniform, and pass hisself off as a Air Force officer. So he could hang out a regular washline of hot paper. That was one idea he told me. (Never thought much of it myself. He was smart, I don't deny, but he didn't *look* the part. Like no Air Force officer.) Other times, he mentioned this friend of his. Perry. A half-Indian fellow he used to cell with. And the big deals him and Perry might pull when they got together again. I never met him—Perry. Never saw him. He'd already left Lansing, was out on parole. But Dick always said if the chance of a real big score came up, he could rely on Perry Smith to go partners.

"I don't exactly recall how Mr. Clutter first got mentioned. It must have been when we were discussing jobs, different kinds of work we'd done. Dick, he was a trained car mechanic, and mostly that was the work he'd done. Only, once he'd had a job driving a hospital ambulance. He was full of brag about that. About nurses, and all what he'd done with them in the back of the ambulance. Anyway, I informed him how I'd worked a year on a considerable wheat spread in western Kansas. For Mr. Clutter. He wanted to know if Mr. Clutter was a wealthy man. Yes, I said. Yes, he was. In fact, I said, Mr. Clutter had once told me that he got rid of ten thousand dollars in one week. I mean, said it sometimes cost him ten thousand dollars a week to run his operation. After that, Dick never stopped asking me about the family. How many was they? What ages would the kids be now? Exactly how did you get to the house? How was it laid out? Did Mr. Clutter keep a safe? I won't deny it—I told him he did. Because I seemed to remember a sort of cabinet, or safe, or *some*thing, right behind the desk in the room Mr. Clutter used as an office. Next thing I knew, Dick was talking about killing Mr. Clutter. Said him and Perry was gonna go out there and rob the place, and they was gonna kill all witnesses—the Clutters, and anybody else that happened to be around. He described to me a dozen times how he was gonna do it, how him and Perry was gonna tie them people up and gun them down. I told him, 'Dick, you'll never get by with it.' But I can't honestly say I tried to persuade him different. Because I never for a minute believed he meant to carry it out. I thought it was just talk. Like you hear plenty of in Lansing. That's about all you *do* hear: what a fellow's gonna do when he gets out—the holdups and robberies and so forth. It's nothing but brag, mostly. Nobody takes it serious. That's why, when I heard what I heard on the earphones—well, I didn't hardly believe it. Still and all, it happened. Just like Dick said it would."

That was Floyd Wells' story, though as yet he was far from telling it. He was afraid to, for if the other prisoners heard of his bearing tales to the warden, then his life, as he put it, "wouldn't be worth a dead coyote." A week passed. He monitored the radio, he followed the newspaper accounts—and in one of them read that a Kansas paper, the Hutchinson *News*, was offering a reward of one thousand dollars for any information leading to the capture and conviction of the person or persons guilty of the Clutter murders. An interesting item; it almost inspired Wells to speak. But he was still too much afraid, and his fear was not solely of the other prisoners. There was also the chance that the authorities might charge him with being an accessory to the crime. After all, it was he who had guided Dick to the Clutters' door; certainly it could be claimed that he had been aware of Dick's intentions. However one viewed it, his situation was curious, his excuses questionable. So he said nothing, and ten more days went by. December replaced November, and those investigating the case remained, according to increasingly brief newspaper reports (radio newscasters had ceased to mention the subject), as bewildered, as virtually clueless, as they had been the morning of the tragic discovery.

But *he* knew. Presently, tortured by a need to "tell somebody," he confided in another prisoner. "A particular friend. A Catholic. Kind of very religious. He asked me, 'Well, what are you gonna do, Floyd?' I said, Well, I didn't rightly know—what did he think I ought to do? Well, he was all for me going to the proper people. Said he didn't think I ought to live with something like that on my mind. And he said I could do it without anybody inside guessing I was the one told. Said he'd fix it. So the next day he got word to the deputy warden—told him I wanted to be 'called out.' Told the deputy if he called me to his office on some pretext or other, maybe I could tell him who killed the Clutters. Sure enough, the deputy sent for me. I was scared, but I remembered Mr. Clutter, and how he'd never done me no harm, how at Christmas he'd give me a little purse with fifty dollars in it. I talked to the deputy. Then I told the warden hisself. And while I was still sitting there, right there in Warden Hand's office, he picked up the telephone—"

The person to whom Warden Hand telephoned was Logan Sanford. Sanford listened, hung up, issued several orders, then placed a call of his own to Alvin Dewey. That evening, when Dewey left his office in the courthouse at Garden City, he took home with him a manila envelope.

When Dewey got home, Marie was in the kitchen preparing supper. The moment he appeared, she launched into an account of household upsets. The family cat had attacked the cocker spaniel that lived across the street, and now it seemed as if one of the spaniel's eyes might be seriously damaged. And Paul, their nine-year-old, had fallen out of a tree. It was a wonder he was alive. And then their twelve-year-old, Dewey's namesake, had gone into the yard to burn rubbish and started a blaze that had threatened the neighborhood. Someone—she didn't know who—had actually called the Fire Department.

While his wife described these unhappy episodes, Dewey poured two cups of coffee. Suddenly, Marie stopped in the middle of a sentence and stared at him. His face was flushed, and she could tell that he was elated. She said, "Alvin. Oh, honey. Is it good news?" Without comment, he gave her the manila envelope. Her hands were wet; she dried them, sat down at the kitchen table, sipped her coffee, opened the envelope, and took out photographs of a blond young man and a dark-haired, dark-skinned young man—police-made "mug shots." A pair of semi-coded dossiers accompanied the photographs. The one for the fair-headed man read:

Hickock, Richard Eugene (WM) 28. KBI 97 093; FBI 859 273 A. Address: Edgerton, Kansas. Birthdate 6-6-31. Birthplace: K.C., Kans. Height: 5-10. Weight: 175. Hair: Blond. Eyes: Blue. Build: Stout. Comp: Ruddy. Occup: Car Painter. Crime: Cheat & Defr. & Bad Checks. Paroled: 8-13-59. By: So. K.C.K.

The second description read:

Smith, Perry Edward (WM) 27-59. Birthplace: Nevada. Height: 5-4. Weight: 156. Hair: D. Brn. Crime: B&E. Arrested: (blank). By: (blank). Disposition: Sent KSP 3-13-56 from Phillips Co. 5-10 yrs. Rec. 3-14-56. Paroled: 7-6-59.

Marie examined the front-view and profile photographs of Smith: an arrogant face, tough, yet not entirely, for there was about it a peculiar refinement; the lips and nose seemed nicely made, and she thought the eyes, with their moist, dreamy expression, rather pretty—rather, in an actorish way, sensitive. Sensitive, and something more: "mean." Though not as mean, as forbiddingly "criminal," as the eyes of Hickock, Richard Eugene. Marie, transfixed by Hickock's eyes, was reminded of a childhood incident—of a bobcat she'd once seen caught in a trap, and of how, though she'd wanted to release it, the cat's eyes, radiant with pain and hatred, had drained her of pity and filled her with terror. "Who are they?" Marie asked.

Dewey told her Floyd Wells' story, and at the end he said, "Funny. The past three weeks, that's the angle we've concentrated on. Tracking down every man who ever worked on the Clutter place. Now, the way it's turned out, it just seems like a piece of luck. But a few days more and we would've hit this Wells. Found he was in prison. We would've got the truth then. Hell, yes."

"Maybe it isn't the truth," Marie said. Dewey and the eighteen men assisting him had pursued hundreds of leads to barren destinations, and she hoped to warn him against another disappointment, for she was worried about his health. His state of mind was bad; he was emaciated; and he was smoking sixty cigarettes a day.

"No. Maybe not," Dewey said. "But I have a hunch."

His tone impressed her; she looked again at the faces on the kitchen table. "Think of him," she said, placing a finger against the front-view portrait of the blond young man. "Think of those eyes. Coming toward you." Then she pushed the pictures back into their envelope. "I wish you hadn't shown me."

Later that same evening, another woman, in another kitchen, put aside a sock she was darning, removed a pair of plastic-rimmed spectacles, and leveling them at a visitor, said, "I hope you find him, Mr. Nye. For his own sake. We have two sons, and he's one of them, our first-born. We love him. But . . . Oh, I realized. I realized he wouldn't have packed up. Run off. Without a word to anybody—his daddy or his brother. Unless he was in trouble again. What makes him do it? Why?" She glanced across the small, stove-warmed room at a gaunt figure hunched in a rocking chair—Walter Hickock, her husband and the father of Richard Eugene. He was a man with faded, defeated eyes and rough hands; when he spoke, his voice sounded as if it were seldom used.

"Was nothing wrong with my boy, Mr. Nye," Mr. Hickock said. "An outstanding athlete—always on the first team at school. Basketball! Baseball! Football! Dick was always the star player. A pretty good student, too, with A marks in several subjects. History. Mechanical drawing. After he graduated from high school—June, 1949—he wanted to go on to college. Study to be an engineer. But we couldn't do it. Plain didn't have the money. Never have had any money. Our farm here, it's only forty-four acres—we hardly can scratch a living. I guess Dick resented it, not getting to college. The first job he had was with Santa Fe Railways, in Kansas City. Made seventy-five dollars a week. He figured that was enough to get married on, so him and Carol got married. She wasn't but sixteen; he wasn't but nineteen hisself. I never thought nothing good would come of it. Didn't, neither."

Mrs. Hickock, a plump woman with a soft, round face unmarred by a lifetime of dawn-to-dark endeavor, reproached him. "Three precious little boys, our grandchildren—there, that's what came of it. And Carol is a lovely girl. She's not to blame."

Mr. Hickock continued, "Him and Carol rented a good-size house, bought a fancy car—they was in debt all the time. Even though pretty soon Dick was making better money driving a hospital ambulance. Later on, the Markl Buick Company, a big outfit there in Kansas City, they hired him. As a mechanic and car painter. But him and Carol lived too high, kept buying stuff they couldn't nohow afford, and Dick got to writing checks. I still think the reason he started doing stunts such as that was connected with the smash-up. Concussed his head in a car smash-up. After that, he wasn't the same boy. Gambling, writing bad checks. I never knew him to do them things before. And it was along about then he took up with this other gal. The one he divorced Carol for, and was his second wife."

Mrs. Hickock said, "Dick couldn't help that. You remember how Margaret Edna was attracted to him."

"'Cause a woman likes you, does that mean you got to get caught?" Mr. Hickock said. "Well, Mr. Nye, I expect you know as much about it as we do. Why our boy was sent to prison. Locked away seventeen months, and all he done was borrow a hunting rifle. From the house of a neighbor here. He had no idea to steal it, I don't give a damn what nobody says. And that was the ruination of him. When he came out of Lansing, he was a plain stranger to me. You couldn't talk to him. The whole world was against Dick Hickock—that's how he figured. Even the second wife, she left him—filed for divorce while he was in prison. Just the same, lately there, he seemed to be settling down. Working for the Bob Sands Body Shop, over in Olathe. Living here at home with us, getting to bed early, not violating his parole any shape or fashion. I'll tell you, Mr. Nye, I've not got long, I'm with cancer, and Dick knowed that—leastways, he knowed I'm sickly—and not a month ago, right before he took off, he told me, 'Dad, you've been a pretty good old dad to me. I'm not ever gonna do nothing more to hurt you.' He meant it, too. That boy has plenty of good inside him. If ever you seen him on a football field, if ever you seen him play with his children, you wouldn't doubt me. Lord, I wish the Lord could tell me, because I don't know what happened."

His wife said, "I do," resumed her darning, and was forced by tears to stop. "That friend of his. That's what happened."

The visitor, K.B.I. Agent Harold Nye, busied himself scribbling in a shorthand notebook—a notebook already well filled with the results of a long day spent probing the accusations of Floyd Wells. Thus far the facts ascertained corroborated Wells' story most persuasively. On November 20 the suspect Richard Eugene Hickock had gone on a Kansas City shopping spree during which he had passed not fewer than "seven pieces of hot paper." Nye had called on all the reported victims—salesmen of cameras and of radio and television equipment, the proprietor of a jewelry shop, a clerk in a clothing store—and when in each instance the witness was shown photographs of Hickock and Perry Edward Smith, he had identified the former as the author of the spurious checks, the latter as his "silent" accomplice. (One deceived salesman said, "He [Hickock] did the work. A very smooth talker, very convincing. The other one—I thought he might be a foreigner, a Mexican maybe—he never opened his mouth.")

Nye had next driven to the suburban village of Olathe, where he interviewed Hickock's last employer, the owner of the Bob Sands Body Shop. "Yes, he worked here," said Mr. Sands. "From August until—Well, I never saw him after the nineteenth of November, or maybe it was the twentieth. He left without giving me any notice whatever. Just took off—I don't know where to, and neither does his dad. Surprised? Well, yes. Yes, I was. We were on a fairly friendly basis. Dick kind of has a way with him, you know. He can be very likable. Once in a while he used to come to our house. Fact is, a week before he left, we had some people over, a little party, and Dick brought this friend he had visiting him, a boy from Nevada—Perry Smith was his name. He could play the guitar real nice. He played the guitar and sang some songs, and him and Dick entertained everybody with a weight-lifting act. Perry Smith, he's a little fellow, not much over five feet high, but he could just about pick up a horse. No, they didn't seem nervous, neither one. I'd say they were enjoying themselves. The exact date? Sure I remember. It was the thirteenth. Friday, the thirteenth of November."

From there, Nye steered his car northward along raw country roads. As he neared the Hickock farm, he stopped at several neighboring homesteads, ostensibly to ask directions, actually to make inquiries concerning the suspect. One farmer's wife said, "Dick Hickock! Don't talk to me about Dick Hickock! If ever I met the devil! Steal? Steal the weights off a dead man's eyes! His mother, though, Eunice, she's a fine woman. Heart big as a barn. His daddy, too. Both of them plain, honest people. Dick would've gone to jail more times than you can count, except nobody around here ever wanted to prosecute. Out of respect for his folks."

Dusk had fallen when Nye knocked at the door of Walter Hickock's weather-grayed four-room farmhouse. It was as though some such visit had been expected. Mr. Hickock invited the detective into the kitchen, and Mrs. Hickock offered him coffee. Perhaps if they had known the true meaning of the caller's presence, the reception tendered him would have been less gracious, more guarded. But they did not know, and during the hours the three sat conversing, the name Clutter was never mentioned, or the word murder. The parents accepted what Nye implied—that parole violation and financial fraud were all that motivated his pursuit of their son.

"Dick brought him [Perry] home one evening, and told us he was a friend just off a bus from Las Vegas, and he wanted to know couldn't he sleep here, stay here awhile," Mrs. Hickock said. "No, sir, I wouldn't have him in the house. One look and I saw what he was. With his perfume. And his oily hair. It was clear as day where Dick had met him. According to the conditions of his parole, he wasn't supposed to associate with anybody he'd met up there [Lansing]. I warned Dick, but he wouldn't listen. He found a room for his friend at the Hotel Olathe, in Olathe, and after that Dick was with him every spare minute. Once they went off on a weekend trip. Mr. Nye, certain as I'm sitting here, Perry Smith was the one put him up to writing them checks."

Nye shut his notebook and put his pen in his pocket, and both his hands as well, for his hands were shaking from excitement. "Now, on this weekend trip. Where did they go?"

"Fort Scott," Mr. Hickock said, naming a Kansas town with a military history. "The way I understood it, Perry Smith has a sister lives in Fort Scott. She was supposed to be holding a piece of money belonged to him. Fifteen hundred dollars was the sum mentioned. That was the main reason he'd come to Kansas, to collect this money his sister was holding. So Dick drove him down there to get it. It was only a overnight trip. He was back home a little before noon Sunday. Time for Sunday dinner."

"I see," said Nye. "An overnight trip. Which means they left here sometime Saturday. That would be Saturday, November fourteenth?"

The old man agreed.

"And returned Sunday, November fifteenth?"

"Sunday noon."

Nye pondered the mathematics involved, and was encouraged by the conclusion he came to: that within a time span of twenty or twenty-four hours, the suspects could have made a round-trip journey of rather more than eight hundred miles, and, in the process, murder four people.

"Now, Mr. Hickock," Nye said. "On Sunday, when your son came home, was he alone? Or was Perry Smith with him?"

"No, he was alone. He said he'd left Perry off at the Hotel Olathe."

Nye, whose normal voice is cuttingly nasal and naturally intimidating, was attempting a subdued timbre, a disarming, throwaway style. "And do you remember—did anything in his manner strike you as unusual? Different?"

"Who?"

"Your son."

"When?"

"When he returned from Fort Scott."

Mr. Hickock ruminated. Then he said, "He seemed the same as ever. Soon as he came in, we sat down to dinner. He was mighty hungry. Started piling his plate before I'd finished the blessing. I remarked on it, said, 'Dick, you're shoveling it in as fast as you can work your elbow. Don't you mean to leave nothing for the rest of us?' Course, he's always been a big eater. Pickles. He can eat a whole tub of pickles."

"And after dinner what did he do?"

"Fell asleep," said Mr. Hickock, and appeared to be moderately taken aback by his own reply. "Fell fast asleep. And I guess you could say that was unusual. We'd gathered round to watch a basketball game. On the TV. Me and Dick and our other boy, David. Pretty soon Dick was snoring like a buzz saw, and I said to his brother, 'Lord, I never thought I'd live to see the day Dick would go to sleep at a basketball game.' Did, though. Slept straight through it. Only woke up long enough to eat some cold supper, and right after went off to bed."

Mrs. Hickock rethreaded her darning needle; her husband rocked his rocker and sucked on an unlit pipe. The detective's trained eyes roamed the scrubbed and humble room. In a corner, a gun stood propped against the wall; he had noticed it before. Rising, reaching for it, he said, "You do much hunting, Mr. Hickock?"

"That's his gun. Dick's. Him and David go out once in a while. After rabbits, mostly."

It was a .12-gauge Savage shotgun, Model 300; a delicately etched scene of pheasants in flight ornamented the handle.

"How long has Dick had it?"

The question aroused Mrs. Hickock. "That gun cost over a hundred dollars. Dick bought it on credit, and now the store won't have it back, even though it's not hardly a month old and only been used the one time—the start of November, when him and David went to Grinnell on a pheasant shoot. He used our names to buy it—his daddy let him—so here we are, liable for the payments, and when you think of Walter, sick as he is, and all the things we need, all we do without . . ." She held her breath, as though trying to halt an attack of hiccups. "Are you sure you won't have a cup of coffee, Mr. Nye? It's no trouble."

The detective leaned the gun against the wall, relinquishing it, although he felt certain it was the weapon that had killed the Clutter family. "Thank you, but it's late, and I have to drive to Topeka," he said, and then, consulting his notebook, "Now, I'll just run through this, see if I have it straight. Perry Smith arrived in Kansas Thursday, the twelfth of November. Your son claimed this person came here to collect a sum of money from a sister residing in Fort Scott. That Saturday the two drove to Fort Scott, where they remained overnight —I assume in the home of the sister?"

Mr. Hickock said, "No. They never could find her. Seems like she'd moved."

Nye smiled. "Nevertheless, they stayed away overnight. And during the week that followed—that is, from the fifteenth to the twenty-first—Dick continued to see his friend Perry Smith, but otherwise, or as far as you know, he maintained a normal routine: lived at home and reported to work every day. On the twenty-first he disappeared, and so did Perry Smith. And since then you've not heard from him? He hasn't written you?"

"He's afraid to," said Mrs. Hickock. "Ashamed and afraid."

"Ashamed?"

"Of what he's done. Of how he's hurt us again. And afraid because he thinks we won't forgive him. Like we always have. And will. You have children, Mr. Nye?"

He nodded.

"Then you know how it is."

"One thing more. Have you any idea, any at all, where your son might have gone?"

"Open a map," said Mr. Hickock. "Point your finger—maybe that's it."

It was late afternoon, and the driver of the car, a middle-aged traveling salesman who shall here be known as Mr. Bell, was tired. He longed to stop for a short nap. However, he was only a hundred miles from his destination—Omaha, Nebraska, the headquarters of the large meat packing company for which he worked. A company rule forbade its salesmen to pick up hitchhikers, but Mr. Bell often disobeyed it, particularly if he was bored and drowsy, so when he saw the two young men standing by the side of the road, he immediately braked his car.

They looked to him like "O.K. boys." The taller of the two, a wiry type with dirty-blond, crew-cut hair, had an engaging grin and a polite manner, and his partner, the "runty" one, holding a harmonica in his right hand and, in his left, a swollen straw suitcase, seemed "nice enough," shy but amiable. In any event, Mr. Bell, entirely unaware of his guests' intentions, which included throttling him with a belt and leaving him, robbed of his car, his money, and his life, concealed in a prairie grave, was glad to have company, somebody to talk to and keep him awake until he arrived at Omaha.

He introduced himself, then asked them their names. The affable young man with whom he was sharing the front seat said his name was Dick. "And that's Perry," he said, winking at Perry, who was seated directly behind the driver.

"I can ride you boys as far as Omaha."

Dick said, "Thank you, sir. Omaha's where we were headed. Hoped we might find some work."

What kind of work were they hunting? The salesman thought perhaps he could help.

Dick said, "I'm a first-class car painter. Mechanic, too. I'm used to making real money. My buddy and me, we just been down in Old Mexico. Our idea was, we wanted to live there. But hell, they don't pay any wages. Nothing a white man could live off."

Ah, Mexico. Mr. Bell explained that he had honeymooned in Cuernavaca. "We always wanted to go back. But it's hard to move around when you've got five kids."

Perry, as he later recalled, thought, Five kids—well, too bad. And listening to Dick's conceited chatter, hearing him start to describe his Mexican "amorous conquests," he thought how "queer" it was, "egomaniacal." Imagine going all out to impress a man you were going to kill, a man who wouldn't be alive ten minutes from now—not if the plan he and Dick had devised went smoothly. And why shouldn't it? The setup was ideal—exactly what they had been looking for during the three days it had taken them to hitchhike from California to Nevada and across Nevada and Wyoming into Nebraska. Until now, however, a suitable victim had eluded them. Mr. Bell was the first prosperous-seeming solitary traveler to offer them a lift. Their other hosts had been either truck drivers or soldiers—and, once, a pair of Negro prizefighters driving a lavender Cadillac. But Mr. Bell was perfect. Perry felt inside a pocket of the leather windbreaker he was wearing. The pocket bulged with a bottle of Bayer aspirin and with a jagged, fist-size rock wrapped in a yellow cotton cowboy handkerchief. He unfastened his belt, a Navajo belt, silver-buckled and studded with turquoise beads; he took it off, flexed it, placed it across his knees. He waited. He watched the Nebraska prairie rolling by, and fooled with his harmonica—made up a tune and played it and waited for Dick to pronounce the agreed-upon signal: "Hey, Perry, pass me a match." Whereupon Dick was supposed to seize the steering wheel, while Perry, wielding his handkerchief-wrapped rock, belabored the salesman's head—"opened it up." Later, along some quiet side road, use would be made of the belt with the sky-blue beads.

Meanwhile, Dick and the condemned man were trading dirty jokes. Their laughter irritated Perry; he especially disliked Mr. Bell's outbursts—hearty barks that sounded very much like the laughter of Tex John Smith, Perry's father. The memory of his father's laughter increased his tension; his head hurt, his knees ached. He chewed three aspirin and swallowed them dry. Jesus! He thought he might vomit, or faint; he felt certain he would if Dick delayed "the party" much longer. The light was dimming, the road was straight, with neither house nor human being in view—nothing but land winter-stripped and as somber as sheet iron. Now was the time, *now*. He stared at Dick, as though to communicate this realization, and a few small signs —a twitching eyelid, a mustache of sweat drops—told him that Dick had already reached the same conclusion.

And yet when Dick next spoke, it was only to launch another joke. "Here's a riddle. The riddle is: What's the similarity between a trip to the bathroom and a trip to the cemetery?" He grinned. "Give up?"

"Give up."

"When you gotta go, you gotta go!"

Mr. Bell barked.

"Hey, Perry, pass me a match."

But just as Perry raised his hand, and the rock was on the verge of descent, something extraordinary occurred—what Perry later called "a goddam miracle." The miracle was the sudden appearance of a third hitchhiker, a Negro soldier, for whom the charitable salesman stopped. "Say, that's pretty cute," he said as his savior ran toward the car. "When you gotta go, you gotta go!"

December 16, 1959, Las Vegas, Nevada. Age and weather had removed the first letter and the last—an R and an S—thereby coining a somewhat ominous word: OOM. The word, faintly present upon a sun-warped sign, seemed appropriate to the place it publicized, which was, as Harold Nye wrote in his official K.B.I. report, "run-down and shabby, the lowest type of hotel or rooming house." The report continued: "Until a few years ago (according to information supplied by the Las Vegas police), it was one of the biggest cathouses in the West. Then fire destroyed the main building, and the remaining portion was converted into a cheap-rent rooming house." The "lobby" was unfurnished, except for a cactus plant six feet tall and a makeshift reception desk; it was also uninhabited. The detective clapped his hands. Eventually, a voice, female, but not very feminine, shouted, "I'm coming," but it was five minutes before the woman appeared. She wore a soiled housecoat and high-heeled gold leather sandals. Curlers pinioned her thinning yellowish hair. Her face was broad, muscular, rouged, powdered. She was carrying a can of Miller High Life beer; she smelled of beer and tobacco and recently applied nail varnish. She was seventy-four years old, but in Nye's opinion, "looked younger—maybe ten minutes younger." She stared at him, his trim brown suit, his brown snapbrim hat. When he displayed his badge, she was amused; her lips parted, and Nye glimpsed two rows of fake teeth. "Uh-huh. That's what I figured," she said. "O.K. Let's hear it."

He handed her a photograph of Richard Hickock. "Know him?"

A negative grunt.

"Or him?"

She said, "Uh-huh. He's stayed here a coupla times. But he's not here now. Checked out over a month ago. You wanna see the register?"

Nye leaned against the desk and watched the landlady's long and lacquered fingernails search a page of pencil-scribbled names. Las Vegas was the first of three places that his employers wished him to visit. Each had been chosen because of its connection with the history of Perry Smith. The two others were Reno, where it was thought that Smith's father lived, and San Francisco, the home of Smith's sister, who shall here be known as Mrs. Frederic Johnson. Though Nye planned to interview these relatives, and anyone else who might have knowledge of the suspect's whereabouts, his main objective was to obtain the aid of the local law agencies. On arriving in Las Vegas, for example, he had discussed the Clutter case with Lieutenant B. J. Handlon, Chief of the Detective Division of the Las Vegas Police Department. The lieutenant had then written a memorandum ordering all police personnel to be on the alert for Hickock and Smith: "Wanted in Kansas for parole violation, and said to be driving a 1949 Chevrolet bearing Kansas license JO-58269. These men are probably armed and should be considered dangerous." Also, Handlon had assigned a detective to help Nye "case the pawnbrokers"; as he said, there was "always a pack of them in any gambling town." Together, Nye and the Las Vegas detective had checked every pawn ticket issued during the past month. Specifically, Nye hoped to find a Zenith portable radio believed to have been stolen from the Clutter house on the night of the crime, but he had no luck with that. One broker, though, remembered Smith ("He's been in and out of here going on a good ten years"), and was able to produce a ticket for a bearskin rug pawned during the first week in November. It was from this ticket that Nye had obtained the address of the rooming house.

"Registered October thirtieth," the landlady said. "Pulled out November eleventh." Nye glanced at Smith's signature. The ornateness of it, the mannered swoops and swirls, surprised him—a reaction that the landlady apparently divined, for she said, "Uh-huh. And you oughta hear him talk. Big, long words coming at you in this kinda lispy, whispery voice. Quite a personality. What you got against him—a nice little punk like that?"

"Parole violation."

"Uh-huh. Came all the way from Kansas on a parole case. Well, I'm just a dizzy blonde. I believe you. But I wouldn't tell that tale to any brunettes." She raised the beer can, emptied it, then thoughtfully rolled the empty can between her veined and freckled hands. "Whatever it is, it ain't nothing big-big. Couldn't be. I never saw the man yet I couldn't gauge his shoe size. This one, he's only a punk. Little punk tried to sweet-talk me out of paying rent the last week he was here." She chuckled, presumably at the absurdity of such an ambition.

The detective asked how much Smith's room had cost.

"Regular rate. Nine bucks a week. Plus a fifty-cent key deposit. Strictly cash. Strictly in advance."

"While he was here, what did he do with himself? Does he have any friends?" Nye asked.

"You think I keep an eye on every crawly that comes in here?" the landlady retorted. "Bums. Punks. I'm not interested. I got a daughter married big-big." Then she said, "No, he doesn't have any friends. Least, I never noticed him run around with anybody special. This last time he was here, he spent most every day tinkering with his car. Had it parked out front there. An old Ford. Looked like it was made before he was born. He gave it a paint job. Painted the top part black and the rest silver. Then he wrote 'For Sale' on the windshield. One day I heard a sucker stop and offer him forty bucks—that's forty more than it was worth. But he allowed he couldn't take less than ninety. Said he needed the money for a bus ticket. Just before he left I heard some colored man bought it."

"He said he needed the money for a bus ticket. But you don't know where it was he wanted to go?"

She pursed her lips, hung a cigarette between them, but her eyes stayed on Nye. "Play fair. Any money on the table? A reward?" She waited for an answer; when none arrived, she seemed to weigh the probabilities and decide in favor of proceeding. "Because I got the impression wherever he was going he didn't mean to stay long. That he meant to cut back here. Sorta been expecting him to turn up any day." She nodded toward the interior of the establishment. "Come along, and I'll show you why."

Stairs. Gray halls. Nye sniffed the odors, separating one from another: lavatory disinfectant, alcohol, dead cigars. Beyond one door, a drunken tenant wailed and sang in the firm grip of either gladness or grief. "Boil down, Dutch! Turn it off or out you go!" the woman yelled. "Here," she said to Nye, leading him into a darkened storage room. She switched on a light. "Over there. That box. He asked would I keep it till he came back."

It was a cardboard box, unwrapped but tied with cord. A declaration, a warning somewhat in the spirit of an Egyptian curse, was crayoned across the top: "*Beware!* Property of Perry E. Smith! *Beware!*" Nye undid the cord; the knot, he was unhappy to see, was not the same as the half hitch that the killers had used when binding the Clutter family. He parted the flaps. A cockroach emerged, and the landlady stepped on it, squashing it under the heel of her gold leather sandal. "Hey!" she said as he carefully extracted and slowly examined Smith's possessions. "The sneak. That's *my* towel." In addition to the towel, the meticulous Nye listed in his notebook: "One dirty pillow, 'Souvenir of Honolulu'; one pink baby blanket; one pair khaki trousers; one aluminum pan with pancake turner." Other oddments included a scrapbook thick with photographs clipped from physical-culture magazines (sweaty studies of weight-lifting weight-lifters) and, inside a shoebox, a collection of medicines: rinses and powders employed to combat trench mouth, and also a mystifying amount of aspirin—at least a dozen containers, several of them empty.

"Junk," the landlady said. "Nothing but trash."

True, it was valueless stuff even to a clue-hungry detective. Still, Nye was glad to have seen it; each item—the palliatives for sore gums, the greasy Honolulu pillow—gave him a clearer impression of the owner and his lonely, mean life.

The next day in Reno, preparing his official notes, Nye wrote: "At 9:00 A.M. the reporting agent contacted Mr. Bill Driscoll, chief criminal investigator, Sheriff's Office, Washoe County, Reno, Nevada. After being briefed on the circumstances of this case, Mr. Driscoll was supplied with photographs, fingerprints and warrants for Hickock and Smith. Stops were placed in the files on both these individuals as well as the automobile. At 10:30 A.M. the reporting agent contacted Sgt. Abe Feroah, Detective Division, Police Department, Reno, Nevada. Sgt. Feroah and the reporting agent checked the police files. Neither the name of Smith or Hickock was reflected in the felon registration file. A check of the pawnshop-ticket files failed to reflect any information about the missing radio. A permanent stop was placed in these files in the event the radio is pawned in Reno. The detective handling the pawnshop detail took photographs of Smith and Hickock to each of the pawnshops in town and also made a personal check of each shop for the radio. These pawnshops made an identification of Smith as being familiar, but were unable to furnish any further information."

Thus the morning. That afternoon Nye set forth in search of Tex John Smith. But at his first stop, the post office, a clerk at the General Delivery window told him he need look no farther—not in Nevada—

for "the individual" had left there the previous August and now lived in the vicinity of Circle City, Alaska. That, anyway, was where his mail was being forwarded.

"Gosh! Now, there's a tall order," said the clerk in response to Nye's request for a description of the elder Smith. "The guy's out of a book. He calls himself the Lone Wolf. A lot of his mail comes addressed that way—the Lone Wolf. He doesn't receive many letters, no, but bales of catalogues and advertising pamphlets. You'd be surprised the number of people send away for that stuff—just to get some mail, must be. How old? I'd say sixty. Dresses Western—cowboy boots and a big ten-gallon hat. He told me he used to be with the rodeo. I've talked to him quite a bit. He's been in here almost every day the last few years. Once in a while he'd disappear, stay away a month or so—always claimed he'd been off prospecting. One day last August a young man came here to the window. He said he was looking for his father, Tex John Smith, and did I know where he could find him. He didn't look much like his dad; the Wolf is so thin-lipped and Irish, and this boy looked almost pure Indian—hair black as boot polish, with eyes to match. But next morning in walks the Wolf and confirms it; he told me his son had just got out of the Army and that they were going to Alaska. He's an old Alaska hand. I think he once owned a hotel there, or some kind of hunting lodge. He said he expected to be gone about two years. Nope, never seen him since, him or his boy."

The Johnson family were recent arrivals in their San Francisco community—a middle-class, middle-income real-estate development high in the hills north of the city. On the afternoon of December 18, 1959, young Mrs. Johnson was expecting guests; three women of the neighborhood were coming by for coffee and cake and perhaps a game of cards. The hostess was tense; it would be the first time she had entertained in her new home. Now, while she was listening for the doorbell, she made a final tour, pausing to dispose of a speck of lint or alter an arrangement of Christmas poinsettias. The house, like the others on the slanting hillside street, was a conventional suburban ranch house, pleasant and commonplace. Mrs. Johnson loved it; she was in love with the redwood paneling, the wall-to-wall carpeting, the picture windows fore and aft, the view that the rear window provided—hills, a valley, then sky and ocean. And she was proud of the small back garden; her husband—by profession an insurance salesman, by inclination a carpenter—had built around it a white picket fence, and inside it a house for the family dog, and a sandbox and swings for the children. At the moment, all four—dog, two little boys, and a girl—were playing there under a mild sky; she hoped they would be happy in the garden until the guests had gone. When the doorbell sounded and Mrs. Johnson went to the door, she was wearing what she considered her most becoming dress, a yellow knit that hugged her figure and heightened the pale-tea shine of her Cherokee coloring and the blackness of her feather-bobbed hair. She opened the door, prepared to admit three neighbors; instead, she discovered two strangers—men who tipped their hats and flipped open badge-studded billfolds. "Mrs. Johnson?" one of them said. "My name is Nye. This is Inspector Guthrie. We're attached to the San Francisco police, and we've just received an inquiry from Kansas concerning your brother, Perry Edward Smith. It seems he hasn't been reporting to his parole officer, and we wondered if you could tell us anything of his present whereabouts."

Mrs. Johnson was not distressed—and definitely not surprised—to learn that the police were once more interested in her brother's activities. What did upset her was the prospect of having guests arrive to find her being questioned by detectives. She said, "No. Nothing. I haven't seen Perry in four years."

"This is a serious matter, Mrs. Johnson," Nye said. "We'd like to talk it over."

Having surrendered, having asked them in and offered them coffee (which was accepted), Mrs. Johnson said, "I haven't seen Perry in four years. Or heard from him since he was paroled. Last summer, when he came out of prison, he visited my father in Reno. In a letter, my father told me he was returning to Alaska and taking Perry with him. Then he wrote again, I think in September, and he was very angry. He and Perry had quarreled and separated before they reached the border. Perry turned back; my father went on to Alaska alone."

"And he hasn't written you since?"

"No."

"Then it's possible your brother may have joined him recently. Within the last month."

"I don't know. I don't care."

"On bad terms?"

"With Perry? Yes. I'm afraid of him."

"But while he was in Lansing you wrote him frequently. Or so the Kansas authorities tell us," Nye said. The second man, Inspector Guthrie, seemed content to occupy the sidelines.

"I wanted to help him. I hoped I might change a few of his ideas.

Now I know better. The rights of other people mean nothing to Perry. He has no respect for anyone."

"About friends. Do you know of any with whom he might be staying?"

"Joe James," she said, and explained that James was a young Indian logger and fisherman who lived in the forest near Bellingham, Washington. No, she was not personally acquainted with him, but she understood that he and his family were generous people who had often been kind to Perry in the past. The only friend of Perry's she had ever *met* was a young lady who had appeared on the Johnsons' doorstep in June, 1955, bringing with her a letter from Perry in which he introduced her as his wife. "He said he was in trouble, and asked if I would take care of his wife until he could send for her. The girl looked twenty; it turned out she was fourteen. And of course she wasn't anyone's wife. But at the time I was taken in. I felt sorry for her, and asked her to stay with us. She did, though not for long. Less than a week. And when she left, she took our suitcases and everything they could hold—most of my clothes and most of my husband's, the silver, even the kitchen clock."

"When this happened, where were you living?"

"Denver."

"Have you ever lived in Fort Scott, Kansas?"

"Never. I've never been to Kansas."

"Have you a sister who lives in Fort Scott?"

"My sister is dead. My only sister."

Nye smiled. He said, "You understand, Mrs. Johnson, we're working on the assumption that your brother will contact you. Write or call. Or come to see you."

"I hope not. As a matter of fact, he doesn't know we've moved. He thinks I'm still in Denver. Please, if you do find him, don't give him my address. I'm afraid."

"When you say that, is it because you think he might harm you? Hurt you physically?"

She considered, and unable to decide, said she didn't know. "But I'm afraid of him. I always have been. He can *seem* so warmhearted and sympathetic. Gentle. He cries so easily. Sometimes music sets him off, and when he was a little boy he used to cry because he thought a sunset was beautiful. Or the moon. Oh, he can fool you. He can make you feel so sorry for him—"

The doorbell rang. Mrs. Johnson's reluctance to answer conveyed her dilemma, and Nye (who later wrote of her, "Throughout the interview she remained composed and most gracious. A person of exceptional character") reached for his brown snapbrim. "Sorry to have troubled you, Mrs. Johnson. But if you hear from Perry, we hope you'll have the good sense to call us. Ask for Inspector Guthrie."

After the departure of the detectives, the composure that had impressed Nye faltered; a familiar despair impended. She fought it, delayed its full impact until the party was done and the guests had gone, until she'd fed the children and bathed them and heard their prayers. Then the mood, like the evening ocean fog now clouding the street lamps, closed round her. She had said she was afraid of Perry, and she was, but was it simply Perry she feared, or was it a configuration of which he was part—the terrible destinies that seemed promised the four children of Florence Buckskin and Tex John Smith? The eldest, the brother she loved, had shot himself; Fern had fallen out of a window, or jumped; and Perry was committed to violence, a criminal. So, in a sense, she was the only survivor; and what tormented her was the thought that in time she, too, would be overwhelmed: go mad, or contract an incurable illness, or in a fire lose all she valued—home, husband, children.

Her husband was away on a business trip, and when she was alone, she never thought of having a drink. But tonight she fixed a strong one, then lay down on the living-room couch, a picture album propped against her knees.

A photograph of her father dominated the first page—a studio portrait taken in 1922, the year of his marriage to the young Indian rodeo rider Miss Florence Buckskin. It was a photograph that invariably transfixed Mrs. Johnson. Because of it, she could understand why, when essentially they were so mismatched, her mother had married her father. The young man in the picture exuded virile allure. Everything—the cocky tilt of his ginger-haired head, the squint in his left eye (as though he were sighting a target), the tiny cowboy scarf knotted round his throat—was abundantly attractive. On the whole, Mrs. Johnson's attitude toward her father was ambivalent, but one aspect of him she had always respected—his fortitude. She well knew how eccentric he seemed to others; he seemed so to her, for that matter. All the same, he was "a real man." He did things, did them easily. He could make a tree fall precisely where he wished. He could skin a bear, repair a watch, build a house, bake a cake, darn a sock, or catch a trout with a bent pin and a piece of string. Once he had survived a winter alone in the Alaskan wilderness.

Alone: in Mrs. Johnson's opinion, that was how such men should live. Wives, children, a timid life are not for them.

She turned over some pages of childhood snapshots—pictures made in Utah and Nevada and Idaho and Oregon. The rodeo careers of "Tex & Flo" were finished, and the family, living in an old truck, roamed the country hunting work, a hard thing to find in 1933. "Tex John Smith Family picking berries in Oregon, 1933" was the caption under a snapshot of four barefooted children wearing overalls and cranky, uniformly fatigued expressions. Berries or stale bread soaked in sweet condensed milk was often all they had to eat. Barbara Johnson remembered that once the family had lived for days on rotten bananas, and that, as a result, Perry had got colic; he had screamed all night, while Bobo, as Barbara was called, wept for fear he was dying.

Bobo was three years older than Perry, and she adored him; he was her only toy, a doll she scrubbed and combed and kissed and sometimes spanked. Here was a picture of the two together bathing naked in a diamond-watered Colorado creek, the brother, a pot-bellied, sun-blackened cupid, clutching his sister's hand and giggling, as though the tumbling stream contained ghostly tickling fingers. In another snapshot (Mrs. Johnson was unsure, but she thought probably it was taken at a remote Nevada ranch where the family was staying when a final battle between the parents, a terrifying contest in which horsewhips and scalding water and kerosene lamps were used as weapons, had brought the marriage to a stop), she and Perry are astride a pony, their heads are together, their cheeks touch; beyond them dry mountains burn.

Later, when the children and their mother had gone to live in San Francisco, Bobo's love for the little boy weakened until it went quite away. He wasn't her baby any more but a wild thing, a thief, a robber. His first recorded arrest was on October 27, 1936—his eighth birthday. Ultimately, after several confinements in institutions and children's detention centers, he was returned to the custody of his father, and it was many years before Bobo saw him again, except in photographs that Tex John occasionally sent his other children—pictures that, pasted above white-ink captions, were part of the album's contents. There was "Perry, Dad, and their Husky Dog," "Perry and Dad Panning for Gold," "Perry Bear-Hunting in Alaska." In this last, he was a fur-capped boy of fifteen standing on snowshoes among snow-weighted trees, a rifle hooked under his arm; the face was drawn and the eyes were sad and very tired, and Mrs. Johnson, looking at the picture, was reminded of a "scene" that Perry had made once when he had visited her in Denver. Indeed, it was the last time she had ever seen him—the spring of 1955. They were discussing his childhood with Tex John, and suddenly Perry, who had too much drink inside him, pushed her against a wall and held her there. "I was his nigger," Perry said. "That's all. Somebody he could work their guts out and never have to pay them one hot dime. No, Bobo, *I'm* talking. Shut up, or I'll throw you in the river. Like once when I was walking across a bridge in Japan, and a guy was standing there, I never saw him before, I just picked him up and threw him in the river.

"Please, Bobo. Please listen. You think I *like* myself? Oh, the man I could have been! But that bastard never gave me a chance. He wouldn't *let* me go to school. O.K. O.K. I was a bad kid. But the time came I begged to go to school. I happen to have a brilliant mind. In case you don't know. A brilliant mind and talent plus. But no education, because he didn't want me to learn anything, only how to tote and carry for him. Dumb. Ignorant. That's the way he wanted me to be. So that I could never escape him. But you, Bobo. *You* went to school. You and Jimmy and Fern. Every damn one of you got an education. Everybody but me. And I hate you, all of you—Dad and everybody."

As though for his brother and sisters life had been a bed of roses! Maybe so, if that meant cleaning up Mama's drunken vomit, if it meant never anything nice to wear or enough to eat. Still, it was true, all three had finished high school. Jimmy, in fact, had graduated at the top of his class—an honor he owed entirely to his own will power. That, Barbara Johnson felt, was what made his suicide so ominous. Strong character, high courage, hard work—it seemed that none of these were determining factors in the fates of Tex John's children. They shared a doom against which virtue was no defense. Not that Perry was virtuous, or Fern. When Fern was fourteen, she changed her name, and for the rest of her short life she tried to justify the replacement: Joy. She was an easygoing girl, "everybody's sweetheart"—rather too much everybody's, for she was partial to men, though somehow she hadn't much luck with them. Somehow, the kind of man she liked always let her down. Her mother had died in an alcoholic coma, and she was afraid of drink—yet she drank. Before she was twenty, Fern-Joy was beginning the day with a bottle of beer. Then, one summer night, she fell from the window of a hotel room. Falling, she struck a theater marquee, bounced off it, and rolled under the wheels of a taxi. Above, in the vacated room, police found her shoes, a moneyless purse, an empty whiskey bottle.

One could understand Fern and forgive her, but Jimmy was a different matter. Mrs. Johnson was looking at a picture of him in which he was dressed as a sailor; during the war he had served in the Navy.

Slender, a pale young seafarer with an elongated face of slightly dour saintliness, he stood with an arm around the waist of the girl he had married and, in Mrs. Johnson's estimation, ought not to have, for they had nothing in common—the serious Jimmy and this teen-age San Diego fleet-follower whose glass beads reflected a now long-faded sun. And yet what Jimmy had felt for her was beyond normal love; it was passion—a passion that was in part pathological. As for the girl, she *must* have loved him, and loved him completely, or she would not have done as she did. If only Jimmy had believed that! Or been capable of believing it. But jealousy imprisoned him. He was mortified by thoughts of the men she had slept with before their marriage; he was convinced, moreover, that she remained promiscuous—that every time he went to sea, or even left her alone for the day, she betrayed him with a multitude of lovers, whose existence he unendingly demanded that she admit. Then she aimed a shotgun at a point between her eyes and pressed the trigger with her toe. When Jimmy found her, he didn't call the police. He picked her up and put her on the bed and lay down beside her. Sometime around dawn of the next day, he reloaded the gun and killed himself.

Opposite the picture of Jimmy and his wife was a photograph of Perry in uniform. It had been clipped from a newspaper, and was accompanied by a paragraph of text: "Headquarters, United States Army, Alaska. Pvt. Perry E. Smith, 23, first Army Korean combat veteran to return to the Anchorage, Alaska, area, is greeted by Captain Mason, Public Information Officer, upon arrival at Elmendorf Air Force Base. Smith served 15 months with the 24th Division as a combat engineer. His trip from Seattle to Anchorage was a gift from Pacific Northern Airlines. Miss Lynn Marquis, airline hostess, smiles approval at welcome. (Official U.S. Army Photo)." Captain Mason, with hand extended, is looking at Private Smith, but Private Smith is looking at the camera. In his expression Mrs. Johnson saw, or imagined she saw, not gratitude but arrogance, and, in place of pride, immense conceit. It wasn't incredible that he had met a man on a bridge and thrown him off it. Of course he had. She had never doubted it.

She shut the album and switched on the television, but it did not console her. Suppose he did come? The detectives had found her; why shouldn't Perry? He need not expect her to help him; she wouldn't even let him in. The front door was locked, but not the door to the garden. The garden was white with sea-fog; it might have been an assembly of spirits: Mama and Jimmy and Fern. When Mrs. Johnson bolted the door, she had in mind the dead as well as the living.

A cloudburst. Rain. Buckets of it. Dick ran. Perry ran too, but he could not run as fast; his legs were shorter, and he was lugging the suitcase. Dick reached shelter—a barn near the highway—long before him. On leaving Omaha, after a night spent in a Salvation Army dormitory, a truck driver had given them a ride across the Nebraska border into Iowa. The past several hours, however, had found them afoot. The rain came when they were sixteen miles north of an Iowa settlement called Tenville Junction.

The barn was dark.

"Dick?" Perry said.

"Over here," Dick said. He was sprawled on a bed of hay.

Perry, drenched and shaking, dropped beside him. "I'm so cold," he said, burrowing in the hay, "I'm so cold I wouldn't give a damn if this caught fire and burned me alive." He was hungry, too. Starved. Last night they had dined on bowls of Salvation Army soup, and today the only nourishment they'd had was some chocolate bars and chewing gum that Dick had stolen from a drugstore candy counter. "Any more Hershey?" Perry asked.

No, but there was still a pack of chewing gum. They divided it, then settled down to chewing it, each chomping on two and a half sticks of Doublemint, Dick's favorite flavor (Perry preferred Juicy Fruit). Money was the problem. Their utter lack of it had led Dick to decide that their next move should be what Perry considered "a crazy-man stunt"—a return to Kansas City. When Dick had first urged the return, Perry said, "You ought to see a doctor." Now, huddled together in the cold darkness, listening to the dark, cold rain, they resumed the argument, Perry once more listing the dangers of such a move, for surely by this time Dick was wanted for parole violation—"*if* nothing more." But Dick was not to be dissuaded. Kansas City, he again insisted, was the one place he was certain he could successfully "hang a lot of hot paper. Hell, I know we've got to be careful. I know they've got a warrant out. Because of the paper we hung before. But we'll move fast. One day—that'll do it. If we grab enough, maybe we ought to try Florida. Spend Christmas in Miami—stay the winter if it looks good." But Perry chewed his gum and shivered and sulked. Dick said, "What is it, honey? That other deal? Why the hell can't you forget it? They never made any connection. They never will."

Perry said, "You could be wrong. And if you are, it means The Corner." Neither one had ever before referred to the ultimate penalty in the State of Kansas—the gallows, or death in The Corner, as the inmates of Kansas State Penitentiary have named the shed that houses the equipment required to hang a man.

Dick said, "The comedian. You kill me." He struck a match, intending to smoke a cigarette, but something seen by the light of the flaring match brought him to his feet and carried him across the barn to a cow stall. A car was parked inside the stall, a black-and-white two-door 1956 Chevrolet. The key was in the ignition.

Dewey was determined to conceal from "the civilian population" any knowledge of a major break in the Clutter case—so determined that he decided to take into his confidence Garden City's two professional town criers: Bill Brown, editor of the Garden City *Telegram*, and Robert Wells, manager of the local radio station, KIUL. In outlining the situation, Dewey emphasized his reasons for considering secrecy of the first importance: "Remember, there's a possibility these men are innocent."

It was a possibility too valid to dismiss. The informer, Floyd Wells, might easily have invented his story; such tale-telling was not infrequently undertaken by prisoners who hoped to win favor or attract official notice. But even if the man's every word was gospel, Dewey and his colleagues had not yet unearthed one bit of solid supporting evidence—"courtroom evidence." What had they discovered that could not be interpreted as plausible, though exceptional, coincidence? Just because Smith had traveled to Kansas to visit his friend Hickock, and just because Hickock possessed a gun of the caliber used to commit the crime, and just because the suspects had arranged a false alibi to account for their whereabouts the night of November 14, they were not necessarily mass murderers. "But we're pretty sure this is it. We all think so. If we didn't, we wouldn't have set up a seventeen-state alarm, from Arkansas to Oregon. But keep in mind: It could be years before we catch them. They may have separated. Or left the country. There's a chance they've gone to Alaska—not hard to get lost in Alaska. The longer they're free, the less of a case we'll have. Frankly, as matters stand, we don't have much of a case anyhow. We could nab those sonsabitches tomorrow, and never be able to prove spit."

Dewey did not exaggerate. Except for two sets of boot prints, one bearing a diamond pattern and the other a Cat's Paw design, the slayers had left not a single clue. Since they seemed to take such care, they had undoubtedly got rid of the boots long ago. And the radio, too—assuming that it was they who had stolen it, which was something Dewey still hesitated to do, for it appeared to him "ludicrously inconsistent" with the magnitude of the crime and the manifest cunning of the criminals, and "inconceivable" that these men had entered a house expecting to find a money-filled safe, and then, not finding it, had thought it expedient to slaughter the family for perhaps a few dollars and a small portable radio. "Without a confession, we'll never get a conviction," he said. "That's my opinion. And that's why we can't be too cautious. They think they've got away with it. Well, we don't want them to know any different. The safer they feel, the sooner we'll grab them."

But secrets are an unusual commodity in a town the size of Garden City. Anyone visiting the sheriff's office, three underfurnished, overcrowded rooms on the third floor of the county courthouse, could detect an odd, almost sinister atmosphere. The hurry-scurry, the angry hum of recent weeks had departed; a quivering stillness now permeated the premises. Mrs. Richardson, the office secretary and a very down-to-earth person, had acquired overnight a dainty lot of whispery, tiptoe mannerisms, and the men she served, the sheriff and his staff, Dewey and the imported team of K.B.I. agents, crept about conversing in hushed tones. It was as though, like huntsmen hiding in a forest, they were afraid that any abrupt sound or movement would warn away approaching beasts.

People talked. The Trail Room of the Warren Hotel, a coffee shop that Garden City businessmen treat as though it were a private club, was a murmuring cave of speculation and rumor. An eminent citizen, so one heard, was on the point of arrest. Or it was now known that the crime was the work of killers hired by enemies of the Kansas Wheat Growers' Association, a progressive organization in which Mr. Clutter had played a large role. Of the many stories circulating, the most nearly accurate was contributed by a prominent car dealer (who refused to disclose its source): "Seems there was a man who worked for Herb way back yonder around '47 or '48. Ordinary ranch hand. Seems he went to prison, state prison, and while he was there he got to thinking what a rich man Herb was. So about a month ago, when they let him loose, the first thing he did was come on out here to rob and kill those people."

But seven miles westward, in the village of Holcomb, not a hint was heard of impending sensations, one reason being that for some while the Clutter tragedy had been a banned topic at both of the community's principal gossip-dispensaries—the post office and Hartman's Café. "Myself, I don't want to hear another word," said Mrs. Hartman. "I told them, We can't go on like this. Distrusting everybody, scaring each other to death. What I say is, if you want to talk about it, stay out of my place." Myrt Clare took quite as strong a stand. "Folks come in here to buy a nickel's worth of postage and think they can spend the next three hours and thirty-three minutes turning the Clutters inside out. Pickin' the wings off other people. Rattlesnakes, that's all they are. I don't have the time to listen. I'm in business—I'm a representative of the government of the United States. Anyway, it's morbid. Al Dewey and those hot-shot cops from Topeka and Kansas City—supposed to be sharp as turpentine. But I don't know a soul who still thinks they've got hell's chance of catching the one done it. So I say the sane thing to do is shut up. You live until you die, and it doesn't matter *how* you go; dead's dead. So why carry on like a sackful of sick cats just because Herb Clutter got his throat cut? Anyway, it's morbid. Polly Stringer, from over at the schoolhouse? Polly Stringer was in here this morning. She said it's only now, after over a month, only now those kids are beginning to quiet down. Which made me think: What if they *do* arrest somebody? If they do, it's bound to be somebody everybody knows. And that would fan the fire for sure, get the pot boiling just when it had started to cool off. Ask me, we've had enough excitement."

It was early, not yet nine, and Perry was the first customer at the Washateria, a self-service laundry. He opened his fat straw suitcase, extracted a wad of briefs and socks and shirts (some his, some Dick's), tossed them into a washer, and fed the machine a lead slug—one of many bought in Mexico.

Perry was well acquainted with the workings of such emporiums, having often patronized them, and happily, since usually he found it "so relaxing" to sit quietly and watch clothes get clean. Not today. He was too apprehensive. Despite his warnings, Dick had won out. Here they were, back in Kansas City—dead broke, to boot, and driving a stolen car! All night they had raced the Iowa Chevrolet through thick rain, stopping twice to siphon gas, both times from vehicles parked on the empty streets of small sleeping towns. (This was Perry's job, one at which he judged himself "absolutely tops. Just a short piece of rubber hose, that's my cross-country credit card.") On reaching Kansas City at sunrise, the travelers had gone first to the airport, where in the men's lavatory they washed and shaved and brushed their teeth; two hours later, after a nap in the airport lounge, they returned to the city. It was then that Dick had dropped his partner at the Washateria, promising to come back for him within the hour.

When the laundry was clean and dry, Perry repacked the suitcase. It was past ten. Dick, supposedly off somewhere "hanging paper," was overdue. He sat down to wait, choosing a bench on which, an arm's length away, a woman's purse rested—tempting him to snake his hand around inside it. But the appearance of its owner, the burliest of several women now employing the establishment's facilities, deterred him. Once, when he was a running-wild child in San Francisco, he and a "Chink kid" (Tommy Chan? Tommy Lee?) had worked together as a "purse-snatching team." It amused Perry—cheered him up—to remember some of their escapades. "Like one time we sneaked up on an old lady, really old, and Tommy grabbed her handbag, but she wouldn't let go, she was a regular tiger. The harder he tugged one way, the harder she tugged the other. Then she saw me, and said, 'Help me! Help me!' and I said, 'Hell, lady, I'm helping *him!*'—and bopped her good. Put her on the pavement. Ninety cents was all we got—I remember exactly. We went to a Chink restaurant and ate ourselves under the table."

Things hadn't changed much. Perry was twenty-odd years older and a hundred pounds heavier, and yet his material situation had improved not at all. He was still (and wasn't it incredible, a person of his intelligence, his talents?) an urchin dependent, so to say, on stolen coins.

A clock on the wall kept catching his eye. At half past ten he began to worry; by eleven his legs were pulsing with pain, which was always, with him, a sign of approaching panic—"bubbles in my blood." He ate an aspirin, and tried to blot out—blur, at least—the brilliantly vivid cavalcade gliding across his mind, a procession of dire visions: Dick in the hands of the law, perhaps arrested while writing a phony check, or for committing a minor traffic violation (and found to be driving a "hot" car). Very likely, at this very instant Dick sat trapped inside a circle of red-necked detectives. And they weren't discussing trivialities—bad checks or stolen automobiles. Murder, that was the topic, for somehow the connection that Dick had been so certain no one could make had been made. And right *now* a carload of Kansas City police were on their way to the Washateria.

But, no, he was imagining too much. Dick would never do that—"spill his guts." Think of how often he had heard him say, "They can beat me blind, I'll never tell them anything." Of course, Dick was a "blowhard"; his toughness, as Perry had come to know, existed solely in situations where he unarguably had the upper hand. Suddenly, gratefully, he thought of a less desperate reason for Dick's prolonged absence. He'd gone to visit his parents. A risky thing to do, but Dick was "devoted" to them, or claimed to be, and last night during the long rainy ride he had told Perry, "I'd sure like to see my folks. They wouldn't mention it. I mean, they wouldn't tell the parole officer—do anything to get us into trouble. Only I'm ashamed to. I'm afraid of what my mother would say. About the checks. And going off like we did. But I wish I could call them, hear how they are." However, that was not possible, for the Hickock home was without a telephone; otherwise, Perry would have rung up to see if Dick was there.

Another few minutes, and he was again convinced that Dick was under arrest. His leg pains flared up, flashed through his body, and the laundry odors, the steamy stench, all at once sickened him, picked him up and propelled him out the door. He stood at the curb retching like "a drunk with the dry heaves." Kansas City! Hadn't he known Kansas City was bad luck, and *begged* Dick to keep away? Now, maybe now, Dick was sorry he hadn't listened. And he wondered: But what about me, "with a dime or two and a bunch of lead slugs in my pocket"? Where could he go? Who would help him? Bobo? Fat chance! But her husband might. If Fred Johnson had followed his own inclination, he would have guaranteed employment for Perry after he left prison, thus helping him obtain a parole. But Bobo wouldn't permit it; she had said it would only lead to trouble, and possibly danger. Then she had written to Perry to tell him precisely that. One fine day he'd pay her back, have a little fun—talk to her, advertise his abilities, spell out in detail the things he was capable of doing to people like her, respectable people, safe and smug people, exactly like Bobo. Yes, let her know just how dangerous he could be, and watch her eyes. Surely that was worth a trip to Denver? Which was what he'd do—go to Denver and visit the Johnsons. Fred Johnson would stake him to a new start in life; he'd have to, if he wanted ever to be rid of him.

Then Dick came up to him at the curb. "Hey, Perry," he said. "You sick?"

The sound of Dick's voice was like an injection of some potent narcotic, a drug that, invading his veins, produced a delirium of colliding sensations: tension and relief, fury and affection. He advanced toward Dick with clenched fists. "You sonofabitch," he said.

Dick grinned, and said, "Come on. We're eating again."

But explanations were in order—apologies, too—and over a bowl of chili at the Kansas City hash house that Dick liked best, the Eagle Buffet, Dick supplied them. "I'm sorry, honey. I knew you'd get the bends. Think I'd tangled with a bull. But I was having such a run of luck it seemed like I ought to let it ride." He explained that after leaving Perry he had gone to the Markl Buick Company, the firm that had once employed him, hoping to find a set of license plates to substitute for the hazardous Iowa plates on the abducted Chevrolet. "Nobody saw me come or go. Markl used to do a considerable wrecked-car trade. Sure enough, out back there was a smashed-up De Soto with Kansas tags." And where were they now? "On our buggy, pal."

Having made the switch, Dick had dropped the Iowa plates in a municipal reservoir. Then he'd stopped at a filling station where a friend worked, a former high-school classmate named Steve, and persuaded Steve to cash a check for fifty dollars, which was something he'd not done before—"rob a buddy." Well, he'd never see Steve again. He was "cutting out" of Kansas City tonight, this time really forever. So why not fleece a few old friends? With that in mind, he'd called on another ex-classmate, a drugstore clerk. The take was thereby increased to seventy-five dollars. "Now, this afternoon, we'll roll that up to a couple hundred. I've made a list of places to hit. Six or seven, starting right here," he said, meaning the Eagle Buffet, where everybody—the bartender and waiters—knew and liked him, and called him Pickles (in honor of his favorite food). "Then Florida, here we come. How about it, honey? Didn't I promise you we'd spend Christmas in Miami? Just like all the millionaires?"

Dewey and his colleague K.B.I. Agent Clarence Duntz stood waiting for a free table in the Trail Room. Looking around at the customary exhibit of lunch-hour faces—soft-fleshed businessmen and ranchers with sun-branded, coarse complexions—Dewey acknowledged particular acquaintances: the county coroner, Dr. Fenton; the manager of the Warren, Tom Mahar; Harrison Smith, who had run for county attorney last year and lost the election to Duane West; and also Herbert W. Clutter, the owner of River Valley Farm and a member of Dewey's Sunday School class. *Wait a minute!* Wasn't Herb Clutter dead? And hadn't Dewey attended his funeral? Yet there he was, sitting in the Trail Room's circular corner booth, his lively brown eyes, his square-jawed, genial good looks unchanged by death. But Herb was not alone. Sharing the table were two young men, and Dewey, recognizing them, nudged Agent Duntz.

"Look."

"Where?"

"The corner."

"I'll be damned."

Hickock and Smith! But the moment of recognition was mutual. Those boys smelled danger. Feet first, they crashed through the Trail Room's plate-glass window, and with Duntz and Dewey leaping after them, sped along Main Street, past Palmer Jewelry, Norris Drugs, the Garden Café, then around the corner and down to the depot and in and out, hide-and-seek, among a congregation of white grain-storage towers. Dewey drew a pistol, and so did Duntz, but as they took aim, the supernatural intervened. Abruptly, mysteriously (it was like a dream!), everyone was swimming—the pursued, the pursuers—stroking the awesome width of water that the Garden City Chamber of Commerce claims is the "World's Largest FREE Swimpool." As the detectives drew abreast of their quarry, why, once more (How did it happen? *Could* he be dreaming?) the scene faded out, and faded in upon another landscape: Valley View Cemetery, that gray-and-green island of tombs and trees and flowered paths, a restful, leafy, whispering oasis lying like a cool piece of cloud shade on the luminous wheat plains north of town. But now Duntz had disappeared, and Dewey was alone with the hunted men. Though he could not see them, he was certain they were hiding among the dead, crouching there behind a headstone, perhaps the headstone of his own father: "Alvin Adams Dewey, September 6, 1879–January 26, 1948." Gun drawn, he crept along the solemn lanes until, hearing laughter and tracing its sound, he saw that Hickock and Smith were not hiding at all but standing astride the as yet unmarked mass grave of Herb and Bonnie and Nancy and Kenyon, standing legs apart, hands on hips, heads flung back, laughing. Dewey fired . . . and again . . . and again . . . Neither man fell, though each had been shot through the heart three times; they simply rather slowly turned transparent, by degrees grew invisible, evaporated, though the loud laughter expanded until Dewey bowed before it, ran from it, filled with a despair so mournfully intense that it awakened him.

When he awoke, it was as though he were a feverish, frightened ten-year-old; his hair was wet, his shirt cold damp and clinging. The room—a room in the sheriff's office, into which he'd locked himself before falling asleep at a desk—was dull with near-darkness. Listening, he could hear Mrs. Richardson's telephone ringing in the adjacent office. But she was not there to answer it; the office was closed. On his way out he walked past the ringing phone with determined indifference, and then hesitated. It might be Marie, calling to ask if he was still working and should she wait dinner.

"Mr. A. A. Dewey, please. Kansas City calling."

"This is Mr. Dewey."

"Go ahead, Kansas City. Your party is on the line."

"Al? Brother Nye."

"Yes, Brother."

"Get ready for some very big news."

"I'm ready."

"Our friends are here. Right here in Kansas City."

"How do you know?"

"Well, they aren't exactly keeping it a secret. Hickock's written checks from one side of town to the other. Using his own name."

"His own name. That must mean he doesn't plan to hang around long—either that or he's feeling awful damn sure of himself. So Smith's still with him?"

"Oh, they're together O.K. But driving a different car. A 1956 Chevy—black-and-white two-door job."

"Kansas tags?"

"Kansas tags. And listen, Al—are we lucky! They bought a television set, see? Hickock gave the salesman a check. Just as they were driving off, the guy had the sense to write down the license number. Jot it on the back of the check. Johnson County License 16212."

"Checked the registration?"

"Guess what?"

"It's a stolen car."

"Undoubtedly. But the tags were definitely lifted. Our friends took them off a wrecked De Soto in a K.C. garage."

"Know when?"

"Yesterday morning. The boss [Logan Sanford] sent out an alert with the new license number and a description of the car."

"How about the Hickock farm? If they're still in the area, it seems to me sooner or later they'll go there."

"Don't worry. We're watching it. Al—"

"I'm here."

"That's what I want for Christmas. All I want. To wrap this up. Wrap it up and sleep till New Year's. Wouldn't that be one hell of a present?"

"Well, I hope you get it."

"Well, I hope we both do."

Afterward, as he crossed the darkening courthouse square, pensively scuffing through dry mounds of unraked leaves, Dewey wondered at his lack of elation. Why, when he now knew that the suspects were not forever lost in Alaska or Mexico or Timbuctoo, when the next second an arrest might be made—why was it he felt none of the excitement he ought to feel? The dream was at fault, for the treadmill mood of it had lingered, making him question Nye's assertions—in a sense, disbelieve them. He did not believe that Hickock and Smith would be caught in Kansas City. They were invulnerable.

In Miami Beach, 335 Ocean Drive is the address of the Somerset Hotel, a small, square building painted more or less white, with many lavender touches, among them a lavender sign that reads, "VACANCY—LOWEST RATES—BEACH FACILITIES—ALWAYS A SEABREEZE." It is one of a row of little stucco-and-cement hotels lining a white, melancholy street. In December, 1959, the Somerset's "beach facilities" consisted of two beach umbrellas stuck in a strip of sand at the rear of the hotel. One umbrella, pink, had written upon it, "We Serve Valentine Ice-Cream." At noon on Christmas Day, a quartet of women lay under and around it, a transistor radio serenading them. The second umbrella, blue and bearing the command "Tan with Coppertone," sheltered Dick and Perry, who for five days had been living at the Somerset, in a double room renting for eighteen dollars weekly.

Perry said, "You never wished me a Merry Christmas."

"Merry Christmas, honey. And a Happy New Year."

Dick wore bathing trunks, but Perry, as in Acapulco, refused to expose his injured legs—he feared the sight might "offend" other beach-goers—and therefore sat fully clothed, wearing even socks and shoes. Still, he was comparatively content, and when Dick stood up and started performing exercises—headstands, meant to impress the ladies beneath the pink umbrella—he occupied himself with the Miami *Herald.* Presently he came across an inner-page story that won his entire attention. It concerned murder, the slaying of a Florida family, a Mr. and Mrs. Clifford Walker, their four-year-old son, and their two-year-old daughter. Each of the victims, though not bound or gagged, had been shot through the head with a .22 weapon. The crime, clueless and apparently motiveless, had taken place Saturday night, December 19, at the Walker home, on a cattle-raising ranch not far from Tallahassee.

Perry interrupted Dick's athletics to read the story aloud, and said, "Where were we last Saturday night?"

"Tallahassee?"

"I'm asking you."

Dick concentrated. On Thursday night, taking turns at the wheel, they had driven out of Kansas and through Missouri into Arkansas and over the Ozarks, "up" to Louisiana, where a burned-out generator stopped them early Friday morning. (A second-hand replacement, bought in Shreveport, cost twenty-two fifty.) That night they'd slept parked by the side of the road somewhere near the Alabama-Florida border. The next day's journey, an unhurried affair, had included several touristic diversions—visits to an alligator farm and a rattlesnake ranch, a ride in a glass-bottomed boat over a silvery-clear swamp lake, a late and long and costly broiled-lobster lunch at a roadside seafood restaurant. Delightful day! But both were exhausted when they arrived at Tallahassee, and decided to spend the night there. "Yes, Tallahassee," Dick said.

"Amazing!" Perry glanced through the article again. "Know what I wouldn't be surprised? If this wasn't done by a lunatic. Some nut that read about what happened out in Kansas."

Dick, because he didn't care to hear Perry "get going on that subject," shrugged and grinned and trotted down to the ocean's edge, where he ambled awhile over the surf-drenched sand, here and there stooping to collect a seashell. As a boy he'd so envied the son of a neighbor who had gone to the Gulf Coast on holiday and returned with a box full of shells—so hated him—that he'd stolen the shells and one by one crushed them with a hammer. Envy was constantly with him; the Enemy was anyone who was someone he wanted to be or who had anything he wanted to have.

For instance, the man he had seen by the pool at the Fontainebleau. Miles away, shrouded in a summery veil of heat-haze and sea-sparkle, he could see the towers of the pale, expensive hotels—the Fontainebleau, the Eden Roc, the Roney Plaza. On their second day in Miami he had suggested to Perry that they invade these pleasure-domes. "Maybe pick up a coupla rich women," he had said. Perry had been most reluctant; he felt people would stare at them because of their khaki trousers and T-shirts. Actually, their tour of the Fontainebleau's gaudy premises went unnoticed, amid the men striding about in Bermuda shorts of candy-striped raw silk, and the women wearing bathing suits and mink stoles simultaneously. The trespassers had loitered in the lobby, strolled in the garden, lounged by the swimming pool. It was there that Dick saw the man, who was his own age—twenty-eight or thirty. He could have been a "gambler or lawyer or maybe a gangster from Chicago." Whatever he was, he looked as though he knew the glories of money and power. A blonde who resembled Marilyn Monroe was kneading him with suntan oil, and his lazy, beringed hand reached for a tumbler of iced orange juice. All that belonged to him, Dick, but he would never have it. Why should that sonofabitch have everything, while he had nothing? Why should that "big-shot bastard" have all the luck? With a knife in his hand, he, Dick, had power. Big-shot bastards like that had better be careful or he might "open them up and let a little of their luck spill on the floor." But Dick's day was ruined. The beautiful blonde rubbing on the suntan oil had ruined it. He'd said to Perry, "Let's pull the hell out of here."

Now a young girl, probably twelve, was drawing figures in the sand, carving out big, crude faces with a piece of driftwood. Dick, pretending to admire her art, offered the shells he had gathered. "They make good eyes," he said. The child accepted the gift, whereupon Dick smiled and winked at her. He was sorry he felt as he did about her, for his sexual interest in female children was a failing of which he was "sincerely ashamed"—a secret he'd not confessed to anyone and hoped no one suspected (though he was aware that Perry had reason to), because other people might not think it "normal." That, to be sure, was something he was certain he was—"a normal." Seducing pubescent girls, as he had done "eight or nine" times in the last several years, did not disprove it, for if the truth were known, most real men had the same desires he had. He took the child's hand and said, "You're my baby girl. My little sweetheart." But she objected. Her hand, held by his, twitched like a fish on a hook, and he recognized the astounded expression in her eyes from earlier incidents in his career. He let go, laughed lightly, and said, "Just a game. Don't you like games?"

Perry, still reclining under the blue umbrella, had observed the scene and realized Dick's purpose at once, and despised him for it; he had "no respect for people who can't control themselves sexually," especially when the lack of control involved what he called "pervertiness" —"bothering kids," "queer stuff," rape. And he thought he had made his views obvious to Dick; indeed, hadn't they almost had a fist fight when quite recently he had prevented Dick from raping a terrified young girl? However, he wouldn't care to repeat that particular test of strength. He was relieved when he saw the child walk away from Dick.

Christmas carols were in the air; they issued from the radio of the four women and mixed strangely with Miami's sunshine and the cries of the querulous, never thoroughly silent seagulls. "Oh, come let us adore Him, Oh, come let us adore Him": a cathedral choir, an exalted music that moved Perry to tears—which refused to stop, even after the music did. And as was not uncommon when he was thus afflicted, he dwelt upon a possibility that had for him "tremendous fascination": suicide. As a child he had often thought of killing himself, but those were sentimental reveries born of a wish to punish his father and mother and other enemies. From young manhood onward, however, the prospect of ending his life had more and more lost its fantastic quality. That, he must remember, was Jimmy's "solution," and Fern's, too. And lately it had come to seem not just an alternative but the specific death awaiting him.

Anyway, he couldn't see that he had "a lot to live for." Hot islands and buried gold, diving deep in fire-blue seas toward sunken treasure—such dreams were gone. Gone, too, was "Perry O'Parsons," the name invented for the singing sensation of stage and screen that he'd half-seriously hoped some day to be. Perry O'Parsons had died without having ever lived. What was there to look forward to? He and Dick were "running a race without a finish line"—that was how it struck him.

And now, after not quite a week in Miami, the long ride was to resume. Dick, who had worked one day at the ABC auto-service company for sixty-five cents an hour, had told him, "Miami's worse than Mexico. Sixty-five cents! Not me. I'm white." So tomorrow, with only twenty-seven dollars left of the money raised in Kansas City, they were heading west again, to Texas, to Nevada—"nowhere definite."

Dick, who had waded into the surf, returned. He fell, wet and breathless, face down on the sticky sand.

"How was the water?"

"Wonderful."

The closeness of Christmas to Nancy Clutter's birthday, which was right after New Year's, had always created problems for her boy friend, Bobby Rupp. It had strained his imagination to think of two suitable gifts in such quick succession. But each year, with money made working summers on his father's sugar-beet farm, he had done the best he could, and on Christmas morning he had always hurried to the Clutter house carrying a package that his sisters had helped him wrap and that he hoped would surprise Nancy and delight her. Last year he had given her a small heart-shaped gold locket. This year, as forehanded as ever, he'd been wavering between the imported perfumes on sale at Norris Drugs and a pair of riding boots. But then Nancy had died.

On Christmas morning, instead of racing off to River Valley Farm, he remained at home, and later in the day he shared with his family the splendid dinner his mother had been a week preparing. Everybody—his parents and every one of his seven brothers and sisters—had treated him gently since the tragedy. All the same, at mealtimes he was told again and again that he must please eat. No one comprehended that really he was ill, that grief had made him so, that grief had drawn a circle around him he could not escape from and others could not enter—except possibly Sue. Until Nancy's death he had not appreciated Sue, never felt altogether comfortable with her. She was too different—took seriously things that even girls ought not to take very seriously: paintings, poems, the music she played on the piano. And, of course, he was jealous of her; her position in Nancy's esteem, though of another order, had been at least equal to his. But that was why she was able to understand his loss. Without Sue, without her almost constant presence, how could he have withstood such an avalanche of shocks—the crime itself, his interviews with Mr. Dewey, the pathetic irony of being for a while the principal suspect?

Then, after about a month, the friendship waned. Bobby went less frequently to sit in the Kidwells' tiny, cozy parlor, and when he did go, Sue seemed not as welcoming. The trouble was that they were forcing each other to mourn and remember what in fact they wanted to forget. Sometimes Bobby could: when he was playing basketball or driving his car over country roads at eighty miles an hour, or when, as part of a self-imposed athletic program (his ambition was to be a high-school gymnastics instructor), he took long-distance jog-trots across flat yellow fields. And now, after helping clear the dining table of all its holiday dishes, that was what he decided to do—put on a sweatshirt and go for a run.

The weather was remarkable. Even for western Kansas, renowned for the longevity of its Indian summers, the current sample seemed far-fetched—dry air, bold sun, azure sky. Optimistic ranchers were predicting an "open winter"—a season so bland that cattle could graze during the whole of it. Such winters are rare, but Bobby could remember one—the year he had started to court Nancy. They were both twelve, and after school he used to carry her book satchel the mile separating the Holcomb schoolhouse from her father's farm ranch. Often, if the day was warm and sun-kindled, they stopped along the way and sat by the river, a snaky, slow moving, brown piece of the Arkansas.

Once Nancy had said to him, "One summer, when we were in Colorado, I saw where the Arkansas begins. The exact place. You wouldn't believe it, though. That it was our river. It's not the same color. But pure as drinking water. And fast. And full of rocks. Whirlpools. Daddy caught a trout." It had stayed with Bobby, her memory of the river's source, and since her death . . . Well, he couldn't explain it, but whenever he looked at the Arkansas, it was for an instant transformed, and what he saw was not a muddy stream meandering across the Kansas plains, but what Nancy had described—a Colorado torrent, a chilly, crystal trout river speeding down a mountain valley. That was how Nancy had been: like young water—energetic, joyous.

Usually, though, western Kansas winters are imprisoning, and usually frost on the fields and razory winds have altered the climate before Christmas. Some years back snow had fallen on Christmas Eve and continued falling, and when Bobby set out the next morning for the Clutter property, a three-mile walk, he had had to fight through deep drifts. It was worth it, for though he was numbed and scarlet, the welcome he got thawed him thoroughly. Nancy was amazed and proud, and her mother, often so timid and distant, had hugged and kissed him, insisting that he wrap up in a quilt and sit close to the parlor fire. While the women worked in the kitchen, he and Kenyon and Mr. Clutter had sat around the fire cracking walnuts and pecans, and Mr. Clutter said he was reminded of another Christmas, when he was Kenyon's age: "There were seven of us. Mother, my father, the two girls, and us three boys. We lived on a farm a good ways from town. For that reason it was the custom to do our Christmas buying in a bunch—make the trip once and do it all together. The year I'm thinking of, the morning we were supposed to go, the snow was high as today, higher, and still coming down—flakes like saucers. Looked like we were in for a snowbound Christmas with no presents under the tree. Mother and the girls were heartbroken. Then I had an idea." He would saddle their huskiest plow horse, ride into town, and shop for everybody. The family agreed. All of them gave him their Christmas savings and a list of the things they wished him to buy: four yards of calico, a football, a pincushion, shotgun shells—an assortment of orders that took until nightfall to fill. Heading homeward, the purchases secure inside a tarpaulin sack, he was grateful that his father had forced him to carry a lantern, and glad, too, that the horse's harness was strung with bells, for both their jaunty racket and the careening light of the kerosene lantern were a comfort to him.

"The ride in, that was easy, a piece of cake. But now the road was gone, and every landmark." Earth and air—all was snow. The horse, up to his haunches in it, slipped sidewise. "I dropped our lamp. We were lost in the night. It was just a question of time before we fell asleep and froze. Yes, I was afraid. But I prayed. And I felt God's presence . . ." Dogs howled. He followed the noise until he saw the windows of a neighboring farmhouse. "I ought to have stopped there. But I thought of the family—imagined my mother in tears, Dad and the boys getting up a search party, and I pushed on. So, naturally, I wasn't too happy when finally I reached home and found the house dark. Doors locked. Found everybody had gone to bed and plain forgot me. None of them could understand why I was so put out. Dad said, 'We were sure you'd stay the night in town. Good grief, boy! Who'd have thought you hadn't better sense than to start home in a perfect blizzard?'"

The cider-tart odor of spoiling apples. Apple trees and pear trees, peach and cherry: Mr. Clutter's orchard, the treasured assembly of fruit trees he had planted. Bobby, running mindlessly, had not meant to come here, or to any other part of River Valley Farm. It was inexplicable, and he turned to leave, but he turned again and wandered toward the house—white and solid and spacious. He had always been impressed by it, and pleased to think that his girl friend lived there.

But now that it was deprived of the late owner's dedicated attention, the first threads of decay's cobweb were being spun. A gravel rake lay rusting in the driveway; the lawn was parched and shabby. That fateful Sunday, when the sheriff summoned ambulances to remove the murdered family, the ambulances had driven across the grass straight to the front door, and the tire tracks were still visible.

The hired man's house was empty, too; he had found new quarters for his family nearer Holcomb—to no one's surprise, for nowadays, though the weather was glittering, the Clutter place seemed shadowed, and hushed, and motionless. But as Bobby passed a storage barn and, beyond that, a livestock corral, he heard a horse's tail swish. It was Nancy's Babe, the obedient old dappled mare with flaxen mane and dark-purple eyes like magnificent pansy blossoms. Clutching her mane, Bobby rubbed his cheek along Babe's neck—something Nancy used to do. And Babe whinnied. Last Sunday, the last time he had visited the Kidwells, Sue's mother had mentioned Babe. Mrs. Kidwell, a fanciful woman, had been standing at a window watching dusk tint the outdoors, the sprawling prairie. And out of the blue she had said, "Susan? You know what I keep seeing? Nancy. On Babe. Coming this way."

Perry noticed them first—hitchhikers, a boy and an old man, both carrying homemade knapsacks, and despite the blowy weather, a gritty and bitter Texas wind, wearing only overalls and a thin denim shirt. "Let's give them a lift," Perry said. Dick was reluctant; he had no objection to assisting hitchhikers, provided they looked as if they could pay their way—at least "chip in a couple of gallons of gas." But Perry, little old big-hearted Perry, was always pestering Dick to pick up the damnedest, sorriest-looking people. Finally Dick agreed, and stopped the car.

The boy—a stocky, sharp-eyed, talkative towhead of about twelve—was exuberantly grateful, but the old man, whose face was seamed and yellow, feebly crawled into the back seat and slumped there silently. The boy said, "We sure do appreciate this. Johnny was ready to drop. We ain't had a ride since Galveston."

Perry and Dick had left that port city an hour earlier, having spent a morning there applying at various shipping offices for jobs as able-bodied seamen. One company offered them immediate work on a tanker bound for Brazil, and, indeed, the two would now have been at sea if their prospective employer had not discovered that neither man possessed union papers or a passport. Strangely, Dick's disappointment exceeded Perry's: "Brazil! That's where they're building a whole new capital city. Right from scratch. Imagine getting in on the ground floor of something like that! Any fool could make a fortune."

"Where you headed?" Perry asked the boy.

"Sweetwater."

"Where's Sweetwater?"

"Well, it's along in this direction somewhere. It's somewhere in Texas. Johnny, here, he's my gramp. And he's got a sister lives in Sweetwater. Least, I sure Jesus hope she does. We thought she lived in Jasper, Texas. But when we got to Jasper, folks told us her and her people moved to Galveston. But she wasn't in Galveston—lady there said she was gone to Sweetwater. I sure Jesus hope we find her. Johnny," he said, rubbing the old man's hands, as if to thaw them, "you hear me, Johnny? We're riding in a nice warm Chevrolet—'56 model."

The old man coughed, rolled his head slightly, opened and closed his eyes, and coughed again.

Dick said, "Hey, *listen.* What's wrong with him?"

"It's the change," the boy said. "And the walking. We been walking since before Christmas. Seems to me we covered the better part of Texas." In the most matter-of-fact voice, and while continuing to massage the old man's hands, the boy told them that up to the start of the present journey he and his grandfather and an aunt had lived alone on a farm near Shreveport, Louisiana. Not long ago the aunt had died. "Johnny's been poorly about a year, and Auntie had all the work to do. With only me to help. We were chopping firewood. Chopping up a stump. Right in the middle of it, Auntie said she was wore out. Ever seen a horse just lay down and never get up? I have. And that's like what Auntie did." A few days before Christmas the man from whom his grandfather rented the farm "turned us off the place," the boy continued. "That's how come we started out for Texas. Looking to find Mrs. Jackson. I never seen her, but she's Johnny's own blood sister. And somebody's got to take us in. Leastways, him. He can't go a lot more. Last night it rained on us."

The car stopped. Perry asked Dick why he had stopped it.

"That man's very sick," Dick said.

"Well? What do you want to do? Put him out?"

"Use your head. Just for once."

"You really are a mean bastard."

"Suppose he dies?"

The boy said, "He won't die. We've got this far, he'll wait now."

Dick persisted. "Suppose he dies? Think of what could happen. The questions."

"Frankly, I don't give a damn. You want to put them out? Then by all means." Perry looked at the invalid, still somnolent, dazed, deaf, and he looked at the boy, who returned his gaze calmly, not begging, not "asking for anything," and Perry remembered himself at that age, his own wanderings with an old man. "Go ahead. Put them out. But I'll be getting out, too."

"O.K. O.K. O.K. Only don't forget," said Dick. "It's your damn fault."

Dick shifted gears. Suddenly, as the car began to move again, the boy hollered, "Hold it!" Hopping out, he hurried along the edge of the road, stopped, stooped, picked up one, two, three, four empty Coca-Cola bottles, ran back, and hopped in, happy and grinning. "There's plenty of money in bottles," he said to Dick. "Why, mister, if you was to drive kind of slow, I guarantee you we can pick us up a big piece of change. That's what me and Johnny been eating off. *Re*fund money."

Dick was amused, but he was also interested, and when next the boy commanded him to halt, he at once obeyed. The commands came so frequently that it took them an hour to travel five miles, but it was worth it. The kid had an "honest-to-God genius" for spotting, amid the roadside rocks and grassy rubble, and the brown glow of thrown-away beer bottles, the emerald daubs that had once held 7-Up and Canada Dry. Perry soon developed his own personal gift for spying out bottles. At first he merely indicated to the boy the whereabouts of his finds; he thought it too undignified to scurry about collecting them himself. It was all "pretty silly," just "kid stuff." Nevertheless, the game generated a treasure-hunt excitement, and presently he, too, succumbed to the fun, the fervor of this quest for refundable empties. Dick, too, but Dick was in dead earnest. Screwy as it seemed, maybe this *was* a way to make some money—or, at any rate, a few bucks. Lord knows, he and Perry could use them; their combined finances amounted at the moment to less than five dollars.

Now all three—Dick and the boy and Perry—were piling out of the car and shamelessly, though amiably, competing with one another. Once Dick located a cache of wine and whiskey bottles at the bottom of a ditch, and was chagrined to learn that his discovery was valueless. "They don't give no refund on liquor empties," the boy informed him. "Even some of the beers ain't no good. I don't mess with them usually. Just stick with the surefire things. Dr. Pepper. Pepsi. Coke. White Rock. Nehi."

Dick said, "What's your name?"

"Bill," the boy said.

"Well, Bill. You're a regular education."

Nightfall came, and forced the hunters to quit—that, and lack of space, for they had amassed as many bottles as the car could contain.

The trunk was filled, the back seat seemed a glittering dump heap; unnoticed, unmentioned by even his grandson, the ailing old man was all but hidden under the shifting, dangerously chiming cargo.

Dick said, "Be funny if we had a smash-up."

A bunch of lights publicized the New Motel, which proved to be, as the travelers neared it, an impressive compound consisting of bungalows, a garage, a restaurant, and a cocktail lounge. Taking charge, the boy said to Dick, "Pull in there. Maybe we can make a deal. Only let me talk. I've had the experience. Sometimes they try to cheat." Perry could not imagine "anyone smart enough to cheat that kid," he said later. "It didn't shame him a bit going in there with all those bottles. Me, I never could've, I'd have felt so ashamed. But the people at the motel were nice about it; they just laughed. Turned out the bottles were worth twelve dollars and sixty cents."

The boy divided the money evenly, giving half to himself, the rest to his partners, and said, "Know what? I'm gonna blow me and Johnny to a good feed. Ain't you fellows hungry?"

As always, Dick was. And after so much activity, even Perry felt starved. As he later told about it, "We carted the old man into the restaurant and propped him up at a table. He looked exactly the same—thanatoid. And he never said one word. But you should have seen him shovel it in. The kid ordered him pancakes; he said that was what Johnny liked best. I swear he ate something like thirty pancakes. With maybe two pounds of butter, and a quart of syrup. The kid could put it down himself. Potato chips and ice cream, that was all he wanted, but he sure ate a lot of them. I wonder it didn't make him sick."

During the dinner party, Dick, who had consulted a map, announced that Sweetwater was a hundred or more miles west of the route he was driving—the route that would take him across New Mexico and Arizona to Nevada—to Las Vegas. Though this was true, it was clear to Perry that Dick simply wanted to rid himself of the boy and the old man. Dick's purpose was obvious to the boy, too, but he was polite and said, "Oh, don't you worry about us. Plenty of traffic must stop here. We'll get a ride."

The boy walked with them to the car, leaving the old man to devour a fresh stack of pancakes. He shook hands with Dick and with Perry, wished them a Happy New Year, and waved them away into the dark.

The evening of Wednesday, December 30, was a memorable one in the household of Agent A. A. Dewey. Remembering it later, his wife said, "Alvin was singing in the bath. 'The Yellow Rose of Texas.' The kids were watching TV. And I was setting the dining-room table. For a buffet. I'm from New Orleans; I love to cook and entertain, and my mother had just sent us a crate of avocados and black-eyed peas, and —oh, a heap of real nice things. So I decided: We're going to have a buffet, invite some friends over—the Murrays, and Cliff and Dodie Hope. Alvin didn't want to, but I was determined. My goodness! The case could go on forever, and he hadn't taken hardly a minute off since it began. Well, I was setting the table, so when I heard the phone I asked one of the boys to answer it—Paul. Paul said it was for Daddy, and I said, 'You tell them he's in the bath,' but Paul said he wondered if he ought to do that, because it was Mr. Sanford calling from Topeka. Alvin's boss. Alvin took the call with just a towel around him. Made me so mad—dripping puddles everywhere. But when I went to get a mop I saw something worse—that cat, that fool Pete, up on the kitchen table gorging crabmeat salad. My avocado stuffing.

"The next thing was, suddenly Alvin had hold of me, he was hugging me, and I said, 'Alvin Dewey, have you lost your mind?' Fun's fun, but the man was wet as a pond, he was ruining my dress, and I was already dressed for company. Of course, when I understood why he was hugging me I hugged him right back. You can imagine what it meant to Alvin to know those men had been arrested. Out in Las Vegas. He said he had to leave for Las Vegas straightaway, and I asked him hadn't he ought to put on some clothes first, and Alvin, he was so excited, he said, 'Gosh, honey, I guess I've spoiled your party!' I couldn't think of a happier way of having it spoiled—not if this meant that maybe one day soon we'd be back living an ordinary life. Alvin laughed—it was just beautiful to hear him. I mean, the past two weeks had been the worst of all. Because the week before Christmas those men turned up in Kansas City—came and went without getting caught—and I never saw Alvin more depressed, except once when young Alvin was in the hospital, had encephalitis, we thought we might lose him. But I don't want to talk about that.

"Anyway, I made coffee for him and took it to the bedroom, where he was supposed to be getting dressed. But he wasn't. He was sitting on the edge of our bed holding his head, as if he had a headache. Hadn't put on even a sock. So I said, 'What do you want to do, get pneumonia?' And he looked at me and said, 'Marie, listen, it's got to be these guys, has to, that's the only logical solution.' Alvin's funny. Like the first time he ran for Finney County Sheriff. Election Night, when practically every vote had been counted and it was plain as plain he'd won, he said—I could have strangled him—said over and over, 'Well, we won't know till the last return.'

"I told him, 'Now, Alvin, don't start that. Of course they did it.' He said, 'Where's our proof? We can't prove either of them ever set foot inside the Clutter house!' But that seemed to me exactly what he could prove: footprints—weren't footprints the one thing those animals left behind? Alvin said, 'Yes, and a big lot of good they are—unless those boys still happen to be wearing the boots that made them. Just footprints by themselves aren't worth a Dixie dollar.' I said, 'All right, honey, drink your coffee and I'll help you pack.' Sometimes you can't reason with Alvin. The way he kept on, he had me almost convinced Hickock and Smith were innocent, and if they weren't innocent they would never confess, and if they didn't confess they could never be convicted—the evidence was too circumstantial. What bothered him most, though—he was afraid that the story would leak, that the men would learn the truth before the K.B.I. could question them. As it was, they thought they'd been picked up for parole violation. Passing bad checks. And Alvin felt it was very important they keep thinking that. He said, 'The name Clutter has to hit them like a hammer, a blow they never knew was coming.'

"Paul—I'd sent him out to the washline for some of Alvin's socks—Paul came back and stood around watching me pack. He wanted to know where Alvin was going. Alvin lifted him up in his arms. He said, 'Can you keep a secret, Pauly?' Not that he needed to ask. Both boys know they mustn't talk about Alvin's work—the bits and pieces they hear around the house. So he said, 'Pauly, you remember those two fellows we've been looking for? Well, now we know where they are, and Daddy's going to go get them and bring them here to Garden City.' But Paul begged him, 'Don't do that, Daddy, don't bring them here.' He was frightened—any nine-year-old might've been. Alvin kissed him. He said, 'Now that's O.K., Pauly, we won't let them hurt anybody. They're not going to hurt anybody ever again.'"

At five that afternoon, some twenty minutes after the stolen Chevrolet rolled off the Nevada desert into Las Vegas, the long ride came to an end. But not before Perry had visited the Las Vegas post office, where he claimed a package addressed to himself in care of General Delivery—the large cardboard box he had mailed from Mexico, and had insured for a hundred dollars, a sum exceeding to an impertinent extent the value of the contents, which were suntans and denim pants, worn shirts, underwear, and two pairs of steel-buckled boots. Waiting for Perry outside the post office, Dick was in excellent spirits; he had reached a decision that he was certain would eradicate his current difficulties and start him on a new road, with a new rainbow in view. The decision involved impersonating an Air Force officer. It was a project that had long fascinated him, and Las Vegas was the ideal place to try it out. He'd already selected the officer's rank and name, the latter borrowed from a former acquaintance, the then warden of Kansas State Penitentiary: Tracy Hand. As Captain Tracy Hand, smartly clothed in a made-to-order uniform, Dick intended to "crawl the strip," Las Vegas's street of never-closed casinos. Small-time, big-time, the Sands, the Stardust—he meant to hit them all, distributing en route "a bundle of confetti." By writing worthless checks right around the clock, he expected to haul in three, maybe four thousand dollars within a twenty-four-hour period. That was half the plot; the second half was: Goodbye, Perry. Dick was sick of him—his harmonica, his aches and ills, his superstitions, the weepy, womanly eyes, the nagging, whispering voice. Suspicious, self-righteous, spiteful, he was like a wife that must be got rid of. And there was but one way to do it: Say nothing—just go.

Absorbed in his plans, Dick did not notice a patrol car pass him, slow down, reconnoiter. Nor did Perry, descending the post-office steps with the Mexican box balanced on a shoulder, observe the prowling car and the policemen in it.

Officers Ocie Pigford and Francis Macauley carried in their heads pages of memorized data, including a description of a black-and-white 1956 Chevrolet bearing Kansas license plate No. JO-16212. Neither Perry nor Dick was aware of the police vehicle trailing them as they pulled away from the post office, and with Dick driving and Perry directing, they traveled five blocks north, turned left, then right, drove a quarter mile more, and stopped in front of a dying palm tree and a weather-wrecked sign from which all calligraphy had faded except the word "OOM."

"This it?" Dick asked.

Perry, as the patrol car drew alongside, nodded.

The Detective Division of the Las Vegas City Jail contains two interrogation rooms—fluorescent-lighted chambers measuring ten by twelve, with walls and ceilings of celotex. In each room, in addition to an electric fan, a metal table, and folding metal chairs, there are camouflaged microphones, concealed tape recorders, and, set into the door, a mirrored one-way observation window. On Saturday, the second day of 1960, both rooms were booked for 2:00 P.M.—the hour that four detectives from Kansas had selected for their first confrontation of Hickock and Smith.

Shortly before the appointed moment, the quartet of K.B.I. agents —Harold Nye, Roy Church, Alvin Dewey, and Clarence Duntz—gathered in a corridor outside the interrogation rooms. Nye was running a temperature. "Part flu. But mostly sheer excitement," he subsequently informed a journalist. "By then I'd already been waiting in Las Vegas two days—took the next plane out after news of the arrest reached our headquarters in Topeka. The rest of the team, Al and Roy and Clarence, came on by car—had a lousy trip, too. Lousy weather. Spent New Year's Eve snowed up in a motel in Albuquerque. Boy, when they finally hit Vegas, they needed good whiskey and good news. I was ready with both. Our young men had signed waivers of extradition. Better yet: We had the boots, both pairs, and the soles—the Cat's Paw and the diamond pattern—matched perfectly life-size photographs of the footprints found in the Clutter house. The boots were in a box of stuff the boys picked up at the post office just before the curtain fell. Like I told Al Dewey, suppose the squeeze had come five minutes sooner!

"Even so, our case was very shaky—nothing that couldn't be pulled apart. But I remember, while we were waiting in the corridor—I remember being feverish and nervous as hell, but *confident.* We all were; we felt we were on the edge of the truth. My job, mine and Church's, was to pressure it out of Hickock. Smith belonged to Al and Old Man Duntz. At that time I hadn't seen the suspects—just examined their possessions and arranged the extradition waivers. I'd never laid eyes on Hickock until he was brought down to the interrogation room. I'd imagined a bigger guy. Brawnier. Not some skinny kid. He was twenty-eight, but he looked like a kid. Hungry—right down to the bone. He was wearing a blue shirt and suntans and white socks and black shoes. We shook hands; his hand was drier than mine. Clean, polite, nice voice, good diction, a pretty decent-looking fellow, with a very disarming smile—and in the beginning he smiled quite a lot.

"I said, 'Mr. Hickock, my name is Harold Nye, and this other gentleman is Mr. Roy Church. We're Special Agents of the Kansas Bureau of Investigation, and we've come here to discuss your parole violation. Of course, you're under no obligation to answer our questions, and anything you say may be used against you in evidence. You're entitled to a lawyer at all times. We'll use no force, no threats, and we'll make you no promises.' He was calm as could be."

"I know the form," Dick said. "I've been questioned before."

"Now, Mr. Hickock—"

"Dick."

"Dick, we want to talk to you about your activities since your parole. To our knowledge, you've gone on at least two big check sprees in the Kansas City area."

"Uh-huh. Hung out quite a few."

"Could you give us a list?"

The prisoner, evidently proud of his one authentic gift, a brilliant memory, recited the names and addresses of twenty Kansas City stores, cafés, and garages, and recalled, accurately, the "purchase" made at each and the amount of the check passed.

"I'm curious, Dick. Why do these people accept your checks? I'd like to know the secret."

"The secret is: People are dumb."

Roy Church said, "Fine, Dick. Very funny. But just for the moment let's forget these checks." Though he sounds as if his throat were lined with hog bristle, and has hands so hardened that he can punch stone walls (his favorite stunt, in fact), persons have been known to mistake Church for a kindly little man, somebody's bald-headed, pink-cheeked uncle. "Dick," he said, "suppose you tell us something about your family background."

The prisoner reminisced. Once, when he was nine or ten, his father had fallen ill. "It was rabbit fever," and the illness lasted many months, during which the family had depended upon church assistance and the charity of neighbors—"otherwise we would've starved." That episode aside, his childhood had been O.K. "We never had much money, but we were never really down-and-out," Hickock said. "We always had clean clothes and something to eat. My dad was strict, though. He wasn't happy unless he had me doing chores. But we got along O.K.—no serious arguments. My parents never argued, either. I can't recall a single quarrel. She's wonderful, my mother. Dad's a good guy, too. I'd say they did the best for me they could." School? Well, he felt he might have been more than an average student if he had contributed to books a fraction of the time he'd "wasted" on sports. "Baseball. Football. I made all the teams. After high school I could have gone to college on a football scholarship. I wanted to study engineering, but even with a scholarship, deals like that cost plenty. I don't know, it seemed safer to get a job."

Before his twenty-first birthday Hickock had worked as a railway trackman, an ambulance driver, a car painter, and a garage mechanic; he'd also married a girl sixteen years old. "Carol. Her father was a minister. He was dead against me. Said I was a full-time nobody. He made all the trouble he could. But I was nuts about Carol. Still am. There's a real princess. Only—see, we had three kids. Boys. And we were too young to have three kids. Maybe if we hadn't got so deep into debt. If I could've earned extra money. I tried."

He tried gambling, and started forging checks and experimenting with other forms of theft. In 1958 he was convicted of house burglary in a Johnson County court and sentenced to five years in Kansas State Penitentiary. But by then Carol had departed and he'd taken as a bride another girl aged sixteen. "Mean as hell. Her and her whole family. She divorced me while I was inside. I'm not complaining. Last August, when I left The Walls, I figured I had every chance to start new. I got a job in Olathe, lived with my family, and stayed home nights. I was doing swell—"

"Until November twentieth," said Nye, and Hickock seemed not to understand him. "The day you stopped doing swell and started hanging paper. Why?"

Hickock sighed, and said, "That would make a book." Then, smoking a cigarette borrowed from Nye and lighted by the courteous Church, he said, "Perry—my buddy Perry Smith—was paroled in the spring. Later on, when I came out, he sent me a letter. Postmarked Idaho. He wrote reminding me of this deal we used to talk over. About Mexico. The idea was we would go to Acapulco, one of them places, buy a fishing boat, and run it ourselves—take tourists deep-sea fishing."

Nye said, "This boat. How did you plan to pay for it?"

"I'm coming to that," Hickock said. "See, Perry wrote me he had a sister living in Fort Scott. And she was holding some heavy change for him. Several thousand dollars. Money his dad owed him from the sale of some property up in Alaska. He said he was coming to Kansas to get the dough."

"And the two of you would use it to buy a boat."

"Correct."

"But it didn't work out that way."

"What happened was, Perry showed up maybe a month later. I met him at the bus station in Kansas City—"

"When?" said Church. "The day of the week."

"A Thursday."

"And when did you go to Fort Scott?"

"Saturday."

"November fourteenth."

Hickock's eyes flashed with surprise. One could see that he was asking himself why Church should be so certain of the date; and hurriedly—for it was too soon to stir suspicions—the detective said, "What time did you leave for Fort Scott?"

"That afternoon. We did some work on my car, and had a bowl of chili at the West Side Café. It must have been around three."

"Around three. Was Perry Smith's sister expecting you?"

"No. Because, see, Perry lost her address. And she didn't have a telephone."

"Then how did you expect to find her?"

"By inquiring at the post office."

"Did you?"

"Perry did. They said she'd moved away. To Oregon, they thought. But she hadn't left any forwarding address."

"Must have been quite a blow. After you'd been counting on a big piece of money like that."

Hickock agreed. "Because—well, we'd definitely decided to go to Mexico. Otherwise, I never would've cashed them checks. But I hoped . . . Now listen to me; I'm telling the truth. I thought once we got to Mexico and began making money, then I'd be able to pay them off. The checks."

Nye took over. "One minute, Dick." Nye is a short, short-tempered man who has difficulty moderating his aggressive vigor, his talent for language both sharp and outspoken. "I'd like to hear a little more about the trip to Fort Scott," he said, soft-pedaling. "When you found Smith's sister no longer there, what did you do then?"

"Walked around. Had a beer. Drove back."

"You mean you went home?"

"No. To Kansas City. We stopped at the Zesto Drive-In. Ate hamburgers. We tried Cherry Row."

Neither Nye nor Church was familiar with Cherry Row.

Hickock said, "You kiddin'? Every cop in Kansas knows it." When the detectives again pleaded ignorance, he explained that it was a stretch of park where one encountered "hustlers mostly," adding, "but plenty of amateurs, too. Nurses. Secretaries. I've had a lot of luck there."

"And this particular evening. Have any luck?"

"The bad kind. We ended up with a pair of rollers."

"Named?"

"Mildred. The other one, Perry's girl, I think she was called Joan."

"Describe them."

"Maybe they were sisters. Both blond. Plump. I'm not too clear about it. See, we'd bought a bottle of ready-mix Orange Blossoms—that's orange pop and vodka—and I was getting stiff. We gave the girls a few drinks and drove them out to Fun Haven. I imagine you gentlemen never heard of Fun Haven?"

They hadn't.

Hickock grinned and shrugged. "It's on the Blue Ridge Road. Eight miles south of Kansas City. A combination night-club-motel. You pay ten bucks for the key to a cabin."

Continuing, he described the cabin in which he claimed that the foursome had stayed the night: twin beds, an old Coca-Cola calendar, a radio that wouldn't play unless the customer deposited a quarter. His poise, his explicitness, the assured presentation of verifiable detail impressed Nye—though, of course, the boy was lying. Well, wasn't he? Whether because of flu and fever or an abrupt lessening in the warmth of his confidence, Nye exuded an icy sweat.

"Next morning we woke up to find they'd rolled us and beat it," said Hickock. "Didn't get much off me. But Perry lost his wallet, with forty or fifty dollars."

"What did you do about it?"

"There wasn't nothing to do."

"You could've notified the police."

"Aw, come on. Quit it. *Notify* the police. For your information, a guy on parole's not allowed to booze. Or associate with another Old Grad—"

"All right, Dick. It's Sunday. The fifteenth of November. Tell us what you did that day from the moment you checked out of Fun Haven."

"Well, we ate breakfast at a truck stop near Happy Hill. Then we drove to Olathe, and I dropped Perry off at the hotel where he was living. I'd say that was around eleven. Afterward, I went home and had dinner with the family. Same as every Sunday. Watched TV—a basketball game, or maybe it was football. I was pretty tired."

"When did you next see Perry Smith?"

"Monday. He came by where I worked. Bob Sands' Body Shop."

"And what did you talk about? Mexico?"

"Well, we still liked the idea, even if we hadn't got hold of the money to do all we had in mind—put ourselves in business down there. But we wanted to go, and it seemed worth the risk."

"Worth another stretch in Lansing?"

"That didn't figure. See, we never intended coming Stateside again."

Nye, who had been jotting notes in a notebook, said, "On the day following the check spree—that would be the twenty-first—you and your friend Smith disappeared. Now, Dick, please outline your movements between then and the time of your arrest here in Las Vegas. Just a rough idea."

Hickock whistled and rolled his eyes. "Wow!" he said, and then, summoning his talent for something very like total recall, he began an account of the long ride—the approximately ten thousand miles he and Smith had covered in the past six weeks. He talked for an hour and twenty-five minutes—from two-fifty to four-fifteen—and told, while Nye attempted to list them, of highways and hotels, motels, rivers, towns, and cities, a chorus of entwining names: Apache, El Paso, Corpus Christi, Santillo, San Luis Potosí, Acapulco, San Diego, Dallas, Omaha, Sweetwater, Stillwater, Tenville Junction, Tallahassee, Needles, Miami, Hotel Nuevo Waldorf, Somerset Hotel, Hotel Simone, Arrowhead Motel, Cherokee Motel, and many, many more. He gave them the name of the man in Mexico to whom he'd sold his own old 1949 Chevrolet, and confessed that he had stolen a newer model in Iowa. He described persons he and his partner had met: a Mexican widow, rich and sexy; Otto, a German "millionaire"; a "swish" pair of Negro prizefighters driving a "swish" lavender Cadillac; the blind proprietor of a Florida rattlesnake farm; a dying old man and his grandson; and others. And when he had finished he sat with folded arms and a pleased smile, as though waiting to be commended for the humor, the clarity, and the candor of his traveler's tale.

But Nye, in pursuit of the narrative, raced his pen, and Church, lazily slamming a shut hand against an open palm, said nothing—until suddenly he said, "I guess you know why we're here."

Hickock's mouth straightened—his posture, too.

"I guess you realize we wouldn't have come all the way to Nevada just to chat with a couple of two-bit check chiselers."

Nye had closed the notebook. He, too, stared at the prisoner, and observed that a cluster of veins had appeared in his left temple.

"Would we, Dick?"

"What?"

"Come this far to talk about a bunch of checks."

"I can't think of any other reason."

Nye drew a dagger on the cover of his notebook. While doing so, he said, "Tell me, Dick. Have you ever heard of the Clutter murder case?" Whereupon, he later wrote in a formal report of the interview, "Suspect underwent an intense visible reaction. He turned gray. His eyes twitched."

Hickock said, "Whoa, now. Hold on here. I'm no goddam killer."

"The question asked," Church reminded him, "was whether you'd *heard* of the Clutter murders."

"I may have read something," Hickock said.

"A vicious crime. Vicious. Cowardly."

"And almost perfect," Nye said. "But you made two mistakes, Dick. One was, you left a witness. A living witness. Who'll testify in court. Who'll stand in the witness box and tell a jury how Richard Hickock and Perry Smith bound and gagged and slaughtered four helpless people."

Hickock's face reddened with returning color. "Living witness! There can't be!"

"Because you thought you'd got rid of everyone?"

"I said whoa! There ain't anybody can connect me with any goddam murder. Checks. A little petty thievery. But I'm no goddam killer."

"Then why," Nye asked hotly, "have you been lying to us?"

"I've been telling you the goddam truth."

"Now and then. Not always. For instance, what about Saturday afternoon, November fourteenth? You say you drove to Fort Scott."

"Yes."

"And when you got there you went to the post office."

"Yes."

"To obtain the address of Perry Smith's sister."

"That's right."

Nye rose. He walked around to the rear of Hickock's chair, and placing his hands on the back of the chair, leaned down as though to whisper in the prisoner's ear. "Perry Smith has no sister living in Fort Scott," he said. "He never has had. And on Saturday afternoons the Fort Scott post office happens to be closed." Then he said, "Think it over, Dick. That's all for now. We'll talk to you later."

After Hickock's dismissal, Nye and Church crossed the corridor, and looking through the one-way observation window set in the door of the interrogation room, watched the questioning of Perry Smith—a scene visible though not audible. Nye, who was seeing Smith for the first time, was fascinated by his feet—by the fact that his legs were so short that his feet, as small as a child's, couldn't quite make the floor. Smith's head—the stiff Indian hair, the Irish-Indian blending of dark skin and pert, impish features—reminded him of the suspect's pretty sister, the nice Mrs. Johnson. But this chunky, misshapen child-man was not pretty; the pink end of his tongue darted forth, flickering like the tongue of a lizard. He was smoking a cigarette, and from the evenness of his exhalations Nye deduced that he was still a "virgin"—that is, still uninformed about the real purpose of the interview.

Nye was right. For Dewey and Duntz, patient professionals, had gradually narrowed the prisoner's life story to the events of the last seven weeks, then reduced those to a concentrated recapitulation of the crucial weekend—Saturday noon to Sunday noon, November 14 to 15. Now, having spent three hours preparing the way, they were not far from coming to the point.

Dewey said, "Perry, let's review our position. Now, when you received parole, it was on condition that you never return to Kansas."

"The Sunflower State. I cried my eyes out."

"Feeling that way, why did you go back? You must have had some very strong reason."

"I told you. To see my sister. To get the money she was holding for me."

"Oh, yes. The sister you and Hickock tried to find in Fort Scott. Perry, how far is Fort Scott from Kansas City?"

Smith shook his head. He didn't know.

"Well, how long did it take you to drive there?"

No response.

"One hour? Two? Three? Four?"

The prisoner said he couldn't remember.

"Of course you can't. Because you've never in your life been to Fort Scott."

Until then, neither of the detectives had challenged any part of Smith's statement. He shifted in his chair; with the tip of his tongue he wet his lips.

"The fact is, nothing you've told us is true. You never set foot in Fort Scott. You never picked up any two girls and never took them to any motel—"

"We did. No kidding."

"What were their names?"

"I never asked."

"You and Hickock spent the night with these women and never asked their names?"

"They were just prostitutes."

"Tell us the name of the motel."

"Ask Dick. He'll know. I never remember junk like that."

Dewey addressed his colleague. "Clarence, I think it's time we straightened Perry out."

Duntz hunched forward. He is a heavyweight with a welterweight's spontaneous agility, but his eyes are hooded and lazy. He drawls; each word, formed reluctantly and framed in a cattle-country accent, lasts awhile. "Yes, sir," he said. "'Bout time."

"Listen good, Perry. Because Mr. Duntz is going to tell you where you really were that Saturday night. Where you were and what you were doing."

Duntz said, "You were killing the Clutter family."

Smith swallowed. He began to rub his knees.

"You were out in Holcomb, Kansas. In the home of Mr. Herbert W.

Clutter. And before you left that house you killed all the people in it."

"Never. I never."

"Never what?"

"Knew anybody by that name. Clutter."

Dewey called him a liar, and then, conjuring a card that in prior consultation the four detectives had agreed to play face down, told him, "We have a living witness, Perry. Somebody you boys overlooked."

A full minute elapsed, and Dewey exulted in Smith's silence, for an innocent man would ask who was this witness, and who were these Clutters, and why did they think he'd murdered them—would, at any rate, say *something*. But Smith sat quiet, squeezing his knees.

"Well, Perry?"

"You got an aspirin? They took away my aspirin."

"Feeling bad?"

"My legs do."

It was five-thirty. Dewey, intentionally abrupt, terminated the interview. "We'll take this up again tomorrow," he said. "By the way, do you know what tomorrow is? Nancy Clutter's birthday. She would have been seventeen."

"She would have been seventeen." Perry, sleepless in the dawn hours, wondered (he later recalled) if it was true that today was the girl's birthday, and decided no, that it was just another way of getting under his skin, like that phony business about a witness—"a living witness." There couldn't be. Or did they mean— If only he could talk to Dick! But he and Dick were being kept apart; Dick was locked in a cell on another floor. "Listen good, Perry. Because Mr. Duntz is going to tell you where you really were . . ." Midway in the questioning, after he'd begun to notice the number of allusions to a particular November weekend, he'd nerved himself for what he knew was coming, yet when it did, when the big cowboy with the sleepy voice said, "You were killing the Clutter family"—well, he'd damn near died, that's all. He must have lost ten pounds in two seconds. Thank God he hadn't let them see it. Or hoped he hadn't. And Dick? Presumably they'd pulled the same stunt on him. Dick was smart, a convincing performer, but his "guts" were unreliable, he panicked too easily. Even so, and however much they pressured him, Perry was sure Dick would hold out. Unless he wanted to hang. "And before you left that house you killed all the people in it." It wouldn't amaze him if every Old Grad in Kansas had heard that line. They must have questioned hundreds of men, and no doubt accused dozens; he and Dick were merely two more. On the *other* hand—well, *would* Kansas send four Special Agents a thousand miles to pick up a small-time pair of parole violators? Maybe somehow they *had* stumbled on something, somebody—"a living witness." But that was impossible. Except— He'd give an arm, a leg to talk to Dick for just five minutes.

And Dick, awake in a cell on the floor below, was (he later recalled) equally eager to converse with Perry—find out what the punk had told them. Christ, you couldn't trust him to remember even the outline of the Fun Haven alibi—though they had discussed it often enough. And when those bastards threatened him with a witness! Ten to one the little spook had thought they meant an *eye*witness. Whereas he, Dick, had known at once who the so-called witness must be: Floyd Wells, his old friend and former cellmate. While serving the last weeks of his sentence, Dick had plotted to knife Floyd—stab him through the heart with a handmade "shiv"—and what a fool he was not to have done it. Except for Perry, Floyd Wells was the one human being who could link the names Hickock and Clutter. Floyd, with his sloping shoulders and inclining chin—Dick had thought he'd be too afraid. The sonofabitch was probably expecting some fancy reward—a parole or money, or both. But hell would freeze before he got it. Because a convict's tattle wasn't proof. Proof is footprints, fingerprints, witnesses, a confession. Hell, if all those cowboys had to go on was some story Floyd Wells had told, then there wasn't a lot to worry about. Come right down to it, Floyd wasn't half as dangerous as Perry. Perry, if he lost his nerve and let fly, could put them both in The Corner. And suddenly he saw the truth: It was *Perry* he ought to have silenced. On a mountain road in Mexico. Or while walking across the Mojave. Why had it never occurred to him until now? For now, now was much too late.

Ultimately, at five minutes past three that afternoon, Smith admitted the falsity of the Fort Scott tale. "That was only something Dick told his family. So he could stay out overnight. Do some drinking. See, Dick's dad watched him pretty close—afraid he'd break parole. So we made up an excuse about my sister. It was just to pacify Mr. Hickock." Otherwise, he repeated the same story again and again, and Duntz and Dewey, regardless of how often they corrected him and accused him of lying, could not make him change it—except to add fresh details. The names of the prostitutes, he recalled today, were Mildred and Jane (or Joan). "They rolled us," he now remembered. "Walked off with all our dough while we were asleep." And though even Duntz had forfeited his composure—had shed, along with tie and coat, his enigmatic drowsy dignity—the suspect seemed content and serene; he refused to budge. He'd never heard of the Clutters or Holcomb, or even Garden City.

Across the hall, in the smoke-choked room where Hickock was undergoing his second interrogation, Church and Nye were methodically applying a more roundabout strategy. Not once during this interview, now almost three hours old, had either of them mentioned murder—an omission that kept the prisoner edgy, expectant. They talked of everything else: Hickock's religious philosophy ("I know about hell. I been there. Maybe there's a heaven, too. Lots of rich people think so"); his sexual history ("I've always behaved like a one-hundred-percent normal"); and, once more, the history of his recent cross-country hegira ("Why we kept going like that, the only reason was we were looking for jobs. Couldn't find anything decent, though. I worked one day digging a ditch . . ."). But things unspoken were the center of interest—the cause, the detectives were convinced, of Hickock's escalating distress. Presently, he shut his eyes and touched the lids with trembling fingertips. And Church said, "Something wrong?"

"A headache. I get real bastards."

Then Nye said, "Look at me, Dick." Hickock obeyed, with an expression that the detective interpreted as a pleading with him to speak, to accuse, and let the prisoner escape into the sanctuary of steadfast denial. "When we discussed the matter yesterday, you may recall my saying that the Clutter murders were almost a perfect crime. The killers made only two mistakes. The first one was they left a witness. The second—well, I'll show you." Rising, he retrieved from a corner a box and a briefcase, both of which he'd brought into the room at the start of the interview. Out of the briefcase came a large photograph. "This," he said, leaving it on the table, "is a one-to-one reproduction of certain footprints found near Mr. Clutter's body. And here"—he opened the box—"are the boots that made them. Your boots, Dick." Hickock looked, and looked away. He rested his elbows on his knees and cradled his head in his hands. "Smith," said Nye, "was even more careless. We have his boots, too, and they exactly fit another set of prints. Bloody ones."

Church closed in. "Here's what's going to happen to you, Hickock," he said. "You'll be taken back to Kansas. You'll be charged on four counts of first-degree murder. Count One: That on or about the fifteenth day of November, 1959, one Richard Eugene Hickock did unlawfully, feloniously, willfully and with deliberation and premeditation, and while being engaged in the perpetration of a felony, kill and take the life of Herbert W. Clutter. Count Two: That on or about the fifteenth day of November, 1959, the same Richard Eugene Hickock did unlawfully—"

Hickock said, "Perry Smith killed the Clutters." He lifted his head, and slowly straightened up in the chair, like a fighter staggering to his feet. "It was Perry. I couldn't stop him. He killed them all."

Postmistress Clare, enjoying a coffee break at Hartman's Café, complained of the low volume of the café's radio. "Turn it up," she demanded.

The radio was tuned to Garden City's Station KIUL. She heard the words ". . . after sobbing out his dramatic confession, Hickock emerged from the interrogation room and fainted in a hallway. K.B.I. agents caught him as he fell to the floor. The agents quoted Hickock as saying he and Smith invaded the Clutter home expecting to find a safe containing at least ten thousand dollars. But there was no safe, so they tied the family up and shot them one by one. Smith has neither confirmed nor denied taking part in the crime. When told that Hickock had signed a confession, Smith said, 'I'd like to see my buddy's statement.' But the request was rejected. Officers have declined to reveal whether it was Hickock or Smith who actually shot the members of the family. They emphasized that the statement was only Hickock's version. K.B.I. personnel, returning the two men to Kansas, have already left Las Vegas by car. It is expected the party will arrive in Garden City late Wednesday. Meanwhile, County Attorney Duane West . . ."

"One by one," said Mrs. Hartman. "Just imagine. I don't wonder the varmint fainted."

Others in the café—Mrs. Clare and Mabel Helm and a husky young farmer who had stopped to buy a plug of Brown's Mule chewing tobacco—muttered and mumbled. Mrs. Helm dabbed at her eyes with a paper napkin. "I won't listen," she said. "I mustn't. I won't."

". . . news of a break in the case has met with little reaction in the town of Holcomb, a half mile from the Clutter home. Generally, townspeople in the community of two hundred and seventy expressed relief . . ."

The young farmer hooted. "Relief! Last night, after we heard it on the TV, know what my wife did? Bawled like a baby."

"Shush," said Mrs. Clare. "That's me."

". . . and Holcomb's postmistress, Mrs. Myrtle Clare, said the residents are glad the case has been solved, but some of them still feel others may be involved. She said plenty of folks are still keeping their doors locked and their guns ready . . ."

Mrs. Hartman laughed. "Oh, *Myrt!*" she said. "Who'd you tell that to?"

"A reporter from the *Telegram.*"

The men of her acquaintance, many of them, treat Mrs. Clare as though she were another man. The farmer slapped her on the back and said, "Gosh, Myrt. Gee, fella. You don't still think one of us—anybody round here—had something to do with it?"

But that, of course, was what Mrs. Clare did think, and though she was usually alone in her opinions, this time she was not without company, for the majority of Holcomb's population, having lived for seven weeks amid unwholesome rumors, general mistrust, and suspicion, appeared to feel disappointed at being told that the murderer was not someone among themselves. Indeed, a sizable faction refused to accept the fact that two unknown men, two thieving strangers, were solely responsible. As Mrs. Clare now remarked, "Maybe they did it, these fellows. But there's more to it than that. Wait. Some day they'll get to the bottom, and when they do they'll find the one behind it. The one wanted Clutter out of the way. The *brains.*"

Mrs. Hartman sighed. She hoped Myrt was wrong. And Mrs. Helm, said, "What *I* hope is, I hope they keep 'em locked up good. I won't feel easy knowing they're in our vicinity."

"Oh, I don't think you got to worry, ma'am," said the young farmer. "Right now those boys are a lot more scared of us than we are of them."

On an Arizona highway, a two-car caravan is flashing across sagebrush country—the mesa country of hawks and rattlesnakes and towering red rocks. Dewey is driving the lead car, Perry Smith sits beside him, and Duntz is sitting in the back seat. Smith is handcuffed, and the handcuffs are attached to a security belt by a short length of chain—an arrangement so restricting his movements that he cannot smoke unaided. When he wants a cigarette, Dewey must light it for him and place it between his lips, a task that the detective finds "repellent," for it seems such an intimate action—the kind of thing he'd done while he was courting his wife.

On the whole, the prisoner ignores his guardians and their sporadic attempts to goad him by repeating parts of Hickock's hour-long tape-recorded confession: "He says he tried to stop you, Perry. But says he couldn't. Says he was scared you'd shoot him too," and "Yes, sir, Perry. It's all your fault. Hickock himself, he says he wouldn't harm the fleas on a dog." None of this—outwardly, at any rate—agitates Smith. He continues to contemplate the scenery, to read Burma-Shave doggerel, and to count the carcasses of shotgunned coyotes festooning ranch fences.

Dewey, not anticipating any exceptional response, says, "Hickock tells us you're a natural-born killer. Says it doesn't bother you a bit. Says one time out there in Las Vegas you went after a colored man with a bicycle chain. Whipped him to death. For fun."

To Dewey's surprise, the prisoner gasps. He twists around in his seat until he can see, through the rear window, the motorcade's second car, see inside it: "The tough boy!" Turning back, he stares at the dark streak of desert highway. "I thought it was a stunt. I didn't believe you. That Dick let fly. The tough boy! Oh, a real brass boy. Wouldn't harm the fleas on a dog. Just run over the dog." He spits. "I never killed any nigger." Duntz agrees with him; having studied the files on unsolved Las Vegas homicides, he knows Smith to be innocent of this particular deed. "I never killed any niggers. But *he* thought so. I always knew if we ever got caught, if Dick ever really let fly, dropped his guts all over the goddam floor—I knew he'd tell about the nigger." He spits again. "So Dick was afraid of me? That's amusing. I'm very amused. What he don't know is, I almost did shoot him."

Dewey lights two cigarettes, one for himself, one for the prisoner. "Tell us about it, Perry."

Smith smokes with closed eyes, and explains, "I'm thinking. I want to remember this just the way it was." He pauses for quite a while. "Well, it all started with a letter I got while I was out in Buhl, Idaho. That was September or October. The letter was from Dick, and he said he was on to a cinch. The perfect score. I didn't answer him, but he wrote again, urging me to come back to Kansas and go partners with him. He never said what kind of score it was. Just that it was a 'sure-fire cinch.' Now, as it happened, I had another reason for wanting to be in Kansas around about that time. A personal matter I'd just as soon keep to myself—it's got nothing to do with this deal. Only that otherwise I wouldn't have gone back there. But I did. And Dick met me at the bus station in Kansas City. We drove out to the farm, his parents' place. But they didn't want me there. I'm very sensitive; I usually know what people are feeling.

"Like you." He means Dewey, but does not look at him. "You hate handing me a butt. That's your business. I don't blame you. Any more than I blamed Dick's mother. The fact is, she's a very sweet person. But she knew what I was—a friend from The Walls—and she didn't want me in her house. Christ, I was glad to get out, go to a hotel. Dick took me to a hotel in Olathe. We bought some beer and carried it up to the room, and that's when Dick outlined what he had in mind. He said after I'd left Lansing he celled with someone who'd once worked for a wealthy wheat grower out in western Kansas. Mr. Clutter. Dick drew me a diagram of the Clutter house. He knew where everything was—doors, halls, bedrooms. He said one of the ground-floor rooms was used as an office, and in the office there was a safe—a wall safe. He said Mr. Clutter needed it because he always kept on hand large sums of cash. Never less than ten thousand dollars. The plan was to rob the safe, and if we were seen—well, whoever saw us would have to go. Dick must have said it a million times: 'No witnesses.'"

Dewey says, "How many of these witnesses did he think there might be? I mean, how many people did he expect to find in the Clutter house?"

"That's what I wanted to know. But he wasn't sure. At least four. Probably six. And it was possible the family might have guests. He thought we ought to be ready to handle up to a dozen."

Dewey groans, Duntz whistles, and Smith, smiling wanly, adds, "Me, too. Seemed to me that was a little off. Twelve people. But Dick said it was a cinch. He said, 'We're gonna go in there and splatter those walls with hair.' The mood I was in, I let myself be carried along. But also—I'll be honest—I had faith in Dick; he struck me as being very practical, the masculine type, and I wanted the money as much as he did. I wanted to get it and go to Mexico. But I hoped we could do it without violence. Seemed to me we could if we wore masks. We argued about it. On the way out there, out to Holcomb, I wanted to stop and buy some black silk stockings to wear over our heads. But Dick felt that even with a stocking he could still be identified. Because of his bad eye. All the same, when we got to Emporia—"

Duntz says, "Hold on, Perry. You're jumping ahead. Go back to Olathe. What time did you leave there?"

"One. One-thirty. We left just after lunch and drove to Emporia. Where we bought some rubber gloves and a roll of cord. The knife and shotgun, the shells—Dick had brought all that from home. But he didn't want to look for black stockings. It got to be quite an argument. Somewhere on the outskirts of Emporia, we passed a Catholic hospital, and I persuaded him to stop and go inside and try and buy some black stockings from the nuns. I knew nuns wear them. But he only made believe. Came out and said they wouldn't sell him any. I was sure he hadn't even asked, and he confessed it; he said it was a puky idea—the nuns would've thought he was crazy. So we didn't stop again till Great Bend. That's where we bought the tape. Had dinner there, a big dinner. It put me to sleep. When I woke up, we were just coming into Garden

City. Seemed like a real dead-dog town. We stopped for gas at a filling station—"

Dewey asks if he remembers which one.

"Believe it was a Phillips 66."

"What time was this?"

"Around midnight. Dick said it was seven miles more to Holcomb. All the rest of the way, he kept talking to himself, saying this ought to be here and that ought to be there—according to the instructions he'd memorized. I hardly realized it when we went through Holcomb, it was such a little settlement. We crossed a railroad track. Suddenly Dick said, 'This is it, this has to be it.' It was the entrance to a private road, lined with trees. We slowed down and turned off the lights. Didn't need them. Account of the moon. There wasn't nothing else up there—not a cloud, nothing. Just that full moon. It was like broad day, and when we started up the road, Dick said, 'Look at this spread! The barns! That house! Don't tell me this guy ain't loaded.' But I didn't like the setup, the atmosphere; it was sort of *too* impressive. We parked in the shadows of a tree. While we were sitting there, a light came on—not in the main house but a house maybe a hundred yards to the left. Dick said it was the hired man's house; he knew because of the diagram. But he said it was a damn sight nearer the Clutter house than it was supposed to be. Then the light went off. Mr. Dewey—the witness you mentioned. Is that who you meant—the hired man?"

"No. He never heard a sound. But his wife was nursing a sick baby. He said they were up and down the whole night."

"A sick baby. Well, I wondered. While we were still sitting there, it happened again—a light flashed on and off. And that really put bubbles in my blood. I told Dick to count me out. If he was determined to go ahead with it, he'd have to do it alone. He started the car, we were leaving, and I thought, Bless Jesus. I've always trusted my intuitions; they've saved my life more than once. But halfway down the road Dick stopped. He was sore as hell. I could see he was thinking, Here I've set up this big score, here we've come all this way, and now this punk wants to chicken out. He said, 'Maybe you think I ain't got the guts to do it alone. But, by God, I'll show you who's got guts.' There was some liquor in the car. We each had a drink, and I told him, 'O.K., Dick. I'm with you.' So we turned back. Parked where we had before. In the shadows of a tree. Dick put on gloves; I'd already put on mine. He carried the knife and a flashlight. I had the gun. The house looked tremendous in the moonlight. Looked empty. I remember hoping there was nobody home—"

Dewey says, "But you saw a dog?"

"No."

"The family had an old gun-shy dog. We couldn't understand why he didn't bark. Unless he'd seen a gun and bolted."

"Well, I didn't see anything or nobody. That's why I never believed it. About an eyewitness."

"Not *eye*witness. Witness. Someone whose testimony associates you and Hickock with this case."

"Oh. Uh-huh. Uh-huh. Him. And Dick always said he'd be too scared. Ha!"

Duntz, not to be diverted, reminds him, "Hickock had the knife. You had the gun. How did you get into the house?"

"The door was unlocked. A side door. It took us into Mr. Clutter's office. Then we waited in the dark. Listening. But the only sound was the wind. There was quite a little wind outside. It made the trees move, and you could hear the leaves. The one window was curtained with Venetian blinds, but moonlight was coming through. I closed the blinds, and Dick turned on his flashlight. We saw the desk. The safe was supposed to be in the wall directly behind the desk, but we couldn't find it. It was a paneled wall, and there were books and framed maps, and I noticed, on a shelf, a terrific pair of binoculars. I decided I was going to take them with me when we left there."

"Did you?" asks Dewey, for the binoculars had not been missed.

Smith nods. "We sold them in Mexico."

"Sorry. Go on."

"Well, when we couldn't find the safe, Dick doused the flashlight and we moved in darkness out of the office and across a parlor, a living room. Dick whispered to me couldn't I walk quieter. But he was just as bad. Every step we took made a racket. We came to a hall and a door, and Dick, remembering the diagram, said it was a bedroom. He shined the flashlight and opened the door. A man said, 'Honey?' He'd been asleep, and he blinked and said, 'Is that you, honey?' Dick asked him, 'Are you Mr. Clutter?' He was wide awake now; he sat up and said, 'Who is it? What do you want?' Dick told him, very polite, like we were a couple of door-to-door salesmen, 'We want to talk to you, sir. In your office, please.' And Mr. Clutter, barefoot, just wearing pajamas, he went with us to the office and we turned on the office lights.

"Up till then he hadn't been able to see us very good. I think what he saw hit him hard. Dick says, 'Now, sir, all we want you to do is show us where you keep that safe.' But Mr. Clutter says, 'What safe?' He says he don't have any safe. I knew right then it was true. He had that kind of face. You just knew whatever he told you was pretty much the truth. But Dick shouted at him, 'Don't lie to me, you sonofabitch! I know goddam well you got a safe!' My feeling was nobody had ever spoken to Mr. Clutter like that. But he looked Dick straight in the eye and told him, being very mild about it—said, well, he was sorry but he just didn't have any safe. Dick tapped him on the chest with the knife, says, 'Show us where that safe is or you're gonna be a good bit sorrier.' But Mr. Clutter—oh, you could see he was scared, but his voice stayed mild and steady—he went on denying he had a safe.

"Sometime along in there, I fixed the telephone. The one in the office. I ripped out the wires. And I asked Mr. Clutter if there were any other telephones in the house. He said yes, there was one in the kitchen. So I took the flashlight and went to the kitchen—it was quite a distance from the office. When I found the telephone, I removed the receiver and cut the line with a pair of pliers. Then, heading back, I heard a noise. A creaking overhead. I stopped at the foot of the stairs leading to the second floor. It was dark, and I didn't dare use the flashlight. But I could tell there was someone there. At the top of the stairs, silhouetted against a window. A figure. Then it moved away."

Dewey imagines it must have been Nancy. He'd often theorized, on the basis of the gold wristwatch found tucked in the toe of a shoe in her closet, that Nancy had awakened, heard persons in the house, thought they might be thieves, and prudently hidden the watch, her most valuable property.

"For all I knew, maybe it was somebody with a gun. But Dick wouldn't even listen to me. He was so busy playing tough boy. Bossing Mr. Clutter around. Now he'd brought him back to the bedroom. He was counting the money in Mr. Clutter's billfold. There was about thirty dollars. He threw the billfold on the bed and told him, 'You've got more money in this house than that. A rich man like you. Living on a spread like this.' Mr. Clutter said that was all the cash he had, and explained he always did business by check. He offered to write us a check. Dick just blew up—'What kind of Mongolians do you think we are?'—and I thought Dick was ready to smash him, so I said, 'Dick. Listen to me. There's somebody awake upstairs.' Mr. Clutter told us the only people upstairs were his wife and a son and daughter. Dick wanted to know if the wife had any money, and Mr. Clutter said if she did, it would be very little, a few dollars, and he asked us—really kind of broke down—please not to bother her, because she was an invalid, she'd been very ill for a long time. But Dick insisted on going upstairs. He made Mr. Clutter lead the way.

"At the foot of the stairs, Mr. Clutter switched on lights that lighted the hall above, and as we were going up, he said, 'I don't know why you boys want to do this. I've never done you any harm. I never saw you before.' That's when Dick told him, 'Shut up! When we want you to talk, we'll tell you.' Wasn't anybody in the upstairs hall, and all the doors were shut. Mr. Clutter pointed out the rooms where the boy and girl were supposed to be sleeping, then opened his wife's door. He lighted a lamp beside the bed and told her, 'It's all right, sweetheart. Don't be afraid. These men, they just want some money.' She was a thin, frail sort of woman in a long white nightgown. The minute she opened her eyes, she started to cry. She says, talking to her husband, 'Sweetheart, I don't have any money.' He was holding her hand, patting it. He said, 'Now, don't cry, honey. It's nothing to be afraid of. It's just I gave these men all the money I had, but they want some more. They believe we have a safe somewhere in the house. I told them we don't.' Dick raised his hand, like he was going to crack him across the mouth. Says, 'Didn't I tell you to shut up?' Mrs. Clutter said, 'But my husband's telling you the God's truth. There isn't any safe.' And Dick answers back, 'I know goddam well you got a safe. And I'll find it before I leave here. Needn't worry that I won't.' Then he asked her where she kept her purse. The purse was in a bureau drawer. Dick turned it inside out. Found just some change and a dollar or two. I motioned to him to come into the hall. I wanted to discuss the situation. So we stepped outside, and I said—"

Duntz interrupts him to ask if Mr. and Mrs. Clutter could overhear the conversation.

"No. We were just outside the door, where we could keep an eye on them. But we were whispering. I told Dick, 'These people are telling the truth. The one who lied is your friend Floyd Wells. There isn't any safe, so let's get the hell out of here.' But Dick was too ashamed to face it. He said he wouldn't believe it till we searched the whole house. He said the thing to do was tie them all up, then take our time looking around. You couldn't argue with him, he was so excited. The glory of having everybody at his mercy, that's what excited him. Well, there was a bathroom next door to Mrs. Clutter's room. The idea was to lock the parents in the bathroom, and wake the kids and put them there, then bring them out one by one and tie them up in different parts of the house. And then, says Dick, after we've found the safe, we'll cut their throats. Can't shoot them, he says—that would make too much noise."

Perry frowns, rubs his knees with his manacled hands. "Let me think a minute. Because along in here things begin to get a little complicated. I remember. Yes. Yes, I took a chair out of the hall and stuck it in the bathroom. So Mrs. Clutter could sit down. Seeing she was said to be an invalid. When we locked them up, Mrs. Clutter was crying and telling us, 'Please don't hurt anybody. Please don't hurt my children.' And her husband had his arms around her, saying, like, 'Sweetheart, these fellows don't mean to hurt anybody. All they want is some money.'

"We went to the boy's room. He was awake. Lying there like he was too scared to move. Dick told him to get up, but he didn't move, or move fast enough, so Dick punched him, pulled him out of bed, and I said, 'You don't have to hit him, Dick.' And I told the boy—he was only wearing a T-shirt—to put on his pants. He put on a pair of blue jeans, and we'd just locked him in the bathroom when the girl appeared—came out of her room. She was all dressed, like she'd been awake some while. I mean, she had on socks and slippers, and a kimono, and her hair was wrapped in a bandanna. She was trying to smile. She said, 'Good grief, what is this? Some kind of joke?' I don't guess she thought it was much of a joke, though. Not after Dick opened the bathroom door and shoved her in . . ."

Dewey envisions them: the captive family, meek and frightened but without any premonition of their destiny. Herb *couldn't* have suspected, or he would have fought. He was a gentle man but strong and no coward. Herb, his friend Alvin Dewey felt certain, would have fought to the death defending Bonnie's life and the lives of his children.

"Dick stood guard outside the bathroom door while I reconnoitered. I frisked the girl's room, and I found a little purse—like a doll's purse. Inside it was a silver dollar. I dropped it somehow, and it rolled across the floor. Rolled under a chair. I had to get down on my knees. And just then it was like I was outside myself. Watching myself in some nutty movie. It made me sick. I was just disgusted. Dick, and all his talk about a rich man's safe, and here I am crawling on my belly to steal a child's silver dollar. One dollar. And I'm crawling on my belly to get it."

Perry squeezes his knees, asks the detectives for aspirin, thanks Duntz for giving him one, chews it, and resumes talking. "But that's what you do. You get what you can. I frisked the boy's room, too. Not a dime. But there was a little portable radio, and I decided to take it. Then I remembered the binoculars I'd seen in Mr. Clutter's office. I went downstairs to get them. I carried the binoculars and the radio out to the car. It was cold, and the wind and the cold felt good. The moon was so bright you could see for miles. And I thought, Why don't I walk off? Walk to the highway, hitch a ride. I sure Jesus didn't want to go back in that house. And yet— How can I explain this? It was like I wasn't part of it. More as though I was reading a story. And I had to know what was going to happen. The end. So I went back upstairs. And now, let's see—uh-huh, that's when we tied them up. Mr. Clutter first. We called him out of the bathroom, and I tied his hands together. Then I marched him all the way down to the basement—"

Dewey says, "Alone and unarmed?"

"I had the knife."

Dewey says, "But Hickock stayed guard upstairs?"

"To keep them quiet. Anyway, I didn't need help. I've worked with rope all my life."

Dewey says, "Were you using the flashlight or did you turn on the basement lights?"

"The lights. The basement was divided into two sections. One part seemed to be a playroom. Took him to the other section, the furnace room. I saw a big cardboard box leaning against the wall. A mattress box. Well, I didn't feel I ought to ask him to stretch out on the cold floor, so I dragged the mattress box over, flattened it, and told him to lie down."

The driver, via the rear-view mirror, glances at his colleague, attracts his eye, and Duntz slightly nods, as if in tribute. All along Dewey had argued that the mattress box had been placed on the floor for the *comfort* of Mr. Clutter, and taking heed of similar hints, other fragmentary indications of ironic, erratic compassion, the detective had conjectured that at least one of the killers was not altogether uncharitable.

"I tied his feet, then tied his hands to his feet. I asked him was it too tight, and he said no, but said would we please leave his wife alone. There was no need to tie her up—she wasn't going to holler or try to run out of the house. He said she'd been sick for years and years, and she was just beginning to get a little better, but an incident like this might cause her to have a setback. I know it's nothing to laugh over, only I couldn't help it—him talking about a 'setback.'

"Next thing, I brought the boy down. First I put him in the room with his dad. Tied his hands to an overhead steampipe. Then I figured that wasn't very safe. He might somehow get loose and undo the old man, or vice versa. So I cut him down and took him to the playroom, where there was a comfortable-looking couch. I roped his feet to the foot of the couch, roped his hands, then carried the rope up and made a loop around his neck, so if he struggled he'd choke himself. Once, while I was working, I put the knife down on this—well, it was a freshly varnished cedar chest; the whole cellar smelled of varnish—and he asked me not to put my knife there. The chest was a wedding present he'd built for somebody. A sister, I believe he said. Just as

I was leaving, he had a coughing fit, so I stuffed a pillow under his head. Then I turned off the lights—"

Dewey says, "But you hadn't taped their mouths?"

"No. The taping came later, after I'd tied both the women in their bedrooms. Mrs. Clutter was still crying, at the same time she was asking me about Dick. She didn't trust him, but said she felt I was a decent young man. I'm *sure* you are, she says, and made me promise I wouldn't let Dick hurt anybody. I think what she really had in mind was her daughter. I was worried about that myself. I suspected Dick was plotting something, something I wouldn't stand for. When I finished tying Mrs. Clutter, sure enough, I found he'd taken the girl to her bedroom. She was in the bed, and he was sitting on the edge of it talking to her. I stopped that; I told him to go look for the safe while I tied her up. After he'd gone, I roped her feet together and tied her hands behind her back. Then I pulled up the covers, tucked her in till just her head showed. There was a little easy chair near the bed, and I thought I'd rest a minute; my legs were on fire—all that climbing and kneeling. I asked Nancy if she had a boy friend. She said yes, she did. She was trying hard to act casual and friendly. I really liked her. She was really nice. A very pretty girl, and not spoiled or anything. She told me quite a lot about herself. About school, and how she was going to go to a university to study music and art. Horses. Said next to dancing what she liked best was to gallop a horse, so I mentioned my mother had been a champion rodeo rider.

"And we talked about Dick; I was curious, see, what he'd been saying to her. Seems she'd asked him why he did things like this. Rob people. And, wow, did he toss her a tearjerker—said he'd been raised an orphan in an orphanage, and how nobody had ever loved him, and his only relative was a sister who lived with men without marrying them. All the time we were talking, we could hear the lunatic roaming around below, looking for the safe. Looking behind pictures. Tapping the walls. Tap tap tap. Like some nutty woodpecker. When he came back, just to be a real bastard I asked had he found it. Course he hadn't, but he said he'd come across another purse in the kitchen. With seven dollars."

Duntz says, "How long now had you been in the house?"

"Maybe an hour."

Duntz says, "And when did you do the taping?"

"Right then. Started with Mrs. Clutter. I made Dick help me—because I didn't want to leave him alone with the girl. I cut the tape in long strips, and Dick wrapped them around Mrs. Clutter's head like you'd wrap a mummy. He asked her, 'How come you keep on crying?

Nobody's hurting you,' and he turned off the bedside lamp and said, 'Good night, Mrs. Clutter. Go to sleep.' Then he says to me, as we're heading along the hall toward Nancy's room, 'I'm gonna bust that little girl.' And I said, 'Uh-huh. But you'll have to kill me first.' He looked like he didn't believe he'd heard right. He says, 'What do you care? Hell, you can bust her, too.' Now, that's something I despise. Anybody that can't control themselves sexually. Christ, I hate that kind of stuff. I told him straight, 'Leave her alone. Else you've got a buzzsaw to fight.' That really burned him, but he realized it wasn't the time to have a flat-out free-for-all. So he says, 'O.K., honey. If that's the way you feel.' The end of it was we never even taped her. We switched off the hall light and went down to the basement."

Perry hesitates. He has a question but phrases it as a statement: "I'll bet he never said anything about wanting to rape the girl."

Dewey admits it, but he adds that except for an apparently somewhat expurgated version of his own conduct, Hickock's story supports Smith's. The details vary, the dialogue is not identical, but in substance the two accounts—thus far, at least—corroborate one another.

"Maybe. But I knew he hadn't told about the girl. I'd have bet my shirt."

Duntz says, "Perry, I've been keeping track of the lights. The way I calculate it, when you turned off the upstairs light, that left the house completely dark."

"Did. And we never used the lights again. Except the flashlight. Dick carried the flashlight when we went to tape Mr. Clutter and the boy. Just before I taped him, Mr. Clutter asked me—and these were his last words—wanted to know how his wife was, if she was all right, and I said she was fine, she was ready to go to sleep, and I told him it wasn't long till morning, and how in the morning somebody would find them, and then all of it, me and Dick and all, would seem like something they dreamed. I wasn't kidding him. I didn't want to harm the man. I thought he was a very nice gentleman. Soft-spoken. I thought so right up to the moment I cut his throat.

"Wait. I'm not telling it the way it was." Perry scowls. He rubs his legs; the handcuffs rattle. "After, see, after we'd taped them, Dick and I went off in a corner. To talk it over. Remember, now, there were hard feelings between us. Just then it made my stomach turn to think I'd ever admired him, lapped up all that brag. I said, 'Well, Dick. Any qualms?' He didn't answer me. I said, 'Leave them alive, and this won't be any small rap. Ten years the very least.' He still didn't say anything. He was holding the knife. I asked him for it, and he gave it to me, and I said, 'All right, Dick. Here goes.' But I didn't mean it.

I meant to call his bluff, make him argue me out of it, make him admit he was a phony and a coward. See, it was something between me and Dick. I knelt down beside Mr. Clutter, and the pain of kneeling—I thought of that goddam dollar. Silver dollar. The shame. Disgust. And *they'd* told me never to come back to Kansas. But I didn't realize what I'd done till I heard the sound. Like somebody drowning. Screaming under water. I handed the knife to Dick. I said, 'Finish him. You'll feel better.' Dick tried—or pretended to. But the man had the strength of ten men—he was half out of his ropes, his hands were free. Dick panicked. Dick wanted to get the hell out of there. But I wouldn't let him go. The man would have died anyway, I know that, but I couldn't leave him like he was. I told Dick to hold the flashlight, focus it. Then I aimed the gun. The room just exploded. Went blue. Just blazed up. Jesus, I'll never understand why they didn't hear the noise twenty miles around."

Dewey's ears ring with it—a ringing that almost deafens him to the whispery rush of Smith's soft voice. But the voice plunges on, ejecting a fusillade of sounds and images: Hickock hunting the discharged shell; hurrying, hurrying, and Kenyon's head in a circle of light, the murmur of muffled pleadings, then Hickock again scrambling after a used cartridge; Nancy's room, Nancy listening to boots on hardwood stairs, the creak of the steps as they climb toward her, Nancy's eyes, Nancy watching the flashlight's shine seek the target ("She said, 'Oh, no! Oh, please. No! No! No! No! Don't! Oh, please don't! Please!' I gave the gun to Dick. I told him I'd done all I could do. He took aim, and she turned her face to the wall"); the dark hall, the assassins hastening toward the final door. Perhaps, having heard all she had, Bonnie welcomed their swift approach.

"That last shell was a bitch to locate. Dick wiggled under the bed to get it. Then we closed Mrs. Clutter's door and went downstairs to the office. We waited there, like we had when we first came. Looked through the blinds to see if the hired man was poking around, or anybody else who might have heard the gunfire. But it was just the same —not a sound. Just the wind—and Dick panting like wolves were after him. Right there, in those few seconds before we ran out to the car and drove away, that's when I decided I'd better shoot Dick. He'd said over and over, he'd drummed it into me: *No witnesses.* And I thought, *He's* a witness. I don't know what stopped me. God knows I should've done it. Shot him dead. Got in the car and kept on going till I lost myself in Mexico."

A hush. For ten miles and more, the three men ride without speaking.

Sorrow and profound fatigue are at the heart of Dewey's silence. It had been his ambition to learn "exactly what happened in that house that night." Twice now he'd been told, and the two versions were very much alike, the only serious discrepancy being that Hickock attributed all four deaths to Smith, while Smith contended that Hickock had killed the two women. But the confessions, though they answered questions of how and why, failed to satisfy his sense of meaningful design. The crime was a psychological accident, virtually an impersonal act; the victims might as well have been killed by lightning. Except for one thing: they had experienced prolonged terror, they had suffered. And Dewey could not forget their sufferings. Nonetheless, he found it possible to look at the man beside him without anger—with, rather, a measure of sympathy—for Perry Smith's life had been no bed of roses but pitiful, an ugly and lonely progress toward one mirage and then another. Dewey's sympathy, however, was not deep enough to accommodate either forgiveness or mercy. He hoped to see Perry and his partner hanged—hanged back to back.

Duntz asks Smith, "Added up, how much money did you get from the Clutters?"

"Between forty and fifty dollars."

Among Garden City's animals are two gray tomcats who are always together—thin, dirty strays with strange and clever habits. The chief ceremony of their day is performed at twilight. First they trot the length of Main Street, stopping to scrutinize the engine grilles of parked automobiles, particularly those stationed in front of the two hotels, the Windsor and Warren, for these cars, usually the property of travelers from afar, often yield what the bony, methodical creatures are hunting: slaughtered birds—crows, chickadees, and sparrows foolhardy enough to have flown into the path of oncoming motorists. Using their paws as though they are surgical instruments, the cats extract from the grilles every feathery particle. Having cruised Main Street, they invariably turn the corner at Main and Grant, then lope along toward Courthouse Square, another of their hunting grounds—and a highly promising one on the afternoon of Wednesday, January 6, for the area swarmed with Finney County vehicles that had brought to town part of the crowd populating the square.

The crowd started forming at four o'clock, the hour that the county attorney had given as the probable arrival time of Hickock and Smith. Since the announcement of Hickock's confession on Sunday evening, newsmen of every style had assembled in Garden City: representatives of the major wire services, photographers, newsreel and television cameramen, reporters from Missouri, Nebraska, Oklahoma, Texas, and, of course, all the principal Kansas papers—twenty or twenty-five men altogether. Many of them had been waiting three days without much to do except interview the service-station attendant James Spor, who, after seeing published photographs of the accused killers, had identified them as customers to whom he'd sold three dollars and six cents' worth of gas the night of the Holcomb tragedy.

It was the return of Hickock and Smith that these professional spectators were on hand to record, and Captain Gerald Murray, of the Highway Patrol, had reserved for them ample space on the sidewalk fronting the courthouse steps—the steps the prisoners must mount on their way to the county jail, an institution that occupies the top floor of the four-story limestone structure. One reporter, Richard Parr, of the Kansas City *Star*, had obtained a copy of Monday's Las Vegas *Sun*. The paper's headline raised rounds of laughter: FEAR LYNCH MOB AWAITING RETURN OF KILLER SUSPECTS. Captain Murray remarked, "Don't look much like a necktie party to me."

Indeed, the congregation in the square might have been expecting a parade, or attending a political rally. High-school students, among them former classmates of Nancy and Kenyon Clutter, chanted cheerleader rhymes, bubbled bubble gum, gobbled hot dogs and soda pop. Mothers soothed wailing babies. Men strode about with young children perched on their shoulders. The Boy Scouts were present—an entire troop. And the middle-aged membership of a women's bridge club arrived en masse. Mr. J. P. (Jap) Adams, head of the local Veterans Commission office, appeared, attired in a tweed garment so oddly tailored that a friend yelled, "Hey, Jap! What ya doin' wearin' ladies' clothes?"—for Mr. Adams, in his haste to reach the scene, had unwittingly donned his secretary's coat. A roving radio reporter interviewed sundry other townsfolk, asking them what, in their opinion, the proper retribution would be for "the doers of such a dastardly deed," and while most of his subjects said gosh or gee whiz, one student replied, "I think they ought to be locked in the same cell for the rest of their lives. Never allowed any visitors. Just sit there staring at each other till the day they die." And a tough, strutty little man said, "I believe in capital punishment. It's like the Bible says—an eye for an eye. And even so we're two pair short!"

As long as the sun lasted, the day had been dry and warm—October weather in January. But when the sun descended, when the shadows of the square's giant shade trees met and combined, the coldness as well as darkness numbed the crowd. Numbed and pruned it; by six o'clock, fewer than three hundred persons remained. Newsmen, cursing the undue delay, stamped their feet and slapped frozen ears with ungloved, freezing hands. Suddenly, a murmuring arose on the south side of the square. The cars were coming.

Although none of the journalists anticipated violence, several had predicted shouted abuse. But when the crowd caught sight of the murderers, with their escort of blue-coated highway patrolmen, it fell silent, as though amazed to find them humanly shaped. The handcuffed men, white-faced and blinking blindly, glistened in the glare of flashbulbs and floodlights. The cameramen, pursuing the prisoners and the police into the courthouse and up three flights of stairs, photographed the door of the county jail slamming shut.

No one lingered, neither the press corps nor any of the townspeople. Warm rooms and warm suppers beckoned them, and as they hurried away, leaving the cold square to the two gray cats, the miraculous autumn departed too; the year's first snow began to fall.

## 4

## *The Corner*

INSTITUTIONAL DOURNESS AND cheerful domesticity coexist on the fourth floor of the Finney County Courthouse. The presence of the county jail supplies the first quality, while the so-called Sheriff's Residence, a pleasant apartment separated from the jail proper by steel doors and a short corridor, accounts for the second.

In January, 1960, the Sheriff's Residence was not in fact occupied by the sheriff, Earl Robinson, but by the undersheriff and his wife, Wendle and Josephine ("Josie") Meier. The Meiers, who had been married more than twenty years, were very much alike: tall people with weight and strength to spare, with wide hands, square and calm and kindly faces—the last being most true of Mrs. Meier, a direct and practical woman who nevertheless seems illuminated by a mystical serenity. As the undersheriff's helpmate her hours are long; between five in the morning, when she begins the day by reading a chapter in the Bible, and 10:00 P.M., her bedtime, she cooks and sews for the prisoners, darns, does their laundry, takes splendid care of her husband, and looks after their five-room apartment, with its *gemütlich* mélange of plump hassocks and squashy chairs and cream-colored lace window curtains. The Meiers have a daughter, an only child, who is married and lives in Kansas City, so the couple live alone—or, as Mrs. Meier more correctly puts it: "Alone except for whoever happens to be in the ladies' cell."

The jail contains six cells; the sixth, the one reserved for female prisoners, is actually an isolated unit situated inside the Sheriff's Residence—indeed, it adjoins the Meiers' kitchen. "But," says Josie Meier, "that don't worry me. I enjoy the company. Having somebody to talk to while I'm doing my kitchen work. Most of these women, you got to feel sorry for them. Just met up with Old Man Trouble is all. Course Hickock and Smith was a different matter. Far as I know, Perry Smith was the first man ever stayed in the ladies' cell. The reason was, the sheriff wanted to keep him and Hickock separated from each other until after their trial. The afternoon they brought them in, I made six apple pies and baked some bread and all the while kept track of the goings-on down there on the Square. My kitchen window overlooks the Square; you couldn't want a better view. I'm no judge of crowds, but I'd guess there were several hundred people waiting to see the boys that killed the Clutter family. I never met any of the Clutters myself, but from everything I've ever heard about them they must have been very fine people. What happened to them is hard to forgive, and I know Wendle was worried how the crowd might act when they caught sight of Hickock and Smith. He was afraid somebody might try to get at them. So I kind of had my heart in my mouth when I saw the cars arrive, saw the reporters, all the newspaper fellows running and pushing; but by then it was dark, after six, and bitter cold—more than half the crowd had given up and gone home. The ones that stayed, they didn't say boo. Only stared.

"Later, when they brought the boys upstairs, the first one I saw was Hickock. He had on light summer pants and just an old cloth shirt. Surprised he didn't catch pneumonia, considering how cold it was. But he looked sick all right. White as a ghost. Well, it must be a terrible experience—to be stared at by a horde of strangers, to have to walk among them, and them knowing who you are and what you did. Then they brought up Smith. I had some supper ready to serve them in their cells, hot soup and coffee and some sandwiches and pie. Ordinarily, we feed just twice a day. Breakfast at seven-thirty, and at four-thirty we serve the main meal. But I didn't want those fellows going to bed on an empty stomach; seemed to me they must be feeling bad enough without that. But when I took Smith his supper, carried it in on a tray, he said he wasn't hungry. He was looking out the window of the ladies' cell. Standing with his back to me. That window has the same view as my kitchen window: trees and the Square and the tops of houses. I told him, 'Just taste the soup, it's vegetable, and not out of a can. I made it myself. The pie, too.' In about an hour I went back for the tray and he hadn't touched a crumb. He was still at the window. Like he hadn't moved. It was snowing, and I remember saying it was the first snow of the year, and how we'd had such a beautiful long autumn right till then. And now the snow had come. And then I asked him if he had any special dish he liked; if he did I'd try and fix it for him the next day. He turned round and looked at me. Suspicious, like I might be mocking him. Then he said something about a movie—he had such a quiet way of speaking, almost a whisper. Wanted to know if I had seen a movie. I forget the name, anyway I hadn't seen it: never have been much for picture shows. He said this show took place in Biblical times, and there was a scene where a man was flung off a balcony, thrown to a mob of men and women, who tore him to pieces. And he said that was what came to mind when he saw the crowd on the Square. The man being torn apart. And the idea that maybe that was what they might do to him. Said it scared him so bad his stomach still hurt. Which was why he couldn't eat. Course he was wrong, and I told him so—nobody was going to harm him, regardless of what he'd done; folks around here aren't like that.

"We talked some, he was very shy, but after a while he said, 'One thing I really like is Spanish rice.' So I promised to make him some, and he smiled kind of, and I decided—well, he wasn't the worst young man I ever saw. That night, after I'd gone to bed, I said as much to my husband. But Wendle snorted. Wendle was one of the first on the scene after the crime was discovered. He said he wished I'd been out at the Clutter place when they found the bodies. Then I could've judged for myself just how *gentle* Mr. Smith was. Him and his friend Hickock. He said they'd cut out your heart and never bat an eye. There was no denying it—not with four people dead. And I lay awake wondering if either one was bothered by it—the thought of those four graves."

A month passed, and another, and it snowed some part of almost every day. Snow whitened the wheat-tawny countryside, heaped the streets of the town, hushed them.

The topmost branches of a snow-laden elm brushed against the window of the ladies' cell. Squirrels lived in the tree, and after weeks of tempting them with leftover breakfast scraps, Perry lured one off a branch onto the window sill and through the bars. It was a male squirrel with auburn fur. He named it Red, and Red soon settled down, apparently content to share his friend's captivity. Perry taught him several tricks: to play with a paper ball, to beg, to perch on Perry's shoulder. All this helped to pass time, but still there were many long hours the prisoner had to lose. He was not allowed to read newspapers, and he was bored by the magazines Mrs. Meier lent him: old issues of *Good Housekeeping* and *McCall's*. But he found things to do: file his fingernails with an emery board, buff them to a silky pink sheen; comb and comb his lotion-soaked and scented hair; brush his teeth three and four times a day; shave and shower almost as often. And he kept the cell, which contained a toilet, a shower stall, a cot, a chair, a table, as neat as his person. He was proud of a compliment Mrs. Meier had paid him. "Look!" she had said, pointing at his bunk. "Look at that blanket! You could bounce dimes." But it was at the table that he spent most of his waking life; he ate his meals there, it was where he sat when he sketched portraits of Red, drew flowers, and the face of Jesus, and the faces and torsos of imaginary women; and it was where, on cheap sheets of ruled paper, he made diary-like notes of day-to-day occurrences.

*Thursday 7 January. Dewey here. Brought carton cigarettes. Also typed copies of Statement for my signature. I declined.*

The "Statement," a seventy-eight-page document which he had dictated to the Finney County court stenographer, recounted admissions already made to Alvin Dewey and Clarence Duntz. Dewey, speaking of his encounter with Perry Smith on this particular day, remembered that he had been very surprised when Perry refused to sign the statement. "It wasn't important: I could always testify in court as to the oral confession he'd made to Duntz and myself. And of course Hickock had given us a signed confession while we were still in Las Vegas—the one in which he accused Smith of having committed all four murders. But I was curious. I asked Perry why he'd changed his mind. And he said, 'Everything in my statement is accurate except for two details. If you'll let me correct those items then I'll sign it.' Well, I could guess the items he meant. Because the only serious difference between his story and Hickock's was that he denied having executed the Clutters single-handed. Until now he'd sworn Hickock killed Nancy and her mother.

"And I was right!—that's just what he wanted to do: admit that Hickock had been telling the truth, and that it was he, Perry Smith, who had shot and killed the whole family. He said he'd lied about it because, in his words, 'I wanted to fix Dick for being such a coward. Dropping his guts all over the goddam floor.' And the reason he'd decided to set the record straight wasn't that he suddenly felt any kinder toward Hickock. According to him he was doing it out of consideration for Hickock's parents—said he was sorry for Dick's mother. Said, 'She's a real sweet person. It might be some comfort to her to know Dick never pulled the trigger. None of it would have happened without him, in a way it was mostly his fault, but the fact remains I'm the one who killed them.' But I wasn't certain I believed it. Not to the extent of letting him alter his statement. As I say, we weren't dependent on a formal confession from Smith to prove any part of our case. With or without it, we had enough to hang them ten times over."

Among the elements contributing to Dewey's confidence was the recovery of the radio and pair of binoculars the murderers had stolen from the Clutter house and subsequently disposed of in Mexico City (where, having flown there for the purpose, K.B.I. Agent Harold Nye traced them to a pawnshop). Moreover, Smith, while dictating his statement, had revealed the whereabouts of other potent evidence. "We hit the highway and drove east," he'd said, in the process of describing what he and Hickock had done after fleeing the murder scene. "Drove like hell, Dick driving. I think we both felt very high. I did. Very high, and very relieved at the same time. Couldn't stop laughing, neither one of us; suddenly it all seemed very funny—I don't know why, it just did. But the gun was dripping blood, and my clothes were stained; there was even blood in my hair. So we turned off onto a country road, and drove maybe eight miles till we were way out on the prairie. You could hear coyotes. We smoked a cigarette, and Dick went on making jokes about what had happened back there. I got out of the car, and siphoned some water out of the water tank and washed the blood off the gun barrel. Then I scraped a hole in the ground with Dick's hunting knife, the one I used on Mr. Clutter, and buried in it the empty shells and all the leftover nylon cord and adhesive tape. After that we drove till we came to U.S. 83, and headed east toward Kansas City and Olathe. Around dawn Dick stopped at one of those picnic places: what they call rest areas—where they have open fireplaces. We built a fire and burned stuff. The gloves we'd worn, and my shirt. Dick said he wished we had an ox to roast; he said he'd never been so hungry. It was almost noon when we got to Olathe. Dick dropped me at my hotel, and went on home to have Sunday dinner with his family. Yes, he took the knife with him. The gun, too."

K.B.I. agents, dispatched to Hickock's home, found the knife inside a fishing-tackle box and the shotgun still casually propped against a kitchen wall. (Hickock's father, who refused to believe his "boy" could have taken part in such a "horrible crime," insisted the gun hadn't been out of the house since the first week in November, and therefore could not be the death weapon). As for the empty cartridge shells, the cord and tape, these were retrieved with the aid of Virgil Pietz, a county-highway employee, who, working with a road grader in the area pinpointed by Perry Smith, shaved away the earth inch by inch until the buried articles were uncovered. Thus the last loose strings were tied; the K.B.I. had now assembled an unshakable case, for tests established that the shells had been discharged by Hickock's shotgun, and the remnants of cord and tape were of a piece with the materials used to bind and silence the victims.

*Monday 11 January. Have a lawyer. Mr. Fleming. Old man with red tie.*

Informed by the defendants that they were without funds to hire legal counsel, the court, in the person of Judge Roland H. Tate, appointed as their representatives two local lawyers, Mr. Arthur Fleming and Mr. Harrison Smith. Fleming, seventy-one, a former mayor of Garden City, a short man who enlivens an unsensational appearance with rather conspicuous neckwear, resisted the assignment. "I do not desire to serve," he told the judge. "But if the court sees fit to appoint me, then of course I have no choice." Hickock's attorney, Harrison Smith, forty-five, six feet tall, a golfer, an Elk of exalted degree, accepted the task with resigned grace: "Someone has to do it. And I'll do my best. Though I doubt that'll make me too popular around here."

*Friday 15 January. Mrs. Meier playing radio in her kitchen and I heard man say the county attorney will seek Death Penalty. "The rich never hang. Only the poor and friendless."*

In making his announcement, the county attorney, Duane West, an ambitious, portly young man of twenty-eight who looks forty and sometimes fifty, told newsmen, "If the case goes before a jury, I will request the jury, upon finding them guilty, to sentence them to the death penalty. If the defendants waive right to jury trial and enter a plea of guilty before the judge, I will request the judge to set the death penalty. This was a matter I knew I would be called upon to decide, and my decision has not been arrived at lightly. I feel that due to the violence of the crime and the apparent utter lack of mercy shown the victims, the only way the public can be absolutely protected is to have the death penalty set against these defendants. This is especially true since in Kansas there is no such thing as life imprisonment without possibility of parole. Persons sentenced to life imprisonment actually serve, on the average, less than fifteen years."

*Wednesday 20 January. Asked to take lie-detector in regards to this Walker deal.*

A case like the Clutter case, crimes of that magnitude, arouse the interest of lawmen everywhere, particularly those investigators burdened with unsolved but similar crimes, for it is always possible that the solution to one mystery will solve another. Among the many officers intrigued by events in Garden City was the sheriff of Sarasota County, Florida, which includes Osprey, a fishing settlement not far from Tampa, and the scene, slightly more than a month after the Clutter tragedy, of the quadruple slaying on an isolated cattle ranch which Smith had read about in a Miami newspaper on Christmas Day. The victims were again four members of a family: a young couple, Mr. and Mrs. Clifford Walker, and their two children, a boy and a girl, all of whom had been shot in the head with a rifle. Since the Clutter murderers had spent the night of December 19, the date of the murders, in a Tallahassee hotel, Osprey's sheriff, who had no other leads whatever, was understandably anxious to have the two men questioned and a polygraph examination administered. Hickock consented to take the test and so did Smith, who told Kansas authorities, "I remarked at the time, I said to Dick, I'll bet whoever did this must be somebody that read about what happened out here in Kansas. A nut." The results of the test, to the dismay of Osprey's sheriff as well as Alvin Dewey, who does not believe in exceptional coincidences, were decisively negative. The murderer of the Walker family remains unknown.

*Sunday 31 January. Dick's dad here to visit Dick. Said hello when I saw him go past* [the cell door] *but he kept going. Could be he never heard me. Understand from Mrs. M* [Meier] *that Mrs. H* [Hickock] *didn't come because she felt too bad to. Snowing like a bitch. Dreamed last night I was up in Alaska with Dad—woke up in a puddle of cold urine!!!*

Mr. Hickock spent three hours with his son. Afterward he walked through the snow to the Garden City depot, a work-worn old man, stooped and thinned-down by the cancer that would kill him a few months hence. At the station, while waiting for a homeward-bound train, he spoke to a reporter: "I seen Dick, uh-huh. We had a long talk. And I can guarantee you it's not like people say. Or what's put in the papers. Those boys didn't go to that house planning to do violence. My boy didn't. He may have some bad sides, but he's nowhere near bad as that. Smitty's the one. Dick told me he didn't even know it when Smitty attacked the man [Mr. Clutter], cut his throat. Dick wasn't even in the same room. He only run in when he heard them struggling. Dick was carrying his shotgun, and how he described it was: 'Smitty took my shotgun and just blew that man's head off.' And he says, 'Dad, I ought to have grabbed back the gun and shot Smitty dead. Killed him 'fore he killed the rest of that family. If I'd done it I'd be better off than I am now.' I guess he would, too. How it is, the way folks feel, he don't stand no chance. They'll hang them both.

And," he added, fatigue and defeat glazing his eyes, "having your boy hang, knowing he will, nothing worse can happen to a man."

Neither Perry Smith's father nor sister wrote him or came to see him. Tex John Smith was presumed to be prospecting for gold somewhere in Alaska—though lawmen, despite great effort, had been unable to locate him. The sister had told investigators that she was afraid of her brother, and requested that they please not let him know her present address. (When informed of this, Smith smiled slightly and said, "I wish she'd been in that house that night. What a sweet scene!")

Except for the squirrel, except for the Meiers and an occasional consultation with his lawyer, Mr. Fleming, Perry was very much alone. He missed Dick. *Many thoughts of Dick,* he wrote one day in his makeshift diary. Since their arrest they had not been allowed to communicate, and that, freedom aside, was what he most desired—to talk to Dick, be with him again. Dick was not the "hardrock" he'd once thought him: "pragmatic," "virile," "a real brass boy"; he'd proven himself to be "pretty weak and shallow," "a coward." Still, of everyone in all the world, this was the person to whom he was closest at that moment, for they at least were of the same species, brothers in the breed of Cain; separated from him, Perry felt "all by myself. Like somebody covered with sores. Somebody only a big nut would have anything to do with."

But then one mid-February morning Perry received a letter. It was postmarked Reading, Mass., and it read:

Dear Perry, I was sorry to hear about the trouble you are in and I decided to write and let you know that I remember you and would like to help you in any way that I can. In case you don't remember my name, Don Cullivan, I've enclosed a picture taken at about the time we met. When I first read about you in the news recently I was startled and then I began to think back to those days when I knew you. While we were never close personal friends I can remember you a lot more clearly than most fellows I met in the Army. It must have been about the fall of 1951 when you were assigned to the 761st Engineer Light Equipment Company at Fort Lewis, Washington. You were short (I'm not much taller), solidly built, dark with a heavy shock of black hair and a grin on your face almost all the time. Since you had lived in Alaska quite a few of the fellows used to call you "Eskimo." One of my first recollections of you was at a Company inspection in which all the footlockers were open for inspection. As I recall it all the footlockers were in order, even yours, except that the inside cover of your footlocker was plastered with pictures of pin-up girls. The rest of us were sure you were in for trouble. But the inspecting officer took it in stride and when it was all over and he let it pass I think we all felt you were a nervy guy. I remember that you were a fairly good pool player and I can picture you quite clearly in the Company day room at the pool table. You were one of the best truck drivers in the outfit. Remember the Army field problems we went out on? On one trip that took place in the winter I remember that we each were assigned to a truck for the duration of the problem. In our outfit, Army trucks had no heaters and it used to get pretty cold in those cabs. I remember you cutting a hole in the floor-boards of your truck in order to let the heat from the engine come into the cab. The reason I remember this so well is the impression it made on me because "mutilation" of Army property was a crime for which you could get severely punished. Of course I was pretty green in the Army and probably afraid to stretch the rules even a little bit, but I can remember you grinning about it (and keeping warm) while I worried about it (and froze). I recall that you bought a motorcycle, and vaguely remember you had some trouble with it—chased by the police?—crackup? Whatever it was, it was the first time I realized the wild streak in you. Some of my recollections may be wrong; this was over eight years ago and I only knew you for a period of about eight months. From what I remember, though, I got along with you very well and rather liked you. You always seemed cheerful and cocky, you were good at your Army work and I can't remember that you did much griping. Of course you were apparently quite wild but I never knew too much about that. But now you are in real trouble. I try to imagine what you are like now. What you think about. When first I read about you I was stunned. I really was. But then I put the paper down and turned to something else. But the thought of you returned. I wasn't satisfied just to forget. I am, or try to be, fairly religious [Catholic]. I wasn't always. I used to just drift along with little thought about the only important thing there is. I never considered death or the possibility of a life hereafter. I was too much alive: car, college, dating, etc. But my kid brother died of leukemia when he was just 17 years old. He knew he was dying and afterwards I used to wonder what he thought about. And now I think of you, and wonder what you think about. I didn't know what to say to my brother in the last weeks before he died. But I know what I'd say now. And this is why I am writing you: because God made you as well as me and He loves you just as He loves me, and for the little we know of God's will what has happened to you could have happened to me. Your friend, Don Cullivan.

The name meant nothing, but Perry at once recognized the face in the photograph of a young soldier with crew-cut hair and round, very earnest eyes. He read the letter many times; though he found the religious allusions unpersuasive ("I've tried to believe, but I don't, I can't, and there's no use pretending"), he was thrilled by it. Here was someone offering help, a sane and respectable man who had once known and liked him, a man who signed himself *friend*. Gratefully, in great haste, he started a reply: "Dear Don, Hell yes I remember Don Cullivan . . ."

Hickock's cell had no window; he faced a wide corridor and the façades of other cells. But he was not isolated, there were people to talk to, a plentiful turnover of drunkards, forgers, wife-beaters, and Mexican vagrants; and Dick, with his light-hearted "con-man" patter, his sex anecdotes and gamy jokes, was popular with the inmates (though there was one who had no use for him whatever—an old man who hissed at him: "Killer! Killer!" and who once drenched him with a bucketful of dirty scrubwater).

Outwardly, Hickock seemed to one and all an unusually untroubled young man. When he was not socializing or sleeping, he lay on his cot smoking or chewing gum and reading sports magazines or paper-back thrillers. Often he simply lay there whistling old favorites ("You Must Have Been a Beautiful Baby," "Shuffle Off to Buffalo"), and staring at an unshaded light bulb that burned day and night in the ceiling of the cell. He hated the light bulb's monotonous surveillance; it disturbed his sleep and, more explicitly, endangered the success of a private project—escape. For the prisoner was not as unconcerned as he appeared to be, or as resigned; he intended taking every step possible to avoid "a ride on the Big Swing." Convinced that such a ceremony would be the outcome of any trial—certainly any trial held in the State of Kansas—he had decided to "bust jail. Grab a car and raise dust." But first he must have a weapon; and over a period of weeks he'd been making one: a "shiv," an instrument very like an icepick—something that would fit with lethal niceness between the shoulder-blades of Undersheriff Meier. The weapon's components, a piece of wood and a length of hard wire, were originally part of a toilet brush he'd confiscated, dismantled and hidden under his mattress. Late at night, when the only noises were snores and coughs and the mournful whistle-wailings of Santa Fe trains rumbling through the darkened town, he honed the wire against the cell's concrete floor. And while he worked he schemed.

Once, the first winter after he had finished high school, Hickock had hitchhiked across Kansas and Colorado: "This was when I was looking for a job. Well, I was riding in a truck, and the driver, me and him got into a little argument, no reason exactly, but he beat up on me. Shoved me out. Just left me there. High the hell up in the Rockies. It was sleeting like, and I walked miles, my nose bleeding like fifteen pigs. Then I come to a bunch of cabins on a wooded slope. Summer cabins, all locked up and empty that time of year. And I broke into one of them. There was firewood and canned goods, even some whiskey. I laid up there over a week, and it was one of the best times I ever knew. Despite the fact my nose hurt so and my eyes were green and yellow. And when the snow stopped the sun came out. You never saw such skies. Like Mexico. If Mexico was in a cold climate. I hunted through the other cabins and found some smoked hams and a radio and a rifle. It was great. Out all day with a gun. With the sun in my face. Boy, I felt good. I felt like Tarzan. And every night I ate beans and fried ham and rolled up in a blanket by the fire and fell asleep listening to music on the radio. Nobody came near the place. I bet I could've stayed till spring." If the escape succeeded, that was the course Dick had determined upon—to head for the Colorado mountains, and find there a cabin where he could hide until spring (alone, of course; Perry's future did not concern him). The prospect of so idyllic an interim added to the inspired stealth with which he whetted his wire, filed it to a limber stiletto fineness.

*Thursday 10 March. Sheriff had a shake-out. Searched through all the cells and found a shiv tucked under D's mattress. Wonder what he had in mind (smile).*

Not that Perry really considered it a smiling matter, for Dick, flourishing a dangerous weapon, could have played a decisive role in plans he himself was forming. As the weeks went by he had become familiar with life on Courthouse Square, its habitués and their habits. The cats, for example: the two thin gray toms who appeared with every twilight and prowled the Square, stopping to examine the cars parked around its periphery—behavior puzzling to him until Mrs. Meier explained that the cats were hunting for dead birds caught in the vehicles' engine grilles. Thereafter it pained him to watch their maneuvers: "Because most of my life I've done what they're doing. The equivalent."

And there was one man of whom Perry had grown especially aware, a robust, upright gentleman with hair like a gray-and-silver skullcap; his face, filled out, firm-jawed, was somewhat cantankerous in repose, the mouth down-curved, the eyes downcast as though in mirthless reverie—a picture of unsparing sternness. And yet this was at least a partially inaccurate impression, for now and again the prisoner glimpsed him as he paused to talk to other men, joke with them and laugh, and then he seemed carefree, jovial, generous: "The kind of person who might see the human side"—an important attribute, for the man was Roland H. Tate, Judge of the 32nd Judicial District, the jurist who would preside at the trial of the State of Kansas versus Smith and Hickock. Tate, as Perry soon learned, was an old and awesome name in western Kansas. The judge was rich, he raised horses, he owned much land, and his wife was said to be very beautiful. He was the father of two sons, but the younger had died, a tragedy that greatly affected the parents and led them to adopt a small boy who had appeared in court as an abandoned, homeless child. "He sounds soft-hearted to me," Perry once said to Mrs. Meier. "Maybe he'll give us a break."

But that was not what Perry really believed; he believed what he'd written Don Cullivan, with whom he now corresponded regularly: his crime was "unforgivable," and he fully expected to "climb those thirteen steps." However, he was not altogether without hope, for he too had plotted an escape. It depended upon a pair of young men that he had often observed observing him. One was red-haired, the other dark. Sometimes, standing in the Square under the tree that touched the cell window, they smiled and signaled to him—or so he imagined. Nothing was ever said, and always, after perhaps a minute, they drifted away. But the prisoner had convinced himself that the young men, possibly motivated by a desire for adventure, meant to help him escape. Accordingly, he drew a map of the Square, indicating the points at which a "getaway car" could most advantageously be stationed. Beneath the map he wrote: *I need a Hacksaw Blade 5″. Nothing else. But do you realize the consequences if you get caught (nod your head if you do)? It could mean a long stretch in prison. Or you might get killed. All for someone you don't know. YOU BETTER THINK IT OVER!! Seriously! Besides, how do I know I can trust you? How do I know it isn't a trick to get me out there and gun me down? What about Hickock? All preparations must include him.*

Perry kept this document on his desk, wadded and ready to drop out the window the next time the young men appeared. But they never did; he never saw them again. Eventually, he wondered if perhaps he had invented them (a notion that he "might not be normal, maybe insane" had troubled him "even when I was little, and my sisters laughed because I liked moonlight. To hide in the shadows and watch the moon"). Phantoms or not, he ceased to think of the young men. Another method of escape, suicide, replaced them in his musings; and despite the jailer's precautions (no mirror, no belt or tie or shoelaces), he had devised a way to do it. For he also was furnished with a ceiling bulb that burned eternally, but, unlike Hickock, he had in his cell a broom, and by pressing the broom-brush against the bulb he could unscrew it. One night he dreamed that he'd unscrewed the bulb, broken it, and with the broken glass cut his wrists and ankles. "I felt all breath and light leaving me," he said, in a subsequent description of his sensations. "The walls of the cell fell away, the sky came down, I saw the big yellow bird."

Throughout his life—as a child, poor and meanly treated, as a footloose youth, as an imprisoned man—the yellow bird, huge and parrot-faced, had soared across Perry's dreams, an avenging angel who savaged his enemies or, as now, rescued him in moments of mortal danger: "She lifted me, I could have been light as a mouse, we went up, up, I could see the Square below, men running, yelling, the sheriff shooting at us, everybody sore as hell because I was free, I was flying, I was better than any of *them*."

The trial was scheduled to start on March 22, 1960. In the weeks preceding that date the defense attorneys frequently consulted the defendants. The advisability of requesting a change of venue was discussed, but as the elderly Mr. Fleming warned his client, "It wouldn't matter where in Kansas the trial was held. Sentiment's the same all over the state. We're probably better off in Garden City. This is a religious community. Eleven thousand population and twenty-two churches. And most of the ministers are opposed to capital punishment, say it's immoral, unchristian; even the Reverend Cowan, the Clutters' own minister and a close friend of the family, he's been preaching against the death penalty in this very case. Remember, all we can hope is to save your lives. I think we stand as good a chance here as anywhere."

Soon after the original arraignment of Smith and Hickock, their advocates appeared before Judge Tate to argue a motion urging comprehensive psychiatric examinations for the accused. Specifically, the court was asked to permit the state hospital in Larned, Kansas, a mental institution with maximum-security facilities, to take custody of the prisoners for the purpose of ascertaining whether either or both were "insane, imbeciles or idiots, unable to comprehend their position and aid in their defense."

Larned is a hundred miles east of Garden City; Hickock's attorney, Harrison Smith, informed the court that he had driven there the previous day and conferred with several of the hospital's staff: "We have no qualified psychiatrists in our own community. In fact, Larned is the only place within a radius of two hundred and twenty-five miles where you'll find such men—doctors trained to make serious psychiatric evaluations. That takes time. Four to eight weeks. But the personnel with whom I discussed the matter said they were willing to start work at once; and, of course, being a state institution it won't cost the county a nickel."

This plan was opposed by the special assistant prosecuting attorney, Logan Green, who, certain that "temporary insanity" was the defense his antagonists would attempt to sustain in the forthcoming trial, feared that the ultimate outcome of the proposal would be, as he predicted in private conversation, the appearance on the witness stand of a "pack of head-healers" sympathetic to the defendants ("Those fellows, they're always crying over the killers. Never a thought for the victims"). Short, pugnacious, a Kentuckian by birth, Green began by pointing out to the court that Kansas' law, in regard to sanity, adheres to the M'Naghten Rule, the ancient British importation which contends that if the accused knew the nature of his act, and knew it was wrong, then he is mentally competent and responsible for his actions. Furthermore, said Green, there was nothing in the Kansas statutes indicating that the physicians chosen to determine a defendant's mental condition must be of any particular qualification: "Just plain doctors. Medical doctors in general practice. That's all the law requires. We have sanity hearings in this county every year for the purpose of committing people to the institution. We never call anybody in from Larned or psychiatric institutions of any kind. Our own local physicians attend to the matter. It's no great job to find whether a man is insane or an idiot or an imbecile . . . It is entirely unnecessary, a waste of time to send the defendants to Larned."

In rebuttal, Counsel Smith suggested that the present situation was "far graver than a simple sanity hearing in probate court. Two lives are at stake. Whatever their crime, these men are entitled to examination by persons of training and experience. Psychiatry," he added, pleading with the judge quite directly, "has matured rapidly in the past twenty years. The Federal courts are beginning to keep in tune with this science as related to people charged with criminal offenses. It just seems to me we have a golden opportunity to face up to the new concepts in this field."

It was an opportunity the judge preferred to reject, for as a fellow jurist once remarked, "Tate is what you might call a lawbook lawyer, he never experiments, he goes strictly by the text"; but the same critic also said of him, "If I were innocent, he's the first man I'd want on the bench; if I was guilty, the last." Judge Tate did not entirely deny the motion; rather, he did exactly all the law demanded by appointing a commission of three Garden City doctors and directing them to pronounce a verdict upon the mental capacities of the prisoners. (In due course the medical trio met the accused and, after an hour or so of conversational prying, announced that neither man suffered from any mental disorder. When told of their diagnosis, Perry Smith said, "How would they know? They just wanted to be entertained. Hear all the morbid details from the killer's own terrible lips. Oh, their eyes were shining." Hickock's attorney was also angry; once more he traveled to Larned State Hospital, where he appealed for the unpaid services of a psychiatrist willing to go to Garden City and interview the defendants. The one man who volunteered, Dr. W. Mitchell Jones, was exceptionally competent; not yet thirty, a sophisticated specialist in criminal psychology and the criminally insane who had worked and studied in Europe and the United States, he agreed to examine Smith and Hickock, and, should his findings warrant it, testify in their behalf.)

On the morning of March 14 counsels for the defense again stood before Judge Tate, there on this occasion to plead for a postponement of the trial, which was then eight days distant. Two reasons were given, the first was that a "most material witness," Hickock's father, was at present too ill to testify. The second was a subtler matter. During the past week a boldly lettered notice had begun to appear in the town's shop windows, and in banks, restaurants, and at the railroad station; and it read: H. W. CLUTTER ESTATE AUCTION SALE * 21 MARCH 1960 * AT THE CLUTTER HOMESTEAD. "Now," said Harrison Smith, addressing the bench, "I realize it is almost impossible to prove prejudice. But this sale, an auction of the victim's estate, occurs one week from today—in other words, the very day before the trial begins. Whether that's prejudicial to the defendants I'm not able to state. But these signs, coupled with newspaper advertisements, and advertisements on the radio, will be a constant reminder to every citizen in the community, among whom one hundred and fifty have been called as prospective jurors."

Judge Tate was not impressed. He denied the motion without comment.

Earlier in the year Mr. Clutter's Japanese neighbor, Hideo Ashida, had auctioned his farming equipment and moved to Nebraska. The Ashida sale, which was considered a success, attracted not quite a hundred customers. Slightly more than five thousand people attended the Clutter auction. Holcomb's citizenry expected an unusual turnout—the Ladies' Circle of the Holcomb Community Church had converted one of the Clutter barns into a cafeteria stocked with two hundred homemade pies, two hundred and fifty pounds of hamburger meat, and sixty pounds of sliced ham—but no one was prepared for the largest auction crowd in the history of western Kansas. Cars converged on Holcomb from half the counties in the state, and from Oklahoma, Colorado, Texas, Nebraska. They came bumper to bumper down the lane leading to River Valley Farm.

It was the first time the public had been permitted to visit the Clutter place since the discovery of the murders, a circumstance which explained the presence of perhaps a third of the immense congregation—those who had come out of curiosity. And of course the weather was an aid to attendance, for by mid-March winter's high snows have dissolved, and the earth beneath, thoroughly thawed, has emerged as acre upon acre of ankle-deep mud; there is not much a farmer can do until the ground hardens. "Land's so wet and nasty," said Mrs. Bill Ramsey, the wife of a farmer. "Can't work nohow. We figured we might as well drive on out to the sale." Actually, it was a beautiful day. Spring. Though mud abounded underfoot, the sun, so long shrouded by snow and cloud, seemed an object freshly made, and the trees—Mr. Clutter's orchard of pear and apple trees, the elms shading the lane—were lightly veiled in a haze of virginal green. The fine lawn surrounding the Clutter house was also newly green, and trespassers upon it, women anxious to have a closer look at the uninhabited home, crept across the grass and peered through the windows as though hopeful but fearful of discerning, in the gloom beyond the pleasant flower-print curtains, grim apparitions.

Shouting, the auctioneer praised his wares—tractors, trucks, wheelbarrows, nail kegs and sledgehammers and unused lumber, milk buckets, branding irons, horses, horseshoes, everything needed to run a ranch from rope and harness to sheep dip and tin washtubs—it was the prospect of buying this merchandise at bargain prices that had lured most of the crowd. But the hands of bidders flickered shyly—work-roughened hands timid of parting with hard-earned cash; yet nothing went unsold, there was even someone keen to acquire a bunch of rusty keys, and a youthful cowboy sporting pale-yellow boots bought

Kenyon Clutter's "coyote wagon," the dilapidated vehicle the dead boy had used to harass coyotes, chase them on moonlit nights.

The stagehands, the men who hauled the smaller items on and off the auctioneer's podium, were Paul Helm, Vic Irsik, and Alfred Stoecklein, each of them an old, still-faithful employee of the late Herbert W. Clutter. Assisting at the disposal of his possessions was their final service, for today was their last day at River Valley Farm; the property had been leased to an Oklahoma rancher, and henceforward strangers would live and work there. As the auction progressed, and Mr. Clutter's worldly domain dwindled, gradually vanished, Paul Helm, remembering the burial of the murdered family, said, "It's like a second funeral."

The last thing to go was the contents of the livestock corral, mostly horses, including Nancy's horse, big, fat Babe, who was much beyond her prime. It was late afternoon, school was out, and several schoolmates of Nancy's were among the spectators when bidding on the horse began; Susan Kidwell was there. Sue, who had adopted another of Nancy's orphaned pets, a cat, wished she could give Babe a home, for she loved the old horse and knew how much Nancy had loved her. The two girls had often gone riding together aboard Babe's wide back, jogged through the wheat fields on hot summer evenings down to the river and into the water, the mare wading against the current until, as Sue once described it, "the three of us were cool as fish." But Sue had no place to keep a horse.

"I hear fifty . . . sixty-five . . . seventy . . .": the bidding was laggardly, nobody seemed really to want Babe, and the man who got her, a Mennonite farmer who said he might use her for plowing, paid seventy-five dollars. As he led her out of the corral, Sue Kidwell ran forward; she raised her hand as though to wave goodbye, but instead clasped it over her mouth.

The Garden City *Telegram*, on the eve of the trial's start, printed the following editorial: "Some may think the eyes of the entire nation are on Garden City during this sensational murder trial. But they are not. Even a hundred miles west of here in Colorado few persons are even acquainted with the case—other than just remembering some members of a prominent family were slain. This is a sad commentary on the state of crime in our nation. Since the four members of the Clutter family were killed last fall, several other such multiple murders have occurred in various parts of the country. Just during the few days leading up to this trial at least three mass murder cases broke into the headlines. As a result, this crime and trial are just one of many such cases people have read about and forgotten. . . ."

Although the eyes of the nation were not upon them, the demeanor of the event's main participants, from the court recorder to the judge himself, was markedly self-aware on the morning of the court's first convening. All four of the lawyers sported new suits; the new shoes of the big-footed county attorney creaked and squealed with every step. Hickock, too, was sharply dressed in clothes provided by his parents: trim blue-serge trousers, a white shirt, a narrow dark-blue tie. Only Perry Smith, who owned neither jacket nor tie, seemed sartorially misplaced. Wearing an open-necked shirt (borrowed from Mr. Meier) and blue jeans rolled up at the cuffs, he looked as lonely and inappropriate as a seagull in a wheat field.

The courtroom, an unpretentious chamber situated on the third floor of the Finney County Courthouse, has dull white walls and furnishings of darkly varnished wood. The spectator benches can seat perhaps one hundred and sixty persons. On Tuesday morning, March 22, the benches were occupied exclusively by the all-male venire of Finney County residents from which a jury was to be selected. Not many of the summoned citizenry seemed anxious to serve (one potential juror, in conversation with another, said, "They can't use me. I can't hear well enough." To which his friend, after a bit of sly reflection, replied, "Come to think of it, my hearing's not too good either"), and it was generally thought that the choosing of the jury would take several days. As it turned out, the process was completed within four hours; moreover, the jury, including two alternative members, was extracted from the first forty-four candidates. Seven were rejected on pre-emptory challenge by the defense, and three were excused at the request of the prosecution; another twenty won dismissal either because they opposed capital punishment or because they admitted to having already formed a firm opinion regarding the guilt of the defendants.

The fourteen men ultimately elected consisted of half a dozen farmers, a pharmacist, a nursery manager, an airport employee, a well driller, two salesmen, a machinist, and the manager of Ray's Bowling Alley. They were all family men (several had five children or more), and were seriously affiliated with one or another of the local churches. During the *voir dire* examination, four of them told the court that they had been personally, though not intimately, acquainted with Mr. Clutter; but upon further questioning, each said he did not feel this circumstance would hinder his ability to reach an impartial verdict. The airport employee, a middle-aged man named N. L. Dunnan, said, when asked his opinion of capital punishment, "Ordinarily I'm against it. But in this case, no"—a declaration which, to some who heard it, seemed clearly indicative of prejudice. Dunnan was nevertheless accepted as a juror.

The defendants were inattentive observers of the *voir dire* proceedings. The previous day, Dr. Jones, the psychiatrist who had volunteered to examine them, had interviewed them separately for approximately two hours: at the end of the interviews, he had suggested that they each write for him an autobiographical statement, and it was the act of composing these statements that occupied the accused throughout the hours spent assembling a jury. Seated at opposite ends of their counsels' table, Hickock worked with a pen and Smith with a pencil.

Smith wrote:

I was born Perry Edward Smith Oct. 27 1928 in Huntington, Elko County, Nevada, which is situated way out in the boon docks, so to speak. I recall that in 1929 our family had ventured to Juneau, Alaska. In my family were my brother Tex Jr. (He later changed his name to James because of the ridicule of the name "Tex" & also I believe he hated my father in his early years—my mother's doing). My sister Fern (She also changed her name—to Joy). My sister Barbara. And myself. . . . In Juneau, my father was making bootleg hooch. I believe it was during this period my mother became acquainted with alcohol. Mom & Dad began having quarrels. I remember my mother was "entertaining" some sailors while my father was away. When he came home a fight ensued, and my father, after a violent struggle, threw the sailors out & proceeded to beat my mother. I was frightfully scared, in fact all us children were terrified. Crying. I was scared because I thought my father was going to hurt me, also because he was beating my mother. I really didn't understand why he was beating her but I felt she must have done something dreadfully wrong. . . . The next thing I can vaguely recall is living in Fort Bragg, Calif. My brother had been presented a B.B. gun. He had shot a hummingbird, and after he had shot it he was sorry. I asked him to let me shoot the B.B. gun. He pushed me away, telling me I was too small. It made me so mad I started to cry. After I finished crying, my anger mounted again, and during the evening when the B.B. gun was behind the chair my brother was sitting in, I grabbed it & held it to my brother's ear & hollered BANG! My father (or mother) beat me and made me apologize. My brother used to shoot at a big white horse riden by a neighbor who went by our place on his way to town. The neighbor caught my brother and I hiding in the bushes and took us to Dad & we got a beating & brother had his B.B. gun taken away & I was *glad* he had his gun taken away! . . . This is about all I remember when we lived in Fort Bragg (Oh! We kids used to jump from a hay-loft, holding an umbrella, onto a pile of hay on the ground). . . . My next recollection is several years later when we were living in Calif.? Nevada? I recall a very odious episode between my mother and a Negro. We children slept on a porch in the summertime. One of our beds was directly under my mother and father's room. Everyone of us kids had taken a good look through the partly open curtain and seen what was going on. Dad had hired a Negro (Sam) to do odd jobs around the farm, or ranch, while he was working somewhere down the road. He used to come home late in the evening in his Model A truck. I do not recall the chain of events but assumed Dad had known or suspected what was happening. It ended in a seperation between Mom & Dad & Mom took us kids to San Francisco. She run off with Dad's truck & all of the many souvenirs he brought from Alaska. I believe this was in 1935 (?). . . . In Frisco I was continously in trouble. I had started to run around with a gang, all of which were older than myself. My mother was always drunk, never in a fit condition to properly provide and care for us. I run as free & wild as a coyote. There was no rule or discipline, or anyone to show me right from wrong. I came & went as I pleased—until my first encounter with Trouble. I was in & out of Detention Homes many many times for running away from home & stealing. I remember one place I was sent to. I had weak kidneys & wet the bed every night. This was very humiliating to me, but I couldn't control myself. I was very severly beaten by the cottage mistress, who had called me names and made fun of me in front of all the boys. She used to come around at all hours of the night to see if I wet the bed. She would throw back the covers & furiously beat me with a large black leather belt—pull me out of bed by my hair & drag me to the bathroom & throw me in the tub & turn the cold water on & tell me to wash myself and the sheets. Every night was a nightmare. Later on she thought it was very funny to put some kind of ointment on my penis. This was almost unbearable. It burned something terrible. She was later discharged from her job. But this never changed my mind about her & what I wished I could have done to her & all the people who made fun of me.

Then, because Dr. Jones had told him he must have the statement that very afternoon, Smith skipped forward to early adolescence and the years he and his father had lived together, the two of them wandering all over the West and Far West, prospecting, trapping, doing odd jobs:

> I loved my father but there were times when this love and affection I had for him drained from my heart like wasted water. Whenever he would not try to understand my problems. Give me a little consideration & voice & responsibility. I had to get away from him. When I was sixteen I joined the Merchant Marine. In 1948 I joined the army—the recruiting officer gave me a break and upped my test. From this time on I started to realize the importance of an education. This only added to the hatred and bitterness I held for others. I began to get into fights. I threw a Japanese policeman off a bridge into the water. I was court-martialed for demolishing a Japanese cafe. I was court-martialed again in Kyoto, Japan, for stealing a Japanese taxicab. I was in the army almost four years. I had many violent outbursts of anger while I served time in Japan & Korea. I was in Korea 15 months, was rotated and sent back to the states—and was given special recognition as being the first Korean Vet to come back to the territory of Alaska. Big write up, picture in paper, paid trip to Alaska by air, all the trimmings. . . . I finished my army service in Ft. Lewis, Washington.

Smith's pencil sped almost indecipherably as he hurried toward more recent history: the motorcycle accident that had crippled him, the burglary in Phillipsburg, Kansas, that had led to his first prison sentence:

> . . . I was sentenced to 5 to 10 years for grand larceny, burglary and jailbreak. I felt I was very unjustly dealt with. I became very bitter while I was in prison. Upon my release I was supposed to go to Alaska with my father—I didn't go—I worked for a while in Nevada and Idaho—went to Las Vegas and continued to Kansas where got into the situation I'm in now. No time for more.
>
> He signed his name, and added a postscript:
>
> "Would like to speak to you again. There's much I haven't said that may interest you. I have always felt a remarkable exhiliration being among people with a purpose and sense of dedication to carry out that purpose. I felt this about you in your presence."

Hickock did not write with his companion's intensity. He often stopped to listen to the questioning of a prospective juror, or to stare at the faces around him—particularly, and with plain displeasure, the muscular face of the county attorney, Duane West, who was his own age, twenty-eight. But his statement, written in a stylized script that looked like slanting rain, was finished before the court adjourned for the day:

> I will try to tell you all I can about myself, though most of my early life is vague to me—up until about my tenth birthday. My school years went quite the same as most other boys my own age. I had my share of fights, girls, and other things that go with a growing boy. My home life was also normal, but as I told you before, I was hardly ever allowed to leave my yard and visit with playmates. My father was always strict about us boys [his brother and him] in that line. Also I had to help my dad quite a lot around the house. . . . I can only remember my mother and dad having one argument that amounted to anything. What it was about, I don't know. . . . My dad bought me a bicycle once, and I believe that I was the proudest boy in town. It was a girl's bike and he changed it over to a boy's. He painted it all up and it looked like new. But I had a lot of toys when I was little, a lot for the financial condition that my folks were in. We were always what you would call semi-poor. Never down and out, but several times on the verge of it. My dad was a hard worker and did his best to provide for us. My mother also was always a hard worker. Her house was always neat, and we had clean clothes aplenty. I remember my dad used to wear those old fashioned flat crown caps, and he would make me wear them too, and I didn't like them. . . . In high-school I did real well, made above average grades the first year or two. But then started falling off a little. I had a girl friend. She was a nice girl, and I never once tried to touch her anyway but just kissing. It was a real clean courtship. . . . While in school I participated in all the sports, and received 9 letters in all. Basketball, football, track and baseball. My senior year was best. I never had any steady girl, just played the field. That was when I had my first relationship with a girl. Of course I told the boys that I'd had a lot of girls. . . . I got offers from two colleges to play ball, but never attended any of them. After I graduated from school I went to work for the Santa Fe railroad, and stayed until the following winter when I got laid off. The following spring I got a job with the Roark Motor Company. I had been working there about four months when I had an automobile wreck with a company car. I was in the hospital several days with extensive

head injuries. While I was in the condition I was in I couldn't find another job, so I was unemployed most of the winter. Meantime, I had met a girl and fallen in love. Her dad was a Baptist preacher and resented me going with her. In July we were married. All hell broke loose from her dad until he learned she was pregnant. But still he never wished me good luck and that has always gone against the grain. After we were married, I worked at a service-station near Kansas City. I worked from 8 at night till 8 in the morning. Sometimes my wife stayed with me all night—she was afraid I couldn't keep awake, so she came to help me. Then I got an offer to work at Perry Pontiac, which I gladly accepted. It was very satisfactory, though I didn't make a lot of money—$75 a week. I got along good with the other men, and was well liked by my boss. I worked there five years. . . . During my employment there was the beginning of some of the lowest things I have ever done.

Here Hickock revealed his pedophiliac tendencies, and after describing several sample experiences, wrote:

I know it is wrong. But at the time I never give any thought to whether it is right or wrong. The same with stealing. It seems to be an impulse. One thing I never told you about the Clutter deal is this. Before I ever went to their house I knew there would be a girl there. I think the main reason I went there was not to rob them but to rape the girl. Because I thought a lot about it. That is one reason why I never wanted to turn back when we started to. Even when I saw there was no safe. I did make some advances toward the Clutter girl when I was there. But Perry never gave me a chance. I hope no one finds this out but you, as I haven't even told my lawyer. There were other things I should have told you, but I'm afraid of my people finding them out. Because I am more ashamed of them (these things I did) than hanging. . . . I have had sickness. I think caused from the car wreck I had. Spells of passing out, and sometimes I would hemhorrage at the nose and left ear. I had one at some people's house by the name of Crist—they live south of my parents. Not long ago I had a piece of glass work out of my head. It came out the corner of my eye. My dad helped me to get it out. . . . I figure I should tell you the things that led to my divorce, and things that caused me to go to prison. It started the early part of 1957. My wife and I were living in an apartment in Kansas City. I had quit my job at the automobile company, and went into the garage business for myself. I was renting the garage from a woman who had a daughter-in-law named Margaret. I met this girl one day while I was at work, and we went to have a cup of coffee. Her husband was away in the Marine Corps. To make a long story short, I started going out with her. My wife sued for divorce. I began thinking I never really loved my wife. Because if I had, I wouldn't have done all the things I'd done. So I never fought the divorce. I started drinking, and was drunk for almost a month. I neglected my business, spent more money than I earned, wrote bad checks, and in the end became a thief. For this last I was sent to the penitentiary. . . . My lawyer said I should be truthful with you as you can help me. And I need help, as you know.

The next day, Wednesday, was the proper start of the trial; it was also the first time ordinary spectators were admitted into the courtroom, an area too small to accommodate more than a modest percentage of those who applied at the door. The best seats had been reserved for twenty members of the press, and for such special personages as Hickock's parents and Donald Cullivan (who, at the request of Perry Smith's lawyer, had traveled from Massachusetts to appear as a character witness in behalf of his former Army friend). It had been rumored that the two surviving Clutter daughters would be present; they were not, nor did they attend any subsequent session. The family was represented by Mr. Clutter's younger brother, Arthur, who had driven a hundred miles to be there. He told newsmen: "I just want to get a good look at them [Smith and Hickock]. I just want to see what kind of animals they are. The way I feel, I could tear them apart." He took a seat directly behind the defendants, and fixed them with a gaze of unique persistence, as though he planned to paint their portraits from memory. Presently, and it was as if Arthur Clutter had willed him to do it, Perry Smith turned and looked at him—and recognized a face very like the face of the man he had killed: the same mild eyes, narrow lips, firm chin. Perry, who was chewing gum, stopped chewing; he lowered his eyes, a minute elapsed, then slowly his jaws began to move again. Except for this moment, Smith, and Hickock too, affected a courtroom attitude that was simultaneously uninterested and disinterested; they chewed gum and tapped their feet with languid impatience as the state summoned its first witness.

Nancy Ewalt. And after Nancy, Susan Kidwell. The young girls described what they saw upon entering the Clutter house on Sunday, November 15: the quiet rooms, an empty purse on a kitchen floor, sunshine in a bedroom, and their schoolmate, Nancy Clutter, surrounded by her own blood. The defense waived cross-examination, a policy they pursued with the next three witnesses (Nancy Ewalt's father, Clarence, and Sheriff Earl Robinson, and the county coroner, Dr. Robert Fenton), each of whom added to the narrative of events that sunny November morning: the discovery, finally, of all four victims, and accounts of how they looked, and, from Dr. Fenton, a clinical diagnosis of why—"Severe traumas to brain and vital cranial structures inflicted by a shotgun."

Then Richard G. Rohleder took the stand.

Rohleder is Chief Investigator of the Garden City Police Department. His hobby is photography, and he is good at it. It was Rohleder who took the pictures that, when developed, revealed Hickock's dusty footprints in the Clutter cellar, prints the camera could discern, though not the human eye. And it was he who had photographed the corpses, those death-scene images Alvin Dewey had continuously pondered while the murders were still unsolved. The point of Rohleder's testimony was to establish the fact of his having made these pictures, which the prosecution proposed to put into evidence. But Hickock's attorney objected: "The sole reason the pictures are being introduced is to prejudice and inflame the minds of the jurors." Judge Tate overruled the objection and allowed the photographs into evidence, which meant they must be shown to the jury.

While this was being done, Hickock's father, addressing a journalist seated near him, said, "The judge up there! I never seen a man so prejudiced. Just no sense having a trial. Not with him in charge. Why, that man was a pallbearer at the funeral!" (Actually, Tate was but slightly acquainted with the victims, and was not present at their funeral in any capacity.) But Mr. Hickock's was the only voice raised in an exceedingly silent courtroom. Altogether, there were seventeen prints, and as they were passed from hand to hand, the jurors' expressions reflected the impact the pictures made: one man's cheeks reddened, as if he had been slapped, and a few, after the first distressing glance, obviously had no heart for the task; it was as though the photographs had prised open their mind's eye, and forced them to at last really *see* the true and pitiful thing that had happened to a neighbor and his wife and children. It amazed them, it made them angry, and several of them—the pharmacist, the manager of the bowling alley—stared at the defendants with total contempt.

The elder Mr. Hickock, wearily wagging his head, again and again murmured, "No sense. Just no sense having a trial."

As the day's final witness, the prosecution had promised to produce a "mystery man." It was the man who had supplied the information that led to the arrest of the accused: Floyd Wells, Hickock's former cellmate. Because he was still serving a sentence at Kansas State Penitentiary, and therefore was in danger of retaliation from other inmates, Wells had never been publicly identified as the informer. Now, in order that he might safely testify at the trial, he had been removed from the prison and lodged in a small jail in an adjacent county. Nevertheless, Wells' passage across the courtroom toward the witness stand was oddly stealthy—as though he expected to encounter an assassin along the way—and, as he walked past Hickock, Hickock's lips writhed as he whispered a few atrocious words. Wells pretended not to notice; but like a horse that has heard the hum of a rattlesnake, he shied away from the betrayed man's venomous vicinity. Taking the stand, he stared straight ahead, a somewhat chinless little farmboyish fellow wearing a very decent dark-blue suit which the State of Kansas had bought for the occasion—the state being concerned that its most important witness should look respectable, and consequently trustworthy.

Wells' testimony, perfected by pre-trial rehearsal, was as tidy as his appearance. Encouraged by the sympathetic promptings of Logan Green, the witness acknowledged that he had once, for approximately a year, worked as a hired hand at River Valley Farm; he went on to say that some ten years later, following his conviction on a burglary charge, he had become friendly with another imprisoned burglar, Richard Hickock, and had described to him the Clutter farm and family.

"Now," Green asked, "during your conversations with Mr. Hickock what was said about Mr. Clutter by either of you?"

"Well, we talked quite a bit about Mr. Clutter. Hickock said he was about to be paroled, and he was going to go West looking for a job; he might stop to see Mr. Clutter to get a job. I was telling him how wealthy Mr. Clutter was."

"Did that seem to interest Mr. Hickock?"

"Well, he wanted to know if Mr. Clutter had a safe around there."

"Mr. Wells, did you think at the time there was a safe in the Clutter house?"

"Well, it has been so long since I worked out there. I thought there was a safe. I knew there was a cabinet of some kind. . . . The next thing I knew he [Hickock] was talking about robbing Mr. Clutter."

"Did he tell you anything about how he was going to commit the robbery?"

"He told me if he done anything like that he wouldn't leave no witnesses."

"Did he actually say what he was going to do with the witnesses?"

"Yes. He told me he would probably tie them up and then rob them and then kill them."

Having established premeditation of great degree, Green left the witness to the ministrations of the defense. Old Mr. Fleming, a classic country lawyer more happily at home with land deeds than ill deeds, opened the cross-examination. The intent of his queries, as he soon established, was to introduce a subject the prosecution had emphatically avoided: the question of Wells' own role in the murder plot, and his own moral liability.

"You didn't," Fleming said, hastening to the heart of the matter, "say anything at all to Mr. Hickock to discourage him from coming out here to rob and kill the Clutter family?"

"No. Anybody tells you anything about that up there [Kansas State Penitentiary], you don't pay any attention to it because you think they are just talking anyway."

"You mean you talked that way and didn't *mean* anything? Didn't you mean to convey to him [Hickock] the idea that Mr. Clutter had a safe? You wanted Mr. Hickock to believe that, did you not?"

In his quiet way, Fleming was giving the witness a rough time; Wells plucked at his tie, as though the knot was suddenly too tight.

"And you meant for Mr. Hickock to believe that Mr. Clutter had a lot of money, didn't you?"

"I told him Mr. Clutter had a lot of money, yes."

Fleming once more elicited an account of how Hickock had fully informed Wells of his violent plans for the Clutter family. Then, as though veiled in a private grief, the lawyer wistfully said, "And even after all of that you did nothing to discourage him?"

"I didn't believe he'd do it."

"You didn't believe him. Then why, when you heard about the thing that happened out here, why did you think he was the one that was guilty?"

Wells cockily replied, "Because it was done just like he said he was going to do!"

Harrison Smith, the younger half of the defense team, took charge. Assuming an aggressive, sneering manner that seemed forced, for really he is a mild and lenient man, Smith asked the witness if he had a nickname.

"No. I just go by 'Floyd.'"

The lawyer snorted. "Don't they call you 'Squealer' now? Or do they call you 'Snitch'?"

"I just go by 'Floyd,'" Wells repeated, rather hangdog.

"How many times have you been in jail?"

"About three times."

"Some of those times for lying, were they?"

Denying it, the witness said that once he'd gone to jail for driving without an operator's license, that burglary was the reason for his second incarceration, and the third, a ninety-day hitch in an Army stockade, had been the outcome of something that happened while he was a soldier: "We was on a train trip guard. We got a little intoxicated on the train, done a little extra shooting at some windows and lights."

Everyone laughed; everyone except the defendants (Hickock spat on the floor) and Harrison Smith, who now asked Wells why, after learning of the Holcomb tragedy, he had tarried several weeks before telling the authorities what he knew. "Weren't you," he said, "waiting for something to come out? Maybe like a reward?"

"No."

"You didn't hear anything about a reward?" The lawyer was referring to the reward of one thousand dollars that had been offered by the Hutchinson *News*, for information resulting in the arrest and conviction of the Clutter murderers.

"I seen it in the paper."

"That was before you went to the authorities, wasn't it?" And when the witness admitted that this was true, Smith triumphantly continued by asking, "What kind of immunity did the county attorney offer you for coming up here today and testifying?"

But Logan Green protested: "We object to the form of the question, Your Honor. There's been no testimony about immunity to anybody." The objection was sustained, and the witness dismissed; as he left the stand, Hickock announced to everyone within earshot, "Sonofabitch. Anybody ought to hang, he ought to hang. Look at him. Gonna walk out of here and get that money and go scot-free."

This prediction proved correct, for not long afterward Wells collected both the reward and a parole. But his good fortune was short-lived. He was soon in trouble again, and, over the years, has experienced many vicissitudes. At present he is a resident of the Mississippi State Prison in Parchman, Mississippi, where he is serving a thirty-year sentence for armed robbery.

By Friday, when the court recessed for the weekend, the state had completed its case, which included the appearance of four Special Agents of the Federal Bureau of Investigation in Washington, D.C. These men, laboratory technicians skilled in various categories of scientific crime detection, had studied the physical evidence connecting the accused to the murders (blood samples, footprints, cartridge shells, rope and tape), and each of them certified the validity of the exhibits. Finally, the four K.B.I. agents provided accounts of interviews with the prisoners, and of the confessions eventually made by them. In cross-examining the K.B.I. personnel, the defense attorneys, a beleaguered pair, argued that the admissions of guilt had been obtained by improper means—brutal interrogation in sweltering, brightly lighted, closet-like rooms. The allegation, which was untrue, irritated the detectives into expounding very convincing denials. (Later, in reply to a reporter who asked him why he had dogged this artificial scent at such length, Hickock's lawyer snapped, "What am I supposed to do? Hell, I'm playing without any cards. But I can't just sit here like a dummy. I've got to sound off once in a while").

The prosecution's most damaging witness proved to be Alvin Dewey; his testimony, the first public rendering of the events detailed in Perry Smith's confession, earned large headlines (UNVEIL MUTE MURDER HORROR—Cold, Chilling Facts Told), and shocked his listeners—none more so than Richard Hickock, who came to a startled and chagrined attention when, in the course of Dewey's commentary, the agent said, "There is one incident Smith related to me that I haven't as yet mentioned. And that was that after the Clutter family was tied up, Hickock said to him how well built he thought Nancy Clutter was, and that he was going to rape her. Smith said he told Hickock there wasn't going to be anything like that go on. Smith told me he had no respect for anyone who couldn't control their sexual desires, and that he would have fought Hickock before allowing him to rape the Clutter girl." Heretofore, Hickock had not known that his partner had informed police of the proposed assault; nor was he aware that, in a friendlier spirit, Perry had altered his original story to claim that he alone had shot the four victims—a fact revealed by Dewey as he neared the end of his testimony: "Perry Smith told me he wished to change two things in the statement he had given us. He said everything else in that statement was true and correct. Except these two things. And that was that he wanted to say he killed Mrs. Clutter and Nancy Clutter—not Hickock. He told me that Hickock . . . didn't want to die with his mother thinking he had killed any members of the Clutter family. And he said the Hickocks were good people. So why not have it that way."

Hearing this, Mrs. Hickock wept. Throughout the trial she had sat quietly beside her husband, her hands worrying a rumpled handkerchief. As often as she could she caught her son's eye, nodded at him and simulated a smile which, though flimsily constructed, affirmed her loyalty. But clearly the woman's control was exhausted; she began to cry. A few spectators glanced at her, and glanced away, embarrassed; the rest seemed oblivious of the raw dirge counterpointing Dewey's continuing recitation; even her husband, perhaps because he believed it unmanly to take notice, remained aloof. At last a woman reporter, the only one present, led Mrs. Hickock out of the courtroom and into the privacy of a ladies' room.

Once her anguish had subsided, Mrs. Hickock expressed a need to confide. "There's nobody much I can talk to," she told her companion. "I don't mean people haven't been kind, neighbors and all. And strangers, too—strangers have wrote letters to say they know how hard it must be and how sorry they are. Nobody's said a mean word, either to Walter or me. Not even here, where you might expect it. Everybody here has gone out of their way to be friendly. The waitress over at the place where we take our meals, she puts ice cream on the pie and don't charge for it. I tell her don't, I can't eat it. Used to be I could eat anything didn't eat me first. But she puts it on. To be nice. Sheila, that's her, she says it's not our fault what happened. But it seems to me like people are looking at me and thinking, Well, she must be to blame somehow. The way I raised Dick. Maybe I did do something wrong. Only I don't know what it could have been; I get headaches trying to remember. We're plain people, just country people, getting along the same as everybody else. We had some good times at our house. I taught Dick the foxtrot. Dancing, I was always crazy about it, it was my whole life when I was a girl; and there was a boy, gosh, he could dance like Christmas—we won a silver cup waltzing together. For a long time we planned to run away and go on the stage. Vaudeville. It was just a dream. Children dreaming. He left town, and one day I married Walter, and Walter Hickock couldn't do step one. He said if I wanted a hoofer I should've married a horse. Nobody ever danced with me again until I learned Dick, and he didn't take to it exactly, but he was sweet, Dick was the best-natured little kid."

Mrs. Hickock removed the spectacles she was wearing, polished the smeared lenses and resettled them on her pudgy, agreeable face. "There's lots more to Dick than what you hear back there in the courtroom. The lawyers jabbering how terrible he is—no good at all. I can't make any excuses for what he did, his part in it. I'm not forgetting that family; I pray for them every night. But I pray for Dick, too. And this boy Perry. It was wrong of me to hate him; I've got nothing but pity for him now. And you know—I believe Mrs. Clutter would feel pity, too. Being the kind of woman they say she was."

Court had adjourned; the noises of the departing audience clattered in the corridor beyond the lavatory door. Mrs. Hickock said she must go and meet her husband. "He's dying. I don't think he minds any more."

Many observers of the trial scene were baffled by the visitor from Boston, Donald Cullivan. They could not quite understand why this staid young Catholic, a successful engineer who had taken his degree at Harvard, a husband and the father of three children, should choose to befriend an uneducated, homicidal half-breed whom he knew but slightly and had not seen for nine years. Cullivan himself said, "My wife doesn't understand it either. Coming out here was something I couldn't afford to do—it meant using a week of my vacation, and money we really need for other things. On the other hand, it was something I couldn't afford not to do. Perry's lawyer wrote me asking if I would be a character witness; the moment I read the letter I knew I had to do it. Because I'd offered this man my friendship. And because —well, I believe in the life everlasting. All souls can be saved for God."

The salvation of a soul, namely Perry Smith's, was an enterprise the deeply Catholic undersheriff and his wife were eager to assist—although Mrs. Meier had been rebuffed by Perry when she had suggested a consultation with Father Goubeaux, a local priest. (Perry said, "Priests and nuns have had their chance with me. I'm still wearing the scars to prove it.") And so, during the weekend recess, the Meiers invited Cullivan to eat Sunday dinner with the prisoner in his cell.

The opportunity to entertain his friend, play host as it were, delighted Perry, and the planning of the menu—wild goose, stuffed and roasted, with gravy and creamed potatoes and string beans, aspic salad, hot biscuits, cold milk, freshly baked cherry tarts, cheese, and coffee—seemed to concern him more than the outcome of the trial (which, to be sure, he did not consider a suspenseful matter: "Those prairiebillys, they'll vote to hang fast as pigs eat slop. Look at their eyes. I'll be damned if I'm the only killer in the courtroom"). All Sunday morning he prepared to receive his guest. The day was warm, a little windy, and leaf shadows, supple emanations from the tree boughs that brushed the cell's barred window, tantalized Perry's tamed squirrel. Big Red chased the swaying patterns while his master swept and dusted, scrubbed the floor and scoured the toilet and cleared the desk of literary accumulations. The desk was to be the dining table, and once Perry had finished setting it, it looked most inviting, for Mrs. Meier had donated a linen tablecloth, starched napkins, and her best china and silver.

Cullivan was impressed—he whistled when the feast, arriving on trays, was placed upon the table—and before sitting down, he asked the host if he might offer a blessing. The host, head unbowed, cracked his knuckles as Cullivan, with bowed head and palms together, intoned, "Bless us, O Lord, and these thy gifts which we are about to receive from thy bounty, through the mercy of Christ, our Lord. Amen." Perry murmuringly remarked that in his opinion any credit due belonged to Mrs. Meier. "She did all the work. Well," he said, heaping his guest's plate, "it's good to see you, Don. You look just the same. Haven't changed a bit."

Cullivan, in appearance a cautious bank clerk with depleted hair and a face rather difficult to recall, agreed that outwardly he hadn't changed much. But his interior self, the invisible man, was another matter: "I was coasting along. Not knowing God is the only reality. Once you realize that, then everything falls into place. Life has meaning—and so does death. Boy, do you always eat like this?"

Perry laughed. "She's really a terrific cook, Mrs. Meier. You ought to taste her Spanish rice. I've gained fifteen pounds since I got here. Course I was on the thin side. I'd lost a lot of weight while Dick and me were out on the road riding all to hell and gone—hardly ever eating a square meal, hungry as hell most of the time. Mostly, we lived like animals. Dick was always stealing canned stuff out of grocery stores. Baked beans and canned spaghetti. We'd open it up in the car and gobble it cold. Animals. Dick loves to steal. It's an emotional thing with him—a sickness. I'm a thief too, but only if I don't have the money to pay. Dick, if he was carrying a hundred dollars in his pocket, he'd steal a stick of chewing gum."

Later, over cigarettes and coffee, Perry returned to the subject of thievery. "My friend Willie-Jay used to talk about it. He used to say that all crimes were only 'varieties of theft.' Murder included. When you kill a man you steal his life. I guess that makes me a pretty big thief. See, Don—I did kill them. Down there in court, old Dewey made it sound like I was prevaricating—on account of Dick's mother. Well, I wasn't. Dick helped me, he held the flashlight and picked up the shells. And it was his idea, too. But Dick didn't shoot them, he never could've—though he's damn quick when it comes to running down an old dog. I wonder why I did it." He scowled, as though the problem was new to him, a newly unearthed stone of surprising, unclassified color. "I don't know why," he said, as if holding it to the light, and angling it now here, now there. "I was sore at Dick. The tough brass boy. But it wasn't Dick. Or the fear of being identified. I was willing to take that gamble. And it wasn't because of anything the Clutters did. They never hurt me. Like other people. Like people have all my life. Maybe it's just that the Clutters were the ones who had to pay for it."

Cullivan probed, trying to gauge the depth of what he assumed would be Perry's contrition. Surely he must be experiencing a remorse sufficiently profound to summon a desire for God's mercy and forgiveness? Perry said, "Am I sorry? If that's what you mean—I'm not. I don't feel anything about it. I wish I did. But nothing about it bothers me a bit. Half an hour after it happened, Dick was making jokes and I was laughing at them. Maybe we're not human. I'm human enough to feel sorry for myself. Sorry I can't walk out of here when you walk out. But that's all." Cullivan could scarcely credit so detached an attitude; Perry was confused, mistaken, it was not possible for any man to be that devoid of conscience or compassion. Perry said, "Why? Soldiers don't lose much sleep. They murder, and get medals for doing it. The good people of Kansas want to murder me—and some hangman will be glad to get the work. It's easy to kill—a lot easier than passing a bad check. Just remember: I only knew the Clutters maybe an hour. If I'd really known them, I guess I'd feel different. I don't think I could live with myself. But the way it was, it was like picking off targets in a shooting gallery."

Cullivan was silent, and his silence upset Perry, who seemed to interpret it as implying disapproval. "Hell, Don, don't make me act the hypocrite with *you*. Throw a load of bull—how sorry I am, how all I want to do now is crawl on my knees and pray. That stuff don't ring with me. I can't accept overnight what I've always denied. The truth is, you've done more for me than any what you call God ever has. Or ever will. By writing to me, by signing yourself 'friend.' When I had no friends. Except Joe James." Joe James, he explained to Cullivan, was a young Indian logger with whom he had once lived in a forest near Bellingham, Washington. "That's a long way from Garden City. A good two thousand miles. I sent word to Joe about the trouble I'm in. Joe's a poor guy, he's got seven kids to feed, but he promised to come here if he had to walk. He hasn't shown up yet, and maybe he won't, only I think he will. Joe always liked me. Do you, Don?"

"Yes. I like you."

Cullivan's softly emphatic answer pleased and rather flustered Perry. He smiled and said, "Then you must be some kind of nut." Suddenly rising, he crossed the cell and picked up a broom. "I don't know why I should die among strangers. Let a bunch of prairiebillys stand around and watch me strangle. Shit. I ought to kill myself first." He lifted the broom and pressed the bristles against the light bulb that burned in the ceiling. "Just unscrew the bulb and smash it and cut my wrists.

That's what I ought to do. While you're still here. Somebody who cares about me a little bit."

The trial resumed on Monday morning at ten o'clock. Ninety minutes later the court adjourned, the case for the defense having been completed in that brief time. The defendants declined to testify in their own behalf, and therefore the question of whether Hickock or Smith had been the actual executioner of the Clutter family did not arise.

Of the five witnesses who did appear, the first was the hollow-eyed Mr. Hickock. Though he spoke with a dignified and mournful clarity, he had but one contribution to make that was relevant to a claim of temporary insanity. His son, he said, had suffered head injuries in a car accident in July, 1950. Prior to the accident, Dick had been a "happy-go-lucky boy," had done well in school, been popular with his classmates and considerate of his parents—"No trouble to anybody."

Harrison Smith, gently guiding the witness, said, "I will ask you if, after July, 1950, you observed any change in the personality and habits and actions of your son, Richard?"

"He just didn't act like the same boy."

"What were the changes you observed?"

Mr. Hickock, between pensive hesitations, listed several: Dick was sulky and restless, he ran around with older men, drank and gambled. "He just wasn't the same boy."

The last assertion was promptly challenged by Logan Green, who undertook the cross-examination. "Mr. Hickock, you say you never had any trouble with your son until *after* 1950?"

". . . I think he got arrested in 1949."

A citric smile bent Green's tiny lips. "Remember what he was arrested for?"

"He was accused of breaking into a drugstore."

"Accused? Didn't he admit that he broke into the store?"

"That's right, he did."

"And that was in 1949. Yet now you tell us your son had a change in his attitude and conduct after 1950?"

"I would say so, yes."

"You mean that after 1950 he became a *good* boy?"

Hard coughs agitated the old man; he spat into a handkerchief. "No," he said, studying the discharge. "I wouldn't say that."

"Then what was the change that took place?"

"Well, that would be pretty hard to explain. He just didn't act like the same boy."

"You mean he *lost* his criminal tendencies?"

The lawyer's sally induced guffaws, a courtroom flare-up that Judge Tate's dour gaze soon extinguished. Mr. Hickock, presently set free, was replaced on the stand by Dr. W. Mitchell Jones.

Dr. Jones identified himself to the court as a "physician specializing in the field of psychiatry," and in support of his qualifications, added that he had attended perhaps fifteen hundred patients since 1956, the year he had entered a psychiatric residency at Topeka State Hospital in Topeka, Kansas. For the past two years he had served on the staff of Larned State Hospital, where he was in charge of the Dillon Building, a section reserved for the criminally insane.

Harrison Smith asked the witness, "Approximately how many murderers have you dealt with?"

"About twenty-five."

"Doctor, I would like to ask you if you know my client, Richard Eugene Hickock?"

"I do."

"Have you had occasion to examine him professionally?"

"Yes, sir . . . I made a psychiatric evaluation of Mr. Hickock."

"Based upon your examination, do you have an opinion as to whether or not Richard Eugene Hickock knew right from wrong at the time of the commission of the crime?"

The witness, a stout man of twenty-eight with a moon-shaped but intelligent, subtly delicate face, took a deep breath, as though to equip himself for a prolonged reply—which the judge then cautioned him he must not make: "You may answer the question yes or no, Doctor. Limit your answer to yes or no."

"Yes."

"And what is your opinion?"

"I think that within the usual definitions Mr. Hickock did know right from wrong."

Confined as he was by the M'Naghten Rule ("the usual definitions"), a formula quite color-blind to any gradations between black and white, Dr. Jones was impotent to answer otherwise. But of course the response was a letdown for Hickock's attorney, who hopelessly asked, "Can you qualify that answer?"

It was hopeless because though Dr. Jones agreed to elaborate, the prosecution was entitled to object—and did, citing the fact that Kansas law allowed nothing more than a yes or no reply to the pertinent question. The objection was upheld, and the witness dismissed. However, had Dr. Jones been allowed to speak further, here is what he would have testified: "Richard Hickock is above average in intelligence, grasps new ideas easily and has a wide fund of information. He is alert to what is happening around him, and he shows no sign of mental confusion or disorientation. His thinking is well organized and logical and he seems to be in good contact with reality. Although I did not find the usual signs of organic brain damage—memory loss, concrete concept formation, intellectual deterioration—this cannot be completely ruled out. He had a serious head injury with concussion and several hours of unconsciousness in 1950—this was verified by me by checking hospital records. He says he has had blackout spells, periods of amnesia, and headaches ever since that time, and a major portion of his antisocial behavior has occurred since that time. He has never had the medical tests which would definitely prove or disprove the existence of residual brain damage. Definitive medical tests are indicated before a complete evaluation can be said to exist. . . . Hickock does show signs of emotional abnormality. That he knew what he was doing and still went ahead with it is possibly the most clear-cut demonstration of this fact. He is a person who is impulsive in action, likely to do things without thought of consequences or future discomfort to himself or to others. He does not seem to be capable of learning from experience, and he shows an unusual pattern of intermittent periods of productive activity followed by patently irresponsible actions. He cannot tolerate feelings of frustration as a more normal person can, and he is poorly able to rid himself of those feelings except through antisocial activity. . . . His self-esteem is very low, and he secretly feels inferior to others and sexually inadequate. These feelings seem to be overcompensated for by dreams of being rich and powerful, a tendency to brag about his exploits, spending sprees when he has money, and dissatisfaction with only the normal slow advancement he could expect from his job. . . . He is uncomfortable in his relationships to other people, and has a pathological inability to form and hold enduring personal attachments. Although he professes usual moral standards he seems obviously uninfluenced by them in his actions. In summary, he shows fairly typical characteristics of what would psychiatrically be called a severe character disorder. It is important that steps be taken to rule out the possibility of organic brain damage, since, if present, it might have substantially influenced his behavior during the past several years and at the time of the crime."

Aside from a formal plea to the jury, which would not take place until the morrow, the psychiatrist's testimony terminated Hickock's planned defense. Next it was the turn of Arthur Fleming, Smith's elderly counselor. He presented four witnesses: the Reverend James E. Post, the Protestant chaplain at Kansas State Penitentiary; Perry's

Indian friend, Joe James, who after all had arrived by bus that morning, having traveled a day and two nights from his wilderness home in the Far Northwest; Donald Cullivan; and, once again, Dr. Jones. Except for the latter, these men were offered as "character witnesses" —persons expected to attribute to the accused a few human virtues. They did not fare very well, though each of them negotiated some skimpily favorable remark before the protesting prosecution, which contended that personal comments of this nature were "incompetent, irrelevant, immaterial," hushed and banished them.

For example, Joe James, dark-haired, even darker-skinned than Perry, a lithe figure who with his faded huntsman's shirt and moccasined feet looked as though he had that instant mysteriously emerged from woodland shadows, told the court that the defendant had lived with him off and on for over two years. "Perry was a likable kid, well liked around the neighborhood—he never done one thing out of the way to my knowledge." The state stopped him there; and stopped Cullivan, too, when he said, "During the time I knew him in the Army, Perry was a very likable fellow."

The Reverend Post survived somewhat longer, for he made no direct attempt to compliment the prisoner, but described sympathetically an encounter with him at Lansing. "I first met Perry Smith when he came to my office in the prison chapel with a picture he had painted—a head-and-shoulders portrait of Jesus Christ done in pastel crayon. He wanted to give it to me for use in the chapel. It's been hanging on the walls of my office ever since."

Fleming said, "Do you have a photograph of that painting?" The minister had an envelope full; but when he produced them, ostensibly for distribution among the jurors, an exasperated Logan Green leaped to his feet: "If Your Honor please, this is going too *far* . . ." His Honor saw that it went no further.

Dr. Jones was now recalled, and following the preliminaries that had accompanied his original appearance, Fleming put to him the crucial query: "From your conversations and examination of Perry Edward Smith, do you have an opinion as to whether he knew right from wrong at the time of the offense involved in this action?" And once more the court admonished the witness: "Answer yes or no, do you have an opinion?"

"No."

Amid surprised mutters, Fleming, surprised himself, said, "You may state to the jury why you have no opinion."

Green objected: "The man has no opinion, and that's *it.*" Which it was, legally speaking.

But had Dr. Jones been permitted to discourse on the cause of his indecision, he would have testified: "Perry Smith shows definite signs of severe mental illness. His childhood, related to me and verified by portions of the prison records, was marked by brutality and lack of concern on the part of both parents. He seems to have grown up without direction, without love, and without ever having absorbed any fixed sense of moral values. . . . He is oriented, hyperalert to things going on about him, and shows no sign of confusion. He is above average in intelligence, and has a good range of information considering his poor educational background. . . . Two features in his personality make-up stand out as particularly pathological. The first is his 'paranoid' orientation toward the world. He is suspicious and distrustful of others, tends to feel that others discriminate against him, and feels that others are unfair to him and do not understand him. He is overly sensitive to criticisms that others make of him, and cannot tolerate being made fun of. He is quick to sense slight or insult in things others say, and frequently may misinterpret well-meant communications. He feels he has great need of friendship and understanding, but he is reluctant to confide in others, and when he does, expects to be misunderstood or even betrayed. In evaluating the intentions and feelings of others, his ability to separate the real situation from his own mental projections is very poor. He not infrequently groups all people together as being hypocritical, hostile, and deserving of whatever he is able to do to them. Akin to this first trait is the second, an ever present, poorly controlled rage—easily triggered by any feeling of being tricked, slighted, or labeled inferior by others. For the most part, his rages in the past have been directed at authority figures—father, brother, Army sergeant, state parole officer—and have led to violent assaultive behavior on several occasions. Both he and his acquaintances have been aware of these rages, which he says 'mount up' in him, and of the poor control he has over them. When turned toward himself his anger has precipitated ideas of suicide. The inappropriate force of his anger and lack of ability to control or channel it reflect a primary weakness of personality structure. . . . In addition to these traits, the subject shows mild early signs of a disorder of his thought processes. He has poor ability to organize his thinking, he seems unable to scan or summarize his thought, becoming involved and sometimes lost in detail, and some of his thinking reflects a 'magical' quality, a disregard of reality. . . . He has had few close emotional relationships with other people, and these have not been able to stand small crises. He has little feeling for others outside a very small circle of friends, and attaches little real value to human life. This emotional detachment and blandness in certain areas is other evidence of his mental abnormality. More extensive evaluation would be necessary to make an exact psychiatric diagnosis, but his present personality structure is very nearly that of a paranoid schizophrenic reaction."

It is significant that a widely respected veteran in the field of forensic psychiatry, Dr. Joseph Satten of the Menninger Clinic in Topeka, Kansas, consulted with Dr. Jones and endorsed his evaluations of Hickock and Smith. Dr. Satten, who afterward gave the case close attention, suggests that though the crime would not have occurred except for a certain frictional interplay between the perpetrators, it was essentially the act of Perry Smith, who, he feels, represents a type of murderer described by him in an article: "Murder Without Apparent Motive—A Study in Personality Disorganization."

The article, printed in *The American Journal of Psychiatry* (July, 1960), and written in collaboration with three colleagues, Karl Menninger, Irwin Rosen, and Martin Mayman, states its aim at the outset: "In attempting to assess the criminal responsibility of murderers, the law tries to divide them (as it does all offenders) into two groups, the 'sane' and the 'insane.' The 'sane' murderer is thought of as acting upon rational motives that can be understood, though condemned, and the 'insane' one as being driven by irrational senseless motives. When rational motives are conspicuous (for example, when a man kills for personal gain) or when the irrational motives are accompanied by delusions or hallucinations (for example, a paranoid patient who kills his fantasied persecutor), the situation presents little problem to the psychiatrist. But murderers who seem rational, coherent, and controlled, and yet whose homicidal acts have a bizarre, apparently senseless quality, pose a difficult problem, if courtroom disagreements and contradictory reports about the same offender are an index. It is our thesis that the psychopathology of such murderers forms at least one specific syndrome which we shall describe. In general, these individuals are predisposed to severe lapses in ego-control which makes possible the open expression of primitive violence, born out of previous, and now unconscious, traumatic experiences."

The authors, as part of an appeals process, had examined four men convicted of seemingly unmotivated murders. All had been examined prior to their trials, and found to be "without psychosis" and "sane." Three of the men were under death sentence, and the fourth was serving a long prison sentence. In each of these cases, further psychiatric investigation had been requested because someone—either the lawyer, a relative, or a friend—was dissatisfied with the psychiatric explanations previously given, and in effect had asked, "How can a person as sane as this man seems to be commit an act as crazy as the one he was convicted of?" After describing the four criminals and their crimes (a Negro soldier who mutilated and dismembered a prostitute, a laborer who strangled a fourteen-year-old boy when the boy rejected his sexual advances, an Army corporal who bludgeoned to death another young boy because he imagined the victim was making fun of him, and a hospital employee who drowned a girl of nine by holding her head under water), the authors surveyed the areas of similarity. The men themselves, they wrote, were puzzled as to why they killed their victims, who were relatively unknown to them, and in each instance the murderer appears to have lapsed into a dreamlike dissociative trance from which he awakened to "suddenly discover" himself assaulting his victim. "The most uniform, and perhaps the most significant, historical finding was a long-standing, sometimes lifelong, history of erratic control over aggressive impulses. For example, three of the men, throughout their lives, had been frequently involved in fights which were not ordinary altercations, and which would have become homicidal assaults if not stopped by others."

Here, in excerpt, are a number of other observations contained in the study: "Despite the violence in their lives, all of the men had ego-images of themselves as physically inferior, weak, and inadequate. The histories revealed in each a severe degree of sexual inhibition. To all of them, adult women were threatening creatures, and in two cases there was overt sexual perversion. All of them, too, had been concerned throughout their early years about being considered 'sissies,' physically undersized or sickly. . . . In all four cases, there was historical evidence of altered states of consciousness, frequently in connection with the outbursts of violence. Two of the men reported severe dissociative trancelike states during which violent and bizarre behavior was seen, while the other two reported less severe, and perhaps less well-organized, amnesiac episodes. During moments of actual violence, they often felt separated or isolated from themselves, as if they were watching someone else. . . . Also seen in the historical background of all the cases was the occurrence of extreme parental violence during childhood. . . . One man said he was 'whipped every time I turned around.' . . . Another of the men had many violent beatings in order to 'break' him of his stammering and 'fits,' as well as to correct him for his allegedly 'bad' behavior. . . . The history relating to *extreme* violence, whether fantasied, observed in reality, or actually experienced by the child, fits in with the psychoanalytic hypothesis that the child's exposure to overwhelming stimuli, before he can master them, is closely linked to early defects in ego formation and later severe disturbances in impulse control. In all of these cases, there was evidence of severe emotional deprivation in early life. This deprivation may have involved prolonged or recurrent absence of one or both parents, a chaotic family life in which the parents were unknown, or an outright rejection of the child by one or both parents with the child being raised by others. . . . Evidence of disturbances in affect organization was seen. Most typically the men displayed a tendency not to experience anger or rage in association with violent aggressive action. None reported feelings of rage in connection with the murders, nor did they experience anger in any strong or pronounced way, although each of them was capable of enormous and brutal aggression. . . . Their relationships with others were of a shallow, cold nature, lending a quality of loneliness and isolation to these men. People were scarcely real to them, in the sense of being warmly or positively (or even angrily) felt about. . . . The three men under sentence of death had shallow emotions regarding their own fate and that of their victims. Guilt, depression, and remorse were strikingly absent. . . . Such individuals can be considered to be murder-prone in the sense of either carrying a surcharge of aggressive energy or having an unstable ego defense system that periodically allows the naked and archaic expression of such energy. The murderous potential can become activated, especially if some disequilibrium is already present, when the victim-to-be is unconsciously perceived as a key figure in some past traumatic configuration. The behavior, or even the mere presence, of this figure adds a stress to the unstable balance of forces that results in a sudden extreme discharge of violence, similar to the explosion that takes place when a percussion cap ignites a charge of dynamite. . . . The hypothesis of unconscious motivation explains why the murderers perceived innocuous and relatively unknown victims as provocative and thereby suitable targets for aggression. But why murder? Most people, fortunately, do not respond with murderous outbursts even under extreme provocation. The cases described, on the other hand, were predisposed to gross lapses in reality contact and extreme weakness in impulse control during periods of heightened tension and disorganization. At such times, a chance acquaintance or even a stranger was easily able to lose his 'real' meaning and assume an identity in the unconscious traumatic configuration. The 'old' conflict was reactivated and aggression swiftly mounted to murderous proportions. . . . When such senseless murders occur, they are seen to be an end result of a period of increasing tension and disorganization in the murderer starting before the contact with the victim who, by fitting into the unconscious conflicts of the murderer, unwittingly serves to set into motion his homicidal potential."

Because of the many parallels between the background and personality of Perry Smith and the subjects of his study, Dr. Satten feels secure in assigning him to a position among their ranks. Moreover, the circumstances of the crime seem to him to fit exactly the concept of "murder without apparent motive." Obviously, three of the murders Smith committed *were* logically motivated—Nancy, Kenyon, and their mother had to be killed because Mr. Clutter had been killed. But it is Dr. Satten's contention that only the first murder matters psychologically, and that when Smith attacked Mr. Clutter he was under a mental eclipse, deep inside a schizophrenic darkness, for it was not entirely a flesh-and-blood man he "suddenly discovered" himself destroying, but "a key figure in some past traumatic configuration": his father? the orphanage nuns who had derided and beaten him? the hated Army sergeant? the parole officer who had ordered him to "stay out of Kansas"? One of them, or all of them.

In his confession, Smith said, "I didn't want to harm the man. I thought he was a very nice gentleman. Soft-spoken. I thought so right up to the moment I cut his throat." While talking to Donald Cullivan, Smith said, "They [the Clutters] never hurt me. Like other people. Like people have all my life. Maybe it's just that the Clutters were the ones who had to pay for it."

So it would appear that by independent paths, both the professional and the amateur analyst reached conclusions not dissimilar.

The aristocracy of Finney County had snubbed the trial. "It doesn't do," announced the wife of one rich rancher, "to seem curious about that sort of thing." Nevertheless, the trial's last session found a fair segment of the local Establishment seated alongside the plainer citizenry. Their presence was a courteous gesture toward Judge Tate and Logan Green, esteemed members of their own order. Also, a large contingent of out-of-town lawyers, many of whom had journeyed great distances, filled several benches; specifically, they were on hand to hear Green's final address to the jury. Green, a suavely tough little septuagenarian, has an imposing reputation among his peers, who admire his stagecraft—a repertoire of actorish gifts that includes a sense of timing acute as a night-club comedian's. An expert criminal lawyer, his usual role is that of defender, but in this instance the state had retained him as a special assistant to Duane West, for it was felt that the young county attorney was too unseasoned to prosecute the case without experienced support.

But like most star turns, Green was the last act on the program. Judge Tate's level-headed instructions to the jury preceded him, as did the county attorney's summation: "Can there be a single doubt in your minds regarding the guilt of these defendants? No! Regardless of who pulled the trigger on Richard Eugene Hickock's shotgun, both men are equally guilty. There is only one way to assure that these men will never again roam the towns and cities of this land. We request the maximum penalty—death. This request is made not in vengeance, but in all humbleness. . . ."

Then the pleas of the defense attorneys had to be heard. Fleming's speech, described by one journalist as "soft-sell," amounted to a mild churchly sermon: "Man is not an animal. He has a body, and he has a soul that lives forever. I don't believe man has the right to destroy that house, a temple, in which the soul dwells. . . ." Harrison Smith, though he too appealed to the jurors' presumed Christianity, took as his main theme the evils of capital punishment: "It is a relic of human barbarism. The law tells us that the taking of human life is wrong, then goes ahead and sets the example. Which is almost as wicked as the crime it punished. The state has no right to inflict it. It isn't effective. It doesn't deter crime, but merely cheapens human life and gives rise to more murders. All we ask is mercy. Surely life imprisonment is small mercy to ask. . . ." Not everyone was attentive; one juror, as though poisoned by the numerous spring-fever yawns weighting the air, sat with drugged eyes and jaws so utterly ajar bees could have buzzed in and out.

Green woke them up. "Gentlemen," he said, speaking without notes, "you have just heard two energetic pleas for mercy in behalf of the defendants. It seems to me fortunate that these admirable attorneys, Mr. Fleming and Mr. Smith, were not at the Clutter house that fateful night—very fortunate for them that they were not present to plead mercy for the doomed family. Because had they been there—well, come next morning we would have had more than four corpses to count."

As a boy in his native Kentucky, Green was called Pinky, a nickname he owed to his freckled coloring; now, as he strutted before the jury, the stress of his assignment warmed his face and splotched it with patches of pink. "I have no intention of engaging in theological debate. But I anticipated that defense counsel would use the Holy Bible as an argument against the death penalty. You have heard the Bible quoted. But *I* can read, too." He slapped open a copy of the Old Testament. "And here are a few things the Good Book has to say on the subject. In Exodus Twenty, Verse Thirteen, we have one of the

Ten Commandments: 'Thou shalt not kill.' This refers to *unlawful* killing. Of course it does, because in the *next* chapter, Verse Twelve, the penalty for disobedience of that Commandment reads: 'He that smiteth a man, so that he die, shall be surely put to death.' Now, Mr. Fleming would have you believe that all this was changed by the coming of Christ. Not so. For Christ says, 'Think not that I am come to destroy the law, or the prophets: I am not come to destroy, but to fulfill.' And finally—" Green fumbled, and seemed to accidentally shut the Bible, whereupon the visiting legal dignitaries grinned and nudged each other, for this was a venerable courtroom ploy—the lawyer who while reading from the Scriptures pretends to lose his place, and then remarks, as Green now did, "Never mind. I think I can quote from memory. Genesis Nine, Verse Six: 'Whoso sheddeth man's blood, by man shall his blood be shed.'

"But," Green went on, "I see nothing to be gained by arguing the Bible. Our state provides that the punishment for murder in the first degree shall be imprisonment for life or death by hanging. That is the law. You, gentlemen, are here to enforce it. And if ever there was a case in which the maximum penalty was justified, this is it. These were strange, ferocious murders. Four of your fellow citizens were slaughtered like hogs in a pen. And for what reason? Not out of vengeance or hatred. But for money. *Money*. It was the cold and calculated weighing of so many ounces of silver against so many ounces of blood. And how cheaply those lives were bought! For forty dollars' worth of loot! Ten dollars a life!" He whirled, and pointed a finger that moved back and forth between Hickock and Smith. "They went armed with a shotgun and a *dagger*. They went to rob and kill—" His voice trembled, toppled, disappeared, as though strangled by the intensity of his own loathing for the debonair, gum-chewing defendants. Turning again to the jury, he hoarsely asked, "What are you going to do? What are you going to do with these men that bind a man hand and foot and cut his throat and blow out his brains? Give them the *minimum* penalty? Yes, and that's only one of four counts. What about Kenyon Clutter, a young boy with his whole life before him, tied helplessly in sight of his father's death struggle. Or young Nancy Clutter, hearing the gunshots and knowing her time was next. Nancy, begging for her life: 'Don't. Oh, please don't. Please. Please.' What agony! What unspeakable torture! And there remains the mother, bound and gagged and having to listen as her husband, her beloved children died one by one. Listen until at last the killers, these defendants before you, entered her room, focused a flashlight in her eyes, and let the blast of a shotgun end the existence of an entire household."

Pausing, Green gingerly touched a boil on the back of his neck, a mature inflammation that seemed, like its angry wearer, about to burst. "So, gentlemen, what are you going to do? Give them the minimum? Send them back to the penitentiary, and take the chance of their escaping or being paroled? The next time they go slaughtering it may be *your* family. I say to you," he solemnly said, staring at the panel in a manner that encompassed and challenged them all, "some of our enormous crimes only happen because once upon a time a pack of chicken-hearted jurors refused to do their duty. Now, gentlemen, I leave it to you and your consciences."

He sat down. West whispered to him, "That was masterly, sir."

But a few of Green's auditors were less enthusiastic; and after the jury retired to discuss the verdict, one of them, a young reporter from Oklahoma, exchanged sharp words with another newsman, Richard Parr of the Kansas City *Star*. To the Oklahoman, Green's address had seemed "rabble-rousing, brutal."

"He was just telling the truth," Parr said. "The truth can be brutal. To coin a phrase."

"But he didn't have to hit that hard. It's unfair."

"What's unfair?"

"The whole trial. These guys don't stand a chance."

"Fat chance they gave Nancy Clutter."

"Perry Smith. My God. He's had such a rotten life—"

Parr said, "Many a man can match sob stories with that little bastard. Me included. Maybe I drink too much, but I sure as hell never killed four people in cold blood."

"Yeah, and how about hanging the bastard? That's pretty goddam cold-blooded too."

The Reverend Post, overhearing the conversation, joined in. "Well," he said, passing around a snapshot reproduction of Perry Smith's portrait of Jesus, "any man who could paint this picture can't be one hundred percent bad. All the same it's hard to know what to do. Capital punishment is no answer: it doesn't give the sinner time enough to come to God. Sometimes I despair." A jovial fellow with gold-filled teeth and a silvery widow's peak, he jovially repeated, "Sometimes I despair. Sometimes I think old Doc Savage had the right idea." The Doc Savage to whom he referred was a fictional hero popular among adolescent readers of pulp magazines a generation ago. "If you boys remember, Doc Savage was a kind of superman. He'd made himself proficient in every field—medicine, science, philosophy, art. There wasn't much old Doc didn't know or couldn't do. One of his projects was, he decided to rid the world of criminals. First he bought a big island out in the ocean. Then he and his assistants—he had an army of trained assistants—kidnaped all the world's criminals and brought them to the island. And Doc Savage operated on their brains. He removed the part that holds wicked thoughts. And when they recovered they were all decent citizens. They *couldn't* commit crimes because that part of their brain was out. Now it strikes me that surgery of this nature might really be the answer to—"

A bell, the signal that the jury was returning, interrupted him. The jury's deliberations had lasted forty minutes. Many spectators, anticipating a swift decision, had never left their seats. Judge Tate, however, had to be fetched from his farm, where he had gone to feed his horses. A hurriedly donned black robe billowed about him when at last he arrived, but it was with impressive sedateness and dignity that he asked, "Gentlemen of the jury, have you reached your verdicts?" Their foreman replied: "We have, Your Honor." The court bailiff carried the sealed verdicts to the bench.

Train whistles, the fanfare of an approaching Santa Fe express, penetrated the courtroom. Tate's bass voice interlaced with the locomotive's cries as he read: "'Count One. We the jury find the defendant, Richard Eugene Hickock, guilty of murder in the first degree, and the punishment is death.'" Then, as though interested in their reaction, he looked down upon the prisoners, who stood before him handcuffed to guards; they stared back impassively until he resumed and read the seven counts that followed: three more convictions for Hickock, and four for Smith.

"—and the punishment is death"; each time he came to the sentence, Tate enunciated it with a dark-toned hollowness that seemed to echo the train's mournful, now fading call. Then he dismissed the jury ("You have performed a courageous service"), and the condemned men were led away. At the door, Smith said to Hickock, "No chicken-hearted jurors, they!" They both laughed loudly, and a cameraman photographed them. The picture appeared in a Kansas paper above a caption entitled: "The Last Laugh?"

A week later Mrs. Meier was sitting in her parlor talking to a friend. "Yes, it's turned quiet around here," she said. "I guess we ought to be grateful things have settled down. But I still feel bad about it. I never had much truck with Dick, but Perry and I got to know each other real well. That afternoon, after he heard the verdict and they brought him back up here—I shut myself in the kitchen to keep from having to see him. I sat by the kitchen window and watched the crowd leaving the courthouse. Mr. Cullivan—he looked up and saw me and waved. The Hickocks. All going away. Just this morning I had a lovely letter from Mrs. Hickock; she visited with me several times while the trial was going on, and I wished I could have helped her, only what can you say to someone in a situation like that? But after everybody had gone, and I'd started to wash some dishes—I heard him crying. I turned on the radio. Not to hear him. But I could. Crying like a child. He'd never broke down before, shown any sign of it. Well, I went to him. The door of his cell. He reached out his hand. He wanted me to hold his hand, and I did, I held his hand, and all he said was, 'I'm embraced by shame.' I wanted to send for Father Goubeaux—I said first thing tomorrow I'd make him Spanish rice—but he just held my hand tighter.

"And that night, of all nights, we had to leave him alone. Wendle and I almost never go out, but we had a long-standing engagement, and Wendle didn't think we ought to break it. But I'll always be sorry we left him alone. Next day I did fix the rice. He wouldn't touch it. Or hardly speak to me. He hated the whole world. But the morning the men came to take him to the penitentiary, he thanked me and gave me a picture of himself. A little Kodak made when he was sixteen years old. He said it was how he wanted me to remember him, like the boy in the picture.

"The bad part was saying goodbye. When you knew where he was going, and what would happen to him. That squirrel of his, he sure misses Perry. Keeps coming to the cell looking for him. I've tried to feed him, but he won't have anything to do with me. It was just Perry he liked."

Prisons are important to the economy of Leavenworth County, Kansas. The two state penitentiaries, one for each sex, are situated there; so is Leavenworth, the largest Federal prison, and, at Fort Leavenworth, the country's principal military prison, the grim United States Army and Air Force Disciplinary Barracks. If all the inmates in these institutions were let free, they could populate a small city.

The oldest of the prisons is the Kansas State Penitentiary for Men, a turreted black-and-white palace that visually distinguishes an otherwise ordinary rural town, Lansing. Built during the Civil War, it received its first resident in 1864. Nowadays the convict population averages around two thousand; the present warden, Sherman H. Crouse, keeps a chart which lists the daily total according to race (for example, White 1405, Colored 360, Mexicans 12, Indians 6). Whatever his race, each convict is a citizen of a stony village that exists within the prison's steep, machine-gun-guarded walls—twelve gray acres of cement streets and cell blocks and workshops.

In a south section of the prison compound there stands a curious little building: a dark two-storied building shaped like a coffin. This establishment, officially called the Segregation and Isolation Building, constitutes a prison inside a prison. Among the inmates, the lower floor is known as The Hole—the place to which difficult prisoners, the "hardrock" troublemakers, are now and then banished. The upper story is reached by climbing a circular iron staircase; at the top is Death Row.

The first time the Clutter murderers ascended the staircase was late one rainy April afternoon. Having arrived at Lansing after an eight-hour, four-hundred-mile car ride from Garden City, the newcomers had been stripped, showered, given close haircuts, and supplied with coarse denim uniforms and soft slippers (in most American prisons such slippers are a condemned man's customary footwear); then armed escorts marched them through a wet twilight to the coffin-shaped edifice, hustled them up the spiral stairs and into two of the twelve side-by-side cells that comprise Lansing's Death Row.

The cells are identical. They measure seven by ten feet, and are unfurnished except for a cot, a toilet, a basin, and an overhead light bulb that is never extinguished night or day. The cell windows are very narrow, and not only barred but covered with a wire mesh black as a widow's veil; thus the faces of those sentenced to hang can be but hazily discerned by passers-by. The doomed themselves can see out well enough; what they see is an empty dirt lot that serves in summer as a baseball diamond, beyond the lot a piece of prison wall, and above that, a piece of sky.

The wall is made of rough stone; pigeons nest inside its crevices. A rusty iron door, set into the part of the wall visible to the Row's occupants, rouses the pigeons whenever it is opened, puts them in a flap, for the hinges creak so, scream. The door leads into a cavernous storage room, where on even the warmest day the air is moist and chilly. A number of things are kept there: stockpiles of metal used by the convicts to manufacture automobile license plates, lumber, old machinery, baseball paraphernalia—and also an unpainted wooden gallows that smells faintly of pine. For this is the state's execution chamber; when a man is brought here to be hanged, the prisoners say he has "gone to The Corner," or, alternatively, "paid a visit to the warehouse."

In accordance with the sentence of the court, Smith and Hickock were scheduled to visit the warehouse six weeks hence: at one minute after midnight on Friday, May 13, 1960.

Kansas abolished capital punishment in 1907; in 1935, due to a sudden prevalence in the Midwest of rampaging professional criminals (Alvin "Old Creepy" Karpis, Charles "Pretty Boy" Floyd, Clyde Barrow and his homicidal sweetheart, Bonnie Parker), the state legislators voted to restore it. However, it was not until 1944 that an executioner had a chance to employ his craft; over the next ten years he was given nine additional opportunities. But for six years, or since 1954, there had been no pay checks for a hangman in Kansas (except at the Army and Air Force Disciplinary Barracks, which also has a gallows). The late George Docking, Governor of Kansas from 1957 through 1960, was responsible for this hiatus, for he was unreservedly opposed to the death penalty ("I just don't like killing people").

Now, at that time—April, 1960—there were in United States prisons one hundred and ninety persons awaiting civil execution; five, the Clutter killers included, were among the lodgers at Lansing. Occasionally, important visitors to the prison are invited to take what one high official calls "a little peek at Death Row." Those who accept are assigned a guard who, as he leads the tourist along the iron walkway fronting the death cells, is likely to identify the condemned with what he must consider comic formality. "And this," he said to a visitor in 1960, "this is Mr. Perry Edward Smith. Now next door, that's Mr. Smith's buddy, Mr. Richard Eugene Hickock. And over here we have Mr. Earl Wilson. And after Mr. Wilson—meet Mr. Bobby Joe Spencer. And as for this last gentleman, I'm sure you recognize the famous Mr. Lowell Lee Andrews."

Earl Wilson, a husky, hymn-singing Negro, had been sentenced to die for the kidnaping, rape, and torture of a young white woman; the victim, though she survived, was left severely disabled. Bobby Joe Spencer, white, an effeminate youth, had confessed to murdering an elderly Kansas City woman, the owner of a rooming house where he lived. Prior to leaving office in January, 1961, Governor Docking, who had been defeated for re-election (in large measure because of his attitude toward capital punishment), commuted the sentences of both these men to life imprisonment, which generally meant that they could apply for parole in seven years. However, Bobby Joe Spencer soon killed again: stabbed with a shiv another young convict, his rival for the affections of an older inmate (as one prison officer said, "Just two punks fighting over a jocker"). This deed earned Spencer a second life sentence. But the public was not much aware of either Wilson or Spencer; compared to Smith and Hickock, or the fifth man on the Row, Lowell Lee Andrews, the press had rather slighted them.

Two years earlier Lowell Lee Andrews, an enormous, weak-eyed boy of eighteen who wore horn-rimmed glasses and weighed almost three hundred pounds, had been a sophomore at the University of Kansas, an honor student majoring in biology. Though he was a solitary creature, withdrawn and seldom communicative, his acquaintances, both at the university and in his home town of Wolcott, Kansas, regarded him as exceptionally gentle and "sweet-natured" (later one Kansas paper printed an article about him entitled: "The Nicest Boy in Wolcott"). But inside the quiet young scholar there existed a second, unsuspected personality, one with stunted emotions and a distorted mind through which cold thoughts flowed in cruel directions. His family—his parents and a slightly older sister, Jennie Marie—would have been astounded had they known the daydreams Lowell Lee dreamed throughout the summer and autumn of 1958; the brilliant son, the adored brother, was planning to poison them all.

The elder Andrews was a prosperous farmer; he had not much money in the bank, but he owned land valued at approximately two hundred thousand dollars. A desire to inherit this estate was ostensibly the motivation behind Lowell Lee's plot to destroy his family. For the secret Lowell Lee, the one concealed inside the shy churchgoing biology student, fancied himself an ice-hearted master criminal: he wanted to wear gangsterish silk shirts and drive scarlet sports cars; he wanted to be recognized as no mere bespectacled, bookish, overweight, virginal schoolboy; and while he did not dislike any member of his family, at least not consciously, murdering them seemed the swiftest, most sensible way of implementing the fantasies that possessed him. Arsenic was the weapon he decided upon; after poisoning the victims, he meant to tuck them in their beds and burn down the house, in the hope that investigators would believe the deaths accidental. However, one detail perturbed him: suppose autopsies revealed the presence of arsenic? And suppose the purchase of the poison could be traced to him? Toward the end of summer he evolved another plan. He spent three months polishing it. Finally, there came a near-zero November night when he was ready to act.

It was Thanksgiving week, and Lowell Lee was home for the holidays, as was Jennie Marie, an intelligent but rather plain girl who attended a college in Oklahoma. On the evening of November 28, somewhere around seven, Jennie Marie was sitting with her parents in the parlor watching television; Lowell Lee was locked in his bedroom reading the last chapter of *The Brothers Karamazov*. That task completed, he shaved, changed into his best suit, and proceeded to load both a semi-automatic .22-caliber rifle and a Ruger .22-caliber revolver. He fitted the revolver into a hip holster, shouldered the rifle, and ambled down a hall to the parlor, which was dark except for the flickering television screen. He switched on a light, aimed the rifle, pulled the trigger, and hit his sister between the eyes, killing her instantly. He shot his mother three times, and his father twice. The mother, eyes gaping, arms outstretched, staggered toward him; she tried to speak, her mouth opened, closed, but Lowell Lee said: "Shut up." To be certain she obeyed him, he shot her three times more. Mr. Andrews, however, was still alive; sobbing, whimpering, he thrashed along the floor toward the kitchen, but at the kitchen's threshold the son unholstered his revolver and discharged every chamber, then reloaded the weapon and emptied it again; altogether, his father absorbed seventeen bullets.

Andrews, according to statements credited to him, "didn't feel anything about it. The time came, and I was doing what I had to do. That's all there was to it." After the shootings he raised a window in his bedroom and removed the screen, then roamed the house rifling dresser drawers and scattering the contents: it was his intention to blame the crime on thieves. Later, driving his father's car, he traveled forty miles over snow-slippery roads to Lawrence, the town where the University of Kansas is located; en route, he parked on a bridge, dismantled his lethal artillery, and disposed of it by dropping the parts into the Kansas River. But of course the journey's true purpose was to arrange an alibi. First he stopped at the campus house where he roomed; he talked with the landlady, told her that he had come to pick up his typewriter, and that because of the bad weather the trip from Wolcott to Lawrence had taken two hours. Departing, he visited a movie theater, where, uncharacteristically, he chatted with an usher and a candy vendor. At eleven, when the movie let out, he returned to Wolcott. The family's mongrel dog was waiting on the front porch; it was whining with hunger, so Lowell Lee, entering the house and stepping across his father's corpse, prepared a bowl of warm milk and mush; then, while the dog was lapping it up, he telephoned the sheriff's office and said, "My name is Lowell Lee Andrews. I live at 6040 Wolcott Drive, and I want to report a robbery—"

Four officers of the Wyandotte County Sheriff's Patrol responded. One of the group, Patrolman Meyers, described the scene as follows: "Well, it was one in the morning when we got there. All the lights in the house was on. And this big dark-haired boy, Lowell Lee, he was sitting on the porch petting his dog. Patting it on the head. Lieutenant Athey asked the boy what happened, and he pointed to the door, real casual, and said, 'Look in there.'" Having looked, the astonished officers summoned the county coroner, a gentleman who was also impressed by young Andrews' callous nonchalance, for when the coroner asked him what funeral arrangements he wished to have made, Andrews replied with a shrug, "*I* don't care what you do with them."

Shortly, two senior detectives appeared and began to question the family's lone survivor. Though convinced he was lying, the detectives listened respectfully to the tale of how he had driven to Lawrence to fetch a typewriter, gone to a movie, and arrived home after midnight to find the bedrooms ransacked and his family slain. He stayed with the story, and might never have altered it if, subsequent to his arrest and removal to the county jail, the authorities had not obtained the aid of the Reverend Mr. Virto C. Dameron.

The Reverend Dameron, a Dickensian personage, an unctuous and jolly brimstone-and-damnation orator, was minister of the Grandview Baptist Church in Kansas City, Kansas, the church the Andrews family attended regularly. Awakened by an urgent call from the county coroner, Dameron presented himself at the jail around 3:00 A.M., whereupon detectives, who had been strenuously but abortively interrogating the suspect, withdrew to another room, leaving the minister to consult privately with his parishioner. It proved a fatal interview for the latter, who many months afterward gave this account of it to a friend: "Mr. Dameron said, 'Now, Lee, I've known you all your life. Since you were just a little tadpole. And I knew your daddy all his life, we grew up together, we were childhood friends. And that's why I'm here—not just because I'm your minister, but because I feel like you're a member of my own family. And because you need a friend that you can talk to and trust. And I feel terrible about this terrible event, and I'm every bit as anxious as you are to see the guilty party caught and punished.'

"He wanted to know was I thirsty, and I was, so he got me a Coke, and after that he's going on about the Thanksgiving vacation and how do I like school, when all of a sudden he says, 'Now, Lee, there seems to be some doubt among the people here regarding your innocence. I'm sure you'd be willing to take a lie detector and convince these men of your innocence so they can get busy and catch the guilty party.' Then he said, 'Lee, you didn't do this terrible thing, did you? If you did, now is the time to purge your soul.' The next thing was, I thought what difference does it make, and I told him the truth, most everything about it. He kept wagging his head and rolling his eyes and rubbing his hands together, and he said it was a terrible thing, and I would have to answer to the Almighty, have to purge my soul by telling the officers what I'd told him, and would I?" Receiving an affirmative nod, the prisoner's spiritual adviser stepped into an adjacent room, which was crowded with expectant policemen, and elatedly issued an invitation: "Come on in. The boy's ready to make a statement."

The Andrews case became the basis for a legal and medical crusade. Prior to the trial, at which Andrews pleaded innocent by reason of insanity, the psychiatric staff of the Menninger Clinic conducted an exhaustive examination of the accused; this produced a diagnosis of "schizophrenia, simple type." By "simple," the diagnosticians meant that Andrews suffered no delusions, no false perceptions, no hallucinations, but the primary illness of separation of thinking from feeling. He understood the nature of his acts, and that they were prohibited, and that he was subject to punishment. "But," to quote Dr. Joseph Satten, one of the examiners, "Lowell Lee Andrews felt no emotions whatsoever. He considered himself the only important, only significant person in the world. And in his own seclusive world it seemed to him just as right to kill his mother as to kill an animal or a fly."

In the opinion of Dr. Satten and his colleagues, Andrews' crime amounted to such an undebatable example of diminished responsibility that the case offered an ideal chance to challenge the M'Naghten Rule in Kansas courts. The M'Naghten Rule, as has been previously stated, recognizes no form of insanity provided the defendant has the capacity to discriminate between right and wrong—legally, not morally. Much to the distress of psychiatrists and liberal jurists, the Rule prevails in the courts of the British Commonwealth and, in the United States, in the courts of all but half a dozen or so of the states and the District of Columbia, which abide by the more lenient, though to some minds impractical, Durham Rule, which is simply that an accused is not criminally responsible if his unlawful act is the product of mental disease or mental defect.

In short, what Andrews' defenders, a team composed of Menninger Clinic psychiatrists and two first-class attorneys, hoped to achieve was a victory of legal-landmark stature. The great essential was to persuade the court to substitute the Durham Rule for the M'Naghten Rule. If that happened, then Andrews, because of the abundant evidence concerning his schizophrenic condition, would certainly be sentenced not to the gallows, or even to prison, but to confinement in the State Hospital for the Criminally Insane.

However, the defense reckoned without the defendant's religious counselor, the tireless Reverend Mr. Dameron, who appeared at the trial as the chief witness for the prosecution, and who, in the overwrought, rococo style of a tent-show revivalist, told the court he had often warned his former Sunday School pupil of God's impending wrath: "I says, there isn't anything in this world that is worth more than your soul, and you have acknowledged to me a number of times in our conversations that your faith is weak, that you have no faith in God. You know that all sin is against God and God is your final judge, and you have got to answer to Him. That is what I said to make him feel the terribleness of the thing he'd done, and that he had to answer to the Almighty for this crime."

Apparently the Reverend Dameron was determined young Andrews should answer not only to the Almighty, but also to more temporal powers, for it was his testimony, added to the defendant's confession, that settled matters. The presiding judge upheld the M'Naghten Rule, and the jury gave the state the death penalty it demanded.

Friday, May 13, the first date set for the execution of Smith and Hickock, passed harmlessly, the Kansas Supreme Court having granted them a stay pending the outcome of appeals for a new trial filed by their lawyers. At that time the Andrews verdict was under review by the same court.

Perry's cell adjoined Dick's; though invisible to each other, they could easily converse, yet Perry seldom spoke to Dick, and it wasn't because of any declared animosity between them (after the exchange of a few tepid reproaches, their relationship had turned into one of mutual toleration: the acceptance of uncongenial but helpless Siamese twins); it was because Perry, cautious as always, secretive, suspicious, disliked having the guards and other inmates overhear his "private business"—especially Andrews, or Andy, as he was called on the Row. Andrews' educated accent and the formal quality of his college-trained intelligence were anathema to Perry, who though he had not gone beyond third grade, imagined himself more learned than most of his acquaintances, and enjoyed correcting them, especially their grammar and pronunciation. But here suddenly was someone—"just a kid!"—constantly correcting *him.* Was it any wonder he never opened his mouth? Better to keep your mouth shut than to risk one of the college kid's snotty lines, like: "Don't say *dis*interested. When what you mean is *un*interested." Andrews meant well, he was without malice, but Perry could have boiled him in oil—yet he never admitted it, never let anyone there guess why, after one of these humiliating incidents, he sat and sulked and ignored the meals that were delivered to him three times a day. At the beginning of June he stopped eating altogether—he told Dick, "You can wait around for the rope. But not me"—and from that moment he refused to touch food or water, or say one word to anybody.

The fast lasted five days before the warden took it seriously. On the sixth day he ordered Smith transferred to the prison hospital, but the move did not lessen Perry's resolve; when attempts were made to force-feed him he fought back, tossed his head and clenched his jaws until they were rigid as horseshoes. Eventually, he had to be pinioned and fed intravenously or through a tube inserted in a nostril. Even so, over the next nine weeks his weight fell from 168 to 115 pounds, and the warden was warned that forced-feeding alone could not keep the patient alive indefinitely.

Dick, though impressed by Perry's will power, would not concede that his purpose was suicide; even when Perry was reported to be in a coma, he told Andrews, with whom he had become friendly, that his former confederate was faking. "He just wants them to think he's crazy."

Andrews, a compulsive eater (he had filled a scrapbook with illustrated edibles, everything from strawberry shortcake to roasted pig), said, "Maybe he is crazy. Starving himself like that."

"He just wants to get out of here. Play-acting. So they'll say he's crazy and put him in the crazy house."

Dick afterward grew fond of quoting Andrews' reply, for it seemed to him a fine specimen of the boy's "funny thinking," his "off on a cloud" complacency. "Well," Andrews allegedly said, "it sure strikes me a hard way to do it. Starving yourself. Because sooner or later we'll all get out of here. Either walk out—or be carried out in a coffin. Myself, I don't care whether I walk or get carried. It's all the same in the end."

Dick said, "The trouble with you, Andy, you've got no respect for human life. Including your own."

Andrews agreed. "And," he said, "I'll tell you something else. If ever I do get out of here alive, I mean over the walls and clear out—well, maybe nobody will know where Andy went, but they'll sure hell know where Andy's been."

All summer Perry undulated between half-awake stupors and sickly, sweat-drenched sleep. Voices roared through his head; one voice persistently asked him, "Where is Jesus? Where?" And once he woke up shouting, "The bird is Jesus! The bird is Jesus!" His favorite old theatrical fantasy, the one in which he thought of himself as "Perry O'Parsons, The One-Man Symphony," returned in the guise of a recurrent dream. The dream's geographical center was a Las Vegas night club where, wearing a white top hat and a white tuxedo, he strutted about a spotlighted stage playing in turn a harmonica, a guitar, a banjo, drums, sang "You Are My Sunshine," and tap-danced up a short flight of gold-painted prop steps; at the top, standing on a platform, he took a bow. There was no applause, none, and yet thousands of patrons packed the vast and gaudy room—a strange audience, mostly men and mostly Negroes. Staring at them, the perspiring entertainer at last understood their silence, for suddenly he knew that these were phantoms, the ghosts of the legally annihilated, the hanged, the gassed, the electrocuted—and in the same instant he realized that he was there to join them, that the gold-painted steps had led to a scaffold, that the platform on which he stood was opening beneath him. His top hat tumbled; urinating, defecating, Perry O'Parsons entered eternity.

One afternoon he escaped from a dream and wakened to find the warden standing beside his bed. The warden said, "Sounds like you were having a little nightmare?" But Perry wouldn't answer him, and the warden, who on several occasions had visited the hospital and tried to persuade the prisoner to cease his fast, said, "I have something here. From your father. I thought you might want to see it." Perry, his eyes glitteringly immense in a face now almost phosphorescently pale, studied the ceiling; and presently, after placing a picture postcard on the patient's bedside table, the rebuffed visitor departed.

That night Perry looked at the card. It was addressed to the warden, and postmarked Blue Lake, California; the message, written in a familiar stubby script, said: "Dear Sir, I understand you have my boy Perry back in custody. Write me please what did he do wrong and if I come there could I see him. Alls well with me and trust the same with you. Tex J. Smith." Perry destroyed the card, but his mind preserved it, for the few crude words had resurrected him emotionally, revived love and hate, and reminded him that he was still what he had tried not to be—alive. "And I just decided," he later informed a friend, "that I ought to stay that way. Anybody wanted my life wasn't going to get any more help from me. They'd have to fight for it."

The next morning he asked for a glass of milk, the first sustenance he had volunteered to accept in fourteen weeks. Gradually, on a diet of eggnogs and orange juice, he regained weight; by October the prison physician, Dr. Robert Moore, considered him strong enough to be returned to the Row. When he arrived there, Dick laughed and said, "Welcome home, honey."

Two years passed.

The departures of Wilson and Spencer left Smith and Hickock and Andrews alone with the Row's burning lights and veiled windows. The privileges granted ordinary prisoners were denied them; no radios or card games, not even an exercise period—indeed, they were never allowed out of their cells, except each Saturday when they were taken to a shower room, then given a once-weekly change of clothing; the only other occasions for momentary release were the far-between visits of lawyers or relatives. Mrs. Hickock came once a month; her husband had died, she had lost the farm, and, as she told Dick, lived now with one relative, now another.

It seemed to Perry as though he existed "deep underwater"—perhaps because the Row usually was as gray and quiet as ocean depths, soundless except for snores, coughs, the whisper of slippered feet, the feathery racket of the pigeons nesting in the prison walls. But not *always*. "Sometimes," Dick wrote in a letter to his mother, "you can't hear yourself think. They throw men in the cells downstairs, what they call the hole, and plenty of them are fighting mad and crazy to boot. Curse and scream the whole time. It's intolerable, so everybody starts yelling shut up. I wish you'd send me earplugs. Only they wouldn't allow me to have them. No rest for the wicked, I guess."

The little building had been standing for more than a century, and seasonal changes provoked different symptoms of its antiquity: winter cold saturated the stone-and-iron fixtures, and in summer, when temperatures often hurtled over the hundred mark, the old cells were malodorous cauldrons. "So hot my skin stings," Dick wrote in a letter dated July 5, 1961. "I try not to move much. I just sit on the floor. My bed's too sweaty to lie down, and the smell makes me sick because of only the one bath a week and always wearing the same clothes. No ventilation whatever and the light bulbs make everything hotter. Bugs keep bumping on the walls."

Unlike conventional prisoners, the condemned are not subjected to a work routine; they can do with their time what they like—sleep all day, as Perry frequently did ("I pretend I'm a tiny little baby that can't keep its eyes open"); or, as was Andrews' habit, read all night. Andrews averaged fifteen to twenty books a week; his taste encompassed both trash and *belles-lettres,* and he liked poetry, Robert Frost's particularly, but he also admired Whitman, Emily Dickinson, and the comic poems of Ogden Nash. Though the quenchless quality of his literary thirst had soon depleted the shelves of the prison library, the prison chaplain and others sympathetic to Andrews kept him supplied with parcels from the Kansas City public library.

Dick was rather a bookworm, too; but his interest was restricted to two themes—sex, as represented in the novels of Harold Robbins and Irving Wallace (Perry, after being lent one of these by Dick, returned it with an indignant note: "Degenerate filth for filthy degenerate minds!"), and law literature. He consumed hours each day leafing through law books, compiling research that he hoped would help reverse his conviction. Also, in pursuit of the same cause he fired off a cannonade of letters to such organizations as the American Civil Liberties Union and the Kansas State Bar Association—letters attacking his trial as a "travesty of due process," and urging the recipients to aid him in his quest for a new trial. Perry was persuaded to draft similar pleas, but when Dick suggested that Andy follow their example by writing protests in his own behalf, Andrews replied, "I'll worry about my neck and you worry about yours." (Actually, Dick's neck was not the part of his anatomy that most immediately troubled him. "My hair is coming out by the handfuls," he confided in yet another letter to his mother. "I'm frantic. Nobody in our family was baldheaded as I can recall, and it makes me frantic the idea of being an ugly old baldhead.")

The Row's two night guards, arriving at work on an autumn evening in 1961, had a piece of news. "Well," one of them announced, "seems like you boys can expect company." The import of the remark was clear to his audience: it meant that two young soldiers, who had been standing trial for the murder of a Kansas railroad worker, had received the ultimate sentence. "Yessir," the guard said, confirming this, "they got the death penalty." Dick said, "Sure. It's very popular in Kansas. Juries hand it out like they were giving candy to kids."

One of the soldiers, George Ronald York, was eighteen; his companion, James Douglas Latham, was a year older. They were both exceptionally personable, which perhaps explains why hordes of teenaged girls had attended their trial. Though convicted of a single slaying, the pair had claimed seven victims in the course of a cross-country murder spree.

Ronnie York, blond and blue-eyed, had been born and raised in Florida, where his father was a well-known, well-paid deep-sea diver. The Yorks had a pleasantly comfortable home life, and Ronnie, overloved and overpraised by his parents and a worshipful younger sister, was the adored center of it. Latham's background was at the opposite extreme, being every bit as bleak as Perry Smith's. Born in Texas, he was the youngest child of fertile, moneyless, embattled parents who, when finally they separated, left their progeny to fend for themselves, to scatter hither and thither, loose and unwanted as bundles of Panhandle tumbleweed. At seventeen, in need of a refuge, Latham enlisted in the Army; two years later, found guilty of an AWOL offense, he was imprisoned in the stockade at Ford Hood, Texas. It was there that he met Ronnie York, who was also under sentence for having gone AWOL. Though they were very unlike—even physically, York being tall and phlegmatic, whereas the Texan was a short young man with foxy brown eyes animating a compact, cute little face—they found they shared at least one firm opinion: the world was hateful, and everybody in it would be better off dead. "It's a rotten world," Latham said. "There's no answer to it but meanness. That's all anybody understands—meanness. Burn down the man's barn—he'll understand that. Poison his dog. Kill him." Ronnie said Latham was "one hundred percent correct," adding, "Anyway, anybody you kill, you're doing them a favor."

The first persons they chose to so favor were two Georgia women, respectable housewives who had the misfortune to encounter York and Latham not long after the murderous pair escaped from the Fort Hood stockade, stole a pickup truck, and drove to Jacksonville, Florida, York's home town. The scene of the encounter was an Esso station on the dark outskirts of Jacksonville; the date was the night of May 29, 1961. Originally, the absconding soldiers had traveled to the Florida city with the intention of visiting York's family; once there, however, York decided it might be unwise to contact his parents; his father sometimes had quite a temper. He and Latham talked it over, and New Orleans was their new destination when they stopped at the Esso station to buy gas. Alongside them another car was imbibing fuel; it contained the two matronly victims-to-be, who, after a day of shopping and pleasure in Jacksonville, were returning to their homes in a small town near the Florida–Georgia border. Alas, they had lost their way. York, from whom they asked directions, was most obliging: "You just follow us. We'll put you on the right road." But the road to which he led them was very wrong indeed: a narrow side-turning that petered off into swamp. Nevertheless, the ladies followed along faithfully until the lead vehicle halted, and they saw, in the shine of their headlights, the helpful young men approaching them on foot, and saw, but too late, that each was armed with a black bullwhip. The whips were the property of the stolen truck's rightful custodian, a cattleman; it had been Latham's notion to use them as garrotes—which, after robbing the women, is what they did. In New Orleans the boys bought a pistol and carved two notches in the handle.

During the next ten days notches were added in Tullahoma, Tennessee, where they acquired a snappy red Dodge convertible by shooting the owner, a traveling salesman; and in an Illinois suburb of St.

Louis, where two more men were slain. The Kansas victim, who followed the preceding five, was a grandfather; his name was Otto Ziegler, he was sixty-two, a robust, friendly fellow, the sort not likely to pass distressed motorists without offering assistance. While spinning along a Kansas highway one fine June morning, Mr. Ziegler spied a red convertible parked by the roadside, its hood up, and a couple of nice-looking youngsters fiddling with the motor. How was the good-hearted Mr. Ziegler to know that nothing ailed the machine—that this was a ruse devised to rob and kill would-be Samaritans? His last words were, "Anything I can do?" York, at a distance of twenty feet, sent a bullet crashing through the old man's skull, then turned to Latham and said, "Pretty good shootin', huh?"

Their final victim was the most pathetic. It was a girl, only eighteen; she was employed as a maid in a Colorado motel where the rampaging pair spent a night, during which she let them make love to her. Then they told her they were on their way to California, and invited her to come along. "Come on," Latham urged her, "maybe we'll all end up movie stars." The girl and her hastily packed cardboard suitcase ended up as bloodsoaked wreckage at the bottom of a ravine near Craig, Colorado; but not many hours after she had been shot and thrown there, her assassins were in fact performing before motion-picture cameras.

Descriptions of the red car's occupants, provided by witnesses who had noticed them loitering in the area where Otto Ziegler's body was discovered, had been circulated through the Midwest and Western states. Roadblocks were erected, and helicopters patrolled the highways; it was a roadblock in Utah that caught York and Latham. Later, at Police Headquarters in Salt Lake City, a local television company was allowed to film an interview with them. The result, if viewed without sound, would seem to concern two cheerful, milkfed athletes discussing hockey or baseball—anything but murder and the roles, boastfully confessed, they had played in the deaths of seven people. "Why," the interviewer asks, "why did you do it?" And York, with a self-congratulatory grin, answers, "We hate the world."

All five of the states that vied for the right to prosecute York and Latham endorse judicial homicide: Florida (electrocution), Tennessee (electrocution), Illinois (electrocution), Kansas (hanging), and Colorado (lethal gas). But because it had the firmest evidence, Kansas was victorious.

The men on the Row first met their new companions November 2, 1961. A guard, escorting the arrivals to their cells, introduced them: "Mr. York, Mr. Latham, I'd like you to know Mr. Smith here. And Mr. Hickock. And Mr. Lowell Lee Andrews—'the nicest boy in Wolcott!' "

When the parade had passed, Hickock heard Andrews chuckling, and said, "What's so funny about that sonofabitch?"

"Nothing," Andrews said. "But I was thinking: when you count my three and your four and their seven, that makes fourteen of them and five of us. Now five into fourteen averages out—"

"*Four* into fourteen," Hickock curtly corrected him. "There are four killers up here and one railroaded man. I'm no goddam killer. I never touched a hair on a human head."

Hickock continued writing letters protesting his conviction, and one of these at last bore fruit. The recipient, Everett Steerman, Chairman of the Legal Aid Committee of the Kansas State Bar Association, was disturbed by the allegations of the sender, who insisted that he and his co-defendant had not had a fair trial. According to Hickock, the "hostile atmosphere" in Garden City had made it impossible to empanel an unbiased jury, and therefore a change of venue should have been granted. As for the jurors that were chosen, at least two had clearly indicated a presumption of guilt during the *voir dire* examination ("When asked to state his opinion of capital punishment, one man said that ordinarily he was against it, but in this case no"); unfortunately, the *voir dire* had not been recorded because Kansas law does not require it unless a specific demand is made. Many of the jurors, moreover, were "well acquainted with the deceased. So was the judge. Judge Tate was an intimate friend of Mr. Clutter."

But the bulkiest of Hickock's mudpies was aimed at the two defense attorneys, Arthur Fleming and Harrison Smith, whose "incompetence and inadequacy" were the chief cause of the correspondent's present predicament, for no real defense had been prepared or offered by them, and this lack of effort, it was implied, had been deliberate—an act of collusion between the defense and the prosecution.

These were grave assertions, reflecting upon the integrity of two respected lawyers and a distinguished district judge, but if even partially true, then the constitutional rights of the defendants had been abused. Prompted by Mr. Steerman, the Bar Association undertook a course of action without precedent in Kansas legal history: it appointed a young Wichita attorney, Russell Shultz, to investigate the charges and, should evidence warrant it, challenge the validity of the conviction by bringing habeas corpus proceedings in the Kansas Supreme Court, which had recently upheld the verdict.

It would appear that Shultz's investigation was rather one-sided, since it consisted of little more than an interview with Smith and Hickock, from which the lawyer emerged with crusading phrases for the press: "The question is this—do poor, plainly guilty defendants have a right to a complete defense? I do not believe that the State of Kansas would be either greatly or for long harmed by the death of these appellants. But I do not believe it could ever recover from the death of due process."

Shultz filed his habeas corpus petition, and the Kansas Supreme Court commissioned one of its own retired justices, the Honorable Walter G. Thiele, to conduct a full-scale hearing. And so it came to pass that almost two years after the trial, the whole cast reassembled in the courtroom at Garden City. The only important participants absent were the original defendants; in their stead, as it were, stood Judge Tate, old Mr. Fleming, and Harrison Smith, whose careers were imperiled—not because of the appellant's allegations per se, but because of the apparent credit the Bar Association bestowed upon them.

The hearing, which at one point was transferred to Lansing, where Judge Thiele heard Smith and Hickock testify, took six days to complete; ultimately, every point was covered. Eight jurors swore they had never known any member of the slain family; four admitted some slight acquaintance with Mr. Clutter, but each, including N. L. Dunnan, the airport operator who had made the controversial reply during the *voir dire,* testified that he had entered the jurybox with an unprejudiced mind. Shultz challenged Dunnan: "Do you feel, sir, that you would have been willing to go to trial with a juror whose state of mind was the same as yours?" Dunnan said yes, he would; and Shultz then said, "Do you recall being asked whether or not you were adverse to capital punishment?" Nodding, the witness answered, "I told them under normal conditions I would probably be adverse to it. But with the magnitude of this crime I could probably vote in favor."

Tangling with Tate was more difficult: Shultz soon realized he had a tiger by the tail. Responding to questions relevant to his supposed intimacy with Mr. Clutter, the judge said, "He [Clutter] was once a litigant in this court, a case over which I presided, a damage action involving an airplane falling on his property; he was suing for damages to—I believe some fruit trees. Other than that, I had no occasion to associate with him. *None whatever.* I saw him perhaps once or twice in the course of a year . . ." Shultz, floundering, switched the subject. "Do you know," he asked, "what the attitude of the people was in this community after the apprehension of these two men?" "I believe I do," the judge told him with scathing confidence. "It is my opinion that the attitude toward them was that of anyone else charged with a criminal offense—that they should be tried as the law provides; that if they were guilty they should be convicted; that they should be given the same fair treatment as any other person. There was no prejudice against them because they were accused of crime." "You mean," Shultz slyly said, "you saw no reason for the court on its own motion to grant a change of venue?" Tate's lips curved downward, his eyes blazed. "Mr. Shultz," he said, as though the name was a prolonged hiss, "the court *cannot* on its *own* grant a change of venue. That would be contrary to Kansas law. I couldn't grant a change unless it was properly requested."

But why had such a request not been made by the defendants' attorneys? Shultz now pursued this question with the attorneys themselves, for to discredit them and prove that they had not supplied their clients with the minimum protection was, from the Wichita lawyer's viewpoint, the hearing's principal objective. Fleming and Smith withstood the onslaught in good style, particularly Fleming, who, wearing a bold red tie and an abiding smile, endured Shultz with gentlemanly resignation. Explaining why he had not applied for a change of venue, he said, "I felt that since the Reverend Cowan, the minister of the Methodist church, and a man of substance here, a man of high standing, as well as many other ministers here, had expressed themselves against capital punishment, that at least the leaven had been cast in the area, and there were likely more people here inclined to be lenient in the matter of the penalty than perhaps in other parts of the state. Then I believe it was a brother of Mrs. Clutter's who made a statement that appeared in the press indicating he did not feel the defendants should be put to death."

Shultz had a score of charges, but underlying them all was the implication that because of community pressure, Fleming and Smith had deliberately neglected their duties. Both men, Shultz maintained, had betrayed their clients by not consulting with them sufficiently (Mr. Fleming replied, "I worked on the case to the very best of my ability, giving it more time than I do most cases"); by waiving a preliminary hearing (Smith answered, "But sir, neither Mr. Fleming nor I had been appointed counsel at the time of the waiver"); by making remarks to newsmen damaging to the defendants (Shultz to Smith: "Are you aware that a reporter, Ron Kull of the Topeka *Daily Capital*, quoted you, on the second day of the trial, as saying there was no doubt of Mr. Hickock's guilt, but that you were concerned only with obtaining life imprisonment rather than the death penalty?" Smith to Shultz: "No, sir. If I was quoted as saying that it was incorrect"); and by failing to prepare a proper defense.

This last proposition was the one Shultz pedaled hardest; it is relevant, therefore, to reproduce an opinion of it written by three Federal judges as the result of a subsequent appeal to the United States Court of Appeals, Tenth Circuit: "We think, however, that those viewing the situation in retrospect have lost sight of the problems which confronted Attorneys Smith and Fleming when they undertook the defense of these petitioners. When they accepted the appointments each petitioner had made a full confession, and they did not then contend, nor did they seriously contend at any time in the state courts, that these confessions were not voluntary. A radio taken from the Clutter home and sold by the petitioners in Mexico City had been recovered, and the attorneys knew of other evidence of their guilt then in the possession of the prosecution. When called upon to plead to the charges against them they stood mute, and it was necessary for the court to enter a plea of not guilty for them. There was no substantial evidence then, and none has been produced since the trial, to substantiate a defense of insanity. The attempt to establish insanity as a defense because of serious injuries in accidents years before, and headaches and occasional fainting spells of Hickock, was like grasping at the proverbial straw. The attorneys were faced with a situation where outrageous crimes committed on innocent persons had been admitted. Under these circumstances, they would have been justified in advising that petitioners enter pleas of guilty and throw themselves on the mercy of the court. Their only hope was through some turn of fate the lives of these misguided individuals might be spared."

In the report he submitted to the Kansas Supreme Court, Judge Thiele found that the petitioners had received a constitutionally fair trial; the court thereupon denied the writ to abolish the verdict, and set a new date of execution—October 25, 1962. As it happened, Lowell Lee Andrews, whose case had twice traveled all the way to the United States Supreme Court, was scheduled to hang one month later.

The Clutter slayers, granted a reprieve by a Federal judge, evaded their date. Andrews kept his.

In the disposition of capital cases in the United States, the median elapsed time between sentence and execution is approximately seventeen months. Recently, in Texas, an armed robber was electrocuted one month after his conviction; but in Louisiana, at the present writing, two rapists have been waiting for a record twelve years. The variance depends a little on luck and a great deal on the extent of litigation. The majority of the lawyers handling these cases are court-appointed and work without recompense; but more often than not the courts, in order to avoid future appeals based on complaints of inadequate representation, appoint men of first quality who defend with commendable vigor. However, even an attorney of moderate talent can postpone doomsday year after year, for the system of appeals that pervades American jurisprudence amounts to a legalistic wheel of fortune, a game of chance, somewhat fixed in the favor of the criminal, that the participants play interminably, first in the state courts, then through the Federal courts until the ultimate tribunal is reached—the United States Supreme Court. But even defeat there does not signify if petitioner's counsel can discover or invent new grounds for appeal; usually they can, and so once more the wheel turns, and turns until, perhaps some years later, the prisoner arrives back at the nation's highest court, probably only to begin again the slow cruel contest. But at intervals the wheel does pause to declare a winner—or, though with increasing rarity, a loser: Andrews' lawyers fought to the final moment, but their client went to the gallows on Friday, November 30, 1962.

"That was a cold night," Hickock said, talking to a journalist with whom he corresponded and who was periodically allowed to visit him. "Cold and wet. It had been raining like a bastard, and the baseball field was mud up to your *cojones*. So when they took Andy out to the warehouse, they had to walk him along the path. We were all at our windows watching—Perry and me, Ronnie York, Jimmy Latham. It was just after midnight, and the warehouse was lit up like a Halloween pumpkin. The doors wide open. We could see the witnesses, a lot of guards, the doctor and the warden—every damn thing but the gallows. It was off at an angle, but we could see its shadow. A shadow on the wall like the shadow of a boxing ring.

"The chaplain and four guards had charge of Andy, and when they got to the door they stopped a second. Andy was looking at the gallows —you could sense he was. His arms were tied in front of him. All of a sudden the chaplain reached out and took off Andy's glasses. Which was kind of pitiful, Andy without his glasses. They led him on inside, and I wondered he could see to climb the steps. It was real quiet, just nothing but this dog barking way off. Some town dog. Then we heard it, the sound, and Jimmy Latham said, "What was that?"; and I *told* him what it was—the trap door.

"Then it was real quiet again. Except that dog. Old Andy, he danced a long time. They must have had a real mess to clean up. Every few minutes the doctor came to the door and stepped outside, and stood there with this stethoscope in his hand. I wouldn't say he was enjoying his work—kept gasping, like he was gasping for breath, and he was crying, too. Jimmy said, 'Get a load of that nance.' I guess the reason he stepped outside was so the others wouldn't see he was crying. Then he'd go back and listen to hear if Andy's heart had stopped. Seemed like it never would. The fact is, his heart kept beating for nineteen minutes.

"Andy was a funny kid," Hickock said, smiling lopsidedly as he propped a cigarette between his lips. "It was like I told him: he had no respect for human life, not even his own. Right before they hanged him, he sat down and ate two fried chickens. And that last afternoon he was smoking cigars and drinking Coke and writing poetry. When they came to get him, and we said our goodbye, I said, 'I'll be seeing you soon, Andy. 'Cause I'm sure we're going to the same place. So scout around and see if you can't find a cool shady spot for us Down There.' He laughed, and said he didn't believe in heaven or hell, just dust unto dust. And he said an aunt and uncle had been to see him, and told him they had a coffin waiting to carry him to some little cemetery in north Missouri. The same place where the three he disposed of were buried. They planned to put Andy right alongside them. He said when they told him that he could hardly keep a straight face. I said, 'Well, you're lucky to have a grave. Most likely they'll give Perry and me to the vivisectionist.' We joked on like that till it was time to go, and just as he was going he handed me a piece of paper with a poem on it. I don't know if he wrote it. Or copied it out of a book. My impression was he wrote it. If you're interested, I'll send it to you."

He later did so, and Andrews' farewell message turned out to be the ninth stanza of Gray's "Elegy Written in a Country Churchyard":

> The boasts of heraldry, the pomp of pow'r,
> And all that beauty, all that wealth e'er gave,
> Await alike the inevitable hour:
> The paths of glory lead but to the grave.

"I really liked Andy. He was a nut—not a real nut, like they kept hollering; but, you know, just goofy. He was always talking about breaking out of here and making his living as a hired gun. He liked to imagine himself roaming around Chicago or Los Angeles with a machine gun inside a violin case. Cooling guys. Said he'd charge a thousand bucks per stiff."

Hickock laughed, presumably at the absurdity of his friend's ambitions, sighed, and shook his head. "But for someone his age he was the smartest person I ever come across. A human library. When that boy read a book it stayed read. Course he didn't know a dumb-darn thing about *life*. Me, I'm an ignoramus except when it comes to what I know about life. I've walked along a lot of mean streets. I've seen a white man flogged. I've watched babies born. I've seen a girl, and her no more than fourteen, take on three guys at the same time and give them all their money's worth. Fell off a ship once five miles out to sea. Swam five miles with my life passing before me with every stroke. Once I shook hands with President Truman in the lobby of the Hotel Muehlebach. Harry S Truman. When I was working for the hospital, driving an ambulance, I saw every side of life there is—things that would make a dog vomit. But *Andy*. He didn't know one dumb-damn-darn thing except what he'd read in books.

"He was innocent as a little child, some kid with a box of Cracker Jack. He'd never once been with a woman. Man or mule. He said so himself. Maybe that's what I liked about him most. How he wouldn't prevaricate. The rest of us on the Row, we're all a bunch of bull-artists. I'm one of the worst. Shoot, you've got to talk about something. Brag. Otherwise you're nobody, nothing, a potato vegetating in your seven-by-ten limbo. But Andy never would partake. He said what's the use telling a lot of stuff that never happened.

"Old Perry, though, *he* wasn't sorry to see the last of Andy. Andy was the one thing in the world Perry wants to be—educated. And Perry couldn't forgive him for it. You know how Perry's always using hundred-dollar words he doesn't half know the meaning of? Sounds like one of them college niggers? Boy, it burned his bottom to have Andy catch up on him and haul him to the curb. Course Andy was just trying to give him what he wanted—an education. The truth is, can't anybody get along with Perry. He hasn't got a single friend on the premises. I mean, just who the hell does he think he is? Sneering at everybody. Calling people perverts and degenerates. Going on about what low I.Q.'s they have. It's too bad we can't all be such sensitive souls like little Perry. Saints. Boy, but I know some hardrocks who'd gladly go to The Corner if they could get him alone in the shower room for just one hot minute. The way he high-hats York and Latham! Ronnie says he sure wishes he knew where he could lay hold of a bull-whip. Says he'd like to squeeze Perry a little. I don't blame him. After all, we're all in the same fix, and they're pretty good boys."

Hickock chuckled ruefully, shrugged, and said, "You know what I mean. *Good*—considering. Ronnie York's mother has been here to visit him several times. One day, out in the waiting room, she met my mother, and now they've come to be each other's number-one buddy. Mrs. York wants my mother to come visit her home in Florida, maybe even live there. Jesus, I wish she would. Then she wouldn't have to go through this ordeal. Once a month riding the bus here to see me. Smiling, trying to find something to say, make me feel good. The poor lady. I don't know how she stands it. I wonder she isn't crazy."

Hickock's uneven eyes turned toward a window in the visiting room; his face, puffy, pallid as a funeral lily, gleamed in the weak winter sunshine filtering through the bar-shrouded glass.

"The poor lady. She wrote the warden, and asked him if she could speak to Perry the next time she came here. She wanted to hear from Perry himself how he killed those people, how I never fired shot one. All I can hope is that some day we'll get a new trial, and Perry will testify and tell the truth. Only I doubt it. He's plain determined that if he goes I go. Back to back. It's not right. Many a man has killed and never seen the inside of a death cell. And I never killed *any*body. If you've got fifty thousand dollars to spend, you could bump off half of Kansas City and just laugh ha ha." A sudden grin obliterated his woeful indignation. "Uh-oh. There I go again. Old crybaby. You'd think I'd learn. But honest to God, I've done my damnedest to get along with Perry. Only he's so critical. Two-faced. So jealous of every little thing. Every letter I get, every visit. Nobody ever comes to see him except you," he said, nodding at the journalist, who was as equally well acquainted with Smith as he was with Hickock. "Or his lawyer. Remember when he was in the hospital? With that phony starvation routine? And his dad sent the postcard? Well, the warden wrote Perry's dad and said he was welcome to come here any time. But he never has showed up. I don't know. Sometimes you got to feel sorry for Perry. He must be one of the most alone people there ever was. But. Aw, the hell with him. It's mostly every bit his own fault."

Hickock slipped another cigarette away from a package of Pall Malls, wrinkled his nose, and said, "I've tried to quit smoking. Then I figure what difference does it make under the circumstances. With a little luck, maybe I'll get cancer and beat the state at its own game. For a while there I was smoking cigars. Andy's. The morning after they hanged him, I woke up and called to him, 'Andy?'—the way I usually did. Then I remembered he was on his way to Missouri. With the aunt and uncle. I looked out in the corridor. His cell had been cleaned out, and all his junk was piled there. The mattress off his bunk, his slippers, and the scrapbook with all the food pictures—he called it his icebox. And this box of 'Macbeth' cigars. I told the guard Andy wanted me to have them, left them to me in his will. Actually, I never smoked them all. Maybe it was the idea of Andy, but somehow they gave me indigestion.

"Well, what's there to say about capital punishment? I'm not against it. Revenge is all it is, but what's wrong with revenge? It's very important. If I was kin to the Clutters, or any of the parties York and Latham dispensed with, I couldn't rest in peace till the ones responsible had taken that ride on the Big Swing. These people that write letters to the newspapers. There were two in a Topeka paper the other day—one from a minister. Saying, in effect, what is all this legal farce, why haven't those sonsabitches Smith and Hickock got it in the neck, how come those murdering sonsabitches are still eating up the taxpayers' money? Well, I can see their side. They're mad 'cause they're not getting what they want—revenge. And they're not going to get it if I can help it. I believe in hanging. Just so long as I'm not the one being hanged."

But then he was.

Another three years passed, and during those years two exceptionally skillful Kansas City lawyers, Joseph P. Jenkins and Robert Bingham, replaced Shultz, the latter having resigned from the case. Appointed by a Federal judge, and working without compensation (but motivated by a hard-held opinion that the defendants had been the victims of a "nightmarishly unfair trial"), Jenkins and Bingham filed numerous appeals within the framework of the Federal court system, thereby avoiding three execution dates: October 25, 1962, August 8, 1963, and February 18, 1965. The attorneys contended that their clients had been unjustly convicted because legal counsel had not been appointed them until after they had confessed and had waived preliminary hearings; and because they were not competently represented at their trial, were convicted with the help of evidence seized without a search warrant (the shotgun and knife taken from the Hickock home), were not granted a change of venue even though the environs of the trial had been "saturated" with publicity prejudicial to the accused.

With these arguments, Jenkins and Bingham succeeded in carrying the case three times to the United States Supreme Court—the Big Boy, as many litigating prisoners refer to it—but on each occasion the Court, which never comments on its decisions in such instances, denied the appeals by refusing to grant the writs of certiorari that would have entitled the appellants to a full hearing before the Court. In March, 1965, after Smith and Hickock had been confined in their Death Row cells almost two thousand days, the Kansas Supreme Court decreed that their lives must end between midnight and 2:00 A.M., Wednesday, April 14, 1965. Subsequently, a clemency appeal was presented to the newly elected Governor of Kansas, William Avery; but Avery, a rich farmer sensitive to public opinion, refused to intervene—a decision he felt to be in the "best interest of the people of Kansas." (Two months later, Avery also denied the clemency appeals of York and Latham, who were hanged on June 22, 1965.)

And so it happened that in the daylight hours of that Wednesday morning, Alvin Dewey, breakfasting in the coffee shop of a Topeka hotel, read, on the first page of the Kansas City *Star*, a headline he had long awaited: DIE ON ROPE FOR BLOODY CRIME. The story, written by an Associated Press reporter, began: "Richard Eugene Hickock and Perry Edward Smith, partners in crime, died on the gallows at the state prison early today for one of the bloodiest murders in Kansas criminal annals. Hickock, 33 years old, died first, at 12:41 A.M.; Smith, 36, died at 1:19 . . ."

Dewey had watched them die, for he had been among the twenty-odd witnesses invited to the ceremony. He had never attended an execution, and when on the midnight past he entered the cold warehouse, the scenery had surprised him: he had anticipated a setting of suitable dignity, not this bleakly lighted cavern cluttered with lumber and other debris. But the gallows itself, with its two pale nooses attached to a crossbeam, was imposing enough; and so, in an unexpected style, was the hangman, who cast a long shadow from his perch on the platform at the top of the wooden instrument's thirteen steps. The hangman, an anonymous, leathery gentleman who had been imported from Missouri for the event, for which he was paid six hundred dollars, was attired in an aged double-breasted pin-striped suit overly commodious for the narrow figure inside it—the coat came nearly to his knees; and on his head he wore a cowboy hat which, when first bought, had perhaps been bright green, but was now a weathered, sweat-stained oddity.

Also, Dewey found the self-consciously casual conversation of his fellow witnesses, as they stood awaiting the start of what one witness termed "the festivities," disconcerting.

"What I heard was, they was gonna let them draw straws to see who dropped first. Or flip a coin. But Smith says why not do it alphabetically. Guess 'cause S comes after H. Ha!"

"Read in the paper, afternoon paper, what they ordered for their last meal? Ordered the same menu. Shrimp. French fries. Garlic bread. Ice cream and strawberries and whipped cream. Understand Smith didn't touch his much."

"That Hickock's got a sense of humor. They was telling me how, about an hour ago, one of the guards says to him, 'This must be the longest night of your life.' And Hickock, he laughs and says, 'No. The shortest.' "

"Did you hear about Hickock's eyes? He left them to an eye doctor. Soon as they cut him down, this doctor's gonna yank out his eyes and stick them in somebody else's head. Can't say I'd want to be that somebody. I'd feel peculiar with them eyes in my head."

"Christ! Is that *rain*? All the windows down! My new Chevy. Christ!"

The sudden rain rapped the high warehouse roof. The sound, not unlike the rat-a-tat-tat of parade drums, heralded Hickock's arrival. Accompanied by six guards and a prayer-murmuring chaplain, he entered the death place handcuffed and wearing an ugly harness of leather straps that bound his arms to his torso. At the foot of the gallows the warden read to him the official order of execution, a two-page document; and as the warden read, Hickock's eyes, enfeebled by half a decade of cell shadows, roamed the little audience until, not seeing what he sought, he asked the nearest guard, in a whisper, if any member of the Clutter family was present. When he was told no, the prisoner seemed disappointed, as though he thought the protocol surrounding this ritual of vengeance was not being properly observed.

As is customary, the warden, having finished his recitation, asked the condemned man whether he had any last statement to make. Hickock nodded. "I just want to say I hold no hard feelings. You people are sending me to a better world than this ever was"; then, as if to emphasize the point, he shook hands with the four men mainly responsible for his capture and conviction, all of whom had requested permission to attend the executions: K.B.I. agents Roy Church, Clarence Duntz, Harold Nye, and Dewey himself. "Nice to see you," Hickock said with his most charming smile; it was as if he were greeting guests at his own funeral.

The hangman coughed—impatiently lifted his cowboy hat and settled it again, a gesture somehow reminiscent of a turkey buzzard huffing, then smoothing its neck feathers—and Hickock, nudged by an attendant, mounted the scaffold steps. "The Lord giveth, the Lord taketh away. Blessed is the name of the Lord," the chaplain intoned, as the rain sound accelerated, as the noose was fitted, and as a delicate black mask was tied round the prisoner's eyes. "May the Lord have mercy on your soul." The trap door opened, and Hickock hung for all to see a full twenty minutes before the prison doctor at last said, "I pronounce this man dead." A hearse, its blazing headlights beaded with rain, drove into the warehouse, and the body, placed on a litter and shrouded under a blanket, was carried to the hearse and out into the night.

Staring after it, Roy Church shook his head: "I never would have believed he had the guts. To take it like he did. I had him tagged a coward."

The man to whom he spoke, another detective, said, "Aw, Roy. The guy was a punk. A mean bastard. He deserved it."

Church, with thoughtful eyes, continued to shake his head.

While waiting for the second execution, a reporter and a guard conversed. The reporter said, "This your first hanging?"

"I seen Lee Andrews."

"This here's my first."

"Yeah. How'd you like it?"

The reporter pursed his lips. "Nobody in our office wanted the assignment. Me either. But it wasn't as bad as I thought it would be. Just like jumping off a diving board. Only with a rope around your neck."

"They don't feel nothing. Drop, snap, and that's it. They don't feel nothing."

"Are you sure? I was standing right close. I could hear him gasping for breath."

"Uh-huh, but he don't feel nothing. Wouldn't be humane if he did."

"Well. And I suppose they feed them a lot of pills. Sedatives."

"Hell, no. Against the rules. Here comes Smith."

"Gosh, I didn't know he was such a shrimp."

"Yeah, he's little. But so is a tarantula."

As he was brought into the warehouse, Smith recognized his old foe, Dewey; he stopped chewing a hunk of Doublemint gum he had in his mouth, and grinned and winked at Dewey, jaunty and mischievous. But after the warden asked if he had anything to say, his expression was sober. His sensitive eyes gazed gravely at the surrounding faces, swerved up to the shadowy hangman, then downward to his own manacled hands. He looked at his fingers, which were stained with ink and paint, for he'd spent his final three years on Death Row painting self-portraits and pictures of children, usually the children of inmates who supplied him with photographs of their seldom-seen progeny. "I think," he said, "it's a helluva thing to take a life in this manner. I don't believe in capital punishment, morally or legally. Maybe I had something to contribute, something—" His assurance faltered; shyness blurred his voice, lowered it to a just audible level. "It would be meaningless to apologize for what I did. Even inappropriate. But I do. I apologize."

Steps, noose, mask; but before the mask was adjusted, the prisoner spat his chewing gum into the chaplain's outstretched palm. Dewey shut his eyes; he kept them shut until he heard the thud-snap that announces a rope-broken neck. Like the majority of American law-enforcement officials, Dewey is certain that capital punishment is a deterrent to violent crime, and he felt that if ever the penalty had been earned, the present instance was it. The preceding execution had not disturbed him, he had never had much use for Hickock, who seemed to him "a small-time chiseler who got out of his depth, empty and worthless." But Smith, though he was the true murderer, aroused another response, for Perry possessed a quality, the aura of an exiled animal, a creature walking wounded, that the detective could not disregard. He remembered his first meeting with Perry in the interrogation room at Police Headquarters in Las Vegas—the dwarfish boy-man seated in the metal chair, his small booted feet not quite brushing the floor. And when Dewey now opened his eyes, that is what he saw: the same childish feet, tilted, dangling.

Dewey had imagined that with the deaths of Smith and Hickock, he would experience a sense of climax, release, of a design justly completed. Instead, he discovered himself recalling an incident of almost a year ago, a casual encounter in Valley View Cemetery, which, in retrospect, had somehow for him more or less ended the Clutter case.

The pioneers who founded Garden City were necessarily a Spartan people, but when the time came to establish a formal cemetery, they were determined, despite arid soil and the troubles of transporting water, to create a rich contrast to the dusty streets, the austere plains. The result, which they named Valley View, is situated above the town on a plateau of modest altitude. Seen today, it is a dark island lapped by the undulating surf of surrounding wheat fields—a good refuge from a hot day, for there are many cool paths unbrokenly shaded by trees planted generations ago.

One afternoon the previous May, a month when the fields blaze with the green-gold fire of half-grown wheat, Dewey had spent several hours at Valley View weeding his father's grave, an obligation he had too long neglected. Dewey was fifty-one, four years older than when he had supervised the Clutter investigation; but he was still lean and agile, and still the K.B.I.'s principal agent in western Kansas; only a week earlier he had caught a pair of cattle rustlers. The dream of settling on his farm had not come true, for his wife's fear of living in that sort of isolation had never lessened. Instead, the Deweys had built a new house in town; they were proud of it, and proud, too, of both their sons, who were deep-voiced now and as tall as their father. The older boy was headed for college in the autumn.

When he had finished weeding, Dewey strolled along the quiet paths. He stopped at a tombstone marked with a recently carved name: Tate. Judge Tate had died of pneumonia the past November; wreaths, brown roses, and rain-faded ribbons still lay upon the raw earth. Close by, fresher petals spilled across a newer mound—the grave of Bonnie Jean Ashida, the Ashida's elder daughter, who while visiting Garden City had been killed in a car collision. Deaths, births, marriages—why, just the other day he'd heard that Nancy Clutter's boy friend, young Bobby Rupp, had gone and got married.

The graves of the Clutter family, four graves gathered under a single gray stone, lie in a far corner of the cemetery—beyond the trees, out in the sun, almost at the wheat field's bright edge. As Dewey approached them, he saw that another visitor was already there: a willowy girl with white-gloved hands, a smooth cap of dark-honey hair, and long, elegant legs. She smiled at him, and he wondered who she was.

"Have you forgotten me, Mr. Dewey? Susan Kidwell."

He laughed; she joined him. "Sue Kidwell. I'll be darned." He hadn't seen her since the trial; she had been a child then. "How are you? How's your mother?"

"Fine, thank you. She's still teaching music at the Holcomb School."

"Haven't been that way lately. Any changes?"

"Oh, there's some talk about paving the streets. But you know Holcomb. Actually, I don't spend much time there. This is my junior year at K.U.," she said, meaning the University of Kansas. "I'm just home for a few days."

"That's wonderful, Sue. What are you studying?"

"Everything. Art, mostly. I love it. I'm really happy." She glanced across the prairie. "Nancy and I planned to go to college together. We were going to be roommates. I think about it sometimes. Suddenly, when I'm very happy, I think of all the plans we made."

Dewey looked at the gray stone inscribed with four names, and the date of their death: November 15, 1959. "Do you come here often?"

"Once in a while. Gosh, the sun's strong." She covered her eyes with tinted glasses. "Remember Bobby Rupp? He married a beautiful girl."

"So I heard."

"Colleen Whitehurst. She's really beautiful. And very nice, too."

"Good for Bobby." And to tease her, Dewey added, "But how about you? You must have a lot of beaus."

"Well. Nothing serious. But that reminds me. Do you have the time? Oh," she cried, when he told her it was past four, "I've got to run! But it was nice to have seen you, Mr. Dewey."

"And nice to have seen you, Sue. Good luck," he called after her as she disappeared down the path, a pretty girl in a hurry, her smooth hair swinging, shining—just such a young woman as Nancy might have been. Then, starting home, he walked toward the trees, and under them, leaving behind him the big sky, the whisper of wind voices in the wind-bent wheat.